THE LOST VALLEY OF
VINCABAMBA

BY
D.R. AMSON

SEVERED**PRESS**

THE LOST VALLEY OF VINCABAMBA

ISBN: 978-1-923165-07-6

CHAPTER 1

Upstate New York, 1954

Rap-tap-tap!

Arthur Ambrose stirred from restless dreams to the high-pitched rapping that echoed throughout his stately home. He sat upright in his grand four poster bed, his mind still swimming in fog as he rubbed sleep from his eyes and tried to comprehend what the noise had been. Outside the wind blew fierce and a barrage of rain splattered against the windowpane.

Has something fallen over in the house? Or perhaps it was the house itself, he wondered. The house was old and creaked with the coming of fall and drop in temperature. A dinner guest had once queried the groaning and creaking of the Ambrose's old house and he had joked that his house was the most haunted in all the United States. He'd suggested that when he'd travelled the world in his younger years and brought back treasures and curios from all four corners of the globe. Vengeful spirits had likewise returned with him, latching on to the mysterious items like leeches. Now they resided within the four walls of his home, a maelstrom of angry spirits from places as diverse as China to Ethiopia. For a second the young lady had become nervous before she realised he had been pulling her leg and playfully chided him for his cruel sense of humour.

He had chuckled at his own joke. He wasn't chuckling now as he sat up in the dark, the coldness of the night seeping into his bones. He listened intently, the sounds from the storm outside making it hard to discern subtle sounds within the house.

Perhaps it was a tree branch swaying in the wind and tapping against a window, or perhaps my own imagination is getting the better of me.

After a few more minutes of listening and finding no other suspect sounds forthcoming, Ambrose settled back down under his thick bed covers, eager to put the strange sound out from his thoughts.

Rap-tap-tap! went the loud, positively angry knocking once again and this time Ambrose sat bolt upright, his body rigid with fear. A flash of lightning illuminated his room and his eyes fell upon the tribal masks he'd brought back from the Ivory Coast, back when he'd been an adventurer. He had always thought of them as beautifully crafted examples of the local traditions and arts from the natives of that land. In the flash of lightning, with dark shadows playing across their features and the spectre of fear on his back, Ambrose now thought they looked ghoulish and positively malevolent.

You're being an old fool, he reasoned with himself as he reached over and turned on his reading light. *There is nothing in my house at night that isn't here throughout the day. No spirits, malevolent or otherwise.*

The reading light lit up the room in a warm glow that dispelled most of Ambrose's fears. The last of his sleep had left him and he put on his glasses and swung his legs out of bed, his feet finding soft, warm slippers where he had left them.

Feeling braver, he paused to listen again. Although he had quelled his fears for the most part, he couldn't deny the knocking was real. After a few breaths, he heard it again and this time he realised what it was; somebody was at the door.

Ambrose glanced at his bedside clock. It was two-thirty in the morning. Who on earth would be beating at his door in the middle of the night during a wretched storm?

Rap-tap-tap! went the incessant knocking again and this time it sounded more desperate in its urgency. The sharp raps reverberated around the house, loud enough to wake the dead.

"Mustaf?" Ambrose called out into the house. "Mustaf, there is someone at the door." He waited for a reply from his manservant and was perplexed when no response was given. Mustaf had perception that was second to none and it was hard to imagine the younger man had not been disturbed by the knocking that had awoken himself.

He licked his lips nervously as he tried to contemplate what the silence meant.

Rap-tap-tap!

"Candy," he called out to his daughter. "Candy, are you awake? I think there is someone at the door."

Ambrose awaited and was once again greeted by a silence that was only broken when the knocking on the door continued once again.

"I'm coming, I'm coming," he called out as he pulled on his night robe and began shuffling down the hallway, turning on lights as he went. He knew that the mysterious knocker wouldn't be able to hear him, not that it mattered. As he walked past the respective bedroom doors of his manservant and his daughter, he decided not to disturb them. After all, he wasn't so old that he couldn't answer his own front door.

Ambrose made his way down the carpeted stairs, flicked on the downstairs light and walked to the oak door. He reached out to pull the latch open just as the *rap-tap-tapping* commenced again. He stilled his hand for a moment as the icy tendrils of fear gripped his heart once more. He suddenly felt with certainty that whatever was beyond his front door would change his life forever.

He wondered what would happen if he refused to open it and recoiled as the ominous knocking continued. Steeling his nerves, Ambrose unbolted the door and pulled it open.

A man younger than Ambrose rushed in, his coat soaked from the cold rain which now dripped with impunity onto the hallway's carpeted floor.

"Thank God you answered when you did," exclaimed the man as he urgently turned and slammed the door shut, pushing the deadbolt back into place with an audible click.

Ambrose was taken aback by the man's forthrightness. "Excuse me, sir. Do I know you?"

The man didn't answer; his back remained to Ambrose as he strode confidently into the lounge, turning on the light as he did so. The man hurried past display cases containing the miscellaneous trinkets of long forgotten cultures and the fossilised remains of the terrible lizards that had ruled the earth long before mankind's reign. The man peeked out from the curtain into the darkness as the rain continued to fall from his clothes.

"It nearly had me. I was nearly a goner."

"It nearly had you? What nearly had you? I'm sorry, but I must insist. Who on earth are you?"

The young man turned to Ambrose and gave a wry smile. Ambrose's blood ran cold. "Don't you recognise me, old friend?"

Ambrose was aghast in disbelief at who stood before him. "My god! Austin, is it really you?"

The man nodded. "For better or for worse, it is."

Ambrose tried to make sense of the situation he now found himself in. "But it's been twenty-four years. I was certain that you were dead. Are you real?"

"I assure you I am standing here before you as certain as you are standing here yourself." He then looked down with a sudden pang of sadness. "Iris, she didn't make it."

An overwhelming feeling of guilt settled over Ambrose. "I am so sorry, Austin. Sorry for your loss. Sorry for abandoning you in that terrible place. I had no choice. You must understand that. I had no choice."

Austin's wry smile returned and he rested his hand on Ambrose's shoulder, giving a small squeeze. "I know, old boy. I understand. I truly do."

Ambrose's shoulders sagged in shame. "You don't hold it against me? Even though I promised to return for you, yet never did?"

"I think your actions have weighed on you for long enough, don't you? What is my scorn, compared to that?"

"I am sorry," Ambrose uttered. He then regained some of his composure and looked over Austin quizzically. "Austin, it's been nearly two and a half decades. You haven't aged a day. How is that possible?"

Austin's reply was cut off by the smashing of glass coming from the back of the house. His expression became tight. "No time for that now. It's in the house."

"What's in the house?" asked Ambrose fearfully.

"I managed to escape Vincabamba, but I was followed, Ambrose. That thing has hunted me down. It wants me dead."

"Thing? What thing? Please Austin, you aren't making any sense."

Austin stealthily walked across the lounge, picking up a poker from the fireplace and wielding it like a weapon. "You know what it is, Ambrose. It was the reason you fled."

Again, a sense of shame and guilt rose in Ambrose and he felt a palpable fear as Austin reached the closed door leading through to the dining room. It was closed, yet beyond it Ambrose could hear *something* moving about.

"Mustaf and my daughter are upstairs. I should wake them," Ambrose suggested.

"There's no time for that," Austin snapped. "If we turn our backs, we're dead. It'll burst through that door and have us. Our only chance is to fight." He reached for the door handle with a trembling hand.

"Austin, this is madness," Ambrose croaked.

"I've been in Vincabamba for so long, Ambrose. I'm tired. This is all I know."

Austin pressed down on the handle as quietly as he could. As soon as the door clicked open it exploded out towards the man in a violent burst of movement. Something big crashed through the door, its skin grey and leathery, its claws long and terrible, its neck long and serpentine.

"Dear God, it can't be! It can't be!" Ambrose cried out in terror.

Austin swung the fire poker at the attacking creature, the terrible lizard that should have been dead thousands of millennia before the first man ever descended from the trees and stood upright. The first time Ambrose had seen this beast twenty-four years ago, he hadn't a clue what it was. Now he knew - a dinosaur! An Elaphrosaurus to be precise. It stood to a height of five feet at the hip, its light, narrow body supported by strong muscular legs. The Elaphrosaurus reeled back from Austin's courageous attempts to club it, appearing far taller than the man it was fighting. Its arms, though short, were armed with cruel claws that reeled in defence as its serpentine neck arched backwards.

"Ambrose, for God's sake, help me man! Don't let me down again!" Austin swiped at the prehistoric beast again and it reared back to avoid the poker before its head snapped forward at the man's hand.

Austin cried out in pain as the dinosaur's teeth latched onto his wrists, causing him to release the poker in blinding pain as he fell backwards, thudding upon the carpet. Ambrose tried to move, tried to help his friend, though his legs would not move. Fear had bolted him to the spot and he hadn't the willpower to move.

The Elaphrosaurus gave a hideous, wicked screech as it realised its prey was now defenceless on the floor. It leapt upon him, pointed teeth sinking into the flesh where Austin's neck met his shoulder. Austin gave a guttural scream as the dinosaur savaged his neck. It pulled back with a jolt, tearing a mouthful of bloody flesh with it. Austin continued to scream as his blood fountained from the open wound and flowed into the carpet. He tried to stem the bleeding with his hand whilst trying to crawl away. His attempts were useless. The Elaphrosaurus kept a foot on Austin's chest, preventing his escape while it threw its head back and swallowed the chunk of red, glistening flesh it had pulled from its victim.

"Ambrose, you have to help me… please…" Austin gurgled as he still feebly tried to resist the feeding dinosaur.

The Elaphrosaurus turned its head to Ambrose, studying him with its beady eyes, as if daring him to try and intervene.

"I'm sorry," Ambrose cried pitifully. "I don't know what to do."

Austin's struggles slowed as he coughed up thick, sticky, crimson blood that ran down his chin in goops. "Save… me…"

The Elaphrosausus gave a final, terrible shriek and a threatening snap in Ambrose's direction before looking down at the bleeding man it had pinned to the floor. Its head darted downwards and its jaws locked around Austin's throat. The man's eyeballs bulged as the dinosaur twisted its neck and tore his throat out. Austin gave a final gargle before his body lay still. The Elaphrosaurus shrieked again, this time in apparent victory as Ausin's blood dripped from its sharp, pointed teeth. It then swallowed another mouthful of flesh before looking back up to Ambrose with those cold, calculating eyes.

"I'm sorry, Austin," Ambrose blubbed. "I'm so sorry."

The dinosaur shrieked in triumph.

***

Arthur Ambrose awoke with a start, fearfully clutching at his rapidly beating heart. It took a few moments to gain control over his breathing as Ambrose took stock of his surroundings. He was still in bed, his room in darkness, the sound of the storm outside ever present. Despite the coldness of the room, Ambrose's back was covered in sweat.

Calming his emotions, Ambrose held his hands out in front of himself. They were old and wrinkled - *when did I get so old?* he ruefully pondered. His hands trembled from the very real fear the dream had distilled in him and he failed to get his appendages under his control.

The bedroom door creaked open, making Ambrose jump as he looked over to see a broad, powerful figure standing in the doorway, silhouetted by the light further up the landing.

"Professor Ambrose, are you okay?" said the man standing in the doorway, with a deep, velvety voice. "I heard you cry out."

Ambrose allowed himself to relax slightly. "Just a dream, Mustaf. Just a dream."

The figure remained in place, stern and immovable as he chewed over Ambrose's words. "Perhaps something to help you sleep?"

Ambrose reached over, turned on his bedside light and put on his glasses. "No, I shan't be sleeping anymore tonight."

"But you must rest," Mustaf pushed.

"I've rested enough, old friend. The time for rest is over. Now is the time for action."

"It's three in the morning, sir. What do you hope to do now that can't wait until morning?"

Ambrose hurriedly pulled his robe on. "I'm heading down to the study. I have some letters to write and telegrams to prepare. If you could make me some coffee, I'd be grateful."

Mustaf nodded. "Of course, sir. May I ask what action it is you feel you must now undertake?"

"I must do something I should have done nearly a quarter of a century ago. I must fulfil a promise to an old friend."

CHAPTER 2

India, 1954

The three men grunted and cursed as they used their machetes to hack away at the undergrowth of the dense, green jungle. The sun sat high in the sky, beating down upon them to put further strain on their toils.

"We're in the wrong location," said one of the men in a southern Irish accent, his body slender and toned, his hair brown and his eyes a piercing green. He spoke as if he were talking to a person who knew they were wrong but wouldn't admit to it.

A grin spread over the stubbled but otherwise boyish good looks of the man leading them. His eyes were blue, his hair a dirty blond. His build was slightly larger than his companion, his body hardened from a lifetime of battling the elements, as well as his fellow man. His body was the result of a life of hardship, bronzed and strong. His face showed none of the weight from the experiences the man had endured. "No, we're not," he said with utmost certainty and the slightest hint of playful mockery.

The third man grunted his exasperation, his face a bright red as he struggled to keep up with his companions. Unlike his two teammates, he was out of shape. His body betrayed a lifetime of eating and drinking that he was now ruefully regretting. "I fear I may have to agree with Pat. By all accounts, the Sun Temple of Yuran Yurin should be located somewhere around one hundred and twenty miles south of here. Where the two rivers of Yuran and Yurin meet. We're nowhere close to where they join."

"Exactly," agreed Patrick "Pat" McGoldric. "We're wasting our time here."

The leading man, Charles "Chuck" Tanner, turned to face his friends. He gave them a winning, cocksure smile as he used the opportunity to catch his breath and wipe the sweat from his brow. "Come on, guys. You just need a little faith in me. Have I ever let you down before?"

"Yes," both Pat and the rotund man, William "Bill" Yates, responded in unison.

Chuck gave an expression of mock surprise and hurt. "Oh yeah? When?" He turned and continued hacking a path through the dense foliage.

"How about the time we spent three months sailing around the South China Sea in circles looking for the mystical Island of Chix-Lui? An island of untold wealth and mermaids you insisted was real?"

Chuck grinned at the memory. "How was I to know that the Island of Chix-Lui was just made up to sell newspapers in the eighteenth century? Are you saying you didn't have a good time visiting Thailand, Malaysia and Vietnam? I remember you breaking a few hearts while we were out there."

"That's not the point," Pat flatly replied.

"How about the time we spent six weeks in the Southern Ocean, searching for the sunken city of Ru'hal, the sea god?" griped Bill. "I don't remember any good times then."

"You don't remember because you spent the whole trip with your head hanging over the side of the boat with sea sickness. Pat and I got some good, quality fishing in." He turned to Pat. "Isn't that right, Pat?"

"Was that on the boat that sank or the one that ran aground on rocks?" Pat shot back.

Chuck laughed. "I never took you both for 'glass half empty' kinda guys. Guess I'm still learning new things about you two, even after all these years." He shrugged. "You guys forget you're talking to the guy who found the Death Shroud of Harapet, the Jewels of Hanaan and the Golden Army of the Sky Emperor."

"How can we forget when you keep reminding us?" Pat sighed.

"And you almost got us killed numerous times during each of those expeditions," added Bill.

Chuck scoffed as he continued to hack at branches and vines. "Almost means nothing, boys. We live in a world of abject certainties. Either you lose it all, or you win big." With a final swing of his machete, Chuck cut a group of vines that fell to the ground and revealed an ancient structure made of brown and golden stone. Chuck grinned from ear to ear when he saw it. His companions stopped in their tracks and looked up in silent awe at the lost temple that had laid undiscovered for over fifteen thousand years. "I give to you, the Sun Temple of Yuran Yurin."

Pat couldn't help but smile as Bill lifted the camera that dangled from his neck and began taking photos of the temple, remarking what an incredible find it was.

"Well?" Chuck chuckled as he elbowed Pat.

Pat returned his grin. "I admit it, when you are on the money, you really are 'on the money.'"

"How did you know it would be here?" exclaimed Bill, continuing to take photographs. "People have been searching for this ruin for hundreds of years and you've found it. You've actually found it."

Chuck grinned but remained elusive with his explanation. "Let's just say that when I was smoking herbs and sharing with the natives on Yurpet I wasn't just promoting my new book." Bill and Pat exchanged a confused glance but before either of them could say another word Chuck's playful demeanour was replaced by abject seriousness. "Right, the easy part is over. Now the real work begins." He studied the structure, taking in all its details. When it came to recollection, Chuck was second to none. He had an eery ability to remember a location with complete clarity. When it came to writing his journals, the publishing of which provided much of the three men's income, he could recollect a temple or tomb with as much detail as any of Bill's photographs.

"Bill, I want you to get back down to the river and wait by the boat for us. There's no telling when we'll need to make a fast escape." Bill nodded. "If we aren't back in two hours, come looking for us."

Bill nodded and took another few photos of the temple exterior, strewn with vines, before traipsing off back through the jungle towards the river. Following the path they had just cut, it would only take about ten minutes to reach their motorboat, where he would hunker down and wait.

"Guess it's me and you going in there, then?" smiled Pat, gesturing to the entrance to the Sun Temple. A dark, foreboding square entry approximately eight feet by eight feet.

Chuck flashed his trademark grin. "You guessed correctly."

The two explorers reached for their flashlights on their belts, twisted them on and slowly made their way into the stone structure.

They both gave an impressed whistle as their respective beams of light moved over the stone surfaces within, revealing various inscribed pictures and stories in an ancient language long forgotten by most men.

"What does it say?" asked Pat, studying the inscriptions.

Chuck spent a little more time moving his flashlight over the ancient writings. "It tells the story of Yuran and Yurin, twin gods who dripped from the sun like liquid gold and created two mighty rivers that would eventually entwine and become one. This temple was constructed to house their earthly idols."

"The Idols of Yuran and Yurin, which legend claims are pure gold," stated Pat with hunger in his eyes. "Said to be priceless."

"As the legend goes."

"Are they here?"

Chuck said nothing, instead he walked deeper into the dank, dark passage. Roots from plants that had grown atop the temple had pushed through the stone blocks and now hung eerily from the ceiling. Eventually they reached the two golden idols of Yuran and Yurin, each about a foot tall. On either side of the small statues were the entrances to narrower passages. "Does that answer your question?" Chuck smiled.

"They're real!" exclaimed Pat, running over to the idols, each placed on a low pedestal. "They're actually real!" He crouched down and picked one of the idols up. "I thought they would have been harder to get to."

"Hey, careful with what you are doing," Chuck warned his friend.

Pat looked up irritably before realising what Chuck meant. Old temples and tombs were filled with traps to catch out the unwary. Before Pat could respond Chuck grabbed him by the backpack and yanked him away from the pedestal just as metal spikes, each four feet in height and just as sharp as they had been fifteen hundred years ago, erupted out from the ground where he'd just been standing.

"Jesus," Pat swore as he dropped his flashlight and the idol he'd been carrying. They both clattered onto the stone floor.

"Like I said, be careful," Chuck glared at his friend. "You were almost a shish kebab."

Pat nodded numbly, ashamed of his amateur behaviour. His shame soon turned to exasperation as he looked down at the smashed remains of the idol. He crouched and picked up his flashlight, shining it over the idol shards in disgust.

"It's pottery," he spat. "It's nothing but pottery, painted gold. The legend is a lie."

"Maybe," Chuck said, pushing the broken shards about with his foot. "Maybe not."

"Why do you say that?"

Chuck moved his light beam over the sharp spikes that had almost ended Pat's life. "People don't tend to make traps unless they are protecting something. We need to move deeper inside the temple."

Pat looked at the two separate passages with uncertainty. "Which way?"

Chuck shrugged. "Shall we flip a coin?"

Pat began searching his pockets for a coin. Chuck ignored him and began walking down the left-hand passage. It didn't go for long until it reached a closed stone door. To the right of the door was a suspect hole amidst the stone blocks. Chuck crouched near the hole and shone his light inside it, trying to ascertain its purpose. Inside the hold was a small lever.

"What's that do?" asked Pat. "You think it opens the door?"

Chuck chewed on his bottom lip. "Maybe."

"Maybe yes, or maybe no?"

"Maybe both."

Pat looked confused. "Are you going to try and pull it?"

Chuck racked his brain, searching for any possible trap. As a rule, he didn't like placing his hand in any ancient contraptions. He'd witnessed firsthand a few people losing hands doing just that. On the flip side, he couldn't see any further way to advance into the temple.

"Let's go back to the idol room," he said after internal deliberations. "Let's see what's down passage number two."

The two men returned to the room with the spike trap and this time went down the righthand passage. It again ended after a short walk at another stone door, only this time there was a striking difference. The small hole was now on the left of the door and on the ground in front of it was a very dead, very rotten explorer. Chuck and Pat both grimaced at the grim discovery as bloated cockroaches the size of rats scurried from the beams of their flashlights. The body was almost a skeleton, only some rotten chunks of meat remained stubbornly attached to the yellowing bones.

"Who was he?" Pat muttered.

"He was careless," Chuck responded before crouching down and searching the skeleton's pockets. He found a wallet and inside was a driver's licence. The information made Chuck's face harden. "I knew this man. Dario Angelo." He pocketed the wallet. "When we return to the world, I'll make sure his folks know what happened to him."

Pat looked down at the skeleton in alarm. "This is Angelo?"

Chuck nodded. Angelo had been in the same line of business as himself, forever exploring the world and seeking to uncover its lost secrets. The two had met several times at various lectures in the museums of the world and had developed a friendly rivalry of sorts. Now he was dead. Angelo had gone missing several months ago and nobody had known where he'd gone. Chuck hadn't been too concerned with the news. He was aware of how expeditions could remove a man from the civilised world for months at a time. Dario was a skilled artefact hunter and Chuck had been certain he'd turn up again, no doubt with a new tale to tell that would rival his own adventures. Chuck had been wrong and compartmentalised the knowledge of his rival's passing for later. There was no time to grieve now.

"I had no idea he was searching for the Idols of Yuran and Yurin," he stated calmly before moving on to examine the hole in the wall.

"Poor bastard," muttered Pat. He spotted something. "Hey, Chuck. Angelo's missing his right hand."

"I've found it," Chuck replied, shining his flashlight into the hole. Pat crouched to see the remnants of Angelo's skeletal hand still clasped to the lever within the hole. He audibly shuddered. "Evidently these levers are rigged. You grab hold and pull, and a blade drops from above, cutting your hand off."

Pat subconsciously began rubbing his wrists. "Yowch."

Chuck nodded, standing up straight and examining the door.

"Then how do we proceed if the levers are booby-trapped? Hey, maybe only one of the levers is booby-trapped and Angelo just got unlucky, you know? Maybe the other one will open just fine."

Chuck paused from studying the images carved into the stone door. "You want to find out?"

Pat remained silent, again rubbing his wrists.

"There's more to it than that. I am certain." Chuck continued to try and make sense of the images and writings covering the walls while Pat remained silent. He knew better than to disturb Chuck when he was thinking; his life could well be dependent on Chuck's deciphering of the ancient puzzle they had stumbled upon. It wouldn't be the first time.

"These pictures, these twin gods, Yuran and Yurin. Their tale is told here again, but some of the details are different."

"How so?"

"It tells of the lone god, Yuran who came from the sun to create a mighty river. The river was indeed mighty, but it wasn't enough to make the lands fertile…"

"Lone god? You mean Yuran and Yurin aren't twins?"

"In order to provide enough water for the people, Yuran approached a mirror and ordered his reflection to aid him. As he was a god, Yuran's reflection obeyed and stepped out from the mirror world. This was Yurin."

"So Yurin is Yuran's reflection? That's very interesting. It doesn't help us in the here and now, though. Does it?"

Chuck said nothing, turning the new information over in his head.

"Perhaps we should return to the other door," Pat suggested. "There were inscriptions there also. Perhaps they'll help shed more light on what we're supposed to do."

"It's no good," Chuck said. "The inscriptions there are the same as the ones in here, only written on the opposite side of the wall."

Pat didn't question how Chuck knew this, all too aware of his friend's ability to recollect with near perfect precision. He remained silent.

"On the opposite side of the wall… like a reflection…" Chuck pondered. "That's it!" he yelled out loud, making Pat jump.

"You've solved it?"

Chuck grinned his cocky grin. "I sure hope so." He then went on to explain how he believed the trap worked. "These two small passages are constructed to be mirror images of each other. They are designed only to be opened by Yuran and Yurin when they seek to return to their earthly bodies. To gain entry we must open the doors as they would."

"Meaning?"

"We need to pull on the levers at the same time. The exact same time."

Pat looked fear stricken as he looked over at the hole with uncertainty. "You are sure?"

Chuck's grin turned to a smirk. "As sure as I'll ever be. Wanna test my theory?"

Pat groaned, looking down at the skeleton of Angelo, then back to the hole in the wall. "You're absolutely sure?"

"When have I ever been wrong?" Chuck grinned.

Pat relented. "Fine, but I pull the lever on the other side. You can have Angelo's."

"How kind of you," Chuck replied.

Chuck waited until Pat had jogged into position in the opposing passage. The passages had been designed in such a way that their voices carried through the ancient blockwork.

"Okay, I'm here," Pat yelled. "You are sure this will work? You're *absolutely* sure?"

Chuck tried to ignore the body of Angelo at his feet. The hapless explorer had believed he had solved the puzzle and look at him now. "I'm completely confident."

"You don't sound confident."

Chuck braced himself as he prepared to put his hand into the hole. His heart rate increased dramatically. "Get ready," Chuck ordered. "We're only going to get one chance at this."

"I mean, I'm hoping to get married one day, settle down and have kids."

Chuck's mind began whirring. *Is this really the right thing to do? Have I missed anything? Any details at all?* "What hand are you going to use?" Chuck called out.

"My right," Pat called back. "Is that right?"

"Okay, I'm going to use my left. That way we'll be more like a mirror image."

"You think that matters?" Pat cried out in disbelief.

"Hell if I know. I'm trying to cover all the bases here. On the count of three. One…"

"I hope you're right about this."

"Two…"

"I won't think any less of you if we call this whole thing off. Maybe reconsider our options?"

"Three!" Chuck reached in and grabbed the lever, trying his best to ignore the bony fingers that had once belonged to his rival. He instantly pulled down on the lever and prayed Pat was doing the same. Relief flooded him as he heard movement from beyond the wall as ancient machinery, pullies and cogs began turning. Not wanting to take any chances, as soon as he was certain the lever had been fully pulled, he pulled his hand out of the dark recess as quickly as he could.

Behind him a grated metal door dropped down, barring his chance to return to the previous room and joining up with Pat.

"A door just closed behind me! I'm trapped!" Pat called in panic from the other room.

"It's happened to me too," Chuck confirmed. "Clearly whoever designed this temple doesn't want us to join back up quite yet."

"So, what do we do?"

The heavy stone door in front of Chuck slowly lifted into the ceiling, making a grinding sound as it did so. A new passage leading downwards lay in front of him. "I guess we continue going down."

Cautiously, ever aware of potential traps, Chuck made his way down the stone passage. He noticed the walls were becoming wetter and wetter. Strange fungi grew upon the wet block walls and bizarre bugs skittered from his light.

Finally he reached the bottom of the passage and it opened up into a vast room, far larger than any chamber Chuck had expected to find here.

The room was about half the size of an American football field and about as tall from floor to ceiling as a two-story suburban house. Shards of sunlight shone in from apertures in the ceiling, illuminating everything in a soft, golden glow. Chuck had emerged on a balcony about halfway up the height of the wall. On the far side of the wall was two gigantic stone carvings of the heads and arms of the gods Yuran and Yurin. They were more detailed and complex than anything Chuck had believed would have been possible of the people from the time this temple was made. Their faces were in opposite corners and their arms stretched down the wall, their hands forming two adjacent platforms. On each of the platforms were pedestals, upon which were the golden idols. The trick was how to get to them.

Two metallic floors were constructed attached to the opposing walls and coming out about a third of the room's width on either side. On them was a grid pattern, four squares wide. Most of the grid squares were black, although some of them were gold plated. Gold plated grids only ever appeared in every other row of grids. The gap between the two grid floors was far too wide to be jumped and to fail a jump would mean instant death. The floor of the chamber was covered in spikes, the same, sharp, four feet high spikes that had sprung from the ground and almost killed Pat earlier.

"Oh Jesus, what fresh hell is this?" moaned Pat as he emerged onto his own balcony further along from Chuck's. He took in the death trap in front of him.

"Looks fun, right?" Chuck called over to him, trying not to let his fear show.

"Oh yeah, looks a right laugh," Pat replied dryly. "Now what do we do? Walk over and take the idols?"

Chuck laughed. "You really think it would be that easy?"

"Of course not" Pat whimpered. "Spikes… why is it always spikes? I hate spikes."

Chuck ignored Pat's protests as he studied the room in as much detail as he could muster. "I think I've got it," he confidently stated.

"There's that word 'think' again. I *hate* that word."

"You keep up this attitude I'll make you wait with the boat next time."

"Promises, promises."

Chuck went on to explain the trap to Pat. The way he saw it, the black grids that made up the majority of the platforms were traps. If they stepped on them they would release and the unfortunate explorer would be deposited unceremoniously onto a bed of spikes. They had to jump from gold grid to gold grid to get to the idols. To complicate matters, Chuck was certain that they would have to jump and land simultaneously. Any deviation would likely cause the golden grids to release also, resulting in their untimely death. Chuck was proven correct when Pat confirmed the pattern of gold grids on his side mirrored his own.

The grid started several feet from the balconies they currently stood on, requiring a perfectly timed leap to begin. The first line of grids was black-black-gold-black on Chuck's and black-gold-black-black on Pat's. Due to there being only one gold square available, their goal was obvious.

"On three," Chuck announced, preparing himself for the jump.

"Ready when you are," Pat sighed as he moved into a 'ready' position.

"One, two, three," both men leapt simultaneously and while in the air Chuck had a moment of terrible doubt. If he was wrong, then the gold platform would give and he'd be impaled on the spikes below. If that was the case, there was now nothing he could do to prevent that cruel fate.

Both men landed with a thud and remained perfectly still, afraid even to breathe as they looked down through the metal lattice of the grid to the evil looking spikes.

"We're alive!" Pat cheered. "We've done it!"

Chuck was surprised at how unsteady his legs were. Sweat stung his eyes and he told himself it was due to the heat and the exertion of the jump. "Don't celebrate yet," Chuck said. "We've still got five jumps to do."

Pat went quiet at the prospect of the leaps. "Let's do this," he said.

The first jump went easy enough. Again, there had only been one gold grid to jump to, so it had been simple enough. The second jump had two potential options. Keeping the mirror image theme in mind they both timed their jumps and landed on the grid closer to their respective walls.

"Nothing to it," chimed Pat.

Chuck was slightly envious of Pat's smaller frame in that instance. Pat had always been the more athletic of them and found climbing and jumping relatively easy. Chuck's larger build was now working against him.

The third jump presented a similar choice of two possible gold grids to leap to. After a moment of conferring they made the jump on the count of three. The third jump was reduced to a singular option again, although due to the pattern it wouldn't be an easy jump. Chuck's current row's grid pattern was black-black-gold-gold. The next pattern was gold-black-black-black. The diagonal nature of the jump made it a longer jump then he was used to, but it looked doable.

"You okay over there?" Pat asked.

"Nothing I can't handle," Chuck replied. "On three. One, two, three!" The two men jumped, Chuck putting his all into it and barely managing to land safely. His momentum nearly made him continue forward and he was forced to drop to his knees to avoid plummeting onto the ever-waiting spikes below. His knees hit the metal lattice hard and Chuck gritted his teeth against the pain.

"Jesus, you sure you're okay?" Pat called over from the other side of the room. "That was close."

"I'm fine," Chuck insisted as he warily stood. "Just a little miscalculation with my speed."

"Please don't miscalculate again. If you fall, I fall. I'd really rather avoid that."

"Noted," Chuck grumbled as he turned and sized up the final jump. His heart sank. The final gold square before he could jump to the waiting hand platform was on the far side of the pattern. His current row went gold-black-black-black. The final row went black-black-black-gold. The gold grid being against the wall. It was a considerably longer jump than the one he had almost fluffed.

Pat could clearly read his friend's apprehension at the last jump. "We can do this on five, if you want."

Chuck felt the cold slither of fear creep up his spine and tried to ignore it as best he could. He didn't have the luxury to let fear in. If he'd entertained fear before, he'd have died long ago. If he allowed it to invade his body now, he'd die in this very room.

"No, we go on three," Chuck shouted back with barely suppressed annoyance. "We always go on three. This is no different."

"Okay," replied Pat. "On three then." He got into his jumping stance.

Chuck remained focussed on the gold platform and blocked everything else out. That platform was all that mattered now. Either he would make this jump or everything he had done up to this point would have been for nothing. He'd end up as nothing more than a skeleton in a crumbling ruin.

Just like Dario Angelo.

He pushed the thought from his mind. Failure was not an option. Chuck took a deep breath and started to count.

"One... two..." he paused, preparing both body and mind for the jump ahead. He breathed out, then in again. "Three!"

Like a coiled spring, the built-up tension in Chuck's body was released and he leapt through the air towards the final gold square. He kept his eyes focused on it as he reached his arms forward, trying to make himself as streamlined as he possibly could.

Clang! His boots landed on the square and his eyes went wide with elation. He had done it. He had risen to the challenge yet again. Chuck's momentum continued to carry him forward, as it had done before. This time he was ready for it and planned to use the wall to stop himself.

Chuck hit against the wall and gave an "oof," as the wind was knocked from his lungs. Before he could regain his breath something black and leathery and vile screeched and attacked his face. Instinctually Chuck jumped backwards, away from the attacking thing. Only when he'd committed to the action of jumping back, his hands held up in a defensive posture, did he realise two things. Firstly, the thing, or rather things that had attacked his face were bats. They must have been sleeping in the wall and when he'd hit the blocks with his body, he'd disturbed them. The panicked animals had taken to air in shock, but they weren't committed to an attack. They now flew off through the large room, seeking escape. Secondly, and more worryingly, his sudden retreat had caused him to step back onto the black square beside the sanctuary of the gold square.

As predicted, the black square immediately swung away on a hinge and Chuck was left falling straight down. He yelled in outrage at such a ridiculous way to die and with flailing arms he managed to grab hold of the golden square. The jolt as he caught himself felt as if it would pull his arms from their sockets. He remained firm in his resolve and kept his grip, dangling above the perilous spike pit.

"Chuck! Hold on!" Pat yelled out in desperation, though there was nothing else to do.

"I wasn't planning on letting go!" Chuck yelled back as he looked down at the waiting spikes. He allowed himself to dangle for a moment, catching his breath and allowing his heart rate to settle to an agreeable amount. He then grunted with exertion as he used his strength to pull himself back up onto the gold square.

"God, that was close!" remarked Pat in giggling glee. "I thought you were done for."

"Not yet," Chuck smiled between pants for breath.

"Goddamn bats! When it gave way on your side, the square next to me released also. For a second, I thought they were all going to go. Scared the crap out of me! It looks like your theory about it all working as a mirrored image is on the money."

Chuck was still trying to recover from his scrape with death. "Good to know," he managed. He took another breath before standing on legs that felt like jelly. Looking across the room he could see the small group of bats fluttering into a crack in the ceiling, feeling a deep animosity towards them. "Let's get a move on."

Chuck couldn't decide whether the platforms made from the statues' outstretched hands were rigged the same as the grid squares so decided it best to act on the side of caution and treat them as if they were. He and Pat timed their jump and landed in unison on the respective palms.

"At last," enthused Pat as he reached down to pick up the gold idol next to him.

"Wait," Chuck ordered, and Pat froze mid-action. "Haven't you learnt anything? On three." The two men counted and then plucked up their respective gold idols with perfected timing.

"My god, it's real. It's solid gold. This thing must be worth a fortune."

Chuck allowed himself a grin. "And we've got quite the story to tell about how we got them, too."

Suddenly a deep rumbling of ancient machinery reverberated throughout the stone walls, growing like a crescendo until blocks in the walls and ceilings started to loosen and drop upon the spikes below. The platforms began to shake from side to side before moving slowly back towards the balconies the two men had entered from.

"My god, the whole place is collapsing," cried Pat as he dropped to his knees to avoid falling from the platform. "What the hell is happening?"

Chuck looked back to see the huge statue arms were extending as if they were alive, carrying the men back to the entry. "Quick, put your idol in your backpack. This whole place is going to come down. The Temple of the Sun was made to house these gold idols. Now we've taken them, the temple's done its job."

Pat obeyed, zipping up his backpack and giving a yelp as a loose block hit the side of his platform with a thud. He cursed. The blocks were large enough that if one hit him, it would surely kill him. He held on tight to the slow-moving stone hand as it moved over to the far wall they had entered from. "Can't these things move any faster?" Pat lamented.

"Hold on tight, we're nearly there."

Soon the entire room was collapsing and as they finally approached the balconies that led to safety a large piece of debris fell from the roof and hit the arm of the statue that held Pat. He screamed in terror as he was forced to jump to the waiting balcony, only just making it. Chuck followed Pat's lead and jumped as soon as the hand that carried him was close enough.

"Run," yelled Chuck, trying to be overheard over the collapsing temple. Pat didn't need telling twice and had already disappeared into his passage. Chuck ran into his own passage, leaving the crumbling grand room behind him.

The shaking did not cease and Chuck sprinted as fast as he could. It was apparent the passage and the entire ruin was collapsing around them. Dirt, rocks and blocks rained down around him and all he could do was sprint and hope for the best. Soon he was back into the room with the lever puzzle. The door that had closed to stop him from retreating earlier had once again risen and he didn't stop for a second as he kept running.

The entire ceiling of the room with the spike trap was falling and Chuck had to duck and swerve to avoid being crushed. He didn't realise when it happened, but he was suddenly aware of Pat frantically running beside him.

"Run, run, run," Chuck yelled as daylight shone in from the exit.

"We're almost out," cried Pat as he wheeled his arms and forced himself to move faster.

They were almost out when Chuck spotted the huge carved stone that acted as the entrance's lintel beginning to fall. "Watch out and keep moving as fast as you can. We can make it!"

Both men leapt together as they narrowly managed to fly through the gap, the lintel stone crashing to the ground behind them. They'd manged to avoid being crushed by mere seconds, yet they couldn't stop running yet.

"We've got to get away from the structure," Chuck shouted.

"Agreed," cried Pat and both men darted to the relative safety of the jungles as the Temple of the Sun, a ruin which had stood undisturbed for over fifteen centuries, collapsed into the mud and was rendered little more than a pile of rubble.

CHAPTER 3

Chuck and Pat sat in the mud laughing and panting as they recovered from their experiences within the Temple of the Sun. Dust from the collapsed ruin settled over them.

The jungle fell silent for a time, no doubt the surrounding wildlife had been shocked into silence by the din of the ancient structure collapsing. Shortly the sounds of insects and birdcalls resumed.

"We did it, we actually did it," cheered Pat.

"We sure did," Chuck laughed.

Pat pulled the gold statue from his backpack and grinned as he kissed it. "My god, it's more beautiful than I could have ever dreamed. This'll make us rich, Chuck. Rich!"

Chuck chuckled as he checked on his own idol. "The Smithsonian will pay a hefty donation to our group for these, that's for sure."

"The Smithsonian? You're thinking small potatoes, Chuck. A private buyer will pay ten times what the museums can."

Chuck rolled his eyes and zipped his statue back up. "Be that as it may, they're going to a museum. They're for the world to see. I'm all for making a profit, but I didn't go through all that just so these idols could be locked up in another vault and never seen again. If that was the case, what would be the point?"

"Uh, the money?" Pat laughed.

"We're doing okay for money, what with the sales on the items we get, plus what we make on my journals."

Pat snorted. "Okay doesn't buy me a mansion."

Chuck laughed as he stood. "I guess not. Come on, let's get back to Bill. He'll be worrying."

Pat agreed and zipped up his idol before following Chuck into the jungle. The two men walked along the path they had previously cut through the dense underbrush and after ten minutes the sounds of the river could be heard.

"The sooner we're gone from here the better," Pat chatted idly as he swatted at the cloud of biting flies that flew above his head. "I'm getting eaten alive here."

"We'll be back in civilisation before you know it," Chuck laughed, swatting at his own flies.

Stepping out from the trees, the two men spotted Bill waiting in their motorboat about fifty feet away. He was sat stiff with an anxious look upon his face as the boat bobbed up and down in the water. Chuck strode confidently towards his companion.

"Hey, don't look so worried," Chuck smiled. "We survived yet another scrape with death."

"That's great," said Bill, though he sounded less than thrilled. His face remained tight. He paused for a moment, as if deliberating what to say next. "Did you find the Idols of Yuran and Yurin?"

"Sure did," smiled Chuck. "The whole damn temple nearly fell on our heads as we took 'em. Have I got a story for you."

"Where are they?" asked Bill.

Chuck stopped approaching the boat, as did Pat. Something was wrong, he could sense it. He searched Bill's gaze, trying to understand what the problem was. Bill's features weren't just tight, they were positively strained. "You okay, buddy?"

"I'm sorry," Bill apologised.

"Sorry for what?"

A thick English accent spoke from behind Chuck. "He's sorry for not warning you about us." Chuck wheeled around with lightning speed and reached for his revolver. He froze before he pulled it from its holster, realising the man in front of him already had a revolver trained on him. If that wasn't enough, on either side of the man a mercenary stood, assault rifle already raised and pointing directly at Chuck's chest. Pat hadn't even tried to reach for his revolver, instead he raised his hands in an act of surrender. "I wouldn't do that, if I was you," the man smugly stated to Chuck. "Not unless you want more holes in you than a pin cushion." The man's deep voice dripped with malice and superiority.

For a second Chuck entertained the notion of making a move. He quickly dismissed the idea as suicide before slowly raising his hands. "Alexandre DeShard," Chuck spat, as if the very name left a bad taste in his mouth.

DeShard looked satisfied with Chuck's response. "Glad you remember me. It's been some time since we last met. I wasn't sure if you'd forgotten our last encounter." The man was tall, with jet black hair, a neatly trimmed short beard and piercing blue eyes.

Several other people emerged from hiding in the trees and two more rifles were pointed towards Chuck and Pat's direction. Chuck recognised the various members of DeShard's team. There was Hilda Klein, the daughter of a German SS soldier who had inherited not only her father's fair features, but also his proclivity for cruelty and violence. Her eyes seemed to be enjoying the confrontation with their old adversaries even more than DeShard.

There was Grigore Dragos, a stern Romanian who was a mountain of a man. Like DeShard he had black hair and a beard, though his hair was long and thin, and his beard was unkempt. He was DeShard's chief organiser and bodyguard.

Beside Dragos was Joe Hill, a slimy, unlikable ball of a man from Chicago who acted as DeShard's dogsbody. He was suffering in the heat even more than Bill had been, though he would never dare admit it to his superiors. Like Hilda, he shared a sadistic streak, although he was more the type to prefer watching rather than getting involved himself. His nose was bulbous and red from alcohol abuse and his hair looked greasy as it stuck to his scalp.

Finally, there were the two mercenaries who had their firearms trained on Chuck. They looked like local militia, an observation that was confirmed when they made utterances to one another in Hindi. Bill made a distressed noise and

Chuck slowly turned to see a fifth mercenary sitting up in the boat beside him. The mercenary had a rifle trained on Bill's head and Bill had his shaking hands held up high as he tried to contain the tears that were running down his cheeks.

"Sorry, Chuck. They jumped me while I was waiting for you," Bill miserably explained.

"That's okay, Bill. Don't worry about it," Chuck called over to him. He then turned back to DeShard as Bill was led to stand next to him. The mercenary who had been in the boat took both Chuck and Pat's sidearms before joining his comrades. "Of course I hadn't forgotten you," Chuck smiled. "The last thing I remember is you crying for help as those Voodoo Priests in Haiti buried you alive in an unmarked grave. I thought you were dead. Glad to see you're doing okay, I was quite concerned for your health."

DeShard's smile wavered slightly. "Your concern is appreciated. If only you had been concerned enough to aid me as those priests threw mud atop my coffin."

Chuck gave an exaggerated shrug. "What can I say, I don't like to disturb religious practices."

"Very ethical of you. Fortunately my associates were able to locate me before I ran out of oxygen."

"Thank God for small mercies."

"Do you know what it does to a man? Being buried alive, I mean."

"I can see it didn't make you a nicer person."

"Very droll, Mister Tanner. Very droll. It makes a man stare his own mortality in the face. To become intimate with death in a manner you can't imagine."

"Intimate with death, huh?" Chuck glanced over towards Hilda who stood with her arms behind her back. "Is your girlfriend okay with that?"

"Pig," scowled Hilda as she marched forward and slapped Chuck hard across the face. She then stepped back beside DeShard.

"Most amusing," sneered DeShard. "In the darkness of that coffin there were times I wasn't sure I hadn't died. Sometimes I thought I was in hell already. I must confess a part of me wonders if I ever was rescued from that shallow grave. Perhaps this is my afterlife. How would I know, after all?"

Chuck leaned forwards and spoke with a secretive tone. "Let me take a swing at you, you'll soon realise you're alive when you're on the receiving end of a beat down."

DeShard chuckled. "I think not. Being unsure of the world around me gives me the courage to act with impunity. To take my pleasures when I can, to enact my will on others and to never feel guilt for my actions."

"These are all things that you did before you were put in the ground so I'm struggling to see how the experience changed you that much."

"That village in Haiti. When I'd suitably recovered, I returned there with armed men and I burnt it. I burnt it to the ground. I ordered the deaths of men. Of women. Of children." DeShard was clearly enjoying gloating over his crimes and Hilda moved towards him, putting her arm around him approvingly. The vile man chuckled. "There were no survivors. The last of the women and children, as they tried to escape, called me *'move lespri sou li.'* The demon. Fitting, don't you think?"

Chuck said nothing, clenching his jaw to hide his anger at DeShard's callous cruelty.

"Yes, that experience certainly changed me. When our business has been conducted here, I'll enjoy seeing how the experience changes you."

"I'm looking forward to digging the hole," chortled Joe wickedly.

DeShard grinned in amusement, as did Hilda. Dragos remained as always stern and passive, observing everything through a lens in impartiality.

DeShard cleared his throat. "Now, let's get down to business. Hand over the Idols."

"Screw you," Chuck snarled and spat at DeShard's feet.

DeShard rolled his eyes. "Oh, please don't make me shoot you and take them from your lifeless corpses. I am so hoping to end you in a more amusing way, and I don't want to risk bullet holes in my new statues. It'll affect the resale value." He reached out his hand and waited.

"Best do as he says," Pat reasoned, slowly taking his backpack off. "These things aren't worth dying for."

Chuck bit his lip as he contained his rage. He took a deep breath and let his anger ebb a little. "You're right," he agreed with his friend. He then turned back to DeShard. "You want them, you can have them."

"Glad to see you finally see sense," DeShard smiled.

Pat begrudgingly handed his pack over to Hilda. She took it, unzipped it and peered inside. She leered at the statue in glee before zipping the bag back up. "They were telling the truth. There is an idol in the bag."

"And the other is in yours?" DeShard asked Chuck.

"There is." He reached out and handed the bag to DeShard. DeShard took it but Chuck failed to release his grip.

"Aren't you the least bit curious how I did it?"

DeShard eyed Chuck with caution. "Did what?"

"How I found the Temple of the Sun. It's been lost for fifteen hundred years. Nobody could find it, but I did. Aren't you the least bit curious how? Or are you purely in this game for the money, like I pegged you for all along?"

DeShard smiled and slowly lowered his pistol. "Of course not. Although I appreciate these relics primarily for their monetary value, I am still a lover and student of history. I'll admit I am confounded. How did you manage to find the temple?"

"It was the natives of Yurpet."

"Yurpet?"

"A small village, very old. About a hundred and fifty miles north of here."

"I am very much aware of Yurpet," DeShard responded. "A small village community high up in the mountains. Very rural. Their history goes back over a thousand years." DeShard was clearly enjoying showing off his knowledge. "But how would they know where the Temple of the Sun stood? Legend has it that it stood where the rivers of Yuran and Yurin meet. That's a hundred and twenty miles from here. And its construction predates their settlement by half a millennium."

"It's amazing what you learn when you share a little tea with the locals," Chuck grinned. "I learnt that several hundred years ago, when the rains failed to come the Yurpet built a dam to divert the water of the River Yuran and irrigate their crops. When they did this, they unwittingly changed the flow of the river for hundreds of miles, completely changing the layout of the southern jungles. The dam in their mountain had the consequence of changing the flow of the river so much so that it now met its twin River Yurin a hundred and twenty miles further north than it had done before their dam had been built. I spent over a week poring over maps, trying to ascertain where the original rivers would have met. It wasn't easy, but I'm no quitter."

"Remarkable," said DeShard, sounding impressed. "Yours truly is a rare talent. Such a shame you had to come up against me."

"That's not my only talent," smiled Chuck.

"Any others that would interest me?"

"Just one; distraction!"

DeShard looked down in horror as he realised that while listening to Chuck's story he had allowed the adventurer to get in too close. Before he could react, Chuck yanked hard on the backpack they both held, pulling DeShard awkwardly off his feet. The ruthless man cried out in shock as Chuck deftly twisted him around, ran his hand up his arm and pulled the revolver from his grip.

DeShard's cohorts gasped in horror as Chuck wrapped an arm around his opponent's neck and squeezed whilst pushing the barrel of the pistol against the man's head.

The five mercenaries started shouting at him in Hindi, their weapons raised and pointing at his head. Hilda, Dragos and Joe had also pulled out their pistols and demanded Chuck release DeShard at once. Pat and Bill lowered their hands, uncertain what their next move should be.

"Everyone calm down," Chuck ordered with authority, all remnants of his easy-going nature gone. The shouting and the pointing of firearms continued unabated. Chuck increased the pressure of the pistol against DeShard's head. "Tell everyone to calm down," he yelled into DeShard's ear.

DeShard struggled for breath. "Everyone calm down," he managed. His team reluctantly obeyed; the panicked shouting of orders stopped. Hilda glared at Chuck with a look of utmost hatred. Dragos remained calm though determined to find the most satisfactory end to this standoff.

"Okay, that's good. That's *real* good. Everyone is calm? Nobody's going to shoot anybody?"

"You're a dead man," DeShard croaked though strained breaths.

"Just like you," Chuck retorted as he began taking walks backwards, keeping DeShard held by the throat and with the pistol pushed against his head.

"You're going nowhere," Hilda hissed, looking as if she were about to fire. Chuck made sure to keep DeShard between them. Of all the guns pointed towards him, hers was the one he deemed most likely to be fired.

Chuck increased pressure against DeShard's head once again, causing his captive to cry out in pain. "Better tell your girlfriend to relax, DeShard. I'm sure you'd hate for this to get messy. Tell her."

"Lower your guns," DeShard ordered his companions. Begrudgingly they obeyed. "Mister Tanner doesn't want to hurt anybody. Do you, Mister Tanner?"

"Me? I'm an honest to God pacifist," Chuck replied. "That's good. Drop 'em. I don't want anyone to get any further ideas."

DeShard gave a quick nod and the mercenaries and his companions placed their guns on the ground. Chuck watched them all intently, wary of any sudden movements.

"Now, I want Joe to hand Pat back his backpack."

"I can do it," snapped Hilda, raising the bag that she still held tightly.

"Nuh, uh, uh. I want Joe to do it. Joe?"

Joe looked from DeShard to Chuck to Hilda, panic in his eyes. He hated being at the centre of the action. He much preferred others doing the heavy lifting. It was Joe's cowardly nature that Chuck was counting on to stop him trying anything fancy.

"Alexandre, tell your boy to cooperate."

"Do it," DeShard grimaced.

Filled with uncertainty and fearful of how his actions would be judged later, Joe took the backpack from Hilda and held it aloft. Pat warily snatched it away and quickly pulled it back over his shoulders. "I have it," he replied.

"Bill, take mine, will you? My arm's getting kinda heavy. The last thing I want is for my arm to get tired. I'm sure you'd hate that too, wouldn't you DeShard?"

"Indubitably," DeShard muttered.

Bill followed Chuck's instructions and took the bag from his arm.

"Now get in the boat, both of you. We're getting out of here." Chuck began slowly dragging DeShard towards the river, never taking his eyes off the hostile crowd eager to fill him with lead.

Pat and Bill climbed aboard and Pat untied the boat from a tree they'd used to dock. Bill manned the motor.

"We're good to go," Pat informed Chuck.

Chuck noticed he was now backtracking through mud and knew the river and his boat was only a couple of feet away. He kept ever watchful, ensuring none of DeShard's cohorts had picked up their weapons.

"DeShard, it's been a real pleasure," Chuck said into his captive's ear before shoving the man forward and turning for the boat.

Chuck had planned on DeShard falling, caught off guard by the sudden push. He'd underestimated his foe. DeShard deftly twisted as he stepped, his hand shooting into his vest pocket and darting out with his fist closed around a combat knife.

Chuck barely had time to react as the knife swiped upwards towards his gut. Instinctually he blocked with his right arm, the one holding the pistol. The knife connected with the back of Chuck's forearm, cutting deep and drawing blood as it slashed upwards, from his elbow to his wrist. The sudden blow to his arm made Chuck's fist clench and the pistol went off. The barrel had been pointed upwards, towards DeShard's leering face. The man screamed and fell backwards as the bullet tore up through his left cheek, grazed the front of his eye and skimmed his brow as it sailed off into the sky.

DeShard fell to the ground, screaming in agony as Chuck leapt into the boat as fast as he could, all too aware the shooting was about to start.

"Go, go, go!" he yelled.

Bill didn't need telling, the boat already accelerating with maximum revs. Chuck lost his footing and fell to the deck, holding his wounded arm tight to stop the bleeding.

"You did it," Bill laughed, bordering hysterics. "You actually did it."

"We're not out of trouble yet, boys," Pat said grimly.

On the muddy bank DeShard was still crying out in pain, holding his ruined face as blood flowed through his fingers onto the muddy riverbank.

The five mercenaries ran to the bank, rifles in their hands and began firing upon the fleeing motorboat. The boat's occupants ducked as bullets whizzed around them.

"You are hurt, my love," Hilda stated as she ran and knelt beside her lover.

"Boss, are you okay?" Joe whined.

"Do I look okay, you idiot?" DeShard roared in anger. His hand reached out and grabbed Joe by his collar, pulling the flabby man towards him. Joe squealed in terror.

"What do you want to do?" asked Dragos plainly.

DeShard pushed the whimpering Joe away in disgust and Hilda helped him to his feet. He kept his left hand over the bleeding, ruined eye. "I want those statues!" he yelled at the top of his lungs.

Dragos passed the order on to the mercenaries and they ceased fire. They ran to an area of the bank where they had concealed two motorboats behind the dense foliage. Four of the mercenaries jumped into the first boat and started the engine, giving chase.

**

"Heads up, here they come!" yelled Pat as he watched the mercenary-laden boat give chase and begin closing the distance between them. He cursed and ducked as gunfire rang out and bullets zoomed past his head.

"Don't these guys ever give up?" Chuck mumbled as he lay on the deck, wrapping a bandage from the emergency medical box around his arm and fastening it with a safety pin.

"Evidently not," Pat grumbled.

"Bill, is this the fastest this tub will go?"

Bill nodded pitifully as he kept his hand on the throttle and tried to stay as low as possible. More gunshots rung out. "This doesn't look good, Chuck. Their boat is faster than ours. They're gaining on us."

Chuck checked the pistol he had snatched from DeShard. It held nine bullets, not that it mattered. Rifles beat pistols hands down in situations like this. He wracked his brain, trying to come up with a solution.

"We're coming to the split in the river," Bill informed him.

"Go left," Chuck ordered.

"Left?" whined Bill. "That's the rapids and the fall. We'll be killed."

"You got any better ideas?"

Bill said nothing and steered the boat to the left while avoiding the incoming gunfire the best he could.

"I sure hope you know what you are doing," said Pat.

Despite the chaos of the bouncing boat on the rapids jolting them left and right and the bullets flying above their heads, Chuck managed to grin. "I never do," he laughed.

Pat groaned at Chuck's light-hearted response.

"We're losing them," yelled Bill over the sound of the roaring white water.

Chuck and Pat both sat up and checked behind them. This fast part of the river had numerous sharp twists and turns, compounded by harsh jagged rocks. It took Bill all his concentration to avoid dashing the boat against these rocks. A single mistake would reduce their boat to kindling.

"They've given up," Pat remarked hopefully.

Chuck shook his head. "No, they won't give up that easily. They've just slowed down to help navigate these rocks."

"As should we," Bill moaned, ever suffering.

"If we slow down, we die. I want you to speed up, as fast as you can."

"But that's suicide," Bill complained. "Even if I avoid all these rocks, the waterfall is a short way ahead. It's over fifty feet. We won't stand a chance."

"Trust me."

Bill exchanged a nervous glance with Pat and kept the engine on full tilt. The boat's hull glanced off a submerged rock, jolting the three men suddenly.

"We're nearly at the fall," Bill said a few minutes later, the speed and turbulence of the water almost immeasurable. "What's your big idea?"

Chuck desperately scanned the shoreline. "There! Head for that, as fast as you can, otherwise the river's current will carry us past it."

Bill glanced at the small muddy patch between two harsh looking rocks. He squeezed the throttle just a little bit more.

"We're going to wreck ourselves!" Pat gasped.

"Brace for impact," Chuck shouted as the speeding boat hit the muddy bank and hurtled up out of the water and slid across the bank, skimming over several sharp rocks that left large gashes in the bottom of the hull. The boat lurched to the right as it slowed, finally coming to a stop as it hit a tree.

It took a few moments for the three men to come to terms with the fact they were still alive. Pat stood up on shaky legs. "Great, you've wrecked the boat!" he cried out in exasperation. "They're going to be able to see us from the river and follow us in. We're done for! Was this your great plan?" Pat turned to confront Chuck, only to see a very dazed Bill pull himself up. Pat's anger was instantly replaced by confusion. "Where's he gone?"

Chuck sped through the jungle, doubling back along the river as fast as he could, ignoring the branches and prickled vines that whipped at his face. He knew Pat was right. The mercenaries would be able to pull up and track them on foot. They were heavily armed so there was no way they'd be able to beat their enemies in a confrontation. Which meant Chuck and his friends only had one chance of getting out of this alive.

Listening intently over his own laboured breathing, Chuck could hear the motor of the mercenary boat. He fell flat to his stomach atop a large rock and waited. He pulled out DeShard's pistol and took aim.

The four mercenaries were avoiding the rocks as carefully as they could, their boat's forward momentum purely the will of the river, the motor propeller only being used to waver left and right.

One soldier manned the engine, the other three stood, rifles at the ready and prepared to open fire at a moment's notice.

"Sorry, boys. Looks like this is one paycheck you won't be collecting." He then pulled the pistol trigger rapidly nine times. He didn't bother saving any bullets. If his shots didn't hit home he'd be done for anyway.

One of Chuck's shots hit the man steering the boat, causing him to scream in pain and drop down out of sight. If the wound was mortal, Chuck couldn't tell. He immediately slid back behind the large rock he had lain on as the three men still standing opened fire in his direction. Chuck didn't dare move, his face in the mud and his hands over his head as a barrage of bullets struck the rock where he had been moments ago.

Realising their quarry had moved out of range, the three mercenaries suddenly realised they had more pressing issues to deal with. One of the men checked on their fallen ally. Another went to take over steering duties. That was when he noticed, with abject horror, that eight of Chuck's bullets had slammed into the engine, rendering it as nothing but scrap.

Panic stricken, the three men began yelling at each other in Hindi as they realised they were now at the mercy of the unforgiving waterway.

Chuck dared to peek his head out and watch as one of the men tried in vain to steer the boat as it slammed into jagged rocks and flipped upside down. The four men toppled into the water and struggled to stay afloat. One of them was dashed against a flat boulder, the impact silencing him and the current swiftly pulled him under.

***

"We need a plan for what to do when those soldiers catch up to us," Pat desperately urged Bill.

Bill pointed to the roaring river, as if dumbstruck by what he was seeing in the churning waters. "You mean *those* soldiers?"

Pat turned in time to see three bobbing heads and the remnants of the mercenaries' boat float past, bouncing from rock to rock.

"The hell?" Pat uttered as he traipsed across to the muddy bank and watched as the helpless men were pulled down the river, almost certainly to their doom.

"Do I ever fail you?" Chuck self-congratulated himself as he took a bow from atop a large boulder.

Pat couldn't help but smirk. "We were lucky," he retorted.

Chuck jumped down from his perch and swaggered over. "I make my own luck," he said with a wink.

Pat shook his head with an amused snort as he turned to look at Bill moving away from their own boat's wreckage.

"Chuck, you have more lives than a cat," Bill exclaimed.

"Nah, I just have the one. I'm just really attached to it," Chuck laughed.

Pat grew serious. "What's the plan now? We're lost in the middle of nowhere without any transport and there's no telling if DeShard and his cronies are out looking for us."

Bill swatted at a cloud of gnats that had begun forming around his head. "And I'm still being eaten alive by these god-forsaken bugs."

Chuck grinned. "Come on, boys. Weren't either of you in the Scouts? There's nothing like a short hike to get the blood pumping. We've still got both statues?"

Pat and Bill both lifted their packs up in the affirmative.

"Great, we'll be the heroes of the Smithsonian. Now, the nearest towns will likely be to the west of here. Let's head out." He began enthusiastically marching off through the underbrush.

"West is that way," Pat informed the wayward man.

"I knew that!" claimed Chuck, changing the direction of his march. "Of course I knew that. I was just getting my bearings."

Pat and Bill rolled eyes at each other. "Of course you did."

Bill crushed a biting gnat against his neck as he followed Chuck into the foliage. "You really think we'll be able to hike it back to civilisation?"

"Nothing to it," Chuck assured him. "Give it a couple of days, maybe three, and we'll be making friends with the locals and sampling the regional delicacies in no time."

CHAPTER 4

Harriet Palmer sat back in her chair as she finished reading the final page of Chuck's handwritten journal. She wore a buttoned-up blouse and glasses, her brunette hair tied in a professional bun.

"You finally got through it all, then?" asked Chuck, leaning back in his own chair, his feet up on his desk.

They were in the small office space rented under the company name, "Tanner and Associates Archaeological Recovery," in Queens, New York. The "associates" being Pat, Bill and Harriet herself as their secretary and editor. Chuck, Pat and Bill would go between taking jobs either through being hired by individuals to retrieve lost artefacts or undertaking their own jobs searching for treasures most of the world thought of as little more than myths and legends. It was these latter jobs Chuck relished; they were always the more challenging and infinitely more interesting.

Sitting at their own respective desks were Pat and Bill, going through paperwork that had accumulated during their absence. The three men wore work suits, Chuck and Pat's being grey, Bill's being brown. Their respective hats hung from the hatstand in the corner of the room. Harriet had kept all their affairs in order while they had been gone and spent her time curating Chuck's assorted treasures, approaching prospective buyers and typing up and editing his journals in a manner in which they could be published.

"Yes, I finished it last night, actually."

"What time?"

"Around midnight?"

Chuck grinned. "Didn't you have anything better to do?"

Harriet suppressed a smile. "Since you've been back, me and the boys have been working all hours God sends arranging for the idols to be sold to the Smithsonian. It's not easy agreeing a sum for 'priceless' artefacts that seems fair to all."

Chuck sighed. "Perhaps we should have just left them on the museum's doorstep and be done with it."

"Believe me, I pushed for that option more than once," said Pat.

Chuck smirked.

"Where have you been for the last two days? We could have done with your, shall we say, unique method of commerce."

Chuck's face went sombre. "I was taking care of a private affair."

Harriet's heart skipped a beat as she realised she'd put her foot in her mouth. "You mean Dario Angelo? How were his family when you broke the news?"

"About how you'd expect," Chuck replied flatly, betraying no emotion.

Harriet hung her head in respect for a few seconds before getting back to the point at hand. "These new journals are going to need some serious editing before I can approach a publisher with them."

"How come? Every word in there is true."

"Regardless, some of it is so fantastic people will think you made it up. You'd lose credibility. And then there's DeShard... I can't use his name. He'd be able to sue us for libel and he'd probably win."

"So that bastard really is on the scene again?"

Bill washed down a mouthful of glazed doughnut with his coffee so he could respond to Chuck's query. "He is. I've reached out to a number of sources. By all accounts DeShard is back in the relic hunting game. He's had quite a bit of success, truth be told."

"Then why hadn't we heard he was back sooner?" Chuck sighed with annoyance. "I thought for sure we'd seen the last of him in Haiti."

Pat spoke up. "All his sales have been to private buyers who wish to remain anonymous. He commands a very heavy price for his services and has a high success rate. His name is only mentioned in the highest of circles. With the money he makes procuring artefacts for the wealthy few, he manages to keep his name out of the papers and away from the public at large. He doesn't need to sell journals to make a buck."

Chuck grinned. "If he's so secretive, how did you come by this information? Have you been dining at the Country Club again?"

Pat gave a knowing smile. "I have to take my dates somewhere."

Chuck gave a short laugh. During the war Pat had been an expert in intelligence acquisition and creating networks of people to feed him information. Pat had been civilian since the war had ended, same as Bill and himself, though Pat's ability to gather intelligence never lessened.

Harriet continued. "And then you go on to mention you hiked through the jungle for four weeks before coming across a small rural village. How you state you stayed alive in the jungles of India for so long without equipment begs belief."

Chuck reached over to Bill's desk and plucked a glazed doughnut from its box. "We'd have found civilisation sooner if someone hadn't lost the compass."

"I can't be blamed for that," Bill grumbled.

"Don't put that on me," Pat added.

Chuck yawned and stretched, the movement making a myriad of small, still healing scratches suffered during their recent jaunt in India, hurt. "Okay, you win. Make whatever changes you need to. Is that it?"

"Your mail is over there," Harriet gestured to a pile of unopened letters. "I suggest you use this downtime to go through them."

"Why should I when you've already done so?" Chuck winked and Harriet averted her gaze as she blushed. "Anything interesting?"

"There's bills, invites to charity galas, exhibit opens..."

"The usual then."

"There is one interesting letter, actually. From a Mister Ambrose."

"Ambrose?" Chuck turned the name over in his mind, trying to recall where he'd heard it before.

"Yes. Arthur Ambrose."

Chuck sat upright, his expression now one of focus and interest. "Arthur Ambrose? *The* Arthur Ambrose?"

"Who's he?" Bill asked, feigning interest as he reached for another doughnut.

"Who is he?" Chuck was incredulous. "Only the most legendary explorer of the tens and twenties."

"He was pretty famous, then?"

"To put it mildly! He's the reason I became interested in relic hunting in the first place. I'd spend hours reading his journals as a kid. Apparently, he fought a mummy once."

"An Egyptian mummy?" Pat said. His words dripped with disbelief. "The man's been watching too many movies."

Chuck defended his childhood idle. "He actually published his journal containing the mummy incident before the Basil Karloff movie."

"If he used to be such a big shot, how come we've never heard of him?" asked Bill between further mouthfuls of doughnut and coffee.

"You guys weren't in the relic game until after the war. At the start of the thirties Ambrose went quiet. Then, in the forties he shifted his focus to digging up dinosaur bones."

"Dinosaur bones?" enquired Pat. "What, he got bored of tombs and temples, then?"

Chuck shrugged. "Who knows? A man's got the right to change his mind, I suppose." He turned back to Harriet. "What does Mister Ambrose want?"

"*Professor* Ambrose has requested a meeting with you at the earliest opportunity," she smiled.

Chuck's eyebrows rose as he tried to contain his excitement. "Has he now? Any idea why?"

"He doesn't say."

"What else does he say, then?"

"Only that it is urgent and he thinks it will be in your interests to indulge him."

Chuck grinned as he stroked his chin to show his intrigue. "Does he now? Well then, I best not disappoint him."

***

Harriet responded to Ambrose's letter with a phone call confirming Chuck's visit. Two days later Chuck caught a train north and after three hours stepped off the carriage and breathed in the cool, fresh air of the more rural region north of New York City. He supposed any air felt fresh compared to New York.

He caught a cab and after a forty-minute journey he was deposited by the grand iron gates at the front of the Ambrose Manor.

Chuck gave an impressed whistle to himself as he walked the long, gravel driveway, hands in his pockets. Despite it being late morning there was still a chill in the air and a slight fog hung close to the ground. Chuck took in the details of the well-manicured hedgerows, rose bushes, flower beds and lawns as his footsteps made the gravel crunch beneath him.

Ambrose Manor itself was a sight to behold. Chuck guessed it had been constructed in the mid-nineteenth century; its gothic architecture was striking, the numerous windows were nearly all arched and stone gargoyles, mottled with moss and lichen, perched high up on their vantage points.

Chuck walked up the three stone steps to the oak front door and rapped three times using the cast-iron knocker. He waited.

After a few seconds the sounds of a deadbolt being pushed aside could be heard and the heavy door opened. A tall, broad shouldered Arabian man wearing an expensive suit and sporting a well-trimmed beard answered. He regarded Chuck for a moment before smiling politely.

"You must be Mister Charles Tanner. My name is Mustaf Maaroufi. Please, come in. You are expected." He opened the door wider and stepped aside so Chuck could enter.

Chuck again whistled to express how impressed he was with the entry hallway. The ceilings were high and the walls were all wood panelling. Lining them were various photos and artefacts from adventures Ambrose had undertaken in his youth. "This is a nice place. I'm impressed."

"This house has been in Professor Ambrose's family for six generations. Please, follow me."

Chuck followed Mustaf to a reception area where he took off his hat, sat on a plush sofa and waited. Mustaf made Chuck some tea and then went to raise the professor, leaving Chuck alone for a few minutes.

As he drank the tea, welcoming its warming effects, Chuck walked around the reception room casually inspecting the various treasures and relics that hung from the walls and filled several display cases.

Some of the relics he recognised from their fame and the stories behind their recovery. Some of the artefacts were so obtuse he failed to identify the cultures they had originated from.

Half the cases were filled with the artefacts of ancient civilisations that fascinated him greatly. The other half were filled with carefully placed bones and fossils of prehistoric animals that had existed long before the rise of man. Although Chuck could appreciate the scientific value of such specimens, they hardly held his interest so he returned to the man-made relics.

"See anything you like?" asked a smooth, silky voice and Chuck turned in surprise at the person standing at the door.

The young woman, in her mid-twenties, cut quite the figure. She wore expensive designer shoes that accentuated the shape of her long legs. She wore a tight, tartan skirt that began just beneath her knees and finished at her waist, a thin white belt holding it in place. A form fitting grey turtleneck sweater graced her top half and showed off the curves of her classical hourglass figure. An elegant silver pendant hung from her neck and a delicate watch adorned her wrist.

On her right ring finger was an odd-looking ring of curious design. It appeared to be made of silver and the band was stylised as if it were a braided piece of rope. The face on it represented some mythical beast, similar to a lion, with a red and blue gemstone representing its respective eyes. It looked old, unique and out of place adorning the glamourous young woman's hand. It looked familiar to Chuck, though his mind was presently focused on other things.

Her face was a thing of beauty, lips red and puckered, skin soft and clear with a slight tan. Her eyes were green and piercing and her hair was a golden blond that hung halfway down her back. A bang rested down the right side of her face and Chuck desperately wanted to brush it back and cup her cheek.

Everything about this enigmatic young woman dripped class and wealth and Chuck forgot where he was for the moment, intoxicated by the woman's beauty and the aroma of her perfume. He swallowed dryly as she reached into her clasp handbag, pulled out a cigarette and lighter and lit it. She inhaled deeply and blew out a fine jet of smoke.

"You want one?" she asked. Her voice was seductive in its very tone and Chuck felt he could have listened to her recite the phonebook in awe.

Chuck caught his breath and regained his senses. "No thanks, I don't smoke." He placed his cup down on the coffee table.

The woman gave a disappointed shrug and walked over to one of the reception sofas. She sat, crossed her legs and took another pull on her cigarette. Every movement she made showcased her grace and class. She tapped excess ash into an ashtray on the table as she looked Chuck up and down, no doubt apprising him as he had done so her. "You're the adventurer Father keeps going on about; Charles Tanner." It wasn't a question, rather a statement of fact.

"I am," Chuck smiled, sitting on the adjoining couch. He leaned back, allowing himself to relax. "And please, call me Chuck."

"Chuck?" the woman raised a single eyebrow, as if she'd heard something funny.

"You said you are Professor Ambrose's daughter? May I ask what your name is?"

The woman inhaled on her cigarette again, taking all the time in the world to give her answer. "Candy. Candy Ambrose."

Chuck pulled a perplexed face as he considered her name. "You know, that sounds familiar to me. Do I know you?"

Again, that look of amusement. "You think you've met me and managed to forget me? You'd be the first. You probably know me by reputation. If you've bought a New York newspaper you've no doubt seen my face."

The penny dropped and Chuck smacked his fist into his palm. "That's it! You're *that* Candy Ambrose. City famous socialite. If there's a party among the city's rich and famous, you'll be there, hanging off the arm of a movie star or future captain of industry. They say you're quite the party girl."

Candy said nothing, instead enigmatically blowing out smoke. "That's what they say," she responded at last.

"I had no idea you were the daughter of Professor Ambrose."

Candy shrugged and inhaled again. "What do you mean by that?"

Chuck blinked. "Nothing. It's just, you and your father are *very* different people."

Candy eyed Chuck coldly. "And how would you know that about me? From a newspaper article?"

Chuck looked down with discomfort. "No. Apologies, I didn't mean any offence."

"I would hardly take any notice of what you read in the newspapers. I think you'll find they are often as fictional as your journals."

Before Chuck could respond Mustaf entered the room. He eyed them both before addressing Chuck. "I see you've met Professor Ambrose's daughter. Please, come with me. The Professor is ready for you."

Chuck glanced back at Candy. She had turned her head as if in boredom as she inhaled from her cigarette again. "It was a pleasure meeting you," Chuck said.

She gave a short, curt smile. Nothing more.

***

Mustaf opened the door to the study and gestured for Chuck to walk inside. He then closed the door, leaving Chuck alone with Ambrose, who sat at a grand, oak desk. The room was filled with all manner of books, artefacts, globes, maps and obscure treasures, alongside artist renditions of prehistoric animals and collections of fossils. The potential for what Chuck could find in this single room made his pulse quicken with excitement. On the desk, given pride of place was the skull of a dinosaur, completely intact. Chuck didn't know much about dinosaurs, though the sharp teeth lining the skull's jaws told him it hadn't been vegetarian.

Ambrose, in a robe, rose to his feet and spread his arms welcomingly as he grinned. He looked old and frail, a far cry from the dashing hero Chuck remembered from his childhood.

"Mister Tanner, welcome, welcome," Ambrose smiled as he walked around his desk and clasped Chuck's hand. The two men firmly shook hands and Chuck was pleasantly surprised to find Ambrose's handshake stronger than he would have guessed. "I'm so grateful that you made the trip. How was your journey?" The older man walked back to his chair behind his desk and gestured Chuck to sit on the chair opposite.

"The journey was fine, and please, call me Chuck. I must admit I was intrigued by your letter. You were something of a childhood hero of mine. I read all your journals. They're what led me into this line of work."

Ambrose kept grinning. "Good to know I inspired you. I've kept up with your career also. You've made some astounding discoveries."

Chuck was flattered that his old hero was aware of him. "Like I said, you inspired me. Can I ask you something, though?" he leaned in with a conspiring tone. "Did you really once fight a mummy?"

Ambrose chuckled as memories he hadn't dwelled on for years resurfaced in his mind. He shrugged. "That's what the journals say," he smiled.

"I knew it!" Chuck snapped his fingers, taking Ambrose's lack of denial as proof the event had occurred.

Ambrose leaned back in his chair. "Tell me, do you still follow my career, Chuck?"

Chuck looked down at his hands. "Honestly, not for a long while now. What with the war and all, I lost track of a lot of things."

"You fought?"

"I was still seventeen when Pearl Harbour attacked. Two months later, on my eighteenth birthday I enlisted and fought in the Pacific Conflict."

Ambrose ruefully shook his head. "That war saw the worst that humanity has to offer. I wish it had been the last, but Korea has happened since. One day I pray we shall learn from our mistakes and stop repeating history. And to stop repeating the past, we must learn from it. That's why I followed the path I did. I was too young to fight in World War One, though I remember its horror all too well. I remember people only slightly older than myself returning with the gravest of injuries. That's if they returned at all…"

The two sat in silence for a while before Ambrose stood and offered Chuck a drink. Chuck agreed and Ambrose pulled a bottle of malt whiskey and two glasses from a desk drawer and poured their drinks. He had a mischievous glint in his eye as he sipped his whiskey. "Mustaf doesn't approve of my drinking. He says it's not good for me."

"Who wants to live forever?" Chuck sipped his own drink.

"Precisely," Ambrose chuckled.

Chuck placed his glass on the oak desk. "What made you shift interest from archaeology to palaeontology?"

Ambrose considered his answer carefully. "There are experiences that men endure that change the course of their lives forever. I'm sure you understand this, having fought against your fellow man."

"I do," Chuck replied.

"I was undertaking a very challenging expedition that was far more demanding than anything I had ever experienced before. I was searching for an artefact of such legendary status that people have long since dismissed it as mere fantasy. I was searching for the Stone of Qualbec."

"The Stone of Qualbec?" Chuck repeated the professor in disbelief.

"You've heard of it?"

"I have."

"Tell me what you know."

"Qualbec was an ancient king of the Incas who allegedly descended from the sky, a king in his own right from times immemorial. He resided in the lost city of Vincabamba and brought with him a piece of the underworld, a stone with power over death. All those in its influence were said to gain the power of immortality and were immune to hunger and disease."

"So the legend tells," Ambrose smiled.

"But it's a myth. Fantasy. It isn't real. Scores of adventurers have searched for Vincabamba and none have returned with a shred of evidence as to its existence."

"I thought you of all people would appreciate that in our line of work the lines between reality and fantasy often blur."

"I believe there are many secrets of the ancient world hidden from us. I don't believe in fairytales."

Ambrose steepled his fingers. "I found it. Vincabamba. I know where it is."

Chuck took a moment to collect his thoughts, digesting what it was Ambrose was telling him. "You found Vincabamba?"

"I did."

"And the Stone of Qualbec? You found that too?"

Ambrose's smile faded. "That, I did not find."

"It isn't real?"

"I believe that it is, but Vincabamba holds many dangers. Dangers that I could not overcome. Dangers that left me the sole survivor of my party."

"What dangers? Traps?"

"Not the ancient boobytraps, though I assure you that there are plenty of those."

"Then what?"

"Vincabamba is more than just an ancient Incan city. It is, in actuality, a sprawling land, isolated on all sides by vast mountain ranges. This isolation has allowed a wholly unique ecosystem to thrive. An ecosystem filled with savage creatures the like of which cannot be found anywhere else in the world."

Chuck glanced down at the prehistoric skull on Ambrose's desk. "You mean dinosaurs?"

"I can see you are a very perceptive man, Mister Tanner. Yes, the terrible lizards still roam our Earth and Vincabamba is where they lurk."

"That's ridiculous. There's no way…"

"You've seen things during your own adventures, have you not? Things the deans and lecturers of academia would call preposterous?"

Chuck couldn't deny there was truth in that statement. He'd witnessed many things that science couldn't or wouldn't accept. "Why have you brought me here, Professor Ambrose? Cut to the chase."

"I want you to lead an expedition back to Vincabamba. To finish what I started. To discover the resting place of the Stone of Qualbec and bring it back to civilisation so that the whole world may marvel at it."

Chuck was unsure. "This sounds like quite a stretch."

"Imagine if I am proven correct. Imagine if you were the man to finally recover this lost treasure for mankind. Imagine if even half the powers attributed to it are true."

Chuck stroked his chin. "You'll be paying me for this?"

"I will. All expenses and a generous completion fee."

"And what's the catch?"

"Catch?"

"There's always a catch. What's in this for you?"

Ambrose took a sip of his whiskey, savoured it before swallowing. "I'll be coming with you."

"No way, it's too dangerous. You've said yourself how dangerous this place is. I can't be worrying about an old man."

"I'm not as fragile as I look, I assure you. And I'll be bringing along my own team of people."

"I like to keep my expeditions small, usually only me and my two men."

"Believe me, the more people we bring the safer we'll be."

Chuck crossed his arms, liking the deal less and less by the minute. "Who are these people?"

"I have four people in mind to join us. Associates of mine."

"You don't want to name them?"

"You'll meet them when the expedition is under way. I'm sure you can understand why I want to keep things as secret as possible. We'll be traveling by boat. It's too easy for us to be tracked if we use air travel. I'm also liaising with a man at our destination. A local. He's assembled a team of ten strong men, locals who will travel with us as guides and labourers."

"I don't like it. It's too many people." Chuck shook his head. "And you won't even tell me where we're heading?"

"The walls have ears, Mister Tanner. A great many people would kill to know where this treasure is hidden. I shan't divulge any further information until our voyage is under way. This is a once in a lifetime offer, Mister Tanner. I assure you, you won't regret it."

Chuck couldn't dispel his uneasy feeling, though the thoughts of him being the man to find the Stone of Qualbec made his mouth water. "Why now? Why after all this time do you want to return to Vincabamba? There's more to this than you're letting on."

Ambrose hesitated, his face tight. He stood, arms behind his back as he pensively walked to his window and peered out as he contemplated Chuck's query. His shoulders sagged a little. "You are correct, of course. There is something I've been hiding from you. Something I've been loath to admit, even to myself. I mentioned that when I was last in Vincabamba, back in nineteen-thirty, I was the sole surviving member of the expedition. That my colleagues all died. This is untrue. My dear friend Austin Kiplard and his wife, Iris, did not die." Ambrose fell silent.

"Then what did happen to them?" Chuck pressed.

Ambrose turned and Chuck could see the tears forming in his eyes. "I left them there."

"You *left* them there?"

Ambrose returned to his chair and sat as tears began making their way down his cheeks. He suddenly looked far older and frailer than he had previously appeared. When he spoke, his voice trembled. "We were attacked... by a prehistoric monster. It was so vicious, so singular in its intent to kill us all. We were separated whilst running through the jungle. The dinosaur ran me down. Would have killed me. Austin distracted it. He saved my life, ran into the jungle towards his wife with the prehistoric horror hot on his heels. I could hear him calling out for me. Pleading for my aid." Ambrose's face darkened, as if the man was overcome by an inner rage. "I ran. I abandoned him like a coward, and I ran so fast. I didn't look back. I left that wretched valley and I abandoned my best friend to die." Ambrose looked down and his tears dripped upon his desk. He said nothing, unable to bare his shame.

Chuck remained quiet for a long time, re-evaluating what he thought of his childhood hero and waiting for the professor to break the silence. When he realised the old man hadn't the strength, he spoke gently. "You think this is a rescue mission?"

Ambrose remained silent, unable to meet Chuck's gaze.

"That was a long time ago, Ambrose. In all likelihood your friend and his wife died on that day. I'm not saying that what you did was right. It wasn't, and I can see you know that. But I'm not going on a suicide mission just because you have a guilty conscience."

Ambrose inhaled deeply and tried to control his emotions the best he could. He finally looked up straight into Chuck's eyes. "I've never told anybody that story. Never. I've admitted to you what my motivations are for this expedition, but I assure you they are my own. Regardless of why I wish to return to that valley, the fact remains. The Stone of Qualbec, possibly the greatest discovery a man such as yourself could ever find, is located in Vincabamba and I am offering it to you because I believe you are the man to succeed where I failed so long ago. Think hard before you tell me your decision."

Chuck took another sip of his whiskey. Then another, before finally downing the whole thing. He studied the glass as he weighed up the opportunity before him. Ambrose didn't press him, instead waiting patiently and studying every micro expression on Chuck's face.

"Okay," Chuck said at last. "I'll lead your expedition, but I have three caveats."

Ambrose's features softened and he relaxed back into his chair. "Name them."

"One, I want a third of the payment up front. Second, I want to bring in two additional men of my own, outside of my usual team, and three, I want me and my boys to get the public recognition we deserve when we bring that stone back."

A smile played on Ambrose's lips. "Done."

Chuck grinned and offered his hand. Ambrose took it and the two men shook. "Then you've got yourself a deal."

CHAPTER 5

After shaking hands, Chuck and Ambrose negotiated the exact terms of the payment and an hour later Chuck left and caught the train back to Queen's. He explained how the discussion had gone to Harriet, Bill and Pat who listened to every word with vested interest. Pat agreed to the expedition immediately, though Bill took more persuading. He'd still not fully recovered from India and felt the whole affair was too good to be true. Chuck offered to buy him a steak dinner to celebrate and Bill finally relented.

Harriet would tend to their responsibilities and keep the business running while they were gone, as well as type up and edit Chuck's latest journals.

The next day they received a telegram from Ambrose informing them of their intended departure at the New York docks in two weeks' time. Chuck queried the need to use a boat rather than simply flying and Ambrose's answer was simple - discretion. It would be harder to keep the news of their expedition from enquiring minds if they travelled by plane and Ambrose kept secrecy at the forefront of his mind. The Stone of Qualbec was too valuable not to draw attention from other would-be treasure hunters.

Now with a set deadline, Chuck set to work reaching out and convincing the two additional men he wanted for the job.

Chuck met the men in a dive bar on the East Side and by the time he arrived both men had already downed several bottles of beer. He had served with them during the war, alongside Bill and Pat, and there was no one he trusted more with his life.

Dillon Carver from Harlem was something of an opportunist. He'd earned the nickname "The Black Viper" in the army boxing league due to his skin colour and the speed at which he struck his opponents. He'd liked the nickname so much he'd had it tattooed onto his left, solid, muscular arm. After the war he returned to the sport, mainly in the backrooms of bars like the one they currently occupied. Rumour had it that Dillon sometimes worked as a debt collector for unsavoury people and Chuck believed it. When he wanted, Dillon's imposing frame and booming voice could intimidate anyone. Chuck knew the real Dillon, though. The man was as gentle as they came when it came to people he liked and Chuck supposed everyone had to make their daily bread somehow, so he never questioned Dillon on the rumours. When he saw Chuck enter the bar Dillon immediately beamed his big, toothy grin and raised a bottle.

Beside him was Grant Baxter, a slim though toned man from somewhere called Eton in England. His features were good looking, though his face was long and his skin was pasty. Not that he ever had any trouble with the ladies, far from it. As soon as most women heard his accent they were putty in his hands. He'd even stolen a broad or two from Chuck back in the day. He had a small, well-kept moustache and eyes that glinted with intelligence. Chuck had no idea how Grant made his money and the topic had never come up in conversation.

Grant's English sensibilities made him feel that any conversation regarding money was in poor taste. Due to his upper-class accent and mannerisms, Chuck couldn't rule out the possibility that Grant was living off an inheritance from back home. During the war Grant had been the most skilled sniper and rifleman Chuck had ever seen. Every time he pulled the trigger in combat, a man had died. He had earned the respect of everyone in his unit time and again and always kept his cool, as if he were able to compartmentalise his emotions perfectly as soon as the crap hit the fan.

After the war the five men, Chuck, Pat, Bill, Grant and Dillon, had split into two. Grant and Dillon had worked with Chuck several times but were always adamant they didn't want to work for him. Chuck could respect that, every man had to walk his own path in the game of life.

After a few more beers and a catchup, Chuck laid Ambrose's deal on the table, though he changed the details regarding "dinosaurs" and "a magical stone" to "hostile wildlife" and "valuable artefact." The two men hadn't seen the kind of things the boys at *Tanner and Associates Archaeological Recovery* had seen and weren't so open-minded.

Grant was intrigued but apprehensive, asking a myriad of questions. Dillon had no such qualms and as soon as he learned of the generous paycheque, he agreed. Grant relented and accepted the proposal shorty after. The two men were like brothers and Chuck knew that if he could get Dillon to agree, Grant would undoubtedly follow.

The three men continued drinking until closing, when Chuck staggered to the exit in a drunken daze. Grant and Dillon knew the bar manager and were being invited to drink in the backroom. Three girls had joined their table and were currently onto their third bottle of wine.

"Hey, Chuck, wanna arm-wrestle before you go?" Dillon laughed, his arm around one of the girls.

"No thanks, I need to use my arm to hail a cab. I'll be in touch, gentlemen." Chuck then stumbled out into the night and made his way back home.

***

Two weeks passed and all preparations were made. The five men met up in the early hours of a Thursday morning, suitcases in hand and their coats buttoned up against the harsh cold. The sun wouldn't rise for another hour and a half and a thick mist rolled in off the black waters.

"Did Chuck mention that he met Candy Ambrose and didn't even recognise her?" Pat laughed with Grant and Dillon. Both men turned and looked at Chuck in disbelief.

"No way," roared Dillon, in fits of laughter.

"She's not your type?" mocked Grant.

"Unlike you guys, I don't spend all my time reading the gossip columns like a bunch of women," Chuck retorted.

"No, you just skip right to the funnies," Grant shot back in an instant.

Chuck decided to change the subject. Grant's wit was as sharp as his aim. "This is the boat they said. Professor Ambrose and his men should be here any minute."

Sitting in the water beside them was a small vessel named 'The Cylopea.' It looked as if it had seen better days and was certainly no luxury yacht. Much of the paint on its dark, rusted hull was flaking off. In the eery lights and the mist it appeared like a ghost ship. The ship had a crew of eight and the captain, an old seadog by the name of Edgington, refused to let them come aboard until Ambrose showed up.

"He better turn up soon," Bill shivered, his teeth clattering together. "I'm freezing. I say we give them five more minutes."

"They'll be here. Relax," Chuck asserted.

As if on cue two cars turned onto the docks, bathing the five men in their headlights. "Better late then never," Pat grumbled as he shielded his eyes.

The car pulled to a stop beside them and after a moment the back door opened and the occupants climbed out. First to step out was Mustaf, who quickly helped Ambrose himself out of the vehicle.

"He's a big fella," grinned Dillon. "I wonder if he boxes."

Next was a small, unimposing man with short brown hair and round glasses. After him was a taller, older man with combed white hair and a stern look on his face.

Chuck walked over and greeted the professor. "Good to see you again, Ambrose."

"Likewise, my boy. Likewise."

Chuck introduced Ambrose to his team before turning to the two new men the professor had brought along. "Who are your men?" They both looked like academics, more used to the lecture halls of universities than the hostile realities of the jungle. He hoped they would be able to cope with what was ahead.

Ambrose indicated to the older man first. "Mister Tanner, I would like you to meet my good friend Stanley Crowley. A leading mind in the field of palaeontology. No matter what we encounter in Vincabamba, I trust Professor Crowley's expertise in ancient animals to serve us well."

"Pleased to meet you," said Chuck, shaking Crowley's hand.

"This young man is Nathaniel Childs. He's an expert journalist, archiver and photographer. He'll be helping me keep a record of everything we encounter out in the valley."

"Pleased to meet you," Nathaniel stuttered, betraying his nervous demeanour. Chuck returned the greeting.

"Have you got all the bags from the trunk?" Ambrose called over to Mustaf. He nodded and closed the trunk back up before carrying the suitcases over to the waiting boat. Captain Edgington was descending the gangplank towards the group of men and two idling cars.

"I thought you said you were bringing four additional men," Chuck recalled. "You've only brought three."

Ambrose sighed. "I'm afraid my last team member is still idling in the back of the car. She's done nothing except complain about the cold and being up so early since we set off."

"She?"

Ambrose walked back over to the car he and Mustaf had travelled in and leaned inside. "Come along, my dear. We're all waiting on you."

Chuck felt his heart speed up as a shapely leg stepped out of the car. He turned to his assembled team, each of them gawping with their mouths hung open like drooling schoolboys.

"I'm coming, I'm just buttoning up my coat," said the silky voice of Candy Ambrose as she emerged from the car. Her eyes passed between each of the men staring at her, clearly used to drawing such a reaction from members of the opposite sex. Her eyes fell on Chuck and she gave a slight nod. "Mister Tanner, nice to meet you again."

Chuck was at a loss for words and watched, his mouth hanging open like the others as Mustaf escorted Candy aboard the boat. Captain Edgington eagerly greeted her as she passed him.

Chuck's team began murmuring to themselves and quietly laughing with each other. Chuck found the turn of events no laughing matter and turned angrily to Ambrose.

"What's the big idea, Ambrose? There's no way your daughter can join us on this trip."

"Mister Tanner, why in heaven not?" Ambrose asked.

"Why not? Look at her. We need people with skills and knowhow. Not pampered princesses whose idea of hardship is asking a man to get her another drink from the bar."

Ambrose became stern. "Mister Tanner, I assure you that my daughter is more capable than you realise. She is a well-trained medic and botanist. I told you I had my team and you accepted. Don't worry, she isn't your responsibility, she's mine and her place on the expedition is non-negotiable."

Chuck bit his tongue and looked back to the boat. Candy was standing on the deck, silhouetted in the dock lights and looking like a ghostly apparition in the fog. Already Grant, Pat and Dillon were by her side making small talk. He turned back to Ambrose. "Fine, but I want it noted that I don't like it one bit." He then turned and marched towards the gangplank. Before he could ascend to the boat he was met by Captain Edgington.

"Captain, I trust you are well and ready to embark," smiled Ambrose, stepping up beside Chuck.

The old captain puffed on his pipe. "Eh, as ready as I'll ever be, I suppose. Can't say I approve of a woman being on board. It's bad luck."

Chuck gave Ambrose a look that said, *"I told you so!"*

"Come now, don't tell me you are superstitious, dear fellow," Ambrose chortled.

Edgington's expression remained unchanged. "There's been rum happenings afoot. Bad luck is the last thing we need."

"Rum happenings? Like what?" Chuck asked.

"People have been creepin' onto the boats in the dead of night."

"Mere thieves and chancers, I am sure," Ambrose replied.

"It's more than that. They don't take nothing. Just creep about."

Chuck's bad feeling became worse. "Have they been aboard your boat?"

"Aye. Didn't take nothin' though. At least, not that I can figure. Made a damn mess of the bridge."

"Mindless vandals," Ambrose grumbled.

"Aye." The captain began walking back up the gangplank.

"This could be a problem," Chuck warned.

"You mean the vandals?"

Chuck became exasperated by Ambrose's inability to see the obvious. "They weren't vandals. They were spies."

"Spies? Sent by who? And for what purpose?"

"I don't know who sent them but think about it for a moment. This voyage has been kept secret. Hell, even I don't know where we're heading. You don't think it's a bit of a coincidence that men have broken aboard this boat and searched the bridge, where the charter book is? This boat has been chartered for our destination for two weeks. Someone wanted to know where we were heading. This could complicate matters greatly."

Ambrose could see what Chuck meant. His face hardened. "But who would have sent them? How could anyone know about this boat?"

"I've known for nearly two weeks. As have my team."

"As have mine," Ambrose admitted grimly.

"I trust my men with my life. Do you trust yours?"

"Implicitly."

"Then we have an even bigger problem than I feared, because someone we trust may be working against us."

Ambrose gave a nod. "Then we must put our trust in ourselves all the more."

"Agreed."

"If what you say is true, then my hiring of a boat to keep our mission secret was all for naught," Ambrose lamented before making his way up the gangplank to the boat. He paused and turned back to Chuck. "Bolivia," he stated.

"Excuse me?"

"That's where we are heading. Vincabamba is in Bolivia."

Chuck considered this for a moment before cracking a smile. "At least it'll be warmer than here."

CHAPTER 6

Alexandre DeShard watched from his upper window as his latest potential client exited his own front door and walked away down the driveway. His fists were balled so tight his knuckles were white and his jaw clenched tight. He watched as the potential client took a left and walked off down the road. He then walked back to his mahogany desk and sat, still seething with anger. He opened a drawer, pulled out a white hand mirror and studied his visage.

The scar left from the bullet back in India was deep and wide. It started midway up his left cheek and didn't end until it met his dark hairline. The only thing breaking the vicious line scorched into his face was the black material of his eye patch. His eye had been unsavable and DeShard was now partially blind. He considered this the ultimate insult from that fool, Chuck Tanner and the desire for revenge burnt deep. Every time DeShard saw his reflection his anger for the man grew, the scar and eyepatch serving as permanent reminders of DeShard's own failure.

Tentatively he reached up to the eyepatch and lifted it to study his ruined eye. He grimaced, looking at the white and red pulp that remained. It looked ugly and he felt a deep loathing for himself.

There was a knock on the door to DeShard's study and he quickly flicked the eyepatch back into place before returning the mirror to its drawer. "Come in," he commanded.

The door opened and Hilda Klein strode in, her face locked in a permanent scowl, her ugly personality detracting from her natural beauty. "How did it go with the client?" she asked bluntly.

"Mister Beckett has decided he no longer requires my services."

Hilda couldn't disguise her surprise. "Why is this?"

DeShard felt his fury grow. "Why? Why?" he bellowed, standing and grabbing for a newspaper he had folded on his desk. He marched over to Hilda, forcing her to take a step back in alarm and shoved the newspaper at her. "This is why."

Hilda unfolded the newspaper and read the front page. It read, "LOST GOLDEN IDOLS OF YURAN AND YURIN AQUIRED BY SMITHSONIAN: A VICTORY FOR EARNEST HISTORIANS EVERYWHERE."

"I'm a failure. A laughingstock! All because of that fool, Tanner!"

"This article doesn't mention you," Hilda pointed out.

DeShard's anger grew even more as he flailed his arms in outrage. "It doesn't need to mention me! It mentions the idols, that's enough. These old fools gossip like a bunch of old women! My employer would have told others that he'd hired me to find the idols for him. God knows how much they like to gloat in the reading rooms, bars and steam rooms of private establishments. The idols turning up in the museum is proof enough that I failed my employer. Faith has been lost, my reputation is in tatters."

"It was only one job," Hilda replied.

DeShard lashed out, grabbing Hilda by the throat with a single, strong hand and squeezing. Her body went rigid as she dropped the newspaper and tried to lessen his grip as she struggled to breathe.

DeShard pulled Hilda towards him, so close her face was barely more than an inch from his. He reached up with his other hand and lifted his eyepatch. "And this is only one eye. Are you saying I shouldn't be bitter about this, also?"

"Please... hurting me..." Hilda gasped, her face turning red as her struggles began to grow weaker. DeShard enjoyed seeing her struggle for breath, enjoyed knowing her life was in his hands. If he chose, he could apply just a little more pressure and Hilda's life would be snuffed out with no more effort than it took to blow out a candle.

"Ahem, Mister DeShard, sir," came the deep voice of Grigore Dragos from the doorway. "Mister Buchannon and his man, Mister Daniels, are downstairs waiting."

DeShard stared at Dragos, considering what he had said. He then turned his eyes back to the struggling Hilda and released his grip. She fell to her knees, holding her throat and taking deep, desperate breaths. Her face had turned beetroot red and her eyes watered. She looked up at DeShard with hatred and feelings of betrayal. As she gasped for breath her chest heaved in a way that made DeShard smile. "Make him wait a further fifteen minutes. Then show him up."

***

The study door opened fifteen minutes later and Dragos showed in Jeffery Buchannon, a tall, skinny, older gentleman and George Daniels, his balding, overweight manservant. He smiled at them as they entered, Dragos closing the door behind them and leaving the three men alone.

DeShard had used the fifteen minutes to compose himself and swallow his anger and now he felt in control of his emotions again. He smirked in amusement as the two men realised there was only one chair available for them to sit. He knew it would be Buchannon who would sit in it, though the dynamics of the two visitors' relationship with each other would be determined by the interaction that would follow.

"You haven't another chair by any chance, have you, old boy? For old George, here?" Buchannon asked.

"Afraid not," DeShard smiled; it was an obvious lie.

Buchannon blinked. "I see." He turned apologetically to Daniels. "I'm sorry, old boy. Do you mind if I sit?"

Daniels eyed DeShard, unimpressed. "Of course not, sir."

Buchannon gave an awkward smile and sat, visibly uncomfortable with the situation.

DeShard was most amused by this interaction. It seemed that Buchannon was every bit as weak and feckless as he had believed him to be from their previous meetings at Buchannon's home. His relationship with Daniels appeared to be one of friends, rather than employer and employee. DeShard hated when people treated their underlings as equals and couldn't understand why anyone would sink so low.

"Mister Buchannon, thank you for coming today." DeShard spoke in a way to deliberately cut Daniels out of the conversation. He couldn't care less what the paunchy man thought of their arrangement.

Buchannon was an avid collector of rare and exotic trinkets from past empires, and it was well known that Professor Ambrose had in his private collection several items Buchannon was more than eager to get his hands on. Buchannon's animosity for Ambrose only grew when Ambrose outbid him on a three-thousand year old vase from the Shang Dynasty. There were only six such vases known to exist and Buchannon already had five of them. He'd desperately wanted to finish his collection and had forever been bitter that Ambrose had ended that dream, despite the massive sums Buchannon offered to try and buy it from him.

It was that aspect of Buchannon that had drawn DeShard's attention. Buchannon's wealth was completely inherited, the man had never worked a day in his life and had no idea of the value of a dollar. He spent his days frequenting dens of vice, gambling and drinking away his life and gaining a reputation for acting like a spoiled, petulant child when he didn't get his own way. He was the perfect man for DeShard to approach.

It seemed Daniels was Buchannon's only long-term acquaintance and, much to DeShard's chagrin, was more level-headed than his employer.

"Thank you for inviting me. Have things progressed smoothly?" Buchannon asked.

"They have. My sources have confirmed that the boat Ambrose has hired is chartered for a port city in northern Chile, Arica. Reaching out to men in the region, I believe that I have located the party of men who are going to act as guides and labourers for Ambrose's expedition."

Buchannon grinned. "That's fantastic, DeShard. How in heavens did you do it?"

DeShard gave a sly smile. "I have my means."

"I bet you do," said Daniels, gruffly. DeShard ignored him.

"George, old boy. Alexandre here is our friend and has provided us with an amazing opportunity. Please show some manners."

"Don't worry about it," DeShard chuckled.

"When does Ambrose's boat set sail? Odd he didn't just book a flight."

"No doubt Ambrose wishes to keep his latest expedition as secret as he possibly can. As for when his boat leaves, it already has." DeShard checked his watch. "Some four hours ago."

Buchannon became alarmed. "Then what are we waiting for? We must hurry after them. Beat them to this great treasure. This 'Stone of Quebec'."

"It's Stone of 'Qualbec', and please, don't panic. With your generous funding I'll be able to charter a private plane to depart in three days. We'll be in Arica long before Ambrose."

"Not a problem. Money is no object. I want that stone, to stick it to that old man once and for all. I'll get the last laugh yet."

DeShard's smile widened. "I'm sure you will. And I am grateful to be the one to make this happen for you. Regarding money, I must say your attitude is refreshing. There are too many skinflints out there, these days. I suspect most of New York's favoured sons are more paupers than princes."

"I can assure you that I am not one of those. I can't take it with me, and all that."

"Quite right. Considering information from Arica, it appears that the guide Ambrose has employed has assembled a team of ten strong men. I suggest we beat him at his own game and employ twenty."

"Twenty?" Buchannon repeated, stroking his chin. "You really think we need such a large party?"

"Remember, we have no idea where Ambrose is heading on to once he reaches Chile. We should be prepared for every eventuality. Even violence."

Buchannon went a shade whiter than he already was. "Violence, you say?"

DeShard gave what he hoped was a reassuring laugh and leaned back in his chair. "Do not fear, that potentiality is exactly why I plan to employ professional soldiers. If ever there is any danger, you will be well protected from it."

DeShard's promise seemed to calm the older man down. He gave a smile. "That's a relief."

Daniels leaned in towards Buchannon. "Are you sure this is worth the effort?"

DeShard shot a venomous glare at the underling, his nostrils flaring in rage. He breathed in deeply, keeping himself composed and professional. "Maybe you should reconsider this expedition," he bluffed. "We can let Ambrose have this artefact for his collection. Perhaps the curiosity shops of New York are better suited to your sensibilities."

"Nonsense," Buchannon snapped before reaching into his pocket and pulling out his chequebook. "I'm not going to let this chance at beating that old codger at his own game go past me. You tell me what numbers I need to write, Mister DeShard. I trust you will get everything in order for our great adventure to begin."

DeShard relaxed and smiled. "I assure you, Mr Buchannon, this will be an adventure you won't forget."

***

The short, rotund, wicked looking man raking leaves from the front lawn paused and gave Buchannon and Daniels the evil eye as they walked past him, heading for the front gate.

"You really embarrassed me in there, George old boy," Buchannon said in short manner.

Daniels was taken aback. "Embarrassed you? How, sir?"

"Questioning whether this jaunt is the right thing to do. Of course it is! I want that stone, man. I want to rub it in that senile old fool Ambrose's face."

Daniels shrugged. "It just seems like a lot of effort to spite someone you only have a passing acquaintance with."

"You seem to have forgotten about how he humiliated me at that auction. That vase should have been in my collection."

"You mean, your collection which is currently packed up in storage?"

"What I chose to do with my belongings is none of your concern, George old boy. Mister DeShard has gone to a lot of trouble to give me this opportunity and I am not one to look a gift-horse in the mouth."

"What opportunity?" scoffed Daniels. "The opportunity to fully fund his expedition?"

Buchannon stopped walking and jabbed a finger into Daniels's chest. "Don't you take that tone with me."

Daniels licked his lips as he tried to formulate his argument. "Sorry, sir. It's these people. I don't trust them. I don't want them taking advantage of you, is all."

Buchannon's face warmed. "You don't need to trust them, George old boy. Trust me." When Daniels still looked undecided, Buchannon slapped his arm with enthusiasm. "Come on, old boy. It'll be an adventure. Something we've sorely been lacking lately. It'll be one for the photo album. We'll top up our tans, dance with some local girls. Have fun! What do you say? You know I'll be lost on my first day there without you."

Daniels couldn't help but grin. "You probably wouldn't be able to get to the airport on time without me."

Buchannon laughed. "Good man, you're probably right! So, you'll come?"

"I will," Daniels laughed.

Buchannon embraced his friend. "Good man, good man. Now let's get home to pack, then a drink to bid New York a temporary farewell."

"Okay, okay. You win. But not too much to drink. We'll need to set some affairs in order tomorrow."

"You see?" Buchannon beamed. "What would I do without you?"

***

From his study window DeShard watched as Buchannon and Daniels embraced before walking off, laughing as they went. His eyes then went to Joe Hill. Joe was muttering angrily to himself as he continued doing a poor job of raking the lawn of leaves in the wind.

The door knocked and then Hilda entered, now sporting a loose-fitting designer scarf to hide the bruises on her neck. "How did it go?" she said. She had no fear, wearing the same, demanding scowl she always did as if the incident earlier had never happened. DeShard liked that about her and was well aware that Hilda could give as good as she got, if ever she felt the proclivity to do so. DeShard decided he'd lock his bedroom door tonight, in case Hilda gained a taste for revenge later on.

"It went as well as I could have hoped for. I have the money. Twice as much as we'll spend on this expedition."

Hilda's face remained unreadable behind its mask of aggressiveness. "That is good."

DeShard allowed himself to smile. "That Buchannon really is as foolish as people say he is. If he thinks I'll let him take possession of the Stone of Qualbec, he's certifiable. I'll be taking that Stone, and I'll enjoy stepping over Tanner's dead body to get it."

"Tell me," asked Hilda. "What is more important to you? Retrieving the Stone of Qualbec or killing Chuck Tanner?"

"The Stone of Qualbec could well be the greatest, most mysterious artefact of all time. On the other hand, Mister Tanner humiliated me and took my eye. I see no reasons why either motivation should be exclusive."

"And Buchannon?"

"The South American wilderness is a dangerous place. There are lots of ways an untrained, unprepared man like that can get himself killed."

Hilda's eyes widened and she allowed herself a wicked smile as the thought of Buchannon's betrayal and death excited her. "Let me do it. I know you want to kill Tanner for what he did to you, but please, let me kill Buchannon and his manservant."

"Why would you ask this? Have you a vendetta against our good friend, Mister Buchannon?"

"No vendetta. I never even knew of the man until you found him a few days ago."

"Then why?"

Hilda's smile became ever more sly. "Everyone else will be having fun. I want some fun, too."

DeShard smirked. "My love, sometimes your sadistic temperament scares even me. Yes, you may kill Buchannon, but only when I have the Stone in my hands. I'd hate for our benefactor to come to an untimely end if we could still make use of him."

CHAPTER 7

Professor Ambrose's chartered boat, the Cyclopea, headed south from New York and followed the coastline of the United States before continuing south past Cuba and onwards into the Caribbean Sea.

Life on board the Cyclopea passed pleasantly. Chuck's men got on well with Captain Edgington and his crew, especially when they learnt the captain never sailed anywhere without copious amounts of alcohol in his stocks and a deck of cards. Every night music and laughter filled the messdeck. Grant had found an accordion aboard and played it like a professional, much to the surprise of everyone, making him a firm favourite amongst the crew. Dillon was also especially popular as he constantly challenged others to arm wrestling matches, the boxer's competitive edge showing through. A crewman even stitched a special shirt for Dillon with the name "Black Viper" across the back. Dillon loved it and took to wearing it at all times. Everyone vied for an arm-wrestling match between Dillon and Mustaf, something the Arab man was vehemently against.

The comradery between the men was fortified by the fact that all bar two of Edgington's men had served in the war, cueing tales of heroics and adventures as well as more sombre stories of some of the tragedies they had witnessed and the friends they had lost.

Ambrose's party, although friendly enough, seemed to keep more to themselves for the most part, with the exception of one. Candy Ambrose became a firm favourite amongst the men, for obvious reasons, and found herself the life and soul of the party every night. Many of the war stories told were instantly outdone by another as the men vied for her attention. Candy herself encouraged this behaviour, dancing, singing and indulging in the drink. Her presence irked Chuck more than he would have liked, feeling she was a dangerous distraction. The crew weren't the most orderly of fellows and Chuck became concerned that there were accidents waiting to happen. He had to give it to Edgington, however. As much as the man drank and gambled, he never seemed to lose control of his faculties. His crew held the utmost respect for him and would always immediately jump to attention whenever he gave an order.

Chuck didn't begrudge his men treating the journey like a pleasure cruise. Their cabins were cramped and uncomfortable and shared between two and the restrooms were communal so there was no privacy. Chuck felt they had every right to let off a little steam. He knew they would be professional and able when the time came.

On the nights when Chuck hadn't the stomach for more alcohol, he would slip away from the revelry of the messdeck and read beneath the stars. He had brought on board several dogeared copies of Arthur Ambrose's published journals he'd held since he was a kid. Reacquainting himself with them, he was astounded at some of the feats Ambrose had pulled off throughout his adventures. He'd forgotten more than he'd realised and found himself falling in love with his chosen path in life all over again.

He kept the journals secret from the others, all too aware of the cutting jibes he'd receive from Pat, Grant and Dillon if they discovered he was shying away from a good time to read a book from his childhood.

As Chuck became more friendly with Ambrose throughout the voyage, he came to see more and more of the man the professor used to be and the more he saw the similarities between Ambrose's present and younger self, the harder he found it to believe Ambrose's story of abandoning his friends out of cowardice. There simply had to be more to the story, the way Ambrose had told it just didn't seem to gel with the type of man Ambrose appeared to be. Chuck was certain there was some truth in Ambrose's version of events, but he decided there had to be more to it.

***

On the sixth night of travel, Chuck read the memoirs of his childhood hero under the stars of the Caribbean sky. The seas were calm and the boat bobbed atop the waves. He'd found a spot by the lifeboats where nobody seemed to frequent and decided it was as good a place as any for some private time. Below he could hear the sounds of music and laughter originating from the messdeck. He tried to ignore it as he read of Arthur Ambrose's times in Brazil, wondering if it was during this adventure that Ambrose came to learn of the location of Vincabamba.

He looked up as light fell across him. The door to the lower decks had opened, momentarily raising the volume of the messdeck's din before closing again. Two figures, unaware of Chuck's presence, walked towards the side of the boat.

One of the figures was a sailor Chuck recognised as Nick Taylor, a young man originally from Boston. The second figure, propped up by Nick, was Candy Ambrose. She laughed and stumbled as she was guided to the railing, her blonde hair blowing in the gentle breeze.

Chuck's jaw clenched as he tried to refocus on his reading. They didn't need to know he was there and if he revealed himself, he would expose his quiet spot to the rest of the crew. He hoped they would soon rejoin the others so he didn't need to listen to their tittering.

"I've never known a broad dance like you dance," Nick laughed as he steadied his companion.

"That's nothing," Candy giggled as she held onto the railing and looked out to sea. She felt somewhat nauseous, though the fresh sea air was making her feel better. "You should see me in the Palladium Ballroom in Broadway."

"I really would love to," Nick laughed, resting his hand on Candy's.

Candy smiled. "Let's get back to the others or else they'll start talking."

"Let them talk," Nick said. "If anyone says anything untoward, I'll clock 'em on the jaw."

Candy grinned at that. "My knight in shining armour. You're sweet." She kissed Nick on the cheek. "I feel better now, thanks for escorting me. Let's get back to the others."

"How about another kiss before we go back? A proper one."

"Maybe another night, when I'm not feeling so tipsy?"

Nick made his best puppy-dog eyes. "Not even a stinking kiss?"

"Please, let's go back," Candy repeated and went to leave. Nick gripped her wrist and remained static, his face turning less friendly. "Ow, Nick, you're hurting me," Candy complained.

"You don't need to pretend," Nick urged her. "I see the way you look at me."

Candy continued to struggle, making pained noises as Nick's grip remained strong. "How do I look at you?" she grimaced.

"Like you want me," Nick said with absolute confidence. "It's okay, you don't have to play the long game with me. I want you too."

"I think you've got the wrong idea," Candy said, but Nick wasn't listening, his mind made up.

"Just one little kiss, that's all I want. One little kiss."

Candy screwed up her face in defiance as Nick took a step into her personal space. "Nick, please…" she attempted again.

Hearing enough, his anger risen to new heights, Chuck stood up from his sanctuary amidst the lifeboats. "Didn't you hear the lady? She said she wasn't interested," he barked with authority.

Nick released his grip on Candy's arm and took a step back, shocked at Chuck's sudden appearance, seemingly from nowhere. He raised his hands defensively. "Hey, now, you've got the wrong idea. Me and the lady here, we were just talking." His eyes flitted over to Candy, who was backing away from him, nursing her sore wrist and staring daggers his way. "Tell him, Candy. Tell him how it is."

Chuck strode forward, getting between Candy and Nick, puffing his chest out and clenching his fists. "Candy doesn't need to say a thing, I heard everything. I heard you being a creep to her. Weren't you ever told 'no' as a child? I suggest you back out of here, if you know what's good for you."

Nick's fear turned to anger. "You don't know what you're talking about and you've no right talking to me that way. Why, I should…"

"Should what?" Chuck snapped. "If you're going to do something, then do something."

Nick's shoulders sagged and he looked defeated. He turned as if to leave before suddenly swinging back around with a wide right hook. Chuck instinctively blocked the clumsy punch with his left forearm before throwing a right hook of his own. Unlike Nick's attack, Chuck's punch was fast and powerful and clocked the crew member clean in the eye. Nick spun around as he fell to the floor. He quickly scooted back, a hand over his struck face as he pulled himself up by the railings. "Are you going to try that again?" Chuck asked, his voice deadly serious.

"I'm sorry. I made a mistake," he muttered, the adrenaline in his system making him jittery.

"Don't apologise to me. Apologise to the lady," Chuck ordered.

"I'm sorry, Candy. I shouldn't have done that."

"Now get out of here, before I really get mad."

With a final look at them both, Nick turned and hurried back inside the door leading to the lower decks.

Chuck flinched as Candy rested a hand on his shoulder, half expecting another attack. "Thank you," Candy said appreciatively.

Chuck turned and eyed her up and down. "You need to be more careful," he berated her. "It's hardly a surprise, the way you carry on."

Candy placed her hands on her hips as her face darkened. "And what, exactly, do you mean by that?"

"The way you're always dancing. Always leading people on, being over friendly."

"Being 'over friendly?'" Candy shouted in disbelief. "I'm just letting my hair down, like everyone else on this boat."

"Well, you're not exactly the same as everyone else on this boat, are you?"

"You mean because I am a woman?"

"That's exactly what I mean. And not just any woman. You're a rich daddy's girl who dines in fancy restaurants and goes to fancy dance halls. You have no idea what makes the working man tick, yet you suppose the whole world bend to your sensibilities. Not everyone is your friend and not everything is a game."

"You think I am treating this expedition as a game?"

"Aren't you? Why are you even here? You have no experience in these things. You're nothing but more luggage for us to drag from place to place. Worse than that, you're a distraction."

Candy bit her bottom lip, her eyes teared up and with a swift movement she slapped Chuck across the face. It stung, though he didn't show it. He kept his eyes on her, his opinion of her unyielding. "You know nothing about me," she spat.

The door to the lower decks opened and another of the crew came outside to light a pipe. Chuck immediately turned his attention to the rolling waves as the crewman bid them good evening. Candy made quick small talk with him, her racing emotions suddenly gone, replaced by a veneer of friendliness and happiness. Chuck couldn't understand how she managed it. He was so angry right now that his arms were shaking. He knew that if the crewman tried to engage him with conversation he'd say something he'd regret. The crewman lit Candy's cigarette for her and she indulged him with comments about how nice the night sky looked. He then bid them both goodnight and leisurely walked towards the front of the boat.

Chuck turned to Candy, his voice now lowered, all too aware of the other man on deck. "Why, you can just turn it on, can't you?"

Candy exhaled a breath of smoke and watched it carry on the wind. She regarded Chuck coldly. "Excuse me?"

"Your blood was boiling a second ago and yet when that crewman showed up you were cool as a cucumber. Like you were a completely different person."

Chuck's tone was accusatory, as if Candy had committed some grave sin, though he didn't know what it was.

"Like I said, you really don't know me at all, Mister Tanner. Nobody does. Not you. Not the crew. Not the men I dance with across New York. Not even my father knows the real me. They only see facets of my personality."

Chuck leaned over the rail, chewing over what Candy had just said. "A different Candy to suit each person's tastes."

Candy shrugged. "If you like."

Chuck's voice lost its harsh edge, becoming gentler. "Sounds lonely."

"I'm used to it; it makes things easy. Most people only see what they want to see, anyway. I simply choose not to shatter their illusion."

"Is that what I see when I look at you? An illusion? Something that's not there?"

"Depends," Candy raised an eyebrow, the corner of her mouth rising with it. "What do you see?"

Chuck turned around and leaned backwards on the railings as he studied Candy's visage. He chose his words carefully and when he spoke there was no malice or sarcasm in them, only honesty. "A pampered princess, a woman who's never been told 'no.' A woman whose beauty means that every door she approaches is opened for her. Who is looking for some excitement in a world she finds dull. Who's never known hardship."

"Hmm," Candy regarded Chuck's words thoughtfully as she tapped cigarette ash into the sea. "I suppose there is some truth in that."

"There's more?"

"Despite what you may have read about me in the papers, I'm not some empty-headed good time girl. I've been educated in the finest institutions."

"I'd expect nothing less," Chuck smiled with a hint of humour.

Candy chuckled gently. "I am a fully trained botanist and medic. I have been on several botany expeditions in my life, none nearly as glamourous as the tabloids would describe. I've written a handful of published papers on plant life, have catalogued two unique species of flowers and saved a man's life."

Chuck was impressed. "You've saved a man's life?"

Candy inhaled another lungful of smoke before again blowing it into the wind. "Yes, on my second expedition. He tripped and fell down a ravine. None of the men in the group were able to get down to him, the ravine being quite narrow. I managed. I administered field surgery and kept him from falling into shock for two whole days on my own, without food or water, until a rescue harness could be fetched and he was pulled out of there.

"For whatever reason the papers didn't see this incident as newsworthy. They prefer to talk about the latest industrial heir I'm sharing dinner with."

"That's rough," Chuck said. "That they portray you in a way that isn't the real you."

Candy laughed. "Let them say what they will! Mister Tanner, haven't you realised what I am saying to you?"

"I told you before, call me Chuck. What *are* you saying to me?"

"That they are *all* me. The botanist, the medic, the socialite. They're all Candy Ambrose, daughter of famed adventurer and palaeontologist, Arthur Ambrose."

"Is that why you are here, now? To be the daughter of Arthur Ambrose? To follow in his footsteps?"

Candy considered the question for a long time. "In part. Did you know that my mother died when I was very young?"

Chuck looked down at the waves and nodded. "I was aware your mother had passed away."

"Eleanor Ambrose, she'd been on almost as many expeditions as my father. She never wanted the fame though. She asked to be kept out of my father's published journals. I wish she hadn't done that."

"Why not?"

"Like I said, she died when I was young. I don't know how; father says an accident but won't go into details. I don't remember her. I have photos of her and I have heard people who did know her describe her as the wit of the city, but did they really know her? Really?"

"Why do you think they didn't?"

"I've been told that she was a lot like me. Multifaceted. I know of the Eleanor Ambrose of New York. I know nothing of Eleanor Ambrose: adventurer."

"Your father knew her."

"He doesn't talk to me about her. I've tried, lord knows. He always shuts off when I bring her up in conversation. He gets this faraway, sad look in his eye. I think it hurts him too much to remember her, so I've stopped asking. That's why I wear this ring." Candy raised her hand, showing Chuck the silver ring he'd noticed before. The beast's face on the silver band glinted in the moonlight.

"That caught my eye when I first met you. It doesn't seem to suit you. It looks old and worn, may I see it?"

Candy grinned and pulled her hand away. "I'll never take it off. It was a treasure of my mother's, found in an ancient ruin in Iran. It's a protective spirit of some kind."

"It was important to her?"

Candy shrugged as she regarded the piece of ancient jewellery. "I don't know. Probably not. But it is one of the few items of hers I have. It's precious to me, that's what counts."

"I guess everyone is multifaceted, when it comes down to it," Chuck observed earnestly.

Candy flicked her spent cigarette overboard and turned to face Chuck, taking a step towards him. He found her perfume intoxicating. "Now that I've bared my soul to you, will you answer a question of mine?"

"I can do that."

"What were you doing? Amidst the lifeboats? Were you hiding? You seem so outgoing, so sociable. I have always been surprised whenever you've ducked out of the revelries down below."

Chuck grinned. "You noticed I wasn't there, huh?"

Candy looked down, smiling. "Of course." She looked back up, her eyes meeting his. "Will you answer my question?"

"I've been reading."

"Reading? Reading what?"

"It sounds corny, but I've been rereading your father's journals. He was a hero of mine from when I was a kid. I'd read his works for hours."

"And now you are rereading them? For what reason?"

Chuck shrugged. "I guess I'm trying to equate the man on this boat with the man in those journals. They seem similar, but distinct."

"It troubles you that they seem different?"

Chuck shrugged. "I just want to understand the man I am following."

Candy gave a grin. "It's like I said. Everyone is multifaceted. Me, my father, everyone in this whole, wide, beautiful world." She reached up, touching Chuck's chest, feeling his heartbeat. "Even you."

Chuck suddenly felt the impulse to lean in and kiss Candy. It would be so easy, their faces only inches apart. Her eyes were wide with longing and her lips were slightly parted, red and plump. His legs began to tremble and he found himself thinking what a joke it was that after all the things he had experienced in his life, now should be when he felt afraid. He leaned down closer to her, strands of her hair on the breeze tickled his face. Candy tilted her head back, her eyes beginning to close.

Chuck leaned in further, certain Candy wanted him to kiss her and then the door to the lower decks opened and Bill came stumbling out, worse for wear. Chuck froze in place and by the time he could comprehend what was happening, Bill had run up beside him, leaned over the railing and emptied the contents of his stomach into the Caribbean Sea.

Chuck quickly placed a hand on Bill's back, steadying him as the rotund man heaved again. "Easy, Bill. Easy." He looked up and saw that Candy was already at the open door, bathed in the light from within.

"It was nice talking to you, Chuck. I'll see you in the morning. Goodnight."

"Goodnight," Chuck stuttered, at a loss of what else to say. With that, Candy went inside and closed the door, leaving Chuck and Bill alone. He soothed his friend as Bill slid down into a sitting position. "Are you okay, now?" Chuck asked with concern.

"I'm okay," Bill hiccupped. "I drank too much. I'm sorry."

"Don't be sorry," Chuck laughed. "It can happen to the best of us."

"Not that," said Bill, shaking his head. "Sorry about disturbing you and Miss Ambrose."

"Oh that?" Chuck tried to laugh off Bill's observation, surprised his friend was still in the frame of mind where he'd noticed what he had disrupted. "That was nothing. We were just talking. One of the crewmen got a little handsy, I had to clock him one."

"I see," Bill mumbled, his head nodding and his eyes barely able to stay open. "I'm still sorry though. She's quite the girl, don't you think?"

Chuck smiled. "I think you are right. She's quite the girl."

CHAPTER 8

The next morning Chuck was sat in the messdeck eating his breakfast as people around him nursed their hangovers. He looked up as Candy entered the mess, collected her tray and scooped eggs and waffles onto her plate. She then sat down opposite Chuck, eyeing the nearby crewman who stood and left, his meal finished.

"I wanted to thank you for last night," she smiled.

"Don't mention it," Chuck replied.

"I really enjoyed our conversation, but I don't want rumours to start spreading."

"I thought you didn't care about what people whispered behind your back."

She sipped her coffee. "Usually I'm not forced to remain in close quarters with those who gossip."

"Well don't worry about it," Chuck smiled. "Of all people, Bill isn't one to spread rumours. That's if he can even remember what he saw."

Candy raised an eyebrow. "And what did he see?"

"Nothing. Nothing at all."

Candy nodded thoughtfully. "That can't happen again."

Chuck tried not to show his disappointment. "Nothing did happen."

"I know... but something could have. I may appear playful, but I must also remain unattainable. If I begin having inappropriate relationships with members of this expedition it could cause complications. I've made that mistake before."

Chuck bristled. "You make a habit of inappropriate relationships, then?"

"That's not what I meant."

"Then I'm the one who is inappropriate?" He kept his voice low but firm.

"You're misunderstanding me."

Chuck stood to leave. "No, I think I understand you just fine."

"You haven't finished your breakfast."

"Suddenly I've lost my appetite."

***

It took a further six days for the Cyclopea to arrive at Arica, the temperature increased the further south they sailed. Chuck mentioned the incident regarding crewman Nick Taylor to Captain Edgington. Edgington glared at the crewman and his noticeable black eye and told Chuck to leave it to him. For the rest of the voyage he was kept below decks, peeling potatoes, carrying out tedious maintenance of the ship and mopping all the floors. Nick remained sullen and quiet, knowing better than to cause more trouble.

Chuck felt like a heel for allowing his wounded pride to get the better of him in the messdeck and tried to apologise. Candy showed just how true to her words she intended to be, never allowing herself to be in a situation where

Chuck could talk to her in private. She was polite and courteous when they did speak with others around, though their conversations were never more than surface level. After the first day, Chuck took the hint and left Candy to her own devices, deciding that if she wanted to speak to him again, she'd make it happen.

Chuck had bigger things to be concerned with than Ambrose's daughter and when it appeared the voyage was nearing its end the professor invited Chuck and his men to a meeting without the crew. There the group pored over various maps Ambrose held. Several of them showed the route that would be taken from Arica to the Bolivian border and then several larger scale maps of the mountains they would need to traverse. One of them was marked with an 'X' and Ambrose confirmed that was their destination.

Ambrose then pulled a tobacco tin from his breast pocket and popped the lid. He took out a small, folded piece of paper. It looked aged and delicate and Ambrose took great care as he unfolded it.

"Gentlemen, I would like to show you my map of Vincabamba," Ambrose said with great pride.

The faded map showed an area of land isolated on all sides by mountains. Technically it wasn't a valley at all. The area was about twice as long north to south as it was wide east to west. A river ran through its bottom third and the surrounding mountains encroached into the valley at the midway point from the west. These mountains stretched two thirds the distance across, almost cleaving the isolated land in two. In the north-west corner of the map the drawing of a temple could be made out. South of it was a body of water.

"This is the valley in its entirety?" Chuck asked.

"It appears to be," Ambrose confirmed. "Though I haven't been able to verify its accuracy myself."

"It looks old," Dillon stated.

"That's because it is," Ambrose explained. "Almost four hundred years to be exact."

Dillon gave an impressed whistle.

"Where did you get it?" asked Chuck.

"I found it in a small village not too far south of Arica. It was drawn by a Spanish explorer. The locals shared their knowledge with him. He drew this."

"And they stated this is where the Stone of Qualbec is?"

Ambrose nodded. "We enter the valley from the south." He then moved his finger to the temple in the north-west corner. "This is the City of Vincabamba. No doubt just ruins now. The natives stated this was where the Stone of Qualbec resides."

Chuck studied the map and stroked his chin. "How far north did you get when you visited this place?"

Ambrose's smile vanished as he pointed to the southern portion of the map. "We made it only slightly north of the river."

"The wildlife, is it that aggressive?" asked Bill with a gulp.

Dillon laughed. "Ain't gonna be nothing there more aggressive than me!"

Grant and Pat joined in with Dillon's bravado while Mustaf rolled his eyes.

"That's enough," Chuck ordered his men. They instantly went silent. "You guys are probably the toughest hombres I've ever had the pleasure to meet, but don't become overconfident. There are animals in this valley that can kill a man like that." He snapped his fingers. "I want you all to listen to the information Professor Ambrose has for you like your lives depend on it. They do."

Chuck's men remained silent and looked questioningly over to Ambrose. The professor nervously cleared his throat, thanked Chuck and then told of his experience. Chuck expected titters of laughter and was proud when none of his men made light of Ambrose's experience. Looking across the room, Chuck noticed a look of shock on Candy's face. *Surely this isn't the first time she's heard this, is it?*

***

After their plan and route had been decided upon, the revelries on board continued and Ambrose's party let their guards down and joined in the fun. On the final night Dillon finally got his wish of arm-wrestling Mustaf. After four hours of straining it was finally ruled a stalemate.

The sky was clear and the seas were calm as the Cyclopea pulled into dock at Arica. The crew helped them with their bags and for the one night they stayed at a local hotel, trying the local foods. After that Edgington bid Ambrose and Chuck farewell and he and his men returned to their boat. Ambrose informed Chuck that after the expedition was a success, he would charter a plane for their return as the need for secrecy would have passed.

Chuck grinned as he slipped a small blade into his boot prior to their meeting with their guides. "Why on earth do you need that?" Ambrose said critically.

Chuck gave a conspiring wink. "I always stow an extra blade in my boot, just in case."

"In case of what?"

Chuck laughed. "You never know. You take your safeguards, I'll take mine."

That night they met with their local guide and the men they could be traveling with. Emanuel Chavas was a small-framed man in his forties with a thick moustache and black, bushy hair. He wore a thin, brown shirt and shorts. The top few buttons on his shirt were open, revealing his hairy chest. The ten men who would be working beneath him were Diago, Jose, Pablo, Lucas, Joaquin, Mateo, Felipe, Juan and the brothers Vincente and Javier. They all wore clothes similar to their boss and were all in their twenties, with the exception of Mateo, who looked to be in his fifties.

Emanuel wore a cheery expression, had a relaxed demeanour and offered to show the expedition party the sights of the town for the night they were there. Before that though was the important matter of sorting through their supplies. Ambrose had given Emanuel a list of equipment he required and the guide hadn't disappointed. The list mainly consisted of rifles, sidearms, and the necessities required to traverse the jungles and mountains. Chuck and his men looked appreciatively over the weapons, especially Grant who chose a rifle that he immediately declared was his and nobody else was to touch it.

In the morning the group left, traveling east into the jungle in three old jeeps. Chuck travelled in the same jeep as Candy and Ambrose and he chuckled as Candy complained about the journey.

"If the roads are this bumpy, why'd they bother making them?" she muttered.

Chuck had to give it to her, since she'd stepped foot off the boat, her demeanour had changed. Gone were the designer skirts and tops, as if she'd shed the skin of the person she was in New York. Now her hair was tied up in a no-nonsense bun and she wore shorts and shirt like everyone else. Her eyes looked intelligent and observant, and she helped her father study maps of the region.

"How far is it?" Chuck asked, over the roaring of the jeep engine.

"We travel by jeep into Bolivia," Ambrose yelled back, the bumps in the road causing him much displeasure. "We should be driving for three days. After that, the jeeps can't take us any further. We'll need to travel by foot for two weeks."

"Two weeks?" Chuck exclaimed.

"The area we are heading to is very remote and the environment is very harsh."

"I can handle it, Professor. But can you and your team?"

"I can handle it fine," Candy snapped.

"I was thinking more about your father and Professor Crowley. I mean, you two aren't exactly spring chickens."

Ambrose grinned and placed a hand on Chuck's shoulder. "Your concern is admirable, but I assure you there is plenty of life in us yet."

***

As unpleasant as the driving portion of the journey had been, trekking through the jungles was much worse. The wall of green that they had to cut through was the densest jungle Chuck had ever seen. Progress was slow and arduous, the jungle itself fought them for every step. Chuck and his men, alongside Emanuel and the labourers who weren't carrying equipment led with machetes, while the others followed.

Throughout the hike, Nathaniel Childs took every opportunity he could to take photos of the plants and animals they saw. "Keep up, or we'll leave you behind," Chuck berated him.

"Mister Tanner, taking photos was why I was brought along. Have you any idea how many potentially new specimens, unknown to science, I have photographed so far?"

"No, I haven't. Have you any idea how easy it is for stragglers to become lost in bush as thick as this?"

Nathaniel said nothing, returning to taking photos the instant Chuck was distracted by something else.

Due to their team's numbers, there was no fear of any larger predators engaging them. The same couldn't be said for the smaller fauna. Biting insects made the trek almost unbearable and there were a couple of close encounters with snakes and smaller crocodiles.

On one of the nights Candy woke the whole camp up with her screaming and nobody could blame her when it was revealed a wandering spider had crawled into her tent.

"I hate spiders," she cried, her skin crawling from the encounter.

"He was just being friendly," Chuck playfully mocked her. "Perhaps we can keep him as a pet."

"Very funny," Candy fumed.

***

"Not far to go now," puffed Ambrose, checking his map. "Another couple of days and we'll be there." The land was more and more mountainous by the day, a constant rise and dip of steep hills. One wrong step could result in a broken ankle.

"I sure hope so," Emanuel said as he wiped sweat from his brow. "We only have enough supplies to allow us to keep travelling for another two weeks. If we can't find this place soon, we'll be forced to turn around."

"We're close," Ambrose insisted. "I'm certain of it."

***

A day later the trees thinned out enough for the team to get a real sense of their bearings. They were on the crest of a foothill and before them they could see the land descend again into thick jungle. Beyond this jungle, rising high, a massive mountain range stretched before them. Ambrose laughed like a giddy schoolboy. Chuck and Pat exchanged glances.

"Are you okay?" Pat asked.

Ambrose turned around; a wide grin painted on his face. Candy said nothing, as in the dark as everyone else. "Never better, my lad. Never better."

Chuck looked around, hoping someone else would step up and ask the obvious. Nobody did so it fell to him. "Do you mind telling me what's got you so excited?"

"That!" Ambrose exclaimed.

"The mountain?"

"Beyond that mountain is the valley of Vincabamba."

"Beyond *that* mountain? You are sure?"

Ambrose looked annoyed by Chuck's question. "Of course I am sure. I remember it as if I was last here only yesterday."

"*That* mountain?" Chuck said again as a low, doubtful murmuring began emanating from the group. "Ambrose, I hate to break it to you, but there is no way we can climb that mountain."

"No need to go over it, Mister Tanner. We'll be going *under* it. There's a cave. Come, we mustn't dawdle. We are so close." With renewed energy, Ambrose began marching into the trees, his path unwavering and the rest of the group exchanged glances once again before following the professor into the dense foliage.

***

"At least we don't have to climb," Bill huffed to Chuck as he swatted at the flies buzzing around his head. He cursed as a mosquito bit the back of his neck. "Damn it, aren't you suffering with these bugs?"

"Not nearly as much as you," Chuck laughed. "It's all that junk you eat. Must make you tasty to them." He then turned his attention to Pat. "Hey Pat, how are you faring?"

Pat shrugged as he hacked at a particularly stubborn vine. "About as well as can be expected. This has been some trek. It's worse than India. I sure hope Ambrose isn't leading us on a wild goose chase."

"Me too," Chuck agreed.

***

At noon the next day the group made their way to the sheer, rocky cliffs of the mountain before them. Strange birds and lizards Chuck had never seen before cawed and scurried on small, overgrown ledges beyond their reach.

"These animals are simply incredible," Nathaniel gushed as he pulled out his camera and began taking photos of the exotic animals.

Stanley Crowley called to his colleague, pointing to a section of cliff. "Nathaniel, take a photo of that one over there. No, not the bird, the lizard. I'm fairly certain it is of a genus that was believed to have gone extinct over a hundred million years ago." Nathaniel eagerly obeyed.

"Some of these plants belong to a similar epoch. Incredible," Candy remarked, running her fingers over a nearby leaf.

Ambrose brimmed with pride as he sat on a nearby rock to catch his breath. "All this pales in comparison to the wonders that lurk beyond this mountain," he stated.

Mustaf, Emanuel and Emanuel's men took stock of the area. Emanuel's man Mateo looked ill at ease by the spectacle before them.

"Hey, old man. Are you okay?" Emanuel asked.

Mateo kept his eyes on the strange animals before them. "We shouldn't be here," he muttered. "This place is cursed."

"It is unexplored, senor. Not cursed."

Mateo spat. "I don't like it."

Emanuel lowered his voice so the foreigners couldn't hear him. "You took the money and told me you weren't superstitious. Now we are here your bravery deserts you?"

"I am brave," Mateo glared. "But I am not a fool. Those animals are from the Underworld. We should go no further."

Chuck, Bill and Pat stood with their hands on their hips, surveying the colossal mountain. Grant and Dillon saddled up behind them.

"I don't see no cave," Dillon said.

"I know," Chuck sighed.

"If there isn't a cave, how are we going to get to the other side?" asked Bill nervously.

"We won't. Not with the supplies and equipment we have at hand," Chuck replied.

Grant gave a mischievous smile and took aim with his rifle. "I suppose if we can't go any further, we can at least have us some target practice and bag a couple of souvenirs." Dillon laughed at that.

Chuck turned around to the Englishman, no humour on his face. "No discharging of weapons unless absolutely necessary, do you hear me?"

Grant's smile vanished and he lowered his rifle. "I hear you. Just a joke."

Chuck wasn't in a joking mood. He walked over to Ambrose. "So where is this cave of yours?" he barked, allowing his tone to keep its harsh edge.

Ambrose wasn't bothered by Chuck's lack of patience. He began scanning the rockface in more detail. "It's around here, somewhere. Now, just a minute..." he stood and began walking slowly to the east. Mustaf stayed close by him, helping him search.

Pat moved in close to Chuck as they let the professor take a meandering lead. "Chuck, if this is all for nothing, I swear..."

"Don't worry," Candy pushed herself into their conversation. "My father knows what he's doing. His memory hasn't failed him yet."

"I sure hope you are sure," Chuck said.

"Of course I am sure. You've read his journals; you should be sure too." She then moved ahead, joining Mustaf and her father.

It took forty minutes for the cave to be found, not by Ambrose, but by Emanuel's men. "Senor, the cave, it is here," Emanuel called, beckoning the rest of the group to an aperture in the rock. The group gathered around as two of Emanuel's men, Pablo and Joaquin, pulled back hanging vines that had covered the cave entrance. "Is this the cave, Professor?"

Ambrose approached the cave, a smile upon his lips as he studied the entrance. It was about ten feet wide and seven feet high and with noticeable straight edges. "This is the one. I'm certain of it."

"It looks manmade," Chuck noted.

"Hmm, it does, doesn't it," Ambrose agreed.

"It stinks," Emanuel said as he peered into the darkness. "Like rotting meat."

"It is cursed," Mateo announced to everyone. "The scent of death lingers. If we continue, death is all we shall encounter."

"Stop that nonsense," Emanuel ordered his man. "It's probably just some animal."

"Could be a predator of some kind has made itself a home in there," Grant whispered into Chuck's ear. "Perhaps Dillon and I should go in first, make sure it's safe."

Chuck nodded. "Good idea..." Chuck trailed off as a deep, guttural roar emanated from the darkness beyond the cave threshold. Everyone started backing away from the cave with a sense of concern. "What the hell was that?"

"Sounded big," said Dillon, raising his rifle. He then yelled to Ambrose and Emanuel's men who were closer to the cave. "Everyone get back."

The party backed away with more urgency. "Probably just a bear," Emanuel suggested.

Suddenly a dark shape, impossibly large and covered with hair, sprinted from a cave and made directly for the nearest group of people. It was indeed a bear, though like no bear anyone had ever seen before. The lumbering beast was twice as large as any grisly and moved with a speed that belied its size. Its face was savage and rage-filled, sharp yellow canines bared as it gave another almighty roar.

Before anyone could react, it gave a swipe of its muscular paw, knocking a screaming Mateo off his feet and sending him flying into a growth of thickets.

"Fire!" bellowed Dillon and began unloading rounds into the lumbering beast. Grant fired without hesitation and Chuck and his men joined him. Emanuel pulled his pistol and emptied it into the bear's hide as his men darted for cover. Mustaf quickly rounded up Ambrose and Candy and guarded them, rifle at the ready in case the barrage of gunfire didn't stop the monster before them.

The giant bear roared its defiance as bullets tore into it, fountains of blood smearing its dark brown fur. It roared and snapped in fury, the bullets stopping it from charging forward.

The bear gave a pained roar, tiling its head back and Grant pulled his trigger, the bullet he fired slamming into the bear's throat. The bear howled in pain and confusion as the bullets continued before falling to the ground dead. Its death had been as quick to come as its appearance.

The men waited in silence for the dust to settle and for the adrenaline to ebb. Eventually the sounds of the jungle returned.

"Emanuel," called one of the labourers. "It's Mateo, he's hurt."

Emanuel and the other labourers ran to their fallen comrade, as did Candy. "Make way, I have medical training," she stated as the labourers parted for her. She crouched beside Mateo, who lay on his back. The old man did not look in a good way. Three deep lacerations crossed his chest and he looked as if he had several broken bones. His breathing was pained and rasping, and blood trickled from his lips.

"Can you save him?" Emanuel asked.

Candy couldn't hide her fears. "He's in a bad way. I can ease his pain, but I fear he has internal bleeding."

Emanuel took a deep breath and nodded. "Please, do your best."

As Candy worked on the gravely wounded man, Chuck and Ambrose's men gathered around the fallen beast.

"I ain't ever seen a bear like that," Dillon remarked.

"I didn't think they got that big," Bill commented.

"Damn thing stinks," Pat complained.

Professor Crowley was of a different opinion as he ran over to the animal and pulled back its lip, revealing a yellowed canine eight inches long. "Beautiful, absolutely beautiful. Nathaniel, get photos of this animal, now."

"Careful, Prof. It might still have some life in it," Dillon warned.

"Do you know what it is?" asked Chuck.

Crowley took out a small tape measure and began putting it against the bear's features before recording the measurements in a small book. "Gentlemen, I believe that what we are looking at is a Cave Bear. Thought to have gone extinct over twenty thousand years ago."

"I guess this bear didn't get the message," Chuck said.

Crowley examined the huge paw and long, curved claws. "I guess not. Absolutely remarkable."

"Don't forget that this 'remarkable' specimen may have cost a man his life," Chuck said bitterly.

"Gentlemen, I want to thank you for joining me this far, but I must tell you something before we continue. Beyond that cave is a land filled with ancient, extinct animals. This you know. What I must impress upon you is that there are animals whose ferocity and size makes this fellow look like a teddy bear. The land of Vincabamba will be filled with dangers we cannot imagine. Dangers that don't exist anywhere else in the world. I want you to know that I won't hold it against any of you if you wish to remain by this cave entrance."

Chuck looked amongst the assembled members of the group and gave a determined smile. "Okay, looks like we're heading in to Vincabamba."

CHAPTER 9

The air inside the cave was cool and would have been a welcome reprieve from the heat outside if not for the stench. Remnants of the bear's previous meals littered the cave floor. Bones scattered around, many of them still with chunks of rotting meat still attached.

"God, that stink," Candy exclaimed. "I think I'm going to be sick."

Pat tried to act as if the smell wasn't bothering him and managed to force a smile. "You should try sharing a tent with Bill."

"I heard that," Bill mumbled as Pat and Candy shared a small laugh.

Grant and Dillon kept their rifles drawn, following the torchlight of the others, ready for any other surprises the cave may have in store for them.

"Stay close to me," Mustaf said to Ambrose as he warily stepped deeper into the darkness. Beyond the entrance to the cave it widened out and the ceiling had risen to the degree that it was positively roomy.

Emanuel and seven of his men came in once the mouth of the cave was announced as safe, carrying the trunks of equipment between them. Two of his men, Pablo and Felipe, had chosen to remain outside with the wounded Mateo. By some miracle Candy had managed to stitch Mateo's wounds, bandage him and relieve much of his pain. Chuck still didn't think the old man would survive, he was in a bad way and the journey back to civilisation would likely be more than he could take. Still, he'd been impressed by the deftness in which Candy had acted to save the man, her skills better than any field surgeon he had encountered before.

Being mindful to step around the bones, eventually the evidence of the bear's presence diminished until the wet rocky walls were all that surrounded them.

The group reached a fork in the cave and Chuck shone his flashlight down both paths. "Professor, which way is it?" he called back to Ambrose, who was chattering away with Crowley.

Upon hearing his name, Ambrose jogged forward to Chuck, Mustaf staying close behind him. Ambrose stroked his chin as he regarded the two paths open to them. "When I came here last, I entered the valley from the left path, though I fear that option won't be available to us this time."

"Why the hell not?"

"It collapsed," Ambrose said simply.

"It collapsed?" Chuck exclaimed. Bill and Pat started nervously checking the structural integrity of the cave ceiling.

"Yes, but don't worry about that. I am confident that we can get through if we follow the right path."

"And how would you know that?"

Ambrose shrugged. "Just a hunch, Mr Tanner. Just a hunch."

The group moved forward following the right path. It twisted and turned but never once did it threaten to tighten around them.

"Chuck, look at this," Bill called and Chuck looked where Bill was focusing his light. A part of the cave had Incan characters carved into it. "What does it say?"

Chuck scrutinised the lettering. "It says..." he paused as he studied it a little longer. "Those who follow this path will descend to the Underworld, where spirits dwell and the dead know no rest."

"Charming," Pat commented.

They all carried on a little further until they reached a stone door, covered in runes and characters Chuck didn't recognise.

"This is it," Ambrose beamed. "The way to Vincabamba. We are so close."

Beside the door was a lever and Ambrose reached over and pulled it down, even as Chuck called on him to wait a minute.

The sound of ancient machinery rumbled behind the cave walls and the door slowly slid open. Chuck and Pat braced themselves for a trap, having experienced too many in the past to be complacent now.

"Nobody move," Chuck ordered and everyone froze. Chuck listened carefully, trying to pick up on the most miniscule of sounds; a turning cog of a jet of air which would reveal a trap had been sprung. He heard nothing, just the quiet breathing of his companions and the dripping of water from the stalactites that hung from the ceiling. He relaxed. "It's okay. We're okay." He then turned to berate the professor. "Ambrose, do me a favour and next time you see a lever, speak to me before pulling it. Okay?"

Ambrose stifled a mischievous smirk. "Right you are, Mister Tanner."

Chuck glanced at Pat. "You with me. The rest of you, hold back until we know it is safe."

Ambrose protested Chuck's order. "This is my expedition, I should go."

"And I'm the guy you hired to lead it. If you don't want to follow my advice that's fine. I'll take my men and we'll go home."

Ambrose looked flustered.

"How dare you talk to Professor Ambrose like that?" Mustaf roared in fury. Pat, Grant and Dillon immediately stepped forward, prepared in case things got physical.

"I've been hired to lead you people and that's just what I intend to do," Chuck snapped, staring Mustaf in the eye. "Professor Ambrose, am I still in your employ and leading this expedition?"

Ambrose looked down at his feet. "Yes, you are still in my employ."

"Then let me do my job."

Mustaf was furious at how Chuck had spoken to Ambrose but the professor talked him down and the two of them skulked away from the beckoning stone door.

Chuck turned to Pat. "Now that the drama is over, let's see what's behind door number one."

***

Chuck and Pat stepped through the door and the cave opened up into a large, stone room, about a hundred by a hundred feet. The ceiling was high, about twenty feet up and in the centre to it was a large square hole allowing rays of sunlight to filter down, lighting the ancient room.

Incan characters and writings adorned all four walls and Pat gave an impressed whistle as he took in the stone chamber. Behind them they could hear the quietened conversations of the rest of the group.

In the centre of the room was a stone pier, approximately six feet high. It was adorned with various precious stones. Further out, towards the corners of the room were an additional four piers, although these only had precious stones on two sides respectively.

"What do you think these are for?" Pat queried.

"Hell if I know," Chuck shrugged as he cautiously walked across the centre of the room to the other side, where a tighter corridor led on a little way before a metal gate barred further progress. In front of the metal gate was what looked like a pressure pad.

"I get the feeling standing on that would be a bad idea," Pat whined.

Chuck crouched down and examined it. "It's already been pressed."

"You think that the mechanism for this place is broken?"

"Could be."

When they were certain there were no other traps, Chuck and Pat returned to the waiting group and explained the situation.

"We got lots of bullets," Dillon grinned. "We could shoot our way through that gate."

"And cause such a ruckus as to have the whole mountain drop on our heads?" Chuck pointed out. Dillon looked sullen that his idea had been shot down.

"With your permission, Mister Tanner, may I examine the piers?"

Reluctantly Chuck nodded his head.

"I'm coming with him," Mustaf stated. Chuck didn't bother to fight him on it. He continued to examine the room as the professor examined the stone piers before walking over to the gate. He moved his flashlight over it, examining it in more detail. A gemstone was mounted in the centre of the gate and above it were further Incan characters.

"Only a guiding light can illuminate your path," Ambrose muttered.

Chuck snapped his fingers. "I think I got it!" he then ran to the nearest pier and with all his might tried to twist it. Sure enough, with some effort the pier rotated.

"They rotate?" Pat said in surprise.

Chuck didn't answer, immediately running to the next one and rotating it just so. Then he ran to the other two and twisted them.

"May I ask what you are doing?" asked Ambrose.

"You said it yourself," Chuck gave his trademark grin. "We need a guiding light." He then ran to the final pier in the centre of the room and twisted it just so before standing back.

Everyone's eyes widened at the majestic light show Chuck had created. The sunbeams coming from the hole in the ceiling were focussed and directed by the central pier before being refracted towards its surrounding brethren. Due to how Chuck had lined them up, further beams of light refracted off the stones on the corner piers, creating laser focussed beams of light between them all. A final beam of light shone directly down the passage and hit the gemstone on the metal gate.

"That's quite a visual," Pat smiled.

The sound of stone grinding on stone emanated from the pressure plate in front of the gate and Chuck quickly jogged over to see what had happened. "The plate, it's no longer pressed down." He then shone his light through the gate, noting the passage descended downwards. "I'm going to stand on it," Chuck called back to the others.

"Are you sure that's a good idea?" Pat called back nervously.

"Have you got any better ideas?" Chuck waited for a response. There was none. "Everyone stay back. When I stand on this pad, there's no telling what could happen." He looked down at the pad, building his courage. "One," he whispered to himself. "Two… three," he stepped forward onto the pad and it sank several inches and once again the sound of ancient mechanical movements could be heard.

Chuck braced himself for the worst. He was relieved when the gate slid up into the roof. He chuckled to himself to release his tension. "Nothing to it."

A click from behind startled Chuck and he turned around to see a huge boulder fall from the ceiling through a previously unseen trapdoor. It hit the ground with a thunderous thud and rolled down towards him.

"I'm downhill," Chuck lamented. "Of course I'm downhill."

The boulder was wide enough that there was no option to hug a wall and let it pass by and at the size it was, it would crush the life out of anyone it hit in an instant, and worse yet, it was picking up speed. Chuck turned and ran blindly down the passage, the heavy rumble of the rolling boulder reverberating off the passage walls and making his ears hurt.

He chanced a look behind and cried out in fear as the boulder gained on him. Sprinting as fast as he could, Chuck pumped his arms and breathed deep to give himself as much of an edge as possible. He looked back behind; the boulder was now even closer.

This can't be how it ends, Chuck thought as he doubled his efforts, rueing the day he ended up flattened like so much roadkill. Keeping his eyes ahead to facilitate his speed, Chuck noticed the passage dead end with a pit. His eyes darted up and down, trying to see the way out of this deathtrap. *There has to be a way out! There's always a way out!*

Chuck noticed a chain dangling from the ceiling above the pit and he made it his goal. It would be a wide jump, but he felt he could manage it.

The rumbling of the huge boulder was getting closer and closer, and Chuck pulled out all the stops, running faster than he had ever run before. He reached the edge of the pit and then jumped, his body flying over an abyssal darkness without a visible limit. The boulder tumbled off the edge into the blackness, eventually hitting a stone floor far below.

Chuck was no longer paying attention to the boulder, his entire existence now completely reliant on him grabbing hold of the hanging chain or else falling to his doom.

He outstretched his arms as much as he could, his fingers grasping, and...

Chuck caught hold of the chain and his hands clamped tight around it. His momentum caused him to jerk, like a worm on a hook and it felt as if his arms were going to be pulled out of his sockets.

He dangled for a moment as he swung, contemplating his next move. The encompassing darkness of the pit beneath him seemed to be goading him to lose his grip. Chuck yelled out in anguish, trying to hold on, his palms slick with sweat.

Something clicked, as if his weight on the chain had activated another aspect of this trap and Chuck held his breath, waiting to see what would happen next. With a deep rumbling the wall before him began lowering like a drawbridge, revealing the path forward and completely spanning to cover the pit beneath him so that one would never know the pit was there at all. With a loud boom the drawbridge rested at last.

Chuck allowed himself to dangle limply and catch his breath before gaining the confidence to let go of the chain, landing on the stone drawbridge only a foot or so beneath him. He sat down, trying to recover from the shocking ordeal he'd just endured.

"Chuck, are you okay?" called Pat as he came running down the passage, Ambrose and Mustaf close behind him.

"Never better," Chuck stuttered, his heart still beating hard against his ribs. "Nothing to it."

CHAPTER 10

It took the best part of the day for the team to traverse the winding caves, leaving the ruins behind them. The dimensions of their route never threatened to close in and evidence of an ancient culture was carved and painted on the bare-rock walls.

Eventually the cave widened out and light at the end of the tunnel signified the end of their subterranean trek. Chuck, Pat, Bill, Grant and Dillon led the way as they approached the exit, unsure what they'd be walking into.

Stepping out into the bright sunlight, Chuck found himself instantly longing for the cooling darkness of the cave. They had emerged into another jungle, just as dense as the one they had left behind and far more alien. Though no expert, Chuck could tell the plants were more exotic and unique than anything on the other side of the mountain. Candy's eyes almost popped out on stalks as she began reciting the Latin names of plant life that had been believed to have been extinct epochs ago.

Professor Crowley and Nathaniel Childs shared in her enthusiasm, joining her and discussing their observations. All the while Nathaniel's camera worked overtime, capturing everything. A dragonfly with a six-foot wingspan buzzed past them and Crowley looked on in awe.

Chuck had to admit their enthusiasm was infectious. This jungle was unlike anything he'd ever seen before. The sounds and smells were all completely out of time. And if Ambrose's valley existed, it lent all the more credence to Ambrose's claim that the Stone of Qualbec was indeed real and close by. As excited as Chuck was, he didn't for a second forget about the potential dangers present. Normal jungles were death traps themselves. According to Ambrose, this jungle was far more dangerous, with an unknowable number of threats.

"Grant, Dillon, Pat, Bill," he called. "Walk perimeter, try and get the lay of the land." He then turned to the chattering researchers. "You guys pay attention to your surroundings. We don't know how safe we are."

"I must say, I feel like a child at Christmas, but I'll try to contain myself," laughed Crowley as he turned back to study a collection of vines covered in sticky, broad leaves. Standing beside him, Candy tried to hypothesise what genus it was.

Chuck kept an uneasy eye on them, not liking how seemingly oblivious the academic members of the expedition were to their broader surroundings. Professor Ambrose approached him, watching Candy like the proud father he was. "I'd forgotten how wonderous this place is."

"You are certain this is your valley?"

"Absolutely. There is no doubt."

"Then we need to be mindful of danger. Let's not forget the reason you ran from this place all those years ago."

Ambrose's face grew serious. "I assure you, I have not forgotten the events that transpired last time I was here."

Chuck nodded. "Okay, so what is the plan? Where's the City of Vincabamba?"

Ambrose smiled, pulled out his tobacco box, popped off the lid and unfolded the worn and weathered map. "We have entered the valley from the south. Vincabamba is in the far, north-west corner, behind a ridge of mountains. Our best bet is to travel north-east, to bypass the mountains, and then head west until we reach the city."

Chuck studied the map in more detail than he had on the boat, trying to compare the crude drawings of mountain ranges to the towering mountains surrounding them. "What is the scale of this map?"

"It's not entirely to scale. We should be able to reach the city in about three to four days, judging from my last visit."

Chuck pointed to a meandering line that cut across the valley from east to west roughly a third of the way up. "How wide is this river? Can we cross it easily?"

"The river has a very strong current. It'll be hard to cross anywhere other than here." Ambrose pointed. "When I was last here there was a bridge spanning the river in this location."

"Any idea who made it?"

Ambrose shrugged. "Not a clue."

"I see…" Chuck's train of thought was disrupted by high pitch screaming and he turned in horror to see the vines the researchers had been studying suddenly spring to life and ensnare Professor Crowley. Crowley pleaded for help as the vines attempted to hoist him high into the trees, only the joint weight of Candy and Nathaniel stopping him from being lost completely.

Mustaf immediately ran over to give his aid, as did Chuck and his men, hacking at the tenacious vines with machetes and knives. They had little success, prickles on the vines cut into the would-be rescuers' flesh and pierced Crowley's skin, making him howl in pain.

"Emanuel," Chuck called, the guide running over to him, desperate to know how he could help. "Get your men to light some torches. If we can't hack this thing to pieces, we'll burn it!"

Emanuel nodded and quickly began barking orders to his men in Portuguese. Chuck hoped they got the message, his attention now fully on keeping the monstrous plant from lifting Crowley up into the canopy. He ignored the cuts and scratches the long prickles slashed into his forearms.

Emanuel and his men came running into the fray, flaming torches at the ready and they began holding the flames against the tendril-like vines. Instantly the plant withered, trying to escape from the heat. Soon its leaves began catching fire and its movements became more panicked.

"I've got him," shouted Dillon, who had managed to pull Crowley from the vine's grip the moment its snare on him loosened. Bill jumped to Dillon's side and together they pulled Crowley out of harm's way. Everyone else released the flailing plant.

"Keep the torches on this thing," Chuck ordered Emanuel. "I want it to burn."

Soon enough the flailing of the vines ceased and they hung limply from the canopy as the fires consumed it.

"Is it dead?" asked Candy, stepping close to Chuck as he watched the plant blacken in the fire.

"Isn't that your field of expertise?" he shot back.

Candy shrugged. "I've neither seen nor heard of anything like this in all my time as a botanist. It's incredible."

"I get the feeling that before the end of this trip, our views on what is or is not credible is going to change."

Candy agreed. "I think you are right."

***

Without much daylight left in the day it was decided that the group set up camp at the mouth of the cave and begin the journey northwards at daybreak. Emanuel and his men sat in a tight group, ominously whispering to each other.

Candy had placed band-aids over the deeper lacerations Professor Crowley had suffered and he immediately retired to his tent, looking far frailer than he had mere hours ago. He was covered in multiple cuts from the prickles of the vine as well as suffering bruises from its attack. His wounds were all superficial and would heal, though he was clearly profoundly shaken over the incident. Chuck couldn't blame him – it's not every day you are nearly eaten by a plant. Something like that would likely stay with a man.

Candy was certain the plant had been trying to devour the professor and showed a piece of severed plant to prove her hypothesis. "See these here?" she said to the group while pointing to small openings at the base of each prickle. "I believe the plant deliberately ensnares animals, squeezes them and then harvests the blood using these openings to gain nourishment."

"Ghastly," uttered Mustaf with a shudder.

"So even the plants want to eat us here?" bemoaned Bill. "What have you gotten us into this time?"

Chuck gave a slight smile. "Nothing we can't handle. Isn't that right, boys?"

Grant and Dillon gave a cheer.

Chuck grinned then turned his focus first to Nathaniel, who was busy maintaining his camera, and then to Pat and Ambrose.

Pat was scrutinising the map and asking about the various topical features of the valley.

"You guys okay, over there?" he asked them.

"Just planning the route," Pat responded, keeping his eyes on the drawing while Ambrose explained certain features on it.

Chuck turned back to Candy. "You really proved yourself today," he smiled.

Candy returned his smile. "I didn't know I had to prove myself to anybody."

"You don't," Chuck stuttered. "That's not what I meant. I mean… if you hadn't grabbed hold of Crowley when you did, then that plant…"

"I'm thinking of naming it the Vampire Vine," she stated proudly.

"Vampire Vine?"

"Why not?" she giggled playfully. "It's a vine that drinks blood. What would you call it?"

Chuck looked bemused at the section of vine beside them. "I guess 'Vampire Vine' is pretty good."

"To think we discovered it almost immediately. It makes one wonder what we'll find tomorrow."

Chuck liked Candy's optimism. He wished he shared it. "It certainly does."

***

"Everyone, stop moving. Stay where you are," warned Chuck and everyone immediately halted their progress. Emanuel's men whispered to each other and tried to get a good view of what the party leader had found.

The group had set off at daybreak and cautiously headed in a north-eastern direction, hoping to meet with the bridge around noon the following day. The hiking was tough, though no more so than the jungle they had already been traveling. It certainly was stranger, though. Ferns and flowering shrubs were in abundance, as were palm trees and conifers. Grass was present, though most of the earth beneath their feet was either bare or covered in small, curling weeds.

Ambrose's team "ooh'd" and "ahh'd" at the natural wonders they were witnessing. Chuck ordered Bill to keep an eye on them, a task his friend protested before falling back to walk amongst them. Chuck smiled to himself. Bill was always the first to complain, yet he'd always carry out any task without fail. Bill's protests weren't legitimate, he just communicated through the language of griping. Fortunately, Chuck didn't think Bill would have too much issue enforcing his orders. Mustaf was a man constantly erring on the side of caution and acted as Ambrose and Candy's full-time bodyguard. He couldn't help wondering how Ambrose had inspired such loyalty.

Crowley and Nathaniel still had the shock of the encounter with the Vampire Vine in mind, especially Crowley, who was covered in band-aids and still winced as he walked. They weren't as over-eager as they had been, which suited Chuck just fine. A cautious party was a safe party. He found himself wondering how Emanuel's man, Mateo, was doing. He prayed he was okay, though his prediction of the man's ultimate fate was pessimistic. Even if he held off long enough for them to return from the valley, would he be able to survive the arduous trek back to civilisation?

Crowley stopped and ordered Nathaniel to take a photograph of a small lizard that scurried up a branch, its hind legs far longer and more powerful than its short forelegs. Its leathery skin was a greenish hue and its small head was situated at the end of a long, flexible neck. It chirped, turning its head at the explorers before rising onto its hindlegs so it could get a clearer look at them.

"My god, a dinosaur," Crowley whispered in awe. "A true to life, living dinosaur. You were right, Ambrose. This place is a marvel without equal."

"You thought I was lying?" Ambrose chuckled, watching the tiny dinosaur. It couldn't be more than two feet in length, including its long, whip-like tail. It chirped again, sounding like a bird and displaying tiny, serrated teeth.

"Not lying, it's just, until I saw it with my own two eyes, I was afraid to let myself believe."

Bill squinted at the small animal. "Are you sure it's a dinosaur? I thought dinosaurs were big. Is it a baby, or something?"

"Not a baby," Crowley advised him. "This is a Compsognathus, fully grown. It's believed it would have fed mainly on insects."

Bill leaned in closer, studying the creature as it looked back at him, bobbing and turning its head. "Huh, if this is the size of the dinosaurs, I suddenly feel a lot more at ease. Even I could take on this little guy."

The Compsognathus chirped again and then sprang onto Bill's face. He instantly dropped his rifle and fell onto his back, screaming and rolling in the mud as he desperately tried to pull the biting, clawing dinosaur from his face.

Chuck and his men immediately came running in alarm to see what had happened. Before they reached the panicking Bill, Mustaf was standing over him. He dropped to one knee and jabbed down with his hand open. His powerful fingers wrapped around the tiny carnivore and it let out a high pitched screech as it realised it was under attack. The Compsognathus turned its attention to biting and scratching Mustaf's hand. Mustaf's face betrayed none of the pain it was inflicting on him as he tossed it with an almighty over arm throw. The Compsognathus screeched again as it bounced in the mud and leapt to its feet. It bared its teeth in defiance as Chuck ordered Grant to take it out.

Grant took aim, but before he could pull the trigger a fast-moving brown blur hit the dinosaur hard from above before taking to the air it had descended from. "The hell?" he yelled in confusion.

"Up there," yelled Ambrose and everyone with a rifle pointed it to where the professor had indicated.

On a high up branch sat a brown, leathery-winged creature with a mouth full of bloodied teeth. Beneath it, the bloodied, decapitated remains of the Compsognathus lay. The bizarre bird-like creature cawed at the people watching it before spreading its wings to an impressive five feet span and again taking flight, its prize hanging limply in its talons. Nathaniel quickly snapped a few photos before it disappeared from view.

"What the hell was that?" Chuck exclaimed.

"Dimorphodon, if I'm not mistaken," Ambrose said. Professor Crowley agreed with him. "An ancient, flying reptile."

Chuck turned his attention to Bill who now sat up, looking sorry for himself. Bill's face was now covered in a criss-cross of shallow scratches. "How are you doing?"

"Fine," replied Bill, glumly. "It stings like hell, though."

Chuck offered a hand and pulled his friend up. "I sent you back here to look after these people, not the other way around," he joked, hoping to lighten the mood.

"Sorry. It won't happen again," Bill mumbled, looking at his feet. Candy came over and offered to dress some of Bill's deeper scratches and Chuck called a short break to allow her to carry out the work.

He sat against a tree and drank from his water canteen. Grant and Dillon approached him, speaking in hushed tones.

"I don't think we should stop for long," Grant hissed.

Chuck made sure nobody from Ambrose's team was listening before leaning in closer to his two war-buddies. "Why not?"

"Can't you feel it?" whispered Dillon, his face like stone. "Someone or something is watching us."

Chuck tried to get a feel for what the men meant but couldn't feel anything. It didn't matter, he trusted Grant and Dillon's perception with his life. "How long?"

"About an hour now. Moving parallel to us, in the trees," stated Dillon.

"We haven't wanted to draw attention to it and force it to act," added Grant. "Not until we know we'll get a clear shot at it."

"Agreed. What is it? One of Ambrose's dinosaurs?"

Dillon and Grant looked at each other and shrugged, their expressions non-committal.

Chuck thanked them and then discreetly informed the rest of the group, making sure they all stayed extra wary and stuck close together, without drastically changing how they acted. He knew that when the time was right, either he, Pat, Grant or Dillon would make the shot.

***

Once their short break was over, the group continued pushing through the hostile jungle. A further three hours had passed before Chuck ordered everyone to halt before he slowly moved forwards on his own.

"What has he seen?" asked Dillon.

Pat shrugged before crouch-walking to Chuck, his eyes scanning everything, all too aware something was still hunting them. "What is it?" he asked Chuck.

Chuck looked startled by Pat's sudden appearance beside him before his eyes fell to the ground. "That rock by your foot, give it to me."

Pat obliged, handing Chuck the rock about the size of a globe. It was heavier than it looked, causing Chuck to grunt as he hurled it forward with both hands.

The entire team watched the rock arch through the air and hit the ground several feet in front of Chuck. The ground around it caved in and Pat jumped back in alarm as mud and sticks fell, exposing a pit ten feet wide.

Chuck remained where he was, listening to a howling from somewhere beyond the trees, as if a troop of monkeys were moving through the canopy. He waited until the howls died down before gingerly approaching the pit, his men beside him.

The pit was deep, almost eight feet and at the bottom were sharpened stakes standing upright in the mud. Anyone who fell in the pit would certainly meet a grisly end, impaled on the wooden spikes.

"Spikes," Pat whined, remembering the Temple of the Sun in India. "Why is it always spikes?"

Chuck ignored him and called for Ambrose. The professor pushed through the small crowd that had gathered around the spike trap.

"Gosh, that's quite a hole," Ambrose commented.

Chuck wasn't in the mood for Ambrose's enthused personality. "Quite the hole? You're telling me. Are you hiding something from me?"

"How dare you?" Mustaf growled, stepping up beside the professor.

Ambrose straightened his shirt indignantly. "And what would I be hiding from you?"

"When I took this job, you warned me of the wildlife we would be encountering here. You said nothing about natives. This trap has clearly been dug for us. It could have worked if whoever dug it hadn't been as sloppy as they were getting rid of the mud." He indicated various piles of mud and clay, freshly dug and heaped behind trees.

"I've told you everything I know," Ambrose insisted.

Chuck didn't believe him. He grabbed the professor by the collar and drew him closer. "Don't lie to me."

"Chuck, that is my father!" Candy cried in outrage.

Mustaf's powerful hand was suddenly around Chuck's throat. They all remained in place, all aware that if they began to fight there was a good chance they could fall into the pit. Grant caught Chuck's eye and Chuck instantly knew what he was asking. *"Shall I draw my gun?"* Chuck gave an almost imperceptible shake and was glad Grant got the message. The last thing he needed right now was for this to escalate to firearms.

"Chuck, please," cried Candy in desperation.

Chuck moistened his lips as he considered his next move. "Answer me truthfully, Professor. When you were last here, did you encounter natives?"

"He already answered…" Candy pleaded.

Ambrose looked at his daughter, raised his hand, telling her to stand down. "I didn't see any natives, but I knew they were here."

Chuck released his grip, though his anger remained. Mustaf drew back his hand but remained at Ambrose's side. "Elaborate. Please," he said in short manner.

Ambrose hung his head in shame. "I'm sorry for misleading you. I knew you'd be more hesitant if you knew. I'd hoped we wouldn't encounter them. Last time I was here, with Austin and Iris, we heard them. We heard their war drums. There was evidence they stole from our camp. I never saw them, but Iris did. What she described was more an ape than a man. A hulking, hair-covered beast with a hideous, ape-like face."

"Sounds like my ex," Dillon laughed. He soon shut up when Chuck shot him a warning glare. This was no time for jokes.

Chuck returned his glare to Ambrose. "You should have told me. I need to reconsider my role in your expedition." He then walked away, Pat following close behind him.

"What do you want to do?" Pat asked.

"I don't know. The old man lied to us. This complicates things. If he's lied about this, what else could he have lied about?"

"You think he's lying about the Stone of Qualbec?"

"Could be. Although I hope for his sake he isn't."

Emanuel approached the two men, hat in his hands.

"Emanuel, how can I help you?" Chuck asked.

"The men want to know what you plan to do. They say that if you leave, they'll follow with you."

"Why would they follow me? I'm not the one paying them."

"It's not about that. You weren't the only one the professor neglected to tell about the natives. They can see that you are the true leader of this group. They will follow your judgement."

"So, if I decide to turn back Ambrose's entire expedition is over, huh?"

"Excuse me." Chuck turned to see Candy standing uncomfortably. "Mister Tanner, may I speak with you in private?"

"Sure, and it's Chuck." He told Pat to wait while he walked a small distance away with Candy. "How can I help you?"

"I'm sorry about my father keeping things from you, truly. I can see he regrets it. You know of him, he's really not a bad man."

"Truth is, I'm starting to wonder exactly what kind of man your father is."

"But you've read his journals. You know he's good."

"Journals written by himself," Chuck said bitterly. "Who knows how much truth is in them?" He went to walk away and Candy touched his forearm, halting him. She looked up at him with wide, imploring eyes.

"Please don't lose faith in him. If not for my father, then stay for me."

"For you?"

"Yes, remember how we spoke on the boat? Of me wanting to understand my mother. I may never get another chance to walk in her shoes and live the life she shared with my father."

"I can't willingly risk the lives of men so you can get a little closure."

"It's more than that. I'm frightened."

"Of this place? You should be."

"Not just that. I'm afraid that if you turn back and your men and Emanuel's men follow you, my father will persist in his expedition. He'll go alone if need be."

"That's on his head. If he wants to die out here alone, it's not on me."

Candy looked down solemnly. "He wouldn't die alone. You know I can't allow that. I'd stay with my father. As would Mustaf."

"Even if it was suicide?"

Candy sighed. "It might not be. I'm trying to be more like you, ever optimistic." She let her fingers slide down Chuck's forearm, across the back of his hand before moving away from him and returning to her father. Chuck watched her go, wanting to run after her, wanting to wrap his arms around her and kiss her on the lips. She certainly had something about her.

"What did she say?" Pat asked.

Chuck shook his intrusive thoughts aside. "She was asking us to stay. She says that if we leave the professor will continue on without us."

"And she'll go with him?"

"Right. What do you think we should do?"

Pat considered their options. "He has omitted some details, but he was on the money when it came to this valley. Could be the Stone of Qualbec is here. Are we really going to hike all the way back home without ever knowing?"

Chuck couldn't help but grin. "I wouldn't dream of it."

***

"Hold on a second, I gotta go," Dillon grinned four hours later, as the group came into a clearing.

"Stay close," Chuck said, keenly listening to the sounds of the forest.

Dillon looked sheepishly over to where Candy was standing. "No can do, I wouldn't do that to the lady," he laughed.

Chuck rolled his eyes. "Just stay alert, okay?" He then announced to the rest of the group that they were taking a break, a fact everyone was happy with. Emanuel's men set down their heavy loads and began passing out biscuits and water to the others.

Dillon pushed past several trees as he looked for somewhere discreet to squat. "Jackpot," he smiled to himself as he found the perfect upturned log to hide behind. In his hand he held toilet roll alongside a small pack of sunflower seeds.

He set his rifle down, placed the toilet roll beside it and ripped the top off the pack of sunflower seeds. He placed a couple in his mouth before unbuckling his pants, lowering them and squatting.

As he waited for things to happen he listened to the sounds of the jungle. It had suddenly grown silent, as if nature herself were holding her breath. The hairs on the back of his neck stood up on end as the feeling of being watched became inescapable.

"Hello?" he called out before sitting in silence, his body tensing. He almost went back to what he was doing when he heard a branch snap somewhere in front of him. "If someone is there, show yourself," he ordered.

A dark shape, similar to a man exploded out of a nearby bush and ran at him at top speed, arms raised and primal features set in a mask of hate. The Ape-Man roared as he bounded towards his intended victim, arms raised and something in his hands.

Dillon's body froze in fear, he wanted to reach for his rifle but knew he wouldn't have time to aim.

The Ape-Man was upon him and-

Bang!

The sound of a gunshot rang out and the Ape-Man fell backwards, dead before it even hit the muddy ground.

Dillon stood up, pulling his pants back into place. "What took you so long?" he yelled.

Grant emerged from the trees behind Dillon's resting place, smoking rifle resting on his shoulder. He grinned. "I wanted to make sure you'd finished your business first," he joked.

Dillon cracked up with laughter as the rest of the party warily converged onto the location to look over their fallen adversary. Emanuel and his men crossed themselves and whispered prayers as they looked upon the ghastly visage of the Ape-Man. It was just as Ambrose had described; its body covered in a thick, brown, matted hair. Around its waist and groin was a covering of leaves.

Grant's aim had been impeccable, a single bullet hole had struck the creature where its heart would be. It would have died before even being aware of its fate.

Yellowing, curved canines and incisors indicated a diet consisting at least partly of meat. Its small, brown eyes were set beneath a heavy brow and now gazed emptily to the sky.

"It looks awful," Candy shuddered.

"It doesn't smell no better, either," added Pat.

"That might be me," laughed Dillon.

Chuck kept his eyes on Ambrose. "This is what we are dealing with? At least now we know."

Ambrose gave a determined nod, though his fear seeped through.

Chuck looked down at the Ape-Man's hands; clasped in one was a stone hatchet. One swipe would have been all that was needed to split a man's head in half.

The team had been aware of the Ape-Man stalking them for some time and Grant and Dillon had come up with the plan of Dillon separating himself from the group to lure it out. Predators couldn't help but attack the isolated members of the herd first, they'd surmised.

Chuck hadn't been happy with the plan but accepted they needed to do something. Dillon was more than happy to test out his acting. His trust in his friend's shooting ability meant he couldn't even see the risk in the endeavour.

"This creature is over seven-feet tall and intelligent. It made that hatchet; it dug that hole for us." Chuck spoke to the entire group. "We are in enemy territory. Everyone be ready for action and keep yourself armed." He looked to Candy. "And I mean *everyone.*" He then turned to Ambrose. "Professor, how many of these creatures do you think there are?"

Ambrose looked doubtful. "I couldn't say. All I can confirm is that there were a lot more than one set of drums being beaten last time I was here."

"Understood," Chuck nodded. "And it would have taken more than one of these things to dig out that spike-pit."

"I can still feel it," Dillon uttered.

"Feel what?" asked Bill.

"The feeling of being watched. This fellow wasn't alone, mark my words. Now we've drawn first-blood. There's gonna be hell to pay."

Beyond the trees the howling of apes began to rise like a cacophony before quieting, replaced by the sounds of lumbering movement.

CHAPTER 11

Within the modest, tan-coloured tent, Felipe soaked a sponge in a small bowl of water before gently placing it on the forehead of Mateo. The old man had been swimming in and out of consciousness and lucidity since he'd been injured by the great bear the morning before. He now had a fever and his bandages were in need of changing. Felipe carefully changed them as Mateo groaned in pain, intermittently yelling to demons that only he could see. He was thankful when he was done and stepped out of the claustrophobic environment.

A small way away, Pablo stood leaning against a tree, a lit cigarette in his mouth and his rifle in his hand. "How is he?" he asked between inhalations.

"Not good," Felipe said, ruefully shaking his head. "Perhaps it would be kinder to put him out of his misery. I don't think he's going to make it. His wounds are deep and starting to show signs of infection."

"That would be a sin," Pablo responded, sadly offering the cigarette to his friend.

Felipe gratefully accepted the smoke. "The sin was coming here in the first place. Mateo knew that. Now look at him."

"You really think that cave is the entryway to the Underworld?"

Felipe shrugged. "I don't know, but I am certain that bear was a demon from hell."

Pablo thought on those words. "Maybe we should leave."

"And abandon the others?" Felipe was shocked at the suggestion. "That would be murder."

"Assuming any of them are still alive."

"You better pray they are. The dead don't pay their ledgers."

Pablo thought on this and sighed. "You're right there."

They were both suddenly caught off guard as a man came walking out from the trees. He was tall and fair skinned, with jet black hair, a trim beard and an eye patch.

Both men suddenly stood alert, Pablo pointing his rifle at the stranger. "Who are you?" he yelled.

The eye-patch man chuckled, his demeanour relaxed as he held up his hands to show he meant no harm. "Gentlemen, please. I've travelled far to reach here. I'm looking for a Mister Tanner."

"Could he be an evil spirit?" gasped Felipe.

"Don't be ridiculous," Pablo chastised his friend. "Identify yourself or I blow your head off."

The man kept his relaxed expression. "My name is Mister DeShard. Has Mister Tanner mentioned me?"

The two labourers exchanged an uncertain glance. "Not that I recall," said Pablo.

DeShard hid how much it irked him that Tanner hadn't even mentioned his name to those he travelled alongside. "Mister Tanner and I are friends. We've had many adventures together, which is why I'm here now. His friend back in New York is very sick. I've journeyed to tell him, to get him home at once."

"It would take you two weeks at the earliest to get back. You're lying."

DeShard looked dismayed. "I assure you; I am not. Please, this is of the utmost importance. If you can tell me where Mister Tanner is, I'll be able to deliver my message to him."

"I think he's telling the truth," surmised Felipe. "He knows Mister Tanner. He's a fellow adventurer."

Pablo kept his rifle trained on DeShard a little longer before slowly lowering it. "Mister Tanner and the rest of the team have headed off through the cave, a little further up."

"Really? When did they head through?"

"Around midday yesterday."

DeShard smiled. "Fantastic, thanks so much for all your help. But tell me, why have you two remained here?"

Felipe spoke up. "We were attacked by a great bear that lived in the cave. It was killed, its body is still outside the cave. We've set up camp here in case the smell of its carcass attracts scavengers."

"Good thinking."

"Mister DeShard, please. Our friend is gravely wounded and we have done all we can for him. Have you any medical expertise or supplies that will be able to aid him?"

DeShard stroked his chin, deep in thought. "I can offer one solution to your problem." He then turned to the trees and nodded. Immediately the sounds of automatic-rifle fire flared up and Pablo and Felipe were hit by a barrage of bullets. They jerked like marionette puppets in a bizarre dance as the bullets ripped through flesh, bone and vital organs and blood sprayed from them. The firing stopped as the bodies of the two men hit the ground.

DeShard wistfully smiled. "Hopefully that has helped." He then placed his hands behind his back and made his way towards the tent.

From the trees emerged DeShard's usual entourage; the blood-thirsty femme-fatale, Hilda Klein; the quiet, deadly lieutenant, Grigore Dragos; the sadistic, rotund fool, Joe Hill. Alongside them was Jeffrey Buchannon, the petty, self-proclaimed rival of Professor Ambrose, his man servant and friend, George Daniels and also Christobal Hernandez, the brutal, efficient leader of a team of twenty equally hardened mercenaries. Hernandez was a violent, death-dealing man who chomped on his cigar while scanning the surroundings for any other threats. The rifle in his hands was still hot from firing and across his bare, muscular chest were two crossing straps. Off each strap hung several grenades that Hernandez was eager to use. Many of Hernandez's twenty men were in the process of changing their rifle magazines, the need to reload being the only reason they had stopped firing on the two labourers.

DeShard peeked his head into the tent, where he found Mateo pleading for help. He stepped away from it, holding his nose and grimacing. "Hernandez, deal with this, if you please."

Hernandez nodded "Si," and walked to the tent. He glanced inside, covering his nose at the odour within. He then pulled one of his grenades from his chest, pulled the pin and tossed it into the tent. He casually walked away and seconds later the grenade exploded, shredding the tent and reducing Mateo to charred mincemeat.

"That was rather 'over-kill,' wouldn't you say?" sighed DeShard.

Hernandez grinned. "You do your job and I'll do mine." He then walked back to his comrades.

"You know where they went?" smiled Hilda, stepping alongside DeShard, loving the thrill of the hunt and the spilling of blood.

DeShard flashed a smile. "Those fools told me where to head. Not far from here is a cave. That's the route into Vincabamba. We've made good time. They aren't much more than a day in front of us. Tanner is almost mine."

Soon they reached the cave entrance, the remains of the Cave-Bear still where it fell. "Goodness, the size of this beast," Hilda exclaimed, her excitement ever-growing.

DeShard knelt before the bear, studying it in detail. "Remarkable." He then looked up at Buchannon and Daniels who looked on in awe. "Quite an amazing specimen, wouldn't you agree?"

Buchannon and Daniels nervously glanced at the creature. "Yes, quite amazing."

If DeShard noticed their lack of enthusiasm, he didn't show it. "Gentlemen, we are on the threshold of history. I want to thank you personally, Mister Buchannon, for making this possible. I promise you won't regret making this expedition of ours a reality."

Buchannon managed a half-smile. "Quite right, old boy."

DeShard returned a wicked sneer as he barked orders at the mercenaries before leading their team into the cave. Hilda pouted like a jilted lover as she was forced to leave the dead bear behind.

When he was certain nobody else could hear them, Daniels whispered into Buchannon's ear. "Sir, did you see what they did there? To those men? That was murder. Cold blooded murder."

"Of course I saw, do you think I am blind? I nearly vomited as I walked past what was left of them."

"Is this really something you want to be a part of?"

"I don't know…" Buchannon mumbled. "We're in the wilderness. The rules are different out here, I suppose. That man was armed, after all."

"It was murder, sir. No matter where we are."

Buchannon sighed as he descended into the darkness of the cave. "I know, old boy. I know…"

CHAPTER 12

Chuck's men kept rifles drawn at all times, constantly watching for movement in the trees, aware of the hulking Ape-Men that could be lurking within them.

"Time's getting on," Pat noted. "In a few hours we'll lose daylight. We'd better start looking for somewhere to camp for the night."

"There's something I can agree on," chimed Bill.

Chuck nodded. "We'll head on another half hour, then set up for the night."

He stopped suddenly as the sound of something very big could be heard moving through the trees. "Everyone stand still," he ordered, trying to ascertain the location of the movement. The group listened as they could hear trees creak their protest as they were passed by some lumbering giant.

"The Ape-Men?" Bill asked.

Chuck shook his head. "No. It sounds bigger. Pat, Bill, with me. The rest of you form a tight group."

Nobody needed telling twice and the main group tightened their ranks while Chuck, Pat and Bill followed the noise into the trees.

"If it sounds bigger, why are we following it?" Bill whined. "I'm not eager to be some primal beast's lunch."

Pat grinned at his friend. "Don't worry, if it's another of those teeny-tiny dinos, I'll give you fair warning."

Bill pouted, his scratches from earlier suddenly stinging.

Chuck emerged into a large clearing and his mouth dropped open in amazement. The clearing held a waterhole and standing beside it, drinking from the still water was the largest, most majestic looking animal he had ever seen. Its hide was scaley with a dark green hew. It stood on four tree trunk-sized legs and at the very end of a long, slender neck was a small head that sipped gently from the water. At its back end was a long, slender tail of equal proportions to its neck. The colossal dinosaur had to be at least sixty feet in length and sixteen feet high at the hip. It gave a low, rumbling call, like an oversized cow between gulping down mouthfuls of water.

"Bill, get Ambrose's team here right away," ordered Chuck and Bill quickly ran back to the others. Chuck noticed Pat watching him. "They're going to want to see this."

"Stupendous!" cried out Crowley in wonder as he stepped close to Chuck. "It's the most beautiful thing I have ever seen."

"That's all well and good, Professor, but what is it? Is it dangerous?"

"Dangerous? I would think not, so long as we keep our distance. What we are looking at is an Apatosaurus. It's a strict herbivore."

Chuck relaxed somewhat at the knowledge the long-necked dinosaur wouldn't make a snack of him or any of his people. He was all too aware that didn't make it safe, though. He'd seen the damage a stampeding elephant could do and understood that any large animal represented a potential threat.

"Incredible, isn't it?" Candy grinned as she took photos with her small camera.

Chuck smiled uneasily. "It really is something."

Candy touched his arm. "I'm glad you chose to stay."

"So am I." Chuck's smile grew more genuine.

Crowley stepped out from the trees with Nathaniel close behind him. "Set up the camera there, put in a wide lens. I'll put myself in the shot for scale purposes."

Nathaniel nodded, pulling out a tripod and setting up for the shot.

"Be careful out there," Chuck warned them. "You're pretty exposed."

"We'll be fine," grinned Crowley. "Just a few photos. We shan't even be getting close to the animal."

Suddenly Ambrose was standing beside Chuck, watching the gentle behemoth as it drank with tears in his eyes. "I just wanted to thank you for making this happen," he said. "And I am sorry. For lying, I mean."

Chuck scratched the back of his head, searching for the right words to say. "Let's just agree to a clean slate from here on in. With no secrets." He held out a hand to Ambrose, who clasped it and shook vigorously.

"Agreed."

Out on the field in front of the Apatosaurus, Nathaniel fumbled with his various camera equipment and accidently dropped his bag into the mud. "Oh, bother," he cried, crouching to pick it up. He sighed as he tried to wipe the mud from it.

"Nathaniel, please hurry," urged Professor Crowley, trying not to lose his patience with the cameraman's fumbling. "Opportunities like this are a once in a lifetime event."

"I'm being as quick as I can," Nathaniel replied, wiping his muddied hand on his shirt.

Crowley turned back around to observe the spectacle before him. "Breathtaking," he smiled under his breath.

The Apatosaur raised its head suddenly and bellowed in alarm. Crowly suddenly felt miniscule besides the colossal creature; small and fragile.

Back amongst the trees, Chuck noticed the change in behaviour the Apatosaurus was displaying. "Something is wrong," he yelled. "Something has spooked it. Crowley, Nathaniel, get back here."

Grant and Dillon had their rifles aimed and were hunkered down, as if in a warzone. "There's something out there," Dillon asserted.

"Where?" asked Chuck, sweeping left to right with his own rifle.

"It was fast," was all Dillon could say.

"There," yelled Grant. "Coming from the right, heading straight for Crowley."

Chuck saw the dinosaur and shuddered at its speed and power. "Crowley, get out of there!"

Crowley struggled to stay on his feet as the Apatosaurus bellowed and stomped its feet, causing the ground to shake. "Where? I don't see anything." He then looked right and came face to face with a nightmare.

The dinosaur sprinting towards him was easily as tall as a man and as fast as any ostrich, its two powerful legs propelled it across the mud. The dinosaur's body was a reddish-tan colour, its snout long and filled with curved, sharp teeth. Its arms were long and ended with three, sharp curved claws, yet they paled into insignificance compared to the eight-inch retractable sickle-shaped claw present on each of its feet. Everything about the dinosaur screamed agility and power, especially its legs and long tail, which were solid muscle. Although Crowley couldn't see from his angle, the dinosaur's body length was well over twelve feet in length, from snout to tail. The dinosaur's reptilian, green eyes had locked onto him, its mouth was agape and its arms spread wide as it charged at him, releasing an unholy screech.

Crowley cried out in terror as he dropped to the ground in fear. He held an arm up to defend himself, knowing it would be useless.

Gunfire rang out and rifle bullets tore into the murderous creature, sending it sprawling to the ground as blood sprayed from it.

Crowley looked on in shock as the dinosaur remained in the mud, still breathing but mortally wounded from the bullet wounds. A pool of blood seeped out beneath the twitching creature. "Raptor," Crowley managed to say. "It's a Raptor."

"We got more incoming!" yelled Dillon as he opened fire on another of the deadly dinosaurs.

"What did you say they are?" Chuck yelled to Ambrose.

"They appear to be Raptors of some kind, though larger than any yet discovered. They are fierce, deadly hunters with a keen intelligence." He shook his head in despair. "And they hunt in packs."

"Run, get back to the trees," called out Grant as he emptied a magazine into another of the pursuing carnivores, causing it to shriek as it was riddled with bullets.

Crowley ran as fast as he could, the sounds of roars, screeches and the snapping of jaws sounding all around him as gunfire rung out from the trees.

He ran past the much younger Nathaniel, who was struggling to run with all his camera equipment. "Drop it, man, run for your life," Crowley yelled to him.

"Do you realise the scientific value of the photos I have taken?" called back Nathaniel. "I can't just abandon them!" He dropped part of his stand and cursed, turning to pick it up. As he did so a shadow fell over him and he looked up in time to see the powerful Raptor leaping down upon him. Before he could react the predator crashed down upon him, its retractable claws raking against his stomach and instantly disembowelled him as the claws on its hands dug deep into his shoulders. Nathaniel crumpled like a house of cards without time for a scream as the Raptor bit deep across his face and continued eviscerating him with constant rakes of its powerful legs.

Candy looked away in horror as the fighting continued. Dillon tried to take out the dinosaur that had killed Nathaniel, but it proved too fast and darted to the side.

Crowley reached the trees and Chuck gave the order for everyone to fall back as the Raptors darted in amongst the trees to give chase. One nearly pounced upon Chuck before he spotted it and put it down with half a magazine.

"This is bad," Grant yelled to him. "They're too fast and too many."

"We just need to stick together!" Chuck yelled back, shooting at and missing a Raptor that ran behind a wall of greenery.

***

Emanuel ordered his men to maintain order and help resist the prehistoric predators and they all did so, pulling out sidearms to combat the threat they now faced. A Raptor leapt at one of the men, his shots fired too wide to hit it as it clamped its jaws around his arm. He cried out in pain before being silenced by a kick from the Raptor's hind leg which went straight through his stomach and out his back, sending blood and viscera over the green backdrop of the jungle.

"Jose!" yelled the next nearest man, Lucas. He turned his pistol on the Raptor and unloaded his magazine. The Raptor demonstrated its intelligence, seemingly already well aware of what a gun was. It ducked behind the still standing Jose, who was already dead and swaying on his feet in a kind of death-trance. Lucas's bullets slammed into Jose's back, sending more blood spraying into the air. None hit their intended target.

Lucas gulped in terror as his pistol clicked on empty and he immediately went to reload. The instant he looked down the Raptor pounced, slashing out with its eight-inch claw, drawing it down and across Lucas's torso.

Lucas dropped down to his knees in shock as he tasted blood rise in his throat and pour from his mouth. He looked down to see bright red intestines spilling out and onto the muddied ground. Unable to fully process what he was witnessing, he reached down and tried to pull his intestines back inside him. The organs were too slick and slippery, causing them to constantly slide from his blood-soaked hands.

The Raptor watched Lucas's struggles, almost as if enjoying the sight, before ending the man with a swift kick to the chest. The vicious, powerful kick sent Lucas sliding across the ground, his intestines trailing in the mud behind him. The Raptor gave a victorious screech before its brains were blown out by several rounds from Emanuel's rifle. He crossed himself as he saw what was left of Lucas and Jose before returning to the fight. Men were still yelling; guns were firing and dinosaurs were still screeching their contempt.

***

"Stay behind me!" Mustaf ordered Ambrose and Candy as he dropped to one knee and opened fire on a Raptor that was charging them. The dinosaur screeched in pain as he took out its legs and it fell to the ground with a heavy thud. He quickly shot another three rounds into the thing's snapping head before ignoring it, steadying himself for the next attack.

A Raptor burst from the trees immediately to his left and charged at Ambrose. Mustaf cried out in frustration, surprised the savage dinosaur had managed to get so close without him noticing it. The Raptor leapt for Ambrose as the professor turned to escape, the momentum from the dinosaur's attack sending him face first into the mud. Ambrose cried out in horror as the Raptor pinned him with its weight and savaged his backpack, sending strips of material into the air.

Mustaf pulled his rifle around to take the animal out. The Raptor seemed to notice this manoeuvre and whipped out at the large man with its powerful, muscular tail. Mustaf was sent sprawling to the ground, the rifle knocked from his hands and lost amongst the ferns that peppered the ground.

"Damn you," Mustaf yelled in fury. The Raptor turned to face him, the crying Ambrose beneath its feet all but forgotten. The dinosaur screeched and snapped in rage as Mustaf pulled out his machete. "Come on, you monster! Fight me!" The Raptor snorted, bared its teeth and bobbed its head, sizing up the weapon as it prepared to leap at its foe.

Behind the dinosaur, Candy screamed for her father, unsure what to do. She was soon silenced by the high-pitched screech of another Raptor that emerged from between the trees and trained its vision on her. She froze, unsure what to do.

"Run!" yelled Mustaf at the top of his lungs. "Run and don't look back!" He then yelled and charged the Raptor that confronted him as it screeched and leapt.

Candy couldn't look back at the ensuing fight, couldn't look back at her father whimpering in the mud, as she quickly clambered to her feet and ran as fast as she could. The Raptor that had spotted her gave another screech and gave chase, its padded footsteps and guttural snorts filling her ears.

Candy knew that if she looked back the dinosaur would have her. She ducked and weaved between trees and branches as all around her, close but hidden by the surrounding trees, others were enduring their own battles. Bullets whizzed, men screamed, dinosaurs screeched. It was as if the entire world had suddenly descended into pandemonium.

The Raptor was catching up to her, snapping at her heels. Candy knew she couldn't outrun it forever. She spotted a hollowed out fallen tree-trunk to her left and without any thought, for there was no time for thinking, she leapt into it. She landed hard and kept scurrying on her hands and knees, ignoring the pain in her knees as she crawled frantically into the darkness of the log.

The Raptor screeched furiously as it attempted to follow, charging full speed into the opening. Rotten bark crumbled and split from the force of its attack as the Raptor hissed and snapped and clawed, eager to get at the trapped girl.

Candy screamed again and pushed herself deeper into the narrowing log. She didn't have much more room to squeeze herself into and the Raptor's powerful, rapid movements were causing the bark to crumble beneath its efforts, allowing it to push itself deeper and deeper inside.

Candy cried out, tears streaming from her eyes as she began clawing at the caked mud and moss at the end of the log, trying to make even the smallest amount of space to help her get more distance from the manic reptile. The

Raptor hissed and snapped some more, its fetid breath, smelling like raw meat, washed over her. It had nearly reached her and continuously snapped at her legs. Candy screamed before delivering the hardest kick she could muster at the dinosaur's face. If the Raptor felt any kind of pain from the kick to the snout it didn't show it. Instead, it reacted with impossible speed and clamped its jaws around her boot. Candy screamed again as she was dragged towards the death-dealing creature.

***

Standing shoulder to shoulder with Dillon, Grant and Pat, Chuck emptied another magazine into one of the attacking dinosaurs, sending it to the ground in a spray of blood and viscera.

"We're burning through ammo, man," Dillon yelled out.

"How many more of these things are there?" cried out Pat.

Somehow, through the gunfire and the ringing in his ears, Chuck heard Candy scream. He quickly reloaded his rifle and yelled into Dillon's ear. "I'm going to check on the others. You guys keep formation and blow these mothers to kingdom come."

"Sir, yes sir!" Dillon yelled back over the sound of Grant firing.

Chuck turned and ran. A Raptor spotted the moving target and gave chase, leaping over the bodies of its brethren, single-mindedly pursuing its prey. Dillon spotted it and let rip; a hail of bullets tore into the Raptor's side, knocking it down. It didn't get up again.

Controlling his breathing, Chuck ran through the jungle, ready to fire upon anything that didn't look immediately human. This was no longer a hazard zone, but a war zone. That meant shooting first and asking questions later.

He stopped, panting for breath as he tried to discern Candy's screaming again from all the chaotic noise. Nearby he heard small arms fire and turned to see Bill had just unloaded into the open maw of a charging Raptor, the beast now drowning in its own blood, twitching. They made eye contact and Chuck gave him a nod, glad to see his friend was still alive. Bill returned the sentiments. They both then turned upon hearing Candy's screams again, this time filled with the utmost desperation.

Chuck sprinted in the direction of the screams with Bill close behind him. They soon came upon a fallen log with the rear-end of a Raptor sticking out the entrance. Candy's screams emanated from within the bark as the Raptor continued to strive to push itself deeper inside the tight space.

Chuck guessed where the Raptor's middle was and opened fire. Chunks of bark flew into the air alongside jets of blood. The dinosaur stopped moving as blood began to seep out the bottom of the fractured timber.

"Give me a hand, quick," Chuck yelled and ran to the hind-end of the dinosaur, dropped his rifle and clasped the creature's tail. Bill followed suit and the prehistoric beast was pulled free from the dead tree. Its middle had been almost completely cut open from the rifle rounds and its guts seeped out.

Eventually the entire dinosaur was pulled free, its jaws still clamped tight on a walking boot.

As soon as there was space, Chuck crouched by the log opening and called inside. "Candy? Candy, are you okay?" He could see Candy huddled in the back of the log, weeping. "I'm coming in to get you, okay?" he said before clambering into the log. Outside, Bill kept guard, prepared should another Raptor attack at any moment.

Chuck reached out to touch Candy's shoulder. In the darkness of the log, he couldn't see if she was hurt or not. He shook her gently. "Candy? Candy, are you okay? Are you hurt?"

Candy's eyes peeked out from above her shoulder, red and puffy. They took a moment to register her rescuer and then she leapt at him. Chuck widened his arms as best he could, allowing Candy into his embrace and he held her tight as she wept into his chest.

"Oh, Chuck. You saved me!" she exclaimed amidst sobs.

"It's okay," Chuck whispered tenderly, stroking her hair. "I'm here now. I got you. You're okay."

Candy held him even tighter. "I don't think I'm ever going to be okay again."

***

"See anything?" asked Grant, scanning the quiet trees, searching for movement through the smoke of battle.

Dillon regarded the several dead Raptors sprawled across the ground. "Nothing moving. You think we got them all?"

"Not a chance. Hey, Pat. You see any more of these lizards running through the trees?"

"All quiet on the western front," Pat replied, refusing to move out of his shooting stance until he was absolutely certain the attack had ended.

Chuck slowly came walking towards them, Candy and Bill close behind him. "Glad to see you guys survived."

"You're a sight for sore eyes, too," replied Pat. "Same can't be said for poor Nathaniel, though. He was torn to shreds."

"I lost two men, too," said Emanuel. He cautiously walked past a dead dinosaur, keeping his gun trained on it. "We managed to protect Professor Crowley. Does anyone know where Professor Ambrose is?"

Candy's eyes widened. "I ran," she stuttered. "Father and Mustaf were being attacked. Mustaf lost his weapon. I ran!"

Chuck held her arms to calm her. "It's okay, you did what you had to. Where were they? You said Mustaf lost his rifle?"

Candy nodded. "It was knocked from his hand."

"If he lost his weapon, maybe you shouldn't search with the lady," suggested Grant. "It could be bad."

"What do you mean by that?" snapped Candy. "They're alive. I'm certain of it." She then pulled out of Chuck's grip and ran away through the foliage.

Chuck stared daggers at Grant, who looked away. "You really need to work on your tact," he snapped before following Candy's path. "Hey Candy," he called. "Candy, wait up, don't go running alone. Those Raptors are likely still close by."

"Father!" he heard Candy call and so doubled his efforts. Sure enough, he found Candy crouched by her father. Ambrose sat on a rock, his entire front covered in mud and blood ran from his nose. He looked like he'd been through hell.

"Ambrose, thank God you are alive," smiled Chuck. "Where is Mustaf?"

Ambrose pointed and Chuck followed his finger, holding his breath at what he saw.

Around twenty feet away Mustaf sat upon the remains of a Raptor, killed not with bullets, but with well-aimed strikes of a blade. Sitting upon the body, the giant that was Mustaf breathed deeply, as if praying or in deep meditation as he tried to come to terms with what he had endured. His shirt had been shredded, revealing the solid muscle beneath his rich, brown skin. Three deep cuts ran across his chest, the defiant act of his fallen enemy. Sitting as he did, Mustaf appeared larger than life, as a legendary warrior from a time long ago, splattered with the blood of his enemy.

Other men stood beside Chuck, observing the man that had single handedly killed one of the Raptors with a machete and whispered in awe and respect.

When Dillon saw the spectacle, he grinned. "When we're on the way home, I've got to give that man an arm-wrestling rematch."

CHAPTER 13

In the aftermath of the Raptor attack, supplies were counted, as were the fallen. Emanuel confirmed two of his men, Jose and Lucas, were dead. Alongside Nathaniel, that meant they had lost three men in the space of about ten minutes.

Arthur Ambrose reeled from the information, unable to compute that all the violence and shooting had occurred in such a short space of time. Chuck and his men knew better. They had fought in the war and understood that time seemed to slow when your life was on the line.

Fifteen of the Raptors had been killed, although how many more lurked amongst the trees was unknown. Had they all been killed? Were some stalking them, even now? Chuck doubted they'd got them all, but he was hopeful the carnivores had come to realise they'd bitten off more than they could chew when they tackled the humans and retreated.

Fifteen dead Raptors against three fallen men meant a net win for the humans. Looking around the group now, it sure didn't feel like a victory. They had travelled thirty minutes north of the battlefield before setting up camp, hoping the distance would help them avoid any further conflicts with the savage dinosaurs. They had now set up camp in an open area of grassland, the tall grass reaching their knees. Trees still surrounded them, but it was nice not to be constantly hemmed in by dense foliage.

"There's always losses on the battlefield," Grant surmised coldly as he serviced his rifle, preparing for the next conflict to arise. Dillon sat beside him, doing the same and nodding his head. He remained quiet.

"This isn't war," Ambrose retorted, feeling disgusted with himself and responsible for the deaths they had incurred.

"It's always war," Grant replied without looking up. "And besides, we took more of them down than they did us. I call that a win."

Emanuel stood up from his nearby seating position and moved away, disgusted by Grant's point of view. "I'll be sure to tell that to the wives and mothers of those two men I lost today."

Nearby, Professor Crowley wept, trying to understand the tragedy that had befallen them. He'd always been fascinated by the prehistoric world and dedicated his life to uncovering the mysteries of the dinosaurs. That the object of his passion had wrought such misery was hard to accept.

Candy went from person to person, tending to any wounds they had suffered and offering a consoling voice. She'd cried enough and now kept herself busy to avoid dwelling on their terrible reality.

Chuck listened to the various conversations surrounding him as he hung his head, trying to decide what their next step should be.

"I never imagined this," Ambrose said, his voice low and his face downcast. He'd been badly bruised by the Raptor attack and there was a fear his nose was broken. The old man seemed past caring. "I never imagined my expedition would lead to such suffering. If I had, I'd never have come here."

"You knew it was dangerous," Chuck replied. "You told me yourself."

"Yes, of course I knew there was a risk. But still, this? We've lost three men. Possibly four, if Mateo succumbs to his wounds from the bear. This is simply terrible."

Emanuel sat close to them to join in the discussion. "We should leave here and head back to the cave. And we should bring the bodies of our dead with us."

"We haven't the resources for that. The dead will have to remain here."

Emanuel spat at Chuck's feet, outraged. "My men can carry your equipment and your supplies, but they can't carry their friends home?"

"Emanuel, please," said Ambrose, softly placing a hand on the man's shoulder. "We are all devastated by what has happened here, but let's be practical."

Emanuel's shoulders sagged. "If we knew it would be like this, I'd have brought Felipe and Pablo along. We need all the men we can get right now."

"How is the men's morale?" asked Chuck.

Emanuel bitterly laughed. "You mean are they thinking of betraying you and heading home? Don't worry, they won't do that. They are good, loyal men."

Pat walked over and sat beside Chuck. "What are you lot discussing?"

"Whether we should turn back," Chuck informed him.

"Turn back?" he said with surprise. "Why in God's name would you do that?"

"Look around you," Chuck said abruptly.

"The price to pay for the Stone of Qualbec may be too high," Ambrose sighed.

Pat looked positively outraged by the mere suggestion. "What? Are you lot a bunch of quitters?"

"Not quitters, just realists," Chuck said.

"I can't believe I am hearing this. Is it your men, Emanuel? Are they refusing to continue?"

Emanuel shook his head. "Nobody is refusing anything."

Pat then turned to Ambrose. "Then is it you, Professor? Have you lost the stomach for adventure?"

"This isn't adventure," Ambrose retorted.

"Sure it is. There is always the risk of lives being lost. That's why we live the lives we do, to chase that thrill. You either die with adrenaline pumping in your veins or you live to fight another day. Is this so different from that?"

"I would like to continue," said Professor Crowley as he approached them. "For all the terrible things I have witnessed today, they only show how little we understand about the mysteries of nature. How much we still have to learn. I've lived my entire life chasing that knowledge. Nathaniel gave his life for it. I can't turn and hide just because the battle for knowledge is hard. If humanity turned tail every time it encountered hardship, we'd still be living in caves."

"You are sure?" asked Ambrose.

"Yes, old friend. I am sure."

"Well, if the doubt to continue isn't from Emanuel's camp or Ambrose's camp, that leaves you," said Pat, turning to Chuck. "And I can't believe Grant, Dillon or even Bill would turn back unless you said so, so that leaves you."

Chuck glared at his old friend. "What are you suggesting?"

Pat didn't turn away. "Are you a coward?"

Chuck stood, feeling his anger rising. He balled his fists. "What did you say? You think I'm a coward?"

Pat stood and moved back a few steps; hands raised in defence. "Now, calm down. I didn't call you a coward. I merely posed a question."

Chuck took a step towards Pat, his anger unabated. "What do you think?"

"Before this conversation, I'd have thought you were the bravest man I've ever met. I wouldn't work for you or follow you if I thought anything less. We've travelled the world together, discovered countless tombs, temples, ruins and treasures. Never once have you shied away from danger. Until now."

"People are dying!"

"I know, and it's a tragedy. Truly it is. But what is the worse outcome? Those men dying for nothing, or those men immortalised as brave heroes who sacrificed their lives in pursuit of something greater than themselves? For God's sake, remember why we are here in the first place. We're talking about the Stone of Qualbec, here. Potentially the greatest prize there has ever been. It could be the reason this valley even exists in the state it is. Its powers could explain the presence of the creatures we are seeing now." He turned to Ambrose. "Is there a chance of that?"

"I suppose…" contemplated Ambrose.

"You see, the Stone could change our fundamental understanding of how the world works. Who are we to turn our backs on such a momentous discovery?"

"And all the glory that comes with it," Chuck said with animosity. He then turned to Ambrose. "You are certain the Stone is here?"

"I am positive. That hasn't changed," said Ambrose. "What I am doubting is how Austin could have survived in this place."

Chuck took a moment to make a decisive decision. When he spoke, he did so with a booming voice that the entire group could hear. Everyone stopped their current activity to listen to him. "Okay, that settles it. If there aren't any objections, we carry on. Pat's right, we've gone too far and lost too much to just walk away now, when we're on the cusp of history. We'll locate the Stone of Qualbec and we'll bring it back to civilisation. All of us and all of those who have lost their lives shall be heroes. With the riches the Stone will bring us we'll make sure the families of each man lost receives their share. We shall honour their memories."

"You're damn right!" cheered Pat and others assented their approval.

Feeling good now he had a confirmed plan, he asked Ambrose to retrieve his map so that they could plot their route.

Emanuel also stood to leave. "I'm going to take a man and walk perimeter."

"Do you need Grant or Dillon with you?"

Emanuel shook his head. "We should be fine. We're just making sure there's no evidence of the Raptors following us."

"Very good. If you see anything at all, shoot and we'll come running."

Emanuel smiled before walking over to where his men were grouped. "Joaquin, take a rifle and follow me. We're going to make sure we're safe for the night. Diago and Juan, begin setting up tents. Vincente and Javier, make sure all rifles are loaded and do an ammo count. It's important to know exactly how much fire power we have." The men nodded and went to their allotted tasks.

"That was quite the speech," smiled Candy, walking over with a coy smile.

Chuck grinned as he watched Emanuel and Joaquin walk into the tall trees immediately to their south. "The men needed a morale boost."

"Then a hot meal will work wonders."

"Sounds great. There's plenty of underbrush to start a fire. Make my steak medium rare."

Candy giggled. "Don't push it." She then walked to the bundle of kindling Emanuel's men had collected earlier and began making a fire.

Chuck watched her for a while, letting his mind wander to warm, soothing places. He allowed himself to linger in the daydream for a little until Bill sat down beside him.

"It appears you aren't the only person good at making speeches," Bill said, his voice guarded.

"What do you mean?"

Bill motioned to Pat, who was busy talking to Grant and Dillon. "You were about ready to cancel this whole expedition until *he* talked you around."

Chuck shrugged. "I always want to hear the opinions of you and Pat. You know that."

"I know that. I'm sure Pat knows that too."

"What are you suggesting?"

"Nothing," Bill replied, his eyes still on Pat. "Just making an observation."

Chuck was going to question Bill further when Ambrose came back holding the small, folded map. Mustaf was one step behind him, ever the bodyguard. They sat down with Chuck and the map was laid out on the back of a bullet tin. Chuck leaned in close to examine it.

"The bridge is close," Ambrose said. "Closer than I realised." He pointed to where they were in relation to the river. "By my reckoning it is barely fifteen minutes north of here. Five if we run."

"That close?" Chuck was surprised. "We're making progress, at least. No matter how painful it may be."

Ambrose looked sad, remembering those they had lost. "Agreed, we are."

Chuck looked at his watch. "We still have an hour of sunlight with us. I think we should head to the bridge now. If we can pass it today and the Raptors are on our tail, they'll only be able to come at us from one direction. They wouldn't stand a chance."

"Agreed."

"Then it's decided. I'll tell everyone to pack up. We'll be able to leave the southern part of the valley behind us before anything else bad happens."

A loud, guttural roar bellowed from beyond the treeline, the bass in it reverberating in Chuck's chest. Everyone in camp stood and turned to the south, trying to see what the source of the thunderous roar was. Those with sharp minds readied their rifles.

"What was that?" Ambrose asked, afraid of the answer.

From the treeline, shots were fired and Chuck winced as he remembered Emanuel and Joaquin were still in there. "That is the trouble I was hoping to avoid. Everyone, get ready to move, quick."

The trees swayed as something big approached, disturbing flocks of birds that took to the air, cawing in protest. Whatever was beyond the trees had to be gigantic, its movements impossible not to notice as trees snapped under enormous forces.

More gunshots rang out and then Joaquin appeared, running towards them and screaming in panic. Emanuel then appeared behind him; his face stricken with fear as he also made a beeline to the camp. Chuck and his men stood firm, waiting to see what was chasing them.

The trees swayed more rapidly, the sound of a giant creature running towards them, so large it was making the ground shake with booming footsteps.

"Get ready, here it comes!" Chuck shouted to the camp.

Trees parted and the tyrant lizard king himself, a Tyrannosaurus Rex, appeared. Its head was as large as a car, its jaws lined with dagger sharp teeth. The beast's skin was a mixture of greenish hues and its beady eyes centred on Emanuel, who was fleeing as fast as his legs could carry him.

The rifle in Chuck's hands suddenly felt pathetically small as the T-Rex gave another bellowing roar before giving chase. It looked to be built of solid muscle and moved with a speed which belied its size.

Emanuel couldn't help the tears from streaming down his face as he sensed the monster bear down upon him. He cried out in crazed fear as he turned to face his foe. Before he could raise his rifle the T-Rex snapped him up in its powerful jaws and viciously shook him from side to side, ensuring his brutal death. It bit down hard on his middle and the rapid, violent shaking movements sent Emanuel's lower half flying through the air, unceremoniously landing in the long grass some distance away. The T-Rex took no notice of the lost remains as it lifted its head and what remained of Emanuel's top half slid down its gullet.

Chuck hesitated; the sheer size of the beast in front of him made any attempt at defiance feel futile. "We need to run!" he shouted at the top of his lungs. "Head north! There should be a bridge we can cross! It's our only hope."

The rest of the group didn't need telling twice and everyone ran, all equipment and supplies left behind. Grant and Dillon unloaded their rifles into the T-Rex, serving only to enrage it before they also turned tail and ran for the bridge.

The T-Rex roared at the humans, strings of flesh dangling from between its teeth. It then began running after them, its wide strides closing the distance fast.

Behind the rest of the group, Joaquin cried out for help as he realised he'd be the next on the prehistoric killer's menu. The ground around him shook, as if he were in the midst of an earthquake. He knew the truth was not so kind. The shaking was from the impacts of the monstrous dinosaur's feet and that he could feel it so readily meant it was almost upon him.

Like his boss Emanuel had been, Joaquin was no coward and if death was coming for him, he would face it rather than run. Joaquin spun on the spot and pointed his rifle. The titanic terror, as large as a freight train and with as much momentum, widened its mouth to snatch him up. He screamed and pulled the trigger; a flurry of bullets hit inside the T-Rex's wide maw. It roared in pain and frustration, slowing its progress, lifting its head and rearing up to escape the stinging assault it was receiving.

For an instant Joaquin thought there just may be a way for him to survive this nightmare. The T-Rex had no such foolish thoughts and although it had learned to avoid the bullets, its hunger for flesh still drove it to attack.

The T-Rex stomped down on the man, instantly crushing his chest. Joaquin managed to open his mouth to scream, only for a fountain of blood to erupt from between his lips as his lungs and heart were reduced to pulp. The T-Rex took a step back to see what damage it had wrought. Satisfied the human could no longer cause it pain, the T-Rex bent down and snatched the flattened remains of the man up in its jaws. Sensing the prey was already dead, the dinosaur tilted its head back and crunched down twice as the remains of Joaquin were cleaved and crushed and swallowed whole. It then gave a bellowing roar to the sky, the taste of hot blood and flesh spurring it on to continue its attack.

***

"It's fallen behind," Pat yelled to Chuck as they ran. "Joaquin slowed it down!"

"At what cost?" Chuck said as he continued running. "Everyone, keep running as fast as you can! The bridge should be just a little further."

Ambrose cried out in panic and confusion as he was held under the arm of Mustaf, who had decided it would be safer for him to simply pick the professor up rather than allow the old man to run. Crowley had no one so loyal to carry him and puffed, out of breath as he struggled to keep up. Chuck's hand was clamped tight around Candy's wrist, ensuring she stayed close to him and didn't fall behind. Grant and Dillon would intermittently turn and fire upon the pursuing behemoth, though they could tell the futility of their actions.

"I've got a stitch," Bill gasped, holding his side.

"Fight the pain, man," Chuck urged him. "Don't give in."

"Believe me, I don't intend to."

Leading the charge was Juan and he called back to the others with a tone of delirium. "I see it! I see the bridge! We are going to make it!"

The trees to his left exploded as a second T-Rex sprinted from its hidden ambush location, jaws wide and its head tilted. Juan didn't even have time to understand what was happening as the T-Rex's jaws closed on him like a gigantic bear trap. Twelve-inch teeth closed upon his head and shins. His skull cracked like a nutshell, the grey brain matter exploding outwards from the biteforce. His shins snapped like matchsticks and the bottom fourth of his legs were completely cleaved from the rest of him and sent bouncing along the ground.

The giant reptile's momentum sent it stomping across the group's path and it ended up to the right of them. It twisted its body to watch them with its beady eyes as its jaws opened and closed several times, turning Juan's body to mincemeat and creating sickening wet crunching sounds before devouring him with one, mammoth swallow.

Chuck could see that Diago, Vincente and Javier were hesitating, unsure what they should do. "Keep running! Run right past it! If you stop, you'll be killed!" Behind him the first T-Rex roared as it gained again on the group.

"We're not going to make it," Candy cried out as they ran past the second T-Rex, positioning itself to snap at them and give chase.

"We'll make it. I promise."

The trees on either side of them fell away and Chuck could see the mighty, fast-moving river and the wide wooden bridge before them, just as Ambrose had said. Already most of the men were running across it. The bridge wasn't the small crossing he had imagined, however. It was big and sturdy. Big enough that the pursuing T-Rex could follow them on. Whether it would be able to take their weight or not was another thing entirely.

"Run!" cried Pat. "Run as fast as you can!"

Chuck realised that it was only him, Bill, Candy and Crowley who hadn't reached the bridge yet and the thunderous stomping of a T-Rex was becoming all encompassing.

"We're not going to make it," Bill cried. "It's catching up!"

"We're going to make it," Chuck said with confidence he didn't feel. "Just focus on the bridge." He knew that if he let go of Candy he would be able to sprint in front and ensure his survival, but there was no way in hell he was letting go of her.

Candy cried out in terror as the warm, fetid breath of the first T-Rex washed over her. Chuck turned his head to see what was happening and his heart skipped a beat as he saw the T-Rex with its mouth open wide, ready to snap down on Candy and pull her from his grasp. He'd failed to protect her...

Before the T-Rex could snap its powerful jaws closed it was tackled from the side by the second T-Rex. It fell sideways into a roll, the earth rumbling like thunder as eight tons of dinosaur crashed down upon it. It roared its protest as the second T-Rex snapped at it before giving chase, not wanting to share its meal.

The greed of the second T-Rex had saved Candy's life and now all members of the group were running over the wooden bridge. The pursuing T-Rex didn't stop to consider its actions as it blindly charged after them, the bridge cracking and swinging from its ungodly mass.

The fleeing humans, only halfway across the mighty river, all dropped to their stomachs, desperately holding on as the bridge swung left and right, threatening to snap into kindling at any moment. The T-Rex slowed its pursuit as it struggled to remain standing. Its ancient brain recognised the peril it had put itself in, though the available prey overrode its sense of preservation. It kept pushing forward over the protesting bridge, albeit at a more cautious pace.

Chuck looked back in horror, realising it wouldn't be long before the T-Rex reached him. "Crawl," he yelled out. "We've got to crawl."

Even as they crawled, trying their best not to be flung into the fast-flowing waters below, the dinosaur was catching up to them.

"It's going to get us," Candy whimpered as she pushed herself forward on her belly.

"It's not. I made you a promise, remember. You'll be okay."

She managed a tight smile. "Thank you, Chuck. But I think this is out of your hands."

The T-Rex gave a guttural half roar as it stood over the prone forms of Chuck and Candy, its mouth salivating at the prospect of more fresh meat. Candy squeezed Chuck's hand and closed her eyes, waiting for the inevitable.

"We got problems up ahead," yelled Dillon and Chuck looked forward, desperate for anything to distract him from the monstrous carnivore towering above him, about to swallow him whole.

At the other end of the bridge, four Ape-Men howled their evil howls and chattered in sadistic delight at the humans' predicament. They each held a sharpened stone hatchet which they used to start hacking at the supporting vines of the bridge.

"Stop them!" Dillon yelled to Grant, who was using all his energy to avoid falling into the rivers.

"You think I wouldn't if I could?" he yelled back.

One of the ropes was cut and that was all it needed for the entire bridge to collapse. The T-Rex roared in panic as it toppled into the swirling waters below.

"Hold on!" Chuck yelled to Candy as he saw men fall into the churning river ahead of them.

"I'm slipping," she cried in terror as both were suddenly flung from the bridge. Gravity seemed not to exist for a second or two and then all Chuck knew was the noise of water filling his ears and being unable to breathe. He knew he was now at the mercy of the frightful river, and worse, Candy had slipped from his grip, lost to the white-water rapids.

***

The first T-Rex, still on the riverside, watched as its rival and the prey it had chased all fell into the wide expanse of river and were rapidly swept away by its powerful flow. It then raised its head and observed the Ape-Men, howling their victory from the far side of the waterway. Frustrated that it had lost the prey it had been pursuing and that this new prey was out of its reach, the T-Rex roared to the heavens before stomping off back into the jungles to the south.

CHAPTER 14

DeShard kicked at the ashes of the fire that had been built by Tanner's group, trying to get a sense of how long ago the fire had been lit.

"They camped here last night," he stated, his voice echoing in the cavernous exit from the cave system. "Then they would have headed out to the jungle at daybreak."

"Should we set up camp for the night? Night is almost upon us," suggested Dragos while looking out at the strange jungle, now bathed in the red light of the setting sun.

"No, we will continue through the night if need be. Tanner and Ambrose can't be far ahead."

"Please, old boy," sighed Buchannon, sitting on the ground and rubbing his feet. Daniels sat beside him. "It's been an awfully trying day. Can't we set out in the morning?"

Hilda hissed at him, like some hateful feline.

"Why, Mister Buchanon, you surprise me," said DeShard with mock surprise.

"Why do you say that?" Buchannon sighed.

"Mister Tanner and Professor Ambrose are out there right now, exploring the wonders and mysteries this jungle has to offer. We are close, but if we falter in our resolve now, the prize shall be theirs."

Buchannon pulled himself to his feet, looking miserable. "Right you are, old boy. Right you are."

DeShard walked outside and breathed in the warm air, enjoying all the smells it carried. Hernandez and his men were patrolling the nearby area, ensuring the area was secure. He walked up to the mercenary leader, his chest out and his head carried high. He felt supremely in control of the situation, just as he liked it.

"Have you discovered any evidence of which direction Tanner's party went?"

Hernandez looked DeShard up and down before answering. "Some of my men have discovered the route they have used. It is easy to follow. They aren't expecting to be followed so are making no effort to cover their tracks."

DeShard grinned. "Their mistaken sense of security is our opportunity. Very good."

Hernandez went to say something when they were interrupted by one of his mercenaries. "In the trees. Something big is moving."

Hernandez nodded before glancing at DeShard. "Wait here." He then slowly began walking to the trees, rifle at the ready.

Feeling his heart beat in exhilaration, DeShard quickly returned to the cave and picked up his own weapon. Hilda could sense his excitement and her own rifle was quickly in her hands. "What is it, my love?"

"Something big, in the jungle. Could be big game." He then left. Hilda, Dragos and Joe followed close behind him, leaving Buchannon and Daniels to their own devices.

"Are you not eager to join them?" asked Daniels, downing water from his canteen.

Buchannon frowned. "I think I'll stay here."

"It might be exciting. Isn't that why you came here? For excitement and adventure?" There was an accusatory tone to Daniels's words.

"You know, I think I've completely gone off adventure."

***

DeShard spotted Hernandez and a group of his soldiers a few hundred meters into the jungle and made their way to him, as quietly as he could. The mercenaries had clearly seen something and were holding their positions with their rifles trained on the threat.

DeShard sidled his way to Hernandez and whispered. "What have you found?"

Hernandez regarded the eye-patch wearing adventurer and his cohorts before pointing to what had been found. Through the trees, grazing on ferns growing in the shadows of larger trees was a foreboding, heavy set, four-legged animal. Its bulky leathery skin was a dark green and black mottled affair and its head seemed to be completely armoured. A long, spiked crest covered the beast's neck like a protective shield and a large, two-foot long pointed horn was set upon its nose. The bizarre creature looked to be about eighteen feet in length and eight feet in height. It had to weigh between two and three tons and looked ready for a fight.

"An animal of some kind. Perhaps a rhino," Hernandez guessed.

DeShard grinned from ear to ear. "No, no. That's no rhino. That's an honest to God dinosaur."

Hernandez turned to his employer with a slack jaw. "A dinosaur?"

"Yes, it is unmistakable. I'm no expert but I'd guess a Styracosaurus. Apparently, this isolated section of land is a lost world of sorts, where animals long extinct elsewhere continue to walk the earth. No wonder Ambrose took every measure possible to keep this place hidden. The Stone of Qualbec is but one of its wonders."

"It is dangerous?"

"It is a plant eater, but I can't speak for its temperament."

Dragos spoke up. "What do you want to do?"

DeShard smiled. "I think that head would look rather good hanging above the fireplace of my den, wouldn't you say?"

"Mmmm, it would make you such a man to kill such a beast," Hilda purred seductively.

Joe felt his own sadistic streak rising. "Good idea. You can only shoot so many rhinos before it becomes passe."

DeShard smirked and took aim.

"You are sure you know what you are doing?" Hernandez asked. "Make sure you kill it with a single shot." He then signalled his men to back away.

"Of course. There isn't a big game animal I haven't hunted." He aimed his sights at the Styracosaurus's head, the dinosaur remaining blissfully unaware.

DeShard pulled the trigger.

The rifle fired, the shot disturbing small birds in the trees above. The bullet found its mark, hitting the Styracosaurus's head. It chipped the thick skull of the lumbering beast, spilling blood but not putting the animal down. The dinosaur reared up on its hind legs in fury and gave a guttural cry before spotting its attackers. It dropped back to all fours, lowered its head and charged them.

DeShard looked on in horror as the Styracosaurus stampeded straight for him. He quickly let off another round, though if it hit, the dinosaur didn't react. One of Hernandez's mercenaries stood to run from the path of the rampaging beast and the dinosaur spotted him. It deftly changed its heading and charged into him at top speed. The mercenary gave a hideous scream as he was impaled on the two-foot horn through the chest. His arms and legs then went limp and he jerked like a ragdoll as the dinosaur continued its attack.

Another mercenary opened fire; the bullets hit the flank of the dinosaur and caused splashes of blood. The Styracosaurus turned on this new foe, looking all the more monstrous with the dead man still impaled on its face. It reared up and then stomped its entire weight on the second mercenary.

The soldier screamed so much his vocal cords shredded as the bones in his legs were crushed into matchsticks. He frantically tried to draw his sidearm to kill the beast before it could gore him. The Styracosaurus saw this and doubled its attack, stomping its colossal weight on the soldier's upper body again and again until all that remained was a grisly red paste in jungle fatigues. Any identifying features of who the man had been were crushed beyond recognition.

"Damn you," yelled Hernandez as he opened fire on the dinosaur. It turned to him and howled its outrage as the bullets tore it open. It charged at him but was blindsided by another mercenary opening fire. Then another as the trained men flanked it.

Under attack from all sides, the Styracosaurus howled a mournful cry, clueless in how to proceed against this strange assault. It waved its head from side to side, the impaled rag doll of a man finally being thrown free.

Hernandez reached to the belts across his chest and pulled a grenade free. "So long, monster," he snarled as he pulled the pin and tossed the explosive. The grenade went off inches in front of the Styracosaurus's head and it howled a final cry before collapsing on its side, twitching in shock as blood poured from the multiple gunshots and its ruined face.

From the bushes, DeShard watched in satisfaction as the mercenaries formed a tight circle around the dying beast and emptied their remaining bullets into it. When they were done the dinosaur was dead.

DeShard stood from the foliage, clapping his hands. "A marvellous display! Marvellous!"

"Encore!" cackled Hilda.

Hernandez marched towards the adventurer, his face like thunder. Dragos could predict what was going to happen and quickly jumped to DeShard's side, rifle at the ready for any trouble.

Hernandez eyed Dragos with disgust before turning his ire onto DeShard. "I do not take the loss of men lightly," he snapped.

DeShard tried to hide his mirth, as if he were a child. "Me neither, Hernandez. Me neither. This was a great tragedy."

"A tragedy that you caused. Now two of my men are dead."

DeShard stepped closer to the mercenary, his humoured expression now gone. "You'd do well not to forget who pays you and your men."

"I haven't. It's that fool, Buchannon."

"Wrong. It's me. Buchannon has already paid me in full for this expedition. That includes the pay for you and your men. You'd do well to remember that."

Hernandez glared at the adventurer. "Money means nothing if my men are dead."

DeShard gave a twisted grin and put a hand on Hernandez's shoulder. "My friend, you have my word that when this is done, I shall pay you the money you and your twenty soldiers were contracted for. If, due to tragic circumstances, not all your men are alive to collect their pay, I am sure you will see to it their funds get to where they need to be."

Hernandez's face was blank for a moment as he allowed what DeShard had said sink in. He then returned the twisted smile. "I'm sure I am up to that responsibility."

DeShard laughed, glad he had escaped the mercenary leader's animosity. As much as he was loath to admit it, he needed all the men he could get right now. There was no telling what other dangers lurked close by. "I have reconsidered our plan. We'll stay in the cave tonight, as Ambrose did," he informed Hernandez. "At daybreak we'll track Tanner's party down." He cackled. "I can't wait to surprise my old friend." He then regarded the remains of the dinosaur with a sigh. "I had hoped to mount that beast's head in my den. Now it's ruined."

Hernandez laughed. "What can I say, I like to make sure I get the job done."

"Your professionalism is commendable," DeShard laughed.

CHAPTER 15

Candy opened her eyes to the blinding light and coughed up the mud that had settled in the back of her throat. She spat the unpalatable mouthful and groggily wiped her mouth as she tried to make sense of her surroundings.

She was lying half submerged on the edge of a swamp, no doubt the runoff for the river she had plummeted into. She was caked in mud, clay and dead leaves, her once perfectly maintained hair now plastered to her scalp. All around her large, spaced out tree trunks grew from mud banks between the still, stagnant waters. Although spaced apart, their high tops spread out and intermingled with each other, creating a dense canopy that left the area in permanent twilight. Here and there bright shafts of sunlight penetrated, cutting into the gloom.

Candy raised a muddied hand into the nearest sunbeam, its warmth on her skin felt good. She tried to make sense of where she was and how she had got here. She remembered the T-Rex on the bridge. She remembered the bridge giving way and then the rushing of water. Then nothing. Whatever had happened, she'd evidently survived and if the sunlight was telling her anything, it was that she'd been unconscious all night and it was now morning.

Then Candy became terribly aware of another truth: she was alone. She crawled out of the grim water, all her body aching as she clawed at the clay to pull herself up the mud bank. Looking down, she gave a shudder as she spotted a fat leech attached to her bare thigh. Its black body was bloated and fat, engorged from feasting on her blood. Holding down her desire to scream and vomit, Candy reached down and gripped hold of the slimy creature and pulled. With some resistance it came off, its hooked mouth wavering in anger as it attempted to bite into her again. In disgust Candy hurled it into the water. It landed with a 'plop' before swimming away.

Candy cried out in horror as she looked at the bleeding, jagged wound the sucking worm had left behind. She'd need it treating to avoid infection setting in.

Taking a moment, Candy stood and began to hobble in a random direction, giving the stagnant waterways as wide a berth as possible. This whole area was swampland, no doubt a basin for the river. She called out. First for Chuck, then for her father, then for anyone. No one replied. She was in real trouble and she knew it. The beasts that roamed this valley would make short work of her if they found her alone and vulnerable. She had to meet up with the others as soon as possible before something found her first.

Something in the mud caught her eye, just over the next bank and curiosity made her hobble over. She covered her mouth to stifle a scream at what she found.

The T-Rex that had fallen into the river with them lay before her. It was on its side, still and partially buried in the wet clay. Its nostrils and mouth were filled with packed mud and its back was to her. It was undoubtedly dead.

Good riddance, Candy thought as she walked around the colossal animal. Even in death it looked intimidating and its teeth looked as threatening as ever. She felt a sense of revulsion and pity as she thought of Juan, who had met a grisly demise in the great dinosaur's jaws. She could make out pieces of meat still stuck between the teeth and wondered if any of it had once been the unfortunate labourer.

A sound of wet crunching caught Candy's ears, coming from the stomach region of the T-Rex corpse and she cautiously circled it, curious as to what it was. She gave a gasp when she found the source of the sound.

A huge lizard of some kind, with a huge, multi-coloured, patterned sail on its back, stood with its head buried in an open wound on the T-Rex's stomach. It backed out, head covered in blood and a mouth filled with viscera. The creature swallowed its meal, making the wet, crunching noises before returning to the wound for more meat.

Candy was certain she'd seen such a creature in her father's textbooks on prehistoric animals, though for the life of her, she couldn't remember what its name was. At fifteen feet in length, it reminded her of a crocodile, though its snout was far shorter, filled with various sized curved teeth and it held its body higher off the ground. It looked fast and deadly and she did not want to draw its attention.

Candy quietly backed off from the strange creature. *Surely it has enough food to last it a year. It probably wouldn't be interested in me, even if it saw me.*

She stepped back onto a brittle stick and it made a loud snap as her weight crushed it. The creature instantly turned around to face her, with what looked like a piece of liver held between its teeth. It looked surprised by her presence and quickly scarfed down the brown, slick piece of offal before taking an exploratory step towards her. Its nostrils flared as it sniffed the air with keen interest.

Candy held up her hands to ward the creature back, hoping it would turn back to its feast. Instead it darted towards her, running like a lizard and barking similar to a canine. Its jaws opened and closed rapidly as it closed the distance between them.

Candy turned and ran as fast as she could, her heart beating rapidly in her chest as she looked for somewhere to escape to. The sail-lizard was twice as fast as the staggering Candy and would soon be upon her, its cruel jaws more than capable of ripping chunks of flesh from her body. She screamed for help, praying someone nearby would hear her as she spotted a tree with several low hanging branches.

Running with everything she had, Candy jumped up and grabbed hold of the lowest hanging branch, quickly lifting her legs up as the sail-lizard snapped at where she'd been an instant before.

Candy cried out for help again as her feet hooked around the branch and she was at a loss at what to do next. The savage creature snapped and barked, willing her to fall into its attack range.

A gunshot rang out and the creature's left eyeball exploded. The sail-lizard fell to its side, killed without even realising it. Candy remained hanging by her hands and feet, trying to register this new turn of events.

"Candy," called a voice she knew all too well and she allowed herself to drop to the ground.

"Chuck?" she joyfully exclaimed as she saw Chuck running towards her, other men trailing behind him, including Mustaf and her father. Relief was painted on all their faces. Candy ran towards them and didn't stop until she was in Chuck's arms.

"We're glad you're alive," Chuck beamed, holding her tight.

Candy composed herself and hugged her father and Mustaf, flooded with relief, as if the nightmare were over. She soon came to realise their situation was just as perilous as ever.

Everyone was covered in mud and half drowned, and worse they no longer had supplies. All had been abandoned, understandably, in the T-Rex attack and now the only fresh water they had was in their canteens. Guns were also an issue. Only Grant and Dillon had succeeded in holding onto their rifles. Chuck, Pat and Mustaf were down to their sidearms and the labourers, Diago and the brothers Vincente and Javier, hadn't had any firearms to begin with when the attack occurred. Her father and Professor Crowley were equally unarmed. Grant and Dillon also had a pistol each, but they didn't seem keen on giving them up. She supposed the firearms would be better in the hands of hardened soldiers than anyone else, at any rate.

While Crowley and Ambrose kept their minds off the peril at hand by musing over the identity of the beast that had nearly made a meal of her, she thought she heard them agree it was a "Dimetrodon," Candy studied the worn out faces of everyone in the group.

"Is this everyone who made it?" Candy asked, her rush of optimism fading as she came to realise there was one other person who had fallen from the bridge and who was now missing.

Chuck looked away, hiding his pained emotions. "We haven't found Bill yet."

Candy touched his arm, hoping to give comfort. "I see…"

"Help me!" cried a familiar voice, causing Chuck to look up and start running up a nearby mud-bank, Pat and Grant following closely.

"I'd know that voice anywhere!" Chuck whooped. He reached the top of the mud bank and spotted Bill a little distance off, stumbling in the mud and trying to swat away something in the air. Chuck broke into a sprint to help his friend and as he got closer he identified Bill's attacker; a mosquito the size of a small bird.

The mosquito buzzed around Bill's head as it tried to line up an opportunity to bite him. "Get lost," he snarled, batting it with his hand before falling onto all fours.

Seeing its chance, the mosquito hovered in place for a second before darting downwards. Bill spun around, wielding a broken branch as if it were a baseball bat and hit the huge bug with perfect precision. The insect was knocked down into the mud where it wallowed, struggling to escape the mire. Bill brought the branch down on it, over and over in a seething rage until there was nothing left that looked even remotely like an insect.

"Why is it always me who is plagued by these damned insects!" he yelled as he continued to smash the remains of the mosquito. He only stopped when he heard Chuck calling his name and dropped the branch to walk to his friend.

"Hey Bill, still in one piece, I see," Chuck beamed.

"Barely," he responded, stopping to rest.

"Good to see you're okay," smiled Pat, slapping Bill's shoulder.

"Don't let the fact I am still alive fool you," he sighed. "I am far from okay."

***

With everyone who had fallen into the river accounted for, the group huddled together and discussed their next move. By some miracle Ambrose's map was relatively undamaged, the tobacco tin he held it in keeping it dry for the most part, and so they could plot their route.

The swamp they were currently in was indeed a flood basin, against the western edge of the valley walls. It was north of the river, due to the land being lower than the surrounding jungles. The only way out of the swamp and back onto more solid footing was to head north-east until the land inclined back to the level of the valley proper. Once out, they would be in the middle of the valley's length and from there would have to trek far to the east to circumnavigate the mountains that encroached from the west and barred their path to the north from their current standing.

Chuck asked the labourers candidly what their thoughts were, now that their boss Emanuel was dead. The three men, Diago and the brothers Vincente and Javier, talked amongst themselves before stating that if the expedition was continuing, they would remain with the team. The only caveat was that they were seen as equals, rather than workers and that they would get double pay. Ambrose didn't argue and promised triple pay if the Stone of Qualbec was recovered. The men seemed more than happy with this.

With their route planned, the map was folded away and the journey to the north-east began. The walk was hard, the sucking mud making them fight for every step they took. Twice they were attacked by small groups of the giant mosquitos and once they had to avoid an anaconda larger than any had thought possible.

Ideally the group wanted to avoid wading through the waterways, but their hopes were for naught. Grant and Dillon kept their rifles high, not wanting their now filthy firearms to get any dirtier.

Bill voiced his displeasure, all too aware of what horrors could be lurking just below the surface of the brown, algae-covered waters. They always stayed in tight formation, everyone watching for aquatic predators.

One such waterway had to be avoided, adding two hours onto their journey due to being infested with hungry three-foot long piranha. Grant had waded into the water first and would have had his legs stripped to the bone if not for Mustaf quickly pulling him out. He'd suffered a single bite, but that was enough for him to realise how close to death he had been.

Another waterway had massive leeches the size of swine wallowing in the mud along its mud banked edges. A few were spotted swimming through the dark waters. One of the leeches on the water's edge seemed to yawn, opening its maw and revealing rows upon rows of sharp, hook-like teeth surrounding a sphincter-like opening. Again, it was agreed that taking a longer trek would be the wiser route.

***

"How much longer are we going to be in this swamp?" Bill moaned. "I think my boots have gone rotten."

Ambrose pulled out the map to study. "We're almost there. We should almost be out. Just through these trees." He folded away the map and Chuck led the way, pushing shrubs and vines away until he realised he was again on the bank of a vast body of water.

The lake had to span about a hundred and fifty feet, its surface still and covered in lily pads and pond weed. The canopies of the large trees from either side kept much of the lake in shadows, allowing for fungi growth from rotten vegetation.

The rest of the group gathered next to Chuck, taking in the view. There didn't seem to be any way to cross.

Bill sat down on an unturned tree root and huffed. "This is great! Just great! Now what are we supposed to do? Swim?"

"Could we?" asked Pat, considering it as an option.

"It's a bit too far for that," Chuck said. "Plus, who knows what's lurking in here. Our best option is to follow the bank until we find our way around."

"I don't think that will be an option," Ambrose said glumly. "We can't see the edge of the expanse of water in either direction. Looking at the map, I'd say that's because there isn't one. It appears this waterway encircles the entire swamp, like a natural moat, if you will. We're going to need to cross it if we are to continue."

"He could be right," sighed Pat. "Look on the other side. The ground appears more solid. We're on the edge of these wetlands and this is our last obstacle."

"I am not swimming in that water. It could be filled with piranha, or thirty-foot snakes, or eight-foot leeches, or even something worse. We need another option."

"Agreed," said Grant, subconsciously touching where the piranha had bitten him earlier.

Chuck tried to come up with a solution. "Maybe we can make a raft of some kind?"

"My word," said Crowley, moving towards the water's edge. "Gentlemen, I appreciate the urgency of our situation, but look at that. Wonderous."

The group looked out to the other side of the waterway and the herd of large dinosaurs that were making their way down the bank to drink. Some of the lumbering dinosaurs were thirty feet in length. They moved on all fours, their forelegs far smaller than their back legs and looked to weigh around five tons apiece. They called to each other in deep, sorrowful hoots as they dipped their heads into the water to drink. Their most distinguishing features were the single long, curved tubes that ran off the back of their skulls. These tubes were a bright red, in stark contrast to the dark greens and yellows of the rest of them and seemed to be the instrument the dinosaurs used to form their melodious calls to one another.

Chuck had to admit that the dinosaurs were an impressive spectacle to witness. One of the dinosaurs waded deeper into the water, dipped its head under the surface and when it pulled up, its mouth was filled with vegetation that it chewed at its leisure.

"Are they meat eating?" asked Bill, feeling unnerved by the large beasts.

"No, they are herbivores. Parasaurolophus, if I'm not mistaken."

Ambrose agreed. "I never imagined them to be so graceful. It's important to remember that as unfortunate as our encounters have been, there is still much beauty in this valley. It is a scientific treasure trove."

The water in front of the Parasaurolophus exploded and before the beast could retreat to dry land, its neck was in the jaws of the largest crocodile that had ever lived. The Parasaurolophus's eyes rolled in fear as it was pulled deeper into the waters, now frothing and red with blood. The rest of the dinosaur herd hooted urgently and stampeded through the trees, away from the danger, abandoning their unlucky kin to its fate.

The Parasaurolophus bellowed in panic before being pulled under the water, the mighty crocodile, forty feet from snout to tail, rolled, its eight-ton bulk, snapping the struggling dinosaur's neck and drowning it. Another of the giant crocodiles suddenly surfaced, snapped down upon one of the Parasaurolophus's forelegs and with a mighty twist tore the limb off. It swallowed the limb whole before again attacking the carcass.

Across the waterway, Ambrose and Crowley looked on in dismay as the beautiful marvel of nature they had been observing moments before was now reduced to mere mangled flesh within a bloodbath, resulted from extreme violence they had just witnessed.

Crowley cleared his throat. "I suppose the food chain humbles us all…"

Bill stood, watching the grisly scene of the monster crocodiles feeding in terror. "If you think I'm getting on a raft with those things in the water, you're dreaming."

"He's right," Candy agreed. "Those crocodiles would tear apart any raft we could put together as if it were made of matchsticks."

"I know," Chuck nodded. "There has to be another way." A small pterosaur, no larger than two feet across, glided down over the water and Chuck watched it skim the water with its beak before it caught a fish between its pointy teeth. It then flew up to the canopy, where it landed to eat its meal. "That's it," he said, slamming his fist into his open palm.

"What's 'it'?" asked Pat. "You want to fly?"

"No. I want to climb."

***

The plan was a simple one. The large, gnarled trees would be easy enough to climb and their tangle of branches spread out far and wide, intermingling with the branches of the trees growing across the opposite bank. It would be a simple matter to make their way across the branches, so long as everyone watched their footing. Ambrose and Crowley would struggle making the ascent and descent, but the actual crossing would be a piece of cake.

Everyone agreed to the idea and once the optimum tree was decided upon the climb began.

"When this is over, I'm writing my resignation," Bill muttered whilst pulling himself up the branches.

"You'd find it easier if you hadn't eaten so many bagels and doughnuts back in New York," Pat said, rolling his eyes.

"Please don't mention New York bagels," Bill pleaded. "I'd kill for a ham and cream-cheese bagel with sesame seeds, right about now."

Chuck grinned as he slowly began moving horizontally across the branches, the murky water some twenty feet below him. "When we get back, I'll buy you a whole delicatessen. How about that?" Candy's foot slipped and Chuck quickly caught her under the arm. "Careful," he winked to her. "We can go swimming later." She blushed and thanked him before moving with more caution.

"Just one delicatessen?" Bill complained. "When we get back, I want delicatessens for life."

"What is a delicatessen?" Vincente asked his brother.

Javier shrugged. "Who knows?"

"I was always fonder of the pizza," Candy smiled. The group was now approaching the centre of the waterway, halfway towards the opposite bank. The two crocodiles and their prey were no longer visible on the bank, having retreated to deeper waters.

"Now you're talking about pizza? Kill me now!" Bill said, drooling at the thought.

"Concentrate," Chuck said, not wanting his team to get complacent. Grant, Dillon and Pat were making easy work of the climb and were already two thirds of the way across. Then there was Chuck, Candy, Vincente, Javier and Diago, followed by Bill, with Ambrose, Crowley and Mustaf at the rear. Everyone seemed to be doing well, though the old men were taking longer than he'd estimated.

"Concentrate," Bill muttered to himself. "Doesn't he think I'm concentrating?"

Bill screamed as a large buzzing filled his ears, nearly causing him to slip.

Chuck's heart skipped a beat as for a moment he thought his friend had fallen. "Bill, you okay?"

"Yes and no," Bill replied as he swatted at three of the giant, sparrow-sized mosquitos that had appeared and were now hovering around him. "It's these damned bugs again. Why is it always me they go for?"

Chuck made sure Candy was okay to carry on before climbing back to check on Bill. "Need a hand?"

Bill pulled a broken piece of branch loose and began brandishing it like a club. "I just need these things to take a hint." With one hand holding onto the canopy, his swings were slow and clumsy. "Damn these bugs!" he cursed.

"Hold on, I'll see if I can help."

Bill lined up a swing, but before he made it a shape blurred past him and one of the mosquitos was gone. He turned and followed the small pterosaur from earlier, which had snatched one of the bugs out of the air. "Nice going, buddy," Bill called to it. He then turned his attention to the remaining two buzzing mosquitos and readied his club. "Come on, come a little closer…"

Another pterosaur swooped in and snatched up the second mosquito at top speed, before Bill could compute. Then something terrible happened. The flying reptile hadn't given itself enough space to avoid Bill and it crashed into him at full speed. Bill yelled out as he was knocked from the canopy. Being so close, Chuck managed to quickly jump forward and grab his friend's hand.

The pterosaur fell and splashed into the murky water. It started squawking as it attempted to regain flight.

"Don't let go of me," Bill begged as he dangled from the branch, Chuck's grip on his hand the only thing that was saving him and his friend.

"Don't worry, I'm going to pull you up," Chuck said as he heard the raised voices of the others as they realised what was going on. The branch where both men hung was sagging down, their combined weight more than it could take.

"I can't do it," whimpered Bill as he tried to raise his second hand to Chuck. "Chuck, I can't do it." Tears started forming at the corners of his eyes as he realised the danger he was in.

The third and final mosquito began hovering close to Chuck's face, sensing his helplessness. He pulled back his head, trying to shoo it away. "Get out of here," he snarled at the bug.

A rifle was fired and the mosquito exploded into slime. "Got it," Chuck heard Grant state from further along the canopy.

"I need help! I need someone to help me pull him up!" Chuck yelled with all his might, the muscles in his arm burning. He'd be able to pull up Bill with both arms, but if he attempted the manoeuvre it was likely Bill's weight would drag him from his perch. He grit his teeth as he fought to hold on, Bill's hand becoming slippery with sweat.

"We can't get to you," said Pat in full on panic mode. "The branch you are on is starting to split. If anyone else stands on it, it'll snap."

"Oh, God," wept Bill.

Chuck could hear Candy crying but blocked it out. "Okay, Bill, it's just you and me. We've got to do this ourselves, just like old times, right?"

"I don't want to die here, Chuck. Don't let me die here."

"You aren't going to die here. You've just got to help me out, okay?"

"Why can't I hear the bird anymore?" Bill sobbed, his legs kicking violently. "I can't hear the bird, Chuck. Where did it go?"

It took Chuck a moment to realise what Bill was referring to. "You mean the thing that crashed into you?" He glanced down at the dark water below. There was no sign of the pterosaur. "Forget about it. It probably flew back up into the trees."

"I bet it was eaten by those monster crocodiles." Bill was nearing hysterics.

"Don't be ridiculous. Now, I'm going to pull you up, but you need to calm down. Think of all the scrapes we've been in before. Think of all the times I've pulled your butt out of the fire. Is this any different?"

Bill sniffed and regained some semblance of composure. "No."

"No what?"

"No, there's no difference."

"Did you trust me all those other times? When you thought you were a goner and I saved your ass?"

Bill nodded. "I did."

"Do you trust me now?"

"I do."

The branch supporting them sagged and cracked a little more. "Okay, we're running out of time, so it's now or never. I'm going to have to give my all and I need you to help me. Are you ready?"

Bill nodded.

"Okay, on three. One, two, th…"

The water beneath Bill exploded in white as the monster crocodile, forty feet long, emerged like a harpoon shooting for the sky. It looked as if it were defying gravity as its bulk was carried up ever higher and its jaws hung wide open.

Chuck didn't have time to react as the monstrous jaws closed around Bill's waist. Bill screamed and his eyes bulged as blood fountained up from his aghast mouth.

Chuck clenched onto Bill's hand with all his might, refusing to surrender his friend, even as the weight of the crocodile forced it to fall back into the water below. The crocodile's vice-like grip of cruel, pointed teeth and eight tons of mass half cleaved and half pulled the fragile human in half.

Chuck watched in horror as Bill gurgled his last breath, his blood, guts and viscera fell out of the bottom of all that remained of him and rained down onto the waterway. The giant crocodile circled, eagerly waiting as it swallowed Bill's bottom half with a single movement. It looked to be preparing itself for another jump.

Candy shouted something.

Chuck couldn't hear it. He couldn't hear anything over his own beating heart.

Candy shouted again. "You have to let him go."

Chuck blinked. *What is she talking about?* he wondered. *I can't let go of Bill. He's been my friend longer than anyone. He's been with me through thick and thin. If I let him go, he'll fall. How dare she say such a thing?*

"He's gone," Candy yelled again. "You need to let him go!"

Chuck looked back down at the remains of Bill. His head rolled limply on his shoulders; his face covered in the blood that had exploded from his mouth. Beneath his waist, all that remained was ragged skin, torn meat, dangling entrails and dripping blood. In shock he let go.

The top half of Bill fell down towards the water and the waiting crocodile jumped at it, snapping it up and swallowing it before it even hit the water. It then submerged beneath the impenetrable surface, a small swell of water and bubbles the only evidence it had ever been there.

Up in the canopy, Chuck wept.

***

Chuck sat on the grass, his head in his hands as he tried to make sense of the loss of his friend. It still didn't feel real, as if he'd lost an arm. Bill had always been by his side. Now he was dead.

Chuck could barely remember the rest of the climb across the canopy. He couldn't even recall the descent. All he kept remembering was Bill's gruesome death. It kept replaying in his mind and he couldn't get the vision out of his head, no matter how hard he tried.

As a soldier, Chuck had lost friends before. More than he cared to remember. Somehow, he'd always managed to keep going. He was no longer sure that was the case.

The cool touch of Candy's hand on his brought Chuck somewhat back to reality. She was knelt before him, genuine sadness and concern on her face. Her face, still beautiful, even now when smeared with mud and tears. He managed the beginnings of a smile.

"I'm so sorry about Bill," Candy managed. "He was a good man."

"He was my friend," Chuck corrected her. "My best friend."

Candy lowered her head. "I wish I knew what to say."

Seeing her need for him, her desire to heal his rent emotions, made Chuck grow stronger. He had to keep it together, for Candy's sake. The longer they spent in this valley, narrowly avoiding death at every turn, the more he realised he was growing to love her. "I'll be fine. I just need a minute."

Candy nodded her understanding. She began to say something and then a look of horror passed over her face and she began to scream. A shadow fell over Chuck and he went to turn, to see what it was. Something hit him on the back of the head. Something hard. He was then falling face first into the grass.

Everything went black.

CHAPTER 16

Chuck's eyes opened to a world of blurry red, a high-pitched ringing in his ears. Everything seemed tilted and the muddled sounds of fighting surrounded him, somehow far away and close at the same time. Men shouting, guns firing, chaos mixed with panic. *Am I back in the war?* he mused.

Pat came running into Chuck's vision, saw him and quickly approached, his expression stricken with fear. He crouched down and shook Chuck's shoulder. "Chuck, get up," he yelled, anxiously looking around. "I said, 'get up!'"

The red haze lifted and time sped back up, the muffled sounds of fighting suddenly becoming loud and raw. Chuck struggled up with Pat's help. He looked around as his friend steadied him, trying to make sense of what was happening. Dillon and Grant were firing their rifles, Candy and Ambrose were hiding behind the broad frame of Mustaf as he grappled with... something. All around people cried out in terror, their voices drowned out by the deep hollering and chittering of apes.

"It's the Ape-Men! They've ambushed us! One hit you on your head. You okay?"

Chuck touched the back of his head and when he examined his fingers, saw they were glistening with blood. *Not good.* He reached down to his holster and drew his pistol. He started firing at targets. "How long was I down?"

"No more than a minute or two."

The Ape-Men had divided the humans and were now running amongst them, wielding clubs that they were using with savage effect. Already Vincente was down, his body limp and an Ape-Man pulling him away.

A hulking Ape-Man jumped at Chuck, swinging its club high and its face twisted into an evil smirk. Chuck quickly twisted to face it and fired four times into its gut. The Ape-Man howled its outrage as it doubled over and died.

"We need to fall back," Chuck yelled, though he didn't know who could hear him. "We need to regroup or we're going to fall."

A high-pitched scream made him lose all objectivity and Chuck turned his head to see Candy being dragged away by her hair, her legs kicking in protest. Mustaf had fallen, a huge Ape-Man standing astride him in victory, the club it had used to knock him down wet and crimson. Ambrose tried to defend his daughter; another Ape-Man soon put an end to such hopes as it grabbed him under the arms and began pulling him away.

Chuck ran to help Candy and was knocked off his feet by another Ape-Man that jumped down from the tree above, kicking him to the ground. Chuck's pistol was knocked from his grip and the Ape-Man did something akin to laughing as it watched him struggle to stand once more. Chuck kept a hand to his side, fighting the pain from the blow. He picked up a club of his own, a snapped tree branch, and ran at his attacker. The Ape-Man swung its more solid weapon to meet the arc of Chuck's makeshift club. Chuck cried out in anguish and took a step back as his club was reduced to kindling. The Ape-Man advanced, club raised, and Chuck looked around, never one to accept he was out of options.

A rifle fired and a look of confusion passed over the Ape-Man's face before it fell forward. Dillon stood behind it, his rifle smoking. He quickly ran to Chuck, who in turn found his dropped pistol and picked it up. The two men stood back-to-back as more Ape-Men descended from the trees and emerged from the bushes, all baring sharp yellow teeth and baying for murder.

Chuck tried to search past the matted haired creatures, trying to spot others. He could still hear shots and voices but couldn't see who made the noises. "This looks bad," Chuck said pessimistically.

"Ain't the first time we've been caught in a foxhole with no way out," Dillon replied, taking aim at the nearest of their attackers.

Chuck was about to shoot into the crowd of monsters when something came arching over from past the trees and landed by his feet. It was red and emitting copious amounts of red smoke, obscuring his vision. The smoke smelt sweet, like berries. *A new form of attack?* he wondered.

"The hell is that?" Dillon cried out as another of the red smoke bombs came hurtling towards them.

Whatever the red smoke bombs were, the Ape-Men didn't like them. They began howling and hollering, jumping up and down and waving their muscular arms in fear rather than aggression. They looked frantically between one another, unsure what to do and requiring leadership.

Another smoke bomb was thrown amongst them and the Ape-Men jumped in multiple directions, their ranks broken.

"I think something is attacking them," Chuck hazarded a guess.

The red smoke now obscured much of the battlefield where the fighting had occurred, making it even harder for Chuck to discern numbers and locations of both the Ape-Men and the survivors.

Suddenly a figure appeared, smaller than the Ape-Men, covered in a primitive armour constructed of vines and tree bark. It wore a tribal mask carved from wood and painted in reds and yellows. It threw another of the red smoke bombs and then beckoned the two men to follow it. Shrouded as it was in red smoke, the figure looked like some powerful deity from the underworld. In its hands it wielded a crude bow and arrow.

"Should we follow it?" Dillon hurriedly asked. "Could be a trap."

Behind Chuck an Ape-Man howled and jumped at him, club raised high. It was instantly placated by an arrow hitting it square between the eyes. It fell backwards into the curling red smoke. "I'd say we're out of choices," said Chuck and ran towards the figure, careful to avoid the manic Ape-Men who were now swinging their clubs wildly. Dillon quickly followed suit.

Seeing that the two men had got the message, the figure turned and ran with a speed and grace Chuck couldn't match. "Hey, wait for us," he said as he ran.

The figure stopped quickly, raised its bow, already loaded with another arrow, and fired into the back of another Ape-Man. Chuck realised the figure had just saved the life of Javier, who had been about to be battered by the offending savage. Realising he'd been saved, Javier joined their ranks as they ran after the mysterious figure.

"Who's your friend?" called Grant.

Chuck turned to discover Grant and Pat had also joined their small group of survivors and were now running beside them.

"Couldn't tell you, we haven't been formally introduced yet," Chuck said.

The figure ran through the jungle with the utmost confidence, the group of five men following at the fastest pace they could. Chuck realised they were making considerable distance from the place where the Ape-Men had ambushed them and called for the figure to stop. The figure continued running and so Chuck called again and this time the figure complied, stopping on a dime and turning to face them.

The figure looked even more bizarre now that Chuck had a chance to look it over. Tufts of grass had been woven into the bark armour of the mysterious figure's outfit. It was smaller than it had appeared earlier in the heat of battle. Now with some breathing time, the men could tell it was no taller than five and a half feet and with a small frame under its bulky armour. The figure stood defiant, proud and unyielding, waiting to see what the man it had just saved had to say.

"We have to go back," Chuck called. "We still have people back there."

The figure remained unmoving, save for a slight cock of its head. The masked face made it feel inhuman and intimidating, hiding all emotion from the men.

"It probably doesn't understand you," Pat said.

Chuck tried again, taking a step towards their strange rescuer. "We can't leave our people behind."

Taking Chuck's step forward as aggression, the figure quickly raised its bow, aiming an arrow directly at Chuck's chest. He froze, not wanting to incur the strange being's wrath. He had no doubt it would fire the arrow without hesitation if it thought he was hostile. Grant and Dillon in turn raised their respective rifles, creating a standoff between them.

Chuck slowly raised his hands, signalling for his men to lower their weapons. Begrudgingly they obeyed.

"It's okay, take it easy. Nobody's going to harm you. You saved us back there and we are grateful." The figure slowly lowered its bow. "The thing is, there are more of us. Back there. We need to go back, we need to get them."

"People... back there... gone..." the figure said. Its voice was higher than Chuck had expected and clearly female. The strange figure's words were slow and stilted, as if it hadn't used its voice very much.

Chuck blinked, fearing what the figure was implying. He thought of Candy and his heart panged. "You mean dead? How can you be so sure?"

The figure shook its head. "Not dead... but taken. If we return there... we'll be taken too."

Chuck lowered his hands, regarding the perplexing figure questioningly. "Who are you?"

The figure reached up and pulled away the tribal mask, revealing features the men had not expected. The youthful face of a young woman looked back at them, her eyes wide and blue, her hair blonde, wild and untamed. Mud streaked across her features. "I am Flora. I live in this jungle... and if you want to survive... I suggest you follow me." She then turned and began walking away as the group of dumbstruck men exchanged glances before swifty following her.

***

Chuck walked beside the young woman, Flora, as she walked through the jungle's underbrush. Several feet behind them, Pat, Grant, Dillon and Javier murmured to themselves, speculating on Flora's identity.

"Flora, it's nice to meet you. I really am grateful for your help back there, all of us are. Thankyou."

Flora nodded, keeping her eyes forward and her bow at the ready. "It's okay."

"My name is Chuck, by the way."

"Chuck?" Flora stated, as if seeing how the name felt in her mouth. She cocked her head slightly. "What a strange name."

"Right," Chuck smiled. He then went on to introduce the rest of the men. Flora listened, clearly making a conscious effort to remember all the names. "Where are we headed?"

"Home," Flora replied, as if the answer was obvious.

"Home? How far is that from here?"

"Not far. How far is your home?"

Chuck grinned and scratched the back of his head. "Pretty far."

Flora raised an eyebrow but said nothing.

"How did you get here?"

"I don't know. I've always been here."

"Alone?"

"For a while, now. I used to live with my father."

"What was his name?"

Flora shrugged. "I think Auston. I always called him 'father.'"

"You mean Austin? Austin Kiplard?"

Flora froze and blinked, trying to recall the name. "Yes," she finally confirmed before continuing to walk. "That's right, Austin Kiplard."

"Who the hell is Austin Kiplard?" Dillon asked Pat.

"Austin Kiplard was the name of Professor Ambrose's colleague who was left trapped here, back in nineteen-thirty."

"Well, I'll be..."

Chuck studied Flora's face, trying to put an age to her. She couldn't be more then eighteen. "So, you were born here," he surmised. "Where is your father now?"

"He died... a while ago, now." There was no grief in her voice. She was merely recounting fact.

"Your father taught you how to speak, then?"

"Who else?" Flora shrugged, again making it sound as if Chuck were asking ridiculous questions.

"Your English is very good."

"Father taught me well."

"What happened to your mother, Iris Kiplard? She was trapped here too. Is she still alive?"

"Mother died when I was very young. I don't remember her."

"So you're alone?"

"No, not alone. I have King with me."

"Who's King?"

Flora smiled. "King is my friend."

***

An hour later Flora led them to a mighty tree. It grew in the centre of a small clearing, its mere presence causing other trees to give it room. It looked old and solid, well over eight feet wide at the base. Chuck whistled, impressed with the huge treehouse structure constructed amidst its branches. "Now that is impressive," Chuck commented, his eyes following the numerous wooden walkways and balconies jutting out from the tree house proper.

"Looks like someone has had a lot of time on their hands," Pat whispered.

Dillon grinned. "Seeing as we no longer have any tents or shelter, this looks like a slice of heaven."

"Those balconies would make good lookout and sniper positions, too," observed Grant.

Javier nodded. "To think someone could survive out here long enough to build this," he said with reverence.

"This is my home," beamed Flora, brimming with pride. She then began marching to the tree trunk, where a rope ladder hung.

Chuck's group began crossing the ground towards the mighty tree when a loud, deep bellow echoed around them and something big began crashing through the trees, heading towards them at speed.

"Heads up, we have company," said Grant, dropping to one knee and raising his rifle. Dillon did the same while Chuck and Pat drew their pistols.

"Relax," ordered Flora, skipping across the ground, towards the thunderous, crashing sound. "That's just King."

Chuck and Pat lowered their pistols uncertainly. Dillon and Grant kept their rifles up, not willing to take anything on trust.

Trees parted and King bounded into the clearing, bellowing again as it spotted Flora.

"I'm no expert but is that a Stegosaurus?" uttered Pat to Chuck. Chuck nodded, not believing what he was seeing.

The huge, bulky dinosaur, though a herbivore, was no less intimidating because of it. The beast measured over twenty feet from its tiny head to its powerful, spiky tail. It moved four, elephantine legs and its body humped to a height of thirteen feet at its peak. On top of King's dark green body were huge, bright red plates, the largest of which measured an additional six feet high and four feet wide. The four spikes at the end of its tail measured another four feet each and would certainly spell the end to any man who incurred King's displeasure.

Flora bounded up to the prehistoric giant and flung her arms around its thick neck, kissing its head as if it were a pet dog. She looked tiny compared to the massive dinosaur. "Oh King, I missed you," she chimed. The creature bellowed, although the call was somewhat softer than it had been before. "I told you not to worry," Flora smiled. "But then, you always do." King bellowed again, snorting irritably. "Oh, these men? They are my new friends. I saved them from the Tacal."

"The Tacal?" queried Chuck, slowly approaching.

"The creatures that attacked you," Flora explained.

Chuck nodded as he looked up at King. The dinosaur looked even bigger up close. "Can I stroke him?" he asked, tentatively reaching out an open hand.

King snorted and bellowed angrily at Chuck, making him back away.

"Maybe you two should get to know each other first," Flora grinned.

***

Flora invited the five men up into the treehouse, making sure to pull up the rope ladder once they were all up. She then quickly inspected the interior of the house before setting down her bow. "Sometimes things climb up the ladder when I am away," she explained.

Chuck and Pat examined the new shelter they found themselves in, impressed by Flora's remarkable ingenuity. Stacks of arrows for the bow were collected into neat bundles and tied off with dried vines. All had been individually whittled from sticks and branches. There were also several bows present, all carved from wood and using tightly pulled vines as the string. They weren't as well-crafted as manufactured bows, but they seemed good enough.

"You made all these?"

Flora shrugged. "Who else? Father showed me how. He taught me how to boil the vines just right, so they have a little stretch to them. That is crucial to getting the power they need." She then presented the group with a large, folded leaf. She unfolded it to reveal a cluster of edible berries and nuts. "Help yourself," she said. The hungry men did not argue, savouring the sweetness of the fruits. She then provided a curved bowl filled with fresh water which they took turns drinking from.

Chuck continued to observe their surroundings. There was evidence of items that would have been brought in by Austin and Ambrose on their first expedition to the valley. A handful of books, a compass, a rope and a mishmash of other equipment. Much of it looked old and well used, kept out of posterity more than anything else.

Flora had also created a variety of spears, masks and shields, no doubt ready for any eventuality. The tops of the spears were flint stone and when Chuck ran his finger over the edge of one of them he was amazed by how sharp it was.

He then noticed a group of red, scrunched up packages of leaves, each about the size of a fist. "What are those?"

"I call them Dragon Eggs. They're what make the red smoke the Tacal are so afraid of."

"Dragon eggs?"

"That's what father called them. You make them by drying the seeds, then wrapping them in the dried leaves. They burn easy and produce a lot of the red smoke. The Tacal hate it, but I find it quite pleasant. Sometimes I light one in here, just for the fragrance."

Chuck cracked a smile. "That's ingenious. But how do you light them?"

Again, Flora looked at Chuck as if he were a fool. "Using matches, of course."

Pat cocked an eyebrow in disbelief. "You're telling me you still have matches from twenty-four years ago?"

"Of course not. I make my own. Father showed me how."

Chuck and Pat exchanged glances. "How?"

Flora reached into her myriad of clutter and pulled out a piece of rock. She passed it to Chuck, who examined it. "Phosphate rock," he noted. Pat was impressed.

Flora nodded. "You can find it in the mountains just north of here. I scrape powder from it and then use sap to attach it to the ends of sticks." She then showed Chuck some of the handmade matches.

"I can't begin to tell you how impressed we all are at how you've survived here for so long." The rest of Chuck's group voiced their agreement. "We've been in the valley only two days. In that short time we've lost seven men. Your survival is nothing short of incredible."

Flora grinned, clearly enjoying the compliments. "My father taught me well."

Their thoughts were distracted by the sounds of drums in the distance. Grant looked out over the jungle, trying to discern any evidence that would give away the Ape-Men's location.

"That's the Tacal?" Chuck asked.

Flora's face darkened and she nodded slowly. "They don't like me very much."

"We ain't too fond of them either," said Dillon.

"Do you know where their village is?" asked Chuck.

"I do. It's east of here. About three hours walk."

It was closer than Chuck thought. He reached out and grabbed Flora's hand. The move startled her, but she did not pull away. "Flora, is there a chance our friends are still alive?"

"They will be. At least, most of them will be. The Tacal are cruel but not dumb. To kill all their captives immediately would be a waste."

"A waste?"

"Yes, the meat would go bad."

Chuck shuddered at the implications of that statement. "Flora, we need to go to the Tacal village. We need to save our friends…"

"And family," added Javier. "They have my brother."

"Can you show us the way?"

Flora looked torn by Chuck's request. "The Tacal are dangerous. They might end up killing you all. Then it'd be only me and King again."

"Can you help us?" asked Pat. "Can you help us fight them? You have experience we do not. And they fear your Dragon Eggs."

"He's right," agreed Chuck. "We'd stand a much better chance with you by our side. Will you join us?"

Flora bit her bottom lip, torn between remaining in relative safety or extreme danger. She reached into a pouch and brought out a faded photograph. It showed Austin and Iris, alongside a younger looking Ambrose. Beside him was another woman, beautiful and familiar looking. In her arms she held a baby. She studied it, as if asking the faded characters what they thought she should do.

"Who is that?" Chuck asked, pointing to the woman.

Flora shrugged. "I don't know. I never asked and father never said."

"You never asked?" said Pat.

"If father wanted to tell me something, he would have. If he didn't, I didn't need to know it."

Chuck pointed to the image of Ambrose. "You see that man? Do you know who he is?"

Flora stared at the image; her emotions impossible to read. She looked up at Chuck. "Do you?"

Chuck nodded. "That man is travelling with us. The Ape-Men, I mean, the Tacal have him. He knew your father. He was hoping to find him here."

Flora tilted her head. "Really?"

Chuck nodded.

Flora stared at her photo again before folding it up and putting it carefully away. "They are your friends?" She turned to Javier. "Your family?"

They both nodded.

"Then we shall get them back."

CHAPTER 17

Ambrose held onto his daughter as around their holding cage the Ape-Men jeered and leered at them. Their inhuman faces were twisted even more by their sadistic hate. They bore their sharp yellow teeth, stuck out their tongues and made sounds that were a grotesque mimicry of human laughter. Some of them jabbed through the wooden bars with pointed sticks, cruelly jabbing at their human captives and mimicking the cries of pain that resulted.

Flaming torches were held aloft, bringing light in the darkness of the jungle at night and the Ape-Men danced in a frenzy of merriment and cruelty.

The cage the survivors hid within was constructed of gnarled tree branches, tied together with vines. The caged walls gave no protection from the stench of death that hung over the seven-foot tall monsters, their matted fur grimy and flea bitten.

"Father, what are they going to do to us?" sobbed Candy, finding whatever security she could in her father's arms.

"Stay strong, child. We'll be okay. Mister Tanner will come for us," Ambrose comforted her.

In his own corner of the cage, Mustaf sat with his head hung in disgrace. "I'm sorry, Professor. I should have prevented this. I've failed you."

"Nonsense," Ambrose said, reaching out and touching Mustaf's muscular arm. "You've never failed me. Not once."

Vincente and Diago sat close together, looking down in the hopes the Ape-Men would cease their torment. "I saw my brother escape," said Vincente. "He wouldn't abandon me. He'll come for us."

"Your brother probably thinks we are already dead," Diago spat. "And soon he will probably be correct."

Curled up in a ball, Professor Crowley wept as the Ape-Men jabbed at him with sticks. "We're all going to die in here," he sobbed. "None of us are getting home."

"Quiet, man!" Ambrose snapped at his friend. "It's not over until it's over."

A short distance away, Ape-Men beat on drums and their females danced and sung an ungodly tune as a huge fire was fed in the centre of their gathering. At the feet of the Ape-Men the bones of humans and dinosaurs lay in the dirt, filthy and with festering meat still clung to some of them.

"Fascinating," Ambrose muttered as he watched the proceedings. "They seem to be conducting a ceremony of sorts."

The drums grew ever louder, the dancing more intense and the fire ever larger as the ceremonial activities reached a climax.

Candy cried out as she felt something yank at her foot. She turned to see a gaggle of Ape-Man children chittering away in amusement, the largest of them pulling at her ankle. She summoned her courage and kicked out at the little monster, the child sent rolling back into its peers. The other children chittered away in deranged laughter at her struggle.

A portion of the crowd parted and Ambrose stood to get a good look at what was coming. Four burly Ape-Men came walking forward, carrying something between them. His eyes widened as he realised it was the upturned skull of a T-Rex. Two shafts of wood had been pushed through the skull's eyeholes and nostril holes respectively and each Ape-Man was lifting a corner. The skull was being carried nose first and sitting in it, as if it were a throne, was an obese looking Ape-Man, at least half a foot larger than the others. This Ape-Man wore a feathered headdress and clearly held prominence amongst the others. It stood, steadying its feet just behind the jutting out teeth of the skull, raised its muscular arms and howled to the night stars. The crowd of Ape-Men joined the calls of this Ape-Chief, enraptured by its power.

"Looks like that's the leader," remarked Vincente.

"What is he going to do to us?" Crowley asked, not wanting the answer.

The drums then stopped as the skull throne was placed down and the Ape-Chief began chattering and grunting in whatever passed as their language. The Ape-Men listened in silence, none daring to talk over their master.

The Ape-Chief then concluded his speech and pointed to the caged humans and the crowd exploded in rapturous celebration once again.

"Looks like we're the guests of honour," Vincente concluded.

Two large Ape-Men approached the cage, grunting and chattering as they pulled the cage door open.

"Get behind me," Mustaf ordered, jumping in front of Ambrose and Candy.

The Ape-Men regarded him and one of them sneered. The other moved close to Crowley, who tried to shrink away, trying to appear as small as possible. The Ape-Man looked amused by the old man's fear and giggled inanely.

The first Ape-Man called out in loud shrieks before reaching out and grabbing Diago by the ankle. Diago screamed and called for help as he was pulled away from Vincente, twisting and kicking as he struggled to break free from the Ape-Man's tight grip. Vincente attempted to pull Diago back to him and was rewarded with a back-handed smack to the face. He fell backwards, his nose bleeding.

Mustaf leapt to Diago's aid, baring his own teeth and balling his massive hands into fists. The Ape-Men did not treat the big man's defiance as lightly as Vincente's, clearly aware of the threat he could potentially pose. The second Ape-Man pushed Mustaf back, screaming angrily into his face and showing its own teeth, yellow and curved. The creature's fetid breath made Mustaf's eyes water and he backed down, seeing no good outcome from jumping at the monster.

Feeling Mustaf's defiance had been quelled, the Ape-Man followed the other out of the cage and the door was once again closed and locked. Diago continued to struggle as he was dragged by the ankles to the middle of the makeshift amphitheatre and thrown down before the fire.

Diago screamed for mercy as he was tied spread eagle to four stakes on the ground. An Ape-Man emerged from the crowd and the incessant drumming once again commenced. It wore the skull of a Raptor on its head and performed an elaborate dance, intermittently groping at the females as they joined it in their bizarre ritual. In the dancing Ape-Man's hand was a stone hatchet which it swung as if it were a macabre dancing accessory.

The trapped survivors watched with bated breath what was occurring before them. Even the Ape-Men that had been tormenting them now turned their backs, more interested in the demented dance.

"Please," sobbed Diago as he struggled against his restraints. "I don't want to die like this."

The skull-wearing Ape-Man stood behind his head, waving its hatchet for all to see. The crowd drew still as the Ape-Man knelt behind Diago and with its free hand stroked its finger over his forehead. Diago cried and begged for mercy. The Ape-Man said something in its own guttural language before raising the hatchet with both hands and roared with a bloodlust that spread to the others. The entire crowd commenced whooping and hollering as the hatchet was brought down with full force. The stone blade struck Diago's forehead and his skull cracked open like a walnut. Diago's screams and struggles were cut short as blood, brain and skull fragments erupted from the top of his head.

The crowd of Ape-Men cheered, jumping up and down and throwing their hands up in the air. The Skullface Ape-Man dropped its hatchet and rammed a hand into the top of Diago's skull. It pulled out a handful of bloodied brain matter and lifted it aloft, spatters of blood dripping onto the skull it wore. Skullface then proudly carried the grotesque handful of grey matter to the Ape-Chief, who gladly accepted it and bit down into the meat, chewing and slurping noisily. It then roared its approval and the cheers grew ever louder.

The dancing females leapt upon Diago's body, fighting to scoop and claw at the inside of Diago's broken head, greedily eating any brain matter they could get their hands on.

Candy covered her mouth and looked away, shocked at the slaughter she had just witnessed. Ambrose, Mustaf, Crowley and Vincente looked on, unable to escape the horror.

More of the Ape-Men bounded over to the body of Diago, many of them carrying weapons and cutting implements. They descended on his remains like a pack of hyenas, commencing with a frenzy of dismemberment, hacking and cutting. When they were done with the body parts, chunks of flesh and organs that were skewered on sticks and cooking against the heat of the raging fire were all that remained of the unfortunate labourer.

"We have to find a way out of here," Crowley whimpered.

"Agreed," said Mustaf, looking for a way out of the cage. The entirety of the Ape-Men were now engaged in the revelries and the survivors were unwatched. They began kicking at the sides of the cage, searching for a weak point.

Feeling along the wooden bars, Candy found one that was frayed and when she pushed on it, it started to give. It wasn't much, but it was a start. She turned to call for Mustaf to try and force it. No sooner had she turned her head then an Ape-Man's hand locked around her wrist and pulled her arm out of the cage. Candy shrieked in terror as she was forced against the cage wall.

"Let her go!" yelled Ambrose in outrage, as he tried to pull his daughter free from the monster's grip.

"Damn you," cursed Mustaf as he held Candy's trapped arm and attempted to pull away from the Ape-Man. Candy cried out in pain as it felt as if her arm would pull apart.

The Ape-Man laughed at their struggles, its own strength far surpassing that of its prisoners. It gave an evil grin as it produced a stone hatchet and held it high. The implication was obvious.

"Don't look," Ambrose sobbed, pulling at his daughter and wishing he could spare her from this awful fate.

A loud bang assaulted their ears and the top of the Ape-Man's skull exploded. Its eyes rolled into the back of its head and it fell to the ground. As soon as its grip released, Candy pulled her arm back inside before rationalising what had happened.

The survivors felt their hopes grow as Chuck came running towards the cage, Grant close behind him.

"Chuck, I knew you'd come to save us!" Candy exclaimed.

"I'm working on it," he said, drawing out his machete and hacking at the wooden bars of the cage. Grant swiftly joined him.

The Ape-Chief grinned as it watched its subjects dance and play and eat. The humans who had trespassed against them had been defeated. Better yet, they would serve as meat for days to come. This was cause for celebration.

Its tongue ran over its teeth, dislodging a piece of the brain matter it had hungrily chewed moments ago. The Ape-Chief looked over to the cage which contained their captives appreciatively. Its smile turned to a howl of fury as it witnessed the last of the captives squeeze through a hole that other humans had cut into the cage wall.

The crowd of Ape-Men stopped their dancing and chattering at once and turned to see what their chief had seen. Chittering of confusion was soon replaced by the collective baying for blood as the creatures raised weapons and rushed the humans en-masse.

"They're going to get us," cried Candy as she frantically ran from the hoard of Ape-Men. Grant fired indiscriminately into the crowd and individual Ape-Men fell, crying out in agony.

"Not if I can help it," said Chuck. He then turned to Pat. "Ready?"

Pat nodded and began throwing the red smoke bombs with all his might at the crowd. The Ape-Men stopped in their tracks, their lust for blood being replaced by fear and confusion.

Seeing their cue, Dillon and Javier began throwing in more of the red smoke bombs from their hidden positions, blinding and terrorising the Ape-Men further.

The Ape-Chief looked on at the utter pandemonium, trying to understand what was happening. The mass of Ape-Men now ran in all directions, panting and coughing as they inhaled the accursed red smoke which had now spread out over the entire amphitheatre. It hurriedly crawled from its throne and began scampering in the opposite direction of the crowd, its own fear getting the better of it.

Blinded by terror, it didn't even comprehend the swinging tail of the Stegosaurus until it was already impaled upon the six foot spikes.

King bellowed in victory as he shook his tail, sending the split and ruined corpse of the Ape-Chief hurtling into the dense undergrowth. On King's back Flora stood proud, donning her tribal mask and firing arrows into the crowd. Each arrow found its mark in the torso of an Ape-Man and the inhuman beasts fell.

Some of the Ape-Men turned to face her, their rage winning out over their fears. Flora yelled orders to King and the Stegosaurus stampeded forwards into the crowd, crushing countless of the Ape-Men underfoot. Those that found themselves in range of King's tail met a similar fate as their chief. Flora yelled in triumph as she gave in to her own bloodlust, enjoying the carnage and firing arrows with abandon. When the Ape-Men's numbers grew too dense she commenced lighting more of the Dragon Eggs and throwing them into the seething ocean of hairy bodies. They had the desired effect, forcing the Ape-Men that could flee to do so.

A single Ape-Man managed to jump onto King's back and began climbing towards Flora. She didn't notice, concentrating on holding on and firing arrows into the hoard of Tacal. She saw the remains of Diago and the sight spurred her on all the more.

The Ape-Man behind her howled in victory as it raised its hatchet for a killing blow. Flora instinctually turned around and drew a knife fashioned from a dinosaur jawbone. Before the Ape-Man could react to block the attack the bone-knife was thrust upwards into its throat, causing it to make a grim, gurgling sound as dark crimson spurted from the wound, covering Flora with Ape-Man blood. Flora then twisted the blade before pulling it downwards, opening the Ape-Man up. She then kicked its gutted body off from King's back and it fell lifelessly to the ground beneath the feet of its panicking brethren.

Grant gave a whistle as he witnessed the slaughter through the sight of his rifle. "Remind me never to get on *her* bad side."

Dillon and Javier emerged from either side of the jungle, their objective of causing confusion and panic by throwing the Dragon Eggs now complete. Javier cheered when he saw his brother and the two embraced.

"What's going on?" exclaimed Ambrose. "Who is that person riding that Stegosaurus?"

"This is insanity," remarked Crowley.

Chuck was in agreement with him. "I'll explain everything later. For now, we've got to get out of here."

Nobody argued and the survivors ran into the night.

***

THE LOST VALLEY OF VINCABAMBA

Three hours later Chuck ran from the jungle towards the huge tree that supported the treehouse. They hadn't faced any opposition on the way back, but that didn't mean no opposition was on the way.

"My word," said Ambrose as he noticed the large, wooden structure.

Chuck quickly ushered everyone up the rope ladder before finally climbing up himself. He then pulled it up behind him, as Flora had instructed.

Dillon and Grant set up on the balcony overlooking the clearing, ready to take out any of the Ape-Men that may have followed them.

"What do we do now?" Ambrose asked, unsure of what was happening.

"Now we wait," ordered Chuck.

For two hours the group waited in tense silence. "That person riding on the Stegosaurus. Who was it?" asked Ambrose quietly. Chuck remained looking out over the dark jungle with his men, the adrenaline in their systems keeping them awake.

"That would be Flora. I'm pretty sure she is the daughter of your pal, Austin."

"Impossible! How could she have survived here for so long?"

Chuck gave a sideways smile. "You saw her in action. Is it that surprising?"

"Heads up, something's coming," called Grant.

Chuck looked to the jungle and saw what his men had already spotted. Something heavy moved through the trees, causing them to sway and crack. A flock of roosting birds took to the air in fright.

"Hold fire until we can see what it is," ordered Chuck.

The group waited silently until the trees parted and the Stegosaurus named King emerged with the masked Flora sitting on its back.

The men in the treehouse relaxed and Chuck smiled. Flora jumped from the dinosaur and stroked its head, thanking it for its aid. King bellowed back at her before turning around and retreating back amidst the trees. Various wounds were visible on its legs and sides, though none seemed to have bothered it too much.

Chuck lowered the rope ladder and Flora quickly climbed up, as if she had all the energy in the world. She was covered in blood from head to toe and still wore her war mask. Her visage made for a ghastly image. Everyone gathered around in awe of her. The survivors who hadn't formally met Flora yet kept their distance, unsure of the nature of this bizarre warrior.

"Are you bleeding?" Chuck asked her.

Flora shook her head. "It's their blood, not mine."

"Amazing, absolutely amazing," enthused Ambrose, clasping his hands together.

Flora cocked her head, turning it to regard the professor. "You're Professor Ambrose?"

Ambrose smiled encouragingly. "Yes, I am. It's a very great honour to meet you, my dear. I was a friend of your father's."

"Truly?"

"Yes, we were firm friends."

Without warning, Flora whipped off her mask and jumped at the professor. Nobody had time to react before she'd pinned him to the wall by the throat with one hand while the other had drawn and pressed her bone-knife against the bottom of his chin. "You are the man who abandoned my father and left him here to die," Flora snarled, accusingly. "Tell me why I shouldn't cut your throat where you stand."

CHAPTER 18

Vincabamba, 1930

Austin Kiplard wiped the sweat from his brow as he set the timer on the camera before running to stand next to his wife, Iris. Alongside her stood Arthur Ambrose, famed adventurer, his wife Felicity, a woman far smarter than any of them, and her six-month-old baby, Candy. Behind them the lush jungles of Bolivia wavered in the wind.

"Hurry up or you won't be in the photo," Iris laughed as Austin put his arm around her and the camera flashed.

"One for the history books," Austin smiled.

"That's for certain," grinned Ambrose. "You know, I think that it's Candy's six-month birthday."

Iris stroked Candy's cheek while Felicity beamed with pride. "Well, this little princess is certainly a more valuable treasure than some stone."

"The Stone of Qualbec could well be the most powerful and mystical artefact in the history of mankind," smiled Ambrose. "Of course it's not as valuable as my little Candy!"

Austin's smile wavered a little as he walked past Ambrose. "Arthur, a word if I may."

Felicity heard Austin's whisper but pretended she hadn't and continued chatting to Iris as the two men walked a short distance away.

"What's on your mind?" Ambrose smiled.

"You know damn well," Austin said shortly. "I understand the importance of Vincabamba and the Stone of Qualbec, I truly do. But do you not think it can wait?"

"If you know the importance of the stone, you know the answer to that," Ambrose snapped.

"But your wife, Ambrose. Why is she here? We should go back, plan another expedition for a year's time, with better resources and planning."

"It's taken over a year to track down that map. Do you really think we can head back to New York now? After embedding ourselves in this for so long? That's a full year exploring ruins, visiting isolated villages, rubbing shoulders with smugglers. We can't turn back now. Felicity falling pregnant was unfortunate timing, but that is all. She's as committed to this as I am."

"They say the valley is dangerous."

Ambrose laughed. "No worse than any other, I assure you. Don't worry, we can handle it. And anyway, it's important the girl gets the taste of adventure while she is still young."

Austin bit his tongue. "Okay, old boy. If you are sure."

"I have faith in my wife. If she has doubts she would let me know. Now, let me show you the route we need to take…"

***

Felicity hushed her crying baby as Austin and Ambrose stood outside the tent and tried to gain their bearings. They'd entered Vincabamba a day ago via a cave to the south, as the map described. They now had three to four days of travelling north to reach the temple that housed the Stone of Qualbec.

"Are you okay?" asked Iris as she rolled up her sleeping bag and pushed it into her backpack. Because they had travelled without guides or labourers, they only had a small array of equipment. Ambrose had been paranoid that others would steal his prize from him and not wanted to delay in their travel nor ask for aid from locals.

Felicity smiled as she changed Candy. "Yes, thank you. Candy is just proving extra difficult today."

Iris chewed on her bottom lip as she helped Felicity pack.

"I know what you are thinking," Felicity said.

"I didn't say anything."

"You didn't have to. It's obvious. You're wondering why I've continued to be pulled all around South America by Arthur while I was heavily pregnant. You're wondering why I'm still allowing it, now I have a baby."

Iris sighed and spoke with a gentle patience. "Why are you still travelling, still *'adventuring'*, as the boys like to say?""It's not just them who refer to what we do as adventuring. Adventuring is in my blood. It's who I am, beneath all the benefit balls and fancy restaurants. When I'm in New York, mixing with captains of industry and the new millionaire traders of Wall Street, I feel like an actress. Do you understand?"

Iris shrugged. "I'm sure I don't."

"I'm sure you don't. I play my role well, don't I?"

"You always seem happy, be it in New York or out in the field."

Felicity's smile faltered. "The truth is my mask I wear so well is suffocating me. The person I am back in New York, she isn't real. Not that the people I dine and drink with would notice. They're only interested in the stories I have to share, hoping that if I share my tales of adventure and exotic locales then they'll somehow become more interesting themselves through osmosis." She chuckled. "Arthur was the first man to truly understand me. He showed me a world far greater than high society ever could."

"Austin and my own travels have certainly become more interesting since we began traveling with the two of you."

"Now that Austin is so close to what he has dreamed of, the legendary Stone of Qualbec, how can I stand in his way? After all the experiences and freedom he has given me?"

"It's not your fault you fell pregnant."

"Isn't it? Regardless, I want to be a part of this, too. I'm just as guilty as him. If I were to return to New York, knowing the journey for the Stone of Qualbec were taking place without me, I'd probably go mad. I am an adventurer; I won't be satisfied with anything less."

"Not even for the sake of your daughter?"

"Candy will be fine tagging along. I have enough experience to keep her safe. After this, we'll be heading back to New York for the next year, anyway. Journals need writing, artefacts need cataloguing. I'll enjoy a little peace and quiet, though not until this business is put to rest. To return with this business unfinished would be a fate worse than death. Especially after I'd accomplished ninety-five percent of the journey. I wouldn't be able to think of anything else."

Iris sighed. "Perhaps you could have sent Candy back, hired a nanny to look after her until the Stone was found."

Felicity shrugged. "Perhaps. If I'd done that though, Candy would have spent her first six months without her mother, and I can't think of anything worse than that. For all my faults, I dearly love my child and would never abandon her to grow up without me."

Outside the tent, Ambrose sat and listened in silence.

***

Ambrose woke to the sound of Candy crying and looked at his watch. It was early, barely five in the morning. He looked at Felicity, who was covering her ears with her hands.

"Why won't that baby sleep in, just once?" she groaned.

"I'll take her for a short walk," Ambrose suggested, hurriedly pulling on his clothes. "You rest a bit longer."

Felicity sat up and gently smiled. She looked tired. "Thank you," she said and leaned forward to kiss her husband. "Don't wander too far though, and stay safe."

"Will do," Ambrose smiled before scooping Candy up in his arms and making his way out of the tent.

Outside it was already light, the strange jungle making unidentifiable sounds, the insects already buzzing around the flowers. Candy kept crying, though her whines were more to seek attention than anything else. He gently rocked her as he took a morning stroll, breathing in the fresh air.

As he walked, Ambrose contemplated many things. Overhearing Felicity's conversation with Iris had forced him to consider his decisions and priorities. He wondered how much of the traveling Felicity undertook due to his own stubborn refusal to postpone the hunt for the artefact. Candy was now the most important thing in his life, or at least that's what he told himself. Still, if Felicity gave to him the ultimatum of either pursuing the Stone of Qualbec without her joining him or postponing their journey to Vincabamba and returning home empty handed, what would he do? He honestly didn't know. People always said that having children was the greatest adventure one could have, but was this true to someone who had walked in tombs that hadn't seen occupants in over a thousand years?

And if he chose to forgo the Stone of Qualbec to return to New York prematurely, would Felicity resent him for it, as if he had decided to throw in the towel? She loved him for his adventurous spirit, but did his desire to earn her love now threaten their daughter's life by putting her in precarious situations? It seemed they were both anxious to live up to the lifestyle they had seemingly committed to without forethought. Had their lifetime of freedom become its own trap, in a way? Was the option of a simple, domestic life now out of their reach? Would they each respectively love the person the other would become? He looked again at Candy, her crying briefly paused as she yawned. She looked content. Happy. He envied her in that moment. Envied the simplicity of her existence.

Ambrose wondered if he'd been selfish in bringing his daughter along. Felicity seemed confident she could keep their baby safe, but could she really guarantee such a thing? If Candy fell ill now, this tiny, innocent bundle that trusted implicitly in her parents making the best decision for her fell sick, they were weeks away from a hospital.

Ambrose's face went red as he felt anger towards himself. He'd been such a fool, chasing treasures when the true treasure was already in his arms. And why was he so afraid to allow himself to move on in his life? It was natural to change one's habits once a baby was born. He spat as it dawned on him that he and Felicity were both being as foolish as each other. Candy had to be their priority now, to hell with the Stone. It had remained hidden for hundreds of years. It would likely still be waiting if he returned to claim it in a few years time. Hadn't he and Felicity earned a little rest, after all?

They'd only journeyed a day into the valley and so far hadn't encountered any hostile wildlife. He wondered if that was more due to luck than anything else. Evidence of large beasts moving through the trees was all around and he had no way of knowing if the tracks they had found belonged to large herbivores or gigantic predators.

The day before, Ambrose couldn't wait to find out. Now, with the fragile life of his daughter in his hands, a new found appreciation for the responsibility he had all but neglected due to his own ambitions, he hoped he would never discover the nature of the giant animals. In the distance he heard the drums begin. They'd played for the duration of yesterday, their source seemingly far away and yet the nature of the valley allowed the sounds of them to carry on the wind.

Were the natives of this valley peaceful? Again, he now hoped never to find out. He'd encountered more than one tribe of cannibals in his time and still had the scars to prove it. Austin claimed to have seen one of them, though what he had seen sounded more like an upright gorilla than a man.

Austin, he thought. The man had been a good and loyal friend and Ambrose hoped Austin would understand his change of heart.

A scream carried through the trees and Ambrose's blood ran cold.

Felicity!

Ambrose held Candy close to him and broke into a run back to camp. He realised he'd walked further than he'd intended and it took almost five minutes to jog back to camp. He cried out in horror and despair at the sight that befell him.

Both tents were in a shambles, though that wasn't what caught his attention. It was the terrible creature that was dragging the bleeding remains of Felicity out of her tent. It was a lythe creature, five feet high at the hip and with a long, serpentine neck. It looked similar to an ostrich, but with no feathers or beak. Its cruel teeth sank deep into Felicity's calf as it dragged her out a little further, revealing her throat had been torn out. Felicity's eyes stared lifelessly up to the sky, her features frozen into a mask of horror. Placing a foot on Felicity's body, the dinosaur pulled and twisted, and a chunk of muscle from the back of Felicity's calf was ripped away. The creature raised its head and swallowed its grisly meal before spotting Ambrose watching it. It jumped around to face him and gave a high pitched, terrible shriek.

"Arthur, up here," called Austin and Ambrose looked up at a tree behind the vicious predator. On the high branches hid Austin and Iris. Iris looked safe, though was sobbing. Austin's arm was covered in deep lacerations that were bleeding profusely. "You have to get the rifle from my tent," Austin called. "It's our only hope."

The dinosaur twisted its neck to shriek its displeasure at Austin. Ambrose took a step back, trying to plan his next move. He could not believe that the love of his life and the mother of his child now lay dead like so much carrion. It was a cruel and senseless death.

Candy started to cry and the sound drew the dinosaur's ire. It shrieked again and took two swift steps towards Ambrose. Ambrose took the only course of action that seemed sensible; he ran.

He ran as fast as he could, even as branches and vines whipped at his face and his arms, he ran. All the while he used his body to protect Candy from the harshness of the world. The dinosaur didn't pursue him. Instead, it shrieked its horrible shriek before stalking the bottom of the tree where Austin and Iris remained trapped.

"Come back here!" Austin called as Iris cried in horror, realising that they'd been abandoned.

Ambrose's sense of pride and his loyalty to his friends screamed out to him that he was doing the wrong thing, that he had to turn around and help. A deeper, more primal part of him compelled him to keep running. It told him that Candy's life was now completely dependent on him, that her safety was his one and only concern. Everything else fell to the wayside. The Valley of Vincabamba, the Stone of Qualbec, even his friends. To attempt to tackle the dinosaur meant the very real possibility of death and he simply could no longer justify that. He doubted he'd be able to look in the mirror ever again. He also doubted he'd ever tell anyone the shame of his actions; of how he'd callously brought his family to a deadly environment and how he'd realised too late the folly of his ways, only to leave his friends behind.

Ambrose's mind repeated this line of thought over and over as he kept running, never stopping to investigate the strange jungle around him, nor to be mindful of potential predators in the vicinity.

As the sun began to set Ambrose realised he'd run all the way back to the cliffs at the south end of the valley. Catching his breath, his mind raced. He'd abandoned his friends, but it wasn't too late to return, to try and save them. Candy cried out, having not been fed all day and Ambrose knew he truly had no choice at all. It took him two hours to find the cave he had entered the valley from and when he did he fled. He promised himself that when he knew Candy was safe he'd return with men and right his wrong and atone for his sin. For now, he had to just keep running...

CHAPTER 19

Vincabamba, 1954

Flora remained unmoving as Ambrose recounted his tale, the rest of the survivors remaining where they were, afraid that any sudden movements would push her into slashing the professor's throat.

"Is that the truth?" Flora asked slowly.

Ambrose's words dripped with shame. "It is, I swear it. I don't blame you for hating me. Austin must have done. Just know that the revulsion you feel for me is but a fraction of the self-loathing I've felt for myself over the years."

"Evidently my father survived that dinosaur. Why didn't he follow you out of the valley?"

Ambrose caught his breath. "As I fled through the cave, I accidentally caused a cave in. The tunnel we used collapsed."

Flora applied more pressure to the knife at the professor's throat. "You're lying. If that were true, how'd you get back in?"

"There were two paths through the cave we used. Although there was one cave entrance that led to both paths, the outlets of those caves are far apart. The southern mountain is covered in shallow caves. Austin wouldn't have known where that exit was."

"He's telling the truth," sobbed Candy. "He's told you what you want to know, so let him go."

Flora turned to look at Candy, cocking her head slightly. "Who are you?"

"I'm his daughter. I'm Candy."

Flora looked back at Ambrose with barely concealed rage. "You brought her back? Even after everything that happened? So, you learned nothing?"

Ambrose said nothing, his eyes screwed shut.

"Release him. Now," demanded Mustaf.

Flora looked at the big man, then to Candy before finally releasing her grip and letting Ambrose slide to the floor. Mustaf ran to the professor's aid, checking the bead of blood that had formed from a nick of Flora's blade. "You want him, you can have him." Flora then turned and walked out onto one of the treehouse's balconies.

Candy looked emotionally numb as she processed all she had just heard.

"I'm sorry," Ambrose blubbered. "I'm sorry I didn't tell you."

Candy ignored him and began walking to the opposite balcony to Flora. Chuck watched her go.

"There should be repercussions for that girl, after how she has acted. She's dangerous. She looks deranged," Mustaf sneered.

"That girl is more dangerous than the rest of us combined," said Grant. "And she saved the lives of you and the Professor. She saved all our lives. Perhaps you should show her some respect."

Mustaf grumbled but didn't argue the point.

Chuck walked outside into the night air where Candy was standing, looking up at the night stars. "You okay?" he asked.

"Do you remember what I said to you back on the boat?"

"About wanting to understand your mother?"

"Hmm. People always told me that we were alike. I just never realised how alike. She was just as tired of the New York elite as I am. I wanted to try and emulate her footsteps, to get an understanding of her. I tried so hard to understand her. Now I feel like I was tracing her steps without even knowing it all along, without even trying."

"In more ways than one."

Candy smiled wistfully. "You're right. I've actually been in this valley before; can you believe that? It seems crazy to contemplate. I wonder why... why didn't my father tell me the truth?"

"Would you have come here if he had?"

Candy paused. "I guess I'll never know."

"Ahem."

Chuck and Candy turned to see Ambrose waiting sheepishly in the shadows. "Mister Tanner, may I speak with my daughter?"

Chuck glanced at Candy and she nodded. "I'll be inside if you need me." He then walked into the treehouse.

Candy said nothing, waiting for her father to break the silence.

"I never wanted you to find out. About your mother's death, I mean. It was a horrible thing."

"I would have found more solace in a harsh truth than an incorporeal lie. You never once hinted that mother had died in the field."

"I was ashamed. Ashamed that you'd blame me, as I blamed myself."

"Why on earth do you blame yourself?"

"Back then, we were at the height of our careers. We went places nobody else dared and we always walked away unscathed, usually with some trinket or another to fill our pockets. We felt we were untouchable. The dangers of our lifestyle seemed like little more than a game."

"I still don't know why you feel mother's death was your fault. She was her own woman."

"Perhaps, but hearing what she said to Iris that morning, it made me doubt everything. I reconsidered why she was doing the things she did? Out of love for me? Because she didn't want to let me down? We spent so long being adventurers, I think we were afraid of trying to be anything else."

"Don't forget she went on to say she felt as addicted to the adventures as you. New York society did nothing for her anymore."

"She did," Ambrose conceded. "She also stated that she was a good actress. I've always wondered, before she talked about her own desires to live a life of adventure, when she mentioned how she didn't want to let *me* down, as if she ever could. I wonder if that was the mask slipping, if only for a second...."

Candy bristled. "That's a very self-centred viewpoint. You think she did what she did for you? Why? Because she was a woman, she can't follow her own ideals?"

"Not because she was a woman. Because she was in love with me. I don't think I truly understood the power of love back then. I certainly thought I did, at the time. I loved your mother with all my heart, but it was never put to the test. If your mother had approached me before I first arrived in Vincabamba, told me she wanted us both to return to New York, what would I have said?"

"You probably would have sent her ahead and carried on without her."

Ambrose smiled sadly. "You're probably right. My lifestyle, my freedoms, they were my truest love. I would have chosen them over any other option. Until that day when I held you and walked in the same jungle we are in now. Only then did I come to realise I would never value anything or anyone as much as you, my one and only daughter. That's why when the dinosaur attacked, your mother lay dead and Austin and Iris were up in that tree, I had a decision to make. It was between you and the life I'd always led. I chose you."

Candy sighed. "You are an old fool. You chose me, but it was a forced decision. I always felt you kept me at a distance. I've always felt lonely in our home."

"I struggled to face you. I didn't know how to relate and I felt guilty for your mother's untimely end. It was my own ambition that led us here, all those years ago. I am sorry, I should have tried harder. You are so much like your mother, far more than you will ever know, and my last day with her shook my foundations. I doubted I ever truly understood her. I doubt I truly understand you."

"I don't even understand me," Candy sighed. She held out her hand and Ambrose took it. "You should have told me."

"I should have. I'm sorry. I'll try harder to be the father you deserve."

Candy crossed her arms and turned back to the jungle. "Please, I need time to think."

Ambrose hung his head and slowly walked back inside. "When we get back to New York, I'll show you photo albums and newspaper cuttings you haven't seen before. She was a remarkable woman."

Candy waited for her father to go before looking back out over the jungle, all detail lost in darkness. She couldn't help but feel as if her mother's ghost were out there somewhere, watching her.

"Your father is a good man," said a voice. Candy twisted around in shock, trying to locate its source. She looked up and saw a dark figure hunched on the roof. It was Flora. Candy's back stiffened.

"Oh, it's you."

Flora stood up and effortlessly jumped down to the balcony without making a sound. "I think Candy is a silly name."

"I don't think much of your name, if I'm being brutally honest," Candy sniffed.

Flora approached her as if she were a wild animal. "Why are you mad with your father? I'm the one who should be mad at him."

"He's kept things from me. All my life he hid how my mother died and never elaborated on the kind of woman she was. I feel like she is a stranger to me. I feel the same about *him* sometimes. Do I really know him at all?"

Flora smirked, as if Candy had said something ridiculous.

"What's so funny?"

"You are. You say silly things."

"What things do I say that are silly?"

"You say your father is a stranger to you, despite growing up with him all your life. That's silly."

"It's complicated," Candy muttered. "Growing up in the jungle, you wouldn't understand."

Flora shrugged. "I understand that your father gave up everything to protect you."

"Hardly 'everything.'"

"He said that adventuring was his life. It was everything. He gave that up for you… didn't he?" She cocked her head.

"You're oversimplifying things," Candy snapped, losing patience.

"I think you are making things more complicated."

"Before I was born, my father lived an entirely different life alongside my mother. It's that aspect of him I know nothing about. This huge part of his personality."

"Before I was born my father and mother lived in places filled with millions of people. I can't even imagine what that is like. That doesn't mean I didn't know them."

Candy felt a sadness for Flora she hadn't expected. "It must have been tough growing up here."

Flora shrugged. "I've known no different."

"Why are you so quick to forgive my father? He abandoned your parents here, made your life what it is. Aren't you mad at him?"

"Partly, but he explained why he did it. That was all I wanted to learn from him. Father never elaborated on why he ran. He was never angry about it, though. He always said your father was a nice man and that he had his reasons. I just wanted to know what they were."

"Now you do, how do you feel?"

Flora's stomach made a loud, rumbling sound. "Hungry," she laughed, impishly. "How about you? Are you hungry?"

Despite herself, Candy grinned. "I'm famished."

"Do you have frogs where you come from?"

Candy was suddenly a lot less hungry. "We do. We don't tend to eat them, though."

Flora laughed. "You are in for a treat!" She stopped at the doorway and turned, her grin now a soft smile. "I'll take you to her tomorrow."

"Take me to whom?"

"Your mother, of course."

***

The next morning, true to her word, Flora took Candy a small distance from the treehouse to a small, tended section of jungle. Somehow it felt tranquil, as if the chaotic nature of the valley didn't intrude upon it. Three crosses were present, simple constructions of two sticks tied together and then stuck into the ground. Candy guessed they marked graves.

"Mother," smiled Flora, touching the first cross. "Father." She then went to the final and by far the oldest of the crosses. "Your mother."

Candy felt a lump in her throat as she looked upon the modest grave. A short way away, Chuck, Mustaf and Ambrose waited. Ambrose was just as eager to visit Felicity's final resting place as his daughter, but had agreed to let her visit the tiny graveyard first. Flora skipped down the dirt path, ignoring the men as she made her way back to the treehouse. She seemed not to have a care in the world as she ate a fruit plucked from one of the nearby trees. Chuck watched her go before turning and waiting for Candy. He watched as she crouched before the cross made of sticks and began talking. He fought the impulse to go to her and comfort her. This was something Candy had to do alone.

Kneeling on the short grass, tears trickled down Candy's cheeks as she wondered what to say. "Hello, Mother," she said, her voice trembling. "It's Candy, your daughter. It's funny… I went on this expedition to be closer to you… to understand the woman you were. I never, for the life of me, expected to find you here." Her voice began to quiver as she searched for the words that would express her pain, her sorrow and her loneliness. "I miss you," she managed, tears dripping onto the grass. "I know that sounds ridiculous, seeing as I don't even remember you. But I do, I miss you so much it hurts. There has always been a hole in my life. A hole in the shape of you. And I've tried to fill it. I've tried to fill it with so many things. I've learnt as much about you as I could. I've tried to emulate your lifestyle, hoping to understand the woman you were, but nothing has helped. You've always felt like a stranger to me. Some larger than life, legendary character who's destined forever to be a mystery. Yet as far away from me you feel, your shadow has always cast over me.

"Father never really told me about you. I didn't know the circumstances of your death until last night. I thought it was because he was too sad to remember, and there is an element of that. But now I have insight into another reason why he never taught me about you. He was afraid. Afraid even he didn't understand you. And I think that fear is why he's always kept me at an arm's length, also. In my bid to understand you, I've turned myself into you more flawlessly than I could have ever guessed. Now *I* am the mystery. The person whose true identity is part tabloid rumour, part doting daughter, part scientist, part healer, part reveller.

"That's why I stand before you now. To tell you that I love you, and also to tell you 'goodbye.' I can't live my life trying to emulate you anymore. It's time I make my own path and be the woman I am truly meant to be. My search for you is over, my search for myself is just beginning." Candy sniffed and wiped her eyes before kissing her fingertips and gently touching the cross. As she did a brilliant, blue butterfly fluttered in off the wind and landed gently on the cross.

Candy watched it, a feeling of warmth blossoming inside of her, until a slight wind blew and the butterfly once again took to the air.

Candy walked back down the short path. As she passed Ambrose he looked as if he wanted to say something but couldn't find the words. He and Mustaf then walked towards the cross.

Chuck put an arm around Candy's shoulder and she allowed herself to be held against his body as they walked. "Are you going to be okay? Did you say what you needed to say?"

Candy smiled, pushing closer into Chuck. "I'll get back to you on that."

Chuck kissed the top of her head and they continued walking in silence.

***

From the balcony, Dillon grinned as he watched Flora march up to the huge Stegosaurus named King with an armful of fruits and drop them in front of it. King bellowed his satisfaction before partaking in the food. Flora sat on the grass beside the fruits and picked one for herself. She then began chattering away to the dinosaur as if it could understand and respond to her.

Dillon glanced at Grant who rolled his eyes. Dillon laughed before quickly jogging to the rope ladder and climbing down. Flora eyed him curiously as he descended before returning her concentration to the dinosaur. King bellowed again before eating a red fruit out of Flora's hand.

"What's he saying?" Dillon asked as he approached.

"He's saying he thinks you are ugly," Flora said absent mindedly.

"Ouch," said Dillon with mock offence. "Same to you, buddy."

King bellowed again and Dillon looked quizzically at Flora. "Now he says I should chase you away before you attempt to steal his fruit."

Dillon laughed at that. "How do you do that? Understand him, I mean?"

Flora shrugged. "He talks, I listen. It really isn't very hard."

"I guess. How long have you had him?"

"Had him?"

"You know, as a pet."

"King isn't a pet. He is my friend. My only friend."

"Beg my pardon. How long have you known him?"

"Since he was a baby. His mother was killed by a predator and Father recovered his egg."

"Wow, so you two are more family than friends, then."

Flora liked the sound of that and smiled. "Family, I like that. Yes, King is my family." She then embraced the Stegosaurus's head and kissed it hard. King bellowed his annoyance.

"Easy," cautioned Dillon. "Aren't you afraid he could hurt you? I've seen the damage he can do."

Flora stared daggers at him. "He only hurts those I want him to hurt."

"Of course," Dillon stuttered. He stood awkwardly for a second. "Can I pet him?"

"It's not up to me," Flora said.

"Right," Dillon sighed before boldly approaching the dinosaur. "Hi, King. I'm Dillon. Nice to meet you." The Stegosaurus ignored him, more concerned with consuming the last of the fruits Flora had provided it. He reached down and gently touched its head with the palm of his hand. Its skin felt rough and dry. "I'm really doing it," he giggled to Flora, unable to hide his excitement. "I'm actually touching a dinosaur." Flora didn't seem to appreciate what the big deal was so Dillon called up to Grant. "Hey, man, look at this! I'm stroking a dinosaur!"

"Way to go, Dillon," Grant laughed, sounding as if he were humouring a child.

Unperturbed, Dillon grinned at the Stegosaurus. "You and me, we make a good team," he laughed. King bellowed and Dillon liked to think the dinosaur agreed with him. He then turned to Flora. "Do you think he'd let me ride him?"

***

The map of the valley was unfolded and laid out on the floor of the treehouse. Everyone huddled around to get a good view. Chuck pointed to a section of the jungle.

"This is where we are at the moment, would you say that is correct, Flora?"

Flora nodded as she gnawed on a bone, the remnants of a small mammal Grant had successfully shot earlier in the day and they'd had for lunch.

"Are you always hungry?" Candy jokingly mocked.

"I eat when I can," Flora explained. "Never know when I'll get another chance."

Using a pencil, Chuck marked the treehouse location on the map. Ambrose protested the marking of the map, but Chuck ignored him. He pointed to the mountains that encroached into the valley from the west, cutting them off from the north. "This is the mountain range we can see, it's barely a day's walk from here. If we head north until we hit the mountains, we can follow them around. In about two days we'll reach the City of Vincabamba."

"It's a shame those mountains are in the way," sighed Pat. "They're directly between us and Vincabamba. Is there no way we can climb them?"

Flora shook her head. "They are too steep to climb, and terror-birds live on their peaks in huge numbers."

"Terror-birds?" Chuck asked Crowley to clarify.

"Flightless birds, six feet high with razor sharp beaks and a proclivity to use them. I think she means pterosaurs, though."

"Them too," Flora added.

Pat stroked his chin. "Okay, so going over them is a no-go. Perhaps there is a path that leads through?"

"You could go under," Flora said, sounding bored.

"Under?" asked Chuck.

"Through the Fire Cave."

"The Fire Cave?"

"Sure, it's where I get the rocks for my matches."

"You've travelled through it? It goes all the way through?"

"No, but Father read the drawings on the walls. He said the pictures show you can get through."

"Then why did you never use it yourself?"

"Because it travels through the Underworld and promises certain death to all those who attempt to travel it."

"Great," sighed Pat.

"Sounds like an ancient temple or tomb or something," sighed Chuck.

"Aye, and probably boobytrapped to high heaven," Pat lamented.

"We'll take the long way around."

Flora shrugged, not really understanding their hesitancy. "Suit yourself."

"Will you not come with us?" asked Ambrose. "We could certainly use your skills."

"No. I'm not the most popular at Vincabamba. I only go when I have items to trade."

Everyone paused, making sure they'd heard what Flora had said correctly.

"You mean there are *people* living in Vincabamba?" asked Chuck.

"Of course. The Vincas."

"The Vincas? Good heavens," exclaimed Ambrose. "I imagined it was ruins."

Chuck kept his questions focused on Flora, who continued talking as if she were sharing information that should be common knowledge. "Are they Ape-Men?"

"Ape-Men? You mean like the Tacal? No, the Vincas are people, like us. They hate the Tacal."

"But they aren't too fond of you, either?"

Flora pouted. "They make fun of me and call me weird."

"Are they dangerous, though? Will they be hostile to us?"

"I can't see why they would be."

"We're hoping to recover the Stone of Qualbec. To take it away with us. Will they take exception to that?"

"Exception?"

"I mean, will they fight us?"

"Ohhhh."

"Well?"

"No, the Stone is on the mountain above their city. If you ask them, they'll take you to it. Father said that if you are worthy, they'll let you take it."

"Worthy?"

Flora shrugged. "That's what Father said."

"What do you think that means?" queried Candy to the group.

"Perhaps a test of some kind?" pondered Ambrose.

"It certainly changes things. Taking from the dead and taking from the living are two entirely different things," said Pat.

"Agreed," said Chuck. "You say you trade with the people of Vincabamba? You speak their language?"

"A little."

Vincente began speaking in a strange dialect that made everyone turn to face him. After a few seconds Flora responded in the same dialect.

"What was that?" asked Chuck.

"It's a very old language, almost dead," Vincente explained. "Used by our elders as a secret code between themselves. Older than the European tongues we now use. Javier speaks it too. We were taught by our grandmother when we were very young." Javier nodded in confirmation.

"Remarkable," said Ambrose. "This is the same language as the Vincas?"

"There are some differences, but yes, it is the same," Flora said.

Ambrose clapped his hands together and stood. "Then we are good to go. We'll travel north and converse with the Vincas. The Stone will be ours."

"So long as we prove ourselves worthy," muttered Pat. "Let's not forget that part."

"I'm sure that'll be merely a formality," laughed Ambrose, filled with self-assurance.

Chuck wasn't so sure. "If it was so easy, someone would have taken it before. Flora, have you any ideas what we must do to prove ourselves worthy? Any ideas at all?"

Flora shook her head in annoyance. "I told you, didn't I? I don't know."

Chuck crossed his arms, stubbornly. "I don't like it."

Ambrose chuckled. "If we want the stone, what other choice have we got?"

"You are sure you won't come with us?" asked Candy, reaching out and holding Flora's hand. "We'd fare better with you, than without."

Flora glanced down at Candy's silver ring, the ancient treasure with the face of a beast with precious stones for eyes that reminded Candy of her mother. "Where did you get that?"

Candy fingered the worn, silver band. "It belonged to my mother. It is a keepsake I have to remind myself of her."

"Felicity and I recovered it together on one of our earlier expeditions to Iran," said Ambrose. "It's one of a kind, a remnant from a civilisation long since turned to dust. It is worth a small fortune to the right collectors. I gifted it to Felicity and she accepted, but never wore it when we travelled. It was always kept in the family vault. It felt right that Candy should have it."

"I want it," Flora stated as she reached for the ring. "Its eyes are beautiful."

Candy withdrew her hand. "You can't have it. It's mine."

Flora looked angrily to Ambrose.

"Candy…" urged Ambrose.

Candy sighed. "Very well. Take us to Vincabamba. Get us the stone. Then you can have it."

Flora grinned. "Deal."

"Then everything is agreed," said Chuck. "We'll have another night here and in the morning we'll set out for Vincabamba. Soon the Stone of Qualbec will be ours."

CHAPTER 20

Chuck sat on the edge of the balcony and looked out over the jungle as the setting sun bathed everything in a warm yellow glow. Somewhere far out a dinosaur gave a melodious call and was answered by others of its kind. Squinting, Chuck could see a parade of long necked creatures moving through the trees on the horizon. No doubt Ambrose and Crowley would be able to identify them, though Chuck had no desire to ask. He was enjoying his slice of solitude too much. Rarely when traveling did he get a chance to be alone with his thoughts. It felt good. Refreshing.

The air, though still humid, didn't have the claustrophobic feel that it had down on the jungle floor and he was enjoying the chance to rest. The sun on his skin felt good. Tomorrow their quest would continue and in a few days they'd be at the City of Vincabamba. The Stone of Qualbec would be within his grasp. He let his mind wander, thinking of Bill. He'd been friends with Bill longer than anyone and they had saved each other's lives numerous times during the war. To think that Bill's life would end as it did, in the jaws of a prehistoric giant crocodile, seemed preposterous.

Although he didn't want to admit it, Chuck was feeling an emotion he rarely had any time for, regret. The Stone of Qualbec was a treasure beyond value, this was true, and they had come too far just to turn back now. Still, knowing what he knew now, if he could go back in time and Ambrose approached him, would he agree to lead the expedition? *Not a chance,* he told himself. Bill was worth more than any artefact, no matter how rare, valuable and mystical. When he accepted, he didn't think he'd have to give anything up to attain the priceless stone. Now he realised how foolish that was. Everything was a gamble. Everything had a cost. Now that he'd paid the price, he owed it to those lost to claim the prize.

Chuck raised his water canteen to the bright orange disc in the sky. "Here's to you, Bill," he said, then took a sip.

"Am I disturbing anything?" asked Candy as she approached, sipping from her own canteen. She looked relaxed in her mannerisms.

"Nah, just enjoying the view."

"May I join you?"

If it had been anybody else, Chuck would have likely made his excuses and gone inside. "Sure."

Candy sat beside Chuck, closer than was really necessary, and dangled her feet off the edge of the balcony. She stared out across the sun kissed spectacle of the primeval jungle. "It's beautiful, isn't it?"

Chuck couldn't keep his eyes off Candy's features, the soft sunlight causing her skin to glow with a radiance that took his breath away. "Beautiful," he said.

Candy turned and smiled. "You aren't even looking."

"Looking?"

"At the vista."

Chuck caught himself and quickly looked out over the landscape. "Right, the vista." He took another swig of water and looked out over the landscape. He found himself appreciating it in a way he hadn't before. "It is beautiful."

"It's easy to forget how special this place is."

"You mean with the man-eating monsters and such?"

Candy laughed again. "That's exactly what I mean."

"I suppose you and I are now seeing this place from different perspectives."

"Different perspectives? How so?"

"This place has given you what you wanted. You found your mother. It still holds what I am looking for."

"Which is?"

"The Stone of Qualbec, of course."

Candy sighed pleasantly and shuffled closer to Chuck, resting her hand on his. Her hand felt cool to the touch. "Is that really what you are looking for?"

"What else is there?"

Candy shrugged. "The men who have followed you here, Bill, Pat, Grant, Dillon... do you think they've followed a man looking for a trinket? Is that why they've put their lives on the line?"

"You'd have to ask them."

"And my father, is he merely here searching for a mere bauble?"

"He said he wanted to make things right with the past. At the time I didn't know all the details, but now I understand. He had ghosts here. He wanted to confront them."

"How can you be so astute about my father and me yet be so clueless about yourself and your friends?"

Chuck wasn't sure if he was being made fun of. "Perhaps you can tell me, if you have all the answers."

"I think what you are looking for is purpose. I think you all are."

"Purpose?"

"After the war, what was waiting for you when you returned home?"

"Nothing, really."

"You had a period in your life filled with purpose. You were a war hero. You and your friends. Then you came home and that purpose evaporated. So what did you do? You turned to stories from your childhood, stories of adventure and exotic locales and hidden mysteries. So exciting, such purpose. Every job another challenge to overcome. Gambling it all for a reason to gamble it all."

"And my friends?"

"They find purpose in you. You helped lead them to victories in the war. You gave them their purpose. You still do."

Chuck thoughtfully considered Candy's words. "A man needs purpose."

Candy leaned in close to him, her grip on his hand stronger. "A man chooses his own purpose. What will yours be when this business is done?"

Chuck leaned in towards Candy, their faces inches away as he felt his heartbeat speed up. "Maybe I'll stop searching. Maybe I'll wait for that purpose to come to me."

Candy felt herself becoming breathless. "But first you'll gamble it all for a reason to gamble it all?"

"If a man wants anything in this world, he's got to be willing to put his everything on the line."

"Is that what you are doing now? Putting your everything on the line?"

"When I give my everything... you'll know." The two kissed. Chuck's hands stroked across Candy's back, gentle yet firm at the same time. Her own hand pressed into his chest, feeling his breathing and his heartbeat.

Candy gently pulled away, her head giddy and her cheeks flushed red. "Do me a favour?"

"Name it."

"When you gamble everything, make sure you win."

Chuck smiled, running his hand down Candy's thigh. "That's not even a concern." He began kissing her neck.

"No?" Candy's breathing grew deeper, her chest heaving from her excitement.

"I'm feeling lucky."

Candy cupped Chuck's face, searching his eyes. "Feeling lucky?"

Chuck grinned. "You could say, I'm on a winning streak." The two embraced once more, sharing kisses and sweet whispers, the world around them forgotten, if only for a blessed moment.

***

"Looks like love," chortled Crowley as he looked up at Chuck and Candy's canoodling from the ground.

Ambrose grinned. "I dare say you are right."

Mustaf averted his gaze, giving an embarrassed groan.

Crowley gave another chuckle before walking on towards Flora, who was busy talking to King the Stegosaurus. As the three men approached, King gave a bellow, making Flora aware of their presence.

"Your friend is absolutely amazing, a true marvel of nature," Crowley gushed.

"I know," smiled Flora, stroking King on the head.

Ambrose gave a slight sigh, keeping his broad smile as he looked Flora straight in the eyes. "I really wish you would reconsider joining us on our journey back to civilisation."

"Why would I? I've always been here."

"Even so. After we have the stone, I'd like you to leave here with us, return to America."

Flora frowned. "I can't return where I've never been."

Ambrose looked down at his feet. "I know, and I blame myself for that fact. When I ran and left your parents here, I never imagined they would be able to survive, let alone thrive. You are a miracle and my chance to make right the sins of the past."

"How can you do that?"

"I want to bring you back to New York, have you educated. Give you the opportunities to explore the world and see things you couldn't imagine."

Flora was uncertain, thinking about what Ambrose was offering her. "Is it really so big? The world?"

"Larger than you know."

"I'm not so sure. Vincabamba is all I've ever known."

"There is so much more to know, Flora. And have no fear. Candy, Mustaf and I, we'll stand by your side, teach you the ways of things. It's the least I can do. Please let me do this, in your father's memory."

"You think this is what my father would want for me?"

"Indeed, I do."

King bellowed and nuzzled his head against Flora. "Would I be able to bring King?"

Ambrose and Crowley exchanged glances. "I'm afraid not," Ambrose sighed.

Flora put her arms protectively around King's neck. "If King isn't going, neither am I."

"I see," Ambrose sighed.

Mustaf placed a hand on Ambrose's shoulder and stepped forward. "Sir, please may I speak with Flora alone."

Ambrose was surprised by the request but agreed.

"Come walk with me," Crowley urged his friend. "There is a rather interesting bird roosting in one of the trees yonder, that I spotted this morning. I think it could be an Archaeopteryx."

Ambrose raised his eyebrows, intrigued by the prospect. "Archaeopteryx? The missing link between bird and reptile? Why didn't you say so before? Lead on, man. Lead on."

Mustaf watched in silence as the two professors walked across to the opposite side of the clearing and started peering up into the trees. He then addressed Flora, who was eyeing him with curiosity. "Miss Flora, I'd advise you to join Mister Ambrose. It is an opportunity you would be wise to accept. As I did."

Flora cocked her head. "You did?"

Mustaf nodded. "I spent the first part of my life growing up in Morocco, the son of a guide who knew well the ancient city of D'Nar."

"D'Nar? Is it like Vincabamba?"

"No. D'Nar is a dead city. It was built long ago. There has never been a time when man hasn't spoken of it as more than a half-forgotten legend."

"How is that possible?"

Mustaf shrugged. "There are more mysteries on this earth than there are stars in the sky. Vincabamba is one such mystery. D'Nar is another. There were… *things* residing in it."

"Things?"

"Perhaps the builders and rulers of D'Nar. Perhaps the foul creatures that wiped D'Nar's residents out and took it as their own."

Flora was becoming frustrated by Mustaf's cryptic words. "How does this relate to me?"

"My father once accepted a job to take a small group of adventurers to D'Nar to explore its secrets. Most men in the village would never accept such a job, believing D'Nar to be cursed. My father had no money, he was desperate. As a boy of ten, I journeyed with him into that strange place."

"What happened?"

"Death resided in D'Nar, eager to welcome us. The adventurer managed to escape and save my life. My father was not so lucky."

"The adventurer... it was *him*?" Flora pointed to Ambrose.

Mustaf nodded. "He felt awful for what happened. He offered to take me back, put me through the finest schools America had to offer."

"He did?"

"Yes, he is a good man. Foolish, perhaps, but kind. He always wrote me, to ensure that I was keeping up with my studies. When I graduated, I travelled for a year, visiting wonders beyond compare. Then it happened."

"What happened?"

"The professor's wife passed away."

"Killed in Vincabamba."

"Precisely. After that I returned to see how he was doing. The Professor looked haunted, the sparkle in his eye now gone. He had a young daughter and no real clue how to raise her. I offered my services to aid him. It seemed the least I could do. He frequently insists in private that I should move on with my life, that he'll be okay without me... I could never do that."

"That is very kind of you."

"I have now served the Professor for over twenty years. He is my benefactor and has never asked for one wit in return, and he'll never need to. He enriched my life more than even he knows. Several years ago, I revisited my home village. Its people were steeped in poverty, living half-lives, like ghosts. He saved me from that. He allowed me to reach my greater potential. In my time I write classical compositions, sounds that people fall in love to, that people cry to. That people live to. I make a fair living from my music even without the generous wage Ambrose insists on paying me, but I'll never forget what the Professor has done for me."

"I had no idea."

"I am a private man. I write under an assumed name and have no taste for fame. I still have plenty of time to pursue my passions outside of my duties at Ambrose's residence."

"You expect me to live such a life as this?"

Mustaf smiled. "I hope for you to live the life you want, not the one circumstances have forced upon you. You are more than just a bright flame flickering in the darkness; you are a brilliant inferno. Don't let this valley contain you. Be free and leave your mark on the world."

Flora looked away, considering Mustaf's words. "Ok," she said at last. "When all this is done... when you leave this valley... I'll come with you."

Mustaf smiled. "I think that is the correct decision."

***

Ambrose and Crowley squinted to see the nest nestled between the branches of a tree on the edge of the clearing.

"You are sure this contained an Archaeopteryx?" asked Ambrose, shielding his eyes.

"It was certainly something similar," Crowley confirmed. "I can't see it from here, it may have left the area. Perhaps if we climb back into the treehouse, we can view it from one of the balconies." He turned around and froze at the sight that confronted him. A man with dark features and an eye patch stood beside Ambrose, holding a pistol against the professor's temple.

"Getting a view from that treehouse sounds like a wonderful idea," the man sneered in a cultured British accent. Before Crowley could respond a military-looking man stepped out of the foliage beside him. The man held a cigar between his teeth and had two belts laden with grenades across his chest. He rammed the butt of his rifle against Crowley's head and Crowley fell heavily to the ground, his head bleeding.

"There was no need to do that," Ambrose glared at the man.

"No, but it was funny," the eye-patch wearing man gave a wicked laugh.

With the eye-patch wearing man's guard down as he laughed at his own joke, Ambrose shoulder barged into him, causing him to stagger as the aged professor ran towards the tree, shouting at the top of his lungs. "We are under attack!" he yelled.

"Damn him," snarled DeShard as he ordered one of the mercenaries emerging from the trees to recapture the fleeing professor.

From across the clearing, Mustaf watched on in horror. He instantly broke into a sprint, running to the professor's aid.

Flora went to join him when another mercenary jumped from the nearby trees, his rifle aimed at her. "Don't move, Chicka," he ordered. Flora paused for a moment before running at the man. In alarm he fired several shots at the ground before Flora's feet and then again aimed his rifle at her head. Flora got the message and stopped, holding her hands up to show her surrender. Behind her, King bellowed in outrage, restlessly stomping his feet.

Chuck and Candy witnessed what was going on from the balcony. Mustaf had run to the professor's aid but they were both now surrounded by several mercenaries. Flora was being held at gunpoint, as was Crowley, dazed from the strike to his head.

"What's going on?" shrieked Candy, completely blindsided by the events taking place before her.

"DeShard," Chuck grimly stated. "A real nasty piece of work, a crook who has a real dislike for yours truly."

"How did he get here? Why?"

"Your guess is as good as mine. I reckon he's learned about my leading this expedition to get the Stone of Qualbec and has decided to take me out and snatch it for himself. That's my guess, anyways." He quickly ran into the treehouse, where Grant and Dillon were already preparing themselves for a siege.

"We go to sleep for two goddamn hours and this happens," Grant snarled.

"Is that DeShard down there?" Pat grimaced.

"Yeah, and he's got an entire army."

Dillon quicky pulled up the ladder to stop DeShard's men climbing up it while Chuck and Pat quickly recounted to them who DeShard was.

Vincente and Javier picked up a bow each, along with a quiver of arrows and ran out onto the balcony, preparing to fight. Grant, Dillon, Pat and Chuck did the same with their firearms. Grant cautiously stuck his head into harms way to get a bead on how many potential targets there were.

On the ground DeShard watched with amusement as Chuck looked prepared to attempt to resist his obviously superior forces. Hilda, Dragos and Joe had gathered by him while Hernandez shouted orders to his men.

DeShard turned to the nearby trees and called out, "You can come out, now. It is quite safe, I assure you."

"Safe? Those men have guns, old boy," spoke a nervous voice.

Ambrose and Mustaf recognised it at once and turned in shock as Buchannon and his man Daniels stepped out from their hiding places. "Jeffrey Buchannon?" Ambrose exclaimed. "What on earth are you doing here?"

Buchannon still looked nervously up to the treehouse.

"They won't fire," DeShard grinned. "Not while we have the professor. His daughter would never allow it, isn't that right, Ambrose?"

Ambrose's face went red with anger. "How dare you interfere with this expedition?"

Hilda grinned as she marched over to the professor and struck him hard across the face with the back of her hand. Mustaf took a step to stop her but when the guns of several mercenaries pointed his way, he accepted any resistance would be futile and result in a meaningless death. He snarled in impotent fury. Hilda cackled at Mustaf's plight.

"This is revenge, old boy," said Buchannon, growing bolder.

"Revenge? For what?" asked Ambrose.

"You outbid me on that Chinese vase. Stopped me from getting a full collection. That was bad sport, old boy. Very bad sport."

Daniels groaned inwardly at his employer's pathetic motivation.

"All this over a vase? Are you mad?" Ambrose couldn't believe what he was hearing.

"This is about more than just a vase," DeShard roared. "This is about pride, about an eye for an eye. Just as Buchannon has a score to settle with you, so do I with Mister Tanner." He then yelled out to the treetop. "Do you hear me, Tanner? I have a score to settle with you!"

Chuck and Pat exchanged glances. "Should have finished him when I had the chance," Chuck growled.

"Maybe we should surrender," Pat gulped. "They have us outmanned and outgunned. This is bad. Really bad."

"Coward," spat Vincente, keeping his bow at the ready.

"We could probably do a lot of damage if we fought," Grant said. "We have the high ground."

"Just say the word," said Dillon, ready to fully commit himself to whatever Chuck decided.

"Chuck," said a pained Candy. "He has my father down there."

"You have thirty seconds to surrender, or I kill one of my hostages," called out DeShard. He then ordered Joe to start counting slowly to thirty, which the squat man proceeded to do.

On the other side of the clearing, two mercenaries kept their rifles drawn on Flora. One of them looked her up and down, appreciating what he saw. He leered at the young woman. "Where did they find you?"

"This is my home," Flora replied without emotion.

The man took a step closer. "You are a savage? You look very pretty for a savage."

Flora gave a coy smile. "You think I'm pretty?"

Joe had reached the halfway point in his count and the people in the tree debated what their action should be.

The man speaking to Flora lowered his rifle slightly. "I do. Listen, these men here, they are all going to die. There is no reason why you should die with them. Come with us. I'll look after you."

Flora smiled at the offer. Behind her, King bellowed, showing his uneasiness at the situation. "Quiet, King," Flora ordered sternly before smiling again at the man. "I might like that. You would look after me?" She slowly lowered her hands.

The man grinned and stepped closer. "I would look after you *real* good."

The other mercenary wasn't too impressed by his colleague's unprofessionalism. "Hey man, stop messing around. Hernandez will have your head."

The man turned to his colleague and laughed. "Come on, what's he going to do?"

"King, swing!" yelled Flora as she dropped to her belly. The mercenary turned back in confusion as King bellowed and swung his powerful tail at the soldier. The tail cut through the air above Flora and hit the mercenary with full force. He was knocked off his feet; his broken body flew through the air before hitting a tree with enough force to make an audible crunch as every bone in his body broke.

The second mercenary was caught off guard by the attack and before he could aim his rifle, Flora had jumped at him and stabbed him in the gut with her long bone-knife. She looked him in the eyes, her face portraying a savagery he couldn't comprehend as she drew the knife across his gut, opening him up and causing his guts to fall out. The man dropped to his knees in shock and agony, at a loss at what to do.

"The hell?" yelled Hernandez from across the clearing as he witnessed two of his men killed in the blink of an eye. "The girl and her pet, kill them now!"

Rifles opened fire and DeShard and his entourage lost some of their confidence as gunshots rang out. From up on the balcony Grant and Dillon began firing from their rifles and three more of Hernandez's men fell.

Flora sprinted for the trees as bullets shot past her. "Run, King, run!" she yelled as she dived into cover. King bellowed before stampeding off into the trees, knocking several over as he made a quick escape from the battlefield.

"Damn it," Hernandez swore as the jungle girl and dinosaur disappeared from his sights.

"Shall we follow them?" asked one of his men. "Following that beast would be easy."

"No, the real battle is here."

Losing patience, DeShard grabbed Ambrose by the throat and pushed his pistol into the base of his skull. "Now hear me," he yelled up at the treehouse. "If you do not surrender in the next five seconds, I pull the trigger."

Dillon looked over to Chuck. "I say we die fighting."

Pat didn't agree. "Chuck, we need to be smart about this. If we try and fight back, this is going to be a bloodbath."

Candy held Chuck's hand and looked at him imploringly. "Chuck, I don't want to die here. I don't want my father to die here."

"What's it to be?" called up DeShard as he began to put pressure on his pistol's trigger.

Chuck appeared on the balcony, his arms raised. "Okay, DeShard. You win. We surrender."

CHAPTER 21

DeShard paced around the interior of the treehouse, enjoying the sights of his enemies on their knees and their hands bound in rope. Chuck stared defiantly at DeShard as he secretly struggled against the rope that bound his hands behind his back at every opportunity. Behind DeShard his cohorts mocked and ridiculed their captives as they walked amongst them while several of Hernandez's men stood watching, their rifles in their hands. The rest of their number remained on the ground, keeping watch for Flora and King. The darkness of night had set in and the jungle was now shrouded in darkness.

"I like this one," hissed Hilda as she roughly held Dillon's face, admiring his looks.

"Let me out of these restraints and I'll be sure to show you what I think of you," he snarled in response.

Hilda's smile turned to a scowl and she struck him hard across the face before turning to Grant. "I'm sure you know how to treat a lady."

"Indeed, I do," said Grant. "You'll have to excuse my friend. He always has a hard time talking to the clinically insane." He received a backhanded slap that split his lip. He felt it was worth it.

Joe laughed at the two men's comments, which angered Hilda more. "He ain't wrong," he grinned.

"Keep laughing, little man. I'll show you how insane I can be," Hilda warned him.

Dragos kept back from their captives, keeping a watchful eye over everything in the room. He wouldn't let Chuck get the better of them again. In the corner stood Buchannon and Daniels, looking very uneasy with the entire situation.

"Stop bickering, you fools," snapped DeShard before crouching in front of Chuck. He made it obvious how much he detested the man before him and enjoyed their current power dynamic. "I've waited a long time for this. I don't need my moment ruined by your incessant chattering."

Joe looked down in submission while Hilda kept her mouth shut but her cruel, defiant eyes said more than mere words ever could.

"Is this your moment?" said Chuck sarcastically. "How are you enjoying it so far?"

DeShard grinned. "Very much, Mister Tanner. Very much."

"I don't get it, why are you here? To get one over on me? An eye-for-an-eye?"

"Very droll," spat DeShard. He instinctively reached up and touched the patch over his ruined eye. "You and I have unfinished business. You may still get out of this alive, if you play your cards right."

"Let's not kid ourselves," said Chuck. He looked around at the various members of his team, each with a rifle pointed at their heads by men who looked like they'd have no qualms pulling the trigger. "You have no plans letting us get out of here alive."

DeShard feigned surprise. "I'm hurt that you think me so unreasonable. Still, what other choice have you got except to trust me?"

"Mister DeShard," called Vincente from across the room, despite his brother warning him to shut up.

"Speak," DeShard snapped, angered by the labourer's interruption.

"We left three men at the entrance to this valley. Pablo, Felipe and Mateo. Mateo was injured. Please, sir, tell me. What happened to them?"

DeShard looked ruefully at the tied-up man. "I regret to inform you that your friends are dead. Killed by some creature."

"Liar," yelled Chuck in anger. "You killed them! Admit it!"

"Me? Lie? Never. This land is beyond dangerous. We have lost three of our own. How many have you lost?"

"Ten, including the three men killed by you."

DeShard chuckled, which only served to boil Chuck's blood further. "Ten? You people have been careless. This kind of endeavour should always be left to the professionals. You amateurs should stick to viewing the artefacts in museums." He glanced around the captives. "I don't see your rotund friend, Mister Bill Yates here. My sources tell me he was with you when you embarked on this expedition. May I ask where he is?"

Chuck felt a fury greater than any he'd ever known before. His body shook with rage. "You keep Bill's name out of your mouth."

"Oh no, did he die?" DeShard said with mock sorrow. Hilda and Joe cackled in delight at his performance. "So sad, I know you two had been through a lot together. Oh well, at least he'd have made an ample meal for whatever ate him."

"When I get out of these ropes, I'm going to kill you," Chuck snarled. "That's a promise." He thought about the small combat knife he still had hidden in his boot. He weighed up how likely it would be for him to retrieve it and cut his bonds before the mercenary behind him realised what was happening. He decided the odds weren't in his favour, at least not without a distraction.

DeShard smirked and leaned in closer. "And how do you expect to do that? You are in no position to be making idle threats."

Chuck launched himself forward, his forehead clashing hard with DeShard's nose. DeShard yelled out in pain as he fell backwards. The mercenary behind Chuck deftly kicked him onto his stomach and pushed the muzzle of his rifle into the back of Chuck's head.

"Shall I kill him?" asked the soldier, his finger already on the trigger.

"No!" DeShard hurriedly said. "I want the pleasure of dispatching this one myself." He pulled a hanky out of his pocket and held it to his bleeding nose while the mercenary pulled Chuck back into a kneeling position.

"Careful, DeShard," warned Hernandez. "I want paying for this excursion."

Dillon hollered with laughter. "He got you good!" He was silenced by a swift kick to the gut by Hilda. Grant made a move to stand and the mercenary behind him quickly grabbed his collar and jammed a rifle muzzle into the back of his neck.

"Give me an excuse," the soldier snarled.

Hilda gave a mocking laugh, looking down at Grant. "I think I prefer this one. He has spirit."

"Stand down," Chuck ordered Grant, afraid the man would try something that would get himself killed. Grant was clearly reluctant to stop his struggling. "I said, 'stand down,' soldier." Grant gave Chuck a look before relaxing his body.

"Now that the small talk is over, on to business. First, who is that girl who was talking to the dinosaur?"

"Stegosaurus," Crowley corrected him.

"Whatever," hissed DeShard. "She wasn't a part of your team. Who is she? She's the one who built this shelter?"

"She's just a native we befriended."

"A native? Really?" DeShard stroked his beard, checking to see if the bleeding from his nose had stopped. He put his stained hanky away.

"She's the daughter of my old friend, Austin Kiplard," said Ambrose. "She is of no threat to you. She grew up here. Leave her be."

DeShard approached the professor with a look of incredulity. "No threat? She has killed two of my men. She is hardly harmless."

"She was acting in self-defence," Ambrose replied. "Regardless, we have no way of contacting her, or any idea what she will now do. She owes us no allegiance. Likely she won't return."

DeShard turned and glared at Pat, who shrunk in his gaze. "Is this true?"

"It's true," he said, looking to the floor.

DeShard stroked his chin thoughtfully. He then looked over at Hernandez. "Very well, we shan't pursue the girl. She seems little more than a wild animal. Keep your men on guard, though. If she returns, she is to be put down."

Hernandez nodded in agreement.

DeShard returned to Chuck. "Now for the million-dollar question; Where is the Stone of Qualbec?"

Chuck smirked. "What's the matter? You can't find anything without following my footsteps?"

DeShard backhanded him. "Don't play games with me, I know it is in this valley, but where? Where is it?"

"Hell if I know," said Chuck as he spat blood on the floor. "We're just here on safari."

DeShard hit him again. "Don't play games with me. You must know its location. There must be a map or something." He looked over at Ambrose with disdain. "You can't just be following this old fool's memory."

Chuck wasn't ready to give in yet. "You're the treasure hunter. Go hunt."

DeShard pointed his pistol between Chuck's eyes and pulled back the hammer. "If you won't tell me, perhaps someone else will." Joe and Hilda giggled at the prospect of more violence.

DeShard prepared to fire.

"Tell him," Pat said finally.

"Pat, you don't say a goddamn word," Chuck said, angered by Pat's submission.

"If you don't tell him, he'll kill you."

"If I do tell him, he'll kill us all."

Pat looked down. "I can't gamble with everyone's life. There's a map. Ambrose has it."

Chuck yelled for Pat to be quiet and was quickly cut off by DeShard pistol whipping him, sending Chuck once again to the floor, spitting blood.

DeShard stood before the professor with an evil glint in his eye. "Is this true, Professor? Have you been holding out on me?"

Ambrose remained fiercely defiant. "You can have it over my dead body."

"Why is everyone ready to test me today?" DeShard sighed before pistol whipping the professor.

Candy cried out in fear for her father. "Leave him alone!"

Mustaf attempted to stand before the rifle behind his head jabbed into the back of his head, reminding him how easy it would be for the mercenary behind him to blow his head off.

Ambrose cried out and coughed blood. "You're a monster."

"And you are a very stubborn old man," DeShard snarled. "Perhaps you don't care for your own life, but I'll wager you care for the life of your daughter." He then grabbed Candy roughly by the arm and pulled her up. She cried out in pain and fear as DeShard pointed his gun at her face. "Such a pretty face. It'd be a shame if someone put a hole in it."

Candy squeezed her eyes closed, unable to bear looking at the pistol. Her lip trembled in fear.

"You're heartless," Crowley declared.

"Don't you touch her," yelled Chuck as he knelt up again. He glanced up, something catching his eye. It was Flora, her lythe figure climbing over open beams of the treehouse roof. She held her bone-knife in her hand and held a finger to her lips, signalling for Chuck to be quiet. He obeyed, unsure how she would be able to help them. Chances were that anything she attempted would end up getting them all killed. Then again, the chances of any of them getting out of this mess was slim, so it would be better taking as many of these creeps as possible with them in a last stand, rather than wait to be executed.

"Steady on, old boy," said Buchannon from the corner. "Don't you think you are taking this all a bit too far?"

"Too far?" glowered DeShard. "Why, Mister Buchannon, I didn't realise you had such a weak stomach. I assure you, I haven't gone *nearly* far enough."

Buchannon went silent, choosing to stand still, scratching his arm while standing beside Daniels. He dared say nothing further, fearing he'd incur DeShard's wrath.

DeShard turned back to Ambrose. "Well, Professor? What's it going to be?"

"Please, don't hurt my daughter," Ambrose cried. "The map is in my front left pocket."

DeShard grinned as Dragos stepped forward and searched the older man. He retrieved the tobacco tin and opened it. He smiled as he pulled out the map and unfolded it. He then showed it to DeShard, who salivated at having it in his grasp. He released Candy and snatched the map, taking in every detail. "This is it!" He gave a triumphant laugh. "With this map we can find the Stone of Qualbec with ease." He began walking away from his captives.

Chuck looked to a shadowed corner where Flora was now lurking. She had to have had a secret entrance and Chuck was amazed the men on the ground hadn't noticed her. Her knife was still drawn and she focused on the mercenary that stood over Chuck as if she were a jungle predator.

He tensed, waiting for her to make her move. He knew that when the moment came, chaos would erupt.

Flora stalked slowly towards the unknowing soldier, ready to strike.

"Make haste, men. We must embark for the Stone of Qualbec immediately."

"What about the prisoners?" asked Hernandez.

DeShard twisted on the spot, made eye contact with Chuck and grinned. "These riff-raff are beneath my concern. Kill them all."

"You heard him," Hernandez said to his men.

"DeShard!" Chuck shouted as he heard the mercenaries ready their rifles. *Could this really be how it all ends?* he wondered. *If Flora doesn't make her move now, we're finished.*

A dull thud from behind him made Chuck turn around. The other soldiers were looking on in shock. He expected to see Flora making her move. Instead, he saw the mercenary wavering on his feet, a large, primitive spear jutting through his back and out his chest. The man looked down at it uncomprehendingly and tried to speak. He gurgled blood which seeped down his chin, before collapsing to the floor.

The rest of the room looked in utter shock. Flora was paused mid-step with a look of surprise on her face that mirrored the treehouse full of people who looked back at her.

Time seemed to stop for a moment.

Then time ran in fast forward.

"We're under attack!" yelled Hernandez, flicking his rifle to full-auto and holding down the trigger.

Flora was faster than he expected as she skittered across the floor. The treehouse wall behind her exploded in a shower of debris from the torrent of bullets.

Chuck leapt out the way and kept low as more mercenaries tried to get a clean shot at Flora. She moved with deadly efficiency and ducked behind a mercenary. The man realised what was about to happen and yelled for his comrades to stop shooting. His words were unheard of beneath the gunfire that tore through his torso. Blood from the man created a crimson mist as it sprayed finely into the air.

"Stop, stop, stop!" yelled Hernandez to his men. Behind him DeShard and his crew stood at the ready, trying to understand what was going on.

The treehouse fell deathly quiet as the soldiers tried to see where Flora had escaped to. The treehouse was cluttered and the smoke from the rifles had given the attacking girl the opportunity to seemingly vanish.

"Little girl, where are you?" called Hernandez, ready to fill Flora with lead the instant he saw her.

"What is that?" asked Dragos, listening to what was going on outside. The loud rifle fire had left everyone's ears ringing and so they had to take a moment for their normal hearing to return.

"Sounds like gunfire," DeShard said. "From outside."

Hernandez and his men ran to the balcony to see what was happening on the ground, leaving their hostages unguarded.

"What is it, Hernandez?" asked DeShard as he ran to the balcony, his team following him.

"We're under attack," Hernandez said grimly. DeShard ran to the balcony rail and looked down below. He could scarcely believe what he was seeing.

The mercenaries on the ground had taken defensive positions and were fighting off an onslaught of horrific, hulking Ape-Men. They weren't faring so well. Ape-Men howled and died under hails of bullets yet more came to take their place. The Ape-Men screeched their bloodlust as they overwhelmed their targets. One of the Ape-Men wielded a spear and impaled a mercenary on it. He gave a triumphant howl as he lifted the dying man over his head and enjoyed the soldier's lifeblood spurting down over his face.

Another soldier screamed as a hatchet severed his leg below the knee. He fell to the ground and screamed in terror for help. None came as his comrades continued to fight for their own lives. Several Ape-Men set upon him, hacking at his limbs before running into further frays. The soldier was left little more than a trunk with all limbs severed at the joints, twitching in a pool of his own blood.

"My God, what are these things?" Hernandez spluttered as he took aim and started firing at targets.

"I don't know," DeShard said, dumbfounded by the sight below. "I have never seen the like of these things before."

"What shall we do?" whined Joe.

"Do? We fight," ordered Hernandez before pulling a grenade from the belts across his chest. He pulled the pin and threw it towards a group of Ape-Men that had emerged from the treeline. They ignored the small round object, naïve to its purpose. It exploded violently and three of the Ape-Men screamed out as if cursing the humans they fought. One Ape-Man was completely blown apart. Another was thrown from the blast, landing in an unmoving heap. The third was left writhing on the grass in agony. Both its legs had been blown off and blood leaked from its ears.

From the treeline, the Ape-Man with the Raptor skull as a helmet cried out in rage at the spectacle before him. Primitive arrows fired from Ape-Man bows soared through the air and one hit the soldier standing beside Hernandez in the chest. He cried out as he fell. Hernandez ordered his men to concentrate fire on the section of trees the arrows were originating from.

***

Flora stayed hidden for a minute or two and watched as the mercenaries and DeShard's men ran out onto the balcony and began engaging with the Ape-Men. Realising it was now or never she darted out to Chuck and quickly went to work cutting the rope that bound him. He urged her to hurry and as soon as he was free, he began freeing the rest of his allies alongside her.

In the corner Buchannon and Daniels squatted in horror, completely confounded by the situation they found themselves in.

"What should I do with them?" asked Flora as she cut the ropes on Ambrose. "Shall I kill them?"

Ambrose massaged his wrists as he stood. "Forget them. They aren't worth our time."

Chuck picked up the rifles from the fallen guards and handed one of them to Pat. Grant and Dillon recovered their own rifles from the other room.

"Are you okay?" Chuck asked Candy as he freed her.

"I'm okay, but how are we going to get out of here?"

"Good question. Flora?"

Flora shrugged as she freed Crowley, the last of them to be liberated. "Run?"

"Run? That's your plan?" Chuck said in disbelief.

On the balcony outside, DeShard and the others continued fighting, their prisoners completely forgotten. The sounds of gunfire and screams continued unabated.

"We should kill them all while we have the chance," Grant stated.

Chuck looked at Candy, recognising the fear in her eyes. "I'd rather avoid any conflicts we can. If we engage them now there is a good chance we'll lose people. They still have us outmanned and outgunned."

Grant looked frustrated by this decision but couldn't deny Chuck was right. To throw away his life now would be meaningless.

Flora opened an unseen hatch. "Quick, down here."

"If we climb to the ground, we'll be in the midst of the slaughter happening down there," Candy gulped while holding onto Chuck's arm.

"Candy is right, it's almost suicide to drop down into the clearing."

"Beneath this hatch is the branch that supports most of the treehouse," Flora explained. "It reaches close to the edge of the clearing and we should be hidden by the leaves. If we climb it until its end, we'll be able to jump down into the jungle. Then we'll be able to make our escape."

Chuck wet his lips as he thought the plan through. "This branch goes right under the balcony DeShard and his men are on. The leaves might provide a little camouflage, but if one of those men looks straight down, they'll spot us."

Pat nodded. "There's also no cover from below. Anyone who looks up will see us in no time. It's too risky."

Ambrose looked anxiously at Chuck. "Mister Tanner, you are our party leader. We'll follow your decision."

Candy gave a high-pitched scream and everyone turned to see what she had seen. Three Ape-Men had climbed the main ladder up the thick tree-trunk and were now in the treehouse. They wielded hatchets and grinned maniacally when they spotted the humans. They immediately charged.

With no time to fire, Grant lifted his rifle to parry an incoming strike. He then used the weight of his attacker as he rolled backwards and kicked out, sending the Ape-Man sprawling across the floor. Pat opened up his rifle and riddled the hair-covered brute with bullets. The second Ape-Man swung at Mustaf and he jumped back to avoid being disembowelled. It swung again and again he jumped back.

Javier and Vincente jumped back to give the big man room as the third Ape-Man tackled Dillon. Chuck pulled out his pistol and unloaded into the Ape-Man's leering face, turning it to a blood-soaked ruined mess. He turned in time to see Mustaf jump upon the Ape-Man assaulting him. It fell backwards and Mustaf used his weight to pin it to the floor as he rained punches upon its head while screaming at the top of his lungs.

"It's okay, it's dead," Javier said, putting a hand on the big man's shoulder. Mustaf caught himself and stopped. He remained breathless, looking at the shattered head that had once been an Ape-Man.

By some miracle the men on the balcony hadn't heard them, no doubt the sounds of their scuffle indefinable amongst the sounds of the larger battle at hand. The sounds of more Ape-Men scaling the ladder could be heard and Chuck made up his mind.

"Our choice isn't any choice at all. If we stay here, we die. Everyone, in the hatch! Now!"

The group moved fast, Dillon and Grant remaining until last, keeping their rifles trained on the main ladder. Another two Ape-Men appeared. Before they realised the humans were there they were reduced to jerking meat as bullets slammed into them. They fell back down to the ground below, even as more Ape-Men began climbing the ladder.

Before ducking beneath the treehouse, Ambrose looked over at the pitiful Buchannon and Daniels.

"Please, old boy. You can't leave us here. Take us with you," pleaded Buchannon.

Daniels spoke up. "You must believe us; we didn't realise what madmen these people are."

Ambrose shook his head in disgust. "You made your bed, Buchannon. Now lie in it."

With everyone else now traversing the thick branches under the treehouse, Dillon and Grant ducked into the hatch. Before closing it, Grant saw another Ape-Man climb into the treehouse and give a wicked grin as it spied Buchannon and Daniels. The two men screamed as the hulking humanoid approached them.

***

On the ground beneath the treehouse the battle waged, as piles of dead Ape-Men littered the ground. Though they fought fearlessly, the rifles and training of the soldiers made it look as if they would win the day, albeit with significant losses of their own.

"Keep moving," Flora ordered as she moved through the branches as if it were as easy as walking on the ground.

"Everyone, stay close," Chuck ordered.

"My God," uttered Candy as she looked down. "It's a massacre down there."

"All the better we stay out of their way," stated Mustaf.

***

From his perch, the Ape-Man with the Raptor skull helmet -*Skullface* - watched the carnage unfold. Many more Tacal had died than he had expected. The intruders' weapons were powerful indeed. It was a brutal fight, yet the Tacal knew no fear. The intruders had killed their chief and revenge was demanded. Skullface enjoyed watching the slaughter and allowed his mind to wander to the females back at the village. Re-populating would be in order after this battle. He would be a hero and have his pick, but not before he smashed the intruders bones to jelly and slurped on their marrow.

He looked up to the treehouse and observed the group of humans still fighting from the balcony. They were holding strong, yet already they were faltering. Several more Tacal had now entered the treehouse and fights between them and the intruders were weakening the humans' defensive position. Less were on the balcony now, as some ran into the treehouse to stop the Tacal advancing from this new angle.

Skullface grunted as a Tacal warrior howled out in pain and fell from the treehouse. He then noticed movement in the tree beneath the treehouse and leaned forward to make sense of what he was seeing. He growled in anger as he spotted several of the intruders attempting to escape.

Cowards! he thought as he watched them. If they thought they would be permitted to escape, they had another thing coming. He gave a war cry and directed those with bows and arrows to fire upon the cowardly intruders. His orders fell on deaf ears, the Tacal on the battlefield were lost in the rapture of violence and bloodshed, slave to their own lust for violence.

Skullface growled under his breath. It didn't matter. He had one more trick up his sleeve and he was almost ready to let it loose. He reached for a curled horn fashioned from the horn of a Styracosaurus and blew it hard. Behind him the trees rustled and parted.

***

Flora indicated for those following behind her to keep quiet and hurry up. Her frustration was plain on her face. The group were now clutching at the tree branch with their hands and legs and moving on their stomachs. With only three feet of space above the branch, they were forced to crawl slowly, upward jutting branches making their progress painfully slow.

Above the group's heads was the balcony DeShard and his men were standing upon, shooting at targets and avoiding arrow fire. Their footsteps were loud and their fear and confusion was evident. Hernandez and DeShard shouted orders and their respective teams shouted out the impossibility of their situation and the locations of targets. Bullet casings dropped onto the wooden floor with abandon, sounding like a thunderous storm.

Mercenaries shouted in surprise that Ape-Men had now invaded the treehouse and began to engage them. The sounds of hand-to-hand struggles could be heard.

Chuck crawled closer to Flora before looking back at the progress of the others.

"We must go faster," Flora hissed, "or we'll be spotted from above when we move from under the treehouse."

"With all that is going on up there, I doubt they'll notice us," said Pat.

Flora shook her head in irritation. "The Ape-Men can't keep up this attack for much longer." She gestured the mounds of bodies on the ground. Some were human, most were the Ape-Men attackers. "If we're not in the jungle by then, we'll be spotted for sure."

Chuck nodded. "You heard her, people. Let's get a move on."

The group murmured their agreement and Chuck turned to carry on following the lythe jungle girl when the ground started shaking. "Now what?" he sighed with the grim resignation that their escape plan was about to become even more complicated.

The group looked to the south, where trees in the jungle rustled and snapped. "Something's coming," Candy remarked. "Something big."

A group of four Ape-Men came walking into the clearing, pulling on numerous ropes with all their effort. Those that were still attacking the mercenaries turned and looked at what was occurring. The howl of a horn could be heard and the Ape-Men quickly fled back into the jungle.

The surviving handful of mercenaries regrouped against the base of the tree, some using heaps of dead Ape-Men as makeshift barriers to hide behind and await this new menace.

The four Ape-Men heaved again and a mighty Tyrannosaurus Rex came reluctantly stomping out into the clearing. It was older than the two dinosaurs the expedition had encountered the previous day, and far larger. Its body was harnessed and its massive jaws were muzzled by rope made from thick vines. The ropes the four Ape-Men pulled on were attached to various points on the harness and they strained to pull the creature into the battle. The Old Rex's hide was covered in countless scars from tooth and claw and it surveyed the scene before it as an animalistic growl emanated from its throat. Upon its back was an Ape-Man who held a bow and arrow. It clambered onto Old Rex's head before waving the arrow under its nose. Old Rex sniffed the arrow and growled, trying to open its jaws. The Ape-Man aimed up at the tree and fired.

The group looked on in horror as the arrow imbedded itself in the bottom of the treehouse, a mere foot from Ambrose's head. "What is that?" Crowley gulped, realising the arrow was anything but normal.

The arrow had the remnants of several dead baby dinosaurs impaled on its shaft. They looked so young they were likely never hatched.

"That's a bait arrow," Flora said. "It's used to lead captive dinosaurs to attack where you want them to attack."

"And it's been fired at us," Pat moaned. "This is bad."

Candy looked down and shuddered as the jaundice eyes of Old Rex stared right back at her. "It's seen us," she gasped.

"This doesn't change anything," stated Chuck. "We still need to get into the jungle and away from this massacre."

"Like hell it doesn't change anything," cried Pat.

The Ape-Man on Old Rex's head drew a knife and cut the vine-ropes holding on the gigantic muzzle. As he did so, the Ape-Men who had pulled Old Rex to the battlefield dropped their ropes and ran for the trees.

The remaining mercenaries reloaded their rifles and conducted ammo counts while they could. There wasn't many of them left.

In the treehouse a mercenary cried out in pain before being silenced by one of the several Ape-Men who had managed to gain access. The firefight was still raging and several of DeShard's team hadn't yet realised that Old Rex was about to enter the fray.

Old Rex waited patiently for her muzzle to be cut, her eyes remaining fixed on Chuck's team up in the tree. The final vine was cut and the muzzle dropped heavily to the ground. The Ape-Man who had cut it jumped from the beast's head.

Old Rex spotted the leaping Ape-Man and quickly snapped at him, her jaws closing over his chest. The Ape-Man gave what counted as a scream before its chest was crushed by the dinosaur's incomprehensibly powerful bite. Old Rex shook her head once and threw the mangled remains hard against a tree, where they splatted. She then gave an almighty, bellowing roar that made everyone shield their ears before she stomped forward, the smell of blood causing her mouth to salivate.

The mercenaries began opening fire and Old Rex roared in anger as a volley of bullets hit her, causing splashes of blood to mottle her hide. Old Rex quickly stomped towards them, making them her priority as she leaned down to attack.

There were five men left on the ground and their assault on Old Rex didn't last long. Both DeShard and Chuck's groups watched as Old Rex ran into the grounded mercenaries' defensive line.

"We need to keep moving," Flora hissed and the rest of the team obeyed.

Old Rex ducked her head as she ran at full speed into the wall of bullets. Pockmarks of bullet holes appeared on the top of her head but she didn't even slow. One of the mercenaries realised the momentum of the giant carnivore meant that even if she fell she would hit him and so he turned to run. Old Rex's snout hit him with the force of a locomotive and she flicked her head up, sending the man hurtling into the dark jungle. Nobody could see where he landed, but he was doubtless dead from the force of the strike.

The remaining four mercenaries screamed in terror as Old Rex skidded to a halt. She turned her head to view the soldier who had commenced firing into her side. In annoyance, Old Rex lifted her foot and stomped down. The mercenary made a sickening crunching sound as he was crushed like a cockroach.

Old Rex then proceeded to bite down upon the next nearest soldier. He screamed as he was lifted high, his legs kicking as the steak-knife teeth of Old Rex penetrated his middle. Old Rex resisted the temptation to bite down for as long as she could, enjoying the feeling of her helpless prey struggling in her maw. She could not resist long before biting down hard. With a crunch the screams and struggles of the man ceased as blood and gore began flooding over her tongue and out over her chin. Old Rex lifted her head back, opened her mouth and let the remains of the mercenary slide down her gullet. She swallowed greedily, savouring the taste before turning her attention to the remaining two men on the ground.

One of the mercenaries had run for the cover of the jungle and Old Rex decided he wasn't worth the effort. She then turned to the other, who was halfway up the ladder leading to the treehouse. Although he was fleeing for his life, all he'd actually achieved was presenting himself at a convenient bite height. The man screamed as he realised his predicament and Old Rex snapped him up, her jaws clamping upon the ladder as well as the man. She pulled him away from the tree trunk and the ladder snapped. The man's scream turned to a high-pitched shriek as he was crushed between Old Rex's unforgiving jaws and blood spurted from his mouth like a fountain. Old Rex than raised her head and opened her gullet, crunching on the soldier's body several times before swallowing him.

"My God," uttered DeShard, completely humbled by the power and ferocity of the mammoth dinosaur.

Throughout the treehouse interior were the remains of dead Ape-Men and soldiers. Although DeShard's core team was intact, Hernandez's team of seven had been reduced to four. Buchannon was hunched in the foetal position in the corner, weeping over the dismembered remains of Daniels, hacked to death by Ape-Men.

"What are we going to do?" cried out Joe, his face slick with sweat. "We can't fight that thing. It's huge!"

"It's just an overgrown lizard," sneered Hilda. "My love can kill it."

Dragos eyed DeShard, whose usual composure had now evaporated. "Sir, your orders?"

"My orders? Yes, right. Um, Mister Hernandez, I humbly defer to your expertise."

Hernandez surveyed the scene in the clearing with a grimace. "We are safe here. We have killed all the Ape-Men. We have supplies. We wait for that monster to leave." The mercenaries behind him looked relieved by their boss's decision.

"Very good," DeShard agreed before clearing his throat.

Old Rex enjoyed the sensation of eating the man and was now hungry for more. True, there were ample bodies littered at her feet, but she was no scavenger. Old Rex craved prey that wiggled and squealed in her jaws. The dinosaur snarled and stomped around the foot of the tree, seeking the prey amidst the tree branches.

"Heads up," Grant said as he noticed the Tyrannosaurus Rex staring up at them. "Looks like this thing is looking for dessert."

CHAPTER 22

Old Rex emitted a growl in excitement as she moved beneath the thick branch the prey was crawling upon. She let her jaw hang open, revealing chunks of flesh and clothing wedged between her teeth.

Flora was now crawling out in the open, the leaves from smaller branches the only thing providing her cover from the men in the treehouse. Chuck, Candy, Pat, Ambrose, Mustaf and Crowley were also on the exposed section of branch. Vincente, Javier, Grant and Dillon were still beneath the treehouse.

"Keep moving," yelled Flora, speeding up her movements. "If we can get amongst the trees, we can lose it."

"We're hurrying, believe us," Chuck shouted back.

Old Rex stretched upwards and with a massive lunge snapped at Candy. She screamed as the dinosaur's massive jaws closed on protruding branches beneath her. Old Rex then began pulling on the branch, her unimaginable strength causing it to start buckling.

"Hold on!" yelled Chuck as he grabbed hold of Candy's wrist to prevent her from falling. Old Rex shook her massive head from side to side, trying to either dislodge her prey or tear the entire branch down.

Ambrose slipped and cried out as he fell headfirst out of the tree. Mustaf's hand grabbed after him and the big man succeeded in gripping the professor's ankle. Crowley immediately gave his assistance, pulling on Mustaf's shirt.

"Father!" Candy cried.

Old Rex noticed the man hanging down and released her grip on the branch. It sprang up about six feet, nearly causing the rest of the group to slip. Javier nearly lost purchase until Vincente reached out and supported his brother.

"You've always caught me when I fell," Javier said, his heart thumping.

"And I always will, so long as you return the favour," Vincente replied with a smile.

Old Rex kept her eyes on the dangling morsel that was Ambrose and positioned herself ready to snap him up.

Ambrose hung in the air, his arms cartwheeling as his body went into full panic mode. "Pull me up! Pull me up!" he cried.

"Stop struggling," Mustaf said through gritted teeth as he strained to pull the professor to safety.

Dillon was suddenly beside him and reaching down, grabbing the other ankle of the swinging old man. "On three," he said. Mustaf nodded. "One, two..."

Old Rex leaped up, her jaws agape and Dillon and Mustaf instinctually yanked the professor upwards. Old Rex's jaws snapped shut on air where the professor had dangled a mere instant before.

"Thank you both," Ambrose wept, tears streaming from his eyes. "I thought I was done for."

Mustaf looked at Dillon and gave a slight nod. "Thank you for helping me save him."

Dillon grinned. "Don't sweat it. And don't forget you still need to give me a rematch on that arm wrestle. No way can I live with a draw."

Mustaf gave the hint of a smile.

Beneath them Old Rex roared her fury at being denied her meal. She then jumped up again and grabbed at lower hanging branches. The entire large branch began buckling again from the strain the nine-ton monster put upon it as she began backing away, pulling it ever lower.

***

Inside the treehouse, sections of flooring and roof began to give way as the supports the structure was built upon began being pulled out of place by Old Rex's assault.

"What on earth is going on?" DeShard demanded as he steadied himself.

Dragos ran to one of the windows and looked outside with urgency. "It's the dinosaur attacking the tree. If it continues the whole treehouse shall collapse."

DeShard put a hand against the wall to support himself as timber beams began to fall around him. "Don't just stand there, you fool," he yelled at Hernandez. "Get out there and deal with it before we are all killed."

Hernandez didn't like the way DeShard was talking to him and made a mental note to confront him about it later. Now was not the time. He turned to his four remaining soldiers. "With me." The men nodded, trying their best to hide their hesitancy as they followed him outside onto the balcony.

The balcony was splitting down the middle as the violent shaking and pulling of Old Rex on the tree took its toll. "Start firing or we'll all be killed!" Hernandez ordered.

The five men let rip, spraying Old Rex with bullets. In pain, the Tyrannosaurus released her grip on the tree branches, once again causing them to spring upwards. Candy cried out as she was nearly thrown clear of the branch. Chuck managed to hold her steady and she clung to him until the wavering of the branch slowed.

"We're nearly there," said Chuck. "Just a little further." In front of him, Flora was perched on the edge of the branch. A six-foot jump separated her from the top of a smaller tree at the edge of the clearing. From there they'd be able to descend to the jungle floor and escape into the trees.

Hernandez was the first to spot the escaping prisoners clambering through the branches. "So that's what she is after," he snarled and opened fire upon them. Down below, Old Rex roared her fury and stomped beneath the treehouse to avoid the hail of bullets which were beginning to wear her down. She then proceeded to snap at further branches, pulling at them, and shaking the entire tree.

Dillon stopped moving through the branches, bracing himself as rifle bullets flew through the air above him. *This is bad,* he thought. He looked back at Grant, the only man behind him. "What's the plan, brother?"

Grant shrugged. "Same as it always is." He then twisted around and released a volley of fire upwards towards the balcony. The soldiers ducked as they received hostile fire.

Hernandez swore as he ducked under cover. "A curse on these men!" he yelled as he tried to see where the bullets had come from.

At the end of the thick branch Flora had already made the jump to a smaller tree and was now descending. Chuck jumped next and landed in the canopy with far less grace than his guide. Chuck then waited to help the others with the jump. Candy made it well and he caught her waist as she landed.

"Follow Flora down," he told her.

"Aren't you coming?" she said with fear in her voice.

"I'm going to make sure your father and Crowley make the jump. Don't worry, I'll be with you soon."

"Make sure you are," said Candy before leaning in and kissing him hard on the lips. She then started climbing down to the ground.

Next up was Crowley and as he prepared to jump bullets whizzed past him, causing him to falter. He slipped and cried out for help. Chuck caught him by the hand and pulled him up into the canopy.

"A thousand thanks, dear boy," Crowley smiled as he followed Candy.

Next was Ambrose, with Mustaf beside him. "You are ready, Professor?" Mustaf asked.

"As I'll ever be," Ambrose smiled.

Mustaf then effectively threw the professor across the gap and he landed roughly beside Chuck. Chuck caught hold of him and made sure he didn't slip until he recovered. Mustaf effortlessly made the jump and together he and Ambrose began climbing downwards.

Pat, Vincente and Javier were next, and being young, fit men, the jump wasn't too taxing for any of them. They began climbing down as Chuck searched the branch, trying to spot Dillon and Grant amongst the wavering smaller branches.

***

"We're all going to die!" squealed Joe as he clung to the floor.

"Shut up, you coward," screeched Hilda as she struggled to keep her footing.

Dragos stood by the window, hanging onto the wall. "Sir, the structure has failed. If the dinosaur continues its attack, we're going to fall from the tree."

"This isn't the end," DeShard declared as he held on to a fallen beam from the ceiling. "I refuse to let it end this way!"

Old Rex shook her head and pulled and the large branch that supported the treehouse splintered where it connected to the trunk. The body of a dead Ape-Man tumbled from the ruined structure and Old Rex released her grip to snap it up before it hit the ground. The large branch sprung up again, this time with enough force to cause the treehouse to shatter. Old Rex roared in triumph as the treehouse collapsed amidst the branches and large parts of it tumbled to the ground with an almighty crash. The dinosaur roared and stomped through the wreckage of the house, bestial noises mixed with the snapping and cracking of wood as she shuffled through the debris with her snout.

Old Rex gave a small roar of excitement as she uncovered a man beneath the wood piles. He screamed as he was uncovered and Old Rex quickly snapped her jaws around his arm. She lifted the screaming, struggling prey up high into the air, enjoying the vain defiance it put up.

From the canopy Chuck grimly watched the fate of the mercenary the Tyrannosaurus had ensnared. Old Rex threw back her head, tossing the man into the sky before leaping forward and biting down on him in mid-air. His screams instantly stopped, replaced by wet, crunching sounds as he was devoured.

"Doesn't that thing ever feel like its eaten enough?" Pat remarked.

Flora stared hard at him. "Never."

Dillon and Grant held onto the branch for dear life; the devastation caused by Old Rex had nearly caused both to fall and they'd watched as the balcony tore apart beneath its own weight and fell away, taking the soldiers with it. All except one; Hernandez who was now reduced to clinging to the same thick branch as them.

Unable to aim a rifle through the branches, Hernandez resorted to drawing his sidearm and firing haphazardly towards the two fleeing men.

"Damn, hasn't this guy got other priorities?" Dillon remarked as he ducked low to avoid Hernandez's shots.

Old Rex was distracted from sifting through the debris of the treehouse by the gunshots and looked up. Her mouth salivated as she spotted three more of the tiny, tasty creatures up in the tree. She moved beneath them, preparing to jump up and pull on the branch.

"You kill my men!" yelled Hernandez, seething with anger. "I kill all of you!" He continued to shoot towards his enemies.

Grant prepared to return fire when Old Rex once again began pulling on the branches. Losing his footing, he cried out as he fell. He reached out to catch a branch and it snapped from the force of his fall. He was then suspended in thin air for a second before landing flat on his back, knocking his head hard on the ground.

Everything turned to black.

***

"Oh my," Candy cried with dismay. "Chuck, Grant has fallen."

"I see," Chuck responded grimly. His whole body tensed, like a compressed spring waiting for release.

Old Rex continued to bite at the tree branch, trying and failing to find offshoots of branch strong enough for her to pull on. As she did so, her feet stomped in the dirt, mere feet from the unconscious Grant who slowly started to move.

"He's alive!" Ambrose shouted with a mixture of relief and horror. Grant's life looked liable to be snuffed out at any moment. The huge, scarred dinosaur's feet made impact craters all around him and it was only by some miracle that he hadn't already been crushed.

"He's done for," Pat was resigned.

Still unaware of the precariousness of his situation, Grant moaned and touched his forehead.

"The hell he is," Chuck declared and ran out from the jungle cover, sprinting to his fallen friend.

"What is he doing?" said Flora in disbelief. "Is he crazy?"

"You could say that," Pat grumbled.

Candy called after Chuck in distress and a part of him wanted to turn back, to be with her. The part of him that had sworn never to abandon a man without trying the upmost to save him kept him running. Old Rex soon towered above him, her size and bulk far larger and more intimidating than he'd previously realised as he stood almost beneath her.

Old Rex was still too preoccupied trying to chomp into the branch holding the now fighting Dillon and Hernandez to notice the men by her feet.

Hernandez had been too reckless with his bullets, firing through the branches with wild abandon and unsteady feet. It was no wonder his firearm had run empty and so he'd drawn his combat knife and was now taking wide slashes at Dillon. So far Dillon had avoided being cut, using all the footwork skills he'd accrued in the boxing ring. Hernandez's brazen strikes were becoming ever more frantic and desperate.

"Why won't you die?" Hernandez snarled.

Dillon kept his eye on the knife, ready to avoid the next slash and when he did, he succeeded in jabbing Hernandez in the face with his left fist. The mercenary fell back but didn't lose his purchase. The grenades on his ammo belts clinked against each other from his rapid movements, sounding like a collection of beer bottles. Dillon felt emboldened by the punch, his years of boxing giving him the edge and keeping him steady on his feet.

Beneath them, Old Rex kept her eyes on them as she roared and snapped her teeth, willing either of them to fall into her eager maw.

Chuck darted over to Grant, crouched beside him and shook his shoulders. "Grant, wake up. This is no time for a nap."

Grant's eyes slowly opened as he groaned. "Head... hurts..." he said.

"No time to worry about that. We've got to get out of here."

Grant's eyes widened as he saw the gigantic beast behind Chuck, roaring up at the branches of the tree. "You don't need to tell me twice," he stammered as Chuck threw Grant's arm over his shoulder and helped him stand. He had planned to run back to the side of the clearing where the rest of the team waited, though that option now seemed unfeasible. Old Rex was now in their path and her erratic stomping feet could spell a miserable death in a heartbeat.

"We'll go the long way," Chuck said as he started pulling Grant towards the jungle at the clearing's far side. He supposed any cover was better than waiting in the open.

Old Rex glared at the two fighting men on the high branch and turned her head down in frustration, preparing to rear up once again. As she did so she caught sight of Chuck and Grant moving towards the trees across the clearing. Seeing easier prey available, she swiftly forgot the two combatants up in the tree and a deep, rage-induced, basal roar made the very ground tremble.

"Oh no, the Rex has seen them!" Candy shrieked.

"There is nothing we can do for him," Ambrose sighed. He put an arm around his daughter, partly to comfort her and partly out of fear that she may run out after Chuck at any moment.

"I can't watch," Candy cried, burying her face into Ambrose's chest.

The huge dinosaur stomped towards Chuck and Grant, her massive strides easily closing the distance between them. Chuck allowed himself a glance backwards and regretted it. He could see there was no way he would reach the tree-cover in time.

"You should have left me," Grant said, still half delirious from his fall. "Now we're both going to die."

"Shut up and keep running," Chuck said, not daring to look back again.

Old Rex lowered her head and her jaw dropped open, ready to scoop up both the fleeing men in one go. Thick wads of drool dripped from her mouth.

Mustaf clenched his fists as he watched what was happening, the outcome inevitable. "This can't be permitted," he said through clenched teeth.

"I'm open to suggestions," Pat replied.

"Hey, Jungle Lady, is there anything you can do?" asked Vincente as he turned to Flora. "Hey, where'd she go?"

The others turned in surprise. True enough, Flora was nowhere to be seen.

"Has she abandoned us?" Crowley pondered.

The ground shook from the impacts of Old Rex's feet as she closed in on her victims. The vibrations caused Grant to trip and Chuck fell with him. They both turned, prepared to meet their fate.

"Never would have guessed this would be how it ends," Grant smiled.

"At least it isn't a boring death," Chuck supposed.

Old Rex prepared to snap shut on the two men resigned to their fate when suddenly the trees behind them shook and parted and the Stegosaurus named King came bounding out, bellowing with hostile intent. Old Rex was caught off guard and began to bring her head up. She was too slow as King swung his spiked tail and it smashed into Old Rex's face with full force. Old Rex roared in agony as six-foot long spikes impaled her on the left side of her face and sent her crashing to the ground. She struggled to right herself while blood spurted from her deep wounds.

King bellowed in victory as Chuck tried to comprehend what had just happened. He then spotted Flora, sitting high on King's back. She quickly leapt off and landed with grace before running over to him.

"You saved us…" was all Chuck could muster.

Flora kept her eyes on Grant and pulled his other arm over her shoulder so that Chuck and herself could hold him up. "Not yet," she said as they started to move as quickly as they could towards cover.

"Are you an angel?" mumbled Grant, his head spinning.

Flora ignored him, all too aware that the Tyrannosaurus Rex was already back on its feet.

***

"Alright, alright, alright! You go, jungle lady!" Dillon cheered as he watched King save his two friends and then Flora help them escape. With her aid they were moving much faster and King kept his bulk between them and Old Rex. King stood side on to the gigantic predator and swished his tail back and forth as a sign of intimidation. Old Rex was still dazed and shook her head from side to side as she recovered from the unexpected blow.

"Don't get distracted," mocked Hernandez as he suddenly lunged forwards, slashing his combat blade horizontally. Dillon instinctively jumped back to avoid the attack. Before the knife cut his skin he already knew he was too late. Fortunately, his fast reaction spared him from being cut too deep. The knife cut through his shirt and skin, but no further. Although the attack wasn't a mortal blow, it still hurt like hell and caused Dillon to stumble back, struggling not to fall as Grant had. Blood seeped from the wound, staining his shirt red.

Hernandez laughed mockingly as he puffed out his chest, feeling emboldened by the successful attack, insinuating his belts of dangling grenades. "Too bad nobody is here to save you," he leered.

***

Old Rex's primitive mind regained clarity and she growled in outrage at the challenger that had denied her the fleeing prey, and worse, hurt her.

King remained steadfast in his defence of the two humans, now almost at the treeline. He stamped his feet and waved his tail menacingly. Old Rex's blood still dripped from his tail spikes.

Old Rex roared as her ferocity grew and she lunged at the brave Stegosaurus, trying to lock her teeth onto his head. King saw the attack coming and struck again with his tail; the spikes drove deep into Old Rex's thigh and her roar turned more high pitched from the pain inflicted.

King returned to his defensive stance as Old Rex limped back a little, not eager to repeat the same mistake. She raised her head slightly and watched as the humans disappeared into the jungle and her temper hit boiling point. She lunged again, jaws agape. This time she aimed for King's flank and the Stegosaurus didn't have the space to complete a swing before she was within its radius. Old Rex's jaws clamped onto King's thigh and he howled in pain as she shook her head and tore away a huge chunk of flesh.

The bloody flesh between her teeth caused Old Rex to enter a frenzy and she quickly swallowed the mouthful of meat before lunging again for the wide, open wound. King successfully fended her off with another tail strike to her middle, though it lacked the power of the two previous hits and only knocked Old Rex back a little.

From the trees Chuck watched the grim battle play out. "King isn't going to win, is he?"

Flora shook her head, her demeaner remaining cold. "He can't. Not against a predator that size."

Chuck struggled to know what to say. "It's because of us this happened..."

"Don't think King is a fool," Flora lambasted. "He knew before he ran into that clearing that the chances were against him leaving. Still, he saved you anyway. That was his choice." A tear trickled down her cheek and Chuck chose not to acknowledge it, certain that to do so would only attract Flora's mire.

"He's very brave."

"Yes. He is."

Old Rex roared with bloodlust as her mighty jaws closed over King's back. King's torturous howls were hard for everyone watching to hear as he attempted to use his bulk to push Old Rex away. She stumbled a few steps back and tore off one of King's plates as she did so. The wound on King's back bled profusely and the dinosaur turned tail and attempted to run. His eyes were rolling white, lost in a world of fear and hurt as he howled again.

Seeing her chance, Old Rex rammed into the back of King, using her head as a battering ram. King was upended and lost his footing, resulting in the ground shaking as five tons of dinosaur crashed against the earth. Now lying on his side and defenceless, the stunned King looked up in abject horror as he desperately tried to stand. He cried out, his call abruptly ended when Old Rex bit down on his head, her teeth sinking deep into the vulnerable flesh of King's throat.

Whatever life was left in King compelled him to still move his legs. Sensing the death of her foe was at hand, Old Rex steadied a foot on the shoulder of the Stegosaurus and with one almighty pull completely severed King's head. A thick jet of blood erupted from the stump of King's neck, showering Old Rex and making her look like death incarnate. Old Rex crunched down on King's head, enjoying the flavours that spilled out over her tongue before she swallowed it whole.

Flora looked away, unable to watch the mutilation of her beloved friend. Chuck forced himself to keep watching, all too aware that what he was seeing was King's sacrifice to save his and Grant's life. To witness the outcome was his way of honouring King's bravery.

***

Dillon held his wounded gut as he watched King's fate with dismay. Hernandez laughed as he again slashed at Dillon with his knife, forcing Dillon to retreat further away.

"Looks like your pet is dead," Hernandez mocked. "Nobody is coming to save you."

"Shut your damn mouth," Dillon huffed, the pain in his stomach causing a moment of dizziness. Despite his bravado he knew Hernandez was right. He was running out of branch thick enough for him to stand solidly upon and the leaves on the branches meant that nobody on the ground would be able to get a clean shot. Like it or not, he was on his own. "I can go all night."

Hernandez hesitated, seeing the renewed determination on Dillon's face. "Mister tough man, eh?" he snarled before reaching for one of the grenades strapped to his chest. He pulled the pin and grinned. "Let's see how tough you really are."

Hernandez casually tossed the grenade towards Dillon and his mind went into overdrive, trying to think of a solution. He quickly dove backwards. Without time to check where he was leaping, he was reduced to hoping he'd be able to catch a branch to stop himself falling.

The grenade exploded, the blast wave making Dillon cry out as branches and leaves were turned to splinters and confetti. The force nearly made him tumble from the tree and only a last minute, desperate grab for a protruding branch saved him. It looked small and he thought it a miracle it didn't snap under his weight.

Old Rex lifted her bloody snout from the belly of King, distracted from her grisly feast by the sound of the explosion. Her hawk-like vision instantly spotted Dillon dangling by a branch and she stomped over towards him.

Hernandez roared with laugher as he brazenly walked towards the helpless Dillon. "It looks like this is the end of the line for you." He crouched down above the hanging man, his knife in his hand. "But don't worry, it looks like you've made a new friend."

Dillon looked down to see Old Rex beneath him, watching intently, willing him to fall. Her jaws hung slack and her skin was covered in blood and viscera. If she stretched up, she'd be able to pluck him from the branch as if he were low hanging fruit.

"Please… help me…" Dillon struggled.

Hernandez enjoyed watching the desperate man beg. "What was that? You want me to help you? I didn't hear you say 'please.'"

"P-please," Dillon said beneath his breath.

Hernandez leaned in closer. "What was that? Say it like you really mean it."

Seeing his chance, Dillon summoned every ounce of strength he had and pulled himself up with so much force that his body lifted as if it were a rocket. He had been doing chin-ups for as long as he could walk and one more wasn't beyond him, despite his exhaustion. Dillon's head collided with Hernandez's face, sending the mercenary falling backwards and crying out in pain. Hernandez's knife fell from the branches to the ground far below. Dillon succeeded in finding purchase on the branch with a booted foot and hoisted himself up just as Old Rex stretched up and tried to close her jaws upon his legs. She roared in frustration, her warm, moist, fetid breath washed over him and made him want to gag.

Hernandez cursed as the large frame of Dillon fell upon him. Not one to miss an opportunity, Dillon began pummelling Hernandez's face over and over until his nose was broken and bleeding and his teeth were shattered.

"Please," managed Hernandez between bloody rasps. "Please stop."

"You want me to stop?" Dillon exclaimed, the irony of the situation palpable. He leaned in close to the defeated soldier. "But you didn't say 'please.'" He then grinned. "But don't worry. I think you've just made a new friend."

Dillon deftly reached down and with a single manoeuvre tore the pins from several of the grenades strapped over Hernandez's chest. Hernandez gasped in utter terror. He went to plead again for his life to be spared. Dillon didn't have time to listen as he kicked the man from the branch.

Hernandez screamed as he fell into the waiting jaws of Old Rex. Her teeth closed on the falling man like some giant bear trap and his screams ended with a sickening crunch. Old Rex went to crunch again, the joy of the kill all that she knew.

The grenades strapped to Hernandez's chest went off with a concussive force that blew Old Rex's head apart as if it were made of leaves. Blood, bone, flesh and brain rained down over the clearing as the still standing body of Old Rex tried to steady itself. The dinosaur's primitive nervous system took a moment to realise it was dead before it fell heavily to the side, landing with a deafening thud. It remained still as smoke emanated from the bloody remains of Old Rex's bottom jaw and an ever-widening pool of blood spread out over the dirt.

"Eat that!" Dillon cheered from the branch, a feeling of euphoria coursing through his veins.

"He's done it. He's killed it," said Ambrose, flabbergasted.

"That a boy!" cheered Pat. "Never mess with my boy Dillon!"

"We need to check on the others," Candy said. "They could be hurt."

Mustaf nodded. "Let's go."

CHAPTER 23

"He did it," Chuck beamed with pride for Dillon's victory. "He actually killed that monster." He then turned to Flora. His smile dropped.

An Ape-Man held a jagged bone-knife to Flora's throat and snarled at him menacingly. A second held Grant in a similar position. They both bared yellow teeth and gnashed them angrily.

Chuck's hands dropped limply to his sides. "Don't you guys ever quit?"

A shadow emerged from the bushes and stepped forward. Chuck dryly swallowed as he eyed the large Ape-Man before him. It wore a Raptor skull as a mask and helmet and clutched in its right hand was a gnarled wooden club. It looked hard and heavy.

Skullface grunted aggressively, as if talking to Chuck. He took a defensive posture, unsure what was happening.

"What's happening?" Chuck asked warily.

"He wants to take us back to his village as trophies," Flora said. The Ape-Man that held her grunted angrily and pressed its knife tight against her throat.

Chuck kept his attention on Skullface; the big Ape-Man lifted the club, preparing to attack. "And we end up like poor Diago? Thanks, I'll pass."

Risking the ire of the Ape-Man that held her, Flora continued to explain. "His war here has been a total disaster. He needs live sacrifices to appease the others." The Ape-Man behind her pulled back hard on Flora's hair and kicked the back of her legs, forcing her to her knees. She gasped in pain.

Skullface gave what looked like a smile at Flora's suffering, his eyes remaining fixed on Chuck. "You want me, come and get me," Chuck snarled.

Skullface roared, raised the club and jumped at Chuck. The Ape-Man was powerful, but his body telegraphed his movements and Chuck rolled to the side, avoiding being knocked by the club. Skullface immediately swung again, this time in a wide arc, forcing Chuck to jump back further. He'd need a weapon if he were going to survive this.

Searching for anything he could use, Skullface swung again. Chuck leapt back, aware that one blow from the club would likely break bones. The other two Ape-Men watched on in amusement.

This place is like a warzone, there must be something I can use.

Risking a glance behind him, Chuck spotted the hacked-up body of one of DeShard's mercenaries. No doubt he'd been killed by the Ape-Men as he'd attempted to flee. A short distance from his body was a rifle. Chuck's heart raced as he rolled backwards away from the swinging attacks of Skullface and plucked the rifle from the ground. Skullface's evil grin faltered as he realised what it was Chuck had picked up. Chuck aimed from the hip as he pointed the rifle at Skullface's centre of mass.

"Say hello to the modern age," he said before pulling the trigger.

-Click!-

Chuck looked down in horror as he realised the awful truth; the rifle was empty. He pulled the trigger again for good measure and felt himself shrink a little as a second impotent click confirmed the miserable truth of the situation.

Skullface's grin returned, his confidence restored as he raised the club high.

"Can't we talk about this?" Chuck gulped as he jumped back as Skullface attacked.

Chuck managed to avoid the strike, but the club connected with the rifle, knocking it from his hands. Pressing his advantage, Skullface allowed his momentum to carry him forward and he kicked the retreating human hard in the gut. Chuck grunted in pain as he fell to his hands and knees, completely winded. He looked up to see Skullface standing over him. The Ape-Man's large, animalistic frame seemed indomitable and Skullface enjoyed making the human feel small.

Skullface glanced over at the other two Ape-Men who watched and grunted approvingly at their leader's skill as a warrior. Feeling his ego swell, Skullface grunted back at them before looking down at the frail human before him who was still struggling to breathe.

Giving what equated to a mocking laugh, Skullface lifted the club over his head with both hands. He'd decided not to bring back the human alive. The pathetic creature had resisted his will and so would die.

Realising it was now or never, Chuck pulled out the small combat knife he always kept in his boot, disguising the movement in his struggles to breathe. He could tell that Skullface had no intention of taking him back to the Tacal village and that in a few seconds he would be dead. Skullface tensed himself, ready to deliver the death blow and Chuck made his move, driving the knife upwards with both his hands. The knife drove up between Skullface's legs and penetrated up to the handle within the Ape-Man's groin.

Skullface howled in agony, dropping the club and reaching down to protect himself. Chuck pushed upwards with everything he had, driving the knife ever deeper before releasing it as Skullface's hands searched for his wrists.

Skullface continued to howl and shriek as blood ran down his inner thighs, staining his dark brown fur red. Chuck pushed away from his defeated foe and stood. Skullface clutched his groin and fell to his knees, lost in complete suffering.

Chuck nervously glanced at the other two Ape-Men who seemed at a loss as to what to do. They remained holding onto their prisoners and now kept looking questioningly at each other and fidgeting on their feet. Seeing they weren't about to rush him, Chuck bent down and picked up Skullface's dropped club.

Skullface remained kneeling and wavered as shock began to take over his body. He looked up at the human who had appeared so helpless a moment before. Now the human appeared powerful and wilful, a true warrior who had beaten him despite being smaller and exhausted from the preceding battle.

Lifting the club to swing as if it were a baseball bat, Chuck struck Skullface's head with full force, shattering the Raptor skull he wore and smashing his face. Refusing to die, Skullface kept his eyes on Chuck. The strike had knocked out teeth and shattered the eye socket of the Ape-Man and yet still he leered hatefully at Chuck in defiance. Chuck had to admit, the Ape-Man had balls. He lifted the club high over his head and brought it down, splitting Skullface's head clean open. Splatters of blood struck Chuck's face as the Ape-Man's frame went limp and dropped to the ground. Dark blood leaked from the massive head wound of the quivering, hair-covered body. Finally, the Ape-Man was dead.

Chuck glowered over at the other two Ape-Men, their leader's blood still spotted over his face. Despite their primitive features, the fear on their faces was easily readable. "Who's next?" Chuck sneered.

The two Ape-Men looked at each other before simultaneously releasing their holds on their respective prisoners and fleeing into the jungle. Their shrieks of fear could be heard long after they had disappeared from view.

Chuck lowered the club, glad it hadn't come to another fight. Flora rubbed at her sore neck where an Ape-Man's blade had been pressed, before checking on Grant.

"Are you okay?" she asked him, tenderly stroking his forehead as she helped him up.

"Never better," he coughed as he stood on shaky legs.

Chuck smiled with relief, dropped the club and made his way over to his allies.

"Mister Tanner, are you alright?" called Ambrose as the rest of the group ran to check on them.

"Chuck, you're alive!" beamed Candy as she ran into his arms, kissing him on his lips.

Chuck enjoyed the interaction, even though his bruised gut made him wince. Candy looked at him with concern. "Are you hurt?"

Chuck managed his trademark grin. "Just a little beaten up, is all."

Ambrose grinned ear to ear as he shook Chuck's hand. "I'm glad you survived, Mister Tanner. When you ran out into the clearing, I thought you were doomed."

"We all did. That was very foolish," Candy chastised him.

Chuck looked over at Grant who was now sitting on a rock beside Flora while Mustaf and Crowley gave them water. Grant caught Chuck watching him and smiled. Chuck nodded back. "Foolishness had nothing to do with it. I made a promise to my friends back in the war. Never leave a man behind."

"Much appreciated," Grant nodded as he drank some more water while Candy walked over to study the bump on his head.

"Where is everyone else?" Chuck asked, realising four men were now missing from the group. He felt as if he were falling. "Did they make it?" He expected to hear the worst.

"They're fine, just fine," Ambrose said and pointed.

Chuck turned with relief to see the four men making their way over towards them from across the clearing. The brothers Vincente and Javier walked with Dillon held up between them. Pat led the way, watchful for any further threats. Thankfully it appeared the Ape-Men had abandoned their attack. Scores of Ape-

Men bodies littered the ground, amongst the wreckage of the treehouse and the massive carcasses of King and Old Rex.

Here and there were the bodies of DeShard's mercenaries and Pat stopped whenever he passed one to relieve them of their sidearms. Their rifles were all proving useless, the ammunition spent.

Despite his being beaten up and slashed across the stomach, Dillon managed a look of brevity. Chuck slapped him on the shoulder as he was sat down and Candy studied his wound.

"It's not too deep, a bandage and some antiseptic and you should be fine," she informed him.

"I'm not surprised," Dillon laughed. "You can't stab a man who is bullet proof!"

Chuck looked over at the massive, near headless carcass of Old Rex. "You did that?"

Dillon gave a toothy grin. "Nobody messes with my friends and lives. Ain't that right, Grant?"

"Never a truer word," Grant laughed, nursing his sore head.

"So much carnage, so much death," Ambrose muttered, surveying the battlefield.

"Perhaps so, but none of us are laying there," Dillon grinned. "We're unstoppable."

"One of us is laying out there," Flora accusingly stated. "Don't forget what he gave to protect us."

Dillon looked at the lifeless body of King and sadly nodded. "You're right. I'm sorry."

Everyone remained silent as Candy finished bandaging Dillon's wound.

Chuck walked over to Flora and looked across at the carnage before them. "We owe King a debt of gratitude. If not for him then Grant and I would have been done for."

Flora stifled a sob.

"And I'm sorry about your home. It's our fault this happened."

Flora shrugged. "It's just a place." She looked over at Mustaf. "Besides, I was thinking it was time to move on, at any rate."

Mustaf gave a warm smile that said he was glad with her decision.

"You mean you are still coming with us? Even after all this?" asked Ambrose.

"You'll need me to, if you are to succeed in retrieving the Stone of Qualbec."

Ambrose agreed. "Your experience and knowledge will be invaluable."

"At least DeShard's finally done for," said Pat.

As if in response, rifle fire rang out from across the clearing and bullets impacted on nearby trees and shredded leaves on branches. Everyone instantly dropped to the ground.

"Doesn't this ever end?" Pat whined.

"I guess at least some of DeShard's group are still active," Chuck said. "Can anyone make out their exact location and numbers?"

Pat shook his head as more shots fired towards them. "I can't even make out where the shots are coming from."

"Me neither," snarled Dillon. "And if I could, from this location I doubt I'd be able to get a clear shot without exposing myself."

"I'm still not at a hundred percent either," Grant grimaced. "My vision keeps going blurry."

"I can see one, but I'm not sure where the rest of them are," spat Flora.

"Why can't they just leave us alone?" Javier lamented.

Candy looked at Chuck. "What are we going to do?"

"Perhaps discretion is the better part of valour," suggested Mustaf. "There is no need to fight, we can easily escape into the jungle. It is unlikely they will pursue us immediately. There is nothing here to fight for."

"He's right," agreed Pat. "We should head out."

"There will be plenty of ammo and supplies in the wreckage of the treehouse," Dillon said. "It would be a shame to leave it to DeShard's men."

Candy spoke up. "How many of our lives is it worth risking for? We have no idea how many of them are out there."

"We'll follow your lead, as always," said Ambrose.

Chuck thought about their situation and came to a decision. "We'll back out and head north, for the city of Vincabamba. We're not in the position to engage in another fire fight right now."

Everyone agreed and they started crawling away, stopping whenever a burst of fire rang out. Soon the clearing was lost behind a wall of green and Chuck gave the word for people to stand and follow his lead. Pat and Mustaf stayed at the rear, watching for anyone following them. Dillon and Grant were helped by Vincente and Javier to keep their speed up.

Ambrose lamented having lost the map to DeShard as he kept pace with Chuck. "We need to head north-east to circumnavigate the mountains up ahead. If only we still had the map, I could check our bearings."

"No," said Chuck. "DeShard has the map now, assuming he is still alive. He'll know that route. If he has survived, he'll be on our tail the entire way."

"Then what other option is there?"

Chuck turned to Flora. "You said there is a cave that leads through the mountains?"

Flora nodded. "Yes, the Fire Cave."

"You are certain it leads all the way through?"

"Father seemed to think so."

"If Austin believed there was a path through, there will be. He was seldom wrong," said Ambrose.

"But it is a treacherous path," added Flora. "He warned against it."

"Every path through this valley is treacherous," Chuck said bitterly.

"It's quite a gamble," Crowley fretted. "If we are wrong, we could be killed. Even if we aren't killed, we'd still lose time and DeShard's men could get to the Stone of Qualbec before us."

"It is a gamble," Chuck acknowledged. "But one we have to take."

"You are sure?" asked Candy, joining in the conversation. "You've thought about this?"

Chuck grinned. "Candy, I don't dare think about anything. I just follow my gut."

Candy cocked an eyebrow and smiled. "And what is your gut saying now?"

"When I work that out, you'll be the first to know."

To Be Continued in
    The Stone of Qualbec...

Check out other great

Dinosaur Thrillers!

Rick Poldark

PRIMORDIAL ISLAND

During a violent storm Flight 207 crash-lands in the South China Sea. Poseidon Tech tracks the wreckage to an uncharted island and dispatches a curious salvage team—two paleontologists, a biologist specializing in animal behavior, a botanist, and a nefarious big game hunter. Escorted by a heavily-armed security team, they cut through the jungle and quickly find themselves in a terrifying fight for survival, running a deadly gauntlet of prehistoric predators. In their quest for the flight recorder, they uncover the mystery of the island's existence and discover an arcane force that will tip the balance of power on the primordial island. Things are not as they seem as they race against time to survive the island's man-eating dinosaurs and make it back home in one piece.

P.K. Hawkins

SUBTERRANEA

Fall, 1985. The small town of Kettle Hollow barely shows up on any maps, and four young friends are used to taking their BMX's outside of town in an effort to find anything interesting to do. But tonight their tendency to go off by themselves may have saved them, and also forced them into the adventure of a lifetime.While they were away, Kettle Hollow has been locked down by the government, and a portal to another world has opened on Main Street. It's a world deep below the ground, a world where dinosaurs roam free, where giant plants and mutant insects hunt for prey. It's also a world where all their family and friends have been kidnapped for sinister purposes. Now, with time running out before the portal closes, the four friends must brave the unknown to save their loved ones. Time is running out, and in the darkened tunnels of Subterranea, something is hunting them.

Check out other great
Dinosaur Thrillers!

Steve Metcalf
OBJEKT 221

Ruthless multi-national conglomerate Allied Genetics is under siege from a paramilitary force for hire. Allied calls in reinforcements and fortifies their crown-jewel property – an abandoned Soviet military facility in Crimea known during the Cold War as Objekt 221. Fortunately for the future of their research, O221 straddles a stretch of rocky landscape that hides a rift – a portal through time and space. Through this rift, Allied Genetics can travel, at will, to the Cretaceous – 100 million years into Earth's past – and bolster their genetic experiments with dinosaur DNA ... something their competitors want to stop at all costs."Objekt 221" is a story blending numerous science fiction elements such as repurposed military facilities, time travel, rogue corporate armies, dinosaurs and the hint of a super-ancient civilization.

Bestselling collection
PREHISTORIC: A DINOSAUR ANTHOLOGY

PREHISTORIC is an action packed collection of stories featuring terrifying creatures that once ruled the Earth. Lost worlds where T-Rex and Velociraptors still roam and man is now on the menu. Laboratories at the forefront of cloning technology experiment with dinosaurs they do not understand or are able to contain. The deepest parts of the ocean where Megalodon, the largest and most ferocious predator to have ever existed is stalking new prey. Plus many more thrillers filled with extinct prehistoric monsters written by some of the best creature feature authors this side of the Jurassic period.

Checkout other great books by bestselling author

Greig Beck

PRIMORDIA: IN SEARCH OF THE LOST WORLD

Ben Cartwright, former soldier, home to mourn the loss of his father stumbles upon cryptic letters from the past between the author, Arthur Conan Doyle and his great, great grandfather who vanished while exploring the Amazon jungle in 1908. Amazingly, these letters lead Ben to believe that his ancestor's expedition was the basis for Doyle's fantastical tale of a lost world inhabited by long extinct creatures. As Ben digs some more he finds clues to the whereabouts of a lost notebook that might contain a map to a place that is home to creatures that would rewrite everything known about history, biology and evolution. But other parties now know about the notebook, and will do anything to obtain it. For Ben and his friends, it becomes a race against time and against ruthless rivals. In the remotest corners of Venezuela, along winding river trails known only to lost tribes, and through near impenetrable jungle, Ben and his novice team find a forbidden place more terrifying and dangerous than anything they could ever have imagined.

THE FOSSIL

Klaus and Doris have just made the discovery of their lives – a complete Neanderthal skeleton buried in a newly opened sinkhole. But on removing it, something else tumbles free. Something that switches on, and then calls home.Soon the owners are coming back, and nothing will stop their ruthless search for their lost prize. Gruesome corpses begin to pile up, and Detective Ed Heisner of the Berlin Police is assigned to a case like nothing he has ever experienced before in his life. Heisner must stay one step ahead of a group of secretive Special Forces soldiers also tracking the strange device, while trying to find an unearthly group of killers that are torturing, burning, and obliterating their victims all the way across the city.THE FOSSIL is a time jumping detective novella where humans soon find that time can be the greatest weapon of all.* THE FOSSIL first appeared in SNAFU No.1 (2014) as a short story. Due to numerous requests, it has now been expanded and released here in its complete, stand-alone novella form.

Printed in Great Britain
by Amazon

62680808R00107

HOUSE OF
DRAGONS

BY K. A. LINDE

OAK AND HOLLY CYCLE
The Wren in the Holly Library
The Robin on the Oak Throne

ROYAL HOUSES SERIES
House of Dragons
House of Shadows
House of Curses
House of Gods
House of Embers

ASCENSION SERIES
The Affiliate
The Bound
The Consort
The Society
The Domina

RoyalHouses 1

HOUSE OF DRAGONS

K. A. LINDE

BRAMBLE

Originally published in 2020 by K. A. Linde Inc.

First published in the UK 2025 by Tor Bramble
an imprint of Pan Macmillan
The Smithson, 6 Briset Street, London EC1M 5NR
EU representative: Macmillan Publishers Ireland Ltd, 1st Floor,
The Liffey Trust Centre, 117–126 Sheriff Street Upper,
Dublin 1 D01 YC43
Associated companies throughout the world

ISBN 978-1-0350-5938-6 HB
ISBN 978-1-0350-5939-3 TPB

Pan Macmillan does not have any control over, or any responsibility for,
any author or third-party websites (including, without limitation, URLs,
emails and QR codes) referred to in or on this book.

1 3 5 7 9 8 6 4 2

A CIP catalogue record for this book is available from the British Library.

Design © 2025 by Sourcebooks
Map illustration by Devin McCain
Internal images © draco77/Getty Images, ArtVector/Getty Images

Printed and bound in the UK using 100% Renewable Electricity by CPI Group (UK) Ltd

Visit **www.panmacmillan.com** to read more about all our books
and to buy them.

To anyone who ever wanted to ride a dragon.

MAP OF *Alandria*

TOSIN

EREWA

ZAVALA

EARLE RIVER

SAYAIR

BAIN BAY

HERASI

HOUSE OF
SHADOWS

HOLY
MOUNTAIN

GARDIC
SEA

WOOD
LOCH

BRYONICA

ISLE
OF
SONG

ROSEMONT

DRACO
MOUNTAIN

EVERIC
OCEAN

VERT
MOUNTAINS

KINKADIA

DAYE RIVER

CONCHA

STRAIT OF URSI

SOUTH RIVER

IBARRA

VENATRIX

VILAND

EDGEWOOD

TANSY CHANNEL

GENOA

AUDE

MORAN

ELSIANDE

ARCHDALE

GALANTHEA

CORVIAN SEA

N
W   E
S

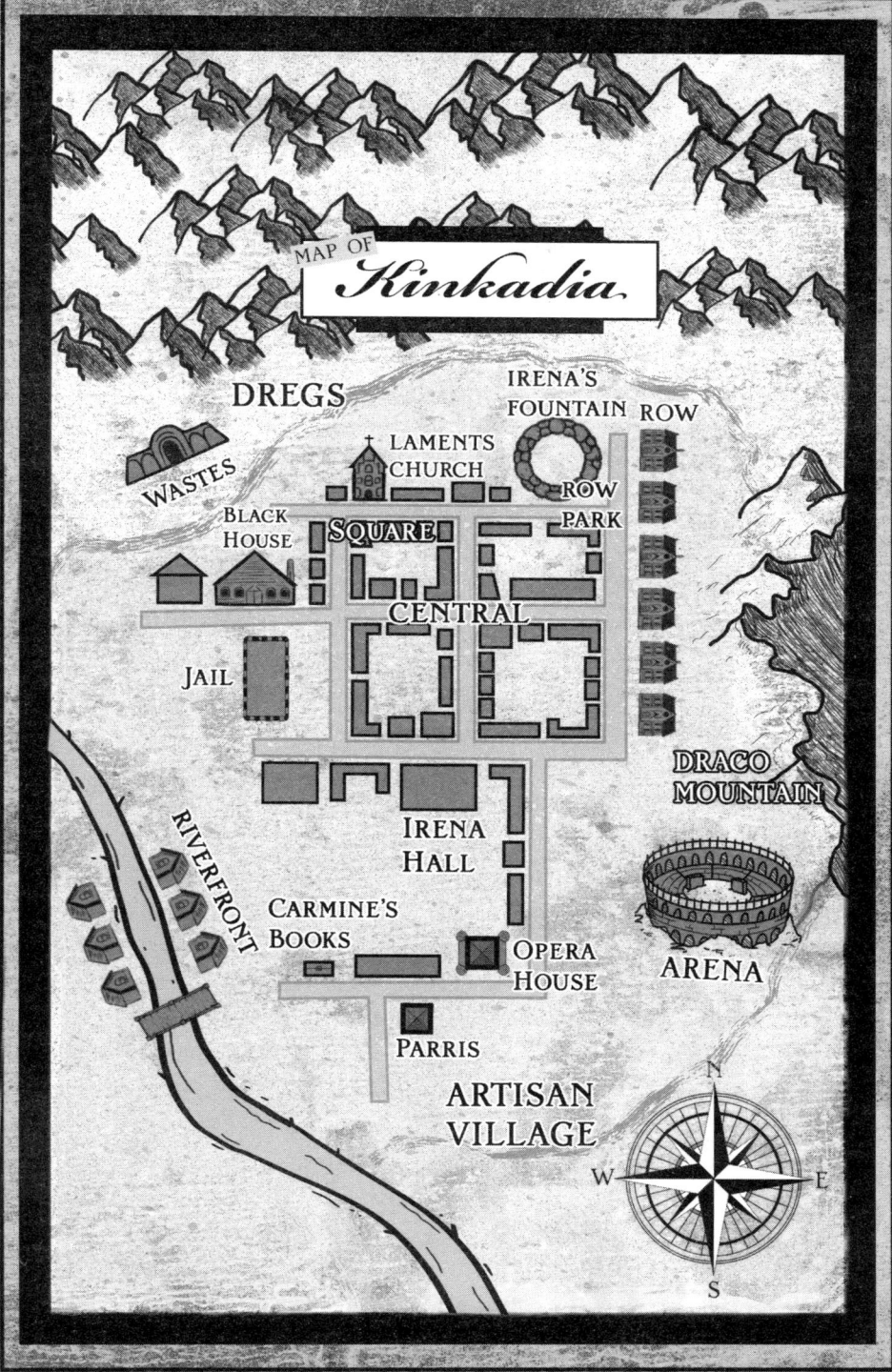

MAP OF *Kinkadia*

DREGS

IRENA'S
FOUNTAIN   ROW

WASTES

LAMENTS
CHURCH

ROW
PARK

BLACK
HOUSE   SQUARE

CENTRAL

JAIL

DRACO
MOUNTAIN

IRENA
HALL

CARMINE'S
BOOKS   OPERA
HOUSE

ARENA

RIVERFRONT

PARRIS

ARTISAN
VILLAGE

N
W   E
S

PRONUNCIATION GUIDE

CHARACTERS

AMOND: Uh-mond

AUDRIA ATHER: Aud-ree-uh Ath-er

AYESHA: Eye-eesh-uh

BASEM NIX: Bay-sum Nix

MASTER BASTIAN: Bast-yun

MASTER CALLIAN: Cal-yen

CHELCIE: Chel-see

CLARE RAHLLINS: Clair Rah-lihns

CLOVER: Clove-er

MISTRESS CRESSIDA: Cruh-see-duh

DARBY: Dar-bee

DARRID: Dare-id

DOZAN ROOK: Doe-zen Rook

ELENEE: Ell-en-ee

ELLERBY EMBERTON: Ell-er-bee Em-ber-tun

EVER: Ev-er

FALLON: Fal-uhn

MASTER FILLION: Fil-ee-un

HADRIAN: Hay-dree-en

HAINFROY: Hain-froy

MISTRESS HELLINA "HELLY": Hell-ee-nuh

IRENA: Ih-reen-uh

ISA: Ee-suh

JAVEL: Jah-vel

KAMARI: Kuh-mar-ee

KENRIS: Ken-ris

KERES: Kerr-is

KERRIGAN ARGON: Care-ih-gen Arh-gone

LORD KIVRIN ARGON: Kiv-rin Arh-gone

MISTRESS LAYLA: Lay-luh

MASTER LORIAN: Lor-ee-uhn

LYAM: Lee-um

MISTRESS MORAN: Mor-in

NODA: No-duh

PARRIS: Pear-is

POSANA: Poe-sohn-uh

PRINCE FORDHAM OLLIVIER: Ford-um
  Ah-liv-ee-aye

ROAKE: Roke

MISTRESS SINEAD: Sih-nayd

LADY SONALI: Suh-nahl-ee

TAIGA: Tay-guh

VALERO: Vuh-lair-o

VALIA: Val-ee-uh

DRAGONS

AVIRIX: Uh-veer-ix

EVIEN: Ev-ee-en

FERRINIX: Fair-ih-nix

GELRYN: Gehl-rin

LUXOR: Lux-er

NETTA: Net-uh

TAVRY: Tahv-ree

TIERAN: Teer-en

HOUSES

The twelve houses of Alandria were split into four groups based on how they perceived the use of magic: Woodloch to the wooded west, Viland to the hills of the east, Tosin to the mountains of the north, and Moran to the rocky south. Though the twelve houses are autonomous, the Society rules over all.

WOODLOCH
MAGIC SHOULD BE USED FOR MIGHT.
(warriors, weapons, armor)

> Galanthea
> Herasi
> Venatrix

VILAND
MAGIC SHOULD BE USED FOR GOOD.
(healing, medicine, art)

> Bryonica
> Concha
> Ibarra

TOSIN
MAGIC SHOULD BE USED FOR EFFICIENCY.
(everyday tasks, mining, travel)

Erewa

Sayair

Zavala

MORAN
MAGIC SHOULD BE USED FOR NOTHING.
(magical artifacts)

Aude

Elsiande

Genoa

WITHIN HOUSE BRYONICA, THERE ARE FOUR ROYAL HOUSES:

House of Stoirm

House of Medallion

House of Drame

House of Cruse

CHAPTER ONE
THE FIGHT

K errigan was losing.

Blood dripped into her eye from a gash at her brow. Her feet danced back and forth on the hard stone floor, light and eager, with her hands protecting her face. Little good it had done.

Her form was in complete contrast to the bruiser before her. He was nearly seven feet tall and built like the haunches of a dragon— massive and muscular. Though he was all power and no finesse.

"You going to dance on your twinkle toes all day, or are we going to fight?" Bruiser grunted.

"I was considering it," she bit back.

He laughed gruffly. "Fine. Make it easy for me, Red."

Bruiser stepped forward, using his limited elemental magic to give him an edge as he rushed toward her. The earth rattled beneath her feet, and she shuffled side to side in an attempt to stay upright. But then he was in front of her, his eyes keen on victory before his fist even shot for her face.

She blocked him with her forearm, taking a bone-crunching amount of pressure. She dodged the second blow and used a trickle of air to shove his fist out of the way. She hated being on the defensive, but she'd never seen Bruiser fight before. She always spent the first couple of minutes discovering her opponent's strengths and weaknesses, assessing the situation to her advantage. Unfortunately, that meant getting punched in the stomach with a giant rock.

All the air gasped out of Kerrigan's lungs as she was propelled backward into the ropes. She collapsed forward onto her knees, coughing spastically. She spat blood onto the floor. An offering to whatever gods were watching.

Her eyes lifted. Bruiser was smirking, holding his hands up to the crowd as if he'd already won the match. Overconfident, arrogant bastard.

She heaved herself back to her feet and kicked the rock he'd thrown off the edge of the ring. Her bright red mess of hair had come out of its braid with that throw, and now, unruly curls framed her narrow face.

At least her gold headband still held. She had no interest in revealing her short, barely pointed ears.

"You still in it?" Bruiser taunted as he sauntered in her direction. He didn't even lift his defenses. He didn't so much as reach for a speck of earth. He was used to using his fists and getting his way. "Poor little thing. I'm going to have to put you to sleep."

"We'll see if you can, Bruiser."

Kerrigan's sight blurred at the edges. The fumes from the Wastes—the deplorable underground crime building where she was currently fighting—sure didn't help matters. The Dragon Ring was on the bottom level and smelled like stale ale and blood and vomit. She preferred it down here to nearly everything up above but, gods, the *smell*.

It was all the worse because her eyes teared up. She looked like an amateur.

A small smile cracked her frightened facade.

Sometimes, looking like an amateur worked to her advantage.

Kerrigan jabbed out with her left hand, swirling the sand on the ground into a tight cyclone. She swung it in an arc before throwing it.

Bruiser's eyes widened in shock as he dove out of the way of the maelstrom. Too slow. The sand yanked him off his feet and threw him halfway across the ring. He rolled over his shoulder and came back up in a crouch. His beady eyes assessed her more strategically than when he'd casually tried to beat her face in.

Kerrigan was losing on purpose.

After nearly a dozen fights, she had learned that no one wanted the fight to end too soon. And *no one* wanted it to end without blood.

The only thing more important than Dozan Rook in these halls—blood.

Blood was the real king of the Wastes.

Bruiser hauled himself up onto his feet again. He shook the sand out of his dark hair and then ran toward her. His feet plodded hard against the packed earth. His hulking figure could make elephants look nimble. Still, she waited with her hands at her sides, ready to strike when he was closer.

Kerrigan lifted her hand and slashed downward, cutting the front of his shirt open. Blood welled dark red against the dull beige of his shirt. He slammed to a halt, staring down in bewilderment at the cut.

Cheers rang out overhead.

The uproarious, drunken crowd was chanting her name, *"Red! Red! Red!"*

"I'll paint *you* red by the end of this," Bruiser taunted. He flexed his muscles.

Kerrigan lifted her hands again and gestured him forward.

A rock slammed into the back of her head. She gasped and crumpled forward, landing hard on her hands. Her magic wavered in her veins as she blinked away the pain. She couldn't see straight.

Not good. *Scales*, that hurt.

Kerrigan wrapped her magic around Bruiser's ankles, yanking hard and fast, felling him like a tree.

He cried out in anger. *Good.* The fight had finally started.

She heard a whoosh and looked up in time to dodge the rock that would have crushed in the back of her skull. She rolled out from under it. Another gasp escaped her lungs. That had been too close.

Another rock crashed into her back as she tried to get up.

"Gods," she groaned as she slammed back into the hard floor.

She rolled away again and came swiftly to her feet. Her back ached already.

Bruiser was smiling as if he were already victorious. He raised his hands to the sky, pumping up the raucous crowd. Kerrigan picked up the air again and slashed fiercely, the first cut through his bicep, the second down his thigh. The third was supposed to hit his cheek, but he somehow flowed around the wind.

Her eyes widened. He'd trained with an air Fae? Doubly not good.

"That's a neat trick," she said.

Bruiser laughed as he weaved away from her and then threw dust right into her eyes. She slammed them shut on instinct, crying out in shock. There were no rules in the Wastes. Certainly none inside the Dragon Ring. But it was dirty play. Dirty, dirty play.

She blinked rapidly, tears welling as the grit ground into her eyes. Concentrating so hard on her eyes, she didn't hear the rock that catapulted into her nose. Something snapped, and she cried out. Blood gushed from the wound.

Her eyes flashed cold death to her opponent. Now she wasn't losing on purpose.

"Say good night, Red," Bruiser said.

Kerrigan lifted her hand. She was barely able to see through the sand in her eyes, but her anger propelled her forward. She froze the air

4

around Bruiser and held him tight in her grasp so that he couldn't even blink without her permission. If she wanted, if she had the strength, she could crush him right where he stood.

Her hand shook, just holding him in place. It took an immense amount of power to be able to do what she was doing. More than she had claimed to have when she started this fight.

She needed to let him go. She needed to dispel her anger and release him. If she didn't, she was going to pay for it later.

"Go back to the underworld you came from," she growled.

She dropped her magic at the same time as she brought her knee up to his balls with a satisfying squelch. He doubled over in pain. She reared back and punched him in his face. He fell backward with the force of her strike. Her knuckles split, and she couldn't stop her hands from shaking.

But there was only one end here: the end where she won.

She stepped over Bruiser's body and kicked him in the temple. A perfectly placed shot to knock him out but not kill him.

The crowd went wild. Cheers and shouts and objects fell from the sky above to litter the Dragon Ring while a man hobbled hastily into the ring and held her arm up.

"Winner goes to Red!"

After the fanfare, Kerrigan stumbled out of the fighting ring and into the back room, where typically, a small weasel of a man waited to give her the earnings from the fight.

That man wasn't there.

In his place stood the owner and proprietor of the Wastes and the biggest crime lord in the city of Kinkadia—Dozan Rook.

"Dozan," Kerrigan said through gritted teeth.

She could barely stand. Her nose ached from that last hit. It was definitely broken. Her back was probably already black and blue. Still, she straightened and held her chin up high. She would never let him see that on her.

"Red," Dozan said with his cocky smirk.

"How can I help you?" she drawled lazily.

"You can take off that ridiculous headband. No one to hide from down here."

Kerrigan frowned and tugged the gold headband free, releasing her bright red hair from its trapping and revealing the delicately pointed ears beneath. The ears that revealed her for what she truly was—half-Fae, half-human.

Full-blooded Fae had sharply pointed ears. And full-blooded Fae was the only *right* thing to be in Kinkadia.

Up above, in the city of Kinkadia, half-Fae were persecuted for their heritage. They were looked down on by the High Fae and much of the ruling class. Many believed that half-Fae shouldn't even exist, especially if they had even a hint of magic. She'd gotten used to hiding her true self. When humans and half-Fae were being beaten in the streets, it was best to remain anonymous.

It was one of the main reasons that she felt so comfortable in the Wastes. No one in this den of iniquity cared whether a person was human, half-Fae, or Fae. They were all too high, drunk, or broke. Unlike above, where she was ridiculed for being *lesser*, the Wastes had only ever drawn her in as their own. She fought here, she made friends here, and despite her past business with Dozan, he protected her within this bed of sin.

"Do you have my winnings?" Kerrigan asked.

"I do indeed."

Dozan slid his hand into the inside of his tailored black suit. The cut accentuated his muscular build. He wore the white shirt with a black vest and jacket, complete with a Wastes red cravat at his neck. His hand was nimble, producing a red velvet bag heavy with gold marks, like the ruthless pickpocket who had taken over the underground.

"Here you are." He set the bag in her hand. It held way more than what she should have earned. His almost golden eyes glittered with defiance, as if waiting for her to suggest that it was too much money.

She did no such thing. She pocketed the bag and ignored the way he ran a hand back through burnished hair that showed more red than brown in the light. Not at all like hers. Not that she would ever admit to paying attention.

"You should consider working bigger fights," Dozan said. "Use more than one element."

Using only one element in the Dragon Ring kept her safe. She did it to keep a target off her back. Half-Fae and humans were notoriously low with magic use, but not her. She had access to all four elements. And the last thing she wanted was anyone else to know about her elemental prowess.

"I appreciate the offer, but no."

"I could make it worth your while," he said silkily. His gold eyes practically glowed in the light.

She swallowed against his infuriating charm.

"I believe that you would," Kerrigan said dryly. "But no."

He stepped toward her. Close enough that they shared breath. She held her ground, tilting her chin in that defiance he so desired. Dozan only did this to unnerve her, and she refused to play his games. She wasn't the same young girl who had landed at his feet five years ago. She'd never be that girl again.

"You know we could practice with your other power," he all but whispered against her lips.

Kerrigan narrowed her eyes. "I have *no* idea what you're talking about."

"Haven't had a dream recently, princess?"

Her body quivered with barely controlled restraint. Her split knuckles ached to ram into his smug face. "I am not a princess."

"Come on, Ker," he breathed softly around the edges of her name. "I find your powers fascinating."

7

"Just because you saved my life five years ago doesn't mean that I owe you a thing," she hissed.

Dozan's eyes dragged across her face, as if he were waiting for her to change her mind. But she would never change her mind. Twice in the last five years, she'd had visions of the future. She had never heard of anyone in all of Alandria ever possessing such a gift. She would know; she had thoroughly perused the library to be sure. Only children's books spoke of such a gift, and in every one, the poor fairy-tale child had been hunted down and slain for their sight. She wasn't stupid enough to think she would be an exception in reality.

But Dozan had been there that unfortunate night and had never let her forget it.

"Fine." Dozan shrugged once, returning to his overly cocky state of being. "What will you do with your winnings?"

"Same as usual."

"Give it all back to me in drinks?"

"Not the worst way to spend the night."

"Not the best," he said, twirling a lock of her bright red hair around his fingers with a lascivious smile before disappearing up the stairs.

CHAPTER TWO
THE WASTES

D ozan was a problem.

He was definitely becoming a problem.

He didn't like it when his things didn't do as they were told. And she refused to be his thing *or* do as she was told. A conundrum that he rarely faced.

Five years ago, he'd saved her life and learned all about her magic and visions. She'd been young and in love. That had been before he had taken over the Wastes, before everything. Then a year ago, she'd had another vision and ended up right back here. He'd gotten her into the fights to give her an outlet. She would thank him if their relationship hadn't gotten even more complicated. If he didn't think that he owned her now.

Kerrigan sighed heavily, pocketed the winnings, and went to her corner. She dropped to her haunches and opened up her bag, pulling out clean clothes. She hastily stripped out of her fighting gear and into a pair of loose pants and a cross-body jerkin that cinched tight at the waist.

Despite what Dozan had said, she tugged her headband back down over her ears and rebraided her hair. She had gotten too used to hiding her slightly rounded, telltale, half-Fae ears. She looked at her wan reflection in the faded glass mirror. She pinched her pale cheeks in an attempt to bring some color back into her skin, but it did little. Her freckles stood out in sharp relief against her complexion. The gash at her eyebrow had stopped bleeding, but she couldn't hide the fact that she'd been in a fight.

Oh well. Nothing to be done.

She left the ring and hastened up the stairs. The Wastes had been built in a deep pit. The Dragon Ring resided on the bottom floor, and as she traveled up to the surface, she passed the spectator seating for the fighting ring, the floor full of addicts high on loch, through the haze of heavily perfumed brothels, and to the gambling levels.

Her bright green eyes scanned the smoke-filled room replete with table after table of card and dice games. Patrons desperate to make it rich threw away their last coins on a lark. The Wastes gambling hall was typically packed, but tonight, Kerrigan could barely move through the press of people. With one hand on her winnings, she finally meandered far enough in that she found her target, stopping before a packed card table playing a crowd favorite, Dragons Up.

The dealer was dressed in the typical red Wastes button-up, black vest, and trousers. Her black hair framed her face, cut off severely at her chin, accentuating her brown complexion and wide dark-brown eyes. Her hands flew across the table, delivering green-and-gold cards.

She tapped her fingers twice as she waited for someone to make a move. But the tilt of her cherry-red lips said she already knew they'd lost.

"Ah, dragons up," she said, her smile turning into a frown. "Better luck next time." She claimed the green-and-gold cards from the man in front of her. She pointed at the next man.

"Crows and scales." He held his hand out flat.

The next man did the same, and on down the line, she pulled cards, added them, and laughed at their misfortune.

Because any loss went right back to the house. Right back to Dozan. And right back to Clover.

Clover looked up as she shuffled the cards by muscle memory. Her eyes lit up at the sight of Kerrigan. "You win?"

Kerrigan nodded, unable to hold back a smirk of triumph.

"All right, you heard the lady. One more hand, and then I'm on break."

The crowd groaned as cards flew from her hands like magic. Which was amazing since Clover didn't have a lick of magic. She was fully human. Not an ounce of the stuff in her veins. Not that it protected her from Fae hatred, but at least she didn't have to worry about accidentally revealing her magic in front of the wrong person like Kerrigan.

Half of the table won this round, and cheers went up all around. A few of those seated tipped Clover big, one man with a pointed wink. Clover reshuffled the deck and gestured to the pit boss before hastening to Kerrigan's side.

"Red!" Clover crushed her long, toned body against Kerrigan as she pulled her into a hug.

"Clove, are you feeling all right?"

Her brown skin was beginning to lose its pallor, and her big brown eyes were bloodshot and red-rimmed.

Clover waved the questions away and fumbled in her pocket for a smoke she'd tinged with loch.

When Kerrigan had first met Clover a year earlier, she had been disgusted with the habit. Loch was an addictive drug on a good day, and she smoked too regularly to not be obsessed with the stuff. But then Clover had accidentally left the cigarettes behind, and debilitating pain had wreaked havoc on her body. The disability had made Kerrigan see the smoking in a whole new light.

With the first puff, everything about Clover loosened. "So how'd it go? You look like shite."

"Thank you very much," Kerrigan said sarcastically. She palmed the pouch Dozan had given her.

"Holy *scales*," Clover said, snatching the bag out of Kerrigan's hand. She pushed up the sleeve of her red button-up and weighed the bag in her hand. "Who'd you swipe this from?"

"Dozan came to see me."

Clover rolled her eyes as she headed toward the bar on the other side of the room. "Of course he did. He has it so bad for you. You should just give in."

Kerrigan rolled her eyes. "No, thank you. Dozan likes to own things, and I won't be owned."

"I'd let him own me," Clover said. She dropped her smoke in a passing drink. Already, she looked so much better, her skin more vibrant and her eyes somehow even wider. As if the smoke had breathed life back into her.

"He already does. You work as a dealer in his gambling ring."

"Well, I meant my body, Kerrigan."

"Red," she muttered. No one here was supposed to know who Kerrigan was. "If you please."

"Right, Red. Sorry. But back to Dozan…"

"Let's not."

"You're no fun."

"You tell me constantly."

Clover rolled her eyes. "Anyway, what are you going to do with your earnings?"

Kerrigan shrugged. "Get you drunk?"

"Get drunk *with* me," Clover said, raising her eyebrows.

"You know I have to go back to the mountain. The tournament starts tomorrow."

Clover sighed heavily and pulled out another smoke. "Fine."

Kerrigan pulled out a few marks from the purse and dropped them on the bar for Clover. "Meet me tomorrow. I'll get you a seat to watch."

"Dragons up," Clover said with a wink.

Kerrigan left her at the bar with her loch and watered-down ale. She headed up another level and out the back way onto the streets of Kinkadia. She breathed in the clean air from the valley and turned her head skyward to take in the twinkling night stars overhead. A dragon passed across the moon, briefly shadowing it. She missed flying. Gods, she seriously missed flying.

She trudged across the cobblestones through the Dregs of the city of Kinkadia. The old familiar walkways were notoriously the worst part of the city. Primarily humans and half-Fae lived in squalor on the north side of the valley where the city was located, bracketed on three sides by an impressively large mountain range and a winding river running diagonally along the southern border.

She should have headed straight for her home in Draco Mountain, but her heart wasn't in it tonight. The mountain had been her home the last twelve years, after she'd been left at the base of the mountain with no note or any belongings. And while she remembered enough from her time before the mountain had swallowed her up, she hated nights like tonight when it all came to the surface.

Like her horrid father who had left her behind so that he didn't have to be responsible for raising a half-Fae.

Her father—Lord Kivrin Argon, the High Fae royal party boy, who had equally destroyed and saved her life.

And she hated him for all of it.

Her heart thundered in her chest as she picked up her pace through the dark, dank streets, accessing her favorite shortcut. A noise sounded behind her, and she stopped in her tracks. Something was wrong.

Then a rock whizzed toward her face. Kerrigan dodged the blow with a gasp. Adrenaline flooded her sore muscles and revitalized her dwindling magic.

Scales, what was going on?

A figure stepped into the center of the alley—Bruiser.

"Hello, Red."

"You again," she grumbled. "Didn't have enough fun the first time?"

Bruiser had cleaned up. He wore a bright white button-up and a fancy black jacket with gold thread. She never would have guessed he could afford that. Not when he was fighting in the Dragon Ring.

But now that her senses were awake, she saw him for the distraction he was. This was an ambush. Three more men slunk out of the shadows.

"You couldn't beat me in the ring, Bruiser, so you brought friends?" Kerrigan placed her hand over her heart. "I'm flattered."

"Shut up, *leatha*," Bruiser spat.

Kerrigan stilled at that word. She didn't flinch. She would *never* let someone see her flinch away from that word again. But anger—deep-rooted fury—settled into her veins and brought forth a fount of magic from the depths of her stores.

"How original," she said, but her voice had lost its humor.

Leatha was a word from High Fae, a dead language, save for the few hundred books within the mountain. It technically meant half-Fae or, sometimes generously, pixie. But that wasn't colloquial usage. That wasn't what Bruiser here had meant when he called her that disgusting word.

Here, it meant, half-breed whore or bitch.

It was not something said in polite company.

"I can't suffer a leatha thinking she can best me," he snarled.

Really, she hadn't asked for this fight. But the ones that came to her, she rarely expected. Right now, the most enjoyable thing in the world would be to crawl into her bed, across from her roommate Darby, and never think of this moment again.

But no, she couldn't allow someone to call her that. She didn't even know how he'd found out that she was half-Fae, but he'd kill her all the same for it. She could see that in his beady eyes. He'd rather she be dead than be beaten by one of her kind. She knew the type. The racist assholes who abused people on the streets because they could, because Fae had all the power.

Today would be different. Bruiser had seen her fight and thought that he was entering a match he could win. He had no *idea* who he was dealing with.

Kerrigan reached down into the core of her magic, and then she unleashed.

She took on the grunts first. A wave of air crushed one into the stone wall at his back. She raised her left hand into a claw. The ground sprouted upward out of the stones around the second man's legs, holding him in place. The third at her back rushed toward her. She snapped her fingers and set him on fire.

She stepped toward Bruiser with passion in her eyes. But he didn't look frightened. He *should* have looked frightened.

He thrust his hand out toward her, clutching a rock tightly in his massive fist.

She froze in place. She couldn't move. Not in the way that she had held Bruiser in the ring with her air magic. This was something else. As if her feet were glued to the cobblestones.

Her head snapped up to meet his eyes. How was he doing this?

She dove deep into her magic, which was already a wavering, stuttering mess. She could feel her well bottoming out. She had only found extra power out of the depths of her emotional pain, but she needed more of it right now.

"You'll get what you deserve, leatha," he crooned as he stepped toward her until he was right in front of her.

She glared at him, and with the last vestiges of her magic, she broke free of whatever spell he'd cast over her.

His eyes bulged in shock and alarm. "How?" he sputtered.

Kerrigan had only enough energy to push his hand out of the way.

The rock he'd been holding on to so tightly dropped and shattered into a million pieces at her feet. And then he turned and fled.

Kerrigan laughed. She wanted to run after him. She wanted to see him suffer for calling her that filthy name. But she was drained. Her magic sat, an empty vessel in her body. At this rate, she wasn't sure if she'd make it back to the Wastes. She stumbled a half a block before she collapsed onto the stones.

"Gods," she muttered.

Her head pounded. Everything hurt.

"No, no, no," she whispered.

It was happening. She knew why she was so weak. Why it felt like all her power was draining out of her.

Another vision was coming.

She'd only had two in five years. Both times, she had ended up incapacitated. The visions worked like a siphon. One minute, she had energy, and the next, it claimed the powers for itself. And she had no control. No way to stop them.

She cried out hoarsely, praying to whatever god would listen that someone would find her. That Bruiser wouldn't come back and claim her weakened body.

Then her sight disappeared, and in its place, a tangle of images flew before her eyes. The arena filled with people cheering for the start of the tournament. Black smoke and darkness. A figure clad in black. She couldn't make out what the person looked like. Who it was. A girl hovering in the sky. Trapped. Screaming. A large crowd in front of a building. The people chanting and cheering like a mob. A figure stepped forward in a black cloak, their features obscured by a red mask. Chaos.

"No," she gasped out as she came back to herself.

Her eyes were glassy, and what she'd seen raced across her mind over and over again.

The first vision had been so clear, and the second had at least made sense. But this? What even was this? And why did it make her want to throw up all over the cobblestones?

Her vision dipped again. Her ears were ringing. She felt like she was going to die here.

A familiar voice sounded through the cacophony in her head. "Here you are."

"Dozan?"

Dozan leaned over her. "Red, how many fingers am I holding up?"

"Six?" she muttered. "Wait…"

He said nothing more, just easily lifted her into his arms. She rested her head against his chest, ignoring all the reasons this was a bad, bad choice. But her vision was black at the edges. She had mere minutes.

"You shouldn't walk alone on the streets in the Dregs after humiliating Basem Nix."

Her eyes wrenched back open, fighting the spiral. "That was Basem Nix?" she croaked in despair. No wonder he'd been wearing that jacket.

Basem had started as a Dregs underling who had reaped the benefits of new trade from the south to haul himself out of the slums. Now, he was a formidable merchant with terrifying, powerful friends. He was not someone she had ever wanted to meet, let alone get on his bad side.

"Why would I be fighting Basem?"

"It was a test, Red. You passed."

She groaned, certain her head was going to split in two.

Dozan was silent as he carried her through the back halls of the Wastes and deposited her into Clover's empty pallet.

Kerrigan was unconscious before her head hit the pillow. Otherwise, she would have reminded someone to wake her for the tournament tomorrow.

CHAPTER THREE
THE TOURNAMENT

Someone was shaking her awake.

Kerrigan groaned. "Just one more minute."

"Kerrigan, are you out of your mind?"

Her eyes flew open to find a tall boy with short blue hair staring down at her. "Hadrian?"

"Yes, it's me, you dolt. What are you still doing in the Wastes?" he demanded. "You were supposed to be at the arena hours ago."

She jolted out of bed, her heart racing like she'd performed a tight roll on a dragon's back. She rubbed her hands over her eyes as she realized where she was. She was in Clover's room. Her room in the Wastes. Oh gods!

"The tournament!" she gasped.

"Yes! You didn't come home last night. We were all worried. I drew the short straw to come here and collect you."

"Can you keep it down?" Clover grumbled from the pallet next to Kerrigan.

"Clover, get up! It's the day of the tournament."

"Scales," Clover gasped, rolling over with wide eyes. "Are we late?"

"Late?" Hadrian asked with a stilted laugh. "We'll be lucky if we make the trek back to the mountain before it starts. Now, get up. Let's go."

With this new information, both girls moved at lightning speed, throwing on fresh clothes and scrambling out of the room.

Gods, how had this happened? She wasn't particularly punctual, but she had never wanted to miss something this important. Then the night before came back to her—the fight, the winnings, Basem Nix.

She winced. She'd fought Basem Nix. *Scales*. That wasn't good. She had never seen Basem in person before, but she sure as hell knew his name. And the echo of it still rang in her ears. He was full-blooded Fae and had money and enough connections to make her shiver. She hoped that she never came across him again.

"This way," Clover said, grasping Hadrian's collar and throwing him toward another set of stairs.

Kerrigan followed at a close clip. They burst out a side door that led into the Dregs, all a little breathless from the climb.

"You are going to be in so much trouble," Hadrian said as they started forward through the crowded streets.

"I know. Don't remind me," Kerrigan grumbled.

"You've always been reckless, but this is next level," he said.

"Hey, leave her alone, pretty boy," Clover cut in.

He shot a seething glare at Clover. "Did you really have to come in that?"

She glanced down at the Wastes uniform she'd donned without thought and then shrugged with a smirk. "You don't like it."

"Leave it," Kerrigan snapped at Hadrian. "I'm tired enough without hearing you two always at each other's throats."

Kinkadia was arranged into six main districts. The largest, technically called Glenwoods, but everyone called it the Dregs, lay to the north and west. Central was full to the brim with markets, merchants, inns, and taverns, especially with all the tourists in town for the tournament. Row to the east was the nicest, most affluent part of the city with wide lanes, freshly manicured parks, and stately mansions for the Fae aristocracy. Riverfront, a new money section of the city, lay southwest, and Artisan Village, filled with artists, was to the southeast.

The final section was the mountain. Draco Mountain towered high above everything. It housed the Society, a talented company of dragon riders and the formal government of the country, as well as her home—House of Dragons.

"I should stop being surprised that you don't care about being Dragon Blessed," Hadrian grumbled.

"I do care," Kerrigan spat back.

"Dragon Blessed is only the greatest honor of a lifetime."

"I know the spiel. The House of Dragons is an elite training program for Fae."

She touched her ears. Fae. Not half-Fae. But no one had argued with her royal father when he'd dropped her off apparently.

"It's more than that. It's our duty to help raise the dragons, to better ourselves, to one day get to return to the world and make a difference, Kerrigan. And you're squandering it all."

Clover rolled her eyes. "It's not like she dropped out of the program."

"She can't drop out," Hadrian said as they finally passed the square at the center of the Central district and turned south, bending toward the arena. "That's not possible."

"I'm not dropping out anyway. I miscalculated the time. I know how important the dragon tournament is."

And she did. It was single-handedly the most important event in all of Alandria. Every five years, the twelve houses came together and presented competitors to enter the tournament. A contestant was chosen out of each house to compete in three tasks. The winner of the event won not only a dragon but a place in the Society, a place in the ruling class. And this year, there were five dragons up for grabs. The most in nearly a century. It was going to be a spectacle to behold.

It was Hadrian's turn to look exasperated. "You're not acting like it."

"Yeah, well…"

Clover punched Hadrian in the arm. "She had a rough night."

"This is too important." He dragged Kerrigan to a stop. She looked into his honey eyes and at his golden-brown skin. Saw the boy who had stood by her side all these years. "You remember what happened five years ago. A human foreigner entered the tournament. She won a dragon and then *left*. She dismantled the entire system. This year has to go off without a hitch, or we're going to have riots in the streets again."

"I know," Kerrigan whispered.

She could hear Hadrian's concern. And she remembered *exactly* what it had been like five years ago. She had gotten caught in those riots and nearly died.

"Are we going to go to the arena or what?" Clover asked through pants.

"Yes," Hadrian and Kerrigan said together.

They finally pushed out of the crowded alleyways and to the entrance of the arena, which loomed in the shadow of the mountain. She panted as she stared up at the giant construction. They were late. They were *so* late.

Hadrian led the way to the box that was reserved for the House of Dragons. He opened the door, looked around once for Mistress Moran, the keeper and guardian of all Dragon Blessed, and then when he saw no one, ushered them inside.

A figure stood pacing anxiously in the darkness. She jumped when the door opened, and her midnight eyes rounded into saucers. "Kerrigan!" she gushed, throwing her arms around her roommate.

"Darby," Kerrigan said with a laugh.

Darby laughed demurely and released her. "Hadrian, here to save the day, as usual. Where was she?"

Hadrian rolled his eyes and then gestured to Clover standing behind her. Clover's hands were in the pockets of her black slacks. She still wore the red button-up shirt and black vest that denoted she worked for Dozan.

"Hi, Clover," Darby said, ducking her chin to her chest at the sight of her long-time crush.

"Hey, Darbs," Clover said with a wink.

"If Mistress Moran sees her in that outfit…" Hadrian said with a sigh, pressing his fingers to his temples. "I should have told you to change."

"Hey, no sweat off my back, sweetheart," Clover said, retreating into street slang as she put up a defensive position against Hadrian.

No matter how often they were together, he always raised her hackles.

"I brought an extra set of clothes," Darby said hastily. She rummaged through her bag and pulled out a frock. She shrugged as she glanced at Kerrigan. "They *were* for you."

"Perfect," Kerrigan cried and snatched the clothes up to give to Clover.

"I'm not sure I'd say it's perfect," Hadrian muttered.

Kerrigan slung an arm around Darby as Clover went to change.

"Did we miss anything?" Kerrigan asked.

"Just a few speeches. We should hurry so we don't miss the dragon presentations."

Though Kerrigan had many reasons to distrust this world, Darby and Hadrian certainly weren't part of that. Together, they were her rock. Hadrian the straitlaced practical type, who always sighed when she ran straight into danger. And Darby her perfectly coiffed and manicured healer, who never fled from the sight of blood and at the same time somehow wanted to be a lady in a royal court.

Darby was truly her opposite in every way. Soft and lithe with midnight skin instead of hard and fit and spattered in freckles.

Long, straight black hair and depthless black eyes while Kerrigan had her mess of tangled curls, and her eyes were so green, they rivaled the emeralds mined in the north. Darby was soft-spoken, ever polite, and the best in their year for all things dancing, etiquette, and propriety.

"Let me see what I can do with your hair," Darby said, settling Kerrigan into a seat.

"And my nose," Kerrigan muttered. "I think it's broken."

Darby sighed. "This will hurt."

"Just do it."

She reached up, pressing her fingers to Kerrigan's nose. A crack sounded out again in the quiet. Kerrigan bit her lip to keep from crying out. It hurt as bad as when she'd broken it.

"I wish I knew how to do more with my healing magic," Darby lamented.

"You've come such a long way. At least my nose won't be crooked."

Darby laughed as she set Kerrigan down to try to control her curls. "I suppose that's a benefit."

Clover stepped out of the shadows in an oatmeal-colored tunic dress with a black belt wrapped tight around her narrow waist, accentuating her curvy figure. A long, tarnished gold chain was tucked into the front.

Kerrigan felt more than heard Darby's breath catch at the sight of Clover. She squeezed her friend's hand.

Darby had confided to Kerrigan that she liked girls years ago. But Kerrigan had never seen Darby have a crush until they started hanging out with Clover a year ago.

"I look like an idiot," Clover said, breaking the silence. She plucked at the dress.

"You look great," Kerrigan reassured her.

Just then, a cheer rose up from the stadium. They jumped at the noise and raced to where the rest of the Dragon Blessed were

23

congregated. Hadrian elbowed his way to the front, and they all gazed out across the sand-strewn arena.

The arena was a long oval construction with graduated stands that went up and up and up. Besides the House of Dragons box at floor level, there was a series of boxes high above the rest of the stadium crowd where the master of ceremonies and the wealthy aristocracy could watch the proceedings.

"What's happening?" Darby asked from Kerrigan's side.

And then they got their answer. A dragon swooped down into the stadium, and another roar rushed through the crowd.

"Avirix," Hadrian whispered.

The House of Dragons, first and foremost, helped raise the young dragons. Every Dragon Blessed knew each dragon by name. Over the years, they had all grown close to certain dragons. The hardest part about leaving the House of Dragons was going to be leaving the *dragons*.

Kerrigan would recognize Avirix anywhere for his bright seafoam-green scales. He was the largest dragon of the five who were part of the tournament this year, but he made up for his scary demeanor by being in perpetual good spirits.

After Avirix left, a bright red jewel soared into the arena. Netta was a nimble flyer. One of the reasons Kerrigan loved her so. They had long been friends, as they shared the same mischievous nature.

"Oh!" Clover gasped when Tieran burst into the arena next.

He was the most beautiful of them all. His scales were midnight blue and glistened in the light. Though he was one of the smallest dragons, he was completely adept at every maneuver. Unfortunately, he was also a total jerk.

Darby reached her hand out with wide eyes as Luxor shot out into the arena with his sapphire-blue scales and muscular form. Luxor was one of Darby's favorites despite the fact that he still didn't understand sarcasm or figures of speech.

But it was Evien that made Kerrigan lean out as she sailed into the arena with her majestic purple scales. Evien, like Kerrigan, loved to fly more than any other. They used to sneak out together and take to the skies. The pain that she wasn't going to be able to do that much longer hit her fresh.

Now that the dragons had been displayed, it was time for the twelve houses to present their potential candidates for the tournament. Anyone over the age of eighteen could submit themselves to be in the tournament as long as they were sponsored by a house. After all the potentials were presented, each would be tested, but only one person would be the final candidate for the tournament from each house.

The representatives of the twelve houses strode into the arena, guided by the sponsor Society member in long, flowing black robes. Each held a banner in their house colors with the coat of arms embroidered in black. When a house was announced, a cheer went up in the crowd from the others of their home. But it wasn't until the four blue-and-silver banners denoting the royal lines of Bryonica flew confidently into the stadium that the entire place seemed to erupt at once.

Kerrigan looked over their faces, wondering if in a different life, she would have known them, would have been one of them. She gritted her teeth and averted her gaze. It hardly mattered now.

"Look at that pomp," Clover muttered in distaste. "A hundred potentials? Absurd."

"It makes perfect, logical sense," Darby said. Her voice was earnest.

"It makes them look desperate," Clover countered. "Twenty to fifty potential competitors are sufficient to guarantee that you find a champion. A hundred is ridiculous."

"It's a show of strength."

"I'd expect that from a warrior house. But Bryonica? They're healers. It's beneath them."

Kerrigan tuned their argument out. Her attention was drawn to what no one else had noticed now that all twelve houses were assembled. Black smoke was spinning into existence at the center of the arena.

Black smoke. Her insides coiled as a memory floated back to her from her vision the previous night.

"Gods, do you see that?" Kerrigan whispered.

Her friends snapped to attention, taking in what was happening.

Hadrian touched Kerrigan's shoulder. "Have you ever seen anything like that?"

"No," she lied. She *had* seen this before, but she had no idea what it meant. Her visions weren't clear. They didn't tell her what was going to happen. Only a hazy idea of images. If this were true, what the hell else had it shown her?

"I thought they had extra security this year," Clover said.

"They do," Darby confirmed.

Kerrigan frowned. The smoke grew stronger, almost solidifying at the center. Even though she had seen this happen in her dream, it was so much different, watching it happen in reality. How was it even possible? Hundreds of barriers around the arena kept anyone from penetrating the grounds. No one should be able to enter without permission from the Society.

The crowd grew restless, talking over the master of ceremonies as he attempted to calm the arena. Society members on the ground reached for their magic, stepping forward to protect their contestants. Others in black robes appeared on the outskirts. Kerrigan recognized the protections they were reinforcing on the perimeter. And still, that black cloud continued to spiral.

As soon as it had come, the smoke disappeared, and standing at the center of the entire arena was a man dressed from head to toe in black. He was tall—impossibly tall—with long, lean legs in fitted black pants. He wore a suit jacket at the height of fashion with a black shirt buttoned high, nearly to his collar, barely exposing his pale, nearly translucent throat. He ran a hand back through his dark-as-night hair and then leisurely surveyed the crowd with eyes that were pure sin.

Kerrigan's throat bobbed as those eyes cast across her box. Gods, he radiated sinister energy. Yet he was the most beautiful person she had ever seen in her life.

"What is the meaning of this?" the master of ceremonies managed to recover his voice to ask.

The man tilted his head slightly and smiled something wicked. "My name is Fordham Ollivier, prince and heir to the House of Shadows. And I have come to enter the dragon tournament and reclaim what was once stolen from us."

CHAPTER FOUR
THE PUNISHMENT

Gods," Kerrigan breathed out.

She ground her hands into her eyes. This couldn't be happening again. It just couldn't. She didn't *want* to see the future. She didn't want to know that things she had seen in her weird dreams and visions would come true. And she had *no* idea what would happen now that they had.

None of them had ever particularly spelled out rainbows and sunshine. It usually meant some bad luck for her and that a lot of people would die.

"Ker, you okay?" Hadrian asked in that calm, authoritative way of his.

Sometimes, the only person who really understood her was Hadrian. Even though they fought and she drove him crazy with her antics, he was always there when she needed him. No matter what.

She slowly peeled her hands away from her eyes. "This is a nightmare."

"They'll figure it out," he said confidently.

They would. Of course. But it spelled disaster.

The last time someone had entered the dragon tournament against the wishes of the Society, thousands of people had died in the protests. If Kerrigan had seen this prince in her vision, she could hazard a guess that he spelled similar disaster.

Clover arched a penciled eyebrow. "Headache?"

Kerrigan nodded. "Now that the ceremony is over, we should probably get you out of here. Don't want Moran to find you here."

"I want to look at the dark prince a little while longer," Clover said with a wink. She nudged Darby, who dipped her chin in embarrassment. "He's quite nice to look at."

Hadrian rolled his eyes. "Is that all you ever think about?"

"Absolutely not," Clover said. "I admire the women too. Look at the head warrior in Galanthea this year, Darbs. I sure do like when they dress up in their gold-plated armor."

Darby coughed into her hand and shot Kerrigan a look of panic. "Clove, come on."

"Hey, Kerrigan," a voice sounded behind her. "Is everything all right?"

She sighed softly and turned to find Lyam hovering nearby. Lyam used to be a part of her inner circle with Darby and Hadrian. They'd been close for years. In fact, he was the first person she'd ever flown with. He had an even bigger rebellious streak than she did. He wanted the skies for himself, and he'd do anything to have it.

But everything had changed in the last year. He'd tiptoed around her. He withdrew from all his rebellions. And he constantly worried about her. He followed her out to the Wastes and tried to drag her back to the mountain. The whole thing was embarrassing enough without him confessing his love for her.

"Everything is fine, Lyam," Kerrigan said.

"You never came back last night. I went looking for you."

She breathed out through her nose. "You didn't have to do that."

"You look like you've been fighting again." He reached up to touch

29

the spot on her eyebrow, but she pulled back, and his hand dropped. His cheeks tinged a soft pink.

Gods, she wished she could go back to when there wasn't this awkwardness between them. When he'd just been the other daredevil in their quartet.

"Lyam! Kerrigan!" Mistress Moran cried.

Both of them snapped to attention. They'd heard that tone one too many times from the keeper of the House of Dragons.

"Yes, Mistress Moran," Lyam said.

"Why am I not surprised that it's *you* two who are in trouble?"

Lyam glanced her direction, a half smile on his lips. He shot her *the look*. She had to stifle a laugh. This was the Lyam that she had grown up with. The one she had always gotten in trouble with. Who she'd weather any storm with.

"You two will follow me to the mountain," Mistress Moran said in exasperation. She turned to Hadrian, who she apparently hadn't realized had disappeared this morning to collect Kerrigan. "Hadrian, darling, would you mind getting everyone else back to duties for the afternoon?"

"Of course," he said, always the mask of decorum.

He rounded up the rest of the Dragon Blessed. Kerrigan noted Clover slipping out past Mistress Moran. She had a knack for disappearing at the right moment.

Mistress Moran snapped her heels together and then marched back toward the mountain. She was dressed in the flowing black robes of the Society and had been the head of the House of Dragons schooling for as long as anyone could remember. Her face had lines in it, and her hair actually had wisps of silver. For a Fae, that was almost completely unheard of.

Kerrigan and Lyam had taken much pleasure in finding ways to add to that over the years. As Mistress Moran constantly reminded them.

Kerrigan grinned as they entered the mountain that was her home. She could weave her way through the maze of corridors and climb her way up into all the dragon eaves. So few were accepting of a half-Fae girl here, but it still felt more like home than anywhere else.

Mistress Moran dragged them both into her office. "You were both out of your beds last night. Explain yourselves."

Kerrigan kept her mouth shut. No explanation would be satisfactory for Moran. Fighting in the Dragon Ring in the Wastes? She might as well tell her that she'd completely lost her mind. Moran might believe her more.

"It's my fault," Lyam piped up.

Kerrigan raised her eyebrows. Since when did Lyam take the fall?

"Explain, Lyam."

"I snuck out last night to go to a tournament party," he said solemnly. "Kerrigan tried to stop me because we had to be here so early. Eventually, she came with me to keep an eye on me. But there was faerie punch."

Mistress Moran's lips pinched.

"Our senses were addled, but it's my fault, not Ker's."

What in the gods' names was he talking about?

"How magnanimous," Mistress Moran said dryly. "Unbelievable, considering the amount of trouble you and Kerrigan get into. But magnanimous all the same for taking the credit for it."

Lyam winced at her words.

"Kerrigan?" Moran asked.

Kerrigan kept her lips sealed. Literally nothing would excuse her.

"Very well. You are both on dragon cleanup duties until the Dragon Blessed ceremony. That's one week and no fussing," Moran said crisply.

Lyam and Kerrigan groaned in unison.

"But, Mistress Moran—" Lyam began.

Moran held her hand up. "I don't want to hear it."

A knock sounded at the door behind them, and then a small figure peered inside. She might have been diminutive in stature, but she was all grace and dominance, a leader of the Society and the last dragon tournament's adjudicator. Also one of Kerrigan's closest allies within the mountain—Helly.

"Mistress Hellina," Moran said, jumping to her feet, "how can I help you?"

"Helly will do, dear," Helly said with a kind smile. Her eyes flickered to Kerrigan. "I need to borrow Kerrigan right away, if you please."

"Of course," Moran said deferentially. "Kerrigan, go with Helly, but do remember your duties."

"Yes, Mistress Moran."

Kerrigan hastened out of Moran's office, and she and Helly began to walk purposefully through the mountain.

Helly looked over at her. "Wipe that grin off your face, dear. I know all about your indiscretions. You hid much of it from Moran, but I know that you've been sneaking out to that heathen den. I know that you've been fighting. I know that you brought one of Dozan Rook's spies into the House of Dragons box."

Kerrigan wilted. "Clover isn't a spy. She's my friend."

"I don't think you know the difference."

"You treat me like I'm still that twelve-year-old girl."

"No, I don't," Helly said. "The twelve-year-old Kerrigan had respect for authority and herself. She got into trouble, but it was all a game of fun. Not this rebellion you have fancied yourself in now. It is not representative of the Society."

"I'm not *part* of the Society."

"You are Dragon Blessed. You represent us. You've been here nearly your entire life. I know you already know all this. I don't know what has gotten into you."

Kerrigan clenched her hands into fists. "You have no idea what I'm going through."

Helly pulled her aside. Her dark eyes were warm with concern. "Then tell me. Surely, we have known each other long enough for you to know that you can tell me anything. You have so often in the past."

"You wouldn't understand."

Helly raised an eyebrow. "Try me."

"I'm a half-Fae, Helly. *Half.* You can't possibly understand how everyone treats me because of who I am. I can't tell people about my abilities." She looked at Helly pointedly. She had been the one, after all, to tell Kerrigan to hide her visions in the first place. "I can't show who I truly am. And even if I could, no one would accept me for it. My father is full-blooded Fae. He's a royal in Bryonica—*your house*—and I'm stuck here because he didn't want me."

She was breathing heavily from her outburst. Only Helly would allow her to speak to her like this without reprimand. All Kerrigan saw was pity in her eyes, and sometimes, that was worse.

Kerrigan straightened again. "At least in the Wastes, no one judges me for these." She touched her short ears. "I can just be me."

"You're right. I can't understand that," Helly said gently. "But I do know you. Things are hard now because of the racial tensions among our people. They will get better. I know they will. And things will get easier for you after the Dragon Blessed ceremony."

Kerrigan wasn't so sure.

In one week, every member of the House of Dragons over the age of sixteen would be a part of the Dragon Blessed ceremony. Each Dragon Blessed would be selected by one of the twelve houses and would leave the mountain behind. For many of the students, it was the only way to advance in the world. Most of the Dragon Blessed had been left at the mountain like Kerrigan, and being selected at the ceremony meant a new life—wealth, security, and a place in this world.

Helly must have seen the doubt on her face. She touched Kerrigan's shoulder and said, "When you're officially a member of a house again, wearing their colors, living under their realm of protection, it will be easier."

Kerrigan deflated. "I wish that I didn't need protection from anyone to be me."

Helly gestured for them to begin walking again. "I hope, one day, that will be the case as well. You are too bright for everyone not to see the light within you. To judge you based on *what* you are rather than *who* you are."

They remained silent the rest of the walk. At least Helly understood even if she didn't *understand*. No one could really since they hadn't walked in Kerrigan's shoes, hadn't seen what it was like to be persecuted for a circumstance of her birth.

Finally, they stopped in front of the Society council chamber. The door was ajar, and she peered inside. Much of the twenty-person high council was already assembled. They were the highest office of the Society governing body, the most coveted seats in all of Alandria.

"What's going on?" she asked in confusion.

"We're holding a tribunal to decide whether to permit Prince Fordham to compete in the tournament."

Kerrigan's eyes rounded. "Do you think they'll allow it?"

"I don't know." The creases around Helly's mouth and eyes said she was worried.

"But he's not part of one of the twelve houses. Surely, he doesn't qualify."

"Everything is different since the last tournament. I doubt he would come here from the House of Shadows if he didn't have a plan in place. We're here to see what it is."

Kerrigan shivered. The House of Shadows. She only knew the haunting stories of the Dark Court, Fae who tortured anyone who crossed their borders. Dark Fae who slaughtered mercilessly on the battlefield and stole babies in the night. They were legend come to life.

"Helly," she whispered, knowing that she had to tell her about her vision. "I had another one."

Helly's face snapped to hers. She drew in close and lowered her voice. "A vision? What happened?"

"I saw him. Fordham."

Helly drew in a sharp breath. "What was he doing?"

"Just materializing in the tournament. Nothing more about him. I also saw a woman floating and screaming, some kind of crowd that had gotten out of hand, and a person in a red mask."

Helly blanched. "A red mask?"

Kerrigan nodded.

The Red Masks were an anti-human, anti-half-Fae hate group. Five years ago, they'd taken to the streets, burning churches and killing humans and half-Fae alike. Kerrigan had nearly been one of them. The Red Masks still haunted her dreams.

"I thought they were gone," Kerrigan whispered.

"I thought so too." Helly released a breath laced in fear. "I will speak to the head of security to keep an eye out. If the Red Masks are going to have a resurgence, then we need to prepare. Those were dark days. As for the rest of your vision, Fordham must be important."

"Yes, but how?"

Helly looked grim. "I suppose we will find out. You remember to be discreet. Don't tell anyone else of this."

"Of course," Kerrigan said hastily. She'd made that mistake once with Dozan. She'd never do it again.

"Good." Helly straightened. "Now, wait here."

"Here?" Kerrigan asked in confusion.

"Yes, oddly enough, I had already decided that your punishment would be to work with Fordham Ollivier."

Kerrigan blanched. "What?"

"Whether or not he makes it into the tournament, you will be his escort."

"But, Helly…"

"A force guides our hands, Kerrigan. We cannot ignore it."

Helly turned and entered the council room. The door closed behind her, and Kerrigan leaned back against the wall to wait. Wait to find out Fordham's fate. Wait to see how tangled it would be with hers.

CHAPTER FIVE
THE DARK PRINCE

An hour later, the doors slammed open.

Kerrigan jumped. She'd been dozing against the opposite wall. Her head started to pound, and she had to blink away her blurry vision.

Prince Fordham Ollivier was standing before her in all his glory.

She'd thought he was beautiful in the arena from a safe distance. Terrifying but handsome beyond measure. Now, this close to him, she felt her body turn to jelly. He was not just good-looking; he was sinister. There was something about his body that made her want to retreat, to curl into a ball and hide from the world. His black hair was swept back off his face. But it was the gray eyes, which caught and held her gaze, that made her shiver. There was something wrong with him. Something terribly twisted inside.

His gaze swept over her and then dismissed her just as quickly as he turned and stormed down the hallway. Without a backward glance or a question of his direction, he just left.

Scales.

Kerrigan jumped from her place against the wall, cursing her right leg for falling asleep underneath her. She shook it out, but that only made it worse. Pins and needles trailed down her leg. She winced with every step.

"Excuse me," she croaked, finally getting her voice back.

He didn't slow down or stop or even look back at her.

She gritted her teeth against her dead leg and pushed herself into a half hobble, half jog. "Excuse me, Prince Fordham."

That got his attention. He pivoted with strict military precision and looked at her with those ever-changing eyes.

"Hi," she said a little breathlessly. "I'm here to be your escort. I'm Kerrigan of the House of Dragons. I'm a Dragon Blessed here in the mountain. Mistress Hellina asked me to escort you to your next assignment."

He stared at her. "You?"

"Me," she agreed.

"Why would they send you? Do they intend insult?"

Kerrigan stiffened at his words. "No. I'm a Dragon Blessed."

"You are half-Fae."

Oh.

Kerrigan straightened and ground her teeth together. She was supposed to be an escort. She'd taken enough lessons on proper etiquette to know how she *should* respond to him. She clenched her fists once and released them.

"Indeed, I am. However, I'm still your escort. Right this way," she said, gesturing the opposite direction he had been walking.

Fordham took two steps forward and looked down at her over the bridge of his nose. She gulped and tried not to be intimidated by him. "They pass me through to be tested and then send me *you*?"

Kerrigan's eyes rounded. "They let you through? But you're not one of the twelve houses. Who sponsored you?"

Fordham shot her a deadly look. "The House of Shadows was once a recognized house of Alandria. I argued my case sufficiently that it should continue to be one. The right was granted along with sponsorship by the council, considering the debt they owe us."

"Debt?"

His eyes flared with anger. She didn't even know what she'd said. "So they no longer teach you our history. I'd expect nothing less from a half-breed."

Kerrigan bristled as he had intended for her to. She was supposed to be on her best behavior, but *he* certainly wasn't. "Excuse me? You know nothing about me," she snapped. All her fear and mesmerizing attention dissipated. "Now, are we going or what? Unless you know exactly where you're going, princeling."

"Do not call me that," he seethed.

Oh, he took offense to princeling but had no qualms with *half-breed*. Typical.

"As far as I can tell, you have no idea where you're going. So I would be *happy* to leave you here and let you fend for yourself. Maybe wandering around for the next few hours would do you some good," she growled.

His look didn't change. She didn't know if he even saw her anger. He looked so puffed up on his own importance.

"I don't want your help," he concluded.

She blew out in frustration. "Well, I don't really want to help you either, but here we are..."

He turned away from her. Looked down the endless hallway with all the interest of someone who wanted to ignore a buzzing fly. "I truly am cursed."

She snorted at his melodrama. "Sure, cursed," she muttered. "Let's get this over with. This way."

Kerrigan headed down the corridor and didn't look back to see if he followed. If he decided to stay behind and get lost, well, that wasn't on her.

Eventually, she heard his faint footsteps trailing behind her. He walked smoothly. If she hadn't been listening for it, she might not have even heard him. That was disconcerting in a place made entirely of stone.

Kerrigan took the final turn and then approached a line of doors. Each one was representative of the twelve houses. There, the potential competitors would be housed until they were called forward for testing. There were more rooms than the twelve, which suggested they used to have a separate purpose, but the twelve each had their emblem stamped into the wooden door. They passed each one soundlessly until they reached the thirteenth door. Unlucky, if you asked her.

There was no stamp on this door. Nothing to suggest it was also part of this ancient ritual. But a Society member waited across the hall before the testing door, and she pointed at Kerrigan when she approached. This was the one.

Kerrigan took a breath and opened the door. The room was suffused with light. A few chairs had been placed inside, and there was a table with parchment, ink, and refreshments. A place to while away the time until the potential was called in. She had never been inside this room before and was mildly disappointed to find it so plain.

"Here you are," she said, masking her disappointment.

She held the door open wider, and Fordham entered with his head held high. Kerrigan debated slamming the door in his face and leaving him to sit alone in silence. She didn't want to be alone with him. It'd be easier to stand outside and wait, like she had for the tribunal. But she was also curious.

Curious about Fordham. If she knew more about him, then perhaps she could figure out how they were connected and *why* she'd had a vision of him.

With a resigned sigh, she followed him into the room and closed the door behind her.

His eyes flicked to her, and his nostrils flared. "Do I need to be watched?"

40

She shrugged. "I'm doing what I was told."

"And you were told to escort me, not wait with me."

Kerrigan ignored him and flopped into a chair by the door. "I'm not going to have Helly mad at me because I didn't do what I was supposed to do."

Fordham glared at her. "Are you always this insufferable?"

"Pretty much."

He looked like he wanted to argue with her. So she smirked up at him and waited for it to come. But he seemed to shake himself out of whatever rage had been forming behind his eyes and turned his back on her.

Damn. He really had decided she was no threat.

He spent an inordinate amount of time pacing the small quarters. So much so that she actually had to close her eyes to stop from getting dizzy. She felt herself drifting again. She hadn't slept enough last night. Not restful sleep at least. It never was restful after a vision. As if it had sapped all her powers straight out of her body and left her with a sense of unease and impending doom.

She jerked awake at the scratch of a quill against parchment. She blinked a few times to adjust to her surroundings and found Fordham seated before the desk. His handwriting was long and elegant, the sound of the quill a lullaby.

"What are you writing?" she asked, straightening so she wouldn't pass out again.

"I thought you'd fallen asleep finally."

"Did you make me go to sleep?" she asked, momentarily terrified.

What sort of abilities did a prince from the House of Shadows have?

He smirked at her suggestion. "And how would I accomplish that?"

"I don't know. Some sort of spell."

He arched an eyebrow.

"You're from the House of Shadows," she said as if that were obvious. "You used dark magic to enter the tournament."

"Did I?" he asked with that same insufferable smirk.

"Black smoke," she reminded him. "I don't even know how the council approved you."

Fordham arched an eyebrow and then said, "Half-Fae simple-mindedness," before returning to his paper.

She clenched her hands into fists. He was goading her, and still she couldn't back down. "We're not like that, you know?"

"And you're a half-Fae," he said with malice in his voice. His quill screeched against the paper, ripping it. His eyes found hers, swirling with darkness. "Do you know what we do with half-breeds where I'm from?"

She gulped but met his stare. "I've heard stories."

"I assure you, it's worse than your imagination has been fed."

Kerrigan glared but sank back into her chair again. This conversation was going nowhere.

"Do they always take this long?" Fordham asked what felt like hours later.

"Oh, so now you want my counsel?"

He scowled at her and returned to the paper. He'd discarded a handful of them already.

She sighed. "I don't know how long it normally takes. There are a lot of potential competitors this year. More than the last time there was a tournament. With five dragons up for grabs, there are better odds of joining the Society. Last time, there were only three, and well, you know."

He arched an eyebrow in question.

"You do know, right?"

He said nothing. Either he was playing coy, or he actually didn't know what had been happening in Kinkadia the last five years.

"Only one Society member attained a dragon and moved forward into the year of training. The Society is eager to have a larger entering class."

"Your perspective is enlightening," he said with a note of sarcasm.

Ah, so he *had* known. She glared right back at him.

A knock sounded on the door, disrupting their standoff. Kerrigan jumped to her feet and wrenched it open. A Society member dressed in their long black robes stood before them— Mistress Cressida.

"Fordham Ollivier, you have been called for testing."

Fordham was already on his feet. Fire danced at his hands as he obliterated whatever he had been writing. He left the last embers to burn and strode toward the woman.

"Wait here for the outcome," Cressida said to Kerrigan. "If he is dismissed, you will escort him out."

Kerrigan agreed then sat back down. Her knee jiggled anxiously as she waited for the outcome. She couldn't stand it any longer. She stood from her seat and paced over to the table. Most of the pages had been burned to a crisp. Only a thin layer of black ash remained behind. But there was one page where the flames had gone out too soon, curling the edges of the paper. He must have released his magic before it could complete his work.

Only a few lines were visible. And she furrowed her brow in confusion as she read them once, twice, three times through.

> *Red rivulets run down his spine.*
> *Her tears gouge canyons into her cheeks.*
> *Black eyes watch, unceasing.*
> *Unceasing.*

Kerrigan shuddered at the imagery. Was this poetry? Did the princeling write dark, vivid poetry?

It felt wrong somehow to read this. She hadn't known what

he'd been doing, but she certainly hadn't imagined him to be an artist. Could someone from the House of Shadows find art in their darkness?

It made her feel a little sick.

She snapped her fingers, and a small flame appeared in her hand. She cupped the remaining page. The fire burned it down to ashes. As if it had never been.

"Kerrigan," Mistress Cressida said.

She whipped around as if she had been doing something wrong. "Yes?"

"Fordham passed through to the tournament. I am going to escort him. He is the last. You can return to the House of Dragons."

"Of course. Thank you."

Mistress Cressida smiled and then continued down the hallway.

Kerrigan was alone once more.

She stepped out into the empty hallway. The sounds of Cressida's footsteps echoed faintly. She should return to the Dragon Blessed, as she had been told to do. She was already in enough trouble as it was. She had to clean up after the dragons for a week, and she was assigned to Fordham, who had been allowed to enter the tournament.

At least in a week's time, she would be through her ceremony and be part of a house. She would get to watch the rest of the tournament from the safety of the crowd. She wouldn't get in trouble for not being there to help with preparations. She'd be a normal member of society once more.

Still, she didn't go back.

Her eyes flicked to the testing door.

What was behind it? No one knew all the secrets of the tournament. Her curiosity was like a living, breathing thing inside her. What would happen if she took one peek? No one would know. It wasn't like they would ever let her compete anyway. Only full-blooded Fae could enter the tournament unless they had a Society sponsor, and even then, with the way things were now, she couldn't imagine anyone ever allowing a human or half-Fae in again.

Kerrigan stepped up to the door. She looked left and right to make sure she was truly alone. Then she opened it and walked through.

CHAPTER SIX
THE TESTING

Kerrigan stepped into darkness.

The door swung shut behind her. She lunged for the handle, but it wouldn't budge. It had locked itself.

Scales, what had she gotten herself into?

There had to be another way out. Just because the competitors all went in and out one door didn't mean there wasn't another way to access it. She'd learned that on dozens of occasions while she snuck through the mountain with Lyam at her side. Always Lyam finding new and more dangerous ways around. Darby and Hadrian coming up in the rear after they scoped ahead. That had been a long time ago. But it didn't change the circumstances now.

She'd gotten herself into this mess. She could get herself out of it.

She snapped her fingers to conjure another small flame and shrieked. She jumped back, the flame going out.

There was something else *in* here.

"Hello, Kerrigan of the House of Dragons."

Kerrigan shuddered. Her heart thundered in her chest at the voice speaking directly into her mind. A dragon. It was just a dragon.

She released her clenched fists and straightened. "Hello?"

It came out more of a question than anything.

"Are you here for testing, child?"

"I…"

Was she?

She had wanted to see what was inside. She wasn't eligible for testing. The Society had rules for the dragon tournament. One, a competitor must be eighteen years or older. Kerrigan had only turned seventeen recently, but still. Two, a competitor must be a member of a house. In a week, she would be, but not today. Three, a competitor must be sponsored. Yeah, she had a lot of doubts that anyone would want a half-Fae competing for a dragon. Especially considering the unspoken rule—*Fae* only.

"I have not known you to be quiet, Kerrigan Argon."

She trembled at the use of her full name. Very few people knew her father was Kivrin Argon. Her other Dragon Blessed friends, of course. You couldn't be friends with someone for longer than a decade without revealing your heritage. But outside of them and Helly, it was a closely guarded secret.

"Might I know who you are?" she squeaked.

Suddenly, the room filled with light. All the bracketed torches ignited at once, and before her stood a great and towering beast. He was easily the size of a house. His shimmering black-and-gray scales were muted in the flickering light. His powerful jaw was level with her face.

It took all her self-control not to scream again.

"Gelryn," she breathed faintly. "Gelryn the Destroyer."

"Aye, young halfling. I am Gelryn of Roan and Fryldran, dragon bound to Master Mexes of Erewa. May his ashes replenish the Great Mother."

Halfling. Kerrigan tasted the word with disgust. Gelryn didn't mean anything by it. He was ancient. One of the oldest dragons in existence. Older even, considering his rider had perished and he had survived. She hadn't heard of any other dragon that had lived through that. One typically meant the fall of the other.

"My apologies, Gelryn," Kerrigan said evenly, slowing her breathing. "I was startled. I didn't know what to expect."

"You are here for testing. I have been expecting you."

She jumped. "You have? But I'm not eighteen."

"The rules of man do not govern me."

He puffed his chest up, and heat radiated throughout the room. She saw him stretch up to his great height. She had seen Gelryn before but not like this. Here, she could see him, the slayer of the Great War. The dragon of nightmares who had razed villages and slain other dragons. The dragon of legends.

"Of course not. I just didn't expect..." She trailed off again. If he had been expecting her, then she was meant to be here. If she had learned anything from her visions, it was that there was a great force guiding her hand. A fate or destiny that led the world on its path. How else could she see the future? "Yes, I'm here for testing."

"Good. Touch my snout, and we will begin."

Kerrigan stepped forward. She had spent much of her life around dragons. She knew their mannerisms and what they found offensive. She didn't think that she had ever touched a dragon's snout. With the young ones, it was too dangerous. They were still learning their fire. And with the older ones, they became sensitive to the touch.

Her fingers trembled, assessing the danger to herself. But Gelryn leveled one large eye at her, and she gently rested her hand on his snout.

Her body convulsed at the first touch. Her eyes slammed shut. And then it felt as if someone had latched on to her ankle and was dragging her deep underwater. She gasped as she forced air in, but all she felt was the tug. Water seemed to fill her lungs. She couldn't breathe. Gods, she couldn't breathe.

Kerrigan began to struggle, to try to escape whatever was happening to her. She didn't want this. She needed air.

"Release your fight, child."

Kerrigan heard Gelryn's voice, but it sounded murky. As if he were far above her. He wanted her to drown. To release and give in to this death. But she'd been hurt too many times to give in to defeat. She would swim. She would kick and flail and reach the surface. This would not be the end.

"Kerrigan!"

His voice actually sounded anxious. Had she ever heard a dragon sound anxious? Not when they were as old as Gelryn. The young ones sometimes. But confidence was their state of being. It made *her* anxious, just hearing that voice.

He wanted her to release. But she couldn't. She couldn't breathe, and she couldn't stop. She was a fighter. If she gave in, then what?

She didn't have an answer. Perhaps this was part of the test. She should be able to release, but she couldn't. She'd fail.

That was fine. She would rather keep the fight within her than give it up for some test. A test she hadn't even planned to enter. She had been drawn to the room. Her curiosity getting the better of her, as always. One day, if she made it out of here, she might learn to repress that particular desire.

"Release from this. You will surely perish if you do not."

Kerrigan shuddered. Perish. If she didn't release, she'd die.

But she couldn't. She looked skyward—or what she assumed was skyward—in this cavern, where she was also somehow underwater. Disoriented, desperate for air, and feverish, she saw a light. Should she swim toward the light? It was a bad metaphor for the end if she did. But there was air up there. Sweet, beautiful air.

It might be the end, but she couldn't stay down here any longer. She couldn't survive it.

She made the decision.

She swam up.

Her head crested the invisible barrier. She inhaled deeply. She could finally *breathe*. There was air in her lungs again. Her head was no longer fuzzy. She felt suddenly weightless. As if she were floating.

She looked down to where the water had been and saw that the divide between above and below was distinct. But she didn't know where *above* was. It didn't feel like death. Though floating in an abyss filled with light wouldn't be the worst way to go. Except that she still *felt* like herself.

None of it made sense.

Where was Gelryn?

As if she had conjured him out of thin air, the dragon appeared before her. She gasped in surprise and then amazement. He was Gelryn, and he was not Gelryn. He was an apparition. Just a distinct ghostlike version of himself. Not the impenetrable, solid dragon she knew.

Kerrigan looked down at her hands and jolted. *She* was a ghost of herself as well. She couldn't exactly see through her hands, but it was close. They had a hazy outline to them. She wasn't solid any longer.

"Where are we?" Kerrigan finally managed to get out. Fear coated her words.

"We are on the spiritual plane." He hesitated, as if in incomprehension. *"You pulled us both through."*

"I did?" she asked. "How?"

"That I do not know."

"Scales," she whispered. "What do I do? How do I get us out? Is this normal?"

"We will assess how to get out when it is time to depart." Gelryn paused over her other questions. *"This has never happened before."*

He said it like an admission.

They were silent at that realization. Kerrigan had done something that no one else had ever done before. That Gelryn knew of at least. All because she had been too stubborn to let go? Or was there another reason?

"Why did this happen?"

"Truly, Kerrigan of the House of Dragons, I do not know."

She was stunned. "You have never entered the spiritual plane?"

"In fact, dragons enter all the time. We are the dominions of the spiritual. The test is to project your essence out onto the spiritual plane so that I might assess your magical prowess."

"And I brought *you* out with me?"

"So it appears."

"Huh. This isn't part of the test then, is it?"

"No." He rumbled in his chest. Fire heating through and then dissipating. *"You appear to be in control of this plane. You were the one who created it."*

"Created it?" Kerrigan asked in confusion.

"Whoever summons the spiritual plane commands it. It would take a great magical user to wrest control of someone else's spiritual work. At present, it seems safer for us both to allow you to control it. This is not how I test my subjects, but it seems prudent to continue—and quickly. The spiritual plane saps your energy. I do not want you to pass out and strand us here."

Kerrigan shivered. "We don't want that."

"No, we do not." Gelryn stretched to his full ghostlike height. *"Show me each of the four elements."*

"I don't have anything to show. I mean, I can probably get a flame in here," she said uneasily.

Magic was a conduit. The elements were its source. It was *possible* to create something out of nothing, but it was draining. That was why, in fights at the Wastes, all four of the elements were provided for the competitors. A lot of Fae couldn't even summon them out of nothing. Only the strongest among them.

She supposed this was why there was testing to begin with. To get the strongest among them to compete to be a dragon rider.

"A small flame will do."

She sighed and then snapped her fingers. He had already seen

51

her do it, but she would oblige him. Nothing happened. She snapped again. Her eyes grew wide and fingers frantic.

"What is happening?"

Gelryn had his eyes closed. He wasn't even watching her. He was swaying slightly, as if to music.

"Gelryn?"

"Now air."

"But nothing happened."

"You do not have control of your magic on the spiritual plane. You only have access to spirit here. It is the energy that moves between us. And when you attempt your magic, you are pulling from the energy to create flame. As you will pull from the energy to create water and air and earth. The energy *is still there, being manipulated. I can sense it even if the flame does not actually ignite."*

"That is…okay," she muttered.

She didn't have words for it. No magic in the spiritual realm. She suddenly felt very exposed. There was energy here that she couldn't see or feel or use, but it was still there. She didn't like it.

"Air," he repeated.

Fire was her easiest by far. Her chosen element, as they expressed in the House of Dragons. Few had fire as their chosen. But it suited her.

Air, however, was what she chose to fight with in the ring. Fire was too flashy and too destructive. Plus, it would pinpoint her as a target if she had that much affinity for the element.

Kerrigan had watched the air Fae train for years by hiding in an alcove in the mountain. She'd hidden the true might of her powers for so long that she had taken to learning in secret so no one else could judge her strength.

She brought her hand up like a blade at hip height. She scooped it inward, as if sweeping the air in a current. She pivoted, flipped her palm, and shot her hand at an upward diagonal. Nothing happened.

She almost laughed. It was ridiculous. That move would have slashed through a competitor's skin with ease in the ring. It did nothing here.

"Strong in fire and air," Gelryn noted. *"Earth next."*

"Is it normal for me to feel nothing?"

"You are not attuned to the spiritual. I would not expect you to be able to feel the energy through the workings. Now earth."

Kerrigan sighed and then continued. Earth was tricky. She had to be grounded to feel the earth beneath her. And she was currently *floating.*

Still, it didn't seem like Gelryn was going to tell her how to get out of here until she finished. She widened her stance in the sky. She dropped into a low squat with her hands between her legs. With a strain that she didn't actually feel but forced into her limbs, she heaved her arms upward as if she were pulling rock straight out of the ground. Her arms shook with the exertion, even though she was simply fighting against air. It was bizarre.

"Good," Gelryn said after a moment. *"Now water."*

Kerrigan swallowed. Water was the opposite of fire. It was smooth and clear and healing. The opposite of who Kerrigan was—erratic, wild, and destructive. It was the element that she always struggled with. Most people had issues with their opposite element. But she had to prove herself here.

Kerrigan reined in her fear. She swiped both of her hands down in a wave stroke, a common move that let a person cup water through their hands and manipulate it like a wave in the ocean. To complete the move, she had to bring the water back up in a figure eight. But her hands were stuck. She buffeted against the energy holding her. She couldn't draw her hands back. She couldn't complete the wave. The energy felt as it were drawing taut.

She gasped and released it instantly. Her breathing was labored, and her fingers tingled.

"What was that?" she panted.

"That was the energy of the spiritual plane."

Kerrigan shivered. "It was fighting me."

"Teaching you." He tilted his head, assessing her. *"There is more than meets the eye. Show me your spiritual attunement."*

"I don't even know what that means."

"The spirit will guide you. Reach out with your soul."

Oh sure. Like that was so easy.

Kerrigan closed her eyes and centered herself as she had in meditations under the mountain. She didn't know how to reach for her soul. But she let her mind go blank. She reached out anyway and something broke.

Suddenly, Kerrigan was tipped upward with her body hovering flat in the air. Something hammered against her skull. A pounding, wrenching darkness.

She screamed. And screamed. And screamed.

She couldn't stop. The pain was endless.

She was going to die here in the clouds on a spiritual plane. She couldn't feel or think or do anything. Just lie there, face up, enduring the endless spasms against her mind and body.

Then it all shifted.

One minute, she was screaming. The next, she was thrust downward through the endless sea, and she crashed back into her body.

She released one more shout of terror, but it came from her own lungs. She crumpled on the floor in the testing room. Gelryn stood mighty and proud before her. And she was a mess. Her body hurt in every place imaginable. Her limbs felt like jelly. Her mind felt as if it had been beaten and returned to her. Sweat coated her body. She couldn't even speak.

"Can you explain what just happened?"

She shook her head. Tears welled at the corners of her eyes. She could barely lift her hand to brush them aside.

"Nor can I."

There he went, sounding worried again.

She coughed and cleared her throat. "What did I open myself up to?"

"You should have revealed the depths of your spiritual magic. You have it, or else you would not have been able to bring us up to the spiritual plane. But it should not have attacked you. Is there anything you know about your powers that could explain this?"

Kerrigan shifted uneasily with a wince.

Yes. The answer was yes. But she wasn't supposed to tell anyone else about her visions. Helly had made that clear. Very clear. If anyone else found out, she would be in danger. People would want to use her.

But Gelryn had seen her magic and energy laid bare. There was something more. She couldn't hide from him.

"Tell me," he commanded.

"I have visions," she got out. "About five years ago, I had my first one. It showed me the future."

"You're a harbinger." His voice was one of awe.

She personally hated the word. She wasn't some prophet. She was just Kerrigan.

"Have you had more than that one?"

She nodded. "One a year ago. And one last night."

He tilted his head. *"What did it show you, child?"*

She shivered at the memory. "Fordham entering the tournament. And...and..." She stumbled over her words as realization hit.

"Yes?"

"A girl suspended in the clouds, screaming."

"Your visions have already come to pass."

"Yes," she whispered. "I also saw a hooded figure in a red mask in front of a crowd."

"You believe this will come to pass as well?"

She pushed her hands into her eyes. "I hope not. I wasn't even supposed to tell anyone about this," she said anxiously. "Helly said that it would put my life in danger."

"And she was right. I would advise you listen to Mistress Hellina of the House of Stoirm, first of her line. She is wise. I see that your threads are entangled. I would not want to see harm come to you, child. But if this is revealed, everyone you know could be in danger."

"I'll be careful," she said.

He bowed his head formally. *"You have passed testing."*

She almost laughed. "What does that mean?"

"You have my permission to continue to the tournament."

"I can't," she said with a sigh. "No one will let me. And I don't want to enter anyway."

"Do you not want a dragon?"

She touched her aching neck. With a shove, she slowly rose to her feet. "I think you all should be free to do what you please."

With a sad smile, she bowed to Gelryn the Destroyer and stumbled out of the testing room.

CHAPTER SEVEN
THE RECOVERY

K errigan should go back to the arena. She should stand with the other Dragon Blessed and watch the contestants be announced. If she didn't, she'd likely suffer another punishment, but she couldn't bring herself to care.

Every muscle in her body ached like it had been beaten into submission. Her head had a dull throb that wouldn't go away. And hunger gnawed at her so fiercely, she felt like she would never be satisfied.

She needed to fix that first. The competitors were brought to a room with a buffet after completing testing. For the first time, she understood why.

She found the room mercifully empty and collapsed into a seat before the table of food. Her hands moved without prompting and grasped a dozen different items to put on a tray. Hearty foods to boost her fatigue and restore her magic. Because right now, she couldn't feel a single drop of the stuff. It was like the feeling after her visions hit her. All her energy completely tapped. She wondered how close she was to blacking out.

Probably too close.

Kerrigan ate and ate and ate.

She ate until her stomach hurt for a whole new reason and the enormous water jug was nearly empty. It still didn't sate her thirst, but it was better than nothing. By the time she finished, she felt as if she could fall asleep right there on the table.

She folded her arms over each other and rested her head on them. What in the gods' names had happened in that training room? Why had she been so curious that she had to walk inside? Had she even been able to ignore the curiosity? It'd felt like something truly was drawing her steps forward. She didn't know what it meant, but she didn't like it. She didn't want to be a puppet on strings.

She had visions about other people. She wasn't *supposed* to have them about herself. Her thread wasn't supposed to entangle with anyone.

"There you are!" Darby cried. "Hadrian, I found her!"

Kerrigan lifted her head and saw spots before her eyes. She blinked them away and saw her friends rushing into the banquet room.

"Where have you been?" Darby gasped, rushing around to Kerrigan's side of the table.

Kerrigan gestured to the feast before her. "Here."

"You should have been at the tournament. They let Prince Fordham through, Ker. It's a nightmare."

"I know," she said. "Helly made me escort him to testing."

Darby shrank back. "You met him?"

"Yeah, he's a jerk."

Hadrian laughed softly as he approached the table. "Hilarious, coming from you, Ker."

"Hey, I'm a lovable jerk!" she said, amazed she could feel this normal after her ordeal.

"You are," Darby said, patting her hand.

"He has a giant chip on his shoulder. And he was mean about me being half-Fae," she said in a whisper.

"That's not surprising," Hadrian said. "Considering the history of the House of Shadows."

"You know the history of the House of Shadows?"

"I don't fall asleep during our history tutoring," Hadrian said pointedly.

"It's all numbers and dates and wars," Kerrigan mumbled.

"I'd rather dance," Darby agreed. "Much more enjoyable."

"What do you know of their history?" Kerrigan prodded.

"I'll tell you if you come with us and get dressed for tonight."

"Tonight?"

Darby sighed. "You do remember that we're going to Sonali's ball, right?"

"I…"

No. She'd forgotten. It felt like a lifetime ago when she'd agreed. Sonali was the second of Stoirm, directly under Helly. Unlike the other eleven houses, House Bryonica was separated into four royal houses that each vied for the throne. The House of Stoirm was the current ruling house under King Mydran and Queen Littany. Since succession didn't go by age but by selection, everyone in Helly's family was first in line. Sonali's family was then second in line. The remaining houses were the House of Medallion, House of Drame, and House of Cruse, each which of functioned in the same manner. Save House of Cruse, which had only one remaining royal line left, and many thought after the disappearance of the princess that the entire line of House of Cruse would fall apart.

Sonali was also Darby's house patron. That Darby had been invited to this party at all made it relatively clear that Sonali was going to choose her for patronage next week at the Dragon Blessed ceremony. It was a real honor.

But Kerrigan had no interest in attending. Not after all this.

"You are coming, right?" Darby asked. Her midnight eyes were wide with the request.

And Kerrigan could deny Darby nothing.

"Of course I am," she said.

She struggled to straighten to her feet, and a groan escaped her lips.

"What happened to you?" Hadrian asked as Darby rushed to get an arm underneath her.

"Just tired."

Hadrian and Darby exchanged a look.

"Fine," Kerrigan grumbled. "I did something that I wasn't supposed to do, and it backfired on me. No one is surprised. Just help me back to our rooms."

Hadrian chuckled, and Darby rolled her eyes. But they each got an arm under her. They walked back like a ridiculous-looking trio and dumped her onto the bed.

"Ugh! Everything hurts. Maybe I can't go."

Darby sighed. "Don't move. Give me a minute."

She vanished, and Hadrian sank down on the bed. "You're a mess."

"Don't I know it." Kerrigan reached forward and tousled his blue hair. It was her favorite thing about her straitlaced friend. "Tell me about the House of Shadows."

Hadrian sighed dramatically. "The House of Shadows are a dark Fae group called the Dark Court. A terrorist sect of people that wants to enslave anyone they deem lesser."

Kerrigan pointed at herself. "Like me."

He winced. "Yes. But you're not lesser, Ker."

"I know that. But that's what he thinks."

"It seems likely that he despises all humans and half-Fae."

"He said that they meant insult by sending me to escort him." She bit her lip. "Do you think they actually meant to insult him?"

"That doesn't seem like Helly's style," Hadrian said as Darby walked back into Kerrigan's room with a bowl of water and her pouch of herbs.

Darby sank onto the floor before Kerrigan and got to work to try to speed up her recovery.

"Well, the other houses and the Society were tired of how the

House of Shadows treated the humans and half-Fae, enslaving and torturing them. So a thousand years ago, they turned against the House of Shadows, sparking the Great War. In the end, the Society won, casting them out forever."

Kerrigan shivered as Darby set her right hand into the bowl of water. This must have been what Fordham meant when he said they owed them a debt. He must think he deserved reparations after a thousand years apart from society.

"If they were cast out, how is Fordham here?"

"That's the real problem. It should have been impossible for him to leave," Hadrian said, his features growing dark.

"Where exactly is the House of Shadows anyway?"

"I don't know. The whereabouts were struck from the record."

"But somebody must know," Kerrigan said.

She could feel whatever Darby was doing was working. Strength was returning to her muscles. Her headache dimmed. She didn't feel like a barren wasteland any longer.

"Surely, somebody knows," Hadrian agreed.

Kerrigan shrugged. "Isn't it weird that there's a place on Alandria that we don't know about?"

"Maybe it's not on the island then," he suggested.

"Then how did he get here? There isn't another continent within four months by boat."

"I don't know. I'm not an expert."

"As much as it pains you," she interjected.

Darby shushed her. "Leave him be."

Hadrian flashed Kerrigan an irritated look. She liked to push him to the point that he dropped the studious little scholar act and the street urchin came back out. Hadrian had survived on the back streets of Kinkadia for years—pickpocketing, stealing food, and squatting—until one day, a Society member had caught him, and instead of handing him over for punishment, he'd been brought in to the House of

Dragons. Underneath his newfound class was the scrappy boy she'd known on sight would be her friend.

"How does that feel?" Darby asked.

Kerrigan tested out her limbs. She still couldn't touch her magic, which made her distinctly uncomfortable, but otherwise, she felt hale. "Better. Thanks, Darbs."

Darby tucked her chin. "Of course. Let's get dressed so that we can go. And leave the work talk here, hmm?"

"Sure," Kerrigan agreed easily.

Hadrian stood then. "I'll meet you at the entrance in a half hour."

"Hour," Darby called after him.

"Fine," he said with an eye roll. "An hour."

⊘⟁⟁⊘

And an hour they needed. Kerrigan felt better, but she still wasn't at a hundred percent.

Darby had forced her into a bath to scrub her skin until it was pink. She'd woven her hair up into an intricate series of braids. Curls fell in precise positions, framing her face. Kerrigan didn't think it was worth the trouble, considering by the end of the night, the humidity would make her hair go *poof*, and suddenly, it would be twice as big as when they'd started.

But she couldn't help but love the style and *wish* it could last the night.

"Oh, hand me that gold shimmer powder," Kerrigan said eagerly.

Darby huffed, "I paid a small fortune for this."

"Then we'd better use it, huh?" Kerrigan saw the hesitation in Darby's eyes. "Never mind," Kerrigan said at once.

Darby was the youngest of seven siblings. Her parents were farmers, north of the valley. And at the end of the day, they hadn't been able to afford a seventh mouth to feed. Her father had packed her up, taken the donkey into the big city, and deposited her on the steps to Draco

62

Mountain. He'd done it out of love. She'd have a much better life here than where she had come from, but that didn't make it any easier.

Darby still felt the pangs of hunger and poverty, just as Hadrian did. Kerrigan had never known such. She had only seen it secondhand on the streets and from her friends. Though she would have preferred to have grown up with someone like Darby's parents. Who had left her out of love, not shame.

"No, no," Darby said with a sigh. "Wear the powder. It will look lovely with your dress."

"Are you sure?"

Darby nodded. "That's why I got it, isn't it?"

Kerrigan took the small pot of powder and gently brushed a hint of it across her lids. Instantly, the sweep of the kohl that winged at the edges and the brush of black paint along her lashes all came together. Her emerald-green eyes looked twice as big as normal.

"Wow," Darby said in awe. "That suits you."

Kerrigan swiveled around and brushed some along Darby's nearly black lids. "It suits us both."

Darby looked at her reflection and smiled shyly. "I suppose it does. Now get in your dress. We're already late to meet Hay."

Kerrigan reached into her wardrobe and retrieved the forest-green dress. She was lucky enough to have made friends with an up-and-coming fashion designer, Parris, who liked to try out all his styles on Kerrigan's frame. He'd sent this one over this morning, and she was dying to see what he'd put together for the Dragon Blessed ceremony.

"You are the only person I know who can primp and preen in a skintight crushed-velvet dress and be just as happy in men's clothing, running her fists through things."

Kerrigan admired her figure in the slim cut of the dress. It had long, breathable lace sleeves and exposed the entire tops of her shoulders. The dress had a slit up past her knee on one side, exposing the milky white of her leg. Scandalous indeed.

"It all feels the same to me," Kerrigan finally said.

"Like I said, the only one."

"I can be multidimensional."

Darby laughed. "You can. But why do you like to fight in that dreadful place?"

Kerrigan sighed. She had come back beaten up one too many times for Darby not to know that she was fighting in the Dragon Ring. Everyone else would be appalled, but Kerrigan didn't want to stop. This was who she was. She liked dressing up in pretty dresses as much as the fighting.

"The world below, in the Wastes, it makes more sense to me," she whispered. "It's more honest."

"More honest?"

Kerrigan shook her head. "It doesn't matter. We should go. We're late."

Darby frowned like she wanted to say more but decided to let it pass. "All right. Put on some shoes."

Kerrigan grabbed the soft gold flats that she preferred and followed Darby from their rooms. They almost made it to the entrance when Kerrigan realized what Darby and Hadrian had failed to tell her.

"What is he doing here?" she hissed at Darby.

Lyam stood next to Hadrian in the glow of the firelight. He fidgeted slightly, an old habit that he'd never been able to break.

"Shh," Darby said. "Be polite. He's still our friend."

Kerrigan groaned. This was not the night she had signed up for.

Hadrian was in the newest fashion in crisp black breeches and a tight black jerkin. His cravat was a soft blue to complement his bright blue hair. Lyam, on the other hand, looked like he'd thrown himself together that moment. As if he hadn't been sure whether he'd come with them. His jacket was askew, and he wasn't even wearing a cravat. A sliver of his neck and chest was exposed from the unbuttoned top of his shirt.

"About time," Hadrian said. "We were going to leave without you."

"No, we weren't," Lyam said with a laugh. His eyes found Kerrigan's, and he flushed. "You look lovely tonight." His eyes darted to Darby. "Both of you."

"Why, thank you, Lyam," Darby said, tactfully taking his arm. *Thank you, Darbs.* "Shall we be off?"

Hadrian offered Kerrigan his arm.

She gratefully placed her hand on his sleeve. "Yes, let's."

CHAPTER EIGHT
THE CELEBRATION

Lady Sonali of House Bryonica, second of the House of Stoirm, had a magnificent mansion on the eastern banks of the valley. Her home was large enough that she had *land* in the city. It was a prominent feature on the Row, the wealthiest area of town for the Fae aristocracy. Beyond the enormous home was a sprawling estate with gardens and a beautiful courtyard. It was a splendor for the rich, while only a few streets over, children lived in poverty. Children like Hadrian had been.

He wrinkled his nose slightly as their carriage drew up to the front of the mansion. "Such extravagance."

"This is our world now," Darby said.

No one contradicted her. Though surely, everyone felt the same discomfort. But this was precisely what they had all been trained for in the House of Dragons. Their education was not merely in history and mathematics and magic. They had all learned the ways of the aristocracy, how to move about them without garnering notice, how to blend in. In six days, many of them would join the upper echelon of society. And parties like this one proved the use of all that knowledge.

A footman helped them out of the carriage, and Darby offered a stiff gold invitation to the man at the door.

"Ah, Miss Darby," he said with a short bow. "Welcome to the House of Stoirm."

Darby beamed in excitement as they were let into the mansion on one invitation. Lyam and Hadrian tried to hide their wide-eyed stares up at the enormous crystal chandelier that hung from the ceiling. The hall stretched on endlessly, filled to the brim with guests in elegant attire. Waiters had silver trays full of bubbly drinks in long-stemmed flutes. They were each offered one at the entrance. Kerrigan took hers greedily. It was going to be way better than the cheap booze she drank in the Wastes with Clover.

"Kerrigan, are you sure you should be drinking that?" Hadrian asked.

She held up her hand. "No lectures tonight, please. Have a few drinks, Hay. Loosen up." She winked and then downed her own glass of bubbly.

The group stuck together as Darby led them through the mansion. She had been here before. She'd been invited over for tea a few times, and her discernment of the surroundings was clear.

Bryonica was the wealthiest of the twelve houses with nearly the entire Viland territory to the eastern coast. The mansions within the capital were the tip of the iceberg. There were four royal houses within Bryonica—Stoirm, Drame, Cruse, and Medallion. Stoirm—which Helly and Sonali were a part of—was the current ruling family. Kerrigan's father's house, Cruse, used to be the ruling line, but nearly everyone had been killed a couple hundred years ago and had fallen out of favor. Drame and Medallion were constantly intermarrying with Stoirm in the hopes of avoiding another war to claim the throne again. It was a big headache as far as Kerrigan was concerned.

A big headache that she had once been a part of. She had vague memories of castles in the Viland hills. Of dinners that lasted for hours as course after course was placed before her. Of banquets and balls set for kings. Even at five, she had been expected to act like any other noble. She didn't dislike the etiquette classes at the House of Dragons because she wasn't any good at them. She hated them because they reminded her of the past.

Kerrigan blinked away the images she had plastered on top of Sonali's home. She didn't want to think about that. She wanted to drink until she *couldn't* think about that anymore.

And then they were before Lady Sonali. She was stunning and the perfect example of a Bryonican noblewoman, dressed in the navy blues of her people, her face unlined, her smile coming easily.

"Darby," she said, holding a hand out. "You made it."

Darby executed a perfect curtsy. "My lady."

Sonali's expression didn't change as her gaze slid over Hadrian, Lyam, and then Kerrigan. Kerrigan, who was accustomed to avoiding the eye of Bryonican nobility lest they see what was hidden underneath—that she had once been one of them.

"I am so pleased you could join us. Come and sit with my ladies."

Darby shot one desperate look at her friends. Kerrigan gestured for her to go. They could fend for themselves.

Kerrigan swept Sonali an exquisite curtsy and then all but hustled the boys out of the hall.

"Shouldn't we stay with her?" Hadrian asked anxiously.

"No. She will be fine with the lady of the house. And *we* should find the harder liquor."

"I like where your mind is at, Ker," Lyam said.

Hadrian groaned. "You two are going to get into trouble, aren't you?"

"Yes," they said at the same time.

She met Lyam's eyes, and they both laughed. She'd forgotten how easy it was to be around him. How it had been before he confessed his feelings. Feelings she didn't reciprocate in the slightest.

She and Lyam pulled Hadrian into a room with an impressive wine cellar. Against one wall was a long bar with every manner of drink available for the evening. Even though these fancy parties were only supposed to serve wine, most parties in the city also had some variety of faerie punch available. Potent alcohol laced with magic. They addled senses, and depending on the spell, they could make you forget the evening, lower inhibitions, cause arousal, and any number of things. Kerrigan had tried them all in small quantities. She was a firm believer in knowing what magic could do to a person and how to escape it. She also liked the feeling of getting out of her head.

"No," Hadrian said when he caught sight of the faerie punch bowls.

"Have wine then," Lyam said, pushing him toward the other side of the room.

Lyam and Kerrigan waited before the row of punches.

He tapped his foot restlessly. "Ker," he said, an anxious note in his voice.

Kerrigan glanced over at him and found him staring at her intently. "Hmm?"

"Can we talk?"

"Talk?"

"Yes. Somewhere private?"

"Right now?"

"Uh, after we get our drinks?"

Panic swept through her. She didn't want to have this talk with Lyam. She'd been avoiding him for practically an entire year. He couldn't think that things had changed.

"I miss our friendship," he said faintly.

Kerrigan softened immediately. Ugh, scales. She missed their friendship too. "Miss having someone to get in trouble with?"

"Looks like you've been doing fine with that on your own."

She shrugged. "It's my specialty."

"Just please, a few minutes?" he asked. His eyes were wide and blue as the ocean.

She wished that she could fall for someone like Lyam. Wished those eyes made her insides squirm. But they didn't. He was more like her brother than anything. And he hated hearing her say that.

"Uh…"

"What would you like?" the woman working the punch asked before Kerrigan could answer Lyam.

Kerrigan looked at each punch. One was pink with slices of watermelon in it. One was bright green with pineapple and cherries. One was bloodred with fresh strawberries on top. She pointed at the last one.

"Don't you want to know which spell is on them?" Lyam asked.

"I'll roll the dice."

The woman poured her a glass of the red liquid, and Kerrigan walked away before she could hear what she'd ordered. Lyam liked to walk on the wild side, but he wasn't reckless with his health. Not after they'd accidentally gotten into the Society's punch stores and hallucinated for days. She figured nothing could be worse than that.

Kerrigan stood at the edge of the room, waiting for Hadrian and Lyam to make their selections and find her. She didn't want to have this talk with Lyam, but it was overdue. Maybe it would be better to get it all out in the open. Hopefully then they'd be able to get past it all.

She sighed and took a sip of her punch. Her insides immediately loosened. Her mind stopped buzzing at a million miles a minute. She knew this feeling. She'd forget the night, forget all her problems. She stared down at the liquid in question and was about to dump the entire contents down her throat when a hand reached out and plucked the drink from her.

"Hey!" she said furiously. "What are you…" She trailed off when she looked up and saw who stood before her.

"Hello, Kerrigan," her father said. "We need to talk."

Kerrigan furrowed her brow and gritted her teeth. "No."

"This way."

Lord Kivrin Argon, first of the House of Cruse, put his hand on the sleeve of her dress and all but pushed her down the hallway. As soon as he could, he dumped the contents of her drink in a plant and discarded the cup.

She glared at him. How dare he! How *dare* he!

"What are you doing?" she hissed.

"Saving you from yourself."

"I don't need saving, Kivrin."

He didn't flinch at his name. That she'd used it instead of Father or Dad. She'd stopped calling him anything else long ago. When he relinquished the right to be her father.

He didn't even seem to care. He opened a door and shoved her inside some sort of music room. A harp was strung against the window. A desk sat against another wall. Lots of plush cushions were in a circle about the room for lessons. Fancy place.

"Why did you drag me in here?" she demanded. "What do you want?"

"We need to talk about the ceremony."

"Why?"

"We need to talk about who is courting your favor."

Again, she repeated, "Why? It's not like *you're* going to pick me."

He looked up at her, startled. "Me? No, of course not."

She sagged in relief. She had always feared that. That after all this time, he'd think he still had some claim, some ownership over her. That she'd be forced back into that sad, lonely castle in Bryonica.

"Who have you been talking to?"

"I don't have to tell you that," she said. "It's confidential."

He ran a hand back through his dark hair, and she realized for the first time that her father looked uncertain. Could he be nervous? It made no sense. He was the playboy prince. He'd abandoned her. Why should he care?

"Have you spoken to Lorian?" he finally asked.

"Master Lorian?" she asked in surprise, wondering why he would be asking about the warrior house. "Of house Venatrix?"

"Yes."

"No, he...he hasn't approached me. Why would he? Isn't he vocally against human and Fae commingling? Hasn't he shredded his own daughter apart for wanting to marry a human? He hates half-Fae. Why would he talk to *me*?"

"All that is true," he agreed. "But he hates something more than that."

She raised an eyebrow. "And that is?"

He met her gaze. "Me."

"You? Because of when you two were in the tournament? He won already."

And you lost. She didn't say it, but she wanted to.

Her father and Master Lorian had been in the dragon tournament together. Lorian was now in the Society, and her father was not. The end. The whole story.

"Yes, he won, and we've had a feud ever since," he said evenly. "I fear that he might have discovered that I am your father."

"And?"

"And he would take you into his household to hurt me."

"Do you hear yourself? Nothing you are saying makes sense. One, wherever I go couldn't possibly *hurt* you, because you abandoned me. You left me at the doorstep of Draco Mountain and walked away. You have no feelings on the matter. And two, Master Lorian would *never* select me when he *hates* half-Fae. He was the person who convinced the Society to put down the rebellions five years ago. I would be a mark on his record. You have lost your mind."

"Kerrigan," he said evenly. "You don't know Lorian like I do."

"And I don't want to. I don't even want to know you. Mind your own business."

"Who?" he got out as she pushed toward the door. "Who are you speaking with?"

She ground her teeth. "Ellerby of Elsiande, if you must know."

Kivrin froze, a look of horror crossing his face. "But you have magic. Elsiande refuses their magic. It would eat you from the inside out."

"I'm aware of their beliefs. But it is not that simple. The younger generations are pushing back on that. They want people to use their magic. Ellerby believes in human and half-Fae rights," she said valiantly. "He doesn't care how much magic I have. And I'd rather have someone like him than someone like you."

Kivrin looked as stoic as ever when she said it. She didn't think she'd wounded him. He didn't have a heart to hurt.

She strode through the door and back out to the party. But she was no longer feeling festive. She couldn't see her friends to tell them where she had gone. Instead, she slunk out a side door and grabbed a carriage back to the mountain.

The ceremony was in six days. She wouldn't have to deal with her father or his delusions about Lorian or any of it ever again. Just six more days.

CHAPTER NINE
THE FLIGHT

You just left!" Hadrian cried.

Kerrigan shrugged. There wasn't anything else to say to this ambush. Hadrian, Darby, and Lyam were all staring down at her as if she had lost her mind.

"You left and told no one," he continued.

"We were worried," Darby added.

"Clearly, I'm fine," Kerrigan said.

"Yes, but we didn't know that," Lyam said.

Kerrigan rose to her feet and sighed. "I had a confrontation with my father."

All three of them sucked in a sharp breath. They knew what that meant.

Darby sighed. "I'm sorry you had to deal with him."

"He's such an asshole," Lyam grumbled.

Hadrian put his hand on her shoulder. All the fight had gone out of him. He always seemed to understand without having to say anything.

But her father made Kerrigan want to scream. She didn't want understanding. None of them could really understand. She needed to get away. Get away from everything in her life that had made this complicated.

"I have to go check on Fordham. He's my responsibility for the next six days," she told them, taking a step back. "I have cleanup later, and then I'll be around. We can do dinner."

Hadrian's eyes were sympathetic. Darby looked sad. She couldn't even really look at Lyam. She'd disappeared in part because she wasn't ready to hear what he had to say. And she'd avoid it as long as she could, just like her father.

Kerrigan hastened out of the House of Dragons' quarters and down toward the base of the mountain where the tournament competitors were being kept. She'd missed their introductions yesterday, so she didn't even know who else was competing alongside Fordham. She'd likely know at least one of them. Offspring of Society members frequently entered the tournament. She'd known Alura of Venatrix and Walston of Bryonica five years ago.

Kerrigan wandered the halls until she came to the line of tournament rooms. Helly had sent a message that morning with instructions to go to Fordham's bedchamber. Servants were assigned to the tournament, and all competitors had access to them, but fear was powerful, and none wanted to go near him. She was to continue her duties to help Fordham through this first week while he was training.

Kerrigan glided down the row of rooms. Some were open with competitors lying on their beds or reading or studying. She could hear the clink of swords from the practice space beyond. Fordham's room was the last one on the left. His door was closed. She wondered if that meant he was in or out.

She sighed and knocked. Nothing happened. She waited before knocking a second time.

"Fordham," she called. "It's Kerrigan. I'm assigned to help you."

The door next to Fordham's opened then, and a woman peeked her head out. Kerrigan froze in place. Her skin heated, and she was sure her cheeks turned pink. She had wondered if she would know someone. She hadn't suspected it would be Audria Ather, third of the House of Drame.

Kerrigan hoped to the gods that Audria didn't remember her from when they had played as kids in Bryonican castles.

"Hello," Audria said with an easy smile on her pink-painted lips.

"Hi," Kerrigan squeaked.

"I believe Fordham left for training this morning."

"Th-thank you."

Audria tilted her head, her blond hair swishing around her shoulders. Her bright blue eyes narrowed. "You look familiar. Have we met?"

Kerrigan remembered to curtsy. "No. I'm a Dragon Blessed. I was assigned to Fordham by Mistress Hellina."

"Oh, I adore Helly. I wish she were administering the tournament this year."

Kerrigan swallowed. "I should be going."

"Of course. Of course. I saw a few other people scurrying around. Everyone thinks he's so terrifying, but he just looks like a man to me." Audria shrugged, a smile lighting her features. "Good luck!"

Kerrigan hastened away from Audria. Another ghost of her past come out to play.

Kerrigan found Fordham exactly where Audria had suggested he would be. He was in the training room, holding a hefty sword in his left hand. He still wore finery, even in training. His black cloak had been discarded on a bench, but his sleek clothing clung to him, exposing powerful thighs and thick biceps.

She swallowed and tried not to think about how attractive he was.

Fordham was stepping easily through his paces. Like he had been sword fighting his entire life. He moved with grace and elegance. A prince he certainly was.

She waited until he finished his last round of movements before striding across the practice room. "Good morning, Fordham."

He whirled his practice sword toward her, placing it under her chin. She stilled but showed no fear. He didn't move. She watched something recede from his gray eyes.

"What do you want?"

"A *good morning* would suffice."

He tipped her chin up, and she felt the steel barely pierce her skin. "What do you *want?*"

"As I mentioned, I've been assigned to you. Since everyone else thinks you're some terrifying monster, I was the person put in charge of your well-being. Lucky me," she spat.

"You don't think I'm a terrifying monster?"

"I think you're an arrogant, overconfident princeling who could deign to learn some manners." She swatted the blade aside. "We don't point these things at other people."

"Don't call me a princeling." He sheathed the sword.

"Fine. An arrogant, overconfident jerk."

His eyes narrowed. "You have a mouth on you."

"I've been told that a few times, yes."

"I don't need anyone to be in charge of my well-being. Definitely not *you*," he sneered.

Kerrigan gritted her teeth. "Well, too bad. That's what I'm here for."

Fordham shrugged as if unimpressed and then began to walk through another set of forms. She didn't recognize these. They were different from the sword training she'd received. She preferred hand-to-hand combat and magical training. Both served her better in the Dragon Ring anyway.

Kerrigan stepped off to the side and watched. If he needed something, well, she was here. That was her duty.

It was another hour before he stalked out of the ring, grabbing a jug of water on the way out. He said not one word to her, but she followed him all the same. He walked straight into his room, and before she could even think to ask him a question, he slammed the door in her face. Gods, he was stubborn.

Kerrigan swore under her breath. He wasn't going to change his mind today. She'd go and do her cleanup with the dragons. Maybe tomorrow he'd want her help.

⚬⚬⚬

He didn't want her help.

Not the next day or the one after that. Or any of the days up to the ceremony.

She was so frustrated with his behavior that on the last day, she decided not to go see him at all. Helly was forcing them together to see if something from her vision came of it. But Kerrigan didn't particularly enjoy being treated like an idiot or receiving taunts about being a stupid half-Fae. He was doing *just fine* on his own as far as she was concerned.

So what if the servants avoided him? Maybe he'd earned it for being such an ass.

Mistress Moran had given her the last day off her punishment. No more cleaning out muck for her. Not when most of the Dragon Blessed were spending the day getting pampered for the ceremony tonight.

Kerrigan's stomach twisted. Tonight was the night. The night she'd join a house and her real life would begin. No more helping to raise the dragons or prodding tutors or etiquette lessons. No more flying.

Her heart constricted at that thought. It was the worst of them all when she thought of leaving the relative safety of Draco Mountain for the relative safety of a house. No flying.

Truthfully, she wasn't supposed to have flown as much as she had. But it was exhilarating, and if it was off-limits, that made it all the more exciting.

While Darby spent the morning soaking in the underground baths, Kerrigan headed up, up, up to the dragon aerie. The wind whipped through the open mouth of the cave entrance. She'd braided her hair back, but it still snagged on her curls, twirling it around her face. She tucked it behind her short, pointed ears. Not that it did much good.

Deciding to ignore it, she stepped inside. Her heart pitter-pattered as she stared at all the gorgeous dragons who were in the aerie that morning. She recognized the five tournament dragons. They stood before Mistress Helly's dragon, Tavry, and seemed to be receiving their own instruction.

Dragons spoke mind to mind, so Kerrigan didn't know what he was saying, but all five dragons were rapt with attention. Even Netta, who was always the most prone to trouble.

Kerrigan skated around the training and walked through the maze of dragons.

A few whispered, *"Hello,"* in her mind as she passed them.

Another dragon offered her a ride. She grinned and kept walking. It felt nice to be up here. She was more at peace here. More like how she felt in the Wastes. The dragons didn't care that she was only half-Fae. Everything *not* dragon was the same to them.

She came back around to the front and saw that the five tournament dragons were now gone. Tavry stood regally at the entrance, his keen gaze locked on the valley below.

"Dragon Blessed Kerrigan of the House of Dragons, it is always a pleasure to have you in the aerie."

Kerrigan bowed her head to Tavry. "Thank you, Tavry. What are you doing with the tournament dragons?"

He inclined his head. *"More training before our own celebration. Do not concern yourself with it. Why are you among us? Is today not the Dragon Blessed ceremony?"*

"It is," she conceded. "And I know that I should be preparing myself for it. As you are clearly preparing your kind. But I wanted one last look over the aerie before I have to leave this place."

Tavry softened at her words. *"You will be greatly missed among the dragons, Kerrigan. You have a true heart. If a mischievous one."*

She laughed. "That seems fair. And thank you, Tavry. I will never forget the time we flew together into a new world. It will be my most cherished memory."

"Would you care to fly through our *world?"*

She brightened. "I thought you were training?"

"I can spare some time for someone who loves flying as much as I do. A rare gift indeed."

Kerrigan straightened. "I would love that."

Tavry waited as Kerrigan climbed up his haunches and onto his back. Tavry was a medium-size dragon, made for swift flying with long, lean limbs. His scales were plum purple, and as she shifted near the light, they gleamed almost metallic. Kerrigan seated herself between Tavry's wings and held on tight. For battle, dragons were fitted with saddles for the comfort and ease of their riders, but on leisure flights, most riders knew how to ride without them.

Tavry didn't wait to ask if Kerrigan was ready. One minute, he was standing on the edge of the opening to the aerie, and the next, he dropped like a stone in the sea.

Kerrigan screamed as they plummeted toward the earth and the great city below. Down, down, down they went. So fast and so far that Kerrigan's eyes watered, tears streaming out behind her.

Then Tavry's wings shot out, and they hovered low over the city. Kerrigan could see the shop workers going about their day. None even seemed concerned that a dragon was flying so close to them. They were used to the movements, especially this close to the mountain.

Tavry climbed back up almost to the clouds, and they soared across the valley. It was much colder than on the ground, but Kerrigan didn't even care. She lay back across Tavry's back and soaked up the sun and the clouds and this incredible life that she had been allowed to live. She hated her father, but if he hadn't given her up, would she have ever had *this*?

"It's amazing," Kerrigan said to Tavry over the wind.

"Truly. You have the heart of a dragon."

It was quite a compliment.

"Thank you," she choked out.

Tavry circled the valley three times before heading back to the aerie. Kerrigan could have stayed out there all day. Forgotten the entire world below and lived among the clouds. But her responsibilities awaited her. As much as she wanted to shirk them, she couldn't.

The House of Dragons had given her a new life.

She couldn't turn away from that even if she wanted to.

"Thank you," Kerrigan said when Tavry finally landed back in the aerie. "I'll always remember this last flight too."

"You are always welcome with me, Kerrigan Argon."

Kerrigan shuddered at the sound of her full name in her mind. Of course the dragons knew.

Still, she dipped into a low curtsy and then retreated from the rooms. A tear trickled from her eye as she left the aerie and flying behind.

CHAPTER TEN

THE CEREMONY

I know. I know," Kerrigan gasped.

Hadrian and Darby were looking at her as if she'd sprouted wings. She waved her hand at them as she hustled into the back of the line.

She was obviously the last of the twenty-three Dragon Blessed who were attending the ceremony today. Mistress Moran shot her a disparaging look before turning back to face the front of the line.

Kerrigan took that opportunity to rest her hands on her knees and take a deep breath.

"Where have you been?" Darby asked, flustered. "You're late. We've been waiting for you."

"I'm here now," she got out.

Truly, she was ready to collapse. Running in these new heeled shoes that Parris had selected for her was not for the faint of heart. But they sure showed off the elegant line of her leg through the slit in her blush silk gown.

Mistress Moran marched forward, directing the lot of Dragon Blessed out of Draco Mountain and through the winding streets of Kinkadia.

"Seriously, where were you?" Hadrian asked, sidling up to her.

Kerrigan shrugged. "Flying."

"Now and not, I don't know, humor me, Ker," he said with an eye roll, "tomorrow?"

Kerrigan ruffled his perfectly kept blue hair. He balked at the touch and swept it back into place. "It was now or never."

"Can I at least put a braid into your curls?" Darby asked with a resigned sigh.

Kerrigan nodded and let Darby work two quick braids into her hair, pulling it off her face and hiding her ears. It didn't matter much to Kerrigan. The dress and shoes and rouge would hide everything well enough. She was used to her hair not being tamed.

"Is it just me, or is it crowded?" Kerrigan asked as they reached the heart of the city.

Irena Hall in the Central district housed the ceremony every year. Since it was a dragon tournament year, it was also coupled with a party for the competitors. It was typically a busy event. Representatives from all twelve houses would show up. Wagers would be made on the competitors. The Dragon Blessed would enter society. But this was beyond that.

"It's not just you," Hadrian said.

He pulled in close to her and Darby. She could sense him reaching for his magic.

She frowned and did the same. It was better to be safe than sorry as far as she was concerned. Darby hardly had a spark, and it was all healing water magic. She wasn't adept at fighting. She'd always shirked the lessons that Kerrigan found interesting and vice versa.

"What's that ahead?" Kerrigan asked.

Hadrian was the tallest. He rose to his toes to look over the crowd. His frown was measured. "It looks like a demonstration."

"A protest?" Darby squeaked in fear.

"Scales," Kerrigan murmured.

She and Hadrian maneuvered Darby between them. Hadrian would do in a fight. He'd grown up with it. Lyam settled back into their unit, effectively closing Darby in. Lyam was more mischief than fighter, but Kerrigan would rather have another person looking out for Darby either way.

"Do you know what's going on?" Kerrigan asked Lyam.

He'd been up with Moran originally.

He gritted his teeth. "They're protesting the tournament."

Kerrigan sighed. It was all beginning again. Just like it had last tournament.

Society members held back the protesters as they passed through the thick of it toward the ballroom. They didn't seem violent at least, but that could change so fast.

A chant rose up out of the crowd. "Tournament is tyranny."

Kerrigan shuddered. Her eyes cast to the left. Her feet stumbled. She gasped as she wavered unsteadily.

She *recognized* the people standing there.

She didn't know them. Not exactly. But she *knew* them. Down to her marrow.

She had seen their faces in a vision. She had watched their anger and their cries. Another part of her vision, and here it was, a reality.

A cold sweat broke out across her skin. She was frozen in place, staring at the faces of the crowd. Hadrian latched on to her elbow and yanked her inside. The doors slammed closed behind them.

"What were you doing?" Hadrian demanded.

"I don't know," Kerrigan muttered.

This was the biggest secret between them. She couldn't tell him or anyone about the visions without endangering their lives. Instead, she looked like an idiot.

"It's dangerous, Ker."

"Sorry. I need to find Helly."

"Mistress Hellina is assisting with preparations for the

competitors," Mistress Moran said, appearing at her side. "She will be here when the ceremony starts. Move along now."

Kerrigan opened her mouth to argue, but Darby took her hand and squeezed. Kerrigan swallowed what she had been about to say and followed. She didn't know what the protesters had been doing in her vision. She didn't know if it had something to do with Fordham or her testing or if the Red Masks would show. She didn't know anything. As much as she hated her visions, she wished they were more specific.

She wanted to go find Helly and deal with this. But this was her night to celebrate. Maybe her last night ever with her friends all together like this. She would tell Helly later. After.

Kerrigan felt more commodity than human.

The Dragon Blessed stood single file atop a small stage overlooking the sea of influential persons. The ceremony was a high honor, but somehow, she still felt like she was on display, for purchase.

Her green eyes drifted across the sea of people. Every one of them was a wealthy, full citizen. More than a few were Society members, though they weren't in their black robes. The room was alight with color for the party after the ceremony concluded. Men in fresh suits and brightly colored robes. Women in elaborate ball gowns with glittering gemstones at their throats and wrists and ears. It was a cacophony.

She found her father standing near the back, a glass of amber liquid in his hand. He was staring not at her but with distaste at another man a few feet in front of him. Even without his Society robes, Kerrigan recognized Lorian's black skin, strong build, and severe features. His wife stood at his side, beautiful and luminous with a medium-brown complexion and a proud tilt of her chin. She didn't see their daughter, Alura, the winner of the last dragon tournament.

Kerrigan kept searching until she found Ellerby. He was a short, aging man with a bald patch at the top of his head. He hunched forward slightly with a curved spine, and he had his customary cane in his hand. People speculated that he was arched so because he refused to use his magic. That not using it withered the person from the inside. Kerrigan had no idea if that was true. People would say anything to condemn someone without magic.

By the time Mistress Moran took the stage, Helly still wasn't in attendance. Kerrigan frowned. She wondered where Helly was. Should she have broken protocol to tell her about the protest being the one from her vision? Unease settled deeper into her bones.

"Ladies and gentlemen, thank you so much for attending the annual Dragon Blessed ceremony," Mistress Moran said. "As you know, we at the House of Dragons take great pride in the young souls that we are able to assist within Draco Mountain. The twenty-three bright minds you see before you have lived and worked inside the mountain alongside Society members and dragons. Their training has been extensive, and we're pleased with the educational advancement of each and every one of our pupils."

The crowd applauded the introduction. Kerrigan's heart lightened at the words. They were likely scripted, but from Moran, they were heartfelt. She'd meant everything she said. Even though Kerrigan had been a thorn in her side, she still was proud of her on this day.

"Thousands of years before we stood on Alandrian soil, dragons ruled the island. Our history was fraught, the battles plentiful. Too many Fae and dragons alike died from those ancient battles. But it was one Fae maiden, Irena, who turned the tide of history. She negotiated a compromise, a truce, with the great dragon Ferrinix. And out of that came the first ever dragon bond. Fae and dragon linked until death. Anyone who would take a bond or bow to the supremacy of the dragon-bound society could live in peace. The Irena Bargain still lives today," Mistress Moran said, quoting their history in hushed, worshipful tones. "And because of Irena's great bravery, the Society rules all of Alandria. From the western forests of Woodloch to the eastern shores of Viland. From the high northern mountains of Tosin all the way to the plains of Moran."

Mistress Moran respectfully bowed her head at the mention of her namesake.

"The houses moved throughout the land, bound to the Dragon Society and its new government, and eventually settled to the twelve that we know and love today. In Woodloch, the warrior houses, Venatrix, Herasi, and Galanthea. In Viland, the healing houses, Bryonica, Concha, and Ibarra. In Tosin, the efficiency houses, Zavala, Sayair, and Erewa. And in Moran, the houses that resist magic's call, Elsiande, Aude, and Genoa."

Each time she called a house, the room applauded for their own.

"And because of the supremacy of the Society, we are able to help those who need it most with this bridge between the two—the House of Dragons." She swept her arm out to gesture to her students. "They are the bridge. They are the future. Let us celebrate them crossing that divide now."

The applause was deafening. Moran's call for their support and their nationalism brought the house down.

Kerrigan beamed with the rest of the crowd. Her feelings of unease dissipated as the ceremony officially commenced. This was what she had been raised for. This was the moment she had been waiting for. Today, she would fulfill her duty to the Society. She would be her own Irena Bargain.

Once the applause died down, Moran continued, "We'll begin with this end." She pointed to where Darby stood at the other end of the room. They'd been immediately separated and put into lines. "Darby."

Darby jolted as if she'd been struck by lightning. Fear blossomed on her face as she took stuttering steps forward to where Moran stood. Kerrigan didn't know why she looked so afraid. She knew who was going to be claiming her and for what house.

"Darby is training to be a healer," Moran told the crowd. "She's dutiful, proficient, and kind. She loves etiquette classes and dancing. Who here has chosen Darby?"

Slowly, a figure materialized out of the crowd. Sonali was dressed in the dark blues of Bryonica. Her gown was regal and beyond reproach. She looked like a princess out of legend.

"I have chosen Darby." She smiled softly and tipped her chin at Darby. "If you will have me?"

"Yes," Darby squeaked.

A small titter of laughter came from the crowd. Darby gulped and looked even more frightened as Sonali strode up the steps of the stage. She gently withdrew a sapphire ring from her own finger and slid it onto Darby's. The house ring of Stoirm. Gods.

"Come," Sonali said gently, and Darby followed her off the stage and into the crowd below.

And so the ceremony continued. Twenty-three of the House of Dragons' best. Kerrigan knew every one of the people selected and cheered for them as they were chosen and moved on. Lyam went to Kenris in Zavala in the north. A peach Zavalan cloth square was placed into the pocket of his suit. He looked positively radiant. His eyes darted back to Kerrigan once before continuing through the crowd. Ayesha went to Genoa, Hainfroy to Venatrix, Elenee to Concha. And on and on.

Until it reached Hadrian, who had gone positively green in the face.

"Hadrian," Moran said.

He stepped forward, and Moran spoke all about his intelligence and studiousness. He'd been courting Javel with Sayair in the north. They had one of the greatest libraries outside of Draco Mountain. It was Hadrian's dream to become a scholar.

But when Javel stepped forward, *another* person stepped forward too.

Fallon of Galanthea.

Kerrigan's eyes widened in shock. This didn't happen. The negotiations were usually complete before the ceremony to prevent this. And to have *Galanthea*, a war house, requesting Hadrian. It was unthinkable. What could they even offer?

Of course, Fallon was different. He'd been part of the last dragon tournament, but he hadn't won. He was attempting to change the makeup of Galanthea. But still...*Hadrian*?

"I have chosen Hadrian," Javel said quickly, glaring at Fallon.

"I have also chosen Hadrian," Fallon added. His voice was smooth and confident. Gone was the terrified boy who had entered the tournament five years earlier.

"This is quite unusual," Moran said diplomatically. She looked to Hadrian with a raised eyebrow as if to say, *Your choice.*

No wonder Hadrian had looked sick. He must have known this was going to happen.

"I..." Hadrian said, looking between the two men who would claim him. "I choose..." He stumbled backward a step and then said everything in a rush. "I choose Fallon."

Moran laughed softly. "Fallon of Galanthea, step forward, please."

Fallon put his hand on Javel's shoulder. An unspoken truce between them for the slight. Then he came to stand before Hadrian. They were nearly eye level, Fallon standing only an inch taller. He retrieved a gold torc from his suit pocket, and with the tenderness of a lover, he wrapped the gold Galanthean collar around Hadrian's throat. His throat bobbed, and then he followed Fallon offstage.

The next three candidates went without fanfare. And then it was Kerrigan's turn. She was the last one onstage. Everyone was staring at her messy red hair and slightly scandalous pink dress as she stepped evenly, carefully on her new high heels to Moran.

Even though she and Moran had had their ups and downs

throughout the years, she gave her an encouraging smile. Kerrigan turned to face the crowd.

"Kerrigan is spunky and spontaneous. She loves weapons training and reading. She is fiercely loyal and fiercely competitive. Who here has chosen Kerrigan?"

Her heart raced as her eyes scanned the crowd for Ellerby. He'd been standing off to the right when it all started. But as the ceremony had gone on and worry crept through her, she'd lost him to her blurry vision and fear.

Now she couldn't find him.

He wasn't there.

CHAPTER ELEVEN
THE OFFER

No one came forward.

Kerrigan's hands were sweating at her sides. Her throat felt like she'd stuffed cotton balls down it. Her body was frozen in place.

And then she heard it. Laughter. People in the crowd were *laughing* at her.

Tears pricked at the corners of her eyes as shame and humiliation followed sharply. Like pinpricks turning to knife wounds. She didn't want to cry. *No*, she couldn't cry. Not here. Not before these people.

Her ears were ringing. This couldn't be right. What had happened? Why would Ellerby have left?

"Now, now," Moran admonished the crowd.

But Kerrigan was still standing there. She was still looking out at the sea of faces. And no one stepped forward. No one claimed her.

One word cut through the crowd—*half-Fae*.

Half-Fae.

Was that the reason this was happening? Had someone decided that half-Fae shouldn't enter a house? Did Ellerby think that? He'd never made it seem that way in the past. He'd always been perfectly fine with her short ears and didn't even care about magic. Everything had calmed down so much in the last five years; she'd been sure it wouldn't matter.

Or was she wrong? Had things just appeared to calm down?

Hadn't she been attacked by Basem Nix in an alleyway for having the audacity to be half and beat him? Hadn't he called her a leatha?

And of course, she'd *known*. She'd certainly known it wasn't great. She hid her magic and her ears enough to know. But it was one thing to know and another thing to *know*.

To be standing on a stage in front of hundreds of people and not be chosen. To be laughed at.

"I…" she muttered.

She needed to get out of here. She didn't want to be their amusement.

Her father stepped forward, and she shook her head once. Because if this wasn't humiliating enough, having her father vouch for her might be worse. She didn't want to be shackled to him for any reason.

She was ready to rush off that horrible stage when the doors to the ceremony room burst open. Everyone wrenched away from Kerrigan's fate to see who had entered.

It was a disheveled Helly, her eyes wide, her hair out of its tight bun.

"The protests have turned into riots. We need more security to hold them back. Quickly!" Helly cried.

The party fell apart in a matter of minutes. Dragon Blessed were left behind by their newly chosen families. Society members burst through the crowd toward Helly. Even Moran, who was hardly a fighter, hastened off the stage.

Kerrigan was left standing all alone. At least now no one was paying attention to her.

She strode away from her friends and off the stage. She didn't know where she was going or what she had in mind. She needed to get *away*. Away from the life she'd thought she knew and the humiliating laughter from the crowd and the slimy feeling of standing onstage and no one choosing her.

But then she heard her name, and she stalled.

Helly ran to her side. "Kerrigan, the protest…"

"Yes," she said at once before Helly could ask the question about her visions. "I wanted to find you when I first got here."

"And the Red Masks?" Helly asked, pitching her voice lower.

"I don't know. I don't know if it's the same protest as what I saw. But it could be, Helly," Kerrigan whispered.

Helly sighed. "At least I know it is one and the same. It must mean that this is the beginning."

"The beginning of what?"

"That, we will see," Helly said evenly. She shook herself. "You were still onstage with Moran when I burst in. Was the ceremony not complete?"

"Oh, it was finished," Kerrigan said viciously.

Helly cocked her head to the side. "What happened?"

"No one chose me."

Helly frowned. "That's impossible."

Kerrigan shot her a deadly look. "I do not jest."

"Helly!" a voice called from the hall. "We need you to direct people."

Helly waved at them. Her gaze was still on Kerrigan. "We will figure this out," she told her confidently. "After this is complete, we will find a place for you."

"Helly!" that voice yelled again.

She sighed and brushed a hand on Kerrigan's shoulder before rushing out after the other Society members. The doors were closed and barred from the inside as the protests raged on in the night beyond.

Kerrigan only made it a dozen feet away from the stage before her friends caught up with her. Hadrian put his hand on her sleeve, but she pulled away. She didn't want comfort like this. If anyone asked about her well-being, she might not be able to hold in her tears. The shape of humiliation still raged through her stomach, and she didn't wish to unleash it until she was well and truly alone.

"Kerrigan, I'm so sorry," Darby whispered.

"We never expected this to happen. Not in a million years," Hadrian said.

"No," Kerrigan agreed. "In fact, it hasn't happened in the nearly thousand years since the inception of the House of Dragons."

"It's bullshit," Lyam snapped, sharp as a whip.

That almost dragged a smile from her features.

"Lyam," Darby admonished.

"It's true," he cut right in. "The whole thing is beneath the House of Dragons and the Society. They should have never let that happen."

"He's right," Hadrian said softly. "I don't know how it could have happened. You had already negotiated with Ellerby. He'd been your choice for months."

"Yeah, and then he disappeared right before my turn came," Kerrigan told them.

Darby blinked in surprise. "He disappeared?"

"Yes. He just vanished. Left the room before he could pick me."

"That's odd."

"Sabotage?" Lyam questioned.

Kerrigan shrugged. "Or a change of heart because of these." She swept aside the braids in her hair and revealed her slightly pointed ears.

Darby bit her lip. "It can't be. That's the lowest of the low."

"You don't know what it's like out there, Darbs."

Hadrian cut in. "We don't. But the Society is honorable. They would never have let that happen. They took you in, knowing you were half."

"And things have changed," Kerrigan reminded them. She gestured to the protests outside. "That isn't normal either."

"But they're not protesting you," Lyam said. "They're protesting the tournament."

"And you do remember the last time people protested the tournament?"

Her friends collectively fell silent. They remembered. They remembered that fateful night. She had come back bruised and bloody. Lucky not to be dead. Her world had never been the same.

"I can't just stand here," Kerrigan finally said. "I need to go see what's happening with the protests."

"What?" Hadrian asked.

"Kerrigan, wait here. The Society will handle it."

Maybe they would, but she hated standing around and feeling useless. She needed to do something. She had enough magic to help the Society if the protests got out of hand. And she wanted to be there to see if her vision came true. If the red-masked figure appeared again.

"There's a back way out," Kerrigan said.

They'd walked every inch of this building in the years before. Younger Dragon Blessed always helped prepare the ceremony, as surely as they had this year.

"Kerrigan, don't go," Darby said.

"Come with me."

Darby shook her head. Kerrigan saw in Hadrian's eyes that he couldn't do it. When she turned to Lyam, she was expecting a similar no from him. He'd lost so much of his edge of adventure in the last year. One day, he'd been her right hand, and the next, he'd confessed his feelings and been determined to protect her.

But what she saw on his face today was what she remembered from so many years in the past. She couldn't help her own face from mirroring it.

"I'll go," he agreed.

"Lyam!" Hadrian and Darby said together.

"We'll be back soon," Lyam told them.

And they were off. They passed through the crowd barred inside, slipped through a side exit into a servants' corridor, and then followed it until they reached a back entrance. Lyam unbarred the door as Kerrigan used her magic to lift the lock. It would be dangerous to leave it without barring the door again, but it was much harder to do magic when she couldn't see. Instead, she flicked her wrist and put a bit of rock against the handle. She spelled it so that if someone tried to open the door, she would be alerted. It was a trick that she'd learned while living in the House of Dragons when everyone wanted to sneak into one another's rooms.

"If something happens, we can rush back," she told Lyam.

He grinned. "We should be quick."

Kerrigan agreed. The pair slunk through the shadows. They couldn't get too close to what was happening. Kerrigan was far from inconspicuous. She was still in her pink party gown, and if that wasn't enough, her red hair was a beacon. Together, they crept along the side of the building and turned the corner to catch sight of what was transpiring.

Kerrigan was almost disappointed to see the Society members working in perfect synchronicity. The humans she'd witnessed were being herded back into orderly lines, save for a few who had clearly acted violently. The Society Guard were hauling about a dozen past Kerrigan and Lyam's hiding spot. Her gaze was trained on those people as she wondered if they were the same ones from her vision. There had to be a reason that she had seen them, seen this whole protest.

The visions showed episodes of importance. They showed what would happen but not why it mattered. But this moment had significance.

"Kerrigan," Lyam hissed through his teeth.

And then she saw exactly what she had been looking for. Not the protesters in her vision but *Clover*.

CHAPTER TWELVE
THE ARREST

Clover was being arrested by the Society Guard.

Kerrigan couldn't fathom it. Clover, who was her closest friend outside the ranks of the establishment, who always saw Kerrigan exactly how she was, who had never seemed violent a day in her life. It was unfathomable.

"You can't do anything," Lyam said. "I know that look in your eye."

"I can't let her go to *jail*," she hissed low as the guards continued toward their location.

The main holding facility for the city of Kinkadia was only a few blocks from here. That was likely where they were being taken. She could guess that they'd spend twenty-four hours there and then pay a fine. Clover didn't have money. Everything she had belonged to Dozan, and Dozan didn't bail out criminals. He was too motivated by greed for that.

If Clover went to jail and couldn't pay her fine, they'd hold her in menial labor until she could. Who knew how long *that* would be? A week? Two weeks? A month?

Kerrigan couldn't let it happen. It was dangerous and irresponsible and utterly foolish, but still, she couldn't stand by and do nothing.

The jail time might actually kill Clover, considering her reliance on loch. The withdrawal alone was one of the biggest killers in Kinkadia.

"Do you at least have a plan?" Lyam groaned.

"Don't get caught?"

"That's not a plan. That's a…"

But Kerrigan never heard him finish. She dragged her magic up to the surface. Way more than she usually utilized at once. Definitely more than she ever showed in the Wastes. Fire was her primary element, but she didn't want to hurt anyone. Instead, she let loose her earth magic, a low rumble through the stones in front of the prisoners.

The guards halted in place in confusion. There were only three of them for the entire lot of insurrectionists. Since they were all chained together in magic-dampening manacles, it wasn't likely that any of them could possibly get away. Not without help.

Kerrigan increased the intensity of the pressure on the stones around them. She broadened the span of the shakes to encompass more and more of the surrounding area.

She heard the call go up in a tremulous shout. "Earthquake!"

The valley of Kinkadia was prone to them. And even though this was a fake one, no one could really tell the difference unless they had the ability to sense magic. Which was incredibly rare. She was lucky that none of those guards could do it. Though guards weren't typically chosen for their magical aptitude. They had the Society to do that.

As everyone feared her fake earthquake, she sent a spear of wind straight to the manacle holding Clover's hands together before her. The manacles opened with a decidedly satisfying *clink*.

Clover's head popped up in shock. She looked left and right, assessing the situation and trying to determine how this had happened. But she was too smart to wait and find out. She dropped the manacles like a ton of bricks and darted through the next alley. A shout went up from the guards, but Kerrigan's magic was still rumbling through the stones. She could feel her magic draining away. It was too much, but her anger fueled its continuation until she was sure that Clover had escaped their clutches.

"Kerrigan, enough," Lyam said, grasping her arm.

And slowly, she released her magic until the stones were silent and she could only feel the rumbling in her mind.

"I cannot believe you did that," Lyam said.

"You can do anything you put your mind to. Don't you know?" she asked with a tilt to her lips. It was something Mistress Moran always parroted to them, even when it felt ludicrous.

"Kerrigan, I have to tell you something."

She shivered in the summer evening. She had forgotten in her anger that she had been avoiding being alone with Lyam.

"What is it?" she asked warily.

"I know."

"You know?"

"About your visions," he whispered.

Kerrigan pulled back, alarmed. That was *not* what she had thought he was going to say. "What? How?"

"I was there a year ago when you confessed your vision to Helly. She told you they were dangerous. That if anyone else knew, if it got out, you'd be killed."

Kerrigan went pale. "You've known all this time?"

He nodded. "I wanted to tell you."

"Then why didn't you?"

"She said if anyone else knew, you could get killed," he repeated. "I wanted to protect you, Ker!"

"Protect me?" she whispered. "That's why you've been following me all this time?"

He shrugged. "Tried to at least. I was worried about you. Worried that a vision would take you, that you'd be alone and vulnerable."

Kerrigan shuddered. That had happened. It had happened the

first time, five years prior. Her sight blurred as she remembered it all. That empty alleyway, the Fae men who had come out of nowhere, the vision that had dropped her to her knees, the first assault that had made her ears ring, and then waking up in Dozan's room in the Wastes. Her entire body had been a bruise, cuts and scrapes littering her skin. He'd applied rudimentary healing skills to it, but he was just a human. Not yet the king of the Wastes. Just a boy, not quite sixteen. Her savior. Such a ludicrous suggestion, knowing him now.

"I'm sorry I didn't tell you."

"It's okay," she said softly, realizing suddenly that it was.

She had wanted so desperately to have someone to share this with. Someone other than Dozan Rook. And now she did.

She opened her mouth to say more, to apologize for the last year of strangeness between them, but it never came. The spell on the back door lock *snapped*.

"Scales," she cried.

She was running back toward the exit with Lyam on her heels. She couldn't let anyone see that they'd left the party. She also couldn't let anyone—a protester or worse—enter through the back and cause trouble. It was now that she understood how reckless her behavior had been, coming out here. A part of her wanted to regret it, but she had saved Clover from the Society Guard. That was worth it at least.

When she and Lyam made it back around to the entrance, her feet slowed. She panted as she saw what had triggered the exit.

"Hadrian," she said on a small laugh. "What are you doing here?"

Darby peeked her head out too. "We decided we couldn't leave you two alone."

Lyam chuckled. "We should all probably get back inside. The riot was put down. It looks like things should go back to normal now."

Darby looked relieved. Hadrian held the door wider.

Kerrigan touched Darby's hand and then Hadrian's shoulder. "Thanks for coming after us regardless."

Hadrian nodded. "Always."

⟡

The party went on as promised. The Society members didn't exactly explain what had happened with the riots. Just that things were under control and it was time to present the tournament competitors.

The adventure had dulled the humiliation of what had happened to her. But as soon as the party resumed, it all rose back to the surface.

She hadn't been chosen. And no one was doing anything about it.

Of course, Helly had said that they would figure it out. Kerrigan knew what that meant. It meant she needed to come up with a plan and quick. Something that she could offer Helly so that she wasn't shunted to the side and forgotten.

Not again. Never again.

It was bad enough that she should have been first of the House of Cruse of Bryonica. That her father had abandoned her rather than legitimize a half-Fae royal. She could not be cast aside a second time. The last twelve years had been nothing but trying to prove herself and her worth to the Society. She would not let all that go in vain.

Tomorrow. Tomorrow, she would have a proposal for Helly. She didn't care that it was the first day of the dragon tournament. She couldn't put it off for more than a day.

Tonight though, she would sulk with a glass of the best wine and watch everyone that she had known and loved the last twelve years enter the civilization that she was no longer going to be a part of.

Kerrigan took another sip of her wine and settled into the corner of the room. She was hardly known for being a wallflower. But tonight was a celebration of the champions and the Dragon Blessed entering society. She was neither. No one was making bets on whether she would get a dragon. No one was trying to woo her to become an ally in the tournament. No one was heaping praises on her for being a newly vested citizen. And the whole thing looked stupendously dull from the outside.

She wanted to leave. It had been an hour of seclusion in the corner. Surely, that was enough time. She glanced to the balcony and all its seductions, planning her escape, when a throat cleared in front of her.

Kerrigan turned back to face the person with a blink of surprise. No one had spoken to her since the party began.

"Master Bastian?" she said, it coming out more like a question.

"Hello, Kerrigan," he said with a slow smile.

Master Bastian had been a Society member for the better part of the last century. He was well respected by his peers. Many thought that he was particularly brilliant. She had always admired his calm repose and his valiant fight for safer measures in the city and rural areas. He had been in a house fire growing up, and a portion of his face had been devoured by the flames. A healer might have been able to save his appearance, but his rural village had been too far from the healing centers.

"How can I help you?" she asked carefully. She liked Bastian, but he'd never really taken much interest in her.

"I came to offer my condolences on what happened earlier."

Kerrigan's face flushed a bright red. "Ah, yes. That was…"

"Unfortunate," he said. "I am sorry for your troubles."

Not enough to fix them.

Though she would never say that out loud. Bastian was being kind. No one else had been kind.

"Thank you, Master Bastian." She demurely lowered her lashes. "I appreciate you coming to speak with me."

"Please, let me know if there is anything that I can do."

She suddenly wondered if there *was* something that he could do. Not here or right now, but later, when she put a plan together. Perhaps Bastian's kindness could be beneficial. She would put him in her back pocket like a card in Dragons Up.

Bastian tipped his head at her and then disappeared back into the crowd.

Kerrigan had had enough of the party. She dropped her drink off on a nearby table and then stepped lightly onto the balcony. The summer heat had dipped uncharacteristically cold while still hanging on to every ounce of humidity. It wasn't a good combination. But it did mean that the balcony was unattended. Or so she had thought.

Her feet stilled when she found Fordham Ollivier leaning his elbows against the railing and staring wistfully out into the city beyond.

"What are you doing here?" she asked.

He slowly turned his head and assessed her. She suddenly felt on display as his gaze dragged up her body and then to her face. There was something in his gray eyes as he drank in her features. A half smile twisted on his mouth.

"Hello, halfling."

She glowered at the word. She should leave him here to rot. And yet…

He looked so miserable. As miserable as she was. It didn't make sense to feel kinship with this princeling. He was an arrogant bastard who likely tortured other people like her.

"Not having fun at your own party?" she asked.

"It's not truly for me. It's for the others."

That was true. Also how she felt.

She leaned next to him. "Did you expect them to cheer you on?"

"No," he said, fastidiously messing with the collar of his black-and-silver cloak. It was elegant and endearing. He looked like royalty, even with his hair all mussed from fussing with it. No one could ever see him as anything else. "And you? What are you doing out here? Making mischief? Here to follow me around like a gnat?"

"Are you always like this?"

"Like what?"

"An asshole?"

His eyes narrowed. "If you must know, yes. It's my best quality."

She snorted. "Great. And here I thought I'd escape your winning personality after all this was over." She sighed and leaned heavily forward again. Letting her guard down in front of him was likely dangerous, but she had so little left to lose. "But it's not over. No one picked me, and now I might have to follow your annoying ass around forever."

"Is that why you are out here?" he inquired. "Did you truly think that a half-Fae would fit with all that?" He gestured to the grand party inside where all the wealthy Fae danced and drank and laughed.

He said it with venom, but she heard the truth of it. Would she ever fit? Had it all been a lie these last twelve years?

"Escape," she whispered. She probably shouldn't have, but the word had slipped out. "I'm out here to escape."

The inquisitive gleam of his gray eyes in the firelight was almost silver.

But she ignored that questioning look and headed toward the side stairs that led down into the garden below. There was a hidden exit through a rusted iron gate. Whoever had thought to put in iron was clearly insane. Not that iron *hurt* Fae. Not exactly. But it was anathema to them. Which was why that exit was rusted and never used. She was surprised that no one had ever commanded it all be replaced.

"Wait," Fordham commanded.

Kerrigan sighed. "What? Are you going to tell me not to go? I thought you'd be pleased that this little *half-breed* was finally leaving the party."

He arched an eyebrow and then untied the cloak at his neck. He slung it off his shoulders and held it out to her.

"What's this?" she asked warily.

"It's a cold night, and you're in pink. This will conceal you."

She stared at it harder. "What's the catch, princeling?"

"Just take it," he snarled.

And the command in his voice sent a different sort of shiver through her body. He was being nice to her. There had to be a reason for it, but she couldn't see why he was doing it. He just was.

She reached out with trembling fingers and took the cloak from him. She swept the fabric around her shoulders, letting the silkiest material she had ever encountered envelop her small figure. It was still warm from his body.

"Thank you," she whispered, but he had already turned away as if he had never done one kind thing for her.

She left swiftly down the stairs, through the iron gate, out of the garden, and into the deep, dark night beyond.

CHAPTER THIRTEEN
THE SHADOW

LYAM

L yam shouldn't have told Kerrigan.

He had known as soon as it slipped past his mouth that he shouldn't have said a damn word about Kerrigan's visions to her. Even though she had seemed almost relieved, it had put another kink in their friendship. A friendship that he very much wanted to become more. And that she very much did not want. He had thought that he could reconcile himself with that. That they could just be friends, as they had always been. But he loved her. He loved her rebellious nature and her quick smile and her sharp wit. He hated how much he loved her. And how it'd ruined the best thing he'd ever had.

He had taken to protecting her, to following in her wake and making sure she got to where she was going. He'd thought he had been more circumspect, but clearly, he hadn't.

And still he couldn't stop.

He watched her exit the ballroom onto the balcony, and he knew what she was up to. They had taken the iron gate out of the gardens one too many times in the past for him not to guess her path.

Especially after what had happened with the ceremony and Clover. Kerrigan would need to leave. And he needed to follow her.

"Excuse me," Lyam said brusquely, interrupting Kenris.

He startled.

Yes, Lyam was a full citizen now, a member of Zavala. But the person who had chosen him deserved more respect than him cutting into the conversation.

But Lyam couldn't care. He was too worried for Kerrigan.

He stepped away from Kenris, sure that he would be in trouble for it later. For now though, he only had one motive.

He hastened out the balcony door and froze when he saw Kerrigan and Fordham standing together. Almost intimate.

Something panged in Lyam's chest at the display. At the quirk of her chin and the faint smile on her lips. And then Fordham gave her his cloak, and to Lyam's dismay, she took it. She took the cloak and fastened it around herself. Then she was gone.

Lyam was stunned. Could Kerrigan possibly want some stuck-up, snobby prince? It was absurd to consider.

He could let her be, but after the night she'd had, she was going to be reckless. He didn't want her to get hurt, and if he could offer some small level of protection, then he would.

Lyam stepped out onto the balcony and into the dim lighting. Fordham didn't turn to look at him. He was still facing out toward the city, oblivious to anyone sneaking up behind him. What was he even doing here? A prince of the House of Shadows with no explanation for why he was entering the tournament. It was suspicious, and he had charmed the committee into letting him enter. Well, he hadn't charmed Lyam.

"You just let her go," he said accusingly to Fordham.

Fordham still didn't look back. "I am not her keeper."

Lyam stepped up to his side and glared at the prince. "It's dangerous out there."

Finally, ever so slowly, Fordham caught his gaze. Lyam tried not to squirm under the depths of those eyes, the way he made him feel so very small. "I'm sure she was aware of that fact. Now leave me be."

Lyam made a derisive noise and then traipsed down the stairs and through the garden. Fordham was an idiot. Lyam really hoped that he lost the tournament and had to return to whatever hellhole had spat him out.

Lyam reached the iron gate and chewed on his lip. Kerrigan usually did this part. Iron didn't affect her. It must have been the half-human side of her that kept it from making her cringe. Iron had been used in the Fae wars to torture enemy combatants and to brand those who were enslaved. It was used for so many horrid things that the sight of it, so innocuous, still made Fae hiss through their teeth. The feeling was protective and instinctual. He could no more cut off his own hand than ignore the cold touch of iron as he dragged the gate open.

He jerked the gate shut behind him with another shudder and then turned toward the Wastes. After seeing Clover get arrested, he knew which direction Kerrigan was going. He took the most likely route, hoping to spot her along the alleyways. He knew Kinkadia like the back of his hand. Together, they had explored every inch of the city. Hadrian had been born here, but what Lyam hadn't had from birth, he made up for with gusto.

No, Lyam, like Kerrigan and Darby, had been given up.

His parents had been fishermen off the coast of the lands of Venatrix. They were drifters, those who were not part of a house, selling their wares at market days along the coast and living off their boat. It was a hard way of life for Fae who weren't part of a house. The system had been set up to help the houses, but his parents hadn't wanted to join. They preferred their nomadic way of life. Except the warrior house Venatrix decided his parents were interfering with house fishermen and destroyed their boat.

They had no other choice but to move into the city and try to find a new life. They never found it. After they'd lost everything, Lyam had been left at Draco Mountain with a promise to join a house and his father's compass, and then he never saw them again.

He liked to think that he'd gotten his sense of adventure from them. That he was always searching for the water again. It was the reason he'd agreed to the first house that would get him on a boat. Not that he wanted to leave Kerrigan behind. Especially now.

Lyam stepped out onto the main thoroughfare that led north toward the Wastes. It was busy for this time of night. The street was crowded with revelers, and the taverns were bursting at the seams. A sign of happy times. He remembered after the last protests that the streets had been emptied and a curfew had been enacted, that no one could leave after nightfall. The winter had been harsh.

He strained his gaze through the crowd and saw a tuft of red hair. "Gotcha," he muttered to himself and followed Kerrigan's hair like a beacon in the night.

They wove through the crowd, deeper and deeper through the city until she abruptly turned left down an alleyway. It moved away from Central and into the darker fringes of the city. The Wastes were only another ten minutes through the Dregs and into Dozan Rook's territory.

Kerrigan could handle herself, but he still worried that something would happen to her, especially in that fine pink dress and a prince's cloak. She didn't exactly blend in with the Dregs. Come to think of it, neither did he.

He usually changed before he snuck out of the mountain to see where she was going. But obviously, coming from the party, he hadn't had the chance. And now he was distinctly aware that no one else was out. He hadn't seen a soul since the main street.

Lyam gulped and pulled out his father's compass, running his finger over the faceplate reassuringly. Kerrigan turned right again, then another right, and then a left. He took that next left and then froze. No one was there. Kerrigan was gone. That wasn't possible. Had he been following too closely? Had she caught on to that fact? That wasn't good. He'd been caught by her once, and he'd thought that she was going to break his nose before she realized it was him.

He backtracked to see if he'd missed her. But no, she wasn't there. He proceeded forward with caution into the alleyway. "Kerrigan?" he whispered. "It's Lyam. I wanted to check on you."

But no answer came.

Only steel.

Lyam gasped, clutching his ribs as a blade slid into his back. He fell to his knees as pain flooded his system. Whoever had stabbed him yanked the blade from his back and came to stand before him. The person was slight with a flicker of white hair appearing from under her black cloak. But instead of a face was a black mask.

"Please," he croaked.

"No, dear boy," a woman trilled.

She brought her face, covered by a black mask, close to his and stabbed him in the heart.

He had wanted to see the sea one more time, and now he never would.

CHAPTER FOURTEEN
THE DEALER

Kerrigan strode into the Wastes, sweeping the hood of Fordham's cloak off her red hair. She was hardly inconspicuous today. Normally, she wanted so desperately to blend in here, to belong. But today, she needed to talk to Clover and knock some sense into her.

But attracting attention in the Wastes was dangerous. And she was attracting *a lot* of attention.

"Hey, baby, you want to go a round?" a male Fae asked, adjusting his crotch for emphasis. As if she wasn't aware that he wasn't talking about a fight in the Dragon Ring.

She rolled her eyes and kept walking.

He followed her when she didn't reply. "What? Think you're too good for me?"

Kerrigan almost laughed. "Yes."

She whipped up an easy wall of air between them and continued forward through the gambling hall. She knew where Clover would be after what had happened. She would want the familiar, and there was nothing more familiar to Clover than the sound of the Dragons Up tables.

Unsurprisingly, Kerrigan found her in front of a cheap tankard of ale, holding a loch cigarette between her fingers and laughing with a handful of regulars.

"Red!" Clover cried as she saw her approaching.

Kerrigan's fury topped out, and she threw the punch before she could stop herself.

Clover toppled off her barstool, landing in a heap on the sticky floor of the gambling hall. "What the…"

"What in the gods' names *were* you thinking?" Kerrigan shouted.

The gaggle of regulars went deathly quiet. In fact, much of the area surrounding their fight had gone silent, everyone waiting and watching to see if the fight would turn into a brawl.

Clover clutched her cheek as she came slowly to her feet. "What was that for, Red?"

"You know exactly what that was for."

Kerrigan clenched and unclenched her fist. Clover looked at it carefully. She couldn't take Kerrigan in a fight. Clover might have a height advantage, but Kerrigan had more muscle, and she had *magic*.

Clover gulped as she realized the extent of Kerrigan's anger. "Why don't you sit down and have a drink on me?"

"I don't want a drink. I want answers."

"Then, perhaps," a voice said, stepping in silkily, "we should take this upstairs."

Kerrigan glared at Dozan. How did he materialize out of nothing? Had he known the second she stalked into the Wastes that she was here? Or was it before then, when she'd left the ceremony? How far did his little spies go?

"Dozan," Clover said, going pale. She bowed her head slightly. "Of course we'll follow you."

Dozan's gaze swept the room. "Nothing to see here. Continue."

Just like that, the rope snapped. Everyone went back to their games and drinks and fondling. It was as if nothing had happened at all.

Kerrigan was still furious. And her fury went deeper than how stupid Clover had been, but it was the only thing that she could fix.

Dozan arched an eyebrow at her. "Shall we?"

She huffed and then strode away. Upstairs meant Dozan's office, and she had been there enough times to know the way. She didn't want to sit back and wait for him to escort her. But he kept an easy pace with her anyway.

"This cloak," he said for her ears only, "where did you get it?"

She glared at him. "I borrowed it."

"It has the sigil of the House of Shadows on it."

"So?" she asked, raising her eyebrows. If he was going to ask questions, she would make him work for his answers.

But Dozan gave nothing away, just released the scrap of material. She didn't look back as she climbed the stairs that led to the king of the Wastes' residence.

A guard stood outside Dozan's office and glared at her, but Dozan swept his hand to the side. The guard allowed the three of them to enter.

Kerrigan dropped into a chair as soon as they entered, but Clover hovered in the corner, as if she were waiting to get in trouble with a teacher in primary care.

"Have a seat, Clover," Dozan said as he folded easily into a massive chair behind his equally massive desk.

Clover gulped and then took a small wooden chair across from Kerrigan. "Ker... I..."

"Why don't we start from the beginning?" Dozan said. "Why are you two fighting on my gambling floor?"

"She was arrested," Kerrigan spat. "She was arrested by the Society Guard."

Dozan raised an eyebrow, but he didn't act like he hadn't known. "She seems to be here and fully intact."

"I escaped," Clover cut in.

"No, you didn't!" Kerrigan roared, coming to her feet. "I let you go. I was there. I saw what had happened, and I went against Society order to get you out of there."

Clover's eyes widened. "Oh."

"Yeah. *Oh.*" Kerrigan paced away. "I cannot believe you were protesting the very ceremony I was attending."

"We weren't protesting the ceremony," Clover said, regaining her composure. "We were protesting the tournament. It's tyranny, Kerrigan. You know it is. It's how they keep us subjugated. By making us think that the tournament is a festive occasion for us and then creating more dragon riders to keep us under their boot."

"That is not true in the slightest," Kerrigan said.

"You'd see that if you weren't already so far up the Society's ass that you can't see your own privilege!" Clover snapped back.

"My privilege?" Kerrigan demanded. "I'm half-Fae. I am hunted and trampled on as much as you are."

"Sure. But it doesn't erase the fact that you're Dragon Blessed. That you have a cushy job, working within the Society system. That they see you as an equal and they see the rest of us as beneath them."

"They do not see me as an equal!" Kerrigan protested.

"Maybe. But you live your life in the mountain, and you come here to slum it when you're bored. It is not the same as having lived this life. We don't have a choice."

Kerrigan rocked back into her chair and took a deep inhale. Clover was right. She was right. Even though her way of life had been turned upside down, Kerrigan still had options. She had Society members who would work with her to find her a place in the system that had been set up. But Clover didn't have that option. At the opening ceremony, she'd had to slink out of the House of Dragons' box before she was caught. This was the life she had to live.

"You're right." Kerrigan blew out a harsh breath. "I'm sorry about throwing that punch. You had every right to protest. But did you have to get violent? Get arrested? It's reckless, Clove. I don't want to see you get hurt."

"I wasn't violent. The Red Masks showed up and started trouble, but *we* were the ones who were arrested," Clover snarled. "Those bastards can rot in hell for all I care. Those Society guards didn't even care that the hate group showed up. They only arrested us after the Red Masks instigated the violence."

All the breath rushed out of Kerrigan's lungs. Her vision flashed before her eyes. "The Red Masks were there?"

Dozan, who'd been uncharacteristically quiet through their argument, leaned forward then. "You have an interest in the Red Masks."

Her eyes flashed to his, and something passed between them that could only be conveyed between confidants. Dozan unfortunately knew about her abilities and her visions. He'd seen her faint only a week ago in that alley and carried her away. He was more than aware of what she was like when she had a vision.

"I do."

"I see."

"Well, I don't see," Clover said.

"They were out the day that I was assaulted five years ago," Kerrigan said faintly.

"What are you going to do about it?" Dozan asked.

"Do about it?" Kerrigan asked.

"You weren't chosen for a house."

Clover gasped. "Is that true?"

"How do you know that?" Kerrigan asked instead. "Do you have spies everywhere?"

He smiled that deadly smile that had won him his kingdom. He stepped around the desk, leaning back against it and crossing his arms. He looked smug as hell. She wished that he wasn't such a problem. That he wasn't handsome and powerful and didn't know all her secrets. She wished she could run far, far away from Dozan Rook.

"Why weren't you chosen?" Clover asked. "I thought every Dragon Blessed graduated and got some amazing apprenticeship with a house member. That they all became full citizens and yada yada propaganda. Didn't someone already pick you?"

Kerrigan deflated as she looked back and forth between them.

"Yes. I had someone. He was there, and then he disappeared in the middle of the ceremony. And no, no one has ever *not* been chosen."

"Disappeared?" Dozan asked at the same time as Clover said, "Gods!"

Kerrigan shrugged. "I don't know. I'm going to figure it out tomorrow when I'm not so mad."

"You don't have to figure it out, Ker," Dozan said, sliding over her nickname like a lover's caress. He stepped forward, gently tucking a loose strand of her red hair behind her slightly pointed ear, revealing it. "You know why you weren't chosen when all the full-blooded Fae were."

She shuddered. At the touch, at the insinuation, at her ear being exposed.

"Do you think it's a coincidence that the Red Masks showed up to a protest on the night the first half-Fae Dragon Blessed was to be selected by a house?"

"That's circumstantial at best," she argued. "It's not because of what I am."

"It could be," Clover said gently.

Kerrigan narrowed her eyes at her friend. "You think they were protesting me?"

"You and me and Clover and everyone who isn't like *them*," Dozan said. "You're a half-Fae to them. Nothing more. You're a leatha."

Clover gasped. "Dozan!"

Kerrigan stilled preternaturally. That word was disgusting. And she never got used to hearing it uttered. That Dozan would use it, even to make a point, turned her stomach.

"You don't belong out there," he said. "You belong in here."

A short laugh escaped her. "In here? You think I belong in the Wastes?"

"Yes," he said simply.

Kerrigan looked to Clover in disbelief. But her friend was nodding along.

Clover agreed with him. "You'd be better off with your own people."

"My *own* people?" Kerrigan said in shock.

Her own people were Bryonican *royalty*. Her own people were the House of Dragons. Yet she had been abandoned by all of them. The Wastes had never abandoned her, but they weren't *her* people just because she was half-Fae. Just because she didn't have to hide herself. Were they?

"You could rule here," Dozan said, spreading his arms wide.

"Rule?" she stuttered.

"Queen of the Wastes," he offered.

Her throat went dry. It sounded so tantalizing. To be at Dozan's side. To have all *this*. But it was impossible. It could never, would never happen.

"You would never give that up."

His eyes grew distant. "With your power and all that you are, you could rule at my side. We'd be unstoppable."

"My power?" she said delicately.

"Yes, you're growing into it. Imagine what it could be. Imagine what the Wastes would look like with you at its helm."

Her power. Her visions. Not *her*. He didn't actually want her to be the queen of the Wastes, to stand at his side. He wanted to use her power and visions. Just like Helly had always warned her about. That if anyone knew what she could do, they would use her or try to kill her. And if Dozan was using her, then there would surely be people lined up to kill her. Because a secret like this couldn't keep if she was his queen.

"Thanks for the offer," she drawled, coming to her feet. "But I'm going to have to pass."

Dozan's eyes glinted dangerously. He was not a man who was told no very often. He had expected her to grovel at his feet, to prostrate before him for the mere suggestion of it. And maybe, five years ago, she would have. He had been the one to save her, and in her youth, she had worshipped him for it.

But five years ago, he had been the son of the king of the Wastes, and within a summer, he had murdered his family to take the throne. She had realized rather quickly that no matter how much she idolized Dozan, he could only love one thing—power.

"Come on, Clover. I should buy you a drink to make up for that black eye you're likely to have," Kerrigan said.

She held her hand out to her friend. Clover warily took it, uncertainly darting her eyes between Dozan and Kerrigan.

"I'd think about this carefully," Dozan told her.

She smiled back just as dangerously as she wrenched the door open. "Oh, I already have."

She slammed the door in his face and went to get rip-roaring drunk with her friend.

CHAPTER FIFTEEN
THE BARGAIN

Getting drunk might not have been the best idea she'd ever had. Her head throbbed as she wandered into the mountain before dawn. She ambled back to her rooms within the House of Dragons, rooms she had shared with Darby for as long as she could remember, and still, it surprised her that her friend was up and packing when she got home. Clothes were strewn everywhere, and a handful of boxes lay at her feet.

"What are you doing?" Kerrigan asked. She removed Fordham's cloak and tossed it against the back of a wooden chair.

Darby jumped. "Kerrigan! There you are."

"You're packing already?"

"Well, yes," she said sheepishly. "Where did you go last night? Hadrian and I looked everywhere."

"To the Wastes."

"Kerrigan, it's dangerous." Darby sighed heavily. "But you don't care about danger. It's in your blood. I shouldn't even be surprised."

"After the catastrophe of last night, probably not." Kerrigan flopped back on her bed and held her head. "I have to go talk to Helly."

119

"Looking like that?" Darby rummaged through Kerrigan's clothes and tossed her pants and a shirt. "Change, and let me brew you something for your head."

"You're a dream, Darbs. Your healing magic should always be used for hangover cures."

Darby snorted as she began to mix something together.

"Seriously, what am I going to do without you?"

The words were supposed to be playful, but they came out mournful. Kerrigan hadn't meant for it to happen, but then the real thought came crashing down. What *was* she going to do without Darby at her side?

"You'll make do," Darby said evenly. "Tell me your plan."

"Well, Helly said that we'll figure something out. I assume that means that she'll want me to stay an extra year," Kerrigan said bitterly. "But I can't do that. There's no way that I can endure another year of meetings with potential houses or get on that stage again with the year below us, *hoping* it'll be different than this year."

"No, that would be impossible." Darby struck the fire starter together once, twice, and on the third time, Kerrigan produced a flame. Darby looked at her ruefully. "And where would I be without you?"

"Still trying to light the fire."

Darby laughed and put the water on to boil. "What do you plan to do about it?"

"I'm going to figure out what happened with Ellerby. Surely, it was a mistake," Kerrigan said doubtfully.

"What if it wasn't?" Darby whispered.

Kerrigan couldn't think of that, so she jested to keep from her terror. "Well, Dozan did offer for me to be his queen."

Darby rolled her eyes. "As if you could ever be someone's puppet queen." She looked slyly at Kerrigan. "Even someone you were *obsessed* with when we were younger."

Kerrigan's cheeks turned red. "I was not obsessed with him."

"Oh, you can't fool me," Darby said, tending to the water as it hissed. She dropped some herbs into it and then handed a mug over to Kerrigan.

"Fine. He was rather handsome when I was twelve."

"He's still handsome," Darby said.

Kerrigan raised an eyebrow.

"Not for me! Obviously, I like girls," Darby said shyly. "But it doesn't matter. He's handsome and a snake. You know better."

Right. Kerrigan knew better.

She finished her drink and then passed it back to Darby. Her headache was much improved. She was going to need to drink less if she wouldn't have Darby as a roommate to put her back together.

Kerrigan quickly changed into the clothes that Darby had picked out and discarded the clothes Clover had let her borrow the night before. Her ceremony dress was still tucked into Clover's small room, forgotten. She hoped to never see it again. Burn it for all she cared.

The mountain was teeming with life. Servants bustled through the corridors, preparing for the first day of the dragon tournament. Society members in their ceremonial black cloaks stood together in twos and threes, discussing what was to come. Though of course, no one knew what the first task would be, save for the three tournament masters this year.

The outside world had looked much the same as she strolled through the streets this morning. Families dressing their children in their best, eager to get into the arena and watch the first task. Street vendors offering specials, filling the air with the scent of cinnamon and clove and even more savory meat pies. The entire world was waiting on a precipice to see what would happen today.

Except for Kerrigan.

Her mind was focused on what was ahead for her own life. The tournament had excited her five years ago. She had thought this time around, she would be watching from the other side. Not a student anxious to become someone but a house member watching with delight for her new people, cheering on their victories and lamenting their failures. The excitement only made her stomach ache more.

She had to find Helly. She had to fix this.

⟨ϺϺϺϿ⟩

Helly stood regally among a group of admiring Society members outside the wing that led to the various levels of living quarters for Society members. This part of the mountain was very unlike where Kerrigan had lived the last twelve years. Her world was so small, so confined. She and Darby had a one-room apartment with two beds big enough for them to grow into over the years. The bathing chambers were shared between all the Dragon Blessed, though final years were allowed their own bathing. The twenty-three of them had seen it as such a luxury to only have to share with one another and not a couple hundred other littlings from five on up.

But the Society quarters were another thing altogether. Instead of the mansions on the Row, they each had their own chambers within the mountain. Depending on seniority, they could have a dozen rooms or more to themselves with full attendants, lavish furniture, lush rugs, and even their own private bathing chamber. The Society quarters were warm and hospitable. A place the esteemed members could find a life, get married, raise children if they chose. An allegiance to the Society first, house second.

Kerrigan cleared her throat as she approached the group of Society members. They turned to her as one, most recognizing her from her time in the castle. By the crinkles of their eyes and tight smiles, she assumed some of them had been at the ceremony last night as well.

"Hello, Mistress Hellina," Kerrigan said, dropping into a curtsy.

"Oh good, Kerrigan," Helly said with a smile. "You are right on time." She looked to the other members. "I will meet you in our box.

I still find it strange that I will be on the other side of the tournament this year."

"We'll see you in there, Helly," one woman said and then gestured for the rest of them to follow her out of the mountain.

"You played that well," Kerrigan said evenly.

"I'm not sure they bought it," Helly said with a shrug. "Come. We have something to discuss, do we not?"

Kerrigan nodded and walked with Helly through the labyrinth of hallways until they came to her rooms. She flicked her wrist to turn the lock, and they entered.

"I don't have long. The tournament starts within the hour, and I must be in attendance. As a previous administrator, it is my duty."

"Of course," Kerrigan said. "You said we'd figure something out for me."

Helly's expression changed to one of sympathy. They took a seat on her settee. "I am truly sorry for what happened yesterday. That should have never been possible. I thought that you had someone secured."

"I did," Kerrigan cut in. "Ellerby of Elsiande was there, but he left right before my name was called. And I want permission to speak to him, to try to reconcile this."

"Kerrigan," Helly said softly. As if she were about to issue a blow. "You're talented, dear girl. So very talented. Honestly, I don't know if you even need a house."

Kerrigan whipped backward as if she had been slapped. "What? What does that even mean, Helly? Everyone has to follow the house system. What you're saying is that I don't need to become a citizen."

"That's not what I'm saying," Helly said evenly, her eyes harsh in the dim light. "I am saying that you could stay here and work for the Society."

"As a servant?" Kerrigan gasped.

"No," Helly said firmly. "Please allow me to finish."

Kerrigan pressed her lips together, but panic was seizing her lungs. Helly thought that she should stay and be a servant to the Society. That she should use her talents, her powers, her *visions* to help the Society. She didn't have to become a citizen, because they could keep her here forever. Where she could never have a life of her own! She never would have suspected it of Helly, who had always been her friend and mentor.

"You have possession of all four elements. You are an excellent dragon rider. The dragons love you. And you have your visions," Helly added simply. "Any house—*every* house—should be clamoring to get your attention, but they aren't."

"Because I'm half-Fae," Kerrigan whispered.

"No," Helly said sharply with a shake of her head. "No, that's not why. Don't ever think that. Because you've done such a good job at hiding how accomplished you are, everyone underestimates you. It's a very safe position to be in."

"It's not safe. It's suicide," Kerrigan croaked. "If I'm not a member of a house, then I don't become a citizen, Helly. I don't get my own life. I don't get to escape what my father did to me!"

And there it was. Her entire life and fears laid out before them like a raw, bleeding wound.

Helly reached forward and pressed her hands to Kerrigan's trembling fingertips. "What Kivrin did to you was wrong, Kerrigan," she murmured. "I am certain he deeply regrets what happened. If you wish to return to Bryonica, then I can speak to him—"

"No! I don't want anything to do with him."

"I wish that I could claim you as my own," Helly said with a soft sigh. "But you know the rules for the Dragon Blessed. A Society member cannot claim you. Too much bias. I think the only choice is for you to come work for me."

Kerrigan despised that rule. It would make so much more sense for Helly to claim her, but it was forbidden. "Work for you? How?"

"You would be a steward of the Society. Not a full member, of course, but you could work alongside us. It wouldn't be the first time that it has happened in our history. Sometimes, tournament champions who don't succeed in becoming a rider will request special privileges to live within the mountain and study alongside our members. They give up their house affiliation and merely become Society."

"I've never heard of this," Kerrigan said warily.

"We don't broadcast it to the public," Helly said. "But you know Master Fillion, who is head of the library systems?"

"Of course."

"He's not a full member. He was allowed to stay almost six hundred years ago now, and he's never left."

Kerrigan's jaw dropped. "He's just a person. Not a rider?"

Helly nodded. "That's right. Mistress Moran is much the same way. Though she would be loath for me to tell you that."

"*Mistress Moran?*" Kerrigan asked in disbelief. "But how?"

"She trained under the last House of Dragons' tutor. And she has been with us for so long, hardly anyone even remembers. It's an option for you, Kerrigan."

Her head was swimming. She had never heard of this. Twelve years in the mountain, and she'd thought she'd discovered most of its many secrets, but she was learning that she knew so very little about how the Society operated. But could that be for her? Could she work for the Society as a nonmember, a noncitizen, and still be fulfilled? Could she do it instead of investing everything to have the life she wanted? One filled with travel, adventure, love, and *home*?

The mountain had been her home for so long. But it wasn't home. Not really. It was a stepping stone to what she could get. And if she agreed to stay here forever, she would never know what else might be.

"I can't," Kerrigan said with a sigh. "It's such a good opportunity, but I think there's more out there for me. And I want to get it. I want to matter. I want to make a difference in the world. I can't do that, staying here, safe under the mountain and the watchful eye of the Society. I can't be a pawn in someone else's game."

"You know I never, ever think of you that way."

"I know. But that doesn't mean it isn't how I feel."

Helly straightened at the words. "What else would you do? There is no contingency plan in place for this. It's this or the streets, and you've never lived on the streets."

"I'd make do," Kerrigan said bitingly.

Dozan's offer sat tantalizingly in front of her. She didn't want to take it. It was going from being one pawn to another, but she wouldn't stay here. That she knew.

"I know you would," Helly said, losing all her heat. "But if what you really want is to make a difference, then what would be the point?"

Kerrigan sighed and put her head in her hands. "Nothing. There'd be no point."

"Stay here with me. You would make a difference with us, Kerrigan. I know you would."

Kerrigan's mind was racing. There had to be a third option. Something she was missing.

"Get me an extension."

Helly's eyebrows rose. "For what?"

"Give me until the end of the tournament to have a house select me."

"You've had a year for this already."

"I know, but I thought I had it secured, and I have to figure out what happened. I need the extra month through the tournament, and if I don't find someone by then…"

"You'll come work for me," Helly said.

"Yes." Kerrigan hated saying the word, but she had to. She could figure this out in a month. She could do it.

Helly held her hand out. "A bargain then?"

Kerrigan gulped and placed her hand in Helly's. This was old magic. She could feel the bond snake up her wrist and join them together. One month until the end of the tournament to find a house to accept her, or she was bound to the Society forever.

CHAPTER SIXTEEN
THE JOB

As much as Kerrigan wanted to get started, Helly had other plans. Even a month of lodging within the mountain wasn't free, and she was no longer officially a Dragon Blessed, which meant that she had to earn her keep. Helly had insisted she continue to assist Fordham, since none of the servants would do it for the length of the tournament, and report to Master Bastian—this year's tournament administrator—for any other duties.

Which was why Kerrigan was currently *running* to get to the champions' area in time to speak to him. Only a half hour remained before the champions would find out the specifics of their first task. She was cutting it close.

By the time she rounded the corner and found Master Bastian standing with the other two administrators to the tournament, Mistress Layla and Mistress Sinead, she was out of breath. All three turned to look at her quick approach.

"What is the meaning of this?" Layla asked, threateningly stepping forward.

Kerrigan halted immediately. The last thing she wanted to do was get on the wrong side of someone from Herasi, the most barbaric of the three warring houses to the west.

"Apologies," Kerrigan said, dipping into a quick curtsy. "I bring a notice from Mistress Hellina."

Bastian's bushy eyebrows rose, but he took the letter she held out before her. He cracked the red wax seal and read the contents. He looked up at her in surprise before passing it to Layla and Sinead.

"This is most unusual," Bastian said.

"A special dispensation from the council is required for this," Sinead said dreamily. She was from Concha, an island off the eastern coast famous for their meditative and holistic healing practices.

"Indeed," Bastian said. "I believe we can arrange that."

It had been Kerrigan's gambit to take this straight to Bastian and not to the council. He was the only person who had offered his help at the party last night. She had hoped that he actually meant it when it came right down to it.

"We cannot proceed without a full council meeting," Layla said curtly.

"There is no time for that," Bastian said. "I give my blessing for this. A conditional acceptance. Rouse the competitors and assemble them in the hall, and then you shall report to me."

"Thank you, Master Bastian."

"Bastian," Layla said, disapproval thick in her voice.

"We will discuss this later," he said with all his resounding authority.

"Lorian will be displeased," Sinead said evenly, almost uncaring.

"Lorian can bring his complaints to me. For now, Kerrigan can complete the instructions I gave her. If the council convenes and decides not to allow her this, we will reconsider."

Kerrigan knew a dismissal when she heard one. She bobbed another curtsy and hastened away before she could hear what Layla and Sinead said to argue against her. Bastian had come through.

One month. She had one month to get a house member to select her and one month to help complete a dragon tournament. She could do this.

Kerrigan slipped down the hallway, knocking on doors and giving instructions. "The administrators want you to assemble in the great hall. Be quick about it."

"Who are you?" one boy asked, turning his nose up at her.

She straightened to her not-considerable height, but still, it was enough. "Who I am doesn't matter. I work for Master Bastian, the head administrator of the dragon tournament. So if I were you, I would listen to me, or would you prefer I report you for insubordination?"

The boy shot her a withering glare and opened his mouth to speak, but then Audria of Bryonica stuck her head out. "Roake, are you causing trouble again?"

"Audria, my dear," he said with an easy smile.

Kerrigan could see how he could likely be charming if he wasn't such an insufferable prick. To Audria's credit, she didn't seem to succumb to it.

"Leave Kerrigan alone."

She remembers my name.

It was a silly thought. And still, she couldn't stop it.

"Kerrigan, is it?" Roake asked.

"Just assemble in the hall," Kerrigan ground out and pushed past him.

Audria gently touched her arm. "Don't mind Roake. He's one of the new lot from Elsiande who isn't trying to get rid of his magic. And he's one of the few truly talented magic users from there in decades. It's gotten to his head. He was the best where he's from, and now he's here, where everyone has magic. I don't think he's quite adjusted."

"He's fine," Kerrigan said with a shrug, anxious to escape. "I should go get the rest."

"I'll take the left side if you take the right."

"You don't have to help me."

Audria's smile broadened, her beautiful eyes widening. "But I want to."

They walked down the hallway, knocking on doors and issuing instructions. It took Audria longer to move down the hall since she actually knew all the competitors, and she seemed to be friends with them all, addressing them by name and making small talk. Kerrigan was quick, efficient. Until she came to Fordham's doorway.

She knocked once. "Fordham."

And then Kerrigan's pulse began to race. Everything around her turned to liquid. Oh gods. She could feel her power pulsing and then slivering out of her like a snake. She knew what it meant, the feeling of helplessness that accompanied one of her visions.

But scales, this couldn't be happening. Not this close together. Five years ago, one year ago, a week ago, and then *now*. No, it didn't make any sense. This was impossible.

She was going to black out at any moment. And if she didn't get into a room, away from the rest of the competitors, everyone would know. They'd know something was different about her. They would find out. Then her life would be in danger.

She did the first thing she could think of as her power all drained like sand through a sieve—she twisted the doorknob to Fordham's room, and she fell forward into the depths.

CHAPTER SEVENTEEN

THE FIRST

One minute, Kerrigan was free-falling into nothing, and the next, strong arms caught her and kept her from face-planting.

"Halfling?" Fordham asked, his tight voice laced with surprise and possibly revulsion.

"Ugh," she groaned.

She wanted nothing more than to push past the pain and the vision that was hovering on the periphery and not have to deal with Fordham right now. But she only had one choice—have everyone witness her pass out or just *him*. She chose him.

"Gods," he growled. He hauled her up and dropped her onto his bed. "What are you doing in my quarters?"

She wanted to say more, but what had been hanging at the back of her mind, stealing the life of her magic, was now crashing over her in full force.

She saw a circle of colors. They drifted around and around, blurring at the edges before settling to reveal the four elements—blue water, green earth, red fire, and yellow air. The elements pulsed and then disappeared. The tournament arena was full to bursting. A fight was taking place with all the competitors. She immediately recognized

Fordham and Audria among them. It almost looked like the Dragon Ring fights, but that didn't make sense. A girl came at Fordham with a bright, glowing arc of blue fire.

The scene shifted. The surroundings were murky. She could only see a competitor coming forward and the sharp glint of a knife.

Then it all disappeared.

Kerrigan slumped backward. Her head pounded from the vision. She could barely focus, but she needed to tell him. More than the breath in her lungs, she had to tell him what she had seen. This wasn't just any vision. This one actually made a bit of sense.

Fordham was leaning over her on the bed, his hand against her throat, as if to check her erratic pulse. His head was dipped low, near to her chest, but at the sound of her voice, he jerked back up. The defiant, dark prince was still there underneath it all, but in that moment, she saw something that almost looked like concern etched on his face. And he looked younger, impossibly younger for someone who had likely committed years of atrocities on her kind.

His eyes were so dark gray, like storm clouds on an ever-approaching rainy evening. A lock of his dark hair had fallen forward across his forehead. Her fingers itched to reach up and brush it aside. An absurd notion. This was Prince Fordham Ollivier.

No matter what her visions had shown her, drawing them together in some tangled weave, she couldn't *feel* anything about this. She could find him attractive. She wasn't *blind*. But that was all.

"What happened?" he asked roughly, jerking back as if he had realized how close together they were.

"You need to listen to me," she said as evenly as she could. "I don't have much time. I'm going to black out."

"Are you ill?"

"No," she told him roughly. "You are about to go to your first task." He opened his mouth to say something, but she didn't want to hear the sarcasm or bite. She didn't have time for it. "It's hand-to-hand combat with the elements. Your first task, you'll only be able to use one."

"How do you know this?" he snarled, his eyes darting around the room as if anticipating the trick.

"Choose air," she told him with as much determination as possible.

"If any of this is true and I can only have one, then it should be fire."

"Air," she repeated.

Her pulse weakened. She could feel herself barely holding on. But she needed to tell him the last part. She needed to tell him about the knife.

"Princeling..."

He rolled his eyes. "You should rest. Something more irritating than normal has happened to your head." He rose to his feet. "I have a tournament to get to, and if I'm late, I won't be able to compete."

"Wait," she whispered. Then slightly louder. "Fordham, please."

He stopped for a brief second at the sound of his full name. But then he strode out of the room.

Gods, no. She knew what she needed, but the exhaustion and magic deprivation took her first. And the darkness claimed her.

⚬ⱲⱲⱲ⚬

Kerrigan awoke in the dark on a hard pallet. She cracked open her eyes and looked around the room in confusion. She blinked to adjust to the dim light coming in from the cracked doorway and slowly rose up to an elbow, fighting back dizziness. This wasn't her room. It wasn't the Wastes.

She cleared her mind, and then her eyes snapped back open. Her vision.

"Scales!"

It all came back to her in a rush. The strangely accurate vision that had been so unlike the ones she'd had in the past. This almost seemed

134

clear. Fordham was going to go into the arena for the first task. He had to choose an element. It was like in the Dragon Ring, which meant he had to choose air. She always used air because people underestimated her, and that gave her an advantage.

She didn't know *why* or even *how* the tournament was the same as what she'd been fighting in the Wastes, but it didn't matter. Either she was being watched, or someone else from the Society frequented the Wastes and had taken the idea from there.

But at this moment, it didn't matter. What mattered was the *knife*.

Kerrigan hoisted herself to her feet, ignoring the dizzy spell that threatened to topple her back onto Fordham's bed. She flushed at that thought and then quickly dismissed it. Everything ached as she ambled back down the competitor hallway, into the main hall, and continued toward the arena.

She had no way of knowing how long she had been out or if her absence was noted. Her first day on the job, and she was already slacking. She would have laughed if it didn't hurt her ribs.

Finally, she came out to the back side of the arena. She heard cheers within. They'd already started. Scales!

"Kerrigan!" a man snapped.

She cringed. "Hello, Master Callian."

Master Callian was a tall, imposing man with light-brown skin and a finely kept beard that he took much joy in. He worked in the greenhouse on the eastern side of the mountain. She had disrupted his work one too many times. Possibly even confiscated some of his herbs for recreational use. He wasn't a fan.

"I am certain this is not where you are supposed to be," Callian said.

"No, sir," she said amicably. "I've been assigned to Master Bastian's care for the length of the tournament, and I have to get inside."

He hmphed. "Well, perhaps Bastian can teach you some manners."

He wrenched a side door open and gestured for her to enter. "You're lucky. I am a secondary administrator to the tournament."

She wouldn't call that lucky, but she was glad she hadn't had to find a way to sneak in. She didn't know the competitors' box like she did the House of Dragons' area.

"Thank you, sir," she said quickly and then hastened inside.

Half of the competitors were standing around, watching the arena. A few of them looked in her direction when she entered with Callian on her heels, but they made no comment. Most of them looked bruised or banged up but were healing. None of them were Fordham.

Kerrigan's gaze swung to the arena and the sun blazing overhead. Gods, it was past high noon. She'd been out for hours. She'd missed almost everything. Her eyes sought out Fordham in the arena, but then she was gently pushed forward.

"Come along, Kerrigan," Callian said.

She followed behind him, and he sat her down next to another young girl she'd never seen before. She was taller than Kerrigan with creamy, fair skin and ash-blond hair. She didn't look up when Kerrigan plopped down next to her.

"You can help Valia keep score and run the finals up to the top box after each match. You know where the top box is?"

She nodded. "Yes, sir."

"Good. Now work. Stay quiet and out of trouble."

She pretended to button her mouth, and Callian glared harder before disappearing back the way he'd come.

"Hi, I'm Kerrigan," she said, extending her hand to Valia. "I don't think I've ever seen you here before."

Valia shook daintily and then withdrew her hand. "I'm a steward of the Society."

"A steward?" Kerrigan asked.

"Yes, we're not servants, but we're not members."

Kerrigan's eyes widened marginally. This was what Helly had

talked about, what she had offered Kerrigan. Was this why this girl was sitting here? A way for them to try to convince her to become this despite the bargain?

She cleared her head. She couldn't get caught up in this. The vision was more important.

Her eyes roamed for Fordham once more, and she found him in the arena, fighting hand to hand against another man wearing the bronze metal of Herasi. She really was going to have to learn all the competitors' names. She watched as Fordham whipped around and then made a cutting motion with air.

She nearly whooped with joy. He'd chosen air. He'd listened to her, even when he didn't agree. And he was good at it. Not as good as her, but he had to be better than his opponent. She wanted to warn him about the knife, but it wasn't like she could do that when he was already out in the arena. And what if the knife was for tomorrow's match or the next?

"What did I miss?" she asked Valia, who was dutifully taking notes.

"The first round was five minutes, timed. It's everyone for themselves, hand-to-hand combat, no magic. The first competitor out is out of the tournament."

Kerrigan gasped slightly. "Just like that?"

Valia didn't seem concerned by the fact. "They had thirteen, twelve with the original houses plus the House of Shadows. This is how they decided who to cut out."

It made sense. Cruel, vicious sense.

"Who left?"

"The competitor from Erewa," Valia said evenly. Her brown eyes cut to Kerrigan. "It was a massacre."

Kerrigan shivered. At the last tournament, Erewa had sent a plant to infiltrate the tournament and attempt to kill the competitors. Apparently, no one had forgotten or forgiven them for that.

"For this round, the remaining twelve were sorted into four teams of three. Each team has to choose one element and otherwise, as you can tell, hand-to-hand combat only."

"How do they win?"

"The contest is timed at an hour. If all three competitors are down before the hour is out, it's a win and three points for the team that wins, zero for who lost. One point for a tie if both teams still have a player in contention at the end of an hour."

Kerrigan listened as Valia explained all the finer minutiae of the individual scoring system. She would have to learn it quickly if she was going to help keep score the next two days. But even as she listened and memorized the scoring system, her heart was in her throat while she watched the actual competitors.

A swift block of air here, a roar of earth there, a timed punch, a sweep of the legs. She wanted to be *out* there. She hadn't really let herself consider the possibility since she had left Gelryn's room and testing behind a week ago. But she had actually passed testing to be in the tournament. She wasn't old enough or part of a house or even full-blooded Fae, but she could have been out there, fighting alongside the other competitors. A dream, a fantasy. Nothing more.

If she had pushed her luck to try to get into the tournament, which seemed highly implausible, they probably would have done to her what they'd done to the Erewa competitor. No one wanted to see a half-Fae in the tournament, disrupting the centuries of competition. Kerrigan was reckless, but she wasn't stupid.

"And that's one point for Noda. She's actually quite good," Valia said under her breath.

"Noda is…"

"Concha in the teal headscarf."

Kerrigan's eyes were drawn to the Concha girl, wearing the soft teal silk of her island homeland. She was doing pretty well against her opponents. She looked like she'd had an air Fae teacher. She moved with the flow of the air, avoiding her opponent's fire and then blasting him in the face, knocking him out of the fight.

Fordham was still dealing with the guy from Herasi. They weren't evenly matched. Kerrigan could see that Fordham was superior in fighting, but Herasi's champion had the brute strength of his flames against air. Had she been wrong to suggest he take air? She had thought that she was doing the right thing. But now she was second-guessing herself. Maybe the vision hadn't been telling her to interfere at all.

But then she saw what Fordham couldn't as the guy from Herasi kept his focus forward—the girl from Aude in a crimson tunic was approaching from behind. She had an arc of blue flame before her like a sword of living flames.

Kerrigan's vision flashed before her eyes. The arc of blue light. The impending destruction. She jumped to her feet before she could think better of it and screamed, "Fordham, behind you!"

Despite the rush of the crowd and the thousands of people yelling all around him, it was as if in that one moment, he heard her. And just her. His dark gaze snapped to the competitors' box for a split second, and then he rolled out of the way. The edges of his black-and-silver sleeve burned away as the other competitor brought the blue flames down toward him.

"Kerrigan," Valia gasped. "We're not supposed to be involved. Protocol dictates—"

"Screw protocol," Kerrigan said, ignoring Valia's concern.

Fordham ducked out of the edge of the Aude champion's flames and sent a blast of air toward the guy from Herasi before concentrating on the girl from Aude. Luckily, Noda had realized what was happening, and she raced forward to help. Both of the third competitors from either team were already out.

Together, Fordham and Noda blasted the other two competitors back. Kerrigan could hear the thud from her seat as they landed heavily on their backs. Bastian waited a full minute before blowing the whistle and announcing Fordham's team as victors.

Kerrigan blew out a breath.

No knife.

That was good. Really good.

He'd made it. He was a total jerk to her, but she was glad that he was still alive. She could tell him about the knife later in the next rounds. Figure out a way to prepare for it. Not that she had ever been able to prepare for anything that happened in her visions before. But things were changing…escalating. She could feel the urgency in them. And she didn't know what that meant. She should talk to Helly about it.

But first, she needed to have *words* with Prince Fordham Ollivier.

CHAPTER EIGHTEEN
THE BOX

Kerrigan stood up to confront Fordham, who was dragging himself off the arena floor with Noda smiling faintly at his side, when Valia slapped a piece of paper against her chest. Kerrigan coughed in surprise.

"Take this to the top box," Valia said. She pointed up to the sky as if the master of ceremonies were in the heavens.

Kerrigan opened her mouth to argue, her eyes tracking Fordham closely, but she had no chance. Just then, Master Bastian appeared before her. He was sweating in his long black robes in the Kinkadian humid heat. He took one look at her and frowned disapprovingly.

"Kerrigan, there you are. You disappeared."

"I was ill," she said softly. "But I feel better now. I was going to take the scores up to the box."

"I am glad you are better. Next time, let us know so a healer can be sent."

"Of course."

If she'd been able to move, she would have certainly sent for a healer. Fordham clearly hadn't thought of it.

"Now hurry along, and come back quickly. We'll discuss your role back inside the shade of the mountain."

Kerrigan glanced once more at Fordham, and then turned toward the steps. She would deal with Fordham when she got back.

She took the steps two at a time, her breathing coming out heavily as the oppressive heat weighed down on her as well. Some of the crowd had already begun to file out of the boxes, but the majority wouldn't leave until the final scores for the day were announced. Then it would be a mad dash back to their homes and to the parties that happened each night. The tournament was in the heart of the festival season. Parties and parades and masquerades were all part of the fun.

Kerrigan finally reached the very tip-top of the arena. She leaned forward, gasping for breath. A stitch had formed in her side. She really wasn't that out of shape, but she was still recovering from the vision.

Finally, when she could straighten again, she stepped into the box for the master of ceremonies. Kerrigan immediately exhaled in relief. By some magic, the box was as cold as a spring night right after the ice melted off the mountains. It cooled the sweat on her neck and sent a soft shiver down her spine. The box itself was lavish beyond measure. Platters of fruit, bread, and cheese were set up on a table along with chilled wine, and attendants were available for any needs. Cushioned chairs sat in rows before the open arena window with the entirety of the arena and the rest of Kinkadia shown before her. This was as good as any view of the city Kerrigan had seen inside the mountain. The entire thing was a far cry from the dusty, drab competitors' box she'd just walked out of. The luxury of the rich at its finest.

She recognized most of the faces, most notably Master Lorian with his family at the front of the box, but that was to be expected. His wealth in Venatrix was only rivaled by his choke hold on the council. To her surprise, her eyes snagged on Darby, seated demurely next to her new mistress. She wore a navy Bryonican dress in the finest silk,

142

embroidered with lace and seed pearls. She looked truly stunning. How Kerrigan had always seen her.

With a wistful sigh, Kerrigan strode up to the attendant beside the master of ceremonies. The attendant nodded gratefully and handed the slip of paper to his master.

Kerrigan backed out of the room as the master of ceremonies wove an elaborate speech about where the teams and contestants had finished on the first day of the tournament. She wanted to escape before the crowds. But as she exited the cool beauty of the top box, another person darted out of it.

"Kerrigan!"

She turned back and found Darby waiting there on the top step. "Darby, what are you doing?"

But Darby's eyes were wide with concern. "I couldn't find you after you left to speak with Helly. I didn't know what had happened to you."

"I'm fine, Darbs," Kerrigan said as her friend flung herself into her arms. "I'm right here. I'm working with the tournament."

Darby pulled back and swallowed. "Good. I'm glad you're safe. Have you seen Lyam? Was he with you?"

"Lyam? No, why would he be? Wasn't he packing to go with Kenris?"

"That's what I thought," Darby said, "but he never showed up. Hadrian hasn't seen him either. Kenris came looking for him, but no one knew where he was. I thought that he must have been with you. But now you're saying he wasn't with you."

"No, he wasn't."

"He wouldn't miss this," Darby said resolutely. "This isn't like him. I think he's missing."

"Missing? Where would he have gone?"

"I don't know." She sounded frantic and a little terrified. "But as wily and adventurous as Lyam is, he has never had us worry about him. We always know where he's going, and he always comes back mostly on time. Kenris is in the box next door, and Lyam's not there. He's been gone for hours."

"Okay. Okay," Kerrigan said softly. "I have to return to the tournament for directions. Why don't we meet back in our rooms, and we can figure out what's going on. There must be a reasonable explanation."

"All right," Darby said. "I'll meet you. And I'll tell Hadrian too. But I don't like this. Lyam loves the tournament. There's no way he'd miss it."

Darby was right. There was no way. Even when they had all made fun of the tournament, the excitement and parties made all the hours and days and weeks cooped up with tutors worthwhile. Lyam wouldn't miss this. Which begged the question, where was he?

Kerrigan squeezed Darby's hand. "I'll meet you."

She hastened back down the stairs as the dam broke and the flood of the crowd burst from the stadium seating. Kerrigan was carried down through the stream of people marching like a herd of cattle. She couldn't even veer to the left to head back down to the competitors' box. There was no escape from the masses, only onward. She couldn't stop moving until she was outside the arena—on the opposite side of where she needed to be.

She sighed heavily. This day was not going at all how she'd thought it would.

"There you are!" a voice called from the crowd.

Kerrigan turned to find a tall figure pushing her direction. Clover materialized then, out of Dozan's red vest and in an all-black tunic and pants. Her bob was as severe as ever.

"I've been looking all over for you," Clover said. "You left way before I woke up this morning. I went to find you in the mountain before the tournament started, but even I couldn't sneak by the guards. They're on high alert."

Clover fell into step with Kerrigan as they picked their way back toward the mountain entrance.

"It's been an interesting morning."

"Tell me about it. Dozan is in a rage in the Wastes. I got out as soon as I could."

"A rage about what?"

Clover shrugged. "Didn't stick around to find out."

"Sounds like Dozan."

"What about you? Did you make your deal with Helly?"

Kerrigan nodded. "Sort of. She offered me a place in the mountain."

Clover wrinkled her nose.

"I know. I asked for a month, until the end of the tournament, to find a house that will accept me."

"You could stay with me," Clover said with a wink.

"You know I don't want to be beholden to Dozan."

Clover sighed. "I know. I don't particularly enjoy it either. You think you can do it? Find a house in a month?"

Kerrigan shrugged noncommittally. "Going to have to try." She brushed a lock of hair behind her ear and then habitually moved it back to hide it once more. "Anyway, Darby is worried about Lyam. He never turned up this morning."

"Ah, Lee is probably drunk somewhere. He's a lightweight," Clover said with a laugh.

"Probably," Kerrigan agreed. "But it's not like him to miss something this important. His new house sponsor showed up and no Lyam? Seems odd. And I don't like the idea that he's missing."

"Yeah. That's not good."

"I can get you into the mountain. Meet me in my rooms. I have to report to the tournament administrator first."

Clover perked up at that. "Why do you have to talk to him?"

"Helly said I still had to work for my keep," Kerrigan admitted. "I'm working for the tournament, since that's my timeline."

"Damn."

"Yep," Kerrigan said, popping the end of the word.

The guards waved them in as they passed back into the shade of Draco Mountain.

"All right, I'll meet you in your rooms," Clover said, veering off in the opposite direction from Kerrigan, who jogged toward the tournament rooms.

She was running behind again. Bastian had told her to hurry back, but she hadn't anticipated getting caught in the melee. She was breathing heavily again when she finally made it into the hall, which was strangely empty. Usually, people were bustling around, enjoying meals, and chitchatting. Voices and the ring of steel could be heard from the training facility. After the beating today, Kerrigan couldn't imagine anyone wanting to train, but to each their own.

Administrators kept rooms near the competitors during the length of the tournament, and Kerrigan headed that direction. She was nearly there when Valia materialized.

"You don't quite know the meaning of hurry, do you?"

Kerrigan bristled. "I got caught in the crowd."

A smile split Valia's face. "I'm kidding. I don't care how long it took you. Bastian is just annoyed and takes it out on me."

"That's frustrating," Kerrigan said. "Should I go speak to him?"

"Better not. I swear it must be a full moon tonight. Everyone is acting so incredibly strange."

"I've noticed that," Kerrigan admitted.

"Anyway, here you go." Valia passed her a note. "I wrote out Bastian's instructions so that you could avoid a few moments of pain."

Kerrigan took the note from the girl. "I appreciate that. My friend is missing, and I really need to figure out where he went off to."

Valia frowned. "I'm so sorry. I hope that you find him."

"Thanks," Kerrigan said, waving the paper at her in retreat. "Me too."

Kerrigan headed back through the hall, and as she was about to enter the corridor that led back to her old apartment, Fordham appeared before her. She didn't even have a chance to think before he slammed her back against the stone wall.

"What the hell?" She struggled against him. But it was no use. He was a good foot taller than her and corded with muscle. She might have the magical advantage, which she drew in close to her body, but she truly didn't want to have to use it. "Release me."

"Who is your contact?"

"My *contact*?" she asked in confusion.

"Who told you to tell me that? How did you know it would be hand-to-hand combat with just one element?"

"No one told me."

It sounded weak, but she couldn't tell him about her visions. Gods, she had been stupid. She had thought the visions were telling her to tell him, to help him. Instead, he was furious and thought she was out to sabotage him.

"You lie."

"I'm not a liar," she growled, shoving against him uselessly. "No one told me. I swear it. I swear it on my mother's grave."

Fordham pulled back slightly at that. "Your mother is dead?"

Kerrigan squirmed out from under him, massaging her aching shoulders. "Yes. Most human women don't survive bearing Fae children."

She didn't know why she had said it. Why she was confiding any of it. Why she was even helping him. Except that her visions kept drawing them back together. That much was clear. And she didn't know what they meant or how to ignore them.

"I was trying to *help* you," Kerrigan said. "And it seems to have worked. You won your match. You're near the top of the leaderboard."

"Yes," he said flatly. "But why would *you* want to help *me*?"

A valid question, all things considered. He had done nothing but insult her since the moment she had met him. And she couldn't tell him the truth, so she'd settle for a half-truth.

"I feel like we're drawn together," she admitted.

His eyebrows rose sharply. "You and I? That's impossible. Why would you think that?"

"I don't know, all right? And I'm aware it sounds ridiculous, but I can't shake the feeling. I thought instead of letting you die today, I would help you."

"You called out to me when Kamari was going to attack me with the flaming sword."

"Kamari? The girl from Aude?"

He nodded.

"Yeah, I did."

"I heard you even though the crowd was screaming, like all of it had turned to background noise."

"Are you saying I'm loud?"

He sighed heavily as if she was such a nuisance. "I meant that perhaps we *are* connected in some way. But I don't understand it, nor do I like it."

"You and me both," she said, crossing her arms across her chest. "And here's a hint, princeling: shoving people against walls and accusing them is not how you make friends."

"You're insufferable."

"Why, thank you." Kerrigan stepped back. "Now, I can't deal with *this*"—she waved between them—"anymore. My friend is missing, and I need to figure out where he's gone."

Fordham's eyes shuttered at that. Everything in him went very, very still. "What friend?"

"Why would you care?"

"Is he about this tall?" Fordham asked, gesturing to a height slightly shorter than his. "Brown hair, tan skin, a little annoying, pompous, self-righteous."

"You're one to talk, you know," she chided.

"Is it him? The one who follows you?"

Kerrigan stopped her jest at those words.

"Yes, that's Lyam. But how do you know?"

"Because he followed you out of the party last night."

"What?" she gasped.

Her heart beat furiously. She hadn't seen him. Normally, she noticed him tracking her, but she hadn't even felt him. Had she been that far into her own head, or had he gotten lost?

For the first time, she wondered if something had *happened* to Lyam.

CHAPTER NINETEEN
THE ACCIDENT

For a moment, Kerrigan was disoriented as she burst into her rooms. Everything in her life had looked almost exactly the same since she arrived in the House of Dragons. Two twin beds with a chest of drawers and an armoire. Over the years, they had accumulated more useless stuff to fill the spaces—old books, sheets of parchment, a kite, a virtual treasure trove of makeup and hair pieces and the like—covering all the nooks and crannies. Now the room was spotless, save for Kerrigan's bed and clothes. Darby had only been in here for a few hours, and already, the place looked empty, except for her three friends crowding the space.

"Whoa," she whispered when she stepped inside.

"Oh, Kerrigan, you made it," Darby said. She looked around the room, flustered.

"You packed quickly."

"I'm supposed to move out tonight," she said. "I would have packed your clothes up, but I didn't know where you were moving."

Except Kerrigan wasn't moving. Not for another month at least.

"No, this is fine," Kerrigan said evenly.

Hadrian sighed and paced another step. "Can we get back to the topic at hand?"

"I still think he's drunk somewhere." Clover lazily leaned back on Kerrigan's bed as if she didn't have a care in the world.

Clover always got so confrontational around Hadrian. It didn't help that he seemed so reticent that Kerrigan was friends with someone from the Wastes.

"He's not just drunk!" Hadrian cried, rising to the bait.

Clover quirked an unconcerned half smile in his direction. "Pretty boy likes to party."

"He does like to party," Darby whispered.

"He does, but that's not…" Hadrian looked at her in distress. "He wouldn't stay out."

"He followed me," Kerrigan interrupted before the conversation could get destructive.

"What do you mean?" Hadrian asked.

"Last night, I left the party early. I snuck out the back gate and went to the Wastes." She gestured to Clover. "We were out all night."

Clover shrugged. "Yeah, but Lyam wasn't with us."

"No, he wasn't."

"How do you know he followed you then?" Hadrian asked.

"Did you purposely lose him?" Darby asked softly.

"No, I didn't even know. Usually, I can tell when he's tailing me, but I couldn't last night. I talked to Fordham, and he saw Lyam leave after me."

"You did?" Hadrian said.

Clover laughed. "So *that's* why you were wearing his cloak last night."

"You were wearing his cloak?" Darby asked, suddenly all too interested.

"No. Yes. Wait, none of that matters." Kerrigan sighed and took a seat next to Clover on the bed. "When I left the party, Fordham gave me his cloak because I was still in my pink dress and very conspicuous. That's all."

"All right," Clover said with a wink.

Kerrigan sighed. "Back to Lyam."

"You never saw him following you?" Hadrian asked.

"No."

"We're going to have to tell someone," Darby whispered.

"Wait…why?" Clover asked.

"Because he's missing," Darby said vehemently. She quickly covered her mouth.

"He's not missing. He hasn't even been gone for twenty-four hours. We have no clue where he went or if he even really followed Kerrigan. He could be anywhere. He could purposely not want to be in the mountain," Clover said with a raised eyebrow. "It's possible to not want to be here, you know."

While her friends bickered, all Kerrigan could think about was the conversation she'd had with Lyam last night. How he had confessed to knowing about her visions and how good she had felt to finally have someone else to confide in about them. Someone who wasn't Dozan Rook or even Helly. Was it a coincidence that the night he'd told her what he knew, he disappeared? All her life, Helly had told her that if anyone else knew about her visions, they would be in danger. *She* would be in danger. And now this.

"I have to tell Helly," Kerrigan finally concluded.

"Kerrigan, you don't have to tell anyone," Clover said.

But Kerrigan rose to her feet. "I know I'm likely going to be in trouble—again—for leaving the party last night. But if Lyam is missing, then we should have the Society Guard out looking for him. We should probably let Kenris know."

"I think it's the right move," Hadrian said, running a hand back through his blue hair.

"Of course you do," Clover snapped.

"Stop," Kerrigan said. "Just stop."

Darby put her hand on Kerrigan's sleeve. "We'll go with you. It'll be okay. We'll find Lyam."

Kerrigan could tell Hadrian must have really been on edge if he couldn't even see that she needed reassurance. Clover got under his skin so easily.

"Thank you."

Darby fought for a comforting smile, but she just looked scared. And Kerrigan was scared, but she couldn't look it. That was how their friendship worked. Kerrigan put on a brave face. She led the way to victory and adventure, as she always had. Today was no different.

"All right," she said, more to herself than anything.

Then the four of them left the room and headed out of the House of Dragons.

Before they even got all the way out, Mistress Moran appeared in the hallway. She looked crumpled. Normally, she was so immaculate, her black robes pressed and clean, her hair a tight bun. But this hardly even looked like her.

"Kerrigan, Darby, Hadrian," she said gently, "I was coming to collect you. I wasn't sure if you had already left to stay in your new homes."

"No," Kerrigan said uneasily. "We have to go talk to Helly."

"I'm afraid that won't be possible," Moran said.

"Why not?" Hadrian asked.

Moran's eyes darted between them. It was a sign of how out of it she was that she didn't even comment on Clover's appearance with the group inside the mountain.

"I came to find you because unfortunately, I have... I have terrible news."

Kerrigan looked at Hadrian and Darby in confusion. "What terrible news?"

"I hate to tell you this, and I know that it is going to come as quite a shock, but Lyam has been found." Moran swallowed hard. "He was found dead."

Darby gasped next to her. Clover's face hardened into something resolute. Hadrian looked thunderstruck, as if he hadn't quite heard her right. But Kerrigan felt all her fears escalate in that moment. A low buzzing filled her ears. As if everything was suddenly and inexplicably underwater. Lyam had told her he knew about her visions. He'd followed her out of the party. And now, he was dead because of her.

"I am so sorry," Moran said. "It's a tragic accident."

"How?" Hadrian asked practically.

"He was robbed, stripped of all belongings. The Society Guard found his body in a less than savory area of the city with a knife wound in his back. Horrible business, horrible."

Darby burst into tears and collapsed right where she was standing, falling into a puddle of taffeta. Clover bent down with her, dropping a caring arm around her shoulders and whispering into her ear. Hadrian looked blank. Like all the wind had been blown out of his sails.

"Knife wound?" Kerrigan managed to get out.

"A slew of them in that area of town, I'm afraid. I wish we could have recovered his father's compass," Moran said sadly.

"What if it wasn't an accident?" Kerrigan asked more firmly.

"I know that you want to find motive in this," Moran said, putting her hand on Kerrigan's shoulder gently. "Lyam was a good, kind boy. He didn't deserve this. But it doesn't mean it was anything but senseless."

Kerrigan didn't believe that.

Maybe it'd be easier if it was just an accident. Just a bad dream that she was bound to wake up from. But it wasn't.

Fate was spinning its wheels, and people she cared about were getting caught in the spokes.

CHAPTER TWENTY
THE FUNERAL

I t was just a tragic accident.

That was what everyone kept saying.

Lyam had been in the wrong place at the wrong time. Everything of value had been stripped from him. A robbery. He'd been in the Dregs, close to the Wastes. Everyone whispered when they said the name. No sensible person would get caught near that den of iniquity.

A tragic accident.

Even though it didn't feel like an accident at all.

Her life had skidded to a halt, yet the world was going on around her. She had been excused from the last two days of task one in the tournament. Fordham had passed through to the next round, but there had been no glint of a knife in the arena. Which would have confused her if she could even concentrate on her vision. She had two weeks until the second task. Two weeks to "recover"—or so everyone told her—but still only a month to find a house.

Not enough time. Not enough time for any of it.

She stood with her feet planted in the dirt as Lyam's body rested on a pyre. Body. His body. It was hard to even think the words. That whatever had made Lyam Lyam had been snuffed out so completely

155

that all that lay on top of the pile of wood was a vessel and nothing more. None of his humor or thirst for adventure or sailing knowledge. Just a body.

Someone had arranged him with his arms wrapped over his chest, his eyes closed, his face serene, his body limp and ready to return to the earth. It didn't even look like Lyam.

Though maybe a touch more than when she had snuck into the depths of the mountain to where they kept him in a cold place to prevent rot. The very thought shuddered through her as her teeth chattered the deeper she crept. She was glad that she hadn't asked Darby or Hadrian to come with her. They'd never have made it this far. She hoped to find a clue, to find anything to tell her *why* this had happened.

But when she got there, she looked down at the body—his skin waxy, his lips blue, the puncture wound deep—and she realized her folly. There was nothing here. Nothing but a wave of grief. She'd fallen to the floor and cried for hours. Lyam was gone. He was really gone.

Darby squeezed her hand, bringing her back to reality. Kerrigan blinked back the weight of that grief. She had heard nothing that the man who was there to bring solace to the grieving said.

"Would anyone like to say anything?" the man finally asked, addressing the crowd.

Hadrian and Darby looked at Kerrigan. They had apparently agreed that she would be the one to do this, to find a place within her to speak words about the person she had lost. But what could she even say? She hadn't prepared for this. But she couldn't send him to rest without at least someone speaking for him.

She stepped forward and cleared her parched throat.

"Lyam was not like you and me," she began softly. Her throat was already closing at the words, but she knew what he would have wanted to say. "Lyam came from very little. His parents were fishermen along the western coast. They had a wonderful life there on the sea. Lyam kept his father's compass with him at all times. He said that it showed him the way back to the water. But due to fishing regulations, his family was forced to give up their life and come to Kinkadia, the city of light. They found no light here."

The crowd surrounding Lyam's funeral pyre shifted uncomfortably at her words. They were not the words anyone had been expecting. But she knew Lyam's truth. The house system had failed him, as it had failed all the Dragon Blessed. And she was not going to sit back and let them burn him without knowing what had happened.

"His parents never found work here. No one would hire unskilled labor. All they'd ever known was the sea, and the sea had been stolen from them. Lyam was dropped off into the care of the House of Dragons, given an opportunity to rise in the ranks. An opportunity his parents had not been afforded. And now, at only seventeen, he was murdered in cold blood," she said, her voice getting angrier. "An injustice so great that I barely have words for it. We have work to do. We need to make this right. For Lyam and for all the families out there, struggling and living in fear. That's what Lyam would want. That's what I want to give him."

Kerrigan met Clover's eyes across the circle near the back, and she was smiling. Kerrigan stepped back and took Darby's hand. Neither of her friends said a word. In fact, no one else said anything.

Then a dragon blew hot fire onto the pyre, and Lyam went up in flames.

Dragon flames were supposed to be the ultimate honor. A sign of great respect for the deceased. Lyam would have wanted dragon fire. He'd loved riding almost as much as she did. But it was too little, too late.

They stood together for a long time as the flames licked at the wood, burning it low. Darby huddled between Kerrigan and Hadrian. Clover came around the pyre and rested her head on Hadrian's shoulder. His arm slung around her to bring her in close to the group. Everyone else left in waves until only the four of them remained.

None of them had to say that they wanted to stay through the night. That they wanted to hold vigil for the loss of their friend. They clustered together and watched the flames burn and burn and burn.

It was hours before Darby finally sank down into the dirt, heedless of the layers of her midnight dress.

"Darbs?" Kerrigan asked gently.

"I can't do it anymore," Darby said, brushing furiously at her wet cheeks. "I can't keep crying. I've cried buckets the last four days. And I'm going to cry more buckets, but I don't want to be sad right now."

Hadrian sank down next to her. "I know what you mean. Lyam was always so happy."

"He was a nuisance," Darby said around a hiccup. "There wasn't trouble he couldn't get into."

Kerrigan glanced at Clover, who tipped her head to the ground. The two of them sat too, forming a small circle with Darby and Hadrian before Lyam's funeral pyre. The sun had already sunk low, brushing a burnished glow across the horizon.

"And you!" Darby said, thrusting her finger in Kerrigan's direction. "You were just as bad."

"Still am," Kerrigan said softly.

"Because you don't think this was an accident," Hadrian said.

Kerrigan slowly shook her head. "No, I don't."

"I liked your speech," Clover said with an arched eyebrow.

"Well, that makes one of you," Kerrigan said.

"What you said was true," Hadrian said.

Clover gasped next to him and nudged his shoulder. "Finally going to admit where you come from, sweetheart?"

He glared at her, momentarily forgetting where they were with her chiding. "I don't *forget* where I came from, but I was given the opportunity to rise above my station—"

Clover held up her hand. "I read the brochure."

"Stop," Darby snapped, uncharacteristically peevish.

Hadrian and Clover's bickering died off immediately with murmured apologies.

"Why don't you think it was an accident? Because he followed you?" Darby asked. "He's followed you a hundred times and never been murdered."

Kerrigan wished that she could explain it. But none of her friends knew about her visions. Only Lyam had known, and he was dead.

"I have a feeling," she said with a shrug. "I don't know how else to explain it. It feels wrong. The whole thing feels like a lie. Lyam wasn't stupid enough to be caught by a robber in the Dregs."

"I wish there were a way to prove it one way or another," Darby said with a sigh.

Kerrigan wished that too, but she didn't see how it was possible. All she had was a hunch, and that wasn't enough for anyone.

⸻

By the time the flames were nearly guttered out, Darby had fallen asleep with her head in Clover's lap. Clover was leaning back against Hadrian as if she belonged there, both of them barely keeping their eyes open.

"Come on," Kerrigan said softly. "Let's get some sleep."

Hadrian gently shook Darby awake. She yawned dramatically and then slowly came to her feet with the others. As a unit, they trudged back to the mountain. Hadrian and Darby had stayed at the mountain the last couple of nights instead of moving in with Fallon and Sonali right away, but Kerrigan knew that wouldn't last. That she wouldn't have them to lean on forever.

"Take my bed," Kerrigan told Clover.

"You sure?" she asked around a yawn.

"Yeah, I'm still not tired."

"You look tired."

Kerrigan laughed once. "Yeah. I can't shut my brain off, I guess."

"Okay. Well, be careful. I want to think that it's just an accident, but if it's not, Red…"

"I know," she whispered. "I won't leave."

Kerrigan didn't have anywhere to be or anything to do. She had restless energy deep in her bones that she couldn't possibly shake. As if it was building. Something was building inside her. Not like her visions, which usually felt immediate, as if right that second, it was going to take her over.

She was edgy. And she didn't know how not to be.

So she walked.

Her feet carried her aimlessly throughout the darkened halls of the mountain. Past barely lit ornate tapestries and ancient metal fighting gear, through the peacefully slumbering dragon chambers, and then to the tournament rooms.

She could lie and say that she didn't have any hope to find a dark-haired boy with gray eyes, but it was a lie. They were connected, and something told her that he couldn't sleep either.

She would be lying again to say she felt no joy at finding out that she was right.

Fordham was seated at a long table in the hall with a leather notebook open before him. He'd shucked off his cloak and untucked his tunic. His dark hair was all a mess from him running his fingers through it, and he looked both contemplative and delectable. Words she should not associate with a prince who had been nothing but cruel to her.

Still, she stepped forward and seated herself at the table across from him. He'd surely heard her steps, but he didn't look up from what he was writing. He scrawled a few more words into the margin before lifting those tempestuous eyes up to meet hers.

"Hello, princeling."

"A little late for you to be wandering the halls, don't you think?" he asked.

"Couldn't sleep," she said with a shrug. "You either?" She gestured to his notebook.

"No."

"Still writing poetry?"

He frowned. "Why are you up?"

"Funeral," she whispered.

His gaze softened for a split second and then returned to its neutral mask. "I heard."

"Yeah," she said noncommittally.

"I didn't realize the streets were that rough in Kinkadia," he admitted.

"They're not," she said at once, defending her home. "Well, they aren't all that great. The Society Guard doesn't care so much about the human side of town. But Lyam wasn't robbed. He was murdered."

Fordham's eyebrows rose. "That fact was not circulated."

"That's because no one believes me."

"And you have proof?"

She sighed. "No, but my gut tells me that there is nothing simple about what happened to him. He was following me out of that party, just like he'd done a dozen times before. He wasn't stupid enough to be caught and robbed like that."

Fordham was silent for a moment before saying, "All right."

"You don't believe me either."

"On the contrary," he said, closing his notebook. "I'm prone to believe that there is something larger happening here."

"You are?"

He leveled her with a look. "You informed me of what was going to happen in the tournament and then passed out in my bedroom."

"Right," she said softly. "About that."

He waved it away. "My gut is also typically right. And it tells me that what you said about Lyam is likely true."

Kerrigan didn't know why she was confiding in this broody princeling. But he was here, and she found herself attracted to him, and something *did* seem to continue to drive them together.

"Yeah, well, I wish we weren't the only ones. I have one month to get a house to accept me, and now I have to figure out what happened with Lyam."

"A house to accept you?"

"I made a deal. I have the length of the dragon tournament to be accepted into a house, or I have to work for the Society in perpetuity."

He frowned at that news. "Would working for the Society be so bad?"

"When the other option is freedom?"

"Point taken," he said dryly. "I've only recently discovered freedom myself."

Kerrigan tilted her head. "How exactly did you get out of the House of Shadows?"

Any humor or lightness left on Fordham's face evaporated. As if he'd forgotten that they were two people alone in the dark and remembered his place in the world.

"I walked out," he said simply and then stood swiftly, tucking his book under his arm.

"Wait," she said, getting to her feet. She reached her hand out. "Fordham."

He strode away purposefully, and her shoulders dropped in dismay. Well, scales.

Right before he reached the corridor that led down to his rooms, Fordham came to a stop and turned back to her. He was silhouetted in the opening. She swallowed.

"If you want to find out what happened to your friend, I could go with you."

162

Kerrigan staggered forward a step in shock. One minute, he'd been pissed and ready to flee from her presence, and now he was offering this? What in the gods' names was going on in his head?

"Why?" she blurted out. "You hate my kind."

"A favor for a favor. You helped me in the tournament, and I will help you with this. Then we are even."

His words were precise and severe. As if this would be the end of their bond. As if helping her would close the loop. He clearly did not like the idea of being in her debt.

She watched him walk away, perplexed. Who exactly was Fordham Ollivier?

CHAPTER TWENTY-ONE
THE DAWN

CLOVER

Clover hadn't been this tired in a long time. Not since the night she had slept among the bones. A small shudder ran down her back, and she pulled out her father's old locket. She should be asleep. Kerrigan had gone off to walk out her anxiety and fear, but Clover didn't have the same nervous energy. Her constant companion was pain.

Even though Kerrigan would kill her, she pulled out a smoke, striking a match to light it and taking a good, long drag. Instantly, her muscles relaxed, and the spasms stopped. Everything felt more like it should. More like before.

Probably, she should finish the cigarette and then get some sleep. Dozan wouldn't care how tired she was tomorrow when she had to deal. He'd dock her pay for being worthless to him. Still, she couldn't sleep.

Maybe it was the empty bed on the other side of the room. The bed that had belonged to Darby for as long as Clover had known Kerrigan. Clover had snuck in more nights than she could count and found the beautiful woman lying in her nightclothes, the white under-things brilliant against her dark onyx skin.

She teased Hadrian to death. They fought like cats and dogs. But sweet, innocent Darby, she was an entire world of different. Clover had never been able to bring herself to make that move. Not when Darby was about to be a lady in a Bryonican aristocracy's household. Darby had been too good for Clover long before that.

Clover flopped back onto Kerrigan's bed and put out the smoke with a sigh when a soft knock sounded on the door. She sat up real quick.

"Kerrigan? You change your mind?" she called.

The door creaked open, and there Darby stood, as if Clover had conjured her up from a dream. "Oh, Clover," she whispered, ducking her chin to her chest. A lantern was clutched in her hand. "I didn't... I thought—"

"Why don't you come on in?"

"You're sure? I was looking for Kerrigan. I didn't know—"

"I'm sure. She went off to wander all night. It's almost dawn. You can come in."

"Oh. All right," Darby said. She stepped daintily inside and closed the door behind her. "It feels odd to be sleeping in different quarters after living here for so long."

Clover sat up on her elbows. "You can sleep here. I don't mind."

"Thank you," Darby said.

She went about the room like it was her own, which it had been up until a few days ago. She found extra blankets and a fresh pillow and bundled up into the bed across from where Clover lay.

"Do you think she was right?"

Clover faced Darby with the lantern light between them. "Do I think Lyam was murdered?"

"He was, wasn't he?"

"Kerrigan has good instincts."

Darby frowned, and Clover decided right then and there that she didn't like it one bit. "We were all about to start our own lives, but I thought it would be like it was, only bigger," Darby admitted. "Like we'd have this new adventure in society and still have this group we always grew up with. That was kind of naive. I see that now."

"Maybe a little naive," Clover conceded. "But why shouldn't you get everything you've ever wanted?"

Darby's eyes landed on her own. Dark as midnight and as earnest as she had ever seen them. "I thought that I was getting that when Lady Sonali picked me."

"Life doesn't always work out the way we want it to," Clover said, rubbing the locket and tucking it back under her shirt.

"Thank you for talking to me. I guess I wasn't quite ready for sleep." Darby punctuated that with a large yawn and then a tinkling laugh. "Or I was, but my brain wouldn't shut off."

"Why don't you try to sleep now?"

"Would you sing to me?" Darby whispered through another yawn, her eyes already closed.

"Sing?"

"Mmm," Darby muttered.

Clover swallowed. She hadn't sung in a long time. Not in five years. Not since her parents had been killed. But she still remembered the tune her mother used to sing as she laid her down to sleep. She hadn't thought of it in so long, and still, it came back to her with ease, the words following close behind.

Sleep, my little darling.
May dreams soothe and obey.
Turn the charm one, two, three times.
Don't leave. I want you to stay.

Sleep, my little angel.
Open the heart, and I'll appear.
Speak my name one, two, three times.
No fear. I'll always be near.

Darby softly snored in the opposite bed before Clover finished the lullaby. It was for the better. She wouldn't see Clover swipe at the tear that had rolled down her cheek.

Clover crept out of bed and carefully tugged the covers under Darby's cheek. She brushed a lock of her dark hair out of her face. She extinguished the lantern and crawled back into bed, trying to forget the memories the lullaby had dredged up.

CHAPTER TWENTY-TWO
THE
DISAPPOINTMENT

ISA

Isa dealt in death.

She enjoyed a good day of espionage like anyone, but the tip of her dagger in a warm body was preferable.

Her hard leather boots were soundless against the stones as she traipsed up to the back of the building. She could have used the front, but she'd rather fewer people knew who she was. A shadow in the night was more fearsome than a girl with a shock of white hair and a pretty little face. Being pretty sometimes helped get her into buildings, but more often than not, it was a nuisance. People assumed a lot about pretty girls. Namely that they were stupid and weren't going to slit you from nose to navel for touching them. For Isa, they were wrong on both counts.

She scaled the small stone wall and landed with ease in the garden on the other side. A black mask obscured her features, but still, she drew her cloak farther forward, putting her face in deeper recess. Now she was ready.

With purpose, Isa stalked through the manor home deep in the heart of Riverfront territory. Wealthy enough to be a solid benefactor but not nearly as much of a nuisance as some of those royal pricks in the Row. New money. The entire estate reeked of it.

Not that she much cared one way or another. As long as she was paid.

She strode forward with the grace of her training and the confidence of someone who feared only one person in her life—her father. And he wasn't here.

A pathetic excuse for a guard stood outside the entrance to the main room.

"I was called," Isa said with disdain evident in her voice.

"He has been waiting for you," the guard said. He turned the knob and announced her presence.

She pushed in before him and lazily strolled into the living area. It desperately wanted to be a four-hundred-year-old Row mansion but didn't quite pull it off. Hardwood in a deep chestnut covered the floor with a collection of recently designed furniture in various neutral shades. Objects of import lined cedar shelves built into the walls, and a man stood at a full glass window display overlooking the river.

"You're late," the man said.

Isa plopped down onto one of the couches. She poured herself a glass of amber liquid out of a crystal decanter and then propped her feet up. "I'm not a dog. I don't come when I'm called."

"You are in my employ."

"And I did what you'd told me. Where's my money?" She took a sip of the bourbon and sighed. At least he'd forked out for the good stuff.

The man never turned to face her, but she could feel his anger emanating off him. "You killed the wrong person and made the mistake of leaving the body for the Society Guard to locate. You failed miserably. You will get nothing."

Isa dropped her feet onto the intricately woven rug. She sure hoped that she'd crushed dirt into the delicate fabric. "No one is going to have any idea that I killed him. I *am* talented at my profession. They will think that it was an accident. I made it look like a robbery."

"But you didn't get the girl!" he cried, finally whirling around to face her.

"One thing at a time, boss," she crooned.

"Do you not understand how any of this works? I hired you to kill one girl. Not to off a full-blooded Fae male on a whim."

"Is that what you think of me?" Isa asked with humor in her voice. "That full-blooded Fae was tracking your girl. If I hadn't noticed his movements, then he would have surely seen me come after the girl. One step at a time. It's a delicate process."

"You are a disappointment," he snarled.

Isa rolled her eyes and finished the liquor. "I'm going to kill the girl."

"You'd better, or you won't be paid."

"Why do you have it out for this girl anyway?"

The man's eyes blazed with anger. "She is a half-Fae bastard. Is that not enough for you?"

"There are plenty of those running around in the Dregs right now. Hell, there are plenty of filthy humans," Isa said with a shrug. "What makes her special?"

He turned back to the riverfront, his body stiff and unyielding. "She is powerful. More powerful than anyone knows. If she comes to her full potential, she could wreak havoc on our entire world."

"No half-Fae is *that* powerful."

"And none ever will be once you're finished with her."

Isa came to her feet. "Then if she's that dangerous, I'm going to have to double my rate."

His jaw set as he glanced at her. "Fine. Just do it, and do it right this time. Dispose of the body, and let no one know when you're done."

Isa smiled, imagining all the money she was going to rake in from this one job. Almost enough to get her own place. Almost enough to escape. Almost enough to finally be free.

"Consider it done."

CHAPTER TWENTY-THREE
THE SEARCH

Y ou've been busy," Fordham said the next afternoon as they strode together out of the mountain.

He'd recently come from the baths, and his dark hair was still wet and slicked back off his face. He wore the same black-and-silver clothing he always wore. Much too fine for Kerrigan, and she had a sharp memory of him handing her his cloak and just how much nicer it was than anything she had ever put on her body.

"What? Did you expect me to nap?" she asked, returning to her chiding demeanor now that they weren't alone under the cover of darkness together.

"How exactly did you get the location of where your friend's body turned up?"

"I bribed a guard," she said simply.

He shook his head but said nothing else as they exited the mountain and headed toward the Wastes. The roads were so familiar. She'd walked them hundreds of times. More times than she could even count with Lyam at her side or trailing in her wake, as if he thought that she wouldn't notice. And now she would never walk them with him again. Not even get annoyed that he was tailing her.

She swallowed back the lump in her throat and continued through the streets. But as fast as she was going, Fordham kept pace with her, even as he stared around the streets as if he had never seen a real city before. He didn't gawk—that would be beneath him—but there was something like awe in his expression.

There were so many questions that she wanted to ask, but she didn't want him to shut down again if she asked about his home. She veered off course, abruptly turning them away from the Wastes and toward the Central district, which housed the square.

"Haven't you been out in Kinkadia since you got here?" she asked him.

He shrugged. "Only once for the ceremony."

"It was night, and you only saw a ballroom," she scoffed. "We're going to need to get you acquainted with my city."

"That's not part of our mission."

"Well, can we at least stop for a meat pie?" she asked. "I know the best place in town."

He narrowed his eyes as if he were trying to find deception in it but finally nodded. "I could use sustenance."

"Princeling, this isn't sustenance. This is living."

Fordham grumbled something under his breath, but he followed her through the winding city streets until they came upon the square. It was more or less the center of Kinkadia, a giant stone-paved square with shops bordering three sides and the ruins of a once-grand church taking up most of the center. Her heart clenched at the sight.

"What happened here?" Fordham asked. His gaze raked over the falling stones and burned-out roof.

"Something tragic," she said softly.

"I didn't think the Fae had a religion other than the Society."

"Most don't," she agreed, turning them away from the church that still made her feel sick to her stomach. "This was a human church for the Laments."

Fordham's eyes widened slightly. "Humans built that? Without magic?"

She nodded. She'd always thought the twenty-story building with its sweeping spires and high, arched bell towers was a truly magnificent sight to see. Even burned and out of use, it still drew quite a crowd of tourists and followers of the Lament.

"Many humans are still in the Laments, but after the protests and riots five years ago, so much of it has had to go underground or on the outskirts of town. Human religions aren't welcome in such public places in Kinkadia. They draw the wrong kind of attention. There are small Lament churches on the outskirts of town, none quite as grand."

Fordham looked perplexed. She wondered more and more what it had been like to live his life in the House of Shadows. By his reaction, he clearly didn't have much interaction with humans.

Kerrigan tilted her head away from the church and stopped in front of a food cart. She ordered two meat pies and tossed coins to the seller. She passed one to Fordham, who took a tentative bite before his eyes doubled in size.

"What is this?" he asked.

She laughed. "Magic."

He finished his pie in two more bites and went back for two more.

"I see you're a fan."

He finished off the next one in record time. "You were not lying about this."

"Nope. The best damn pie in the city. Shredded quail meat with a hint of spice. I don't know what he does, but it's the best."

Fordham ate the third pie slower than the first two as they walked around the square. There were chocolatiers and candlemakers and cheesemongers. A glassblower was showing off her latest creations. A skilled blacksmith worked before a forge. Anything and everything a person could want was for sale in the square. Only the finest quality and generally a few extra coins more than outside the square, but she figured for the experience and the quail meat pie, it was worth it.

"All right, we have veered off course enough. Where was his body found in comparison to this?" Fordham asked. "I cannot think that a dead body would be easily concealed in this neighborhood."

"No," she agreed, coming back to reality. This was about Lyam, not about gallivanting around the city with one wicked prince. "He was found in the Dregs, near the Wastes."

"The Dregs. That sounds pleasant."

"It's a nickname for the neighborhood, because no one actually calls it Glenwoods," she said with an eye roll.

After a twenty-minute walk, it became completely transparent why no one called the neighborhood by its given name, instead going by the Dregs. The street grew narrower and narrower. A smell lingered in the air, as if waste were still being thrown into the streets or there were too many taverns with customers vomiting and pissing nearby. Instead of Fae dressed in their best, musicians playing on the streets, and dances breaking out, there were taverns, taverns, and more taverns. Mostly humans, half-Fae, and some poor Fae lived in these parts. They walked quickly with their heads down, hastening to another job because most had more than one here.

Fordham's brows came together the deeper they walked into the Dregs. He was still in his crisp black-and-silver attire. She should have told him to wear something less conspicuous, but it was too late now.

He said nothing as Kerrigan led the way with ease, stopping when she reached the intersection the guard had given her earlier that day. It was a darkened alcove running off the main thoroughfare of the Dregs. She didn't remember whether she had walked down this street the night of the ceremony. She had been in such a hurry that she'd all but run the entire way. None of her movements came back to her.

"This it?" he asked, stepping into the alley.

"Yes. This is what the guard said."

She followed Fordham down the length of the alley. She tried to see what it must have been like at night, walking down this darkened alcove. It was near a tavern, but everything was in this part of town. The alley opened on both sides. Not exactly great concealment for a robbery.

Fordham stooped down near a pile of refuse and prodded it around.

She wrinkled her nose and came over to look. "Anything?"

He pointed to the left. "Blood. From what I can see, he was stabbed here." He pointed at a footprint that she'd missed completely. One foot had landed in the dirt. It was mostly gone already. "And fell backward into the garbage, where he bled out."

Kerrigan shivered at the thought. "They left him in the garbage?"

"Appears so." Fordham rummaged through the trash and came out with a small gold chain. "This look familiar?"

Kerrigan's jaw dropped. "That's Lyam's compass."

"Looks like he might have had it out or was fiddling with it when it happened. Dropped it into the garbage before whoever did this could get to him."

He passed it to Kerrigan, and she held it reverently.

"Do you think it was a robbery?" she asked, eyes wide.

He stood from where he had been digging through the dirt. "I'm not sure. If it was done quickly in the middle of the night, a robber might have seen the glint of his compass and come after him."

"But then why wouldn't they have taken it?"

"Why indeed?"

Kerrigan sighed in frustration. More questions. No answers. "This feels like a dead end."

"At least you got his compass back."

She bit her lip. "Yes, thank you for that."

He remained silent as she turned away from him and pressed the compass against her chest. Lyam was really gone. He was gone, and she would never know who had killed him. Never know if her hunch was correct, because this was a dead end, and she had no more moves. And gods, she shouldn't even be worrying about this right now. She had to figure out what to do about a house. She only had three weeks now before this was all over, and then she would have to give up on the life she had always wanted.

She loosed a breath and turned back to Fordham. "Why are you helping me?"

"I already told you," he said stiffly.

"Yeah, a favor for a favor. But you've been nothing but cruel to me since you arrived. I wouldn't think you'd want to sully yourself with my presence."

"You helped me despite my behavior toward you," he said coolly. "Why shouldn't I help you?"

"I don't know. I can't figure you out."

"Perhaps you should cease trying."

Kerrigan huffed. "Fine. Do we have time for one more stop?"

"After you," he offered.

♾

"Breaking and entering was not on my list of things to do today," Fordham growled low behind her.

"Mine either," Kerrigan said as she twisted the handle and heard it open with a satisfying click.

"Remind me again why you're doing this."

"Ellerby was supposed to pick me for his house. We'd had it worked out for months," she explained, pushing the door open slightly. She waved him in behind her. "He was there the day of my ceremony, and then right before my turn, he just *left*."

"So?"

"It's suspicious. And I want to ask him why."

"So you're breaking into his home?" he asked in dismay.

"Someone should be here. Why didn't anyone answer?"

"Maybe he's out?" Fordham suggested reasonably.

Kerrigan rolled her eyes. "Ellerby?" she called into the house from the small foyer.

He lived off the Row in a sprawling town house that she had visited before and adored. She'd thought very kindly about taking up residence within this place at one point.

"Hello, Ellerby? Are you home? It's me, Kerrigan."

No one answered. In fact, it was eerily quiet.

"Kerrigan," Fordham said softly. He pointed to a side table by the front door. A stack of letters sat unopened, tied together with a bow, as if they were all going to have to be sent on elsewhere. "I don't think anyone is home."

She frowned. That made no sense. Had Ellerby gone back to Elsiande? He'd talked fondly of his home, but he'd never made it seem like he preferred the stuffy anti-magic south to a life in the city. He only went back on rare occasions. She could count the number of times in the last year on one hand. Without a dragon, travel was perilous. Most people only did it for large events or trade.

"You seem good with clues," she told Fordham. "Could you…" She waved her hand at the letters.

"You want me to go through his mail?"

"Does that offend your princeling sensibilities?"

He scoffed. "You are a wicked little thing."

She couldn't help but smile.

"What are you going to do?"

"I'm going to look around." And then Kerrigan tiptoed through Ellerby's house.

The tiptoeing ended up being pointless. It was truly deserted. Not a soul in sight. It didn't look like anyone had even been inside to clean or tend to anything except the mail. There were even dirty plates in the kitchen. Ashes in the fireplaces. The beds were unmade. The dressers had been thrown open, all the clothes were gone, and it looked like someone had left in a serious hurry.

Why in the gods' names would he have rushed out of town so fast?

Kerrigan crossed her arms and looked around in confusion. Something was wrong here. She could feel it all the way through her body. A tingling sensation, like if she just looked, she would find all the answers. But it didn't make sense. She had no answers.

In fact, it was even more frustrating than assuming Ellerby had changed his mind. Because if he had changed his mind, then he'd run out of town in a hurry after he did it.

She was about to walk back down the stairs to see if Fordham had found anything when she heard a faint creak of the wood floor.

"Hello?" she asked uncertainly.

And then a shadow surged out of the darkness, brandishing an all-too-familiar knife.

Kerrigan saw the knife coming toward her, as it had in her vision, and everything slowed to a crawl. She had thought that it had to do with the tournament, but it had come to this moment.

All Kerrigan's carefully honed instincts clicked into place from years of training in the House of Dragons, coupled with the last year in the Dragon Ring. She should have been frightened. Even terrified. Instead, she kicked into high gear, dodging the edge of the knife. The tip of it barely grazed her arm. Still, she hissed and pulled back from the shadow.

She didn't know who this person was, but they were fast and clearly ruthless. How they'd gotten into Ellerby's home without her knowing was a mystery. Not to mention they were cleverly disguised— dressed head to toe in black fighting garb with a black mask obscuring most of their facial features. They were a nameless, faceless monster.

"What do you want?" Kerrigan spat at the person.

But they didn't respond. They moved in quick, like a viper, and struck. Kerrigan pulled up her magic in time, trying to block their approach, but the person sliced right through her shield as if it were made of butter.

Kerrigan faltered at that, letting her guard down for one painful second. And then the person was in her space, thrusting the dagger toward her. Kerrigan twisted out of the way of the weapon, but she was too slow, and the knife plunged through her shoulder.

She cried out in shock and pain. While she'd averted a killing blow, searing pain still coursed through her body, and she saw double as the agony wrecked her, disabling her reflexes. The assassin became a blur. She could hardly concentrate on them. She'd been beaten to within an inch of her life before. She should have been able to process a little stab through the shoulder, but somehow, she couldn't. She had blocked out the memory of that pain so thoroughly that this blind-sided her.

Then, to her horror, the person did something worse.

They wrenched the knife out of her shoulder.

She saw black. Thought she was going to pass out. Gods, she couldn't collapse. This was what she had trained for.

"Who are you?" Kerrigan croaked as she watched her own death loom before her eyes.

"No one," the throaty female voice said before bringing the blade back down to end it all.

CHAPTER TWENTY-FOUR
THE ASSASSIN

A wave of dark power flooded the bedroom, and both Kerrigan and her assailant were blasted off their feet. Kerrigan collided with Ellerby's bed. Her head hit the metal post with a resounding clang. She groaned and focused on what was happening in front of her. The assassin had landed in front of the balcony doors, her blade flung wide. With the light from the fading sun, Kerrigan could see that the girl was younger than she had appeared in shadow. And to Kerrigan's surprise, the girl was already getting to her feet, leaning down in a crouch, and glaring at who had just attacked her.

"I've come to finish what I started," the girl hissed at them. "You will not stop me."

"Won't I?" a sinister voice growled back.

It took Kerrigan's addled brain a second to realize what had happened. That Fordham stood in the doorway, wreathed in a full black cloak of darkness, the same incredible shadow that had made his grand entrance in the arena. Kerrigan blinked, momentarily mesmerized by it. She didn't know if it was her mind playing tricks on her. She hadn't thought of that darkness since that day, certainly hadn't thought of how he could *use* it against his enemies.

Scales.

"Finish what you started?" Kerrigan croaked.

"The boy was in my way," the girl hissed, tugging her dark hood over her face.

Kerrigan's heart broke into a million pieces. This was Lyam's killer. She had been right. It hadn't been some accidental murder. The assassin had been for her, and Lyam had been in the wrong place at the wrong time.

Fordham lashed out with a rope of flame this time, a tendril of red that slashed around the girl's leg and dragged her back to the ground. Beneath the mask, her eyes widened in alarm and a flash of pain. But she didn't even cry out. As if fire was no match for her. She easily maneuvered away, and as soon as she was free, she wrenched open the balcony doors and slipped outside.

Fordham flung himself after her, but in the span of a few heartbeats, the girl had already scaled the far wall and disappeared out the back.

He came back inside, cursing vividly. "Who the hell was that?"

"Lyam's killer," Kerrigan croaked as she got to her feet.

The memory of all her pain came crashing back down around her, and she fell back in a heap on the floor once more.

"Gods, you're injured," he said, crouching before her.

"She stabbed me in the shoulder," Kerrigan said, pulling back her cloak to reveal the wound beyond.

Fordham inspected it, thoroughly and efficiently with little compassion. She winced through the entire thing.

"How'd you do that?"

"What?"

"The shadows," she said. "It's what you used to get into the tournament."

"Family secret," he said through gritted teeth. "You need to see a healer. This is beyond basic battlefield healing."

182

"Battlefield healing?" she asked, her vision swimming again.

"Never mind." Fordham stood and rummaged through the closet, pulling out an old bedsheet. He tore it precisely into strips, and carefully wrapped her shoulder to stanch the bleeding and secured a makeshift sling for her arm. "There. Can you stand?"

"Um..."

Fordham put his arm around her shoulders and lifted her to her feet. Kerrigan groaned at the pain, even with the bandages and sling.

"My head hit the bedpost."

He ran his hand through the mass of curly hair until Kerrigan yelped in pain. "Yeah, you have a knot. Let's get you back to the mountain."

"No," she said right away.

"No?"

"The Wastes."

He looked at her skeptically. "The mountain has healers. You need to be seen immediately. You've lost a lot of blood."

"I know. The Wastes have healers, and they're closer. Also"—she moved uneasily toward the balcony doors, where she bent down and retrieved the discarded knife—"I have a friend I want to ask about this."

⚬ⱳⱳⱳ⚬

"This isn't a good idea," Fordham growled low as they approached the entrance to the crime lord's lair.

"Probably not," Kerrigan conceded.

But she didn't have another choice. By the time they reached the Wastes, she could barely walk. She never would have been able to reach the mountain in time. Unfortunately, she'd have to put her health in Dozan Rook's hands once more.

"Remind me why I decided to help you again."

"I have no idea. This was your idea."

183

He rolled his eyes. "I am never doing a favor for anyone ever again. Certainly not a halfling."

The words had none of his usual venom though. They were almost friendly. Or maybe he was trying to keep her mad so she wouldn't pass out.

Kerrigan rolled her eyes. "Just get me inside, princeling. I can do the rest."

He shot her a distrustful look. "Why was there an assassin after you anyway?"

"If I'd known, do you think I would have let them stab me?"

"Let them stab you? That's an eloquent way of putting the scene when I walked in and saved your ass."

"I would have been fine."

He narrowed his eyes. "Are you always this overconfident?"

"Yes, she is," a voice said, appearing at the entrance to the Wastes. A dark and broody crime lord, wearing the black and red of his establishment and a frown of displeasure.

"Dozan," she croaked.

His eyes trailed down her body where she clung to Fordham for support, then to the prince of the House of Shadows. She could tell he was not pleased, but he could shove it for all she cared. Word must have traveled fast for him to be here at the entrance when she turned up.

"What have you done with my fighting champion?" he asked Fordham.

Fordham's eyebrows rose at that. "Fighting champion?"

"I'll tell you all about it after I don't have a hole in my shoulder," she grumbled. "Dozan, this is Fordham. Fordham, this is Dozan. He runs the place and is a kind, magnanimous figure who is going to get me a healer for this gods-damned shoulder."

Dozan quirked a half smile at the introduction. He was far from *kind* or *magnanimous*. He was ruthless, irritable, and unyielding, and he hated being bossed around. He always had. Even five years ago, when he'd first brought her back to the Wastes to find her a healer after everything. Her heart twisted at that. She still didn't know why he hadn't left her for dead that first time. He got power out of the equation, but she'd offered nothing when she lay mangled and bloody on the ground.

Dozan raised an eyebrow at Fordham. "You can leave Red here, and we'll take care of her."

To Kerrigan's surprise, Fordham's grip on her tightened. "I think I'll take her to the healer myself." His voice held bite and possessiveness. Even his posture straightened.

If he kept this up, a fight would break out, and she really didn't have the time. This was about that absurd authority that men had to push against to see who was the alpha among them. If she wasn't injured and half falling over, she would hit them both upside the head.

"Stab wound, remember?" she said through gritted teeth. "Can we not do this right now?"

Dozan set his jaw. The look he gave her said that someone was going to pay for this later. But she was as stubborn as he was and didn't care about the cost.

"Follow me," he said tightly.

The crowd parted for him in the Wastes, and they moved past a bar full of regulars, girls in scandalously clad dresses who winked at Fordham as they passed, and past the stairs that led to level after level of debauchery far below. And at the center, on the very bottom floor, was the Dragon Ring. Even this high up, she could hear the cheers of the crowd, their thirst for blood. It made her skin tingle with want.

They didn't head down. No, they headed up to Dozan's quarters. The only area that actually existed *up*. No one was higher than Dozan Rook.

Kerrigan stumbled over the first few stairs. Her feet kept getting stuck under her. Blood loss? She didn't know, but she felt sluggish and clumsy.

Fordham reached for her, and she held up her hand unsteadily. "I can walk."

He sighed as if it were a great inconvenience and then hoisted her into his arms despite her protests. It hadn't been that long ago that Dozan was the one carrying her through the Wastes after her fight with Basem. It felt like an eternity ago.

No one seemed to care about her protests to walk. Dozan opened a door and gestured for Fordham to put her inside. It was stark with nothing but a small pallet and a wash tin nearby. Fordham laid her down onto the bed, which was surprisingly comfortable. Her head lolled back. She hadn't realized how exhausted she was until everything finally stopped and she didn't have to try anymore. She could just lie here and breathe. Maybe sleep.

There was a muffled argument that ensued while she tried to get her bearings, and she only caught pieces of it.

"I won't leave her alone with you."

"You don't have much choice."

"I can take her back to the mountain."

"If you were going to do that, then you wouldn't have even come here."

"She wanted to come here, not me."

"Then trust her judgment."

"Hers. Not yours."

"Only at your own peril." There was a soft pause. "And apparently hers tonight."

"Just get her a healer."

And then the strange conversation drifted off. Kerrigan felt like she was floating off and away. Everything went very fuzzy around the edges.

What felt like minutes or maybe hours later, another man appeared in the room. He wore the red vest and black slacks of one of Dozan's men, but he didn't *look* like one of Dozan's. He looked serene and calm. He must not have been part of a house to be working for Dozan now.

"What are you?" she whispered, reaching up with her uninjured arm toward him.

"My name is Amond," he said. "Now lie back and stay still."

Kerrigan did what he'd told her and waited for the slow work of the healing to take effect. Amond pulled a glowing blue light out of thin air, and Kerrigan's eyes widened in shock.

"What are you doing?" She jolted up at the sight.

"Lie back, please." He gently pushed her back into place.

"That's not how healers work."

He chuckled softly. "It's not how house healers work."

Kerrigan didn't know what he meant. The only healers who could process the craft, who were strong enough in healing, were house healers. Helly was the greatest healer in hundreds of years, more powerful than almost any who had been rumored to come before her, except perhaps the ancients. What would she have to say about this glowing blue light? What *was* the light?

But she didn't ask those questions. She let Amond go to work. Really, she didn't have the energy to fight him off anyway.

He took the light and first cast it across her body from head to toe. "Your shoulder is severe, but you have a cut on your arm and a contusion on your head. Also, you've suffered from a sprained ankle."

She frowned. "Not recently."

"No, it looks many years old. It never healed right."

How could he know that? It hardly even bothered her anymore. She'd jumped off a dragon wrong and rolled her ankle. When the weather was particularly bad, it still irritated her.

Amond said nothing more despite surely seeing the questions in her eyes. He plunged the light into her shoulder. She stiffened in shock and confusion, but it didn't hurt. It didn't feel like anything really. The whole thing was disconcerting. If she concentrated, she could feel a slow trickle of the glowing ball moving around inside her shoulder, almost like a bug under her skin. It made her shudder in revulsion. But Amond only looked at her shoulder a few minutes before removing the light. Immediately, she felt empty, her entire body sagging.

"What the gods?" she said.

But he was already back to work, running the glow across her cut, into her skull—which, *gross*—and then even to her ankle. Each time the glow went through her, she felt like bugs were crawling around inside her, and she wanted to escape, wanted out, but as soon as it was gone, she felt like a loch addict, craving more.

Within minutes, he was done. *Minutes.*

She couldn't fathom it. A healing of this magnitude usually took at least an hour. The magic worked with her natural healing elements and stitched everything back together. Even so, she was usually drained and exhausted after it. As if it had taken as much from her as it had from someone else. The herbal remedies that Darby was proficient at were usually better for anything less problematic, as they didn't exact a price.

"How do you feel?" Amond asked, releasing the blue light as if it had never been.

She slowly shifted into a sitting position and experimentally rolled her shoulder. It felt good. No, better than good. No more pain, no exhaustion, no protrusion on her head. And yes, even her ankle felt good as new.

"What did you do to me?" she gasped.

"I healed you. You look much better."

"Yes, but *how?*"

Amond smiled faintly and then rose to his feet. "I don't believe that you're ready for answers yet, Kerrigan Argon."

She startled at her family name. *No* one used it. Hardly anyone even knew it.

"How…"

"The healing sometimes is a connection," he admitted. "Do not fear. It is against the healer's code to divulge information."

Gods, what had he *seen*?

Fear must have shown in her eyes, because he tentatively reached out and touched her hand. "Not even to Dozan."

"But I don't understand."

"No, many only see what is right in front of them."

"Why do you work for Dozan when you have these abilities?"

"Instead of the mountain?" he asked with no accusation.

She nodded.

"Not all knowledge is equal. Especially not knowledge that disrupts the balance of our society and what is most commonly accepted."

He looked at her purposefully. He knew about her visions. She should have been terrified, but somehow, she wasn't. She trusted that Amond could keep the secret, that it was part of his code. She didn't know if it was because he had healed her or if it was because he kept his own healing secrets hidden. But she understood perfectly what he was trying to impart to her. Her visions would not be a welcome new knowledge inside the mountain. That much she was well aware of.

CHAPTER TWENTY-FIVE
THE KNIFE

She wanted to ask Amond more questions, but Dozan appeared then and dismissed him as if he hadn't done the most miraculous thing she had ever seen.

"Where did you find him?" she asked Dozan.

"Amond?" he asked as if he didn't know. "Around. As I find most of the strays." He stepped into her until there were mere inches between them. He brushed a strand of her hair behind her ear. "Like you."

She stepped back. "Don't."

Anger flared in his irises. "You come to me in your time of need. Always to me. And still, you deny what is right in front of your eyes."

"I don't *deny* anything," she quipped. "I see what you really are."

"And what is that, Ker?"

She grimaced at the nickname. Anyone else could say it, and it hardly bothered her, but she remembered him whispering it over her skin and breathing it into her ear as he held her naked against him. She remembered giving in to this once before and how much of a terribly bad idea it had been.

"Shall I recount our history?" she asked him.

"Allow me," he said, circling her like a hawk. "Five years ago, I

190

saved your life. I brought you here as the broken prince of the Wastes and healed you. Though I had no reason to do so. *You* fell in love with me."

She winced at the bald statement.

"It wasn't love," she growled.

"Fine. Then you were obsessed with me. What was I to do with a twelve-year-old's obsession? Nothing. I was sixteen. You were just a kid. So I sent you away. I sent you back to the mountain."

"Where I belonged," she cut in again. "Then you *murdered* your family and took over!"

Dozan grinned. "I took hold of my birthright."

"That's one way of putting it, Dozan."

"Four years later, you came back to me. You'd had another vision. I was the only one who would understand."

He said the words with such longing. The words she had said to him in the same manner. Her cheeks heated. Her obsession had burned away, but she'd been sixteen then, and he'd turned twenty and become the king of his own empire. More beautiful and more dangerous than ever before. She'd replaced her obsession with desire.

"Should I continue?"

"No," she growled.

She remembered what had happened next and why he was trying to use it against her now.

"I'd love to recount that night for you if you'd like, Ker," he said, stopping behind her and running his finger across her shoulder.

"Let's not," she got out, taking a step away from him. Trying to hide the hitch in her breathing.

Dozan Rook might be her first obsession, her first love, her first *everything*, but she wasn't stupid enough to make him her second too.

"Pity," he breathed, still so close. "Perhaps you'll explain to me why you brought the prince of the House of Shadows into my territory."

She pointed at her shoulder. "Stab wound, remember? He brought *me*."

"What were you doing out with him?"

"Aw, jealous, Dozan?" she asked teasingly.

His jaw was set. "The House of Shadows is not an ally. They hate humans and half-Fae. They torture and kill us for sport. They are even worse than the Society and that damn terrorist organization, the Red Masks. What happened to you in that alley five years ago is the least of what they would do to you. Why exactly do you trust one of their kind?"

Kerrigan took a small step back. Dozan actually sounded worried? No, that couldn't be right. She knew the history of the House of Shadows, how much they hated humans and half-Fae. After all, Fordham had treated her poorly for weeks. In fact, they hadn't managed to say more than a few pleasant words to each other. But he'd still offered to help her after she had helped him. And he hadn't made any kind of move to torture and kill her. He seemed like a sad, broody boy who wrote sad, broody boy poetry.

"Yet he's here," she countered. "Not in the House of Shadows."

"You think that's because of the goodness in his heart? He's here to win a dragon. What is someone from the House of Shadows going to do with a dragon?" he demanded. "What they always did before the walls were put up to protect us—war. If you do not see that, then you are deluded."

It didn't make sense. Why would her visions be pointing her to help Fordham if he wanted to start a war? As far as she could tell, her visions pointed her toward ways to stop catastrophe, not create it.

"I think you're wrong about him."

"Ah," Dozan said, crossing his arms. "And what makes you think so? Is he playing all the right strings for you?"

"As you did?" she spat.

"Mark my words, that prince out there is not what he seems. And he will be the end of you if you let him."

She scoffed.

Dozan might be a lot of things, but he was not prophetic. He didn't like Fordham and clearly hated his people for their history. But he was judging him for all the things others had done. As so many had done to Dozan for his family and their murders. She didn't know *what* Fordham was doing here, but she no longer accepted that his plan was to torture and kill her.

"This isn't the reason I came here," she said, crossing her own arms to match.

"You didn't come to be healed and yell at me? I'm shocked, princess."

She glared at him. "You didn't even ask what happened."

"Does it matter?"

"When an assassin is set out after me, then *yes.*"

"An assassin?" he asked incredulously.

"She already killed Lyam, and she tried to kill me tonight."

He shot her a dubious look. "Who would want you dead that much?"

"That's the question, isn't it?" She had no clue who wanted her dead that much. Plenty of people believed that half-Fae shouldn't have rights, but there wasn't a long line of them who wanted her specifically dead. "I have the assassin's knife."

"You are full of surprises. Let's see it." He held his hand out.

She smiled dangerously. "Fordham has it."

Dozan's face froze in anger. He looked like he wanted to yell at her for her stupidity or possibly throw her back down on the pallet. There was a fine line between pain and pleasure when it came to Dozan Rook.

"Fine," he said and opened the door.

An angry princeling thundered into the small room. His storm-cloud eyes were a hurricane, his body a barely contained ripple of power.

"The knife," she said, holding out her hand before he could say anything that would make Dozan not help them.

"You're healed," Fordham said.

"You actually seem pleased by that fact," Dozan said, his words one second away from striking him down. "I wouldn't have guessed that from your kind."

Fordham looked at Dozan as if he were the scum under his boot. All Dozan's carefully worded criticisms of Fordham's home and character came to the surface in that moment. He looked the imperious prince, hatred flaring across his features at being addressed by a lowly human. But what came out of his mouth...

"My *kind* or not, she was in my care," he snarled at Dozan. "And thus my responsibility."

"You two can bicker all day if you'd like—after we figure out where that knife came from," she snapped, stepping between them.

Fae prince versus human crime lord. She had a guess who would win that fight. Especially after seeing Fordham's dark magic unleashed against the assassin. Dozan had tricks up his sleeve. He ruled here after all. But it wasn't something she wanted to witness. Men!

Fordham slowly retrieved the knife from his cloak and passed it to Kerrigan.

"Thank you," she said as she turned the blade in her palm. It was light, about eight inches long, and as sharp as death. The pommel wasn't fancy, but it had a small bird engraved in the handle. "This is the knife the assassin tried to kill me with. Can you tell us who made it?"

Dozan gripped the handle and twirled the blade in his hand. Show-off. He'd always been skilled at blade work. Kerrigan had taken lessons in the mountain to try to catch up, but he stayed one step ahead of her. As infuriating as it was.

194

"Tendrille steel," he said faintly.

"Well, that explains how she cut through my shield," Kerrigan grumbled.

Tendrille was a pure metal found north in the heart of the Cascade Mountains. Legend said that when the dragons had been exiled from their homeland of Domara, the gods had cast them from the sky and to this world. That act left behind enough tendrille to fill a mountain—the Holy Mountain. The dragons' most sacred site and a place where tendrille would never be mined, making it as precious as it was rare. It was the strongest substance on earth, light as a feather, and immune to magic. Most weapons were made of an alloy with a small percentage of tendrille. They couldn't cut through shields, as this one surely had, but it made them strong and light and valuable.

"Whoever owned this is wealthy," Dozan continued. "Must be to have this much tendrille in this blade." He frowned down at the bird sigil she had seen earlier. "And a raven on the handle."

"What does that mean?" Fordham asked gruffly.

"A raven," she whispered. "Like Rahllins's men?"

"Indeed."

Kerrigan saw Fordham's look of confusion and explained, "Clare Rahllins is a rival gang leader and weapons dealer on the north side of the Dregs. I didn't think that she worked in tendrille."

"Nor did I," Dozan said. "Interesting."

"Do you think she sent the assassin?"

"It's more likely that she sold this blade to whoever sent the assassin," Dozan said.

"Could you find out who that is?"

Dozan's sharp golden eyes met hers. A small smile spread across his sensual lips. His russet hair was almost brown in the dark lighting. "And what will you give me if I could?"

She should have seen it coming, and still, it felt like a punch to the gut. Healing her could be done for free or a small collection from her winnings. He had an incentive to keep his fighters alive. But information? Well, that was something that came for a price.

"What do you want?" she asked with a frustrated sigh. Of course, it could never be this easy. Especially after she had rebuffed him earlier.

"A big fight with all the elements."

She met his triumphant stare. This was what he'd wanted from her for so long. He'd wanted to put her abilities on display in the ring and watch her best his opponents. Not any of these small peanuts fights she had been competing in the last year but a high-stakes, high-profit fight. He wanted to use his little half-Fae girl to destroy anyone in her wake. She'd draw a crowd, that she'd bring him a lot of money, but she'd never wanted that. She hadn't wanted the fame or the money or the target on her back.

"No yields. No tap-outs. A fight to the death."

"Out of the question," Fordham spat.

"Fine," she ground out. "You get us the information. Help us figure out who is trying to kill me *and* why. And I will fight for you. One fight."

Dozan held his hand out, and she put hers in his.

Another bargain struck.

CHAPTER TWENTY-SIX
THE TRAINING

Fordham didn't say a word as they headed back toward the mountain. She fingered Lyam's compass in her pocket. At least one good thing had come out of this. The rest made little sense, and tying her fate to Dozan even more than she already had felt like suicide.

What other choice had she had?

She had less than a month to figure all this out, or else her life was over.

By the time they stepped back inside the cool interior, the exhaustion she'd been fighting off since she'd been stabbed hit her full in the face. She dragged the rest of the way back to her rooms. She turned to face Fordham, prepared to thank him for his help and wish him good night, knowing she'd probably never see him again, despite his assistance with the assassin and Dozan.

But he beat her to it.

"You are not what I expected." His gray eyes no longer held that malice. The tension that permeated him had been released.

She coughed a laugh. "I've heard that before. More trouble than I'm worth?"

"It's not that. You're brave."

She glanced up at him in surprise. His body was close to hers. A lock of his midnight hair had fallen forward. She hadn't expected him to say anything kind.

"Well, I guess we're even now," she told him.

But still he didn't move. He remained in her doorway, his gray eyes swirling and then finally settling. She swallowed hard at that look. She'd always found him attractive, but without all that sinister energy radiating off him, she felt drawn to him like a moth to a flame. Having these feelings would only mean getting burned.

Her heart thudded as their energy mingled, brought together by destiny or time or this very moment after all that danger. And maybe it wouldn't be wrong to want something for herself in the midst of all of this.

"Thank you," she whispered. They were almost touching.

"But you are also stupid," he said.

And there it was.

She sighed and stepped back. Spell broken. "Well, thanks."

"You cannot fight to the death."

"The bargain has already been made."

"You will lose."

"You haven't even *seen* me fight," she snapped at him. "Are you assuming because I'm half-Fae that I'm not capable? Is that what you're saying?"

"The assassin almost killed you. Would it be so hard to believe that a half-Fae cannot fight after you were *stabbed* tonight?"

"She got the jump on me, and she had a knife to break my magic," she snarled. "Being half-Fae has nothing to do with it. You know nothing about me, princeling."

"I know enough to know, *halfling*," he shot back.

"Whatever," she said, dismissing him.

"You need a trainer."

She laughed derisively. "And who is going to train a half-Fae? You?"

"No, that's not what…"

"As I thought. Good night, princeling. Our deal is over. You won't have to worry about me anymore."

"I didn't save your life to watch you die for your own stupidity," he growled.

She whirled around. "I'm not going to die, nor am I stupid."

"No, you're reckless."

"Fine. I'm reckless. But Lyam died because of *me*, and I'm not going to rest and do nothing while his killer is still out there, while they want me dead," she snapped at him.

"And you think he'd want you to throw your life away?"

"He's not here to say otherwise, is he?" Her anger and grief pulled to the surface. Then she released it all. "I don't want to die or throw this all away. But there's no one here to train me to be a better fighter than I already am." She shrugged her shoulders. "I'll take Dozan's help to find that assassin, and then I'll fight the best I can."

He ran a hand back through his hair. "I'm going to regret this."

"What?"

"I can teach you," he offered through gritted teeth. "If you're not too stubborn to learn."

Her body stilled. He was actually *offering*? That didn't make sense. They had each saved the other, and now they didn't have to work together anymore.

"I thought that our bargain was ended," she said.

"This isn't part of the bargain. This is to keep you alive."

"You want to keep a *halfling* alive?"

"Do you want my help or not?" he snapped.

"Yes," she said quickly. She'd seen how he moved against the assassin and in the training ring. He was talented. She'd take his help even to prove she wasn't as weak as he thought.

"We begin at dawn," he said before disappearing into the night without a backward glance.

Prince Fordham Ollivier was not what she had expected at all.

⚬⚬⚬

Kerrigan could have slept straight through morning and on into the evening. If she'd had her way about it, she would have. She'd tossed and turned all night. Dreams of the assassin running her through had kept playing on repeat.

But Fordham knocked on her door at dawn.

Dawn.

He'd said it the night before, but she hadn't wanted to think he was serious. Especially since they had been gallivanting around the city well into the night.

Every part of her screamed to ignore him and fall back into a dreamless slumber, but today was her first day of training. She got up and put on her favorite pair of black pants, carefully bound her chest— she'd learned long ago to do that before any kind of fighting session— and then threw a loose shirt overtop. She braided her hair into a curly plait, wishing she had Darby's magic fingers, and then stepped into the hallway. She looked a wreck, and Fordham looked like a prince.

It truly wasn't fair that he could look like that with only a few hours of sleep. His black-and-silver House of Shadows attire was pristine, his back straight, chin lifted, shoulders pushed back. The only sign that he wasn't happy about the early morning wake-up call was the half-moon bruises under his eyes, which said he'd slept about as well as she had.

"Morning," he said, almost chipper.

"Ugh," she groaned in response.

He gestured down the hallway, and she followed him out of the mountain. He finally stopped in a small grove outside the city. The sun hadn't quite risen, and the final blue-black of night was disappearing as a haze of morning crept onto the horizon. Fordham tossed her some bread and a waterskin.

"You're going to need that," he said. "Don't drink it all."

She mock saluted him as she washed the bread down with water. "What are we doing today? Sword fighting, hand-to-hand combat, elemental prowess?"

"We'll start with a warm-up and see where you are."

"Okay. What's the warm-up?"

"Five-mile run and then a series of strength exercises."

Her eyes bugged. "Five *miles?*"

"To start. We can build you up to more."

"Or not. I only run if someone is chasing me."

"With your nightly activities, I would think that happens more often than not," he quipped. "We have to get you in better physical shape if you hope to make it through this fight. Plus, if Dozan comes up with information on who the assassin is, I don't want to have to pull all the weight."

She rolled her eyes. "Like you're so much better than me because you can run."

"You need discipline," he said, squaring his shoulders off with her and looking her in the eye. "You're lazy and unfocused. If you had half the prowess you proclaim from some street fights, then you would have handled that assassin with ease."

"Fine, princeling. I need discipline. And that means running?" she asked skeptically.

"You know what? Let's get this out of the way." Fordham stripped out of his cloak and laid it in the grass. "Go ahead and try me."

"Try you?" she said. "You want to fight?" She looked around. "Right here?"

"Is that not appropriate for you?"

"Not many people know how much magic I have," she admitted, touching her ears.

"That's good. Then they can underestimate you." He began to circle her.

The hair on the back of her neck stood on end. He stalked her like prey, a slow, steady prowl. The magic in his veins crackled to life. She could practically feel the hum of him brushing against her fair skin.

"They can." A shudder snaked down her skin. This might have been a mistake. Training with someone like Fordham certainly hadn't been her *best* idea. The monster that you knew was still a monster. "They do underestimate me."

"Like me?" he asked silkily.

And somehow, the softness in his voice was worse than all the harsh edges and barbs.

"Uh…yes. Like you."

She brought her magic close into her chest. A gentle thrum of power that suffused her body, bringing it to life, as if all along, she had been going through the motions, and here, like this, she was *real*. She was prepared. Her feet were spaced perfectly apart. Her hands were held in tight fists at her sides. Her awareness was controlled and ready.

Fordham turned the corner, finishing his methodical stroll around her body, and all her perfect planning fell to shit.

He jabbed out lightning fast with one hand, brandishing water magic like it was the air in his lungs. It slashed out, lassoing around her legs. She managed to sidestep, getting thrown onto her back, but it was exactly what he'd been anticipating. One second, he was in front of her, and the next, his feet were dancing through steps so fast that she couldn't even put together the forms. He moved like the wind, as if he'd been born to this. His foot caught her at the same time as a brush of wind catapulted her backward and the earth beneath her feet propelled upward.

She sailed through the air, landing hard on her backside, a solid ten feet from where she had been standing earlier. And Fordham stood there with his arms crossed over his chest and one eyebrow raised.

The whole thing had only taken a matter of seconds. Not minutes, *seconds*. She had never seen anyone move like that before. Not even Fordham, and she had watched enough of his training sessions and seen him in the ring to know that he had never shown off those moves to anyone.

"Are you satisfied?" he asked from his stance overtop her.

She groaned and rubbed her aching back. "Where did you learn to *move* like that?"

Fordham lifted his chin, a twinkle in his gray eyes. "I am the crown prince of the House of Shadows. What did you expect?"

"No idea," she told him honestly. "A pompous jerk with a chip on his shoulder?"

"The chip on my shoulder is earned," he said with almost a little smile at the end.

He held his hand out to her. She put her hand in his and let him haul her to her feet.

"As you have your secrets, I have mine."

"Secrets?" she whispered.

"I didn't see you run to the mountain to convince anyone that Lyam was murdered, that house was abandoned, and there was an assassin after you."

She bit her lip. "No one will even believe me without proof. The knife isn't enough."

"And the empty house?"

"They'll dismiss it. House members come and go all the time."

"Fine," he said begrudgingly. "But there is much at stake these next few weeks. Let's not walk into them unprepared. Discipline is the foundation of the House of Shadows' military protocol. If you can survive the next few weeks, there's hope for you surviving this fight and catching this assassin."

"Five miles?" she asked.

"It's a start."

Fordham took off at a moderate jog, likely more for her benefit than anything.

"Tell me…about the…military protocol," she said between pants.

He wasn't even breathing hard. "The House of Shadows is divided into three primary families."

"Like the…four Bryonican…royal houses?"

He frowned. "Sort of. *Family* is a loose term. It's more like different factions, and people can move between families. My father has ruled the House of Shadows for five hundred years but not continuously. Another faction will rise up, depose my family, and take over for a decade, and then my father will rally enough support to take back the throne."

"That's…barbaric."

He shot her a rueful look. "Challenge is a way of life. The Society rules under absolute power across all of Alandria. Unchecked and unaccounted for. Challenge is put down like a dog. That is not freedom."

Kerrigan peered at him in surprise. "You are…competing to…join…the Society."

"I am." Though he said nothing further about why he had decided to join something he clearly disapproved of.

They ran until they came to the top of a bluff and Kerrigan could run no more. "I need a break."

She all but collapsed onto a nearby stone. She tilted, trying to get the stitch out of her side. It felt quite literally like someone was stabbing her repeatedly. She'd had it happen recently enough to know.

"This is torture."

Fordham paced back and forth in front of her. "It'll get easier."

After her fingers stopped throbbing with the pulse of her erratic heartbeat, she managed to take a sip from her waterskin. "I'm surprised you're talking about home."

He looked off toward the mountains. "You needed to know why discipline was important."

"Right, but you could have told me to suck it up. Instead, you told me about your family…your people."

His gray eyes met hers, cold and unyielding as ever. "Now you will try harder, for you know the cause. I have gone to war. I have seen things you cannot comprehend. It has saved my life." He held out his hand again, hauling her back to her feet. "And it will save yours."

CHAPTER TWENTY-SEVEN
THE BATHS

Three days of discipline training equated to aching muscles, a desperate need to eat anything and everything in her path, and long, *long* hours in the baths, like she was doing right now. Sleeping would have also been a great way to pass the time, but it still evaded her. Every day, she felt like she was going to drop dead from exhaustion and fatigue. As soon as her head hit the pillow, her eyes were *wide* open.

Apparently, near-death experiences did that to a person. Five years ago, she had almost died, and sleep had never really come back. The knife embedding in her shoulder was another thing to add to the list of reasons she couldn't sleep.

She tipped her head back and sank an inch lower into the steaming water. A natural hot spring ran under the mountain and provided bathing water year-round for residences. It was easily one of the best things about living here.

Kerrigan tended to go when everyone else was already asleep. She didn't mind being naked in front of the other girls, but she still wasn't used to showing her ears. Not if she could help it.

Her eyes fluttered closed as the last couple of days slid off her skin.

She wished she could calm her mind as much as the water calmed her body.

It didn't help that she was anxiously waiting to hear from Ellerby. She'd written him a letter and had it mailed to his home in Elsiande. She had no idea when to hope to hear from him or if she even would. Considering the state of his home, she thought it was unlikely. But now she was worried about him.

The whole thing frustrated and confused her. To make matters worse, it put her no closer to finding a house to take her in time. She was going to have to put something together, figure out a way to pull some strings.

If only she could sleep.

Her breathing evened out. Her fingers slipped into the water, the lull of the underground baths pulling her deeper into slumber. It had been days since she'd slept more than a handful of hours. She couldn't resist the pull.

A dream took root almost immediately. A dream unlike any other. This was crystal clear, the images stark and blinding, as if imprinted on her eyelids.

First, a gold medallion broken into three unequal parts. Once the pieces of the puzzle slid together, a symbol appeared—a raven. The same raven that had been on the dagger. The raven took flight, and abruptly, she was looking down on the arena, but it was flooded. A series of platforms was held together by ropes, ladders, and an unsteady framework. The entire thing hovered in the air over the water, and as she watched, the structure *moved*. She found Fordham in the arena. He stood on a rounded bit of scaffolding as he reached out for something in front of him. He couldn't fall or he'd lose everything. A figure appeared behind him, but she couldn't tell who, and with a sharp push, Fordham fell. She reached for him, but already, the dream had shifted.

This time, it was a blur of images flashing hastily before her eyes, as if there was so much, too much, to show in one snap. A warehouse, a length of rope, a dragon flight, a blue drink in a gold goblet, the back of a girl's head with hair the color of ash, the Dragon Ring, Dozan standing over her, a figure in black, and a red mask.

"Kerrigan! Kerrigan!" a voice cried, jolting her awake.

She snapped out of her vision, jerking out of the water and coughing spastically to clear her lungs. She'd fallen all the way under. Any longer, and she might have drowned. She sucked in deep breaths as she tried to make sense of what in the gods' names was happening to her.

"Oh my gods, are you okay?"

Kerrigan cleared her green eyes enough to see who had found her and kept her from drowning. "Audria," she said in surprise.

"Are you all right?" Audria fiddled with a loose lock of her blond hair.

"I'm fine. Thank you," Kerrigan said, suddenly tongue-tied.

Audria was beautiful and royal and a friend from home. A friend she could never be again because Kerrigan didn't want anyone to know where she had come from.

"What are you doing down here?"

"I could say the same to you."

"True," Kerrigan conceded, running a shaky hand back through her red hair.

"But I came to find you. I wanted to talk."

"About what?" Kerrigan asked, retreating in the water, but Audria stepped forward.

"I saw you were training with Fordham."

"Yeah," Kerrigan said warily.

"How's that going?"

"It's grueling. I think he takes pleasure in me being in pain."

"That sounds like the House of Shadows."

Considering what Kerrigan knew about the House of Shadows from Fordham, she would be even more inclined to agree. They weren't brutal to those they thought were beneath them; they were like that to their own too. Brutality was built into their being from a young age. No one could come away from that unscathed.

Audria continued when Kerrigan didn't reply. "What's he like?"

"What do you mean?" Kerrigan crossed her arms over her chest. The last thing she wanted was a line of interrogation from Audria.

"You're the only person he talks to," Audria said with a small shrug of her shoulders. "I've tried to get to know him, but he has no interest in talking."

"I don't know," Kerrigan said softly. "He's exactly what you'd expect."

It was a lie. Fordham wasn't what she had expected at all. Yes, he was brutal, strong, arrogant, but there was something else underneath it all. She didn't know what exactly. She was now discovering it. He didn't have to train her for this fight, and he was anyway. That said something about his character. Maybe he wanted everyone to think he was a brute. Maybe it was easier.

"If he was exactly what I expected, then he wouldn't be training you," Audria said gently. "I don't mean that how it sounded. I'm not…" She cringed again. "I'm not prejudiced. I am completely pro-rights for all marginalized people. I just think that he wouldn't be."

"I don't know why he's training me," Kerrigan admitted.

Why was she still talking to Audria? She couldn't be friends with this girl. No matter how nice she was.

"Okay," Audria said uncertainly. "But just be careful, okay?"

"I can take care of myself."

"I don't know if you heard or knew that someone died recently," Audria said, her voice lowering to a whisper. "It was tragic. He was only seventeen. I heard that he was a pro-rights sympathizer, and now he's dead."

"I do know. He was my friend."

"I'm sorry," Audria said, her blue eyes rounding with worry. "Then you should know that the rumor going around is that Fordham was responsible."

"What?" Kerrigan gasped.

"Apparently, he was the last person to see him alive."

Kerrigan went cold. He *was* the last person to see him alive. But that didn't make him Lyam's murderer. "Fordham didn't do it. Why would he be helping me if he killed Lyam?"

"Well, I don't know. I don't want to speculate."

Except that was precisely what she was doing.

"It doesn't make sense."

"I'm not saying he did it," Audria said quickly. "I've seen you two together a lot, and I was worried. I don't want it to happen to anyone else. Just be careful."

"Thanks," Kerrigan said, retreating once more. This was a lot to take in. She didn't want to think it was Fordham, but she didn't *know* either. "I have to head to bed."

"Oh. Right. Yeah. No problem." Audria smiled, and it was brilliant. All teeth, and her eyes glittered. There were so many layers to Audria Ather. "You know, you really do remind me of someone."

Kerrigan shot her a pained smile and hastened out of the pool. She slid on her clothes and exited the hot springs.

A pounding began in the back of her head and was slowly spreading to her temples.

So others saw what she and Fordham were doing, and they immediately thought the worst of him. It would be easy to do so, considering the history of the House of Shadows. But that didn't seem like the person she had been training with or the person who had saved her from the assassin or carried her to a healer so she didn't bleed out.

She didn't want to think about him betraying her. That he might be a part of all this in some twisted way. It was possible, but her visions kept propelling them together. Even this last one with the tournament had had Fordham in it.

Gods, she needed to sleep—to really sleep. She couldn't process all this. She didn't even know where to begin. Three visions in three weeks? She had no basis for what to do about any of this. She was one person, and the visions were getting more frenetic. She needed someone to tell her what was happening. But she didn't have anyone like that.

She straightened in the empty hallway.

Or did she?

Gelryn slumbered high above in the barely lit eaves. Kerrigan strained her neck to catch a glimpse of the fierce dragon. Even with the dim light, she could barely make out his massive figure.

Her eyes flickered to the set of stairs carved into the side of the mountain. They were used in daylight, when the cavernous rooms were fully lit. It would be supremely stupid to risk them at night, but Kerrigan had training in the morning, so she had no other option.

With a huff, she attempted to summon a small ball of fire to guide her way. The flame sputtered and popped in her hand before guttering. She strained, attempting to force her magic to do what she commanded, but it was no use. The vision had tapped her magic, draining her dry. A little bit of light had never been a feat for her. Flames came the easiest to her, but right now, she couldn't even make a spark.

She straightened her shoulders and moved to the first step. She really wished that she had thought to bring a torch of some sort with her as she climbed the impressive cliffside.

Kerrigan clung to the mountain wall, feeling out each step before she made it. Her legs burned, and her breathing was ragged. Though to her surprise, she saw some marked improvement with all the running Fordham had made her do. Not that she planned to tell him that.

At one point, a rock slipped out from under her foot. Her body crashed sideways, toward the gaping mouth of the opening far below.

She latched on to a chunk of rock and held on for dear life, one leg dangling into the abyss.

She lay flat on her belly and dragged her leg up and over onto the stairs. Her hands shook. If she had fallen, she would have died, and no one would have been the wiser. That was why no one climbed in the middle of the night with no light. She groaned and carefully hauled herself up to her spaghetti legs. She continued up the stairs, nearly collapsing at Gelryn's feet in relief and exhaustion.

One giant eye opened up and stared at her. *"Child, why are you interrupting my slumber?"*

She held up a hand as she caught her breath. "I need…to talk to…someone."

"Talk to a human, and do not bother me again."

"My visions," she gasped out. "They keep happening, and they're getting stronger. I need to find out how to control them or stop them or at least figure out what they mean. You said I was a harbinger, that I am strong in spirit magic, but I don't know what to do, Gelryn. Please, I beg your assistance."

Gelryn's eye had closed once more, and she thought that he had gone back to sleep. That all this had been for nothing. But then he breathed out a wave of heat through his nostrils.

"Let us leave this place."

"Leave?"

"Climb on my back, and we shall depart."

"Are you sure?" she whispered reverently.

The last thing she wanted was to insult Gelryn, who had lost his bonded dragon rider and never taken another, but she had to be sure.

"Kerrigan Argon, do not ask me to repeat myself."

She should have known better. She rose slowly to her feet, wincing at the pain in her legs. She was really going to pay for that tomorrow when Fordham made her run a million miles.

With the strength left in her arms, she pulled herself up and onto Gelryn's enormous back. Dragons weren't this large anymore. He was truly an ancient breed. She felt like a bug on him more than a rider.

Gelryn rose to his haunches, spreading his massive wings. Kerrigan held on with all her might, flattening herself against him, and then he took off, descending deep into the cavern below. She barely suppressed her shriek of terror before he leveled off and then flew upward to one of the exits in the mountain. Then, just like that, they were soaring high above Kinkadia.

She released her death grip on Gelryn's back and pressed herself up into a sitting position. She held her hands out to her sides, enjoying the wind running through her hair. It was easy to forget all her problems when she was up in the clouds. Her last ride with Tavry felt like a lifetime ago, but she remembered thinking it would be her last. She was glad that she had been wrong.

They didn't fly long before Gelryn descended toward another smaller mountain peak. He dropped gracefully onto a summit overlooking the entirety of the valley below and every twinkling light above.

"Whoa," she breathed. "This is beautiful."

"You speak of more visions. Tell me what you have seen."

She spilled her guts, telling him all about her latest visions—the tournament, the raven sigil, and then the bizarre dream she'd had that prompted her to come see him.

"The tournament portions make some sort of sense, but how am I supposed to know what to do with the rest of it? A length of rope? A blue drink? A girl with blond hair?"

"It is as I feared."

"What is?"

"The spiritual magic is controlling you, child, and not the other way around. You need to find a way to harness this ability, or it will destroy you."

"And how am I to do that?" she demanded. "They come on completely unexpected."

"Since our meeting, I have been researching the harbinger ability. Others in the past have been harbingers, but it does not appear that we have seen one in millennia. The recorded histories of that time are few. But even without more information, it is clear to me that the closer your visions are together, the more danger."

"That at least is true. All my visions have spelled danger, usually personal danger."

"I fear that dark times are coming for Alandria. If only one vision was enough to reveal the Red Masks riots, how much danger could be coming if you have already had three visions?"

She frowned. She had not thought about it in magnitudes. "A lot."

"Indeed. We need more knowledge. That is always the answer."

"What can I do? Scour the library?"

"No, child. I fear Fae and humans alike have not been kind to harbingers. Most are seen as mad at best." He looked at her with one wide eye—a warning. *"It appears almost all have been violently killed for their gift."*

She shuddered. "That's marvelous. At least I'm on the right trajectory."

"With your visions coming more frequently, I think it is time that I go home."

He said it with such reverence that there was no question in her mind where he meant. He wanted to go to the Holy Mountain. When dragons had first come to Alandria, the story went that they had been exiled through a portal from another world and left on a mountain of tendrille. There, they would bring their eggs to feel the vibrations of home. She didn't know how much of it was even true, but it was a good story. And many dragons lived and pilgrimaged to the Holy Mountain every year, especially those whose riders were too old to continue participating in the Society culture. They retired to the mountain, and immense amounts of knowledge were still recorded there.

"You think that someone will know about other harbingers?"

"Unlikely," he said truthfully. *"But I hope to find more information from our spiritual leaders. They have walked the plane for generations. I will find control for you, child, if I can."*

She respectfully bowed her head. "Thank you, Gelryn."

"While I am away, you need to stay close to Fordham. He is in your dreams for a reason. Whether for good or evil, we will find out with time."

She cringed. Well, that wasn't exactly comforting. It paralleled what Audria had been alluding to in the caves. Was Fordham here for good or to cause havoc? Kerrigan had come to believe that he was on her side, but she wasn't sure if he was on anyone's, save himself.

"Trust your gut."

"I will," she agreed.

Her gut said he was friend, not foe. She hoped her gut was right.

CHAPTER TWENTY-EIGHT
THE TIP

Fordham punished her with more running. Okay, it wasn't precisely a punishment. He thought that he was helping. But her legs ached for days after her climb up the mountainside, and she couldn't exactly tell him why she hurt so much. She couldn't confide in him about the visions.

At the third-mile mark, Fordham slowed to a walk. Kerrigan happily fell into step beside him. Her chest wasn't heaving quite as badly as it had been, but it wasn't easy either.

"You're improving," he said.

"Does this mean we can move to weapons?"

He shot her a look. "We'll cut this session early. The second task is tomorrow."

"Okay," she said, trying not to sound eager.

She couldn't believe the second task was already here. Half of her time was up, and she hadn't gotten any closer to finding out who had killed Lyam or what house was going to accept her. She had thought Ellerby would be the answer, but he still hadn't responded to her letter. He might never respond. She needed to find a way to get in front of house members who wanted a Dragon Blessed.

Parties were the easiest way to do that, but she'd found Ellerby almost right away and not had to schmooze at any of the parties. Plus, there weren't any more Dragon Blessed parties until *after* the tournament was completed.

"You seem distracted," Fordham said.

"Just two weeks left."

Fordham remained silent, continuing their walk and turning them back toward the mountain. It had seemed so simple when she made that deal with Helly. But then life had gone down the drain, and though she could see the future, she had no idea what was coming next.

"Are you worried about the tournament tomorrow?" she asked.

"Unless you have some insider knowledge about the second task, I have no idea what's coming. There's no reason to worry." He shrugged. "Anyway, I've been through worse."

"Well, that's highly logical," she said with a raised eyebrow.

"This isn't what has you distracted," he said.

"No," she said with a sigh. "Audria came to see me a couple nights ago."

His back stiffened. "About what?"

"You."

He gritted his teeth. "And what did your friend from Bryonica have to say?"

"She's not my friend," she said at once. "But she was worried about me."

"Because of me?"

Kerrigan shrugged. "You are from the House of Shadows."

"Of course."

"There are rumors that you killed Lyam because you are anti-human rights."

He looked at her, and then all the anger bled out of him. To Kerrigan's surprise, he began to laugh. She'd never seen him laugh before. Not really. Not like this. It was full-bodied with his head tipped back and his eyes closed. The display was contagious, and she found she was laughing too. She hugged her belly and tried to stop but failed three times before she got it back under control.

Finally, they both straightened, and Fordham cleared his throat. "Rumors are rumors. It's easy to pin it on me, but why in the gods' names would I be helping you find his killer if it was going to lead you to *me*?"

That was a very good question.

"I said that to Audria, but I just wanted you to know."

"I can handle myself," he said as easily as she always did.

And she let the subject drop. She hadn't believed Audria when she passed that rumor on to her. Kerrigan would have been more worried that she and Fordham were working together if her visions hadn't kept pushing them together. Plus, Gelryn had told her to stay near him. Fordham surely had his own aims for joining the tournament, but they didn't seem to have much to do with her.

◊ⱮⱮⱮ◊

After another long session in the baths, Kerrigan retreated to her room for a much-needed nap. Only two or three hours was all she was getting. It seemed prudent to try to get in as many sessions as she could. Anyway, Fordham was busy the rest of the evening, and she'd already received instruction from Bastian about her role in the tournament tomorrow. A nap sounded wonderful.

But when she returned to her rooms, Clover was seated on her bed.

"Hey! What are you doing here?"

Clover sighed and held up a piece of paper. "Dozan has me sending missives now."

"I thought you were a card dealer," Kerrigan said, taking the letter from her hand.

"I am, but he knows that you trust me. So here I am."

Kerrigan waved away the note of concern and instead broke open Dozan's red wax seal—an arrow through a capital *R*.

The letter held an address, and underneath that:

Tonight at midnight.
   Do try not to get killed, princess.

                              —D.R.

She scowled at the letter. Princess. She hated everything that he called her, but princess was a joke. A stupid joke. Oh, how she regretted confiding in him all those years ago.

"What have you gotten yourself into?" Clover asked.

"There's a weapons deal happening tonight," Kerrigan said. Magic flared to life at her fingertips, and she burned the note to cinders.

"So?"

"I'm going."

"What? Why?"

Kerrigan sighed. "Someone tried to kill me the other night. It was the same person who killed Lyam."

Clover's jaw dropped. "What? When were you going to tell me this? Do Darby and Hadrian know?"

"No. I haven't told anyone yet. I wanted proof."

"You need to tell them, Ker. They need to know."

"I know. I will. I promise."

"How does Dozan factor into this?"

"Well, the assassin got away, and Dozan offered to help me find out who did it."

"Dozan doesn't offer to help people." Clover looked worried. "What did he want in exchange for this information?"

"I agreed to do a fight, a big fight."

Clover groaned. "You said you never wanted to be beholden to him."

"I don't, but this is important. Lyam's death wasn't an accident. No one believed me when I first said it. Not even you. But if I can get proof and take it to the Society, then we can get justice for what happened to him."

"Or you could die!"

"I'm not going to die. I'm bringing Fordham."

Clover's eyebrows rose sharply at that. "*Fordham*, huh? On a first-name basis with the dark prince?"

"Stop it," Kerrigan said, a flush rising to her cheeks.

"I mean, you have good taste. Dozan Rook. Fordham Ollivier. You like them big and bad with muscles and—"

"Please stop!" Kerrigan said, hiding her face. "Fordham and I are not together. I am not interested in him. He is helping me figure out who killed Lyam."

"And what is *he* getting in return?" Clover asked carefully.

"Nothing."

"Don't be naive. No one does anything for free."

"I helped him with the last task. He's returning the favor."

"Seems like a big favor."

Kerrigan shrugged. Clover wasn't wrong. People weren't altruistic. But this was different. "He saved my life from the assassin."

"He *really* had no reason to be helping you. Favor already repaid."

"Yeah. I don't know," Kerrigan admitted.

"Maybe find out."

"Yeah," she whispered. "I should go get him so we can make it to the drop point."

"I wish I could go with you," Clover said. "Dozan told me to come straight back. That he wants me on a table all night."

"It's better that you don't. It's dangerous."

"Just because I don't have magic doesn't mean I'm not capable," Clover snapped.

"I didn't say that," Kerrigan said quickly. "But I'd worry about you."

Clover shrugged. "No sweat."

"Clove, don't." Kerrigan hated when she got defensive and retreated away from her.

"Dragons up, baby," Clover said dismissively. "Come see me tonight after the weapons deal."

"I will," Kerrigan agreed and watched as Clover disappeared through her door.

Kerrigan ground her teeth together. That hadn't gone how she'd wanted, but she really didn't have time. She needed to get Fordham and get the hell out of here.

She changed into all black before heading down the competitors' corridor. Many of the doors were open, and she glimpsed a few competitors stretching or congregating, a few laughing together. Friends. They were friends here.

She ached for that. Darby and Hadrian had moved into their new homes far away in the city. She missed their easy company and even Lyam interrupting them for his antics. She missed it all.

She swallowed back a lump in her throat and passed Audria's room. She was inside, lying on her bed. Roake stood sentinel-like at the entrance. His eyes found hers, and they turned cold.

"What are you doing here again?" he asked.

"Just finding Fordham," she muttered, uncertain of his enmity.

"Yeah, and what exactly are you two always doing together?" He suggestively raised his eyebrows, and her face flushed.

"They're training," Audria cut in. "Or haven't you noticed, Roake?"

He looked back at Audria, and Kerrigan saw his whole face relax. She could see the blatant desire there.

"Why are you training with the dark Fae?" Roake asked.

"Leave her be," Audria said. "No need to harass her for information."

Even though she had done the same thing a few nights ago.

"Good luck tomorrow," Kerrigan told them both and then hurried away.

She knocked once on Fordham's door.

When he didn't reply, she entered without thinking. He sat at the small wooden desk. Papers were strewn in front of him, all of them littered with verses. She could see the rubbish bin was full of crumpled papers, discarded poems that hadn't met his standard.

His head jerked up when she entered. His eyes were raw and open and intense. That darkness had leaked out of him and onto the pages. They bled with his sinister energy. But as soon as he realized who stood before him, he began clearing the papers away.

"What are you doing here?" he asked, the edge still tight in his voice.

She swallowed. She felt as if she had intruded on a moment for him and didn't know how to fix it. Before she could speak, her eyes snagged on a black envelope with gold lettering on the dresser. She picked it up and inspected it, knowing what it was before it revealed itself.

"What's this?" she asked.

His eyes flickered to her in confusion. "A party invitation." He waved his hand away as he continued shoving papers aside. "We get a bunch of them."

She said nothing as she put the invitation back—an invitation to her father's tournament party.

"You had a reason for being here…" Fordham prompted, drawing her away from the letter.

"Right. Dozan," she croaked. "He sent a note. A weapons deal is happening at midnight. If we want to find out who they sold that knife to, we have to go now."

"Tonight?" he hissed.

She nodded.

"But tomorrow is the tournament."

222

"I know."

"You're going to go without me if I don't go, aren't you?"

She bit her lip and shrugged. "Probably."

He finished tucking away all the bleeding pages and hid the contents in a drawer before straightening to his considerable height. He snatched a cloak off a hook and then tipped his head at her. "Then let's go."

They were only a half-mile from the address Dozan had given her when the skies opened up. Dark, heavy clouds had been lingering for two days straight. She had hoped they would hold off for the tournament tomorrow, but no luck. None at all. Rain fell in a deluge, soaking through their clothes and chilling the night air.

"This is madness," Kerrigan grumbled.

"You're the one who wanted to come out here."

"Why are you out here with me?"

He said nothing, and with the rain, she couldn't tell what he was thinking. Not that he was particularly expressive in the first place. Maybe it was Audria's warning, the visions and talk with Gelryn, or Clover's questions, but she couldn't let it go.

She yanked Fordham to a stop under an alcove. "Why *are* you helping me?"

"Do we have to do this right now?"

"The first time, you said it would make us even. But now? There's no reason for you to help me anymore."

He stared at her, his dark eyes intent and irritated. "Why must there be a motivation?"

"Because it doesn't make sense," she yelled over the pounding rain. "Look, I'm glad for your help. I even appreciate the training, despite cursing you in my head."

"Not just in your head."

She shrugged. "Yeah, I hate running. But I don't get it, Fordham. I don't understand why you're helping me."

"You don't trust me," he said simply.

She gulped. No, she didn't. With everything going on, trusting him felt supremely dangerous and supremely stupid.

"Should I?"

His jaw was set. She could almost feel him retreat away from her. "That's good. It's safer if you don't trust me."

"It still doesn't explain…"

"There's someone out there killing humans, half-Fae, and sympathizers. I want to meet them and congratulate them," he hissed, spreading his arms wide. "Is that what you want to hear? What you *expect* from me?"

His voice was laced with venom, and it took everything in her not to step back.

"I didn't say that," she whispered. The wind caught her voice and whipped it away.

"You didn't have to," he accused. "You are the one who has stuck your nose into my business since day one. I did not seek you out. Perhaps it is you who has ulterior motives."

She cringed. Her motives were not innocent, but she couldn't tell him about the visions.

"How about this? We finish this mission, and you never have to see me again." He barreled back out into the rampaging storm.

Kerrigan cursed and dashed after him. His strides were long and measured. She had to jog to keep up with him. She'd never realized how much he slowed his prowl to accommodate her.

"That's not what I want," she gasped, reaching out and gripping his elbow.

"Unhand me, halfling," he said, lethally cold.

She yelped and released him. "I'm sorry, Fordham," she blurted. "I'm sorry, okay? What everyone else has been saying got in my head.

I'm not used to anyone helping me for no reason. Everyone has an angle. Everyone wants something. I didn't expect this."

Slowly, the anger that had unfurled from him was washed away by the storm. "I didn't expect this either."

They stared at each other, and something sparked that hadn't been there before. She'd always found him attractive. She'd never allowed herself to go past that. She hadn't *wanted* to think beyond that. He was dangerous and deadly, yet he was protecting her. And he'd gotten *mad* at her accusations. Her heart thudded in time with the pounding rain, and she felt the tension grow taut between them.

Finally he nodded. She released her breath, and they continued forward in silence.

The address was an old flattop building that might have once housed food stores. The brick facade was crumbling, half of the windows were broken and boarded up, and the front doorway had scorch marks on it. The entire thing looked like one stiff breeze would bring it tumbling down. It was either the perfect place for an illicit weapons deal or a death sentence.

They scouted the surrounding area and found four of Rahllins's lackeys watching the building. One was in front of a ladder that led to the roof. Fordham pointed upward, and she bit her lip but acquiesced. As quick as lightning, Fordham stepped forward, choking the air out of the man's lungs to keep him silent and then putting his fist to the man's temple. He collapsed like a sack of potatoes.

She helped him haul the man deep into the shadows before scaling the rain-slicked, rickety ladder. Fordham went first, and she trailed behind, none too pleased with the creak of the wood. The roof was paper-thin with loose boards littering the top and a giant hole near the entrance where the fire had burned through. It was in even worse shape than she had anticipated.

Without a word, Fordham gestured to the hole, and they crawled forward on their bellies to the edge. She took a small breath and then leaned over the edge to peer down into the dimly lit room below.

A half-dozen men stood on one side behind a woman with raven hair and alabaster skin. There was no doubt in Kerrigan's mind that this was Clare Rahllins. Any minute, she might transform into a raven herself and fly away, so close was the likeness, even from a distance. Across from Clare stood two men and a woman along with a full wagon of covered supplies. Another dozen stood guard around the weapons wagon.

The rain had gone from a flood to a drizzle, but Kerrigan still couldn't hear what anyone was saying.

"We need to get closer," she whispered to Fordham.

He raised his eyebrows, as if to ask how the hell they were going to do that.

She shrugged and inched out a little farther. It would be beneficial to have some sort of advanced hearing, but even Fae couldn't hear that acutely. She had no hope. She tried desperately to make out what Clare was saying.

Crack.

The boards beneath them splintered. She looked at Fordham with wide, panicked eyes before the roof gave way, and they plummeted.

CHAPTER TWENTY-NINE
THE WEAPONS DEAL

K errigan woke tied to a chair.

She struggled against the chafing bonds, but there was no escape. Her chest, arms, and legs were bound so tightly that she could barely breathe, let alone get out of the restraints. Her head hurt like... well, like she'd fallen through a roof. She had no concept of how much time had passed since then, only that the room was now empty, save for Fordham, who was passed out beside her, and a guard with his arms crossed, staring off into space.

A warehouse. A length of rope. Well, that part of her vision hadn't been particularly useful. It would have been nice to know what the warehouse and rope were going to be used for.

"Fordham," she hissed, low and urgent.

But he didn't move an inch. Just sat there with his head back, eyes closed. Very much knocked out.

"Looks like someone is finally awake," the guard said.

He disappeared through the door, and a few minutes later, a woman with raven hair that fell like a waterfall over one eye entered. She was even more beautiful in person. Skin the color of milk and her one visible eye so blue, as if plucked straight out of the ocean. She wore black leather from head to toe and had so much steel on her, she would have dropped like a stone in the sea.

"Well, well, well," she said in a slow, concentrated drawl. Her accent was thick, like those from the north. "What do we have here?"

"Hello," Kerrigan said, hoping for chipper. "It appears there has been a mistake."

"A mistake?" the woman said, chewing on her words. "Yes, there has been a mistake." A knife appeared in her hand as if out of thin air, and it tipped Kerrigan's chin up. "You made the mistake of crossing Clare Rahllins."

"Clare who?" Kerrigan asked innocently, widening her eyes. "I'm sorry. I've no idea what you're talking about."

"And I might have believed you, pretty thing," Clare said, "but for him."

"Him?"

"He is a competitor. That means you must work for the Society," Clare said. "You are here on their business. What do they want with Clare Rahllins?"

The woman was mad. She was referring to herself in the third person, and Kerrigan didn't know how to get out of this one. The last thing she wanted was to get sliced open over a botched weapons deal. She had only been there to find out who they were selling to in hopes of getting a lead on her assassin.

"I really don't want anything with anyone," Kerrigan said hopefully. "If you could untie me, we could go about this in a civilized manner."

Clare snorted. "Civilized?" She wrenched back her black hair, revealing the side of her face that had been concealed. Her left eye was missing, and a scar ran from the edge of the empty socket across to her ear, which was mangled.

The only sign of distress that escaped Kerrigan was a small intake of breath. Clare had clearly shown her this to shock her. And Kerrigan was shocked—that she would hide it. Clare was stunning. All full lips and arched eyebrows and high cheekbones. The scar was just a part of her, and it made her more complete, if less symmetrical.

But who was Kerrigan kidding? She hid her ears all the time. Anything that could create enmity was a thing to hide, though not be ashamed of.

"Yes, please, civilized." She smiled brightly.

Smack.

Kerrigan cried out as Clare's fist connected with her face. Her nose was broken again. Scales!

"How is that for civilized?" Clare spat, straightening.

Kerrigan couldn't even bring her hand to her nose or stanch the bleeding. The blood flowed freely down her face and coated the front of her shirt. Her face throbbed. What had she gotten herself into now?

Clare flicked her head at one of the guards nearby. He hefted a bucket and threw the contents into Fordham's face. He came to, sputtering and coughing.

"What the hell?" he spat out.

"Hello, darling," Clare crooned, twirling a knife again. "Thank you for joining us."

Fordham blinked rapidly, expelling the last of the water from his storm-gray eyes. He took in everything around himself in a matter of seconds—the binding, Clare, and Kerrigan beside him, bleeding.

"We fell through the roof," he said simply.

"Ah, so you do speak. That's a relief. This one," Clare said, pointing her knife at Kerrigan and nicking her jaw, "likes to play dumb."

Kerrigan grunted at the new pain and wrenched her head back.

"I'm not here to play dumb," Fordham said, icy cold. "But I will have to retaliate if you do not untie us immediately."

Clare raised an eyebrow. "Not bloody likely."

Fordham glared at her. "You'll regret this."

"You're in the tournament, and you think I'm dumb enough to tie you up without slipping you some dampening drugs?"

Kerrigan's face paled. "That's illegal!"

Clare quirked a half smile at her. "Thanks for the tip, sugar."

Fordham strained against his ropes, and Kerrigan could practically feel him trying to access his magic, but nothing happened. No black smoke. No fierce elemental abilities. Nothing.

Kerrigan swallowed down her fear and reached for her own powers, hoping that Clare had been stupid enough not to dampen her. To see Kerrigan's slight ears and not find her a threat. But no, when she dove down into her well of energy, there was nothing. The emptiness made her want to vomit all over the walls. There was a reason magic-dampening drugs were illegal. Removing magic from magical users was like severing a limb. People went insane from it. Most couldn't even stomach living. Suicide occurred at a severely high rate.

"What do you want with us?" Kerrigan asked, trying to ignore the yawning chasm within her.

"Want? Nothing. You were the ones spying on Clare Rahllins," Clare said, pointing the knife at her own chest. "It's your turn to tell me who sent you."

"No one sent us," Fordham spat.

Clare pointed at the guard. He punched Fordham in his face, cracking hard against that chiseled cheekbone. He grunted as the man pummeled him in the chest and stomach.

"Stop!" Kerrigan cried. "Stop it! No one sent us! We're telling the truth."

Clare flicked her blade. "If no one sent you, then why were you spying?"

"We weren't spying."

She tipped her head again, and the guard came toward Kerrigan. She froze, caught in a trap. There was nothing she could do. She couldn't tell this woman that she was trying to find out who had attempted to kill her. That an assassin with a knife bearing the raven sigil had attacked her. She would surely kill her to finish the work for the person. It might be better to let Clare think that they were here for the Society. At least then they could extract information from them. But she didn't want to get hit. Not again.

Not *again*.

"Please no," she whispered.

But the man didn't even balk at her whispered words. He just came for her. His first hit was clean, right to her temple. Her vision blurred and wavered. Everything swam. The second knocked into her stomach, and the air whooshed out of her lungs.

She coughed and sputtered, spitting blood on the floor.

"Rahllins," a man said, stepping in the room and momentarily halting the beating.

"You dare interrupt!"

"It's just that the delivery to Black House was interrupted."

Black House. Kerrigan swallowed down blood, thinking about the name of the haunted mansion. What could possibly be delivered there?

Clare growled. "You stay here and work on the interrogation. I'll deal with them."

Clare stormed from the room, ignoring Fordham's shouts of protest. The weasel-faced man stepped inside. For a moment, Kerrigan thought he might be better than having Clare, the vicious snake, but she was wrong.

"Now, why did the Society send you?" he asked, dragging over a stool and staring between the two. "Why is the Society taking an interest in our weapons? What member is in charge of this?"

"We don't work for the Society," Fordham ground out. "We tried to tell you that already."

"Begin," the man said, pointing at Kerrigan. "Perhaps watching her suffer will loosen your tongue."

"She has nothing to do with this," Fordham cried.

His gray eyes found hers, pleading with her to say something, to end this. But what could they say? They were telling the truth. She could rat out Dozan, but that wouldn't save them. Dozan and Clare were enemies on a good day. And today was not a good day.

The next blow cracked across her jaw and then back the other way. She retreated hard within herself as pain exploded across her body. Over and over and over again.

Fordham was yelling something, but her ears were ringing. She couldn't make out what he was saying. The man was hitting her, using her pain to try to get Fordham to talk, but Kerrigan wasn't here any longer. She burrowed deep within herself, losing her sense of identity and her sense of time and her sense of space. She vanished into that nothingness, where there was no pain or fear or torture. A place she hadn't gone to since that night five years ago when she had her first vision. Just like…

Kerrigan's green eyes glittered with excitement. For the first time ever, a human had won the dragon tournament. Cyrene had won! Her success was a huge victory for humans and half-Fae alike, even more so for the cause.

Parades littered the streets. People chanted Cyrene's name. They called her a saint. Kerrigan had tried to convince her friends to join her in cel-ebration. It wasn't every day that you got to witness history. But Darby's parents were in town, Hadrian didn't like crowds, and Lyam had been sent to do chores for his last indiscretion. They'd all agreed she shouldn't go out alone, not after the Erewa bombing in the arena, but she couldn't sit there when the whole world was celebrating Cyrene's victory.

Kerrigan felt a certain thrill that she knew *the human champion. That she had met her and spoken with her and confided in her for the month that she was here. She likely would never see her again, but still, she had met Cyrene Strohm of Doma!*

Kerrigan turned down an empty alleyway, heading toward the square. She wore her favorite white dress and a pink cloak. Bright colors to match the vibrant festivities.

Then a man stepped into the alleyway. Huge with a menacing air about him and sharply pointed ears. Full-blooded Fae.

"Hello there, pretty," he crooned.

Her steps faltered and then stopped. "Hello," she whispered, the fear creeping into her voice.

She took a step back, prepared to run, but when she turned, there were more of them. More Fae, not all male, but every one of them made her skin crawl to escape.

"What's a leatha doing out here, all alone, on a night like this?" the first man addressed her.

She flinched. Leatha. What a horrid word. How dare he call her that!

"I'm heading to the parade. If you'll let me pass…"

"Oh, I don't think so," the man said.

"Please, I don't have any money."

The man stepped forward, pressing his chest against hers. She was only twelve, but she knew to be afraid. Afraid of what he could do to her, afraid of how he could hurt her. She drew her magic in sharp and tight to her chest. She had power, but against this many?

"We don't want money from a leatha," he growled, running a finger down her cheek.

The people behind him laughed and cheered and egged him on. She couldn't hear what they were saying. She could only smell the rank breath of the man and see his dark eyes, almost black, and the abject anger in them. As if she were an affront to him for simply having been born.

"What…what do you want?" she asked, near to tears now.

"Unfortunately, we can't suffer a leatha to live."

Kerrigan lashed out with her magic. Flames erupted, blasting the man backward and destroying his face. He screamed, and others hastened forward to put out the flames. Kerrigan ignored them all and tried to run,

233

run far away from them. Darby and Hadrian had been right. This was a mistake, a terrible mistake.

One of the women latched on to her wrist and yanked. A sharp pop sounded in the alleyway as her wrist dislocated. Then the woman threw her down into the dirty street. Dirt and grime and sewage covered the front of her white dress and dirtied the pretty silk cloak. Her hands were scraped raw from catching herself, and the pain from her wrist was agonizing.

"You leatha bitch!"

A boot connected with her jaw. She was flung backward, stars exploding in her vision. She reached for her powers, but suddenly, as if a whirlpool had drained inside her, her magic was sucked up and emptied. There was nothing there. Nothing at all to save her. She reached and reached, but she was being pulled under and away.

Images flashed before her eyes. The parade at the square on fire. People wearing red masks, flooding the streets. Death. So much death. A portal door within the mountain. A castle in a distant mountain range. Not of this world. A magical battle and dragons, hundreds of dragons flying to aid.

A voice spoke to her. A voice she recognized. Tears sprang to her eyes at the sound of Cyrene speaking to her.

"I have little time, Kerrigan. We are in desperate need of your help. Open the portal this one last time. We beg of you. The fate of our world may rest in your hands."

"Cyrene, I don't know if I'm strong enough."

Cyrene's voice was a caress. "I know that you are or else I would not be able to speak to you now."

"I'm afraid."

"Do you want to know a secret?"

"Yes," Kerrigan whispered.

"We're all afraid. Every minute of every day. But those who master their fear, they're the ones who go on to do great things."

And then her voice was gone. The images were gone.

All Kerrigan felt was the pain. For however many seconds she had had *those images and Cyrene in her head, the Fae had converged on her. They were beating her. They were going to kill her. She was broken. Her limbs couldn't move. She had no magic anymore. Not even a drop.*

She was going to die here. Die before she could ever tell a single soul that Cyrene had spoken to her. That Cyrene's world needed saving.

She opened her eyes, and a scream of protest escaped her. The Fae had donned masks. Red masks. They were part of the images in her head. Had they been true? All she saw was the red masks beating her, kicking her, killing her. Red blood coated her white dress.

Pain overtook her body. Unconsciousness beckoned. Failure. If she left now, she would fail Cyrene, fail everyone. Still, there wasn't anything she could do. She retreated deep, deep, deep into herself. To the dark, empty place where there was no pain, no fear, no torture. Just eternity.

And then something rocked through her. A wave of energy exploded from the core of her body and released outward, like a bomb detonating.

CHAPTER THIRTY
THE SECOND

Kerrigan opened her eyes. Her bonds were severed. Bodies littered the ground before her. Her limbs were heavy, and her pain rushed back to her tenfold. She groaned and turned her attention to Fordham.

He was still conscious, though barely. One eye was swollen shut. His shirt was torn, and there was a long cut from his left shoulder across to his right abdomen. It wasn't deep, but it was still freshly leaking blood.

"What did you do?" he muttered, his one eye wide in shock.

She stood despite her many injuries and began to unknot his bonds. "We have to get out of here."

"What happened?"

"I don't know," she admitted.

It was the truth and not the truth. She had clearly caused some kind of magical explosion despite the fact that her magic had been dampened by whatever drug Clare had given them. And it wasn't the first time she had done it. She had done it five years ago as well. She tamped down that thought until she had time to process it later.

She finished with the bonds on his feet. "You need to get up. We have to flee."

"But—"

"Now," she commanded, hard and unyielding. "Now."

He bottled up all his questions and turned back into the military commander he so obviously had been in his previous life. "Let's move out."

Kerrigan toed the man who had beaten her. He didn't move. She swallowed, uncertain if she had killed them or knocked them out, but she didn't stop to check. Already, Fordham was to the door, holding his ribs.

"This way," he said and then charged down the hallway.

She followed after him, peeking her head into doorways. Everyone they passed was crumpled and unconscious. They didn't have to fight a single soul as they fled the building.

They both halted when they exited and saw the sun rising bright on the horizon.

"The tournament," Fordham gasped.

"Shit," Kerrigan spat.

"We'll have to run back to the arena."

"Can you make it?" she asked him, gesturing to his side.

"I'll have to," he said with fierce determination. "Where the hell are we?"

Kerrigan assessed their surroundings. "I'm not sure exactly. Still north valley. They must have moved us to a more secure location. But we have to follow the mountain."

She pointed to Draco Mountain looming in the distance. Far, *far* in the distance.

Fordham straightened his shoulders and took off at a jog. She could hear him wheezing as she followed after him. Broken rib. If not multiple. Under no circumstances should he be running before seeing a healer, but besides the noise, he didn't stop or slow down at all.

Kerrigan hurt everywhere, and she still couldn't access her magic. She'd been able to have some sort of explosion when she was kidnapped, but she couldn't touch her magic now? That made no sense. And if she couldn't access hers, then Fordham likely couldn't either. He was going to have to walk into the second task without *magic*. Scales.

"Aren't you glad that I made you run?" he quipped.

She glared at him. "If we make it to the tournament, remind me later to kick you."

He laughed humorlessly and then clutched his ribs. "If I make it through this task, remind me to never go on scouting missions with you again."

"Deal," she said with a half quirk of her mouth.

And then they ran and ran and ran.

The sun was high on the horizon. They had so little time to get to the tournament, and there was no way they were going to hold the entire event, waiting for Fordham.

"Almost there," she gasped out as they moved from a run to a final full-out sprint.

She couldn't believe they still had energy left, but there was no other choice. They could hear the master of ceremonies speaking to the crowd and the stadium chanting with pleasure at the start of the second task.

"Where—"

"This way," she told him, back in her element.

And then they were in front of the competitors' door. She yanked it open, and she and Fordham all but fell through. The other nine competitors, three administrators, and Valia turned as one to stare at them, bloody, beaten, and out of breath.

"What in the gods' names has happened?" Bastian asked, striding forward with part anger and part concern.

"We…" Kerrigan began at the same time as Fordham said, "I…"

They looked at each other and then shrugged.

"We fell," Fordham informed Bastian.

Kerrigan's eyes widened. It was the truth and somehow also a terrible lie.

"We went hiking, and we fell."

Bastian looked between them as if he couldn't fathom what was wrong with them. "We will discuss this later. For now, the tournament must go on."

"A healer for certain, Bastian," Mistress Sinead said with wide eyes. "I can work on him."

"There's no time. We've already delayed long enough. Fordham chose to be out all night," Bastian said evenly. "He will have to compete as he is or not at all."

Fordham straightened, ignoring the pain in his ribs. "I will compete."

"Good lad," Bastian said and then ushered him toward the rest of the competitors.

Kerrigan reached out and grabbed his hand, a tingle racing up her arm at the slightest touch.

Fordham turned around in confusion. "What?"

"The raven," she told him. "Get the raven medallion."

"What are you talking about?"

"Trust me," she said earnestly. "Like last time."

He looked at her shrewdly. "All right."

And then Sinead was tugging her away from Fordham and pushing her down into a chair. "I don't know *what* you two were up to, but I need to set this nose and heal your injuries. You could have internal damage."

"I want to watch the tournament."

Sinead brooked no argument. She got to work. After only a few minutes, Kerrigan was so exhausted, she thought she was going to pass out entirely.

"What is happening?" Sinead asked incredulously.

"Healing draws on a person's energy, right?" Kerrigan muttered.

"Of course. It draws on us both."

"I have none. I'm spent."

Sinead stared her down. "And what were you doing that exhausted your magic?"

Kerrigan sealed her lips and stared back at the woman. She wasn't going to tell her a thing.

Sinead sighed. "Fine. I don't want to use all my energy either. It is much easier when it flows through both of us," Sinead said with another pointed sigh. "I will finish your nose and jaw. They're both broken. Then you can go watch the tournament. Once you have had something to eat and drink and rested, we'll have another session."

The next half hour of healing was an effort in self-control. Kerrigan could hear the cries for the competitors and had no idea how Fordham was doing out there, how any of them were doing. But once her jaw and nose were set, her entire body felt so much better.

She thanked Mistress Sinead and then hastened to the box to watch the rest of the event.

Kerrigan gasped when she got a glimpse of the arena for the first time. Even though she had seen images of what would come in her vision, it was nothing compared to seeing the entire arena flooded. A man-made lake now resided within the arena, and overtop were the interlocking platforms. Each of them could move on their own. The ladders and ropes to climb between them weren't connected but dangling, so competitors had to jump to reach them and haul themselves up.

"Gods," she whispered as she came to stand beside Valia, the Society steward.

How was Fordham supposed to climb with broken ribs?

"What happened to you?" Valia asked, knotting her blond hair into a plait at her back.

"Something unfortunate." Kerrigan smiled at the other girl though. "Don't worry. I got a few licks in myself."

"You're absurd."

"Thank you," Kerrigan said, returning to the task. "How does it work?"

"Each competitor has to find and put together three medallion parts and then climb to the top of the platform. The first eight competitors to finish advance to the final."

"That doesn't sound too bad."

"Did you not notice the platforms are moving?" Valia inquired. "And there are Society members stationed around the arena, soaking the various platforms. If someone falls into the water, they're automatically out. No second chance."

Kerrigan shuddered as her vision whipped through her once more. A push and Fordham falling. Gods, he'd be out of the tournament. How was she supposed to warn him of that now that he was already out there, scrambling around on those moving platforms with broken ribs?

"Oh" was all Kerrigan managed.

"Yeah. Oh."

Kerrigan watched Fordham, who somehow, despite his lack of magic and the amount of pain he surely was in, still managed to move through the platforms, hoisting himself up and finding medallion pieces. She watched him pick up a piece and look at it, and then his eyes found hers. It must not have been a raven piece, because with a clench of his jaw, he put it back.

"What is he doing?" Valia asked in shock. "Why would he put the piece back?"

"Maybe it doesn't fit?"

"Unlikely. All the medallions were cut into three pieces."

Kerrigan said nothing. The raven medallion was three uneven pieces. And she had no idea why he needed them, but he did.

A bell sounded from the master of ceremonie's box. Kerrigan jolted.

"What was that?"

Valia pointed to the top, and Kerrigan saw with shock that Audria had already finished. She'd climbed to the top of the platform, and she was standing victorious with a medallion clutched in her hand.

"He put back another piece!" Valia cried. She whirled on Kerrigan. "What is he doing? If he's not careful, he won't finish in time."

Kerrigan shrugged. "I don't know what he's doing."

But she could see that Valia was right. It looked like two or three of the other competitors had already located all three pieces of their medallion and were hastening upward after Audria's miraculous first-place win.

"She'll get to enter the third task first before everyone else."

Kerrigan worried at her lip. Had she made a mistake in telling Fordham about the raven medallion? He'd already be finished and climbing the platform to meet Audria if Kerrigan hadn't told him about the raven. But the visions hadn't been wrong. They were typically painful but not wrong. She had to trust them even if he was likely cursing her name.

Another bell rang out.

"Taiga," Valia said.

Kerrigan paled. Venatrix in second was not good for anything. More warrior house Society members meant more war.

"Come on, Fordham," she whispered under her breath.

Another bell.

"Chelcie of Galanthea."

Kerrigan shuddered. Great. Two warrior houses in the top three.

"They'll both go in after Audria," Valia told her.

Another bell.

"Roake," Kerrigan said softly. The boy form Elsiande who harassed her in the halls and was likely in love with Audria.

"Surprised to see the houses who don't participate in magic doing well this year," Valia mused.

"They still do magic," Kerrigan said. "They think it should be used for other means."

"Like getting rid of it."

Kerrigan shrugged. "Maybe less magic would be better for some people."

Valia's eyes flared wide in anger. "Are you one of those people who think that the Society should have less power? Because they are the only thing keeping this city in check."

"I've lived my entire life in the mountain. I don't think that I'm against the Society, but that doesn't mean that I can't have an opinion on their policies."

Valia opened her mouth to argue, but Kerrigan gasped, cutting her off.

Darrid of Herasi, the competitor that Fordham had humiliated in the last task, was sneaking up on Fordham from behind as he dug through one of the boxes on the platform. Fordham stood, a look of triumph on his face as he slid the third piece of his medallion into place. Darrid was there. And just like in her vision, everything fell apart.

A shove, a scream, hands reaching out.

And then Fordham was free-falling toward the arena water below.

CHAPTER THIRTY-ONE
THE FALL

Fordham fell. His body moved past one, two, three platforms, his momentum carrying him faster and faster and faster toward that impending water. The water that would push him out of the tournament forever.

Kerrigan could hear cheers and boos from the stands. Some were mad that Darrid had pushed Fordham. Others were delighted to see the prince of the House of Shadows fall. But she was focused on him soaring through the air. He had no magic. He couldn't buffer his fall. He couldn't slow himself. He could do nothing but drop.

She put her hands over her eyes, peering out through a slit in her fingers. Her stomach was in knots. There wasn't a single thing that she could do.

"Fordham!" she cried despite herself.

And then, with the dexterity only she had seen him move with, he reached out at the last second and grasped on to the final platform with one hand. There was a sickening snap as something broke or dislocated in his arm. An inhuman snarl ripped from him, reverberating throughout the arena.

He'd saved himself. He'd done it.

Then she saw the real horror. He wasn't holding the medallion. He'd dropped it. It fell slower than him with less mass to carry it down. It drifted toward the water, as if calling itself home.

Fordham's eyes were wide with pain, but still, he managed to reach out and pluck the medallion out of thin air. It dangled on a finger, the length of the ribbon just barely caught. He didn't even dare breathe as he slowly slid it down his finger and clenched the thing in his fist. With a sigh of relief, he slid the medallion over his head and began the arduous process of climbing back up to the lowest platform.

By this time, it was clear that all competitors had found their medallion pieces and were now climbing the slippery platforms to try to be one of the final eight competitors. Fordham was on the bottom rung. To make it through to the final task, he still had to beat two other competitors to the top of the platform.

With another disgusting pop, Fordham wrenched his shoulder back into place. The crowd seemed to make a collective gag at the brutality. But Fordham's military training kept him up, and she saw in his face basic battlefield healing.

She didn't know when everything had changed. Between the first task, when she'd been hoping he'd win because of the vision, and now, when she was a ball of anxiety over the fact that he might *lose*. And he couldn't lose. Not because of her visions but because of him.

"Fordham, come on!" she screamed over the roar of the crowd. "Get moving!"

As if he'd heard her, he began to climb up the soaked platforms.

A bell rang out.

"Darrid," Valia whispered.

"Bastard," Kerrigan grumbled. "Cheating bastard."

"It's not technically against the rules."

Kerrigan huffed and went back to watching Fordham. He was flagging. His breathing was unsteady. His hand kept going to his ribs, as if all this exertion was only exacerbating the issue. His shoulder couldn't be feeling great either. Not to mention neither of them had slept a wink last night unless unconsciousness was considered sleep. She couldn't believe he'd made it this far.

Another bell.

"Noda."

Kerrigan bounced up and down on the balls of her feet. That left four competitors, and only two more could go through. She was so fixated on Fordham's relentless climb up a swaying rope ladder that she didn't notice anything was wrong until the crowd gasped.

She turned and saw a girl—Kamari—sail through the air and land with a splash into the water. Kerrigan winced. That was a long fall. It had to have hurt, and now, she was out.

A bell rang.

"Posana. Only one more spot."

Kerrigan worried on her lip as Fordham and Valero shot to the top of the structure. Two platforms down from the top, they met. Each sized the other up. Fordham looked like a brutalized mess. Valero looked more the image of a prince in that moment. They each lunged for a way up.

Valero got ahold of a ladder as water rained down on them. He slipped, falling to the last rung as the rope shredded his hands. He cried out but managed to hang on. Fordham had gone for a single rope. Not many of the competitors had climbed up the ropes, but Fordham scaled it like he'd been rope climbing his entire life.

Valero noticed Fordham's efficiency and hastened back up the ladder. Fordham hit the platform top first with Valero a second behind him. There was only one more platform to reach and only one way to get there: a black wall about ten feet high.

Each competitor had to run up the face of the slick surface. Most had used their magic to ease their way to the top. Fordham had no magic left.

Valero took a running leap for the edge, but before he could hold on to the edge, Fordham lashed out, grasping Valero by the ankle. He yanked viciously with a pull that dropped Valero to the platform. The whole thing shook with the force of it and then began to move in a tight circle. Valero tried to get up, but Fordham hovered over him now.

A ripple of unease passed through the crowd. Kerrigan could see the ferocity in Fordham's expression. His need to win this. And for a second, looking at the cunning evil in his face, she wondered if she had made the right choice. If he could flip to this in an instant, what could he do to her?

Everyone waited with bated breath for Fordham to end it. For him to kick Valero off the platform or put his foot through his face. To do something to earn the nightmares he'd elicited in those assembled.

But it was the fear on Valero's face that snapped Fordham out of it. He took a step away from him and then ran up the side of the wall with such ease that he might as well have been using magic.

Another bell rang.

"Fordham," Valia hissed.

Valero collapsed backward and brought his hands to his face in miserable defeat. Fordham had broken him with a look—a terrifying, menacing look—but that was all it had taken.

The master of ceremonies exclaimed and cheered for the competitors who were going through to the final task as the platforms slowly drifted toward the arena lake. They fit together like puzzle pieces with perfect notches until they were one solid piece. A walkway was pushed out, connecting the competitors to the arena floor.

Fordham was somehow still on his feet, standing proud and a touch regal. But as soon as he made it inside the cover of the competitors' box, he collapsed into a chair and promptly passed out.

꩜

"He will be fine," Mistress Sinead said, patting Kerrigan's arm a few hours later. "He needs to rest and recover. His injuries were quite severe."

Kerrigan nodded mutely as Sinead exited the room. Kerrigan took the seat next to Fordham's bed, where he had been carried after healing. She'd had her own healing, taken a strict power nap, and eaten enough food for a horse. Her magic had flickered back sometime while Fordham was still knocked out. Sinead had given him some kind of sedative to keep him under.

Kerrigan sighed heavily and leaned backward. What was she going to do now? They both probably needed to sleep it off for a few days. Not go rushing back out into danger. She should leave him to it, but for some reason, she couldn't move. She didn't feel comfortable leaving his side.

Instead, she stood and began to slowly pace his room. His notebook was tucked away against his desk. Her fingers itched to open the book so she could read what he had written, what had made him bleed on the pages. But it felt too private. Now that they were friends, she wouldn't intentionally break his trust.

Her eyes swept to the notebook one more time, and then she retreated. Her curiosity always got the best of her. She couldn't expect him to trust her if she snooped through his things while he was unconscious. She plopped back down into the chair with a sigh.

She felt herself nodding off again when a knock sounded on the door. Kerrigan scrambled uneasily to her feet, ready to tell the person to leave, that he wasn't ready for visitors. But it wasn't another competitor. It was Clover.

"Clove, what are you doing here?" Kerrigan yanked her inside the room and promptly shut the door.

Clover was still wearing Dozan's red button-up and vest uniform. She couldn't have been more out of place.

"Kerrigan," she gasped, throwing her arms around her. "You never came to see me last night. I thought you were dead."

"Clove, I'm sorry."

"What happened?"

Kerrigan sighed and sank back into her chair. She ran a shaky hand through her red hair and then told Clover *nearly* everything that had happened, leaving out the part about her explosion that had helped them escape. She wasn't sure she wanted anyone else to know about that yet. By the end of it, Clover looked horrified.

"You were tortured," Clover whispered.

"Yes," Kerrigan said softly.

She had been tortured, and her magic had unleashed on the building. She didn't know if they were all dead, if she had killed them all. What she did know was that this wasn't the first time it had happened.

That night five years ago, when she had been beaten in the alley and had her first vision, her magic had exploded like that as well. *She had been the one to knock out the Fae who were going to kill her.* And all along, Dozan had let her believe that he had saved her. That she'd been about to die, and he'd killed everyone to keep them from hurting her. Dozan, who had never done anything magnanimous in his entire life. Now she knew the truth. He'd done it because she had power. Power that even she didn't know what it was or how to control it. And then she had been *stupid* enough to tell him about her vision that night.

"What is it?" Clover asked, reading her face all too well.

"Nothing," Kerrigan said with a shake of her head. "But we have to go to Black House."

Kerrigan cringed even saying the words. She knew what Clover's response would be, but it was her only lead from the weapons deal. Her only chance to find out who the assassin was.

Clover paled. "You can't go *in there*, Red."

"Well, not until Fordham is well at least."

Clover looked like she was going to argue further when a groan came from Fordham. Kerrigan rushed to his side. Fordham's eyes opened, and his body went rigid.

"Hey, it's okay. You're okay."

Her face appeared before him, and he scrunched up his brow. "What are you doing in here, halfling?"

Clover opened her mouth to protest the name, but Kerrigan didn't even feel the bite in it anymore.

"Well, princeling," she said, giving the sass right back, "you tried to die."

"Sounds like me," he grumbled.

"Sinead healed you, and you should be better. You need rest. Not like you're going to do that."

"Probably not."

"But you made it through to the final task."

He lifted himself up and swung his legs off the bed.

Kerrigan made a yelp of protest. "What part of rest don't you understand?"

"I've rested," he simply said.

"Your magic."

He blew her hair out of her face with a small puff of air. "Is back." His eyes found Clover's. "What are you doing here?"

"Hello to you too, sweetheart," she said with a grin.

He looked back to Kerrigan. "Are all your friends like this?"

"Pretty much," Kerrigan conceded. "And she's here because we didn't show up at the Wastes last night. Now she's trying to convince me not to go to Black House."

He put his head in his hands. "What's Black House?"

"It's where Clare said they took the weapons last night. I think it must be their headquarters," Kerrigan told him.

Clover shook her head. "It's an old, haunted orphanage where they experimented on children and then drowned them in bathtubs."

Fordham looked up skeptically. "That sounds pleasant."

"It's all superstition," Kerrigan said.

"For a reason," Clover shot back.

"Are you saying there are ghosts?" Fordham asked. "Real ghosts?"

Clover shrugged. "No one goes inside, but the house makes weird noises, and on the Night of the Dead, anyone who walks in there doesn't come out."

Kerrigan laughed. "We'll be fine but only after you're rested."

Fordham rose to his considerable height. "I'm rested," he repeated.

"Sinead said—"

"I'm rested," he growled.

"All right," she said with an arched eyebrow. Then, she stepped forward and kicked him in the shin.

He cursed sharply. "What the hell?"

"Don't scare me like that," she told him.

He looked down at her, and something passed between them. Whatever joking anger had always been there was replaced by something she couldn't explain. That same feeling she'd had in the thunderstorm last night and when she'd reached for him before the start of the tournament. Heat.

Her cheeks flushed, and she looked away.

Clover cleared her throat. "You two are actually going to go into Black House at night?"

"You don't have to come with us if you're scared, Clove," Kerrigan told her.

Clover crossed her arms over her chest. "I'm not scared."

"Then we'll go tonight," Fordham said.

And neither of them disagreed with him. Though neither could keep from shivering at the prospect.

CHAPTER THIRTY-TWO
THE BLACK HOUSE

Despite all her bluster about not being afraid, Kerrigan had never been reckless enough to go into Black House. Certainly not at night. Lyam had dared her on more than one occasion, but even Lyam hadn't followed through with it. The farthest they'd made it was up the creaky stairs to touch the door. And even that felt impossible tonight, with the clouds obscuring the moon and the stars. Darkness swept in, total and absolute.

"This feels like a big mistake," Clover whispered from the front lawn of Black House.

It used to be a reputable area, somewhere between the Dregs and Central, but since it had fallen into legend, the Dregs had swallowed it up.

"It's going to be fine," Kerrigan bluffed.

"You two actually believe there are ghosts?" Fordham asked again in disbelief. Apparently, ghosts were too far-fetched for him. He hadn't heard the entire house rattle on the Night of the Dead.

Clover and Kerrigan looked at each other. They both shrugged. It was as close to a yes as they'd get.

Fordham sighed. "It doesn't look like anyone's been here. There's dust on the front steps."

"Maybe we should go through the back?" Clover squeaked.

"Why don't you be the lookout?" Fordham suggested to Clover.

She visibly relaxed at the suggestion. "Yeah, I'll be the lookout."

Kerrigan followed Fordham to the back side of the enormous black house. The black paint was chipping, some of the windows were busted, and the house groaned loudly in anticipation of their arrival. Goose bumps erupted on her arms, and she tamped down her mounting fear.

"Maybe this is a bad idea," she whispered to Fordham as he took the first step up. She latched on to his arm to stop him. "Maybe I heard what they said wrong."

"You didn't hear wrong." His eyes bored into hers. "Do I have to go in there alone?"

"No," she said. "No, I'll go. You didn't grow up with fear of this place."

"Aren't you lucky I'm here to dispel your fears?"

"I guess," she muttered as he tugged her up the stairs.

Once they reached the wobbly porch, she released him and tiptoed across the boards to the back door. This was as far as she had ever made it at Black House. She had touched the front door, not necessarily the back, where the shadows were darker and deeper.

"There's no one inside," Fordham whispered, peering in the window. "It looks empty."

"Maybe they only house the weapons here?"

Fordham went to the door. "This is a new lock."

"That's promising. Need me to—"

Before she could ask him if he needed help with breaking in, the lock clicked in his hand, and he pressed the door open. Fordham entered first, igniting a small flame in his palm and stepping over the threshold.

Kerrigan gulped. The hair rose on the back of her neck. But she pushed through, determined to master her fear. That was what she had been doing every day of her life since she had spoken with Cyrene. If she could master her fear, she'd do great things. She'd taken that to heart, lived by it. And she needed it now.

The inside of Black House looked like a house. An old, dilapidated, musty, half-destroyed house but still just a house. She straightened her spine and continued forward into a large, empty den. She followed close on Fordham's heels into a formal dining room, complete with an eerie chandelier missing most of its grandeur.

"There's no dust in here," Fordham acknowledged, his voice still pitched low.

Kerrigan blinked and held her own flame out in front of her. Despite the ramshackle exterior, the inside was relatively clean. That was strange.

"None in here either," he said from the next room over.

She heard him stomp around the rest of the floor while she remained in the formal dining room, confused and more than a little creeped out. A phantom breeze brushed across her neck. She shivered and swatted at it, using her magic to stop it, but it didn't stop.

"Fordham," she whispered.

He clomped up the unstable stairs. She cringed.

Suddenly, the temperature dropped precipitously. The farther up the stairs he went, the colder it got. Until her fingers and lips were numb. She breathed out in front of her and could see the fog from her breath. It was the beginning of summer.

"Fordham," she said, louder this time, her voice full of panic.

A giggle rang out behind her. Kerrigan whipped around, but there was nothing there. She felt a tug on her hair. She turned around again, but still, nothing there.

She backed up until her back hit the wall in the dining room. Her chest heaved painfully up and down as her heart rate skyrocketed.

The wind picked up until she felt like she was outside. The torrent whipped her hair into her face and lashed her off the wall. But she held firm, paralyzed by her own fear. She had tried so hard to appear unmoved by all of this. To pretend as if she didn't truly believe. Yet here she was, in Black House, being haunted.

"I mean you no harm!"

She willed her eyes shut and muttered nonsensically to herself as the wind swirled. She heard something break through the noise. Fordham was coming back downstairs.

Just as he reached the last step, the wind disappeared, and Kerrigan felt the presence in the room leave with it.

Fordham strode back in with a shake of his head. "It's empty. The whole place is empty."

"Empty," she whispered.

"It looks like there might have been weapons here once, but they're gone."

"Right."

"And no ghosts," he said with a smile that would have made her knees weak if they weren't already about to collapse. His smile faltered. "What happened?"

"Uh, nothing."

He frowned. "Let's get you out of here. This is a dead end. No closer to finding out who killed Lyam or why they want you dead."

She didn't move. He stepped forward until they were mere inches apart. His hands came to rest on her shoulders. The heat from his body melted the hold that had been on her from the spirits. She sank into his touch, pressing herself into his chest and clutching her still-frigid hands to his shirt.

She felt him tense all over at her abrupt embrace. His hand came down around her and held her against him.

"It's all right. We've both had a long couple of days."

"Thank you for coming with me," she whispered. "I know I accused you of having ulterior motives last night, but..."

255

"It's fine," he said.

"It's not. If I don't want people to judge me for being a half-Fae, I shouldn't judge people for things they can't control."

She tilted her head up to look into those big gray eyes. His flicked between her eyes and then her mouth and back. Her heart stuttered in her chest for a whole new reason. She watched the calculation in his mind. The pull that she could no longer deny. It wasn't just fate and visions that brought them together. She *wanted* to be near him.

But when she thought he might be starting to feel the same, he cleared his throat and released her.

"Come on," he said, turning away from her. "We should get out of here."

Kerrigan shivered, remembering where she was, and hid her disappointment at the loss of his hands on her. Gods, she was in deep, *deep* trouble.

She tucked her arms around her stomach and followed him out of Black House. The place was empty and a dead end. The torture had all been for no reason. She was no closer to finding out the truth.

Clover impatiently tapped her foot as they finally came back out to the street. "Well?"

Kerrigan shook her head. "No weapons. It was empty."

"Yeah, but was it haunted?"

"No," Fordham said at the same time as Kerrigan said, "Yes."

"It was not."

Kerrigan shrugged. "The ghosts only cared about me."

"You *saw* it?" Clover gasped.

"Felt it," Kerrigan corrected. "Why don't I tell you all about it on the way to the Wastes?"

"We're going to the Wastes?" Fordham asked. "What for?"

"We are," she said, pointing between herself and Clover. "You should go back to the mountain. After the last two days, we need to sleep and recoup to figure out our next move."

"And you're going to sleep and recoup in the Wastes?" Fordham asked disbelievingly.

"Wouldn't be the first time," Clover said.

"Yeah, and I need to have a conversation with Dozan Rook," Kerrigan ground out.

Fordham's eyes narrowed. "I should go with you."

She waved him off. "I can handle Dozan."

Clover snorted, and Kerrigan glared at her.

Clover held her hands up. "Sorry."

"I'll see you tomorrow. Training?"

Fordham looked like the last thing he wanted to do was walk away while she headed toward the Wastes, toward Dozan. But he eventually nodded. "Dawn run."

Kerrigan groaned. "I'm so looking forward to it."

He set his jaw before disappearing back toward the mountain.

"Why isn't he coming with us?" Clover asked.

Kerrigan didn't answer as she watched his retreating back. "Should I trust him, Clove?"

Clover produced one of her loch cigarettes. "Nope."

"Yeah, you're probably right."

"But he's *so* damn good to look at."

Kerrigan laughed. "Another problem."

"One at a time, baby," Clover said, slinging an arm over her shoulders. "Dozan first?"

"Yeah," Kerrigan said, turning away from Fordham. "Dozan."

CHAPTER THIRTY-THREE
THE CRIME LORD

Kerrigan should have gone back to the mountain and slept off this healing headache—or tried to, considering sleep still hated her. But she and Dozan had unfinished business, and she couldn't go back until they had it out.

"You sure about this?" Clover asked, stubbing out her smoke.

"Yep," Kerrigan spat.

"You do know it's Dozan Rook, right?"

"Well aware."

"He's not just any guy."

"No, he's not," she snarled.

"Like, I know he wants to bang you, but—"

"Please don't finish that sentence," Kerrigan warned. "I try not to think about that night."

"That bad?"

Kerrigan glared at her. She did not want to have that conversation.

Clover chuckled. "All right. I'll leave you be, but be careful. He's dangerous, Ker."

"I know."

Kerrigan was still learning how dangerous he was after all these years. But it didn't stop her from storming into the Wastes and demanding to see him.

Two guards were stationed in front of his private quarters. She glared at them with such ferocity that they balked at her anger.

"Let me pass. I have to see Dozan."

"No one is to disturb him tonight," the first guard said.

"I'm not just anyone."

"I'd let her through, boys," Clover said, pulling out another smoke with shaking hands. "You don't want to see her get angry."

"We can't. We'd lose our jobs," the second said anxiously.

"You'll lose your jobs if you don't let me through," Kerrigan snarled.

The first narrowed his eyes. "Dozan has company, and he said he wasn't to be interrupted."

Kerrigan rolled her eyes. "I don't care who he's sleeping with."

She brought her magic tight to her and pushed them both out of the way with a blast of air. She was past them and racing up the stairs before they even realized what she had done. She could hear them rushing after her, but she didn't care. She was going to speak with Dozan, and she was going to do it right now.

"Stop!" the second guard yelled, breathing heavily.

Kerrigan should have been exhausted, but running wasn't half as bad after all the training with Fordham. Adrenaline propelled her forward, and she yanked on the handle to the bedroom, pulling it wide. She startled when she saw who was inside.

"You," she hissed.

Clare Rahllins turned slowly, a dagger in her hand. Her raven hair was once again over half of her face, but it didn't cover her surprise. Flames erupted in Kerrigan's hand, and she advanced on the woman who had her tortured.

"Stop," Dozan drawled lazily. His hand was out, and he stepped between them.

259

The guards took that moment to barrel in, breathless. "Sir, we didn't—"

Dozan held up his hand. "It's fine. Return to your post."

They reluctantly eased out of the doorway. Kerrigan advanced another step.

"She *tortured* me," Kerrigan snarled.

"You murdered half of my men," Clare shot back.

Kerrigan winced at that. She hadn't known their fates. She had guessed, but gods, she'd killed them all?

Clare spun on Dozan. "She was working for you?"

"No," Dozan said levelly. "She was working for herself. I would never send someone so sloppy in."

Kerrigan bared her teeth at him. "I'll show you sloppy."

"Red," he warned, his golden eyes boring into her. "Stop."

She wanted to leap forward and attack the woman. Just the sight of her made her blood boil. But Dozan's warning was clear—he was handling it. With effort, she released her flames, though she held her magic close, just in case.

Dozan gestured to Clare. "You can go. I'll be in touch."

Kerrigan pushed herself away from Clare. She stood stiffly, watching the woman with unease. Clare regarded her in the same way. She had made a powerful enemy.

Dozan stepped forward and pulled the door closed behind Clare. He didn't immediately face Kerrigan, just stared at the door for a few precious minutes in silence.

"I can handle Clare," he finally said.

"Handle her?"

"That she doesn't seek revenge on you." His voice was barely a whisper but filled to the brim with power. "Though she refused to tell me who she'd sold those weapons to. I'm sure she knows it's her only bargaining chip."

"So you have nothing."

"I cleaned up your mess," he growled.

She couldn't take it any longer. "You knew," she snarled. "You knew this whole time."

He turned around to face her. His face was, as ever, unreadable. "Knew what?"

"You knew about my magic."

"You told me about your magic."

She stepped forward until she was right in front of him. "Don't play games with me, Dozan. Five years ago, I was beaten to within an inch of my life. You found me. You brought me back here. You told me that you saved me, that you killed those men, that I was safe."

"Did I?" he asked, a glint in his honey eyes.

"Yes," she snarled. "You failed to mention that I used some kind of—I don't know—energy bomb to *kill* all those Fae."

"Do you regret killing the Fae who would have killed you?"

"No," she immediately said, but her stomach twisted. "But you told me that you did it!"

"Did I?" he repeated. He brushed a lock of her hair out of her face, and she slapped his hand away. "Or did I let you come to your own conclusions? You didn't know what had happened. You woke up here, with me, safe. You assumed that I'd killed the Fae who had done that to you and that I'd spirited you away to safety. There was no reason for me to let you think otherwise."

"Other than the truth?"

"The truth? Kerrigan, you were twelve years old and had been badly beaten. It was a mercy that I did not tell you that you had *murdered* a half-dozen Fae. How would you have reacted to that news?"

She stumbled at that thought. How would she have reacted? She never would have recovered. At the time, she had been young and innocent yet jaded. She had seen the world as having done her a great injustice. It was only through that beating and subsequent journey to help Cyrene that she had realized she wanted a bigger

261

purpose in her life, to take action for herself. If she had known she was a murderer…

She shuddered.

"Exactly," Dozan said.

"Don't act like you were simply doing something altruistic," Kerrigan said, taking a step away from him. "Everyone knows that you only act in your own self-interest. That you surround yourself with unique, magical people. I thought it was my visions that you coveted when I returned last year, but I should have known better."

"I covet you," he said baldly.

She laughed at him. "You want my powers. Nothing more. I'm another instrument of the king of the Wastes."

"Is that so bad?" he asked, closing the distance once more. His hand came up under her chin and tilted her head up to look at him. "Is it so bad to be wanted? For your powers, for *exactly* who you are, Kerrigan? I don't want you to be anything else. You don't have to change for me. You can be as brilliant as you are, right here, with me."

His lips dipped down toward hers, but she wrenched back before he could finish. She was not going to fall helplessly into Dozan Rook's arms. She didn't want to play that game.

She slapped him across the face—hard. "Don't you dare presume to kiss me."

He grinned broadly. "I do love your fight."

"You lied to me. You want to use me. You're a scoundrel and an asshole."

"I am what I am, Ker." He whispered her name like a prayer, holding his hands out in front of him.

"I'm done," she spat at him. "I'm just done. The fight is off."

He straightened even further to his considerable height. He went from the supplicating man to the crime lord in the blink of an eye. "You can't walk out on a deal with me."

"Watch me!"

She yanked open the door to his rooms and flung it wide.

Dozan grabbed her wrist. "You're making a huge mistake. No one double-crosses me without facing the consequences."

"Maybe you should have thought about that before you *lied* to me. I promise you that I am a much more formidable opponent than you want to take on," she challenged him.

His eyes glittered with ferocity. A challenge. Oh, how he loved challenges.

"We'll see then, won't we?"

CHAPTER THIRTY-FOUR
THE EXPLOSION

ISA

Y ou have got to be kidding me," Isa growled as she burst into the home of her benefactor.

Her black mask was securely in place, and those she passed hastily scurried out of her way. She was a force today.

She thrust her hand out at the door, and it burst open with a jet of air. She didn't often get angry enough to use her magic. Her greatest triumph was that she was skilled enough not to have to use it if she didn't want to.

"Isa," the man said, once again facing the window.

He wore a red velvet coat, long in the back, with a top hat. His pants were navy blue with a strip of velvet down the side of the leg. He looked ostentatious and ridiculous. A man who had money but no class.

"Tell me that she didn't ruin the weapons deal with Rahllins," she snarled.

"You *were* supposed to kill her," he reminded her coolly, his voice frigid.

"And I would have if she hadn't been working with that House of Shadows competitor. She never goes anywhere alone anymore."

"I didn't promise you an easy target."

"Yeah, well, targeting the competitors would be *beyond* foolish, especially after what happened five years ago."

He slowly turned around, and his eyes swept her. "You're still mad that she got the better of you. I did warn you she would be a worthy adversary."

Isa gritted her teeth. "Not her. Him."

He waved his hand with a flourish. "No matter. I've decided to take matters into my own hands."

No, no, no. She needed that money. It would be enough to get her out of Kinkadia. Maybe not enough to set herself up well, but beggars couldn't be choosers. She'd learned that long ago.

"What the hell does that mean?"

"The deal is off, Isa," he said frankly.

"The deal is not off. I can still get her. Plus, I helped with the weapons. Everything went fine on *my* end," she spat at him.

"And then she ruined it. How did she even know it was happening?"

Isa said nothing. She couldn't tell him that she'd lost a blade. That would damn her. If he told her father...

She shuddered. No, she couldn't go down that route. Losing that blade was as sure as a death sentence.

"We were able to secure the weapons. I've moved them to a safe location, just to be sure. Since that idiotic woman had her in custody and she *still* managed to slip through our fingers."

Isa wanted to be relieved. At least she wasn't the only one who had tangled with Kerrigan and come out empty-handed. But regardless, it didn't look good for her.

"Let me go after her one more time."

"No, it's too soon."

Isa narrowed her eyes and crossed her arms. "I can do this."

He let the tension stretch between them. She hated this moment. The time where she felt as if she had to beg for her chance. She had never failed before. Not like this. And she would prove herself once and for all. Then she would claim that money and leave Kinkadia and her father and her life as an assassin far, far behind.

"Fine," he said, a cool smile gracing his thin lips. "If I don't end her first."

CHAPTER THIRTY-FIVE
THE WEAPONS TRAINING

Dawn came before she knew it. And strangely, the now six-mile run felt more invigorating than she remembered. She still didn't exactly enjoy it, but by the end, she felt renewed, like she'd really accomplished something.

She drained the waterskin once they were back to the mountain. Her legs felt like jelly, and her heart was still racing.

"That was your fastest time," Fordham said, taking a sip from his own waterskin.

"Yeah?"

He nodded. "I think you're ready for weapons."

She straightened. "Seriously?"

"After what you did in Clare's headquarters," he said with a raised eyebrow.

She ducked her chin. They hadn't talked about what had happened when they escaped that place. She didn't know what to say. Well, mostly, she'd taken her anger about it out on Dozan.

"Are you ever going to tell me what that was?"

Kerrigan shrugged. "I don't know what it was."

"Our magic was dampened by whatever drug Clare had used, and somehow, you managed to knock out everyone in that house. I've never seen anything like it."

"Yeah."

"Have you ever done that before?"

She sighed. "Yes. Once before. I don't know what it is. Some kind of energy blast? Some defense mechanism that my body produces when I'm in danger? I'm honestly not sure."

"Were you in danger last time it happened?"

"I almost died in the protests five years ago."

"Protests?" he asked in confusion.

She forgot sometimes that he wasn't from here. "Five years ago, a human won the dragon tournament."

"Cyrene," he said simply. "I met her."

She startled. "You did?"

"Yes, she came through the House of Shadows in the final tournament."

"Oh right," she said, remembering that. "Anyway, after she won, the Red Masks rose to power quickly. They rioted. They burned churches. They sent their minions into the streets to kill humans and half-Fae and sympathizers. It was a bleak time. And I was out one night and attacked by Red Masks. I kind of exploded, like I did the other night."

"Hmm," Fordham said thoughtfully. "It sounds like you need someone to train you in this ability."

"How can someone train me if I don't even know what it is? And how would I find someone to even help?"

He considered it for a minute. "Let me think on it. That power is dangerous. You need to be able to control it."

"Like your black smoke?" she asked carefully.

He sent her an appraising look. "Yes. Just so."

"Are you ever going to tell me about what it actually does?"

"Perhaps," he said with a sly smirk. "But for the time being, we're going to need to find a place to weapons train where the other competitors can't find us."

Kerrigan huffed that he wouldn't tell her about the smoke but eventually gave up. He'd tell her in his own time. "Actually, I know just the place."

⚬⚭⚬

Twenty minutes later, she locked the door to the House of Dragons training room. "This work?"

"Yeah. This is perfect. What is this?"

"It's for the House of Dragons. I spent a lot of time in here for weapons training, but the Dragon Blessed get this month off studies for the tournament. So we won't be disturbed."

It made her heart ache even bringing him here. This wasn't her life anymore. And even though she'd had so many good memories in this room, they were all tainted in sadness now. At least she had sent off letters to Darby and Hadrian like she had promised Clover she would do. They deserved to know what she did about Lyam's murder.

Fordham shucked his cloak off and slung it on a hook at the wall. He walked the length of the weapons trove, testing the weight of a few of the swords before putting them back. He withdrew two practice swords and tossed one to her.

"Not even with steel?" She pouted.

"In battle," he began, ignoring her question, "there are only two options: kill or be killed. There is no point where you can decide to spare your enemy. That will only lead to retaliation and your eventual death."

He brought his sword up and began to step through paces. She matched him. Right foot, then left. Side to side. Back and forth. An easy, gentle movement that she was familiar with.

"You spared Valero."

He held his wooden sword low, swooping gracefully through the

269

next movement. "He's out of the tournament. That was the point of the challenge."

"I have to learn to destroy my mercy?" she asked, mirroring him.

"You must learn to do the opposite of what your opponent expects. The best thing to do would be to learn your enemy, know them better than they know themselves, and exploit their weaknesses."

Fordham lunged forward. She gasped and took a step back, bringing her sword up and barely blocking him. But he was lightning fast, and he'd feinted. The length of his sword slapped hard against her ribs. She doubled over and coughed.

"You favor your left side," he said simply. "I know that because I know you."

"Okay," she croaked, rising to her feet again. "Know your enemy. Got it. But how can I do that if I don't know my opponent?"

Fordham picked back up where he'd left off, and she reluctantly followed him. Though she was more on guard this time. This was a lesson, not basic footwork.

"If you don't know your opponent," he told her, "then you rely on your training. You must understand how others fight, all the potential ways they could attack you, have a mental dictionary of ways that an opponent could hurt you. Then you train every one of those mistakes out of you."

Kerrigan slid into the next movement, considering what he'd said. "You're going to train my mistakes out of me?"

"Yes and no. I'm going to train *every* mistake out of you. So that when an assassin comes at you again, you aren't surprised when they jump out of the shadows." He finished the last sequence and let the sword drop to his side.

This time when he attacked, she was ready.

☙❧

Fordham still beat her every single time they sparred. It was beyond frustrating since she had thought she was pretty good with a sword before this. He was just that much better.

By the third day, she thought she was finally making a bit of improvement. Not that she could win against him, but she wasn't *losing* quite as fast. This was the opposite of how she had been taught. Her teachers had all shown her *how* to fight. Fordham was training her in all the ways *not* to fight. Explaining the ways others fought and twisting it around to show how to break down the movements and counter, how to win. It was exhausting, both physically and mentally.

Especially because Fordham refused to let either of them go through healing.

"The pain makes you stronger," he told her after she asked him again if she could go get a quick healing.

"Right now, it makes me feel terrible."

"You won't always be in a position where you can get healing. You might have to deal with injuries. Healing makes it so that you don't have any way to handle pain. If you've never been hurt before, then the shock of it will be a stumbling block."

"Is that what you mean by battlefield healing? How you were able to pop your shoulder back into place in the tournament and fight through broken ribs?"

His eyes went far away. "Yes. That was not the worst that I'd ever endured."

Kerrigan frowned. She didn't like when he was withdrawn. As if he were imagining a not-too-distant past where he had suffered many horrors.

He blinked, and it was gone. "In a battle, magic is reserved for fighting. It drains you too quickly to use magic to heal. You learn to fix what you can and deal with anything else."

"Okay," she muttered. "No healing."

"You are getting stronger," he told her, taking the practice sword and replacing it. "That is all for today."

Kerrigan took another sip of water and considered how to ask him the next question. She'd decided yesterday that she wanted to do this. She wasn't sure how Fordham would react. But still, she couldn't shake the feeling that he needed this.

"What are your plans tonight?" she asked him, still facing away to hide her blush.

"Plans?" He sounded suspicious. "Do you have a new lead?"

"Unfortunately, no. But…do you want to go into the city with me?"

"Does this involve torture?"

She laughed, finally turning. "Some people might say so. Though I think you'd like it."

Now he looked even more suspicious. "What is it?"

"A surprise."

"I don't like surprises," he told her.

"You'll like this one, princeling." She grinned. "Meet me at the entrance in an hour. Wear normal clothes."

He frowned. "What's normal?"

"Something less princely."

"I'll see what I can do." His eyes were searching hers. "Am I going to regret this later?"

She stepped backward, toward the exit of the House of Dragons' training room. "Depends. Can't you anticipate my next move? Isn't that what you've been training me on?"

"That's precisely why I am skeptical."

"Live on the wild side with me," she said with a wink and then swiftly exited the room, her heart pounding in her chest.

She'd done it. She'd actually asked him out.

CHAPTER THIRTY-SIX
THE ARTISAN VILLAGE

"This is the Artisan Village," Kerrigan informed Fordham an hour later as they walked casually through Kinkadia.

As promised, he'd worn something resembling normal clothing. He'd replaced the black-and-silver princeling garb with an all-black shirt and pants. His cloak was wool and not silk. At a glance, he looked shockingly normal.

But then he'd tilt his chin up just so, and she'd see that he couldn't completely hide who he was, even under cotton and wool and linen.

"There's an opera house just there. They have quarterly ballets as well. And there"—she pointed out another street—"they call that Painters Row, as it mirrors the aristocratic row on the eastern side of the valley, but it's just for artists—drawing, painting, sculpting."

Fordham drowned in the sights like a man dying of thirst in the desert. His eyes took in everything as they made their way through the village, but he never said a word.

"Over there is where my friend Parris lives. He's a fashion designer. Very up-and-coming. Only works with the wealthy, but we met years ago when he was in the House of Dragons. So he still designs for me."

They passed Parris's shop with fashionable dresses in the windows.

"He was a Dragon Blessed?" Fordham finally asked.

"Yes. He was scooped up by a woman in Sayair who saw his talent. They trained together for a few years, and then she helped him open up his own boutique in the village."

"And that's what you could do?"

She swiftly shook her head. "Oh no, I have no real talent like that. Plus, I really don't know what I'm going to do about a house. I haven't heard from Ellerby, and I've been so focused on this assassin and Lyam's murder and training." She sighed. "I don't know what to do."

"You'll find someone. You seem to charm everyone you meet."

She laughed. "Hardly. Most people find me too outspoken. I'm not particularly ladylike."

"Overrated," he said.

And she smiled, turning her face away from him. "Well, a problem for another day. We're here."

"Here?" he asked and looked up at the location they'd stopped in front of.

"Carmine's Books." It was the largest bookstore in the village complete with a large sitting area and stage. Musicians performed on the small stage, and parties were housed inside the store. It was something magical—to be surrounded by books on all sides for an evening.

A sign out front read: *One Night Only—A Magical Poetry Experience Unlike Any Other.*

Fordham's eyes glued to the sign. "You didn't…"

"Didn't what?"

But Fordham seemed to have lost all words.

"Tickets," a man said at the door.

Kerrigan produced her two tickets and passed them to the man, and then she all but dragged Fordham inside. The interior of the bookshop was warm and homey. Candlelight flickered around the room in protected glass cases. Wooden chairs were set up before the stage, which had just one stool and a herringbone wood backdrop.

They were offered drinks, which they took, and then found seats in the middle of the room.

"What is this?" Fordham whispered.

"A poetry reading."

His eyes were warm, the gray almost silver in the candlelight. He placed his hand over hers. Sparks flared at the smallest touch, and she had to make sure that she was still breathing.

"You did this for me?"

She swallowed and nodded. "I saw that you like to write. I thought that you should see that Kinkadia has something to offer other than fighting. It has art and culture and music. It has poetry."

Fordham was speechless. She had known him to grow silent when he was irritated or disdainful, but this was altogether different. This was like watching the moon try to capture the sun—hopeful, endless, and impossible.

Kerrigan smiled at him and withdrew her hand. Fordham still sat in stunned anticipation as the musicians ceased their playing and a woman walked onstage. Carmine gestured exuberantly, sinking into her ample hip, her golden-brown skin almost glowing. And then the reading began.

The poets' verses varied wildly. Most spoke about love and lust and death. They were evocative and endearing. The poets' voices filled with emotion, dripping with enthusiasm. A few were downright erotic. Her cheeks tinted pink at the mere suggestion of what their words implied.

But the best and the most dangerous was the final poet—a young human woman dressed entirely in black and holding a candle before her face.

Red.
The color of blood.
The color of life.
The color of death.

Masks.
To shield the guilty.
To wield the darkness.
To field the hate.

A worm writhing in the dirt
does not know how it can be hurt.
But it can feel the impending doom
as the boot so ever looms.

A spark is the light of the first
who knows what it is to thirst
for a world that will burst into flame
and not burn it down as a game.

Now is the time to rise up
against the boot that would smother our heat.
Now is the time to fill your cup.
To tell the game masters, we will not be beat.

Red.
The blood of our people.
The life of our children.
The death of our existence.

Masks.
The guilty.
The darkness.
The hate.

A hush fell over the crowd as she finished. Then a soft round of applause followed her exit.

Carmine stepped back onto the stage, wiping tears from her eyes. "Thank you, Neslie. That concludes our evening performances. Feel free to mingle. We have music and refreshments."

Fordham looked to Kerrigan. "That was pointed."

Kerrigan frowned. "Indeed."

She had known that the Red Masks were at the Dragon Blessed ceremony, that they were in her vision, but she hadn't seen them since. But if poets were writing about them and reading about them, then they must be gathering forces again. She shuddered at the thought.

"We should go," Fordham said, reading her mood.

"Yes, I think so."

Darkness had truly fallen in the village, but no one would be the wiser. Street performers had come out to dance and sing and play music. Taverns were open, and customers sprawled out onto the steps. A dance had started in the intersection to Painters Row. Merriment was had all around.

"I never knew anything like this existed," Fordham admitted as they passed row after row of dancers.

"Is the House of Shadows so different? No dancing? No music?"

His eyes grew distant. "There is music and dancing, but it's not like this. We have been closed off in our world for a thousand years. No one leaves, and only humans dare to cross our borders—and most do it by accident. We have made our own city our own realm."

"That sounds isolating," she admitted. Though she did not ask the question she wanted to know—how exactly had he gotten out?

"It likely helps that the majority of us do not know any different," he admitted. "They have not seen the streets full like this. They do not know the joy of running for *miles* in any direction. They have not been permitted *life*."

"That's terrible. The stories make the House of Shadows seem like monsters. But this sounds like a horror that should not be bestowed on anyone. To be so isolated would be true torture."

Fordham didn't have to say anything for her to know that he agreed. Especially now, after tonight.

They returned to the mountain. Kerrigan realized she was still a little tipsy from the drinks. Waking up at dawn to run for miles didn't sound tempting in the least. But she enjoyed the lightness in her head as they headed back to their rooms. When they came to the place where their paths diverged, she stopped in anticipation, not quite ready to say goodbye.

But Fordham gently took her hand. "I'll walk you."

Her heart thudded in her chest. He released her hand, and they walked together, side by side, tension brimming between them. She had felt desire and obsession but nothing like *this*. Nothing where her entire insides squirmed and shivered at the mere touch. Suddenly, her mouth was dry. She had no words for how she felt in that moment.

When they reached her door, she expected him to release her and go. But he hovered there before her, and for a moment, she was too frightened of what she would find when she looked up. For all her bluster about not being afraid, about controlling her fear, deep down, she had never been more afraid. She could master herself in life-or-death situations because she had to. But this?

"Kerrigan," he said.

Her body shivered at the use of her name. All this time, he'd never really called her by her name. And now, to hear it from him in this moment, her body turned to mush.

"Look at me," he commanded in that soft, urgent voice of his.

Slowly, she pushed down all her trembling fears and met his gray eyes. They were the same eyes she had been looking into for weeks. The same face that she had wanted to see smile—really smile—so she had brought him for a poetry reading. The man with a dozen layers and a million secrets. She had no hope of unraveling them all, but somehow, she was pulling them back inch by inch. And he was doing the same. Despite her fear—or maybe because of it—she realized just how much she wanted this.

"Who are you?" he asked softly.

"Who am I?"

"You are nothing like I expected."

"Nor are you, princeling."

He brushed a lock of her red curls out of her face, and his finger ran along her jaw. She didn't breathe for the length of that touch. She wanted to move into it, but they were on a precipice. As if at any moment, they could plunge forward into oblivion or be wrenched backward. And she didn't want to be the thing that scared him off.

"I mean it. I was raised to believe that humans and half-Fae were different from full-blooded Fae. No, not just different. They were an abomination. Lower functioning and barely capable of more than servitude. Fae were silenced for even questioning those basic teachings. When you were sent to me that first day, I assumed the Society was trying to slight me for bending their rules and finding a loophole."

"But they weren't," she whispered.

"No, I see now that they actually sent their best."

She laughed shyly. "I wouldn't say their best."

"You are the first human or half-Fae I have ever been allowed more than a passing interest in. And everything I was taught was wrong," he told her plainly.

She swallowed, taken in by his confession. She had known that the House of Shadows had these beliefs, but hearing them told as such made her heart ache. The lies that were spread about her people. It was heartbreaking.

But Fordham's realization was more than moving. It showed that people could change. They had the ability to see others as three-dimensional. And after he saw her as a real person and not lesser, he couldn't unsee it. His world tilted on its axis, and now he had to look at it through a new lens of empathy.

279

That was what she had seen from him over the last couple of weeks. Not a softening expressly to her but a softening of his hardened core beliefs. And she fell for him even more in that moment.

"I'm glad that you came around. It couldn't have been easy."

"No," he said, stepping forward.

She stilled under that gaze. His head dipped lower toward her. She wanted this. She wanted more from him. Her eyes fluttered closed of their own accord, and she hung in midair, heavy with anticipation. His breath fell against her lips, hot and tantalizing. She could practically taste his lips.

But then he withdrew, leaving her hanging suspended.

She opened her eyes in surprise and a little more than embarrassed. Red tinged her freckled cheeks.

"Thank you for this evening," he said formally, withdrawing a step.

"Oh…you're welcome."

"No one has ever done anything like that for me before, and I won't soon forget it."

She wanted to say so much more. She wanted to be bold enough to take that kiss for herself. But she saw something in his moody gray eyes that stilled her. It wasn't fear, but it was taut with tension.

He wasn't ready. For some reason, he still wasn't ready to make that step. He had changed his views of half-Fae enough for her, but even still, he couldn't move past that and give her the kiss that she so desired. This was still too new. Too anathema to his upbringing.

She stepped backward, hid her plain desire from her face. "I'm glad that you enjoyed it."

"I should bid you good night."

She saw the resolution in his eyes, the set of his jaw. The night was over.

"Good night," she muttered wistfully and then reached for the handle.

The door fell open behind her, and she stepped inside, staring into Fordham's gray eyes all the while. A crinkle sounded beneath her feet at the first step. Her brow furrowed in confusion, and when she looked down, she discovered a letter.

"What is it?" Fordham asked.

She reached down and picked it up, immediately recognizing the handwriting. "A letter from Ellerby."

CHAPTER THIRTY-SEVEN
THE SOUTH

Fordham followed Kerrigan into her room as she broke the Elsiande wax seal and opened the letter. "What does he say?"

She read through the letter. It was short with a flourishing signature at the bottom. And it said *nothing*. Not a damn thing.

Dear Kerrigan,

Thank you so much for your entreaty into my well-being. All is well with me. I have returned to the countryside for my health. It is wonderful to be back in my hometown of Archdale, where I can wake up every morning whole and hale and look out across the Corvian Sea.

It does bring me joy to hear from you. As ever, you should have no reason to worry over me. I merely wish to continue the long days I have left in this world with my family—particularly my nephew, Ever—nearby. The city has lost its luster of late.

I do wish to hear from you soon.

Sincerely,
Ellerby Emberton of Elsiande

She cast the letter aside, and Fordham gingerly plucked it off the ground.

"That bad?" he asked.

She huffed, "All he does is rave about his health. He says nothing about why he abandoned me to this fate. Only that he left to return home to be with his nephew."

Fordham read through the letter once, twice, three times before he sighed. "I believe this is a code."

"What?"

"I don't believe he is speaking plainly. I think it is a cry for help."

"What do you mean? He clearly says all is well."

"Yes. He says it multiple times. How often do people write a letter and say over and over again that they are well?"

She shrugged. "I don't get many letters. What do you think he's really saying then?"

"That he was in trouble. He fled the city in haste and has given you explicit directions as to where he went. He reminds you not to worry and that he wanted to be with his nephew. I would suspect his nephew was part of all of this in some way. Then he says he wants to hear from you soon. *Soon*, not again, which is the customary address, is it not?"

She reached for the letter and reread the whole thing. "It is. *Soon* is too immediate. It's not used. I would have never realized that. So, he's in trouble?" she asked.

Fordham nodded.

"Which means we need to get to Elsiande to speak to him. Maybe he knows why Lyam was killed and why the assassin tried to kill me next. Maybe he knows who is doing all this."

"And how exactly do you presume we get to Elsiande? Isn't it a few days' travel by horse?"

She bit her lip and grinned up at him.

"Oh no," he muttered. "That look usually precedes us being tortured."

"I have an idea."

"A bad idea?"

"How do you feel about stealing a dragon?"

※

"If someone catches us, we'll probably be kicked out of the mountain," Fordham reminded her as they crept through the dragon quarters.

"Where's your sense of adventure, princeling?"

"Securely on the ground," he muttered.

She turned around in surprise. "Are you afraid of heights?"

"Heights? No," he said at once. "Falling from extreme heights— like off the back of a dragon, for instance…"

She laughed. "Dragons are perfectly safe, and riding one is the most exhilarating experience of my entire life. You're going to love it. Or at least you'll get used to it since you're trying to get a dragon in a few weeks' time."

"Fine," he muttered.

Kerrigan grinned at him and then continued through the cavernous rooms where she had spent so much of her time growing up. She could name practically every dragon as they passed. Some twitched an eye open at her approach, saw it was her, and then went back to sleep. This place was warm, welcome, and familiar.

"What are you afraid of?" Fordham asked behind her.

"Nothing," she lied quickly.

"Everyone is afraid of something."

"Someone once told me that if you master your fear, you'll do great things. So for most of my life, I've walked right into every fear I've had. I face them and embrace them. I don't want to have any fears holding me back on my way to greatness."

"Hmm," Fordham said.

"What?"

"Well, that doesn't sound like you aren't afraid of anything. It sounds like you've learned to live with your fears every day of your life. Which means you're afraid all the time, of everything, but no one can see it."

Kerrigan stopped walking as a shiver ran down her back. How was it that she had only known him for a few weeks, and already, he saw straight through her like no one else in the world?

"Yes," she breathed, turning to look at him. "But isn't that life?"

"Where I come from, yes," he said softly. "Here though? I don't think everyone else is afraid all the time."

"Everyone else isn't a half-Fae who was abandoned when they were a child and has had to fight for their place in this world every day of their life."

Fordham watched her. He didn't say anything. Didn't try to soothe her. He saw exactly who she was and accepted that.

Kerrigan swallowed and kept moving until they came before the plum-purple dragon she had been looking for. "Tavry," she whispered.

A golden eye opened. *"Kerrigan, this is most unexpected."* His eye swiveled to Fordham. *"Prince Fordham Ollivier of the House of Shadows, it is a pleasure to make your acquaintance."*

Fordham bowed deeply at the waist. "As it is to make yours, great one."

Tavry looked back to Kerrigan. *"I like this one."*

Kerrigan laughed. "So do I."

"I assume you did not disturb my sleep just to introduce me to the prince of the Dark Depths. What is it that you require?"

The Dark Depths. Well, that was different. She wondered what it meant as Fordham stiffened at the words.

"I received a letter from Ellerby of Elsiande, and I am in deep need of a way to get to Archdale as fast as I can."

Tavry looked startled. *"What is the purpose of this visit?"*

She swallowed and persevered. She decided to go with the truth. Anything else, and Tavry would be able to see right through it. "I have been investigating a murder, and I believe that Ellerby has important information to prove what truly happened to Lyam." She rubbed Lyam's compass in her pocket. "I have been following the leads. I was almost killed twice. Whoever did this is going to great lengths to make sure they are not discovered. I will see justice for Lyam."

"*Is this true?*" Tavry's eye fixed on Fordham.

He nodded. "Yes, great one. I have been assisting her in these matters, and Ellerby is our last hope to rooting out a murderer in our midst."

Tavry closed his eye, and Kerrigan thought they were done for. Then Tavry straightened to his considerable height. His wings crested as he lengthened his figure.

"*We must be back by dawn,*" Tavry told them.

Kerrigan calculated the time they had left as she dragged her cloak tightly around her. "It's a three-hour flight on a good day. That will give us hardly any time to find and speak with Ellerby."

"*Then, we must hurry, child.*"

Kerrigan ground her teeth. By dawn. Gods, was that even possible?

She decided not to think about it until they were on their way home. Right now, she was doing the right thing. Rules be damned.

She climbed onto Tavry's back and watched Fordham assess how she'd gotten onto the dragon before making his own ascent. He took a seat directly behind her.

"This is your first time. You should hold on tight," she told Fordham.

"To what?"

"Me."

Fordham's hands came to her waist gently at first, then as Tavry rose to his full height, he wrapped his arms around her waist and pulled her flush against him. Kerrigan tamped down the shivers that spread through her body at his touch.

"*Prepare yourselves,*" Tavry told them.

Tavry reached the edge of the entrance to the dragon cavern. His wings fluttered open. She felt the softest touch of their minds all connecting as one before he flew out of the cave and plummeted toward the ground. Fordham's arms around her waist crushed her ribs and lungs. She pulled him forward with her, flattening them to Tavry's back as they held on for dear life.

A gasp of excitement and exhilaration traveled through her. As they leveled out, tears streamed from her eyes from the wind, and she laughed uncontrollably. Her arms came out to her sides, even as Fordham held her so securely. This was life. Fordham had been right. She was so afraid of everything in her life. But flying? Never flying. This was the real joy she felt in the world. This was what she had been made for. If only she had been born a full Fae, she might have had this life.

That thought sobered her, and she forced Fordham's arms to loosen. "Open your eyes. Look."

She didn't have to turn to know that he'd been squeezing his eyes shut, but at her words, she felt him relax. A soft inhale of breath meant he was finally seeing the world for what it was.

"The world is so…"

"Small," she agreed. "So small up here."

"Beautiful," he finished. "Even in the dark, we can see for miles and miles, and every inch needs to be memorized for eternity."

"The poet *does* come out on something other than paper," she joked.

He said nothing, just held her closer. She leaned back against his broad chest and watched the only world she had ever really known disappear completely in the starlight.

⌬

Kerrigan had lived in a castle in Bryonica until she was five, but her home was Draco Mountain, the city of Kinkadia. She had rarely been out of the city since she was five. This was a whole new adventure.

When Tavry touched down outside the town of Archdale in the craggy, rocky wasteland that was Elsiande, she realized that this was her first time away from home in twelve years. Her feet hit the ground, and she shivered slightly despite the oppressive southern heat. Kinkadia had hit the humid summer heat wave, but Elsiande must have been in it for weeks. She felt like she could drink the air and was certain her hair was twice the size it had been when they started.

Fordham dropped down beside her on unsteady legs. "Well, we made it."

"Yes," she agreed.

"Where to now?"

She shrugged. "I've never been to Elsiande."

Fordham turned her to face him. "I thought you knew where we were going."

"Not exactly," she admitted.

"Gods," he grumbled.

"I mean, I do know where he lives. He told me before. I don't know exactly."

"Then you should hasten. We must leave again within the hour," Tavry reminded them.

Kerrigan frowned. "Let's go."

Together, they traversed the uneven rocks that made up the southern landscape. Their eyes had adjusted to the night, but it was too dangerous to walk without a light illuminating their path, so they held flames in their palms to cut across the rocks.

She was relieved when they left behind the last column of rocks, and she took a deep breath of the salty air. Archdale rested on the shore of the Corvian Sea, at the mouth of a small inlet. They let their fires die out and stared down at the town. The homes were made of the surrounding rock, most only standing a story tall but sprawling, sloping out into the landscape. Each had its own private yard with a fence and cultivated grass and flowers. As they ventured deeper into Archdale, keeping tight to the shadows, they came upon a town square. Two buildings here were multiple stories—an inn and city hall. The whole thing was mesmerizing and confounding. It was absolutely nothing like Kinkadia, where nearly every building was two, three, even four stories high and no one saw grass outside a park or a Row mansion.

"Which way?" Fordham asked.

She shook herself from her fascination and desire to see this during the day and then gestured westward. Ellerby had told her once that he lived on the western banks outside the city. A large Row-style home set into the hillside overlooking the inlet. She doubted there would be many of those.

In fact, the home was very easy to find once they were heading in the correct direction. There were many homes set into the hillside, but most of the them followed the pattern of the city, sprawling one-story stone mansions. Ellerby's home was large, but it went straight up four stories with wide-set windows and enormous gardens. How he ever accomplished true gardens here in this rocky land, she would never know.

Kerrigan debated on going around to the back. He had seemed afraid in his letter, but it hadn't been tampered with. No one would suspect they would borrow a dragon and fly south in the middle of the night.

She opened the gate leading up to his mansion, surprised to find it wasn't locked, and then Fordham followed her to the front door. No lights were on inside. She was not looking forward to breaking in to his home.

With a sigh, she knocked on the front door anyway.

"Everyone is asleep," Fordham whispered.

"I know, but common courtesy."

They waited a moment to see if anyone would answer, and then she reached for the doorknob. Just as she turned it, the thing was twisted sharply and wrenched open. She fell forward with it, and she looked up at the man standing in his dressing robe.

"Ellerby," she said in shock.

"Kerrigan, you made it," he said with a trembling fear in his voice. His eyes darted around the outside of his home. "Someone could be watching. Come in quickly. *Quickly.*"

She gestured to Fordham, and they both stepped into Ellerby's mansion.

CHAPTER THIRTY-EIGHT
THE THREAT

W atching?" Kerrigan asked as Ellerby slammed the door behind them.

"Yes, yes, they've been watching." His hands trembled as he gestured outside with paranoia. "Come. Let's have a spot of tea to calm the nerves."

Fordham glanced at Kerrigan in confusion. She shrugged and followed Ellerby tottering down the hall on his wooden cane. He was nearly as short as Kerrigan, especially since he hunched forward due to his curved spine. She could see that he was balding in the faint light. It hit her then how much she'd missed him—eccentricities and all.

Ellerby's mansion was dark until he reached a formal living room. The heavy curtains had all been drawn over the massive windows, and a dozen candles barely lit the towering interior. A pot of tea was already on a low table at the center of the room with just one cup.

"Have a seat. I'll get more cups."

"I can get them," she said at once.

"No, no, I can still walk," he said, tapping his cane against his leg twice and then disappearing back the way they'd come.

Fordham stepped up to the window and peered through the curtains. "I don't see anyone."

"We saw no one when we came to the house."

"But it doesn't mean that no one is there."

She nodded. "Agreed."

Just then, Ellerby bustled back in with two additional cups and poured them tea. Kerrigan took the proffered cup and sat on a blush settee. Fordham took his own tea, adding both cream and sugar, but remained standing.

"I didn't expect you for weeks," Ellerby confided, sitting down in a brown leather armchair. He took a tentative sip of the tea. "How did you get here so fast?"

"We borrowed a dragon," Fordham said.

Ellerby nearly spat out his drink. "You're House of Shadows, young man, aren't you?"

"Yes, sir." Fordham straightened to his considerable height.

"I didn't have the chance to meet you before I left the city. I assume since you are working with my girl Kerrigan that you are not as prejudiced as history makes it seem."

Fordham eyed Ellerby sharply before glancing back to Kerrigan. "I believe I am no longer representative of my people in that regard."

"Ah," Ellerby said with a bobbing head of acknowledgment.

"But that's not why we're here," Kerrigan butted in before things could get worse. "You left the city so abruptly, in the middle of the ceremony. And then we got your letter. I just don't understand. Why did you leave in the first place?"

Ellerby set his teacup down on the table. "I truly am sorry about that. I had every intention of selecting you at the ceremony and staying through the tournament. But a man approached me the day before the ceremony. He said that he had my nephew, Ever, and that if I didn't do exactly what he said, he would kill him."

Kerrigan shuddered. "What did he tell you to do?"

Ellerby shifted uncomfortably. "He told me to go to the ceremony, and right before you were to be selected, I had to leave. As soon as I was gone, I had to pack up my entire household and return here. Only then would he give my nephew back to me."

"*Did* he return your nephew?" Fordham asked.

Ellerby shivered. "No," he croaked. "No, he still has him as collateral for my silence. It was risky even getting a letter out to you. I assumed it was read by them before it reached you. I had to make it deliberately banal or else they might have suspected and hurt Ever."

"You've risked much in doing so," Kerrigan said gently. Though her insides were squirming.

What could be the purpose in doing this to poor Ellerby? And why would they want her humiliated like that? Could it be that all this was somehow related?

Fordham must have come to the same conclusion as Kerrigan. "We have been attacked since you left. An assassin was sent out for Kerrigan. Do you think this person would want her dead as well?"

Ellerby's eyes rounded in horror. "I didn't know. I'm so sorry."

She waved him off. Words stuck in her throat. They didn't have time to beat around the bush. She needed answers. "Who was the man?"

Ellerby gritted his teeth. "I dare not say. If he found out…"

"My *life* is on the line, Ellerby," she hissed. "He sent someone to kill me. I flew all the way out here based on your letter. Please, we must know the person's name."

"I can't," Ellerby said, trembling as he rose to his feet and moved toward one of the windows. "Ever is still in trouble. They're watching my house."

Fordham stepped forward and put his hand on Ellerby's shoulder. "You have suffered greatly. But the only way that we can help, that we can get Ever back, is for you to trust us. We want this to end. We do not want you to continue to live in fear."

Ellerby looked to Kerrigan. "I truly wanted to select you."

Kerrigan's throat constricted. She hadn't let herself think too much about that fact. Because it was plain now that he couldn't do it. Not while Ever was still absent. "Please," she whispered. "We are running out of time. We must return to the city. Help us stop him."

Ellerby shuddered. "Nix."

"Nix?" Fordham asked in confusion.

But Kerrigan wasn't confused. Her body froze in place. Her thoughts unclouded. Suddenly, everything made sense. Everything made perfect sense.

"Basem Nix," Kerrigan said softly.

"Yes," Ellerby said, latching on to the name. "The one."

"Who is Basem Nix?" Fordham asked.

Kerrigan said nothing. She was still reeling from the new information. The bruiser that she had humiliated at the Wastes fight, who had called her a leatha and sent three of his thugs to ambush her. She hadn't thought of him since that night. But she had seen the way he looked at her when he called her a leatha. He was racist to his core, and he believed that she was beneath him, that she didn't even deserve life. She had seen the same look in the Fae who attempted to kill her that night five years ago.

Hatred didn't make sense. It simply *was*.

"He's a…" Ellerby stumbled on the word.

"Gangster," Kerrigan finished for him.

"Yes. He does not come from money," Ellerby explained, "but due to trade he facilitated through from the south, he quickly rose through the ranks. He made a fortune, but he's not landed money. Row society won't accept him. He has a home in Riverfront, where he has been keeping Ever."

"It's where the new rich live in Kinkadia," Kerrigan said. "They can't get houses on the Row."

"But why would he want to kill you?" Fordham asked.

"He's racist," Kerrigan said simply.

And that was the truth of it. He didn't need another reason to want her dead. Her humiliating him was just icing on the cake.

"He hates half-Fae, and I beat him in a fight the night before the opening ceremonies. Which is likely why he went to you, Ellerby. I'm so sorry."

Fordham frowned. "That explains a lot, but I think I'm still missing a piece. What was he trading?"

Kerrigan shrugged. "I don't know. I never asked about that."

Ellerby sighed heavily and looked like he was going to run. "Magical artifacts."

"What do you mean? What kind of artifacts?" Fordham asked.

"Elsiande is known for the creation of magical artifacts. They're used for any number of sources but primarily to contain magic. The older generations have always wanted to be rid of their magic. As you know, we were founded by house members who believed that magic was flawed. It could do wonderful things, but ultimately, it could do *terrible* things as well. The use of magic brought the world out of balance. They created objects to house their magic, as they no longer wanted it."

"Does that work?" Fordham asked.

"Not really. Not to the extent that most of them wanted it to," Ellerby told them. "And anyway, most of those objects were destroyed in the Great Purge, but over the last several years, the trade of them has become very lucrative."

"Because they're illegal," Kerrigan snapped.

"Yes. Some of them are. It's not uncommon for people to have gemstones filled with an Elsiande honeycomb. A small burst of magic can be filtered into it to be used at a later time, especially during fighting. Those are perfectly legal and rather common. But there are many other kinds of artifacts that can work very powerful magic. Things that no one should get their hands on," Ellerby said faintly. "The Society deemed them too much of a risk and has been slowly collecting and destroying the lot."

"Which makes them even more valuable," Kerrigan said. Her eyes flicked to Fordham. "The weapons deal."

"That's what we saw. Those were no ordinary weapons, and Clare is no ordinary dealer. That's why she interrogated us, thinking we were working for the Society."

"She thought that they had found the new stash of artifacts," Kerrigan put together.

"Yes, and she must be working with Basem to get these artifacts onto the streets."

Ellerby looked faint. "If that's the case, then we're already too late."

"Too late for what?"

"To stop him."

Fordham left Ellerby's side and came to stand with Kerrigan. "On the contrary, I think we finally have a shot."

She looked up at him, filled with determination. "I think you're right. We will do what we can to save your nephew."

Ellerby's eyes filled with tears. "I don't even know if he's still alive."

Kerrigan ground her teeth. "We will get revenge for what he has done to you."

"We need to go," Fordham said. "We have to get back by daybreak."

"Thank you for meeting with us."

Ellerby stepped forward and took her hands. "I am truly sorry. I hope that we meet again on more favorable terms. You are always welcome in my home."

She followed Fordham. They slipped out the back door this time. Neither said a word as they slunk through the streets of Archdale to where they had left Tavry. They found him waiting impatiently. He shook his long, powerful neck.

"We must be off. The time is nigh."

They scrambled onto Tavry, and he burst into the sky before they were even completely situated.

"Did you find what you were looking for?"

"Yes," Kerrigan said. "Unfortunately."

She hugged Tavry's side and tried to keep the terror from overwhelming her.

Basem Nix was a formidable opponent on a good day, but this was above and beyond anything she could have imagined. They had stepped into the middle of a tangled web, and she didn't know what their next move was or where they would land.

⊙ഝ

Dawn blurred bright across the horizon. Kerrigan's heart sank as Draco Mountain came into view. They were late. Tavry had been certain that they would need to be there before daybreak. She hadn't thought they had dawdled, but they had had to navigate an unknown city.

Tavry flew into the aerie with ease, landing effortlessly.

She slid off Tavry's back. "Thank you."

"Don't thank me yet, Kerrigan Argon."

Kerrigan was about to ask why, but then she realized that she didn't need to. Helly stormed toward them. Her carefully placed bun was disheveled, her black robes rumpled. Her eyes spat fire. Kerrigan had never seen her look so angry.

Fordham dropped to his feet next to her, straightening at the sight of Helly. "This isn't good, is it?"

"No," Kerrigan whispered.

"What in the gods' names do you two think you were doing?" Helly all but shrieked as she approached them. "You were both out of your beds, a dragon missing. Do you know what would have happened if the council had been alerted?"

Kerrigan winced. "We were only trying to help—"

"I don't want to hear it!" Helly slashed her hand down to stop her from speaking further. "I don't want a single word out of either of you. We had a deal." She glared at Kerrigan in fury. "What you did was reckless and dangerous, not to mention *theft*."

"*Mistress Helly,*" Tavry began.

But she whirled on her dragon and flung a finger out. "We will talk about this later."

Tavry's wings flared in outrage, and then the beast took to the skies once more.

Helly sighed, rubbing her temple. Kerrigan didn't know anyone who had been in a fight with their dragon. They were bound together. They shared so much that it was hard to stay mad at each other.

"You were *gone*," Helly said, her voice stiffening into pain. "Just like Lyam. You were just gone."

"I'm sorry, Helly, but if you'd let me explain."

"No, I need no explanation. I understand precisely what you did. But have you forgotten what happened with Lyam?" Helly asked, sounding sick to her stomach.

"Of course not."

"What you did is *cruel*, if not simply reckless."

"Mistress Hellina," Fordham began formally.

But it was the wrong move. She turned her anger on him. "And *you*! You could be expelled from the tournament for this. Did you consider that?"

Fordham's jaw set. "No, but we are trying to solve a murder."

"Murder? What murder?" She looked between the two of them. "What happened to Lyam was a tragic accident. Whatever you two have been doing, you're finished."

"Just listen to us!" Kerrigan cried. "An assassin was sent after me. We witnessed an illicit weapons deal. There is more at stake than you know. Basem Nix is trading illegal magical artifacts, and he has Ellerby's nephew."

Helly held up a hand. "That's enough. If you had any of this information, you should have come to the Society with your concerns. We handle criminal investigations in Kinkadia. It is not left to a Dragon Blessed and a tournament competitor. You will cease your operation *immediately* and allow me to handle it from now on."

"Helly, please," Kerrigan cried.

"You are confined to the mountain for the remainder of the tournament," Helly snapped. "Both of you."

Fordham stiffened, clenching his jaw.

"What? But I'm supposed to find a patron," Kerrigan said.

"You should have considered the consequences to your actions," Helly said coldly. "After all the deaths last tournament, I should report you both to the council. Consider this a warning. If I discover you plotting again, I will have to follow through with that."

"Helly—"

"Do you understand?" Helly snapped over Kerrigan's protest.

"Yes," she whispered.

Fordham brusquely nodded his head.

"Then go. You both look like you haven't slept in weeks. I don't want to hear anything else out of you."

Kerrigan didn't see another choice. She swallowed, holding back her mounting anger, and stormed from the room. Fordham was hot on her heels as they left Helly behind. She didn't dare look back. Not once.

"What do we do now?" Fordham asked. "We can't just let this stand."

"No, we can't," she agreed. She rubbed her temples. "I have an idea."

"Is this going to get me expelled from the tournament?"

She squeezed her eyes shut. "You no longer have to be a part of this."

He reached out and dragged her to a stop. "I'm a part of this. We're in this together. What do we do?"

"Do you still have that party invitation? The one that I picked up the other day?"

"I believe so. Why?"

"I have an idea on how we can draw Basem out."

"With a party?"

"Yes."

"And how will we get out when Helly confined us both to the mountain?"

Kerrigan's lips lifted at the edges. "I've lived here my entire life. You think I only know one way in or out?"

CHAPTER THIRTY-NINE
THE PARTY

Curly hair sleeked and pinned to perfection, Kerrigan stood resplendent in a Parris original gown, red velvet that fell to her feet with a fitted bodice and dainty off-the-shoulder sleeves. Her bright red hair had been dyed a temporary chestnut brown, and her features were obscured by a small black mask. Only her emerald-green eyes and cherry-red lips were visible against her pale skin.

"Why do I feel like this is a bad idea?" Hadrian asked from her side as they stepped up to her father's home on the Row.

"Because danger goes against your nature."

"Yes, yes, it does."

"Don't worry so much. I don't look like me," Kerrigan reminded him. "And no one will recognize Fordham. He's wearing a powder-blue suit to match the swirling colors of the Row. Not a single person expects the prince of the House of Shadows to be in powder blue."

Even she had barely recognized him. Though it hadn't stopped her heart from fluttering at the sight of him in something that showed off his broad shoulders and tapered waist. The way the mask concealed all but his perfect, pouty lips.

"But somehow, you are still recognizable," Hadrian grumbled.

Kerrigan laughed and tugged him closer. "Just hand over the invitation when we get there."

Hadrian straightened and cleared his throat as they approached the front of the considerable line to enter Lord Kivrin Argon's residence. Hadrian himself was in a soft mint jacket with dark trousers. His patron, Fallon, had impeccable taste in clothing.

The first thing to do had been clueing everyone else in on what was happening. It was much easier to get Hadrian, Darby, and Clover into the mountain than getting Kerrigan and Fordham out. But once she had them on board, the plan was in motion. Clover staked out Basem's residence and tracked his movements to get a sense of what he did during the day. Darby used her connections to secure a second invitation to the party, which Hadrian delivered to Basem.

Fordham didn't think it was going to work, but he didn't understand the idea of someone starting from the bottom and working their way up. If Kerrigan knew anything about wanting to belong, it was that no one who so desperately wanted to fit in would turn down an invitation to the Row. And to be certain, Clover had found Basem at an off the Row tailor, securing a new evening suit. Checkmate.

He'd be here. Then they'd need to enact phase two of the plan.

They finally reached the front of the line, and Hadrian handed over his invitation. Kerrigan stepped inside with Hadrian and allowed Fordham, Clover, and Darby to extend their own invitations to enter.

Her stomach was in her throat as she stared around at her father's home. She had spent most of her life trying to *avoid* the man who had thrown her out. This went against all her own ideals.

"Breathe," Hadrian whispered. "You don't have to see or speak to him."

Kerrigan swallowed down the rising bile. Hadrian knew, of course. That part of this plan hinged on her being able to keep it together if she ran into her father. She straightened her spine and adjusted her face mask. She could do this.

Fordham, Clover, and Darby entered behind them, and the lot of them moved off into the shadows.

Fordham irritably messed with his own mask. "Is this really necessary?"

"Shush, you. Enjoy the espionage. If I can dress like this," Clover said, gesturing to the gold gown instead of her normal shirt and trousers, "then you can suffer wearing blue."

Hadrian snorted. Kerrigan grinned. Darby rolled her eyes. She was the only one deliberately dressed to draw attention. Her navy Bryonican dress was in the fashion of Sonali's household, and she even wore the lady's crest. Her mask was a shimmery gold lace strip that covered her eyes.

Fordham assessed them all critically. "I see why you are all Kerrigan's friends."

"What's that supposed to mean?" she asked, unable to keep the smile from her lips or the challenge out of her eyes.

"They're nearly as insufferable as you are."

"And what does that make you, princeling?"

He arched an eyebrow. "Suffering."

"Okay, you two, break it up," Clover said. "Let's get back to business."

"Yes," Darby squeaked. "I'm quite put out by this whole"—she lowered her voice—"spying thing."

"Luckily for you, Darbs," Clover said, tossing an arm around her shoulders, "you're just you tonight."

"Follow orders, as we outlined," Kerrigan said. "Everyone is to split up and take a portion of the house. If anyone lays eyes on Basem, be discreet and do not engage. We'll meet up in the gardens in an hour."

"And steer clear of the drinks," Hadrian added.

Clover released Darby and poked playfully at Hadrian. "That's no fun, sweetheart. Just imagine the trouble we could get into."

He cleared his throat and stepped backward. "It's just a suggestion."

"And a good one," Kerrigan agreed. She hugged her friends and then sent them off into the party. "Good luck."

Fordham grasped her arm before she could walk away. "Be careful."

"I will," she said.

He opened his mouth to say more but closed it and released her.

Kerrigan headed deeper into the party. Her father's house was ostentatious on a good day, but somehow, he made all that wealth and extravagance look purposeful instead of out of place. The grandiose affluence of generations of Bryonican royals all on display in one glorious house on the Row. She stepped into a large ballroom, complete with a marble floor, an enormous cherubic painting covering the ceiling, and dozens of guests lining up for the next dance from the string quartet in the corner.

"Would you care to dance?" a gentleman in a silk top hat and a crisp lavender jacket asked.

"Oh, thank you so much, kind sir," she said, layering on a thick accent. She was desperately glad that her ears weren't visible. "But I am looking for my beau."

The man bowed deeply at the waist and then retreated. If someone had asked her to join the dancing, she must look too much like the lady she was masquerading as.

Kerrigan kept to the shadows as she traversed the ballroom, looking for a hint of Basem Nix among the crowd, but she found nothing. She stepped into the next room, which was a second ballroom with a slow serenade playing for the benefit of the dancers. This room was half the size of the last, all polished black granite floor, gilded portraits, and heavy red curtains. A cursory glance said that she would never find Basem in the likes of this place.

She was about to leave when a waitress stepped forward in the navy-and-white Argon livery. A mask covered the whole of her face. "Drink?"

On the tray she held aloft to Kerrigan, there was but one glass left.

Kerrigan inhaled sharply and then covered it with a polite cough. "Allergies," she whispered to the waitress.

The gold goblet was straight out of her last vision and filled nearly to the brim with the same blue liquid. The waitress stood amicably and waited for Kerrigan to make her selection.

With fear creeping into her, Kerrigan took the goblet and inclined her head. "Thank you."

"As you wish," the woman said, tucking the tray under her arm and disappearing into the crowd.

Kerrigan stared down at the blue drink as if it were a bomb that was going to explode any second. Her stomach felt queasy, and she hastily looked around the room to see if anyone had noticed her before ducking out a side entrance and into the gardens. Though she was hardly alone here. At least everyone was preoccupied with stripping out of their evening gowns and taking a dip in the various rectangular pools that waterfalled in tiers down to the main gardens.

But Kerrigan's focus was not on the mostly naked raunchy aspects of her father's party. What had her vision been warning her about by showing her this liquid? Was it poison? It didn't typically show her things that wouldn't hurt her in some way. She couldn't drink it, but she still wanted to know what it was.

She headed down the steps and stopped before a potted plant nearly out of sight. With a backward glance at the rest of the festivities, she emptied half the liquid in the pot.

Nothing happened. What had she been expecting anyway? It was likely a particularly potent brew of the faerie punch. She'd had her fair share of dangerous concoctions in her life. Her heart clutched as she remembered more than one occasion with Lyam where they'd gotten so drunk from the faerie punch that they passed out before they even made it back to their rooms.

Just as she was about to turn her back on the entire ordeal, the pot began to smoke. The dirt had been reduced to ash, and the liquid was actually *disintegrating* the stone.

Her eyes widened in horrified alarm. If it could do this to stone, what would it have done to her stomach? Kerrigan hastily tossed the rest of the liquid, thanking the gods for her visions. Under any other circumstances, she wouldn't have thought twice about taking a sip of an offered drink. Holy scales.

"Careful there," a voice said with a tinkling laugh as a hand clamped down on her wrist. "Don't want to stumble back into the pools."

Kerrigan halted in her steps. She hadn't even realized that she had been walking backward, away from the horror of the poisoned drink. Someone was *here*. They were here, and they knew she was here, and they had tried to kill her. Again.

Was it Basem? Did he somehow know her ploy to get him here and confront him?

"Are you all right?" the girl asked gently.

And that was when Kerrigan realized who was touching her. She hadn't noticed at first with her in a dove-gray gown that hugged all her curves or the blond hair in a perfect, aristocratic coif. But she would know that voice anywhere, especially coupled with the bright blue eyes and pink-painted lips.

It appeared that Audria recognized her as well. "Kerrigan?" she asked in surprise. "What are you doing here?"

"Uh…hi, Audria," Kerrigan said, losing her ability to form coherent sentences around the girl.

"I thought that you were confined to the mountain," Audria whispered. She flicked a lock of Kerrigan's brown hair. "I like the color."

"I…uh…well…"

Audria looped their arms together. "You don't have to tell me. I'd want to get out too." Audria glanced behind her. "I've just ditched Roake actually. Boy is as hard to get rid of as a leech."

Kerrigan laughed lightly as Audria directed them away from the noise of the pools and deeper into the gardens. She should have felt unease creep in as they escaped the party together, but somehow, she couldn't feel that with Audria. The last thing she wanted was for Audria to realize who she had once been, but she couldn't deny that Audria's presence, as terrifying and confusing as it was, felt natural.

"Where are we going?" Kerrigan asked.

"Just trying to keep Roake at bay," Audria said with her easy laugh. "The party is a little much, isn't it?"

Kerrigan nodded despite herself. "Kivrin does like to go over the top."

Audria slanted her eyes toward her. "He does have that tendency."

"I should really get back."

"Are you here with Fordham?"

"Uh…no. I came alone."

Audria looked disbelieving. "Just stay with me a minute longer. I'd like to keep Roake's grubby hands as far from my silk dress as possible."

"Why do you put up with him?" Kerrigan asked.

Audria shrugged. "He's not so bad. Not all the time. But when he's drunk…" Audria sighed and gestured in a *you know what I mean* sort of way.

"Ah."

They entered a small, circular garden lined with benches that would likely be occupied for more devious purposes later in the evening but were as yet unoccupied. Audria sank gracefully into one and patted the chair next to her for Kerrigan to follow. Kerrigan reluctantly did so.

"Can I ask you a question?"

"Sure," Kerrigan said.

"Have you ever heard of the story of the lost princess of Bryonica?"

Kerrigan froze in place. Everything seemed to move in slow motion. Oh gods.

"I think everyone has," she said faintly.

"Of course," Audria said lightly. "Well, I actually *knew* Lady Felicity. We were so young, and we became fast friends. Our parents visited frequently, and when we were together, the world was ours for the taking. We were practically sisters. But then, twelve years ago, Lady Felicity disappeared." Audria turned to look at her. "Lord Kivrin was bereft over his only daughter's apparent vanishing. The entire kingdom searched for her. The capital city, my lovely Rosemont, was turned over to find the small girl, but not a single trace was found. She was *poof*. Gone."

Kerrigan said nothing. Just met Audria's questioning gaze.

"Lady Felicity Argon, first of the House of Cruse, a Bryonican royal, and the lost princess of our people was just gone."

"That must have been upsetting," Kerrigan said around the lump in her throat.

"She was never really gone though, was she, Kerrigan?" Audria asked. "She came here, to Kinkadia, to the House of Dragons, and changed her name. She's you."

Kerrigan felt like a knife had been shoved into her ribs. All these years, she had hidden her past away, avoided those who could ever suspect who she was, and lived this new life. But now, here Audria was, bringing it all to the surface again.

"My name is Kerrigan."

"It is Felicity," Audria insisted.

Kerrigan closed her eyes fiercely. "Kerrigan Felicity Argon," she whispered. "My father never wanted to use my first name after my mother, Keres, died, but the mistresses in the House of Dragons had no such qualms."

Audria's eyes filled with tears, and then she threw her arms around Kerrigan's neck. "I've missed you so much!"

"Audria, you can't…"

But Audria didn't let her finish her thought. Didn't let her tell her not to let anyone else know.

"This changes everything," Audria said, holding Kerrigan at arm's length. "You are Dragon Blessed. You have to be chosen by a house. I will speak to my mother and have her choose you. You can live with us in Bryonica and on the Row, as you were always meant to. We could be sisters in truth!"

"Audria," Kerrigan gasped. Fear settled in where unease had previously been. This was a dream come true but also her worst nightmare.

Audria grasped Kerrigan's hands in her own. "I'm overjoyed. I knew you were familiar, but it wasn't until I saw you here, among your father's things, that it all came together." A tear fell down Audria's face, and she swiped it aside with a laugh. "Our people will be so pleased to have you back. You're no longer lost."

Kerrigan took a deep breath, and then she pulled back from Audria's grasp and her enthusiasm and the desperate hope that she could have a sister.

"What is it?" Audria asked.

"A person can't be lost when they were abandoned."

Audria frowned. "What do you mean?"

"I mean, my father was the one who left me on the steps of Draco Mountain to be in the House of Dragons. No matter how bereft he appeared, he *knew* what he was doing. He abandoned me."

"No," Audria said with a shake of her head. "That can't be true."

"But it is," Kerrigan said, rising to her feet. "Being lost implies that you can be found, that someone wants to find you. Kivrin Argon has known precisely where I have been every day for the last twelve years. How could I want to go back to a life that so easily threw me away?"

Audria stood. "What he did was terrible, but there *are* people who want you. You could have a home and a life. Don't you want that?"

Kerrigan closed her eyes. In fact, the last thing she had ever wanted was to return to Bryonica. But was this different? Was Audria's offer a means to escape the life Helly had set up for her in the Society? Was this actually freedom or more chains?

"I'll think about it," she said, and before Audria could say another word, Kerrigan stumbled out of the clearing and dashed through the gardens.

CHAPTER FORTY
THE TRIO

CLOVER

Clover pulled a drag on her smoke with gusto. She hated this stupid dress and that she had to fit into normal society to come to this sort of event. Truthfully, she would have preferred to be dressed in Fordham's ridiculous powder-blue suit than this monstrosity. How was anyone supposed to exist in this much fabric?

"Is it really smart to be smoking that in public?" Darby asked, appearing outside the crowded ballroom.

"Probably not."

Darby smiled at her shyly and took a step forward. Hadrian practically fell out of the room after her. Darby's face faltered for the briefest minute. Hmm. Had she wanted to be alone?

"Clover!" Hadrian gasped. He stalked toward her and snatched the smoke out of her hand.

"Have a pull on it, pretty boy," she teased. "Might get that foot out of your ass, where it's permanently stuck."

Darby giggled, covering her mouth.

Hadrian dropped the cigarette on the ground and stamped it out. "Are you insane?"

"Not in the least, sweetheart. This party is the definition of depravity. You think a little loch is the worst thing that anyone is doing here?"

Clover took a step into him and winked. He flushed a deep crimson. She ruffled his blue hair, the edgiest thing that had ever happened to this straitlaced boy.

"Want to find out what else is out there?"

He gulped visibly, his Adam's apple bobbing. "We're supposed to look for Basem."

"We can have some fun while we search," she teased, plucking his tie and snaking her fingers down it.

He tugged it away from her. "I have no time for your games, Clover." He turned back to Darby, who looked like she wanted to be anywhere else. "Come on, Darbs. We'll go search elsewhere."

"Darby should stay with me," Clover said without thinking. Darby's head snapped up to look at her. "We can finish this side of the house."

"Darby?" Hadrian asked.

"What? Don't trust her with me? I promise, I have very careful hands," Clover said with another pointed wink.

Hadrian huffed and then stormed off in a fury. Upsetting him was half the joy in her existence.

"You shouldn't tease him so," Darby said softly. "All you do is get him riled up."

Clover kept her eyes focused on Hadrian's retreat. She shouldn't feel pulled toward that prudish, arrogant boy, but somehow, she was. "That's the fun of it."

Darby sighed and then gestured to Clover's bag. "You should have another."

"Another what?"

"Smoke."

Clover raised her eyebrows. "You're condoning my smoking? Just a second ago, you said it wasn't a good idea."

"It's not, but your hands are shaking."

She hastily clasped them behind her.

Darby smiled again shyly. "You feel better when you have one."

Clover did, but she hadn't thought anyone noticed. Kerrigan knew about her condition. She simply hadn't told the others. It wasn't their business. Had Darby figured it out all on her own?

"All right," Clover said, pulling out another smoke and bringing it to her lips.

"Let me." Darby stepped forward and managed a flicker of fire magic to light the smoke.

Darby had never shown much affinity for magic, not like Kerrigan. It must have taken a great deal of concentration to light the cigarette.

Clover took a good, long pull on the smoke, breathing in the healing loch. It might be illegal, but it was the only thing that kept the pain back.

They stood together in silence as she finished her smoke. Darby purposely looked away from her and watched the crowd to see if anyone would appear. No one did.

"Do you…" Darby began and then bit her lip.

"Do I what?" Clover asked, stamping the smoke out on the ground and feeling like a new person.

"Do you like Hadrian?"

"Sure," Clover said with a shrug. She *did* like Hadrian. Maybe more than liked him. It was why she couldn't stop herself from poking at him.

Darby's face crumpled slightly. "I see."

"So what if I do, Darbs?" Clover prodded.

"I just thought you liked…"

Clover waited, but Darby didn't finish. "Say it."

"Girls," Darby finished on a whisper.

"Ah," Clover said, a smirk crossing her features. "I do like girls."

Darby's look of confusion was adorable. Her little nose in the air, her eyes darting here and there, as if she were trying to make sense of it all.

Clover stepped forward until their bodies nearly touched. Darby hiccupped in alarm and stepped back, but there was nowhere to go.

"I like both. I like boys, and I like girls. Actually, I like everyone."

"Everyone?" Darby asked.

"Some people don't grow up feeling like a boy *or* a girl," Clover said, speaking from experience. "Some people grow up feeling like a person. I don't feel binary about the whole thing. I'm open to all sorts of love."

"Oh. Okay." Darby chewed on her bottom lip.

"I'm open to this," Clover said.

Before Darby could say anything, Clover tipped her chin up and pressed their lips together. Darby's lips were so damn soft and sweet. As if she were made of something that much purer. Darby was too damn good for her. That fact had always been known. But standing there at some rich, fancy-ass party, wearing a ridiculous gown, talking about love, she hadn't been able to hold back. All she'd done for the last year around Darby was hold back. And dammit, this would all go down in flames, but she wanted one taste of the sweet elixir before giving it up forever.

Darby stumbled backward a step. Her hand went to her lips. Those perfect, innocent eyes were wide with alarm.

"What's wrong, Darbs?" Clover asked as quiet as a mouse. "Don't you want this?"

"Yes," Darby whispered before she could stop herself.

"Then what's the problem?"

"I can't," Darby said with a worried shake of her head. "Sonali doesn't know. She's been talking marriage prospects."

Clover's face darkened. "Marriage prospects," she said hollowly.

"Yes. She's going to bring in gentlemen after the tournament."

"Gentlemen," she said, her voice rough around the edges. "But, Darby, *you* don't like boys."

"I know," Darby said, her eyes filling with tears. "I cherish this kiss, my first kiss, Clover. I always will. But it can never happen again."

Darby ran away down the stone steps into the garden, her brilliant gown flowing out behind her as she raced away. Clover had always known she would never get to keep someone like Darby. One kiss should have been enough. Instead, all she felt was heartbreak.

CHAPTER FORTY-ONE
THE PAST

R unning wasn't her smartest move.

Kerrigan hadn't been able to stand there and listen to Audria's soothing words, the words she had waited her entire life to hear. They weren't feasible. Nothing Audria had said even made sense. There was no world that Kerrigan could go back to and become Lady Felicity, first of the House of Cruse again. The House of Dragons had shaped her beyond recognition. She wasn't a princess, not even a lady. She was a fighter, a weapon, a survivor.

Tears blurred her eyes, and she ripped off the mask in the garden. She could hardly see where she was going, only that her past had caught up with her and she wanted to forget any of this had ever happened. That it all had the ability to make her cry at all.

A figure blocked her path. She hardly saw him and nearly careened into him.

"Sorry," she gasped, stepping around him to try to find an empty space to grieve her old life.

But the man caught her elbow. "Kerrigan?"

She stilled, her eyes drifting up to meet blue. The last person she wanted to meet tonight. "Kivrin."

He looked around the gardens. No one had yet noticed them. "What are you doing here? How did you even get into my party?" He fingered a lock of her tresses. "What have you *done* to your hair?"

Kerrigan tugged her arm out of his grasp. "Don't touch me."

"This is unacceptable," Kivrin said with fury in his tone. "You were not invited to this event. You should not be attending parties."

"And why not? Are you ashamed of me?" she hissed. "Oh wait, you gave me up. Of course you are. Here's a hint: leave me alone."

"I would leave you alone if you didn't stumble into my events. I want you to leave."

Kerrigan couldn't leave, not yet. She fought for a lie. "I have one week to find a patron or else I will work for the Society for life. I'll give up everything I've worked for."

His eyes softened marginally. "And you thought you'd find one here?"

She inclined her head slightly. "Yes."

"Then you are more foolish than I thought. Why did you not come to me if that was the bargain? I could have helped you find someone."

She laughed at him. "I don't need your help. You've done quite enough."

Kivrin grasped her arm again, towering over her. He should have been intimidating in his grandeur, but he seemed smaller than ever.

"Listen and listen closely," he growled.

But Kerrigan never had to hear what he said, because a hand came down and clamped on Kivrin's shoulder.

"I would release her, good sir."

Fordham Ollivier stood there, standing eye to eye with her father. His mask had been removed, and his stormy-gray eyes raged. He didn't even look ridiculous in the powder blue. He looked like he belonged.

Kivrin let Kerrigan's arm go. "This is how you got into the party?"

317

"I was invited," Fordham said evenly. He gestured to Kerrigan. "Come on. Let's go."

"This is a bad idea," Kivrin said, glancing between them.

"Not any more than you are," Kerrigan spat.

She followed Fordham away from her father. Her chest ached, and she felt like she had been wrung out. She didn't even pay attention to where Fordham was leading until they were in the gazebo at the back of the property, where they had all agreed to meet. Fordham gestured for her to take a seat, which she did, burying her head in her hands.

"What was that all about?" he asked.

"It's complicated."

"That guy was a total dick to you."

Suddenly, she couldn't pretend anymore. She was tired of hiding who she was. After Audria's confession and her dealings with her dad, she couldn't sit by and act like everything was fine.

"That guy is my father," she said, looking up to meet his eyes.

Fordham balked at that. "Kivrin Argon is your father?"

She nodded. "Yes."

"But he's a royal? And you're..."

"Half-Fae?"

"Dragon Blessed," he finished. "Obviously, your father would have to be Fae if your mother was human, but I thought that the House of Dragons was a way to advance in society. I gathered that they took kids off the streets and out of poverty to help them have a second chance in society. If your father is a royal..."

"That's exactly why he abandoned me," she said bitterly. "Most Fae don't grow into their severely pointed ears until they're five or six." She gestured to the sharp points of his own ears. "I was left at the mountain when I was five, right as my shorter ears were beginning to reveal that I wasn't fully Fae."

Fordham stared at her, his face unreadable. She didn't know if he felt the horror that she did when she thought about it. Perhaps this was normal where he was from. Perhaps they would have just killed Kerrigan instead.

Kerrigan didn't wait for him to say something. She barreled forward. "There's a story of the lost princess of Bryonica. Princess Felicity Argon of the House of Cruse was stolen at five years old, and everyone went looking for her, but she was nowhere to be found," Kerrigan said, looking off into the gardens. "But I wasn't lost. I was right here, where my father left me. Now Audria found it all out. She wants her mother to adopt me from the House of Dragons so that everything can go back to the way it was." She choked on the last words. "But it can never go back. Not after what my father did. Besides Helly, who knows what happened, I've avoided everyone from Bryonica. The very last thing I want is to go back to the place that let my father abandon me and be paraded around like some long-lost princess. I would rather work every day in the Society as a forgotten nobody than live that sham of a life."

Fordham sank into the seat next to her and tilted her chin up to look at him. "You don't have to go back."

"I don't know if I have another choice," she gasped. "Once a Dragon Blessed has been chosen, that's that. I don't think I can say no."

"Since when have you ever taken *anything* at face value?"

She hiccupped around a laugh. "Never."

"We'll figure it out. We always do."

"Okay. You're right."

Their eyes locked. Where she had seen nothing only moments earlier, deep emotions swirled through his irises. It startled her. So frequently, he shut down, as if not showing emotions was a defense mechanism. Something trained into him.

"Ford," she whispered hesitantly.

His hand moved from her chin and back into her hair. "What have you done to me?"

"What have I done?" she asked back.

"You have bewitched me so."

And she was lost to him.

His lips lowered to hers, and time froze. He tasted like honey and liquor and oranges. His lips were soft and supple and oh so inviting. His tongue grazed across her bottom lip, and she shivered, opening her mouth to him. He swept in, brushing their tongues together. A soft groan escaped her at that first touch.

Her hands reached for the elaborate jacket, knotting into the material. He reacted by drawing them closer, his hands roaming down her sides to her hips and then against the middle of her back until their bodies were flush. Still, they weren't close enough. She slid forward until she was seated in his lap.

She couldn't breathe, and she didn't even care. This was bliss. This was precisely where she wanted to be. Her hands slipped under the jacket and found the strong contours of his back. Everything felt urgent and necessary and needy. She had no desire to stop this. Didn't think that it was possible to stop this. It was a runaway cart, barreling down a hill. Only a force of will or the gods could impede its descent.

She hadn't had a sip of faerie punch, but her skin felt hot, her breaths came out as gasps, and every brush of his lips sent fire coursing through her. She forgot their mission, the real reason for them being here. She got lost in Fordham Ollivier.

Then he was standing, and she tumbled off his lap, nearly landing on the ground.

An "Oof" escaped her as she tried to right herself. What the gods?

Fordham walked away from her across the gazebo, his hand fisted in his hair. Kerrigan came swiftly back to her feet. Her heart still thudded a quick staccato from their intimate kiss, but now he was gone, and she had no idea what had just happened.

"Ford?" she whispered, a faint, delicate thing that betrayed her hurt.

"I can't do this, Kerrigan."

She swallowed and took a step backward. "Right. Of course not," she bit out.

"You don't understand."

"No, I think I do." Mounting anger lashed at her. "It's because I'm half-Fae, isn't it?"

He turned back to face her. "It's not that."

She laughed without mirth. "Real convincing, princeling."

"Don't."

"Don't what? You kissed me first. And even if you hadn't, this was building. You can't deny it."

"I know," he said, his voice barely above a breath. "I wanted to, but I can't." He looked visibly distressed. "I'm cursed."

She rolled her eyes. "Convenient thing to have never mentioned."

"I did mention it to you," he said. "When we first met, I told you that I was cursed."

"That was a joke!"

"It wasn't. I actually am cursed."

Kerrigan tilted her head in confusion. "What does that even mean? An actual curse?"

"Yes. There is dark magic in the House of Shadows. One of my father's enemies sent a woman to my crib after I was born and cursed me. She said I was cursed to wander perpetually and to hurt all those I care for."

"You're serious."

He looked away again. "I have never cared for anyone. But I cannot deny how I feel for you, and the last thing I want is to hurt you."

"To live is to take that chance."

"It's not a chance," he insisted. "It is a necessity. I will hurt you. It's a promise."

She shivered at his words. It sounded like a promise. It rang with truth. Yet she couldn't bring herself to care. Not when this felt so right. They were so similar in so many ways. He didn't know the whole of it. If he was going to give her his biggest secret, then she would confess hers.

"You are not the only one who is cursed."

He blinked in surprise. "What do you mean?"

"I am also cursed. With visions."

"Visions?" Fordham asked.

"I can sort of see the future. It's not exactly clear, usually just flashes of images that don't even make sense until it happens. It started five years ago. I saw Cyrene's world in jeopardy. Then a year ago, it happened again. I saw that Lament church at the square—you remember it?"

He nodded gravely.

"I saw it burning before it ever happened. And then a few weeks ago, I saw a man materializing out of black smoke in the center of the arena."

He reared back. "You saw me?"

"And I haven't stopped seeing you, Fordham. The visions keep pushing us together. That's how I knew what element you should use that day. It's how I knew you were going to fall in the second task."

"And the raven medallion?" he guessed.

"I don't know what it means, honestly, but if it's in my vision, it's important." She wrung her hands. "I'm not supposed to tell anyone about it. Only Helly and Gelryn know the truth of it…" She bit her lip. "And Dozan."

"Dozan? Why would you tell him?"

"He was there that first night when it happened. I was assaulted in the streets, and in the middle of it, I had my first vision. Dozan nursed me back to health, and when I woke up, I thought he'd taken care of the people who had hurt me, but when I had that energy explosion with you, I realized that *I* was the one who had killed all those people."

Fordham sank back down onto the stone seat. "That's a lot to take in."

"I know. The last person who knew was Lyam, and then he turned up dead," she whispered. "And Basem was there the night I had my vision of you. I'm not sure if it's all connected, if he knows."

"Gods, that's another motive that you didn't mention."

She chewed on her bottom lip. "I know, but I've never told anyone else about my visions, and the one person who found out was just murdered. I don't want that to happen to you too."

Fordham stood and put his hands on her shoulders, gentle this time. "That's not going to happen to me. I'm glad you told me."

"It's good to have it off my chest actually."

"Likewise," he admitted. "Everyone back home knows about my curse. It's common knowledge, but here, I finally feel…"

"Free?"

"Precisely."

"Me too."

He brushed a lock of her hair behind her ear. "I don't know what to do about this."

"I don't either."

She stared up into his eyes, knowing that was a lie. All she wanted was to kiss him again, to feel his perfect lips on hers. Yet she could see that he was being honest. That he believed he would hurt her if they continued forward. She didn't know what to do about that. Her heart ached just thinking about it.

"We'll figure it out," she told him.

He nodded.

"What a touching moment," a voice said from the other side of the gazebo.

Kerrigan and Fordham wrenched away from each other and turned to face the woman. She was dressed in head to toe black with her shock of white hair visible but her face hidden by a black mask.

"You!" Kerrigan yelled at the assassin.

She drew her magic to her and shifted into a defensive stance. She could sense Fordham do so next to her.

"Now, now," the woman said, holding up her hand. "I'm not here to fight. Would I have announced myself if I were?"

"What do you want?" Fordham snarled.

"I'm here to deliver a message."

"From whom? Basem?" Kerrigan asked.

"As a matter of fact," the woman said with a sinister smile. "Basem would like you to meet him in Row Park by Irena Fountain in a half hour, or your little friends will die."

All the color drained from Kerrigan's face. "What did you do to them?"

"Me? I didn't do anything. I'm the messenger, but Basem isn't likely to back down. So chop-chop. Clock is ticking. Oh, and you should go alone if you know what's good for you."

And then the little assassin traipsed away into the dark.

CHAPTER FORTY-TWO

THE HOSTAGES

Kerrigan walked into the park alone. She had a minute to spare when she reached Irena Fountain. The enormous fountain was made entirely of a white rock from the heart of the Vert Mountains far up north. A carving of Irena, the first dragon rider, stood atop the structure with dragon heads at her feet, spewing water into the concentric pools beneath her. The fountain stood on the cusp of the lake at the center of Row Park. And waiting in front of it was Basem Nix himself.

With her head held high, she approached the fountain, counting off the number of goons he'd brought with him while telling her to come alone. Two at the fountain, holding Darby and Hadrian. But not Clover. Was that a good thing or a very bad thing? She counted six along the waterline. Two were trailing her from the entrance to the park. And one more against the tree line. A dozen in total, including Basem. No sign of the assassin.

"Well, well, well," Basem drawled, "look what the cat dragged in."

Kerrigan stopped before him, standing casually in the dress that was far from made for fighting. She gave off the distinct impression of being young and innocent. Not a threat. Of course, Basem already knew she was a threat. That was why he'd kept trying to kill her.

"Hello, Basem. We've been tiptoeing around each other the last couple of weeks. It's time we're finally introduced properly."

Basem laughed, a wet coughing sound that grated on her nerves. "You think you deserve to be properly introduced to me, leatha?"

She showed no outward sign of revulsion. "Ah, just as clever as always with your comebacks. Still upset that I beat you?" she asked sweetly.

The two men behind her stilled. She could sense confusion ripple through the crowd of Basem's men.

"That is hardly what happened," he said through gritted teeth. "And now, you'll pay with your life."

"We'll see," Kerrigan said evenly, forcing a smile. "You seem very bad at killing me."

"Isa was a mistake. I admit that. She's accomplished, but it was too impersonal."

"Ah, want to do it yourself this time?"

"With pleasure." He grinned, revealing a row of uneven teeth.

She had dubbed him Bruiser when fighting him in the ring all those weeks ago, and it still held truth. He might be in a gentleman's coat with a distinguished top hat, but he would never be one of the Fae elite that he envied. Not when he still had the stench of the Dregs all over him.

"How did you find out about the party?"

Basem's cheeks heated at the question. "None of your business."

Kerrigan realized what must have happened, what she hadn't even considered in all their scheming. "They turned you away at the door."

Basem bared his teeth. "Enough talking. Turn yourself over, and I'll release your friends."

She had underestimated him. And just how snobbish her father was. Of course he had turned Basem away. He wouldn't consort with the likes of him. Now, her friends' lives were in jeopardy.

"How do I know that you're going to hold to your word?" Kerrigan asked. "That you'll release them?"

"I have no issue with them," Basem said dismissively. "They're full Fae. They're citizens of a house. One is even part of a royal family."

Darby huffed, "As if I'm going to speak so highly of you after my kidnapping."

"This isn't about you," Basem said with a blaze of fury. "This is about the leatha bitch. I can't suffer you to live. You half-Fae and humans infesting the streets, breeding like rabbits. It's disgusting. You're taking up all the resources. If it weren't for you lot, Kinkadia would be pure."

"And you'd still be on the bottom," Kerrigan spat at him.

She had heard this same rhetoric before time and time again. As if it were the humans' and half-Faes' fault that some Fae were poor and going without. There were so many more humans in poverty that the comparison was laughable at best. Unintelligent and damaging were more like it.

"You're all criminal lowlifes who don't deserve the space in our city."

"Hilarious, coming from you," Hadrian muttered.

Kerrigan grinned at Basem. "Pot, meet kettle."

"You're surrounded," Basem snarled over their jokes. "We have your friends. Turn yourself over to me, and I will release them. This is between me and you, leatha."

"Fine," Kerrigan said with a sigh. "Fine. I know when I'm beat."

Hadrian and Darby looked at her with fear in their eyes.

"Kerrigan, no," Darby cried.

Hadrian reached for her. "You can't do this."

"It's done," Kerrigan said with all the confidence she could muster. "He's right anyway. You two are better than me. This is how it has to be."

They talked over her, but she walked toward Basem. Her heart thudded in her chest, and she calmed her breathing. She needed to keep herself under control if she was going to survive what came next.

Darby and Hadrian had to be safely removed from the picture. That was what was most important.

"Where's your little House of Shadows boyfriend?" Basem taunted. "Decided he couldn't stand a leatha anymore?"

Kerrigan gritted her teeth. "He decided not to help."

"Just what you deserve."

She was nearly to Basem now, where he stood by the edge of the fountain. "Release them," she commanded.

Basem sneered at her, but he gestured to his two men, and they released the two prisoners and shoved them forward into the circle of Basem's ruffians. They took only two stumbling steps forward when a swirl of black smoke circled their feet. One of Basem's men cried out as the smoke intensified, coalescing into something solid. Then suddenly, Darby and Hadrian disappeared, and standing in their place was Prince Fordham Ollivier.

Encircled by a ring of darkness, he looked every ounce the prince that he was. Despite the absurd powder-blue suit, he was magnificent and terrifying. His eyes glowed silvery as the smoke dissipated, and he rose to his considerable height.

"Now, Kerrigan?" he asked with all the calculated calm that she had come to rely on.

And as Basem made a grab for her, she blasted him in the face with a torrent of air. She leaped away from Basem and into Fordham's ring of darkness. They stood back to back, their hands raised, their magic tight to them, prepared for the attack that was surely coming.

"Any chance you can use that shadow trick on us too?" she asked hopefully.

Fordham said nothing, and it was answer enough.

When they planned this rescue mission, Fordham had finally confided in her about his powers. That they allowed him to bend the darkness between places. It was an incredibly dangerous and difficult ability. It ran in his family, but only his father was able to do it with any regularity and not wipe himself out completely. The magic required was so enormous that Fordham hadn't even been sure he would be able to do it today, but they'd both agreed it was worth the risk.

"Great," she muttered. "Twelve against two."

"I'll take those odds," Fordham said.

Basem chuckled his rattling laugh and then produced a small amber orb out of his pocket. It was bigger than the thing she'd shattered in the alley the first time they'd met. Suddenly that meeting made so much more sense. He'd held her long enough with the stone, but it hadn't been strong enough that night. She doubted he'd be that stupid again.

"I don't think you'll survive very long, prince. And I thought we would have become allies. Your people were the greatest human and half-breed haters in the world. You hated them so much that they exiled your entire population, and you still slaughter anyone who comes onto your grounds."

"It is clear we are not allies," Fordham said evenly.

"No, I could never be allies with a leatha lover like you."

"Is that from your stash of magical artifacts from Elsiande?" Kerrigan challenged.

Basem grinned. "You have done your homework."

"That's what you used on me that first night we met."

"Indeed. This is a bit of an upgrade. Would you like to see what it does?"

By the smile on his face and the cheery way he'd asked that, she did *not* want to know. Not if the objects were as valuable as Ellerby had made them seem. They must be able to do some pretty powerful magic.

"Fordham," she whispered.

"I know."

Kerrigan reached deep into her well, prepared to fling her magic wide and make a run for it. But then a disturbance came from the northern part of the park, and a figure walked forward in a red button-up and black slacks.

"I wouldn't do that if I were you," Dozan said, his smooth voice like silk in the heated tension.

"Dozan Rook," Basem sneered. "What are you doing out of the Wastes?"

"Protecting my investment."

Kerrigan recoiled at the statement, even though Dozan was here to help her. He stepped out of the shadows and into the light. With him were a half-dozen other men and women that he employed. Kerrigan had seen most of them around the Wastes over the last year, but she wasn't entirely sure what they all could do. Just that they were powerful and everyone steered clear of them at all costs. Dozan was known for collecting and owning people who were special. She'd never had any interest in being one of them.

"You know, I've left you where you are because you keep control of the Wastes," Basem told him. "But I don't have to let you stay in power there. I'd be happy to burn down the entire Dregs to get rid of shit like you."

Dozan quirked a dangerous half smile. "I would truly like to see you try, Basem." Dozan glanced away from Basem dismissively. His eyes met Kerrigan's. She could see their last argument playing over on repeat, how she had yelled at him, and he had still shown up here for her. "Come, Kerrigan."

"You think I'm letting her out of here? You're crazy." Basem took a step forward. "We could still take you."

"Doubtful," Dozan said flatly. "Now we will be gone."

Basem drew power from his amber orb. "You ready to find out, D?"

Dozan eyed him critically and then slipped his hands into his pockets. "How about I make a proposition? You two solve this where it started. Settle this dispute in the ring. No rules. Anything goes. Fight to the death. The winner gets fifty thousand marks."

Kerrigan choked. Fifty thousand marks was a king's ransom. How in the gods' names was he even going to be able to pony that up to the winner?

"Fifty?" Basem asked greedily. "And I get to kill her anyway?"

"That's right," Dozan said.

"Done. I'm in."

"How about the night before the final tournament task? Kerrigan?"

She looked to Dozan and wondered what he was playing at. He wouldn't let her die in his Dragon Ring. She was his investment after all, and she'd sworn she wouldn't fight for him again. Not after the lies he'd told. It was either fight Basem here or fight him on her terms.

"You don't have to do this," Fordham said at her side.

Yes, she did.

She lifted her chin stoically. "Count me in."

CHAPTER FORTY-THREE
THE GUEST

Kerrigan and Fordham followed Dozan out of the park, leaving Basem and his cronies far behind. No one said a word until Kerrigan saw Clover waiting against the wall on the outside of the park, smoking loch.

"Oh, thank the gods," Clover muttered. She stamped out her smoke and rushed to hug Kerrigan. "Don't ever scare me like that again."

Kerrigan chuckled. "I'm sorry."

"Where are Darbs and Hadrian? Are they okay?" Clover asked, concerned.

"They're back at the party. They're fine," Kerrigan told her. "We got them out." Not that she cared to explain exactly how Fordham had gotten them out. "What the hell happened with you guys? How did Basem even get Darby and Hadrian?"

"The assassin chick," Clover said with a sigh. "She didn't seem to want me. She grabbed Darby and Hadrian and knocked me out. I came to with a killer headache and ran to get Dozan."

"Ugh, Isa," Kerrigan said, tasting the name that Basem had given her for the assassin. "She told you where they were being taken?"

Clover nodded.

"Either she thought you were insignificant, or she's not working directly with Basem."

"She kidnapped Darby and Hadrian!"

"I know. She can do his bidding but not agree with what he's doing." Kerrigan paced away. "Isa could have killed Fordham and me at the party, but she delivered a message and vanished."

"She appears to be on her own side," Fordham agreed.

"Well, whatever side she's on, at least I had enough information to tell Dozan where to find you."

"And you came," Kerrigan said, facing Dozan.

"You're surprised?" he asked cockily.

"It's unlike you."

"In fact, it seems I am constantly saving your life." His eyes were warm as he teased her. "You should not be surprised to know that I don't want you dead."

Kerrigan squirmed at the intensity of that look. Clover coughed behind her, and Kerrigan carefully didn't look at Fordham. The two had already gotten into it, and she had no desire to repeat that.

"And you get your fight," she said.

Dozan's diabolical grin said it all. "That is a bonus."

She scoffed. "As if that wasn't the entire purpose."

"No one backs out on a deal with me, princess."

Fordham stiffened at the pet name.

"I am not a princess," she furiously repeated to Dozan. "Stop calling me that."

"But you are so easy to rile."

Kerrigan huffed and turned from him. "Whatever, Dozan. I guess we'll see the outcome to all this in six days. But you'd better give me the fifty thousand marks when I win."

"I intend to make much more than fifty thousand marks, Red," he said, brushing a lock of her brown-dyed hair out of her face and winking.

She shrugged him off. "Of course you do, you leech."

He just laughed. "Clover, are you coming?"

"Yeah," she said. "Give Darbs and Hadrian my best?"

Kerrigan pulled her into another hug. "Be safe."

"You too."

By the time they checked in on Darby and Hadrian, made sure they got home safe, and returned to the mountain, Kerrigan was beyond exhausted. Fordham didn't look much better. In fact, his face was ashy, and he kept almost tripping over his own feet.

"Are you okay?" she asked softly as they climbed back into the side entrance they'd escaped through earlier that evening.

"The black smoke uses up a lot of my magic when I jump by myself. It took more to retrieve Darby and Hadrian."

"I'm sorry I asked you to do that."

"I offered," he reminded her.

She laughed. "Then I'm sorry that you had to offer. Life would have been easier for you without getting to know me, I think."

"But a hell of a lot more boring."

Her cheeks flushed. "Thanks. You look like you could use some sleep. Maybe we should skip practice tomorrow."

"No," he said automatically. "We need to train harder than ever if you're going to go up against Nix in the Dragon Ring. We'll need a plan of attack. I'll be able to train tomorrow."

"Okay," she said as they came to the crossroads where he would return to the competitors' area.

She bit her lip, desperately wanting to bridge the gap but knowing she couldn't. He truly believed he was cursed. And she didn't want to push him.

She swallowed and stepped back. Stepped away from him instead of toward him. Even though her chest ached and her heart was in her throat and she wanted to do anything *but* walk away from him.

He stood as if on a precipice. That same haunted look in his eyes from the gazebo. The pain of seeing her step back from him. With a resolute expression, he broke eye contact and muttered, "Good night."

"Night," she said, swallowing back her heartbreak.

All she wanted to do was rush back and throw her arms around him. But that couldn't happen. Not now. Maybe not ever.

Kerrigan closed her eyes to fend off the pain and then headed down the hallway. She could traverse the mountain in her sleep. Despite wanting to sleepwalk through her life at the moment, she had to remain alert in case anyone saw her wandering. She had changed out of her party dress before sneaking back in, but it still might raise an alarm that she was out of bed at this hour.

She reached her room without running into anyone but paused at the door when she realized that it was ajar. Her heart rate kicked up as adrenaline coursed through her. Someone was in her room.

She could sense the person now that she was paying attention and not worrying about Fordham's rejection or Helly finding her. Who the hell was in her room? And what did they want?

A minute was all she had to make her decision. She decided against using fire. It would blind both of them when it came down to it. Her eyes were adjusted enough to the dark. She silently pressed the door open.

Her stomach flipped as a figure stood at her dresser. She had a long mane of ash-blond hair. Suddenly, Kerrigan felt like she was in the midst of her vision. The girl with the ash-blond hair. Who was she? What was she doing here?

A sense of foreboding hung over the moment. Something was wrong. Was this person here to finish what Basem had started?

Fear crept through Kerrigan, and she lashed it down into place, but after everything that had happened tonight, she couldn't stop it. She pulled up her magic quick, prepared to strike the assassin in her bedroom. She wouldn't make the mistake she had made the last time in Ellerby's home. She had trained that out of herself. Now she would attack first and ask questions later.

She whipped out with a tendril of air, grasping both of the girl's wrists and twisting them tight together behind her back.

"Who are you?" Kerrigan demanded, stepping farther into the room and turning the girl around to face her.

"Kerrigan?" Valia asked in shock.

Kerrigan dropped her magic at once. A gasp of relief escaped her. It wasn't an assassin or one of Basem's men or anything. It was just Valia.

"Valia!" Kerrigan gasped. "What are you doing here?"

"Gods, Kerrigan, you attacked me!"

"You're in my room at night!"

Kerrigan ignited a flame and set it into the lantern by her bed, illuminating the small, mostly empty space. Valia rubbed her bare wrists. Kerrigan could see a line of red around them.

"I'm sorry," Kerrigan said with a sigh, sinking into her bed. "I'm jumpy right now."

"I noticed that," Valia said indignantly.

"But really, what are you doing here?"

"Helly was looking for you."

"Scales."

"Yeah. I covered for you and told her that you were training late. But I knew you had been sneaking out, and if she found out, the punishment would be severe. I waited to see if I'd have to cover for you again."

Kerrigan frowned. "How did you know I was sneaking out?"

"Because you're really not that good at it," Valia said with a small laugh. "But that's coming from someone who is used to being alone all the time and likes finding ways to avoid notice."

"Well, thanks for covering for me. Do you know what she wanted?"

Valia shook her head. "Not sure. She seemed sad."

"Okay. I'll talk to her tomorrow, I guess."

"Good luck."

"Thanks. I think I'll need it."

Valia headed to the door, and then right before she walked through, she turned back around and looked at Kerrigan. "Where were you tonight anyway?"

Kerrigan laughed, trying for levity. "A party."

"With Fordham?"

She nodded. "You're only young once, right?"

"Right," Valia said softly. "Night."

Kerrigan watched her go with a pang in her heart. How had she ever thought Valia was a threat in her bedroom? It was odd that she'd been in here at all, but nothing was out of place.

She had judged Valia. After this tournament, she was going to make a more concerted effort to befriend the girl. She didn't like that Valia had been left alone all this time.

Kerrigan lay down in her bed and stared up at the ceiling. She put out the light with a snap of her fingers and waited for sleep to take her. After everything that had happened that night and the exhaustion settling into her bones, she thought it would come easily. But it was nearly dawn before sleep finally came, and where sleep was, nightmares followed.

CHAPTER FORTY-FOUR
THE BIG FIGHT

Y ou can do this," Clover said in her best pep-talk voice.

Kerrigan sat with her head in her hands in the locker room the night of the big fight. Her stomach was in knots. Everything was riding on this moment. Her final confrontation with Basem Nix. The same place where this had all started.

"I know I can," Kerrigan said weakly.

"Ker, come on. You need more energy than that."

She did. She really did.

But sleep had eluded her all week. She didn't know if it was fear of the impending fight, which she'd never had before, growing anxiety toward the end of the tournament, or how much exactly depended on getting this right.

"It's so much more than a fight."

"You can't think of anything but what you're about to do out there, Red. Play your part. Beat Basem. Let the rest of the pieces fall into place."

"You're right."

And she was. Kerrigan had worried about what Helly wanted to say after Valia was in her rooms, but she had wanted to apologize for her reaction. She had been more worried than mad, and it had come out poorly. They parted on good terms. Though her punishment hadn't been lessened. Not that Helly knew she wasn't where she was supposed to be. Valia had shown her a new exit that Kerrigan hadn't even known about. It made all this *much* easier.

"Damn straight I'm right. You're going to win this."

Kerrigan watched a man stride in and gesture for her to follow him.

"You're about to be announced. Come with me."

She got to her feet, rolling her shoulders and bouncing back and forth on the balls of her feet. She repeated everything Fordham had been training into her the last couple of weeks. She'd prepared for this. All or nothing.

With an eruption of applause, the announcer stepped into the Dragon Ring. "Welcome, ladies and gentlemen and all manner of bottom-feeding scum in the Wastes. We are here for a momentous night of fighting. Our main event is a winner-take-all, no-rules, no-holds-barred fight to the death!"

The crowd roared at those words. What every spectator wanted to hear.

"Up first, the scrappy and daring fighter, Red!"

Kerrigan took a deep breath, and then she jumped into the ring, holding her hands above her head. The crowd cheered for her.

"Her competitor, the hulking and dominating fighter, Nix!"

Basem slunk into the ring, holding his own fists high. He was shirtless, revealing his massive bulk. He looked every inch the bruiser she had first named him. He had a pouch at each of his sides that dangled from his shorts. The crowd was thunderous for the enormous tree trunk of a man.

"You ready for this, leatha?" Basem snarled at her.

A few *boos* came from the crowd at the slur, but just as many people cheered for the horrible word.

"Oh, I'm ready," Kerrigan said.

She ripped out the headband that obscured her too-small ears, the delicate points that marked her as half-Fae. The exact thing that she had tried to hide for so long. But she wasn't just here to fight Basem Nix. She was here to fight anyone who had ever dared to call her that horrible word. For anyone who had ever dared to look down on her for only being half-Fae. She was doing it for all the half-Fae out there who had ever faced down a bruiser.

She tossed the headband out of the ring and deliberately tucked her red hair behind her ears. "Let's do this."

A chorus screamed at the revelation. A half-Fae fighting a full-blooded Fae in the Dragon Ring wasn't unheard of, but they were usually smaller fights. Nothing this big. Definitely nothing to the death. Dozan was offering a rare treat indeed. Likely as many people in the audience wanted to see her blood spill as those who wanted to see her take down someone like Basem. Bets rained down on the awaited spectacle.

Kerrigan tuned it all out. Just centered herself under the lanterns that illuminated the space. She breathed in through her nose and carefully out through her mouth. *Discipline.* This was what she had been training for. And Basem Nix had no idea.

The announcer called out some other nonsense and then ceded the floor to Dozan. Kerrigan turned her face up. She had been waiting for this. Her vision had shown her in the Dragon Ring with Dozan standing over her, just as he was now. She had walked away from it, but of course, she still ended up here.

Both opponents waited for his signal, tensed and ready.

Then Dozan called out, "Begin!"

Basem grinned and launched toward her. She recalled everything she knew about him from their first fight. Affinity for earth. Small drop of water magic. Used his strength to overpower his enemies. Trained with an air Fae. Ambushes over one-on-one combat.

"Know your enemy, and if you don't know your enemy, anticipate their mistakes."

He stomped his foot, and Kerrigan reflexively stepped to the side. The chunk of rock went flying wide, right where she had been standing. The last time she'd fought, he had pummeled her with rock that she hadn't been able to anticipate. She'd won because she'd gotten mad and unleashed that anger. Not for any real skill. She had been as much brute strength as he was.

Basem continued to volley rocks at her as she nimbly evaded them. "Come out. Come out, girl," he snarled. "You can't run forever."

Truly, she could. She could run until he ran out of magic or collapsed from the effort. But she had no plan to.

The next rock he lobbed at her, she circled around it, using its momentum to slingshot it back to Basem. A sickening crunch erupted throughout the ring as it collided with Basem's chest. He stumbled back one step, and his eyes burned a deep dark brown and went wide with anger.

"I didn't plan to run forever," she taunted right back.

Basem expected her to retaliate with air. That had been her main element at the last fight, so she gave him exactly what he'd expected. She stepped forward and sliced her hand down, the wind listening to her every move as it cut through his chest. He avoided the next one and the next before kicking at the earth under his feet. It ricocheted throughout the arena, and the rock under her own feet erupted upward. She was propelled forward. But instead of being thrown off-balance with the force, she used it to vault upward, do a somersault midair, and then come back at him with an arc of flames.

Basem barely moved enough to bring up a shield of water to turn the flames into steam. Kerrigan landed as gracefully as a cat on her feet on the other side of the ring.

"New tricks," Basem growled as he forced the water to do his bidding.

Kerrigan dispelled it with ease, taking the water he'd thrown at her and bringing it into her magic. He didn't have enough water magic to overpower her. His best bet was still earth.

"Same tricks," she said back as she tossed the water aside. It wasn't her best element either. "I thought this was going to be a fight."

Basem reacted as she'd expected him to—with a vengeance. He went entirely on the offensive, slinging rocks and then trying to trap her with the earth at her feet. She evaded the rocks and propelled the chunk of rock he had caged her with back toward his face. He barely got out of the way in time.

She watched his sloppy footwork and increasingly heavy breathing. He was tiring and fast. No wonder he didn't do his own dirty work. She had never been more thankful for all those runs with Fordham.

Kerrigan matched him pace for pace, using air to fend off his attacks and floating to avoid his wrath. She was going to have to play up the offensive to get the crowd on her side, but this fight was about so much more than that. And she needed to keep it going for longer than she'd like. She would prefer pummeling him and seeing this end.

She avoided another large chunk of rock and landed in a crouch. She narrowed her eyes, feeling the adrenaline pump through her as she waited to make her move.

"You are beneath me," Basem said, kicking up a cloud of dust. "You will always be beneath me." He threw the dust up into her eyes. "You don't deserve to live."

Luckily, she saw his move for what it was and pulled up some water to protect herself before it happened. But she played it up and stumbled backward, scrubbing at her clean eyes. This part was as important as reality. She could warp what Basem saw, use it to her advantage.

"Learn to do the opposite of what your opponent expects."

Basem laughed, and she sensed him approaching her. She held her hands up as if in surrender, to stop him from hurting her. Her eyes flipped up to Clover, who was waiting in the wings. Kerrigan smiled.

When Basem next brought a rock down to end her, she grabbed his fist in her hand, turned it in place, and catapulted him over her shoulder. She opened her eyes enough to watch him collapse back into the rock.

And Fordham's final lesson: *"Kill or be killed."*

"You could never beat me," Kerrigan said, whipping the dirt into a frenzy. "Never. You are weak. You used ambushes and an assassin to try to kill me, and still, you've failed. You will always fail."

She turned her finger, picking Basem off the ground and into the whirling tornado she had created out of the air and dirt. She added fire to it, and he screamed. She flung her hand out, and Basem collided with the wall on the other side of the ring. Her confidence lifted, she advanced, drawing from her reserves, and tried to get up the nerve to end this. She had never killed anyone, not on purpose, but Fordham was right. She had let Basem live once before, and all it'd brought was retaliation. The last thing she wanted was to have a life on her conscience, but she refused to continue to play this game.

Basem heaved on the ground. A slash of fire had burned across his cheek. He met her glare with his own fury. And then something shifted, as if it moved from anger to satisfaction. Like he had her exactly where he wanted her.

"Big mistake, leatha," he snarled.

His hand went to the pouch on his hip and removed the amber orb he'd held the night of the kidnapping.

Kerrigan had no idea what that thing did, but it was a move she hadn't anticipated. She didn't know what it was or what it could do. She couldn't possibly be ready for this.

"Need a magical artifact to win?" she asked. "Pathetic."

"Anything goes," he reminded her.

Without warning, he hurled the small rock at her feet. She jumped back, expecting it to shatter as it had that first night they'd fought, but it rolled harmlessly toward her, knocking into her boot. The crowd was silent with anticipation. Kerrigan took another step away from the thing that might as well have been a bomb.

Her eyes met Basem's for a second, and he smiled. "*Carthai.*"

The world exploded. Kerrigan dropped to her knees, and her hands went to her head. There was ringing in her ears that she couldn't explain. Her vision was blurry, and she was seeing double. But all around her, the rest of the world looked normal.

It hadn't been an actual bomb. Not what she had thought at all. But somehow, it was still making her bleed from her ears. She could hardly see anything in front of her, and the ringing wouldn't stop.

She struggled to get back to her feet, but then there was a boot at her shoulder, kicking her over. She lay on her back and tasted the rusty blood in her mouth. Her eyes watered as she stared up at Basem's giant form. He had a knife in his hand as he leaned his knee into her chest. She gasped as the pressure crushed her ribs and pinned her helplessly to the ground.

The knife came to her throat. He bent down until he was speaking into one of her ruined ears. "I own magic in this city. You never stood a chance."

The edge of the blade cut into her neck. Pain seared through her, bringing her to the edge of consciousness. But she couldn't lose here. She couldn't let her life end with him slitting her throat in the Wastes. Fordham had taught her about pain. He had told her how to survive through pain. Pain made her stronger.

"You think you're so strong?" she croaked, feeling the knife bite into her. She ignored it and forced herself to laugh.

"What's so funny, Red?"

"No matter what happens here, you've already lost," she got out.

"Doesn't look like that to me."

She grinned, going for madness. "Oh, but I'm just the distraction."

Basem's eyes widened.

"You never wondered why my friends didn't come to the fight?

Or why I danced around the ring until you were nearly exhausted? I was here to keep you and your goons in one place. Your house has already been raided." Her eyes were triumphant as she told him, "Ever is gone."

CHAPTER FORTY-FIVE
THE RESCUE

Basem roared, slicing across her neck, "Die, leatha bitch!"

At the same second, Kerrigan used her last bit of energy to pull the amber orb to her. She grasped it in her hand, and the world returned to normal. Her awareness righted itself. Whatever the orb had done to disorient her had evaporated. Even her ears were no longer ringing. Though they were still bleeding.

Her hand went to her throat, trying to stop the blood from seeping out of her. He hadn't pressed down hard enough to kill, just to wound, but she could see he wanted to go in for another shot.

She blasted him backward with all the air, water, fire, and earth she had in her veins, and he flew through the ring and out into the crowd. With a heave, she came unsteadily to her feet. But the fight wasn't over.

As much as she wanted to end his life right here, that wouldn't be justice for what he had done to Lyam. What he had tried to do to her. She needed to get him out of the Wastes. He needed to be arrested and stand trial for his crimes. Death wasn't good enough for him.

She strode forward, still holding the orb in her hand. Basem took one look at her, a fiery red ball of vengeance, and took a step back. The crowd booed him as she advanced. True panic flicked across his features for the first time. And with a look around to see that he had lost favor, he reached into his pouch and withdrew a black orb.

"I'll be seeing you, Red," he said. He threw the orb to the ground, shattering it into a million pieces. The ashy smoke enveloped him, and he was gone.

"No!" she screamed.

But there was nothing she could do. Basem had escaped.

Kerrigan sank to her feet as the announcer came out to declare her the winner. The crowd had a mixed reaction. No one had been killed. One competitor had fled.

She didn't even have the energy to care what they thought. Basem was gone. She had been this close, and he had slipped out of her grasp.

Clover rushed out into the ring and helped her backstage. "What the hell, Red?"

"He escaped."

"You're losing a lot of blood. We need to get you to a healer."

"No," Kerrigan said, straightening. "We have to get to the mountain. Fordham, Darby, and Hadrian got Ever out of Basem's house. If we have Ellerby's nephew, then we have a witness. We have proof. We have to tell Helly."

"Bravo," Dozan said. He stepped into the back room and casually applauded her. "Devious even for you."

She glared at him. "No thanks to you. Basem escaped."

"But you brought him down. He won't be able to show his face in Kinkadia ever again."

"That's not justice."

"It's more than most people get," Dozan said.

"He's right," Clover said. "He's not behind bars, but he can't come after you now. Not when we have proof of what he's done. He'll be hunted by the Society."

Kerrigan sighed. "I know. It's just…half as much as I wanted."

"Run off to your mountain, princess, and see if they give you more justice than I did." Dozan smirked. "Doesn't tonight prove that you belong here with me?"

"Just because we work well together doesn't mean that I belong here."

He stepped forward, exposing her ears once more. "I have never seen you look more magnificent than when you were out there tonight, proud of your heritage. Can you really say that you can do that in the mountain? Anywhere else in fact?"

Kerrigan swallowed, caught in his golden gaze. She ignored the beat of her heart at his words. The rightness in them. She hated that he was right. Hated that he still had a pull over her after all these years.

"I belong where I can do the most good," she told him. "That is not here."

Dozan dropped his hands and shrugged. "We'll see."

Kerrigan turned to Clover. "Come to the mountain with me?"

Clover nodded once, and they headed out of the Wastes and through the Dregs. They were nearly to the mountain when Clover finally sighed.

"So, you and Dozan? You and Fordham?"

Kerrigan blew out an exasperated breath. "I'm bleeding from my neck and my ears, and you want to talk about boys?"

"Men," Clover purred.

"Dozan and I are both fire. We'd burn each other to the ground. And Fordham doesn't want this."

"What's not to want?"

Kerrigan was unable to explain about Fordham's curse. That was his story to tell. "Let's get to Helly and deal with my love life after we save the city."

Clover laughed, and they jogged the remainder of the way inside.

By the time they caught up with Fordham, Darby, Hadrian, and a shaking Ever, Kerrigan's neck wound had soaked through her fighting shirt, and she was feeling woozy.

"What in the gods' names happened?" Hadrian gasped.

Darby stepped forward in horror. "Kerrigan!"

She put her hands up to start the healing, but Kerrigan shook her off.

"Helly. We need Helly. Deal with me later."

"Kerrigan," Fordham said gently. "This is serious. You've lost a lot of blood."

"Please," she forced out.

Her friends shared a look. Taking her to Helly was likely the best bet anyway. The neck wound was beyond Darby's expertise in healing thus far, and Helly was the most accomplished known healer.

Fordham and Hadrian came to either side of Kerrigan to assist her the rest of the way to Helly's quarters. Clover and Darby walking Ever between them. They were almost there when a figure stepped out of the shadows, clutching books to her chest.

"Oh my gods, Kerrigan!" Valia gasped, nearly dropping the books. "What happened to you?"

"Come with us. I only want to explain once," Kerrigan muttered.

Valia's eyes were wide, but she stepped into ranks with Kerrigan's friends and the confused Ever. They stopped in front of Helly's quarters, and Clover unceremoniously banged on the door. After a minute, the door flew open, and Helly appeared, still in her nightgown, as she hastily dragged her black Society robes over them.

"Yes?" she asked, rubbing sleep out of her eyes. Then she saw Kerrigan and gasped. "Kerrigan, what happened? Come in. Come in. Gods!"

Fordham and Hadrian carried Kerrigan across the threshold. Helly tossed pillows off a couch, and they deposited Kerrigan on it. The rest of her friends followed inside with Ever huddled against Darby. Valia seemed to disappear entirely in the shadows.

Helly threw flames from her fingertips to ignite all the lanterns and take them out of darkness. She assessed Kerrigan's injury. "What happened? Were you attacked?"

Kerrigan shuddered as she realized she was so close to losing consciousness. She couldn't do that before she told Helly what had happened. "I was fighting in the ring."

"What?" Helly gasped. "After I strictly forbade you from leaving the mountain?"

"There's more," Kerrigan said, but Helly began her work.

"You've lost a lot of blood. You shouldn't speak. This will hurt." Helly looked around the room. "The rest of you, begin to explain to me what is going on, and who is that young boy?"

"We discovered that Basem Nix had killed Lyam," Fordham began. "But you didn't believe us, so we had to get proof."

"Proof?" Helly said with anger in her voice.

But Kerrigan couldn't say a word. She was using all her strength to stay conscious.

"We staged a meetup, where Basem confessed to trying to kill Kerrigan. He was going to kill her that night, but he agreed to fight her in the Dragon Ring."

Helly scoffed but said nothing.

"And it was really Hadrian's idea," Fordham said, gesturing to him against the wall, "to use the fight as a distraction."

"And get Ever out," Hadrian finished.

Helly's eyes flicked to Ever. "He looks traumatized. Get him from where?"

"From Basem Nix's home," Darby said. "Where, as Ellerby had informed Kerrigan, he was being held captive to keep him quiet."

"What?" Helly gasped.

"While Kerrigan and I were at the fight, keeping Basem and his men busy," Clover said, "Darby, Hadrian, and Fordham infiltrated his home and rescued their hostage. Now you have Ellerby and his nephew, Ever, who will testify to what he did to them."

"And where is Basem Nix now?"

Clover frowned. "He escaped."

"Gods," Helly said in abject horror.

She didn't say anything for a long time, as if she were processing the information and deciding where to go from there.

All the while, she worked on healing Kerrigan's neck. Restoring the blood loss would be a whole other thing that would take time, time that they didn't have.

"Do you believe us?" Kerrigan asked warily. Sleep beckoned.

"I'm furious that you would all take this risk," Helly admitted. "I had the Society watching Basem after you told me about him. We were very close to arresting him for his actions, but now he has slipped from our grasp."

The group withered under her words.

"However, I am glad that you rescued Ever. His disappearance was tragic. I am proud of you lot even if you circumvented Society mandates to do what you did. You've saved an innocent boy's life. That is not a small thing. The tournament is tomorrow. I think you all should get a good night's rest."

"What will we do with him?" Darby asked.

"Valia, would you mind finding him something to eat and a secure room for him to stay in for now?" Helly asked.

"Of course, Mistress," Valia said. She bowed and then ushered the boy from the room.

"Thank you, Mistress Helly," Darby said, curtsying.

Hadrian gave her a slight bow, and they headed out of the room with Clover and Darby.

"I can help Kerrigan back to her room," Fordham offered.

"I appreciate that, Fordham, but I believe my patient should stay here with me tonight. I want to observe her overnight."

"Of course." Fordham looked conflicted but eventually bowed to them both and slipped from the room.

"You have a loyal team behind you."

Kerrigan smiled wanly. "Friends," she corrected. "Loyal friends."

Helly smiled. "You should get some rest. Stay here tonight in the guest room. I don't want you wandering the mountain and undoing all my hard work."

"All right." Kerrigan gingerly got to her feet and followed Helly to her guest room. The bed was at least twice the size of her own with a giant, fluffy comforter and big feather down pillows. It looked like the most inviting place in the world. Maybe she'd finally *sleep*.

Helly left and came back with a bundle of clothes. "These should suffice for the night."

"Thank you."

"Kerrigan," Helly said, gently brushing Kerrigan's curls out of her face. "Can I speak with you about one more thing? I know you're tired."

"Of course." Kerrigan leaned against one of the wooden bedposts.

"I spoke with Audria."

Kerrigan froze. She had completely put Audria's offer out of her mind.

"I know you have been worried about not joining a house. That you think it is your mission to join and become a citizen, to help do good. And I want to let you know that we got it all worked out. Audria will be selecting you tomorrow to join Bryonica."

"Helly…"

"I'm so pleased. You know I wanted to accept you myself," Helly said. "I should have thought of consulting with someone else in the ranks, but Audria is a perfect fit. You can become an Ather, a Bryonican royal again. All will be as it should."

Kerrigan opened her mouth to object, but what other offer did she have? It was this or work for the Society as steward, as Valia did. Not exactly a servant, but nothing more than that either.

"Thank you," she finally got out, choking on the words.

"Tomorrow, this will all be over."

Helly smiled brightly at Kerrigan before leaving her to change and get some sleep. But a pit had formed in her stomach that had nothing to do with her ailments and everything to do with what would come tomorrow. Kerrigan of Bryonica once more.

CHAPTER FORTY-SIX
THE THIRD

Helly awoke Kerrigan early. They dined on a nutritious breakfast of eggs, bacon, and berries. She returned to her rooms to change into comfortable leggings and a loose shirt in lieu of her typical dresses and then headed down to the arena with Valia.

"How is Ever doing?" she asked.

Valia sighed. "He's frightened, but Mistress Moran has taken him under her wing. She seems besotted with the child."

Kerrigan nodded. "Good. She's like that with all the littlings."

"Who do you think is going to win?"

"I really have no idea."

"Fordham, of course," Valia said.

But Kerrigan hadn't had a vision again. She didn't know who was going to win or if Fordham would be in danger. She was walking into this task blind. And it was the most important. The five people who succeeded would get one of the five dragons and be inducted into the Society. A dream come true.

"I hope so."

They stepped into the competitors' box in the arena. The last eight competitors stood in clusters around the room. Fordham stood alone with his arms crossed over his broad chest. Audria laughed with Roake, her blond hair fluttering in the faint breeze. Noda stood with Posana and Chelcie, speaking furtively. Darrid glared at Fordham. Taiga seemed to be trying to get his attention. Everyone but maybe Audria looked stressed. Kerrigan could feel it coming off the room.

"Almost time," Mistress Sinead said reassuringly.

Bastian appeared then, stepping into the box last. His eyes went to Valia, and he nodded at her. She scurried into whatever position they had agreed on.

He clapped Kerrigan on the shoulder. "My dear girl, I heard what you did last night."

"Oh?" she asked warily.

"What an achievement. I'm so proud of you. We haven't apprehended Basem Nix, but we certainly will. I assure you of that." Bastian glowed with approval. "And rescuing a member of my own house, I cannot thank you enough. Having Ever Emberton home safe brings me so much peace."

"Oh, well, of course," she muttered, flustered.

"You have a bright future ahead of you."

"Thank you, Master Bastian."

"Now, on to the tournament!" he cheered and headed toward Valia.

Once Bastian was gone, Fordham came to her side. "Any information for me?" he asked hopefully.

She shook her head. She hadn't had a single vision. Nothing to tell her what was coming. He was going in as blind as she was.

"That's all right. I can win this anyway," he said confidently, his hand going to his raven medallion.

"Have they told you what's going to happen?"

"Last night, before the fight," he confided. "It's a battle of wits. We will be transported around Alandria and have to try to get to this cave network. We can only bring our medallions with us. There's no set amount of time either. We could be out there for days and have to find our own food and water. There will be tasks along the way. If we make it through, then we get to choose a dragon."

Kerrigan had been a part of the last dragon tournament in the final task, though she had sworn to never discuss it. They had even put a spell over the binding to keep her from saying anything. But she knew precisely what would happen once he found that cave network. She hoped he made it.

"Good luck" was all she said.

He reached out and slipped his pinkie around hers. Just the barest gesture, a slight squeeze, and her entire insides melted into goo. She looked up into his bright gray eyes, and her heart fluttered. He quirked a half smile before straightening and joining the rest of the competitors.

Kerrigan moved to the front of the box as music blared and the final eight competitors were paraded around the arena one last time. After today, eight would narrow down to five, and those five would become dragon riders.

A pang of envy flashed through her. She had told Helly that she wanted to make something of herself. That she didn't want to be left behind again. But it was more. She wanted *that*. Fame and glory and to be a part of the lawmaking. From the inside, she could actually enact change—or at least try, which was more than was happening now.

But it would never, ever be. After Cyrene, they'd never allow a half-Fae girl in their ranks. And on some level, Kerrigan hardly blamed them, but that didn't mean she wanted to accept it.

The competitors were in line, and the master of ceremonies gave final instructions. The crowd cheered. The tension in the enormous arena was frothing.

And then came the final bout of information.

"Today, we're testing to see if you are worthy to join the ranks of the great Society. We have already tested your physical and mental prowess in the first two tasks, but this will test your will. To do that, the officiators have agreed to give each competitor a potion that will temporarily remove your access to your magic."

Cheers from the crowd. Shock and disgust from the competitors. Kerrigan remembered the feeling of being without magic. It had been terrifying. Also, she found it ironic that a society built around the biggest and baddest magical wielders would make their competitors no better than the humans they so loathed. Only someone so deep into their own privilege wouldn't see the absurdity of it.

The competitors were escorted out of the arena and deep into the mountain. From here on out, they were beyond the view of the crowd. Anything that happened in the third task was for those competing only. That was the only way they kept the third task mysterious enough.

"Well," Valia said to her right, "now we wait."

Kerrigan bit her lip and prayed to whichever god would listen to watch over Fordham. She hoped that no visions meant that he was going to be safe, but she doubted it. No one was safe in the final task.

⚬⚬⚬⚬⚬

At dusk, the crowd grew restless, Kerrigan among them.

Most knew that the final task didn't typically end that last day, but it made for a long wait to see who would show up. Luckily, the Society had other displays come into the arena—sword fighting, music, dancing, horse racing, and even some dragon flying demonstrations—while they waited on the big spectacle. But by nighttime, even Kerrigan was tired of waiting around.

A good portion of people had gone home. They would return the next morning and hope that they hadn't missed out. Only a few diehards would remain all night in hopes of seeing one of the dragons flying home.

"I need sustenance," Kerrigan told Valia, who was ever vigilant, staring at the horizon.

"Bring me back some hard cheese and goat's milk, if they have it," she requested.

Kerrigan yawned. "Sure thing."

Nerves bit into her the entire walk back to the mountain. She didn't like not knowing what was happening with Fordham, if he was doing all right. She was glad for the distraction of returning to the mountain. They had some food, water, and wine at the table, but it had been sitting out all day. She needed something fresh and couldn't bring herself to ask a servant to do it for her.

She made it inside to the feasting table, which was mostly empty at this hour, and rounded up supplies for herself and Valia. She had a tray full of food and turned to exit the mountain once more when she felt a dizzy spell hit her.

Kerrigan gasped as her vision went blurry, and she felt unconsciousness beckon. "Oh gods."

Hastily, she set the tray down on the ground and pressed her back into the cold stone of the mountain. Blissfully, the corridors were empty, but even if they weren't, she wouldn't have been able to fight off what was happening. A vision was coming whether she wanted it or not. Just before it pulled her through, she hoped that this was the answer to her prayers, and she would find out what was happening with Fordham. She needed good news.

Her vision went dark, and an image appeared of a small girl in boy's clothing, walking the halls of the mountain. Kerrigan startled as she realized it was her. Dream Kerrigan entered an unguarded room. The sentinels who should have been standing watch were distracted at the other end of the hall. Oh gods, she had been in that room. Dream Kerrigan looked up at the shimmery, iridescent doorway and knew what she must do. She drank from a goblet, closed her eyes, and then pressed her hand to the doorway.

Kerrigan gasped awake from the vision. She was drenched in a cold sweat. Her magic was drained, but not nearly as bad as normal.

She kept waiting for unconsciousness to come and for her to slip under, but she felt steadier than she had with any of her other visions.

Everything was different about this vision. Her visions had never been that deliberate. This was breaking the theme of them. They always showed images of what was to come in the future. They never told *her* what to do. The whole thing made her uneasy. Did she follow what the vision had shown her? Or did she run and tell someone what she had seen?

She chewed on her lip a minute as she debated what to do. The longer she thought about going into that portal room, the more certain she was of its inherent rightness. She couldn't turn her back on the dreams now. She had no idea where the portal would take her, but it had told her for a reason, and despite the recklessness, it was her destiny to follow the instructions.

Kerrigan took the bread, cheese, and chunk of meat and stuffed them into the small pouch she kept at her side. After a quick jaunt back into the feast room, she found a water pouch and slung that over her head as well. She was weighed down, but she would rather have the provisions than not. She left the rest of the food behind. Valia would wonder where she had gone off to, but she couldn't wait to run the food back to her.

With a determination set into her very marrow, Kerrigan left for the portal room. It was not a long walk, and within minutes, she was at the end of the hallway. She waited patiently for the two guards standing in front of the room to turn and walk the other way. She didn't know what kind of gods' luck this was, but as soon as their backs were turned, she hustled down the hallway. With her heart in her throat, she turned the doorknob and entered the room, carefully closing the door behind her.

The room itself was enormous, big enough for multiple dragons to comfortably stand in. This was only the Fae entrance. There was a separate tunnel that the dragons could enter through that disappeared deep into the mountain. And standing as large as a house was a giant stone archway, magnificently carved and ornately built. The center of the archway shone with a brilliant iridescence. Just as in her vision, there stood a goblet on a table next to the archway.

Kerrigan warily approached it. She looked into the milky liquid with unease. She knew what this did. It was the same potion the competitors had taken before walking through that portal. But why would she need to take it? She wanted to doubt the dream, but she didn't doubt it.

With a deep breath, she brought the golden goblet to her mouth and consumed a few mouthfuls of the chalky substance. She gagged once around the disgusting liquid, and then she felt the magical effects. Her magic was being drained away. One second, it had been there. The next, it was gone. She felt suddenly bereft, as she had that night with Clare. Her magic was *empty*. With her will, she reached down into that well of power and felt nothing. It was severed. She shuddered in discomfort.

Pushing that aside, she turned to face the portal. She had walked through this once and ended up on the other side of the world. Walking through it again for another vision felt like it was all coming full circle.

She tied her red hair up into a ribbon to keep it out of her face. With trepidation, she pressed her hand to the side of the portal arch, as she had in the vision. The center of the portal shimmered and moved at her touch, and for a moment, she felt as if the portal *read* where she needed to go. The portal opened to darkness, and with her heart in her throat, she stepped through.

CHAPTER FORTY-SEVEN
THE FOREST

A weight settled on Kerrigan's chest in the darkness.

The portal had sucked her through, only vaguely tugging on her, as if it wanted to keep her for itself, and then she had entered this mysterious place.

She didn't instantly recognize her surroundings, as the sun had completely fallen and only the light from the moon and the stars barely penetrated the canopy. Thankfully, the House of Dragons had equipped her with wilderness knowledge. They had taken an expedition around the mountains for a few days when she was younger. Darby stayed home, but Lyam and Hadrian went with her to learn how to start a fire and read trail signs. Growing up in the city, she hadn't had any idea why she would need the knowledge, but she had found the camping trips more fun than being stuck in the mountain.

Now she was thanking Mistress Moran for encouraging her to go out into the woods with Master Faris for these extracurriculars. Without her magic to light a fire, she would have to use that limited knowledge. Of course, she hadn't used stones to light a fire in probably six years, but she knew the mechanics of it. She got to work, finding a few twigs and two stones that she could strike together to get sparks. After what felt like an eternity, she considered giving up, but she couldn't. She was in unfamiliar territory, who knew how far from home, and she was alone. She needed a fire to guide her way and scare off predators, if need be.

With renewed determination, Kerrigan struck the stones together until, miraculously, the brush under her twigs caught fire.

"Yes!" she cheered, blowing on the small flames to encourage them to build and build. And after a few more minutes, she had enough light to see by.

She kept feeding the small fire with twigs and brush. Likely, she would need to find a large stick to use as a torch, but it would be nearly impossible to scout for the rest of the supplies. It would be smarter and safer to build up her fire first and sit around it for the evening, even though the last thing that she wanted to do was wait until morning.

After the fire was built to a considerable height, Kerrigan found an old log and sank down onto it to wait. She felt ridiculous, but the vision had sent her for a reason. There was no use doubting it now.

Sleep had evaded her for weeks, and then suddenly, in this oppressive forest, surrounded by nature, in front of a campfire, she felt the edges of sleep finally come to her. She kept her food and water close to her chest and then snuggled up onto the ground to sleep.

But as soon as she winked out, she jolted awake at the snuffling sound of something *sniffing* her.

Kerrigan froze on the ground, careful not to alert whatever was smelling her that she was awake. A wet nose pressed into her shoulder and hair. She tried not to let her fear show. She had no weapon and no magic. All she had was the fire, which was burning much lower than when she had gone to sleep. It wasn't out yet, but it was close.

The beast trotted down to her feet, and a tusk pressed against her calf. She swallowed and slowly reached for one of the larger sticks still burning in the fire. From the corner of her eye, she could make out the boar that was determining if she was its next meal. Her hand closed around the stick, ignoring the heat radiating off the fire.

The boar's head snapped up, and she quickly brandished the stick at the beast. The creature roared in protest as she slammed the fire end into its eye. She scrambled backward away from it as it screamed and kicked at the dirt. It fixed its good eye on Kerrigan and reared back, preparing to charge. She waved the fire stick in front of her as her only weapon and hoped against hope that it would do enough.

Her heart raced in her chest, and her hands were slick on the wood. It wasn't going to be enough. The beast would attack her and skewer her with one of its massive tusks. She would have been sent here for nothing. She settled into a defensive position and watched as if in slow motion as the beast charged toward her.

"Ahhh!" a voice suddenly screamed from the tree cover, and a body charged at the boar, ramming into it and sending it straight into the fire.

The boar screamed as the fire ate at it and then scrambled backward out of the flames. It looked between her and the stranger dressed in all black and decided to try its luck elsewhere. The beast scampered off into the forest.

"Thank you," Kerrigan said, letting the stick fall to her side. Her heart was still in her throat.

The figure turned to her with wide eyes. "Kerrigan?"

She gasped. "Fordham?"

He looked wild. It was the only way to describe him. His clothes were tattered, his face covered in mud, and he was brandishing a stick that he appeared to have whittled down to a point.

"What are you doing here?"

"What happened to you?" she asked at the same time.

"I've been in this wretched forest for nearly an entire day. I passed my first test, and then it brought me here. There's nothing to eat, and the forest is a maze. There's no way out."

"Wait, you've been here all day without food?"

He nodded.

She rummaged through her bag and brought out some provisions, passing them to him. "Here, eat this."

"Gods," he breathed as he reverently took the food.

"Sit at my fire and eat." She busied herself building the fire back up as Fordham forced himself not to devour every scrap she had given him.

"And this place." He took another bite. "It's haunted."

"I thought you didn't believe in ghosts," Kerrigan joked.

"Not like that. It's dampened everything. I had some berries and ran around in circles for hours. I've been too terrified to eat since then. I don't know what's going on."

And then it clicked. "Noirwood Forest."

"What?"

"We're in Noirwood Forest. It's a black forest off the western coast, where everything you could eat within it is poisonous. We don't know what happened to the woods to make it this way, but travelers who pass within must bring enough provisions to survive without eating or drinking anything in the forest. The berries likely made you hallucinate. You're lucky you didn't die."

Fordham looked back at her blankly. "I'm beginning to think my education about Alandria is woefully incomplete."

Kerrigan frowned. "I'm sorry."

"It's fine," he said, taking a sip from her waterskin. "And you were sent for me?"

"A vision," she admitted.

"Did the vision show you how to get out of here?"

"No. It didn't tell me anything except to walk through the portal."

"Do you still have your magic?"

She shook her head. "But I have this."

Then she produced Lyam's compass. She'd had it with her at all times since they had gone together to the alley where he had been murdered. It had been a trinket, a memory. But right now, she had never been gladder to see it.

He came to his feet. "Well, that's lucky."

She swallowed back the lump in her throat. "Lyam, here to save us after all."

"We should probably set out at dawn," Fordham said. "Together, we can get out of here."

"All right, princeling," she said with a half smile. "But first, we're going to need some pine cones."

Fordham didn't ask, just helped her cover a few pine cones in sap, and then she cracked the two biggest sticks she'd found on a sharp piece of rock, placing the sap-covered pine cones inside and dipping them in the flames.

He looked at her, impressed. "Torches. How did you know how to do that?"

"House of Dragons teaches us more than just etiquette," she said with a grin. She brushed mud off his brow and laughed. "You look ridiculous."

"I ate poisonous berries," he reminded her.

And then they both laughed.

ᏩᎥᎥᎥᏎ

The weight and fear of the night before had dissipated at dawn. They had gotten through a lot together this last month. This was one more adventure.

Together, they tracked through the forest, heading north by the dial on Lyam's compass. Though they saw more eyes peeking out at them and a few howls in the forest, nothing else approached them. And by high noon, they reached the edge of the trees.

Fordham sighed in relief and wiped sweat and mud from his brow. "Thank the gods."

"Second test complete."

"Yeah. Wonder what the third will be if the forest was…"

But he didn't finish. If Fordham Ollivier could be shaken by the Noirwood Forest, then it was an atrocious hellhole that she never wished to venture into again.

A snap jolted both of them to rush farther out of the forest. When they turned around to face the beast that was surely going to attack them, Darrid strode out of the tree line toward them. Kerrigan frowned. Darrid had had a grudge against Fordham from the start. He'd attacked him in the first task and pushed him off the platform in the second. Him being here in the forest was not a cause for celebration.

Kerrigan instinctively reached down into her well of magic to keep her safe before remembering that it didn't work. She had no magic to defend herself against Darrid.

"Ollivier," Darrid said.

"Darrid," Fordham volleyed back, already stepping closer to Kerrigan.

"Fancy meeting you out here."

"What do you want?"

"No pleasantries?" Darrid asked. "Right down to it?"

"What do you want?" Fordham repeated.

"I'd like to know what your leatha whore is doing in the woods with you."

"Don't call her that," Fordham snarled.

Darrid laughed. "You know, I thought that it must just be a dalliance. What would a prince of the House of Shadows want with a half-Fae girl when your people have slaughtered them for millennia? But do you actually *care* for her?"

Kerrigan bristled at his words. She hadn't realized that Darrid was a bigot. They hid in plain sight, ready to use that horrid name and reveal themselves at such inopportune moments.

"We don't need to deal with you," Fordham said. "Be on your way."

"See, I would," Darrid said, revealing a short dagger from his waistband. Kerrigan tensed. "But I don't like you, and the last thing we need is more bastards like you in the Society."

Kerrigan sighed. "You're all so predictable."

"Shut up," Darrid snarled, brandishing the weapon in her direction.

"It's two on one, Darrid," Fordham said evenly. "What do you think you'll accomplish?"

"Oh, is it?" he asked.

And then Kerrigan realized Darrid had been the distraction. Taiga came out of the woods to their left and Chelcie to their right. From high in the tree above Darrid, Posana nocked an arrow and let it loose at their feet, just to let them know that running would be no use.

"There's nowhere to go," Darrid jeered.

"Four against two. That's almost a fair fight," Fordham said confidently. "Look at you, the little gang leader of the wayward competitors."

Darrid stiffened at the words. "We're going to cut you down, Ollivier, and no one will mourn you."

"Fordham," Kerrigan whispered, drawing even closer. "The medallion."

He tensed as if preparing to meet Darrid's attack. But they had been training so long that they both saw it coming. Darrid hadn't been training out his mistakes, and he had *many*.

"Left," Fordham whispered.

"And turn."

"One, two, three."

Darrid ran at them with the knife, but as a seamless unit, Kerrigan and Fordham pivoted left, away from the oncoming assault, missing the arrow from Posana. Fordham broke open the raven medallion and waited for what he had risked his life for.

Suddenly, the sound of wings filled the air. Even Darrid paused at the unholy noise. Birds rushed out of Noirwood Forest and blanketed the sky black. Hundreds, maybe even thousands, of ravens descended on the battling ground outside the forest.

Kerrigan ducked her head to try to shield herself from the attack. But the ravens never touched her or Fordham. And a memory hit her, though she knew not from where, of ravens guiding spirits through the unknown. *Psychopomps*—the word came to her, unbidden.

Spirit guides. Ravens were spirit guides. They directed the dead to the next world, but that wasn't all they could do.

"Trust me," she told Fordham.

She grasped his arm and closed her eyes, and they walked into the raven melee, letting the birds carry them onto the spiritual plane.

CHAPTER FORTY-EIGHT
THE RAVEN FLIGHT

The ravens disappeared, save for one lone bird, as they exited the physical and materialized on a new plane. The raven looked at her, and she shivered with the realization that *this* was what she was here for. Not to survive in the forest but to cross the spiritual plane.

"What did you do?" Fordham gasped.

"I saved us."

She didn't know what she had done. Not really. But she had done it. It felt the same as the time with Gelryn when she had unconsciously pulled him into the spiritual plane. Now here she was again with a raven waiting for her command.

Before Fordham could ask any other questions, she smiled at the bird. "Are you here to guide us?"

The bird cawed knowingly.

Kerrigan ignored Fordham's look of puzzlement. She couldn't doubt herself. Not here. For some reason, she felt perfectly at ease. As if she had been waiting for this very moment, and she knew exactly what to do. "Can you take us to the caves?"

The bird cawed and then was off.

Fordham's eyes were wide. She touched his hand, not quite real, not quite not. "Do you trust me?"

"Yes," he said easily.

"Then trust me."

And with their first step together, they followed the raven across the expanse of the plane.

That first step was the hardest. Her body felt encased in the energy of the plane. But as soon as they started up an easy pace behind the raven, they moved through it like free-flowing water.

She had never seen anything like it. The sky was the bluest blue, and the ground was the greenest green but not naturally so. As if the entire space had a blanket thrown over reality. What they were staring at was the clearest, purest, bluest form of the world below. None of it felt quite like *walking*, per se. At least, she didn't feel the stretch of her muscles or the elements against her skin or get tired in the same way. Though she was certain that this time, her physical body *was* coming with her. It wouldn't have been much of an escape if they'd left their bodies behind for Darrid to ravage.

After a short time, the landscape at their feet began to change. No longer were they on the plane, but right ahead, they could see a raging river.

"That's the South River," she said. "I didn't think we were that close to it from the forest."

"That's what you're concerned with?" Fordham asked.

Kerrigan looked over at him. He was very pale. As if the weight of reality was pressing down on him. "Breathe, Ford. Just breathe."

"I don't understand what's going on." He took a deep breath and released it. "The adjudicators of the tournament told us to bring our medallions for the final test. I assumed it was a weapon."

"It was," she confirmed. "The ravens responded to the call from the medallion. They attacked the other competitors, and we were able to flee."

"Flee," he said blankly. "When I think *flee*, I think running out across the field we were in and finding cover."

"Well, isn't this nicer?"

"I don't know what *this* is," he said, gesturing to the barren landscape that overlay the physical world.

"The ravens were a distraction in the physical world. But for those who have access to the spiritual plane, they're guides."

"I know what the spiritual plane is, but isn't that reserved for dragons? Isn't that half the reason we bond with dragons to begin with? We're stronger together with the use of the spiritual plane and our combined knowledge and might."

"Yes, dragons are connected to the spiritual plane, but they're not the only ones who have access to it. Birds, especially ravens, are traditionally omens of evil or ill intent. Not because the birds themselves are bad but because they escort people from the physical to the spiritual like dragons do. Only ravens shepherd the dead."

Fordham looked ashy. "And are they doing that for us?"

Kerrigan looked up at the bird gliding in the air with no breeze and guiding them through the plane. "I don't think so. I believe it's taking us where I asked it to go."

"How do you know all of this?"

She furrowed her brow. "I don't know, but I just do. I'm not an expert by any means, but I think it's where I draw my energy for my visions and for that blast I had when we were being tortured by Clare. It's where Gelryn pulled you when you were in testing."

Fordham looked startled. "How do you know about that?"

She grinned sheepishly. "I'm nosy. So I got tested."

"You got tested?" he asked in exasperation. "Why does that not even surprise me?"

"It wasn't purposeful. I wanted to know what testing was, but when I stepped inside, Gelryn said he'd been waiting for me."

"Ominous," Fordham muttered.

She laughed. "A little bit. But it ended up being fine. He actually left and went to the Holy Mountain to try to find information on my visions." She shrugged. "I don't know if he'll find anything, but he seemed confident."

"That's good at least. You need to get those under control."

"Hey, they've helped you!"

"They have," he admitted. "I don't want them to control you."

She fell silent. They did control her, and if she didn't find a way to stop them, then they always would. It was why she'd gone to Gelryn in the first place.

They continued trudging through the plane and watched as they crossed over the South River without ever getting wet. The landscape turned rocky, and suddenly, they were in the mountains. The sun was low on the horizon when they began to trek through the Vert Mountains toward the cave system. The bright and vibrant plane turned darker and darker. If she was right about where they were, then they were traveling across days of land in a matter of hours. It was unfathomable.

"I wish we still had those torches," Fordham muttered.

Kerrigan gulped. "Me too."

She heard a dark, rasping noise.

"Do you hear that?" she whispered, shaken by the first sound other than them or their raven in the plane.

"Hear what?"

Kerrigan waited and listened, straining her ears. The noise came again—a low, scratchy groan, as if someone were straining against their bonds or reaching for them in the darkness.

"That," she whispered again urgently.

Fordham furrowed his brow. "Nothing, Ker."

She strained again but couldn't hear anything. The sound still shivered down her spine, but whatever it was, if it had even been real, was gone.

"I guess you're right," she said with a sigh.

The bird cawed then, making Kerrigan jump straight out of her skin. Well, she already had been.

"We're here," Kerrigan said.

"Where is here?"

She shrugged. "I don't know, but we must have made it as far as the raven can take us." She respectfully bowed her head to their guide. "Thank you so much for your assistance."

Fordham likewise bowed, and then with another caw, they both snapped back into their bodies.

Kerrigan jolted into reality, feeling the full weight of her existence settle over her again. She felt heavy, like her limbs were made of lead. "Oof!"

Fordham cursed and dropped to one knee. "Well, that's something. Where are we?"

She looked around at the dip in the mountain pass. "There!" She pointed to an opening in the rock. "I think that must be the cave."

"The raven actually took us here," he said in amazement.

"You should go," she encouraged. "You want to be one of the first five to make it through."

Fordham was about to respond when they heard a battle cry behind them. They both whipped around to find Darrid standing on the high ground, holding up an ax. Where he'd gotten it and *how* he had made it to the cave system at the same time as them was a mystery. His threat was not. With no magic and no weapon, they were defenseless.

"Go!" Kerrigan cried. "He wants to stop you, not me."

"Kerrigan."

"Go!" She pushed him backward. "I'll handle it."

"I won't leave you."

"Don't be an idiot. You taught me well enough. I'll be fine."

He searched her eyes for a lie.

She laughed and pushed him again. "Get out of here."

Fordham took off at a run toward the tunnel. Kerrigan turned back to face Darrid. He looked every inch the Herasi warrior as he charged toward her. She scanned the area for a weapon of some kind, but there was nothing to use, except small, pebble-size rocks. Nothing sharp. Nothing that could go up against a Herasi battle-ax.

"Darrid, stop!" she cried, stepping into a defensive position.

He screamed at the top of his lungs. And at the moment that he brought the ax down to sever her neck, she pivoted out of his way. The ax barely grazed her shoulder. She cried out but had enough strength to slam her hand into his kidney and dash farther away from his weapon. He clutched his side, looking like he might vomit, but he was a soldier after all, and he knew enough not to collapse here.

"Please just stop."

"I'll never stop," he snarled. "He doesn't deserve to enter the Dragon Society."

"Well, I think that's already too late," she said, edging closer to the mouth of the cave that Fordham had entered.

He yelled out another battle cry, held the ax aloft, and charged for her. Her eyes rounded in horror. There was nowhere to go, nothing to do. If she stayed where she was, Darrid would kill her in cold blood.

With her last dash of desperation, Kerrigan turned and fled into the mouth of the cave with a raging Herasi warrior on her tail. As soon as she stepped through, something settled over her, holding her in place. Darrid vanished. The world disappeared. And she was dragged into a nightmare.

CHAPTER FORTY-NINE
THE NIGHTMARE

Kerrigan stood from the floor, but it wasn't a floor. It was a royal ballroom.

She had been to this place. A Bryonican flag hung from the ceiling in striking navy blue and silver. Her dress matched with the square-cut neckline and full sleeves that were in the current fashion. The bodice was tight and the skirt enormous. She even wore uncomfortable heeled shoes and heavy diamonds in her ears and around her neck. Her hair was piled high on top of her head. Not a loose curl in sight.

The ballroom was full of Bryonican Fae, so many that she couldn't possibly recognize them all. But every one of them seemed to recognize her. They smiled and curtsied as she stood at the head of the room.

"Introducing Lord Ashby March, first of the House of Medallion."

Kerrigan startled at the name that she hadn't heard in twelve long years. Her stomach dropped as she realized what was to come next.

"And his betrothed, Lady Felicity Argon, first of the House of Cruse."

A cheer rose up from those assembled in the ballroom. Kerrigan thought she was going to be sick. And it only got worse as March stepped up to her side and offered her his arm.

"My lady," he said demurely, the gesture hiding his cruelty in public.

"March," she whispered, stunned by his presence.

He had grown exceedingly handsome in the twelve years since she had last seen him. He had been an uncomfortably charming young man with enough baby good looks to get away with anything. But now he was a man with sweeping broad shoulders and a face that any woman would swoon over. Still, she saw the boy who had learned at an early age to put bruises where no one would see them.

He grinned devilishly. "Shall we?"

"I…"

But he didn't wait for her response. He'd never cared for a woman's answer to anything. He tugged her close to his side, and they stepped down into the ballroom.

"Lady Felicity, I love that dress," one woman said.

"The height of fashion," a second added.

Another fluttered her eyes at March. "Hello, Ashby."

He grinned at her but continued walking with Kerrigan close at his side. It felt like an interminable distance to reach the end of the room, where her father stood with a golden goblet in his hand. He actually looked the part of a prince and not the elusive party boy he was.

"My beautiful daughter, the day has finally come for you to marry Lord March," Kivrin said proudly. "I have been waiting for this your entire young life. I know this is what you have always wanted."

Always wanted? No, no, it wasn't what she wanted. It had never been what she wanted. Why was everyone looking at her like this was normal? Did no one see her for who she truly was? She wasn't Lady Felicity any longer. She was Kerrigan. She loved fighting and colorful, sleek party gowns and flying and breaking the rules. She loved getting drunk with Clover and sneaking into fancy parties. She loved adventure and her friends, who weren't present, and she loved her own life.

Not this one that had been made for her. Not this one that they had thrown her out of.

She tried to take a step back, but March tightened his grip on her arm.

"This is what we've always wanted too," March said. His gaze was steely. "Isn't it, Felicity?"

"No," she whispered.

A gasp went up through the room. She had never said this before. She had never denied Ashby March anything. But she would never accept this.

His grip turned painful, and she whimpered, "Let me go!"

"Tomorrow, we will be married, Felicity, and all this weak display of disobedience will be gone," he hissed, low and urgent.

Kerrigan looked to her father and Sonali and Audria and all the many people she knew from her time in Bryonica. She saw them wait with bated breath for her response. Saw them all judge her for not wanting the most eligible bachelor in all of Bryonica.

But none of them *saw* her. Not a one. They saw a lady to be wedded off. Not a girl with real feelings and emotions and wants and needs. And she could never live this life. It was the one thing she feared above all others, even more than abandonment—to be trapped forever.

She wrenched her arm free of March's grip. He snarled at her and grabbed for her, but she easily evaded him. He had always been sloppy on discipline. She turned, and like a runaway bride, she ran back through the ballroom as fast as her feet could carry her out and away from that life.

Kerrigan came to, gasping for breath. She put her hands on her knees and sucked in enough life to leave that horrible nightmare behind. She had walked into a faerie illusion. It was designed to warp reality and pull out her deepest, darkest fear. She had survived it—marrying

Ashby March and living a life where no one ever saw her in truth. She had come out on the other side, had risen above the adversity, but it had felt so very real.

Her body trembled with exhaustion from the illusion, but she was no longer helpless. Her magic flared bright and bursting within her, and all her injuries had been healed. She straightened to her full height and found herself before a gaping audience. The cave was large enough to hold the five dragons—Avirix, Netta, Tieran, Luxor, and Evien—as well as their five Dragon Blessed handlers. Standing before them were the four competitors who had made it this far. Audria stood with wide eyes, farther from her. Roake looked shocked at her side. Noda crouched in a corner, a green tint to her visage. Finally, Fordham stood on the other side, pale and shaken.

"Kerrigan?" he asked in shock.

"What is she doing here?" Roake asked indignantly.

Kerrigan looked around the room. "I shouldn't be here. Darrid is going to be coming in right behind me. He was chasing me with a battle-ax."

"The room is sealed," a small but powerful voice said from beside Tieran.

Kerrigan gulped and found Tara, a pale-skinned Dragon Blessed three years younger than her. "What?"

"What do you mean, sealed?" Audria piped up.

"Yeah, we're missing one more competitor," Roake spat. "Darrid will be here in a moment."

"No," Tara said evenly, pushing her dark ponytail over her shoulder. "The room has selected the five competitors who will become dragon riders this tournament."

Kerrigan gaped. "That's not possible."

"She is not a competitor," Roake yelled.

"I mean, I hate to say it, but he's right," Audria said. "She wasn't part of any of this. How could she even be accepted?"

"This room is imbued with powerful magic. Only a competitor could have passed the fear test and entered," Tara said with a small smile for Kerrigan. "Whether she was an *official* competitor matters not. If she has been tested for her magical ability and passed the fear test, then she *is* a competitor, and the room has accepted her as a victor."

"Well, she couldn't have gone through testing," Roake continued.

Fordham glanced at Kerrigan. "But you did. You just told me you did."

She bit her lip. "I did. I didn't mean for any of this to happen, but yes, I was tested by Gelryn. He said I was passed through. I didn't think it meant *this*."

"Then leave," Roake snarled.

"She cannot," Tara said. "We are sealed in until the ceremony is complete. The other competitors will be escorted back to the mountain. We must begin with our champions."

"I don't understand," Noda said softly. "She's taking someone else's spot?"

"No, she is claiming her own spot," Tara said. "And this isn't up for discussion. The magic is powerful. A group of thirteen came together to build this for the competitors. There is no way that a single person could break it down. The only logical conclusion is that Kerrigan is a competitor, and she will now be a part of the final task."

Tara waited to see if anyone else would speak up. But everyone was too shocked by the pronouncement to do much of anything but stare. Kerrigan among them. This wasn't what she had planned. This was far from it. She had been following her visions that told her how to help Fordham. She had sent him ahead so that he would make it and she could hold off Darrid. She never dreamed that she would even be allowed to test for a dragon. Not her—a half-Fae with no house and no prospects.

"That is settled," Tara said. "Kerrigan is our fifth and final competitor. Please form a line, and we will begin."

CHAPTER FIFTY
THE BONDING

Tara brooked no argument. And though Kerrigan was sure this was an elaborate prank, that it couldn't possibly be true, that not even in her wildest dreams had she envisioned herself standing in this moment, she moved into a line with the other four competitors. Audria, then Roake, then Noda, then Fordham, and finally Kerrigan before the five dragons.

She swallowed painfully and stared back at the dragons, unable to fathom that this was real life. Her stomach was topsy-turvy, and her mind was reeling, but if this was real, she wasn't going to give it up for anything.

Five years ago, Kerrigan had stood where Tara was now, and she had spoken these words to Cyrene. It was a duty so honored that Dragon Blessed were spelled to never, ever speak of what happened within. But that didn't mean Kerrigan didn't remember. She knew what was coming even though the other four competitors did not. She was far from ready, but she would serve with honor.

"The final task set forth in the tournament is not for you, our final five competitors, but it is actually for the dragons themselves," Tara said.

"The dragon's choice," Kerrigan whispered.

Tara's smile was magnetic. She knew as much as Kerrigan did. Kerrigan had gone through this as a Dragon Blessed five years ago. The other competitors looked at her in surprise. She had never been able to even speak those words aloud. But finally, she was in a place to speak of her experience.

"Yes, Kerrigan," Tara said, respectfully bowing her head.

Disim, a young brown boy of maybe eleven or twelve years with a shaved head, stepped up next. "A dragon is not complete without the existence of a dragon rider. Only the best competitors can arrive at this point. After all the necessary tasks, the competition has prepared you for the Society and living the remainder of your days with a dragon bound."

Yesmin clasped together her hands, which were black as night, and cleared her throat. Her voice had a slight tremor in it. "It is ultimately the dragon's decision. They must find you worthy."

Kerrigan trembled as the shock of the moment coursed through her. All these memories that she had suppressed because she could never speak of them. This was the real reason that they never wanted someone from the House of Dragons to compete. Dragon Blessed knew too much. They waited in the sidelines to help with the tournament. They worked with the dragons day in and day out for years. And most of all, they knew about the final task for the competition. Dragon Blessed would have an unfair advantage, getting to this point. But it didn't mean a dragon would choose her. She hadn't proven her worth in the competition. She had landed here by accident. Maybe it would all be for naught now.

"We will begin with Tieran," said Tara.

The dragon stepped forward. His midnight-blue scales twinkled in the lantern light inside the cave. He was the smallest of the lot but also the most beautiful, and like any male who had that much beauty, he knew it. She had watched him primp and preen, and the females went crazy for him. But she had never gotten along with him. Not that he was anything like March—he was a dragon after all, and they had keen intelligence and were regal figures—but his attitude always rebuffed her.

Tieran surveyed the five competitors. His golden eye narrowed when it got to Kerrigan and then whipped back to the other four. And he did nothing.

Kerrigan shifted uncomfortably. The last time, each of the three dragons had known immediately which competitor they wanted to bond with. It normally took a few seconds to come to that conclusion. But Tieran looked torn as he judged each of the five people before him.

"Tieran?" Tara prodded after several agonizing minutes.

"I am Tieran of Essex and Thiery. Born of the Holy Mountain. Proud and tenacious with a heart that sings for the skies."

Kerrigan swayed at the sound of his musical voice in her ears. But he stopped again right before he made his choice. She furrowed her brow in confusion.

"My choice is one of honor, for I value it above all else. And thus, this choice is difficult, because honor and power sing different songs."

Kerrigan and Tara caught each other's eyes. Tara shrugged her shoulders in confusion. At least Kerrigan wasn't the only one.

"But the music thrums louder than sense. Thus, I must make my decision against my own judgment. If you will accept, I will be dragon bound to Kerrigan of the House of Dragons."

"What?" she gasped, frozen in place.

Tieran's words swam all around her. Was he saying that he didn't want to accept her but that something about her was louder than his own sense? Well, that sounded like a ringing endorsement.

"I choose you, Kerrigan, if you will accept me."

She wanted to ask, *Why?* Why her? When he didn't even *like* her. She had hardly expected to be in this position, but if she had thought any dragon would pick her, any at all, the very last one on that list would have been Tieran.

Her mouth hung open as everyone awaited her answer.

"Kerrigan, your answer?" Tara whispered.

This was all Kerrigan had wanted all her life. She'd wanted to fly. And if this meant that she could join the Society and fly the rest of her life, then she and Tieran could figure out their differences.

"I accept," she gasped.

"Follow me," Tara said. "From here, your magic will be bound."

Kerrigan stepped forward on heavy feet, away from the rest of the competitors, and up to Tieran's side. Tara walked them to a small pool. A table was set up next to it with five goblets and a book. Tara picked up the book and began to read the binding spell in ancient Fae. Kerrigan wasn't fluent in the old language despite her tutors' attempts to get her to understand it, but she could still *feel* the magic winding around her and Tieran, drawing them together.

One of the goblets was offered to Kerrigan. "Drink from this. You will pass into the spiritual realm, where you and Tieran will meet. When the binding is complete, you will be dragon and rider." Tara touched Kerrigan's hand with a wide, genuine smile. "I'm so happy for you. Good luck."

"Thank you," Kerrigan whispered, staring down into the goblet. It looked like water, as it did in the pool, but it was part of the spell. She looked to Tieran. "Ready?"

"As I'll ever be."

Kerrigan frowned and then downed the drink at the same time as Tieran lapped from the pool. For the second time today, her vision went fuzzy, and then she blacked out.

⁂

For the last five years, Kerrigan had thought constantly about what it would be like to go through the dragon-binding ceremony. Having witnessed it firsthand, she had seen each of the competitors drink from the goblet and then enter a state of sleep, coming to with excitement as the bond set in. She'd imagined every scenario for how the binding was actually accomplished.

But she hadn't envisioned this.

Kerrigan stood on a bridge. It was small and wooden, overtop a bubbling creek that ran through the lawn of an estate. A white marble gazebo stood tall and proud with large columns and a statue of a woman at the center in a scandalously revealing gown. The gardens were massive, even compared to those in Bryonican territory, where the land was fertile and lush. This was a monument to meticulously maintained flora. And the mansion that sat at the top of the hill, all white stone and iron balustrades and glass windows, was the largest single building she had ever seen in her life.

"Tieran," she whispered.

She craned her neck. Tieran was supposed to be here, right? That was part of the binding. Or at least she had thought it was. That they would have to go on some adventure together. Maybe she had just assumed what she wanted to happen, not reality.

Kerrigan uneasily stepped off the bridge and onto the thick dark-green grass. Her eyes shifted to the horizon. She startled, nearly falling over at the sight. There were mountains in the distance. She had grown up in a mountain and had a pretty good idea what the Vert Mountains looked like. Sure, there were other mountain ranges in Alandria, up north in Tosin territory. But without a doubt, she had never seen these mountains in her life. There was nothing like this on Alandria.

She shivered in fear. Where was she? And *why* was she here?

Voices rang out from farther away. Anxiety shot through her, but she was here for a reason. She couldn't stand here in front of a bridge all day.

She swallowed hard and then walked past the gazebo and down a carefully laid stone path.

A man raged from the front of the house. "How dare you think to rise against your betters!"

The man stood in the doorframe. He was enormous, six and a half feet tall, with a cruel, sneering face and golden-tan skin. He wore a strange garment draped across one shoulder and belted at the waist. A circlet of laurel fit onto his golden hair. He was monstrously beautiful.

Screams could be heard from inside the house.

"Stop, Vulsan! You can't do this!"

"Restrain her!" he cried back as he stepped out onto the back patio. His massive hand was fisted into the dark hair of another man. He flung the man forward at his feet as if he were a rag doll. "We will teach you manners."

The man coughed blood onto the white stone floor, injuries from a previous beating visible on his pale skin.

Kerrigan put her hand to her mouth as Vulsan pulled a barbed whip out of thin air and uncoiled it before the other man. She had to stop this. It was beyond barbaric. It couldn't continue.

She stepped forward to intervene, and that was the moment when the man on the ground defiantly lifted his head to look at Vulsan.

Kerrigan gasped.

"Father?" she whispered.

But no one seemed to hear her. Not as she raced across the garden pathway. Not when she screamed as the first lash of the whip came down onto Kivrin Argon's back. Not as she lunged for Vulsan to keep him from harming the father who had abandoned her, who she still couldn't leave to this fate. But all she did was pass straight through Vulsan's form. And all she could do was watch as her father's back was ravaged. He made not one sound. Not one.

Kerrigan put her hand out. She could stop this. She could make Vulsan stop harming her father. She stretched with every last fiber of her being, into that place where the visions and energy bursts came from, into that place she had never willingly touched, but she would here, for this.

And for one small fraction of a moment, Vulsan turned his head. His lips parted, and he *saw* her.

"Who?" he breathed.

A headache seared through her, as hot as a fiery poker to her eyeball. She gasped and collapsed to the ground. Vulsan returned to beating her father. And she could do nothing as blackness rushed up to greet her once more.

✺

"Kerrigan?" Tieran spoke urgently into her mind.

She shuddered awake. The memory of her father's whipping at the hands of that man. It was terrible. She couldn't fathom why her mind had conjured such a thing. She turned her head and vomited onto the stones.

"Are you all right?" Tara asked in concern.

She waved her off. "Fine."

"Okay," Tara said uncertainly. "You two are bound forevermore. You will exit through here and fly home to Kinkadia, where you will have a hero's welcome in the arena."

Kerrigan straightened and followed Tieran away from the watchful eyes of the Dragon Blessed and the rest of the competitors. She glanced up at him and saw mirrored worry in his eyes.

Once they were finally alone, she breathed out heavily. "It didn't work, did it?"

Tieran stretched his lithe limbs. *"No, I don't believe it did."*

"What did you see?"

"The Holy Mountain, where I was born." A shudder ran through his scales. *"It was destroyed."*

Kerrigan shivered. "I saw my father being beaten by this enormous golden man in some foreign world. I don't understand it at all. This wasn't supposed to happen."

"I believe dragons are more informed than Fae about what is supposed

to happen during the bonding. I was told that we would face three challenges together and that we would have to choose each other above all others each time. Then we would be bound."

"Yeah, that didn't happen, did it?"

"No."

Kerrigan sighed. "Scales."

"This is why I wasn't even going to pick you."

Kerrigan glared at him. "Hey, I didn't even sign up for this. It just happened. You could have picked someone else."

"Well, I wanted to."

"Fine, then go back in there and tell them it didn't work! You can have one of the other competitors, and we can put this behind us."

She shouldn't have been mad with Tieran. She knew that. It wasn't his fault that it hadn't worked. She didn't know *what* had gone wrong. But dragon binding was essential between dragon and rider. It was how they communicated and found each other and did all the incredible things that dragon riders had accomplished in the thousands of years since the advent of the Society. Without it, they were nothing.

"I cannot," Tieran said softly. "If I am found defective, then I might never get a rider."

"Yeah," she muttered. "I don't know if they'll even let me have this first chance. They'd never let me try again."

"Then, I believe we're stuck together. However unfortunate."

Great. All that, and she was stuck with a dragon who didn't even want her and a binding that hadn't even worked.

CHAPTER FIFTY-ONE
THE RETURN

Kerrigan and Tieran were silent on the flight back to Kinkadia. As much as her anxiety was fresh, not to mention confusion over the vivid dream she had seen in the botched binding ceremony, she couldn't ignore the brilliance of flying.

She was *flying*. And as long as everything went well, she would get to fly forever. It was what she had always wanted, and it was almost too good to be true.

As the arena came into view, they could hear the cheers erupt at the first sight of them. They were the first dragon pair back. The least expected pair ever. She was not looking forward to the disaster they were about to walk into.

"Do you think they'll know we're not bound?" Kerrigan asked nervously.

"No. I don't think they'll be able to tell. We will just have to be careful."

Kerrigan frowned. Careful. Right. Her specialty.

Tieran did a sweeping loop around the arena to thunderous applause and then came in with a perfect, tight landing at the center of the arena.

"Are you ready?"

She released a breath. "As I'll ever be."

Kerrigan slipped easily from Tieran's back and came face-to-face with Master Bastian, Mistress Layla, and Mistress Sinead. Bastian's mouth was hanging open. Layla's brow was furrowed, and she held her magic tight in outrage. Sinead kept flicking her eyes up and down, as if she couldn't believe what she was seeing.

"Kerrigan?" Bastian finally got out.

She bowed slightly. "Master Bastian."

"What have you done?" Layla snarled. "You are not a competitor. How dare you ride a dragon here."

Tieran leveled his head with Layla and blew a puff of air in her face. *"Careful. She is mine."*

Layla wrenched back, her eyes widening. "Tieran, I meant no offense, but she cannot possibly be your rider."

"She was not a competitor," Sinead said, finally overcoming her shock. "There are rules in place for a reason. She would have had to enter the tournament, be tested, go through all three competitions…"

"Not to mention she is of the House of Dragons," Layla spat. "She isn't even part of a house."

"And she's too young!" Sinead cried.

Another figure approached, bold and furious across the arena. Kerrigan recognized Lorian right away. She straightened her spine. This should be fun.

"What is the meaning of this?" Lorian demanded. "What happened to the dragon's rider?"

"I am Tieran's dragon rider," Kerrigan said boldly.

Lorian scoffed at her. "You? You're nothing but a half-Fae wretch in the House of Dragons. You're no more qualified to be a dragon rider than a human off the streets."

Kerrigan gritted her teeth, but it was Tieran whose fury materialized. *"Kerrigan is my dragon rider. We are bound. You can no more separate us than you from your own dragon, Oria."*

Lorian didn't back down from Tieran's anger though. He matched it. "How dare you threaten my dragon bond. I am a full member of the Society. You are still in training until the Society has recognized you as a dragon capable of a rider match. We will speak to your elders about this foolhardy nature."

"Lorian, please," Helly said, appearing swiftly across the sand-strewn arena. "Do not be too hasty."

"Hasty, Hellina?" Lorian snarled. "After what you allowed to happen at the last tournament? This will not stand. There will be rioting in the streets."

"Is that a promise, Lorian?" Bastian asked carefully.

Lorian glared back at him. "Not at all, Bastian. I am merely stating that a repeat of last tournament's events will result in similar complications."

"She was not a competitor!" Layla cried again. "She is not qualified."

"I was not a competitor," Kerrigan said, meeting all their eyes. "But if you'd let me explain."

"Explain what?" Lorian asked. "I'm sure we'd all love to hear your rehearsed gambit for how you got a dragon, but we have no interest in it. We will hold a council meeting to decide your fate."

"I, for one, would like to hear the girl's story," Sinead said calmly.

"As would I," Helly said.

"Go ahead, Kerrigan," Bastian said encouragingly. "We all need to know what exactly happened."

"This is preposterous!" Lorian said.

Kerrigan could see the worry and fear in Helly's expression. She wanted to tell Helly about the vision that had led her here, but now was certainly not the time.

"When all this started, I met with Gelryn, and he tested me."

A gasp went up from a few of the members present.

"He said he'd been waiting for me. Afterward, he said that

I'd passed through. I didn't think anything of it. I wasn't actively competing."

"Because you're not a competitor," Lorian grumbled.

Kerrigan's cheeks heated. "Then something called to me to join in the final task. I was spirited away to the Noirwood Forest, where Fordham and I barely managed to escape an ambush engineered by Darrid. When we got to the mouth of the cave, he was there again and prepared to kill us both. I held him off so that Fordham could enter, but Darrid ran me into the cave with a battle-ax."

"Gods," Sinead breathed. "The competitors aren't supposed to try to kill each other."

Helly's face paled considerably. "No, they're not."

"From there, well, you all know what happened. I went through the final task and arrived in the room. It sealed itself behind me, and the Dragon Blessed confirmed that I was a competitor because the room accepted me. Tieran chose me, and we were bound," she said, rushing over the lie at the end.

"That's incredibly dangerous, Kerrigan," Helly said gently.

"Preposterous! The entire thing is outlandish. She was *called* to the tournament? She cheated. We cannot let this stand," Lorian argued.

Suddenly, another round of cheers erupted from the crowd. Kerrigan turned with Tieran to see a bright purple dragon soaring in the skies.

"Evien," Tieran said.

Kerrigan had always loved Evien because of how much she adored flying. Not just because she could or had to but because she wanted to. She'd had many a late-night encounter with Evien, who took her out into the night sky. She'd thought she'd never do that again.

Evien pulled up a little too quickly and landed a few yards away from them. But it was clear who her rider was as soon as her lithe form dropped on the sand—Audria.

The three adjudicators left Kerrigan with Lorian and Helly as they went to congratulate Audria on her success. But as soon as they were done, she rushed over to where Kerrigan stood and threw her arms around her.

"We did it, Kerrigan. We're both in the Society."

"Not quite," Kerrigan muttered, breaking from her embrace.

"What? What do you mean?"

She gestured to Lorian. "He doesn't think I qualify. He wants to hold a council meeting about it."

"No," Audria gasped. She pushed Kerrigan behind her as if she could keep her safe from Lorian's attacks. "I vouch for Kerrigan. The room picked her. It wanted her to be in the tournament, and she was tested."

"A council meeting will be held to decide that," Lorian said. "She doesn't qualify. She has no house, and we have never had a half-Fae."

"You never had a human before either, and you let two compete last time," Audria shot back.

"And look at how that turned out," Lorian snapped.

"Just because there are a few loud bigots doesn't mean that we should go backward! We must stay the course, or else people will think that all they have to do is cause enough fuss and we'll take away other people's rights. That is not the Kinkadia that I know and love. And I won't stand by and let you use your prejudice against her."

Kerrigan wanted to duck out of sight. She'd never had someone like Audria, who was so full of privilege, so very Bryonican royalty, stand up for her to completely defend her. She barely even *knew* her.

Lorian opened his mouth to object again, but Audria barreled forward.

"And on the second account, my mother and I have agreed to select Kerrigan into Bryonica under the House of Drame."

Kerrigan's stomach flopped. Even though she had *known* Audria was going to do this, everything had changed. Before, she had been running away from the people who had abandoned her. Now, she had faced Ashby March and realized it was the very last place that she wanted to be. But she couldn't say *no*. Not when her entry to the Society was on the line.

More applause from the crowd revealed a bright red dragon on the horizon.

"*Netta*," Tieran said.

Netta was such a good flyer. She took tight corners and swirled through circles better than any other dragon Kerrigan had flown with. She and Kerrigan had always gotten along because they were both mischievous. Truthfully, she'd hoped to have Netta for herself. But when Netta landed, she couldn't be happier to see Fordham drop from her back right next to her and Audria.

"Congratulations, Fordham," Bastian said, holding his hand out.

Layla looked irritated but not as much as she had been with Kerrigan. "You've earned your spot."

The implication was clear: Kerrigan hadn't.

Fordham shook hands and then pressed through the crowd that had formed between them and to Kerrigan's side. "You did it. I can't believe it, but you did."

Audria huffed, "We're still working on that."

"What's going on?" Fordham asked.

"Lorian wants to hold a council meeting. He doesn't think Kerrigan qualifies. Even though I told him that Kerrigan is now a member of Bryonica."

"She is?" Fordham asked in alarm.

"Yes, she is. So she qualifies," Audria said defiantly.

Lorian ignored her as he held conference with the adjudicators and Helly. More and more Society members were stepping onto the sand to meet the new members and their dragons and were getting sucked into the debate about Kerrigan.

Fordham tugged on her arm to draw her aside. "I thought you didn't want to go back to Bryonica."

"I don't," she admitted solemnly.

"Then don't."

"What other choice do I have?" she demanded. "Lorian doesn't want to let me in. He's only considering it with the other Society members right now because Audria stuck her neck out for me and said that I was Bryonican. If I don't have house backing, there's no way he's going to allow it. He'd send Tieran back before letting a half-Fae with no house enter his Society."

"That's ridiculous. There has to be another way to fix this."

"I don't see one, and I'm queen of finding another way out of things. But I don't think there is here." She swallowed hard. "And worse yet, my fear in the faerie illusion was returning to Bryonica. I don't want to do it, but I've faced it once. I can do it again."

"This isn't another test, Kerrigan. This is your life. Forever."

"I know," she snapped. "Find me another way, because I just don't see it."

Fordham sighed and released her as she brushed past him. Noda and Roake landed next in the arena, releasing the adjudicators to give their round of congratulations. Festivities would begin soon, starting with a parade for the winners of the tournament. But Lorian was still busy arguing his case to the rest of the Society members present.

Finally, it seemed that something had been settled. Lorian strode to where she stood with Fordham and Audria behind her. Helly and Bastian followed him close behind.

"We have come to an agreement," he said bitterly. "If you have the backing of House Bryonica *and* can show proof of your testing and entrance into the tournament, then the council will convene to determine your fate."

Kerrigan wasn't relieved by that ruling, but it was better than nothing. At least she could argue. She was good at that. She had no other choice about Bryonica. "I accept."

Audria jumped up and down. "Yes! I'm so excited."

"Wait," Fordham snapped from her right.

Kerrigan looked at him in confusion. "What?"

"You said if she had the backing of House Bryonica, but what if she had the backing from any house?"

"Any house will do," Bastian agreed.

Helly furrowed her brow. "Why do you ask, Fordham?"

"A thousand years ago, the twelve houses and the Society sealed my people away and named us the Dark Court. We claimed House of Shadows for ourselves. Under the ruling of the council, the House of Shadows was recognized as a house of Alandria."

"So?" Lorian asked impatiently.

Fordham looked directly at her as he said, "Then Kerrigan can join the House of Shadows."

Kerrigan's mouth hung open. Was he offering her a way out? Through his house? It didn't make sense. She'd never thought he would give her something like this.

"No half-Fae would ever join the House of Shadows," Lorian said with a laugh.

"It wouldn't make sense," Audria agreed. "Bryonica is safer for her."

Bryonica didn't see her. Fordham saw her. And Fordham was risking the wrath of his own people by making her one of them. He was doing it for her and no other reason. The out she needed to step away from her own worst nightmare.

"I accept," Kerrigan said.

"Kerrigan, no," Helly gasped.

"I urge you to reconsider," Bastian said. "You don't know what those people are like."

"I know what Fordham is like," Kerrigan said. "And that's good enough for me. I'm joining the House of Shadows, and I will bring my proof to the council meeting. Be ready."

Kerrigan felt powerful as she made the utterance, sealing her fate with Fordham's, but then she smelled the smoke and heard the screams that filled the air.

CHAPTER FIFTY-TWO
THE SMOKE

I t's begun," Lorian said with dread in his voice as he stared at the skyline.

Kerrigan whipped around and saw the waves of smoke coming off the south side of the city.

"That's the Artisan Village!" Audria cried next to her.

"What's happening?" Sinead gasped.

Kerrigan narrowed her eyes. This was the same thing that had happened five years ago at the end of the tournament—riots. Red Masks had gotten emboldened and flooded the streets, murdering innocents. There had been nothing she could do then, but that wasn't the case anymore.

"We need to go help those people," Kerrigan said. "Now!"

"You won't do a thing," Lorian said. "You aren't a Society member yet. The Guard and the Society in the city can handle this."

Kerrigan glared at him, straightening. "I might not be a Society member, but I'm never going to stand by and watch *my* city burn to the ground because you didn't want me out there."

She made eye contact with Fordham and Audria. Noda and Roake looked on, aghast, but hastily jumped back onto their dragons when Audria snapped orders at them.

"We'll swing in from the riverfront," Audria yelled at them, taking command with ease. "We'll bring in as much water from the river as we can and douse the buildings. Let's figure out what we're dealing with and go from there."

Tieran lifted into the air, heading directly for the river. They passed over the Artisan Village. Kerrigan's eyes watered at the sight of one of her favorite parts of the city on fire. Audria swooped in over the river first, drawing water toward her with her magic. Fordham went in next, and Kerrigan flew in tight behind him. She pulled on her reserves and drew and drew and drew water to her, as much as she could manage. She had her sights on the opera house when Tieran headed back toward the city.

"The opera house," she yelled over the wind whipping in her face.

Tieran dove low over the village, and with a deluge, she released the water magic over the burning opera house and nearby buildings. Other Society members had taken up the call. Dragons filled the air, heading for the river.

Kerrigan's eyes searched the ground for the rioters who had started this.

And as Tieran began to bank away from the river, she nudged him forward. "Straight ahead."

"I see them."

Tieran came in low, and just before he reached the wide city street, Kerrigan dropped off his back and landed heavily on the ground. She winced at the pain that flared up her knees. She was going to need to work on that. She'd never made a landing like that before, but she had no more time to consider it. She took off at a run, straight for the line of people in black robes and red masks who were dispersing back into their hidey-holes now that the Society had been called in to break up their fight.

It should have felt like any other fight she had ever walked into, but it felt like more. It felt like every Red Mask who had beaten her that night almost exactly five years ago. She couldn't let them get away with this. She couldn't let their leader go free.

Footsteps sounded behind her, and she didn't have to turn her head to know that Fordham had followed her into the mayhem, as he had been doing for weeks. She didn't slow. He would catch up to her. She kept moving forward, glad for those hours and hours of running so that by the time she reached the first line of Red Masks, she wasn't winded.

Kerrigan used her wind magic to bowl through the first group, and they hastily fled. But she could see the leader up ahead. Their leader was holding up a large, swirling gray orb, much like the amber one Basem had used against her.

This was her chance to get revenge for what those people had done to her. This was her chance to end it. No longer would Red Masks walk her streets. No longer would they terrorize humans and half-Fae. No longer would they try to take away their rights. It could end right here, right now.

The crowd had cleared enough for Kerrigan to slow as she approached the leader of the Red Masks. He turned to face her. He was a large man, the black robes barely covering all his bulk. His hand held the object aloft, and she could see the thick veins where he gripped it in place. The red mask obscured his features, hiding who he was.

"This ends here," Kerrigan shouted at him. "Drop the orb, and no one gets hurt."

A sharp laugh resonated through the stone path. "Is that what you think?"

Kerrigan tried not to let her shock register, but she couldn't completely mask it. "Basem?"

"Who else, leatha?"

Basem was the leader of the Red Masks. Her stomach tilted and gurgled in disgust. Of course, it made sense. She had wondered how he had so much power. Money alone wasn't enough, but a cult following of like-minded bigots to spread his hate speech? That would do it.

"It was you all along. You're the leader of the Red Masks. You killed Lyam. You tried to kill me. And now, when I've exposed who you really are to the Society, you burn down a part of the city and riot against it? You're a monster."

"A monster I might be, but no one ever gets anywhere without breaking a few rules." He held the gray orb aloft. "I almost killed you once. Are you ready to see if I can do it again?"

"You can't beat me without your bag of tricks," she spat.

He shrugged. "Then there's no reason to fight fair."

And at that moment, he thrust the gray orb toward her. Lightning shot out of the eye of the storm. She yelled and threw her body out of the way of the lightning bolt that would have electrocuted her. Fordham dove the other direction, just barely missing being singed, but another building took the brunt of the attack and went up in flames.

"Come out, come out, wherever you are," Basem taunted.

"There's something you don't know this time, Bruiser," she yelled back.

"And what's that?"

Kerrigan looked to the skies and grinned. "I have a dragon."

Tieran burst through the open alleyway that Kerrigan had cleared for him, and before Basem could get another shot off, Tieran slammed his bulk into Basem. He flew backward twenty feet and landed on his back with a crunch, continuing to roll a few times. The gray orb shot from his hand and skittered harmlessly against the cobblestones.

"The orb," she shouted at Fordham as she jumped up and ran for Basem.

Fordham was already on his feet, running to grab the weapon Basem had been wielding. Kerrigan dashed for the man who had done so much damage in her life. She scooped him off the ground with a burst of air magic, cocooning him in a tight cyclone as she wrenched his arms back.

Basem's mask had fallen off in Tieran's attack, and a cut at his eyebrow was dripping blood into his eye. "This…isn't…over!"

"I think it is," she spat at him as Society members flooded the street. "I think it's finally over."

"We can take it from here," a guard said, stepping up to her and putting a hand on her shoulder. "You can let him go."

Kerrigan hadn't realized how tightly she'd been holding on to her magic until she was told she could release it. She set Basem back down onto the ground and took a step backward. A pair of Society members rushed forward, shackling him with magic-dampening cuffs.

"That was great work," said Mistress Corinna, chief of the Society Guard. She inclined her head, and the dying rays of sunlight caught against her red-clay brown skin. "When you go through Society training, come find me. I think you have a real future in law enforcement."

Kerrigan blinked in surprise. *When* she went through Society training. She'd said it as if it were a certainty. Which Kerrigan did not think it was. Not if Lorian had anything to say about it.

"Thank you, Mistress Corinna," Kerrigan said with a small bow.

"We're going to take the Red Mask here to the dungeons under the mountain where he can't do anyone harm ever again." Corinna easily towered over Kerrigan, but when she held her hand out to shake, she did it as equals. "You and I are going to have a talk with the council about what happened here tonight."

CHAPTER FIFTY-THREE
THE RULING

Kerrigan's hair had slipped free of its ribbon. Her pale skin was covered in ash. Her eyes and lungs ached from inhaling the smoke that every inch of her smelled like. Her knees protested her harsh landing. Still, she held her head high as Tieran dropped her off in the arena, and she walked toward the waiting group of council members.

She counted seventeen out of the twenty in total. But even better, behind them stood her friends. Darby waved excitedly. Hadrian bit his lip, clearly anxious about what was to come. Clover was smoking a loch cigarette, brazen as ever. Valia stood next to Bastian, her eyes wide with concern. Kerrigan felt a twinge of regret. She nodded her head at Valia in apology for leaving her without a word, and after Valia smiled in acceptance, Kerrigan focused her attention on the council.

Fordham, Audria, and Mistress Corinna dropped off their dragons and fell into step beside her. Almost a team—at least united in their cause.

Kerrigan was nervous, but she couldn't show it. She came to a stop before Lorian and Helly and Bastian and the fourteen other members who sat on the high council.

"Before you begin," Mistress Corinna said, "I would like to speak freely, if that is all right."

"Go ahead, Corinna," Helly said.

"Most of the Society members responded to the call for aid by flying to put out the fires rampaging the streets. My guards were in the streets, rescuing others from the burning buildings and trying to put down the riot, which had been engineered by a group of Red Masks. Unfortunately, most of them escaped. But Kerrigan entered the riot ring and went up against their leader, unprompted. She could have been injured or even killed, but she showed determination and fearlessness in the face of adversity. She stopped the leader, recovered the illegal magical artifact he had been using to generate lightning-bolt levels of destruction, and apprehended him. We are taking him to the dungeons, currently as a war criminal, and it is thanks to Kerrigan that we are able to do this," Corinna said, point-blank. "She proved herself today, and I would be proud to call her a Society member."

The council members began to whisper back and forth to each other, and Lorian coughed.

"Great. She knows how to disobey orders and enter a war zone that could have gotten many others killed. Just what we need."

"We need free thinkers," Corinna interjected. "People who will jump into action and not stay behind and let others fight their battles."

Lorian reared back at the words, but they weren't wrong. Lorian had a lot of bark but not much bite.

"Kerrigan, do you have anything to add?" Helly asked. "About the incident or your admittance into the competition."

"I think everyone here knows that I belong in the Society at this point," Kerrigan said boldly. "I went through testing with Gelryn. He passed me through. I was accepted into the room. I have a dragon. I defended the city like any Society member should. But not just that, I was doing it long before any of you knew about it. My friend Lyam was killed in the Dregs, and everyone was content to say that it was an accident—wrong place, wrong time, a senseless robbery. That the Dregs are bad, and it was no surprise, just tragic. But why should it have to be? The Dregs don't have to be like that. We can fix them, make people's lives better. Worse than that, Lyam wasn't just killed; he was murdered by Basem Nix."

A gasp went through the crowd. Helly nodded. Lorian pursed his lips.

"I discovered that he had been plotting to kill me as well. I rescued a hostage from his clutches, and the Society was supposed to bring him in on murder charges. Instead, he escaped and burned down the Artisan Village as the leader of the Red Masks! Now, he's in Guard custody thanks to me, and we can finally question him and put an end to this systemic problem." Kerrigan held her hands out before her. "I don't see why it's even a question as to whether I should join unless some of you are just prejudiced against half-Fae." She let the words linger. "And that's not good enough."

Her friends burst into applause, and more applause rang out in the arena. She hadn't realized how easily her voice carried. That so many had been listening to her. But she saw more people nodding along in agreement than looking like they had sucked on a lemon, like Lorian.

Corinna put her hand on her shoulder. "Bravo."

Fordham stepped up to her side and then Audria, surprisingly followed by Roake and Noda. They might have argued against her in the cave, but they were one now. She could feel Tieran's presence heavy behind her. And she no longer felt alone.

"We still need to convene a council meeting to discuss this," Lorian grumbled.

"I believe we have a majority present," Helly said with a coy smile.

"That is not decorum."

"Neither are the circumstances," Bastian said, striding to Helly's side. "I call for a vote on the matter of Kerrigan's entrance into the Society."

"All in favor?" Helly said.

Kerrigan's heart caught in her throat as she counted the hands raised in the air. Half. It was at least half. She kept counting—nine, ten, eleven, twelve. Oh gods! Almost everyone.

"Those opposed?" Helly called out.

Lorian shot his hand up, and four others slowly raised their hands as well. Kerrigan memorized their faces. The council members—Masters Roldan and Dowde and Mistresses Freya and Kopeli—who, for whatever reason, wanted to deny her her future. She wouldn't forget a single one.

"The motion is passed," Bastian commanded. "Kerrigan is our fifth champion."

More applause rang out, and the council joined in with it.

"You all have two weeks off before Society training commences. Go home and visit your families. When you return, a year of training will begin."

Kerrigan looked to the other four people who would be in her training class. They were all from such different worlds, but for the next year, Fordham, Audria, Roake, and Noda would be her constant companions.

"Take a moment, and then the parade will begin," Bastian announced. "Five years ago, we didn't have it, but this year, I believe we have cause to celebrate our victors."

Helly stepped forward, pulling Kerrigan into a hug. "My dear girl, I'm so proud of you."

"I thought you might be mad."

"Why?"

"Because I didn't choose Bryonica."

Helly sighed. "I am disappointed, as I wanted you to be a part of my house, but that is solely selfishness. I know how you feel about it. I hope that you made the right choice."

So did Kerrigan.

Helly released her as Darby, Hadrian, and Clover rushed to her side. Darby grabbed her around the middle, and Hadrian joined in on the hug. He even opened his arm up to leave room for Clover.

"Not interested, sweetheart," Clover teased.

He narrowed his eyes at her. "Get in here, Clove."

She arched an eyebrow. "So demanding."

But she stepped in and joined the hug, all four of them teetering back and forth with excitement. When they finally released Kerrigan, they all beamed with pride.

"You're really a Society member," Darby gushed.

"It's what you always wanted," Hadrian said.

Kerrigan flushed. "It is. It just never felt attainable."

"Look at you, going around and changing the world," Clover joked.

"I meant what I said about the Dregs."

Clover reached instinctively for another smoke. "I know. It's a step."

"We'll get there together."

"Nice to have someone on the inside at least."

Kerrigan laughed. "Not sure how much sway I'll have, but it's a life appointment. I'll spend my life working on it."

"All right. Competitors, line up," Layla yelled, corralling them into position with their dragons.

Kerrigan took up the rear of the line with Tieran at her side. She placed her hand on his flank. "Thank you for your help in the fight. We make a good team."

"We'll see about that. I've heard about this year of training, Kerrigan. I don't know if we'll be able to hack it without the bond."

"But no one will know about that," she said, lowering her voice as they stepped through the arena entrance and out to the parade route.

Hundreds of people lined the street and threw yellow lilies—the flower of Kinkadia—in their path.

"Someone might find out if we're not coordinated."

"Then we'll practice."

He looked unconvinced. *I'm afraid the easy part is behind us.*

Kerrigan gulped. "We'll figure it out. I got in, didn't I?"

"Luck."

She snorted. "As pleasant as ever, Tieran."

"We're going to get caught."

"No, we won't."

And when we do, what will we tell them? That we thought we could make do without the bond? The binding has been in place for dragon riders for ten thousand years.

She groaned. "What would you rather do? Tell them? We both agreed that wasn't possible."

"No, we can't tell them."

"We'll figure it out."

"I am not optimistic."

"What else is new?" Kerrigan asked, waving her hand at the crowd and beaming as she ignored the fear at the pit of her stomach.

If they find out, they won't just tear us apart. They'll kick you out of the Society. You'll be adrift, an outcast. And I'll have to return to the Holy Mountain. A shiver seemed to run through him. *I never want to go back there.*

Kerrigan glanced over at him, concerned. "What happened at the Holy Mountain?"

"Nothing," he snapped.

Kerrigan frowned. She didn't believe him, but he seemed set on not telling her. She plastered the smile back on her face and continued down the parade route. Tried to revel in the joy of winning something she'd never believed she could compete for. Tried to imagine that all this fanfare was really for her.

She tucked her hair behind her ears and displayed her heritage for all to see. She was a Society member now. She might have been hunted and reviled for being half-Fae, but for the first time, she felt truly proud of who she was. She wanted everyone to see.

To soak all this up and hope that Tieran's words weren't prophecy.

CHAPTER FIFTY-FOUR
THE SPIRIT

Kerrigan slept like a baby for the first time in weeks. She slumbered so late that it was early afternoon when a knock finally woke her from the restorative—and thankfully dreamless—sleep. Kerrigan yawned and rubbed at her crusty eyes before heading to the door to peek outside. She'd been expecting Fordham. Yesterday, he'd put off any talk about what they would do the next two weeks and if, like everyone else, they would visit his—now her—house. She figured now would be the time.

What she hadn't expected to find was the dragon tournament handler—Tara.

"Hello, Kerrigan," she said with a smile. "May I come in?"

"Of course." Kerrigan pushed the door open wider, and Tara stepped inside. "I wasn't expecting you."

"No, but I wanted to come and congratulate you personally."

"Thank you," Kerrigan said, shutting the door behind her. "And thank you for what you did."

Tara waved her hand away at Kerrigan. "The room let you through. Whether I had someone hastily close the barrier afterward didn't matter. It's a House of Dragons' secret. The council need not know."

"Well, you didn't have to do it, and I'm grateful."

Tara smiled mischievously. "Well, I for one wanted to see a Dragon Blessed in the Society."

"Will Mistress Moran be a problem?"

Tara held a hand up. "She agreed that closing it after you was the right call. She even read the tournament rule book, and we found the language that would protect you."

Kerrigan breathed out heavily. "That's a relief."

Tara clutched her chest. "And thank you for bringing justice to Lyam."

"I had to."

"I know I'm three years younger, but I've always looked up to you guys. I wanted to be you, and I wanted Lyam to see me," Tara confessed. "I think he would have wanted to see you in the Society. You do justice to his memory."

Kerrigan fingered the compass in her pocket. It had saved her and Fordham's lives in the forest. "I think he's watching over us."

"Me too," Tara said, sniffling. "You're going to do wonderful things."

"I have to get through training first."

"You'll do it. You never back down from a challenge. It's what I really admire about you."

Kerrigan smiled, seeing herself reflected back through Tara. She had been like this with Cyrene five years prior. It felt strange to have anyone look up to her, but maybe it had for Cyrene too.

"You're going to do great things too, Tara."

"Thanks." Tara wiped her eyes and laughed uncomfortably. "I also came to tell you that Gelryn arrived back from the Holy Mountain. He said he had to eat, and then you should visit him."

Kerrigan's eyes rounded. "Scales! I should go!"

Tara laughed. "Yes. Maybe change first though."

Kerrigan laughed at the fact that she was still in tournament clothes. She had passed out immediately as soon as her head hit the pillow and hadn't even had time to change or bathe. She needed to do both.

She thanked Tara one more time before she left, and then Kerrigan grabbed new clothes, went for a quick bath to scrub the tournament off her skin, and went in search of Gelryn. She found him in the same eaves with the impossible climb as she'd had that night she came in search of him about her visions. Her legs burned by the time she made it up to the top, and she nearly collapsed at his feet.

"Kerrigan Argon, now of the House of Shadows, a full Society member, welcome."

Kerrigan bowed dramatically. "A fancy title for the same person."

"Perhaps. Do you feel the same?"

"I don't know. I feel rested, and that's different."

Gelryn laughed, a booming thing that filled the cave. *"You entertain me. Such a rare quality."*

"I am so glad to see you return. I was worried that they weren't going to let me into the Society without your testimony that I had been tested."

"This is your destiny, and no one can deny it to you."

"Well, Lorian sure thinks he can."

"Master Lorian cannot always see what is right in front of him. He has had a clouded past and a fraught history with your father."

"Do you think he knows Kivrin is my father?" Kerrigan shivered at the thought. She had been trying to ignore the binding dream that she'd had of her father. It made no sense, and she worried that asking anyone about it, especially Gelryn, would reveal that she hadn't bonded with Tieran.

"Assuredly. Your secret is no longer a secret."

Kerrigan froze. "What?"

"How long did you sleep, child?"

"All day," she confessed.

"Audria Ather in the House of Drame has proclaimed you the lost princess of Bryonica. You have made waves in their community. I believe that you will be celebrated among them for generations."

Kerrigan thought she was going to be sick. "She told everyone?"

"It appears so. You will have to make peace with your past if you hope to continue into this future."

"What does that even mean, Gelryn?"

"It means that I discovered answers for you in the Holy Mountain."

Kerrigan froze. "You did? You found out about my visions?"

"I spoke with the ancients of my race, the dragons who came before even me, who preserve our history. They told me of others in the past who had access to mystical visions and great spiritual energy. They were called spiritcasters."

"Spiritcasters," she whispered. It felt incredible to finally have a name for what she could do. "Are there any now? Can I meet them?"

"No, the last spiritcaster was from nearly a thousand years ago during the Great War."

"What happened to them?" she whispered.

"They never found a way to master their casting, and they slowly went insane."

Kerrigan shivered at the words. Gods! "That could happen to me?"

"Yes, if you do not learn to control the castings, then they will control you. Already, I believe it is happening with the increased rate of the spiritual energy swirling through you. You must find a teacher to help you learn to spiritcast."

"How can I possibly do that if no other spiritcasters exist? If there hasn't been one in a thousand years."

"You will dedicate the next year of your life to Society training, but through that training, you must also dedicate yourself to your spiritcasting. You will never survive one without the other."

Kerrigan bowed again. "I will do so. Thank you, Gelryn. You have helped more than I could have possibly hoped for."

412

Gelryn blew a puff of air in her face. *"Go now. There is someone waiting for you below."*

"There is?"

Gelryn turned away from her and folded himself up to sleep. Kerrigan sighed and then headed back down the endless stairs. She didn't know who was waiting for her, but she couldn't get over the giddy feeling of knowing that she was a spiritcaster, not just a strange girl who needed to hide her abilities. She was also from a line of great workers, the first in a thousand years.

When she stepped off the last stair, Fordham turned to face her. He looked every inch the prince she had first seen him as. Tall and broad with the soft black silk and thick silver embroidery. The silver House of Shadows seal on his breast. But now she saw so much more than that. Not just the pampered prince but also her friend. The man who had stood by her side through everything, who had kissed her in the open night air, who had told her he was cursed and that they could never be together.

Her heart panged at the sight of him. They had walked the path together through the tournament and come out on the other side. But they couldn't walk *this* path, the one she actually wanted. He might have gone out on a limb for her to have her join the House of Shadows, but it didn't change anything between them. And she could see that in his swirling gray eyes, the same color as that insufferable orb.

"I heard Gelryn was back and thought I might find you here," Fordham said, his hands slipping into the pockets of his pants.

"Are you going to chide me for not going on my morning run?" she joked. She fell into step beside him as they walked away from the dark depths and into the main opening to look out over the city of Kinkadia.

"You needed the sleep."

"Not even going to volley with me. This must be serious."

Fordham frowned and ducked his chin. "I'm sorry for offering you the spot in the House of Shadows."

"Sorry? You *saved* me, Ford."

"They were right. No half-Fae should want to have a place in the Dark Court."

"But I want to."

"You don't even know what you're saying."

"Then tell me."

He looked off into the distance, resigned. "I can't take you back there."

"Fordham, if I'm with you, then I'll be fine. Together, we're unstoppable."

"You don't understand."

"How can I when you're speaking in riddles?" Kerrigan asked.

"I don't know how well *I* will be received back home."

"Why? You came here and got a dragon. You're part of the Society. The first time in a thousand years the House of Shadows has representation in the government. They have to be pleased. It has to look like the first step to rejoining the world."

A lock of hair fell onto his forehead and blew in the breeze as his face hardened further and further with every word she said. "I thought that would be enough to regain my place there, but now, I'm not sure."

"Regain your place?" she asked in confusion. "Is this about your curse?"

"No," he said forlornly. "I'm not who you think I am, Kerrigan."

"You're exactly who I think you are, Ford. I've spent the last month with you. I know precisely who you are."

"I lied."

"About what? You cannot lie with actions." She forced him to look at her. "I know who you are."

"I was exiled," Fordham bit out. "That's why I came to get a dragon and join the Society. I'm no longer welcome in the House of Shadows, and I should never have brought you into this with me."

Exiled. Gods!

"Why? Why didn't you tell me?" she asked, the hurt seeping into her voice despite everything.

His face went dark. "Why should I have told you?"

She took a step back at the viciousness in his voice. "Ford…"

"It was a mistake to invite you to join the House of Shadows, and if you come home with me, I can't guarantee your safety."

"Guarantee my safety? Since when have you ever been able to do that?" she snapped back. "I'm the one who has been running straight into danger. How is this any different?"

He met her own hardened gaze. "Suit yourself, but don't say I didn't warn you. We'll leave tomorrow at dawn."

He strode away from her, leaving her standing before the opening to the mouth of the cave with more questions than answers. She had never dreamed that she would be able to join the Dragon Society, and now here she was. She had done the impossible. She could survive Fordham's exile and the House of Shadows and Society training with the same perseverance.

Nothing was going to hold her back now.

CHAPTER FIFTY-FIVE
THE RED MASK

ISA

Isa slunk through the deepest, darkest shadows of Draco Mountain. She curled into those shadows, and they claimed her as their own. She passed the sleeping guards. The nightshade draught she had given them all had worked wonders, but she wasn't careless, and she wanted to make sure that no one else had come down to see why the screams had ceased. The dungeons were a playroom for the depraved.

She snatched the large brass keys off the guard and then moved silently down the path through the reeking corridors. Finally, she stopped before the last door, the most recently occupied. The man who had once held such esteem was nothing more than a disgrace.

Basem Nix was bolted upright to the dungeon wall. His arms hung limp from where his hands were secured high above his head in magicked manacles. He could barely hold his weight after the beating he'd received from the guards as they extracted his secrets. He'd even pissed himself in the process.

"Tsk. Tsk. Tsk," Isa crooned.

Basem jolted at the sound of her voice. "Who's there?"

"A phantom," she breathed as she came into the light, her black mask covering her face.

He shuddered. "He sent you after all?"

"My father is nothing if not thorough."

"He's a bastard."

She wagged her finger at him. Though she detested the man who had raised her and was doing everything in her power to escape this wretched hellhole, no one else could speak ill of him in her presence. "That's not nice, Basem. I could get you out of here."

She held the keys up as bait. He greedily lunged forward, as she had known he would.

"Then get me out of here!"

"First, I want to know everything you told the Society about our little organization. What did you spill other than your own piss?"

He glared at her. It would have been more formidable if he weren't chained and one eye wasn't swollen shut. "I didn't tell them shit."

"Persuade me."

"They beat me near to death, and I didn't tell them anything. I let them think that I was the leader of the Red Masks. I didn't even give them information on the cache of weapons."

"That's good. What about my identity?"

"As if they'd be able to find you."

She grinned devilishly. "True. What about headquarters?"

"No."

"Our numbers?"

"No!"

"Our plans for the future?" Not that she thought Basem was high enough up to actually know future plans, but she let him think he did.

"No! I'm a Red Mask through and through. I swore a blood oath to the Father."

"I believe it is time for that to be called in," another voice joined in.

Isa slowly disappeared back into the shadows at the sound of her father. Terror shot through her, as it always did when he seemed to materialize out of nothing but thin air. But Basem was now shaking. A putrid smell came from him, and it was clear that he was pissing himself again in fear. He was utterly broken. There was no redemption in him.

Her father appeared then in the dark black robes with red stitching for the highest-ranking members of their organization. Covering his face was the original red mask, a metal alloy that molded to his face when worn and could only be removed by the wearer. So even in death, his identity would be obscured.

"Father," she gasped, sinking to a knee and reverently bowing her head. "I thought you wanted me to finish the job."

Her father held out his hand, and she carefully placed hers in his. He slapped it away as if she were no more than a fly. She retracted in haste.

"The keys, girl," he said with lethal calm.

She swallowed and passed him the guard's keys. "Of course, Father."

The leader of the Red Masks pressed the key into the hole and turned it. The door creaked open, offering Basem the first taste of freedom. But Isa knew better than to think that her father would offer forgiveness. It had been a test. He had wanted her to get the information he required from Basem, to see how far his treachery went, and then come here himself to pass judgment.

"You have disappointed me, Basem," the Red Mask said, stepping into the cell, carefully avoiding the pool of liquid coming out of Basem's pant leg.

"I never meant to, Father. I was only doing your work. The work of the Red Masks."

"False. You were doing your own work. Going against the girl and enacting revolution. I never called for these things. The timing had to be perfect, and you've *ruined* years of work."

"I'm sorry, Father. I'm so sorry."

"You were a brute, Basem. Nothing more. I gave you everything, and this is how you repay me."

"I can do better. I swear I can."

Her father dismissively waved his hand. Basem could be no more or less than what he was. He had been a risk from the start, but he had the zeal. He wanted humans' and half-Faes' heads on a platter. He wanted to eradicate the diseased breed. But his zeal didn't equate to intelligence. And he had proven it with his stupidity in the Artisan Village.

"I can give you one more chance, Basem."

"Yes, thank you, Father. Thank you."

"You must forget your vengeance for the girl Kerrigan. Can you do that?"

"Yes, of course. I can do that, Father."

Isa was shocked. She'd never thought her father would offer mercy. Not to someone like Basem when she had never received it herself.

"I require one other thing."

"Anything," Basem gasped.

"A sacrifice," the Red Mask said.

"Of course. Yes, I offer whatever you require." Basem was in tears now, wetness pouring down his face as he stared at her father with reverence. His last salvation.

The Red Mask scoffed, and then as swift as Isa had ever seen, he sliced open Basem's throat. Basem gargled on his own blood for a few seconds, gasping for breath, but there was nothing he could do, tied up as he was. There would have been nothing he could do regardless. No mercy. Basem had offered himself up as the sacrifice, and her father had taken it.

He cleaned the knife on Basem's shirt and then slipped it back into his sleeve. He stepped out of the cell and turned to face her. "Come, daughter. We have much work to do."

Isa followed in her father's wake, knowing she had no hope of escape now. Not without the money from Basem. But she had to find a way, or one day, she would be the one with the knife at her throat, and her father never showed mercy.

TO BE CONTINUED

BONUS CHAPTER

FORDHAM

The Society council believed he—Fordham Ollivier, crown prince of the House of Shadows—should fear them. They had clearly never met his father. Five hundred years on a throne that he ruthlessly ruled with blood and torture and pain. Holding the entire mountain under control with an iron fist. His son most of all.

Fordham was supposed to be forged in his likeness. The fearsome ruler to take over after his father descended into the dark abyss. Or more likely, when he rose up and committed the patricide that many believed would follow. Instead, he was here.

Exiled to this hell dimension that boasted the Society—the great dragon rider rulers, who had left them to their fate.

But he did not fear them. He would infiltrate their mountain. He would claim a dragon for himself. He would return home to regain his position. And he would do it all while they believed the lie he had woven for them.

"You would have us believe that he means us no harm? The entire House of Shadows could be on our doorstep," a conniving little Fae male with the face of a squashed toad snarled.

"It's just like last time! We could end up without a dragon for…" a Fae female with a high forehead and spectacles bellowed before she was cut off.

"We should vote," Mistress Hellina said.

Thus far, she was the only one who had been kind to him. He hadn't truly anticipated any of them would be. Not when he was doing precisely what they had suggested. In fact, it was worse than what they thought.

He had spun them a tale they wanted to hear. The House of Shadows had once been the thirteenth house of the Society. It was only after the Great War that it had fallen to twelve. As a member of the thirteenth house, he had every right to join under their standard. Five years ago, they had let a human compete under a new banner, and he should be given the same ability especially considering he fit all their other parameters. He was a full-blooded Fae over the age of eighteen with a requisite house. He just needed the Society council to approve the change.

Considering the debt they owed his people, it should have been an easy decision.

And yet…

"This should be a unanimous vote," a Fae man with black skin said.

"This doesn't call for a unanimous vote, Lorian," Helly quipped.

Lorian. Fordham filed the name away. He was going to be a problem. He could already tell.

"We made a mistake five years ago, Hellina," Lorian said. "We shouldn't change the rules unless everyone agrees."

"Stand down," another voice rose up. This Fae man had burns down the side of his face and command that Fordham could respect.

"Bastian," Lorian snarled. "I would expect someone of your status to understand where I'm coming from."

"I do not. The prince has made his case. We will vote," Bastian

422

argued. "It had never come to a unanimous vote and it shouldn't today."

"Agreed," Helly said with a nod at Bastian.

Ah, so those two were working together. Another note to stick in his pocket.

The leader of the council, Presiding Officer Zoh, banged a gavel and called for order. "For all in favor of letting Prince Fordham compete as the thirteenth competitor in the dragon tournament, raise your hands."

Fordham stilled in anticipation. There were twenty council members and the council leader who would vote on his entrance into the tournament. He had done his part. The plan was in motion. He just had to jump this one hurdle and then he would be on his way.

Helly's hand went up first. A smile tugged at her lips, and she just barely nodded her head at him. An ally in this madness. Well, he'd take it.

Bastian's hand went up next. But his gaze was more speculative. Maybe not an ally exactly. He seemed as if he had his own aims, but considering Fordham had his own as well, he could respect that.

Other hands went up, more tentatively, more slowly, but they still went up. His eyes roamed the room full of black robes. The Society members who could determine his fate. And then one more went up, tipping the scales in his favor. He resisted a satisfied smile.

Lorian looked around the room aghast, as if he couldn't believe any of his colleagues would vote for him, let alone a majority.

Presiding Officer Zoh banged his gavel again. "The ruling is concluded. Prince Ollivier will be permitted to compete under the banner of the House of Shadows as the thirteenth house." He paused as if anticipating dissention. "So long as he passes through testing."

Fordham's brow furrowed slightly. Testing? What was testing?

"Congratulations," Zoh said. "You may exit through those doors behind you and proceed to testing."

423

Helly gave him a reassuring smile.

"Thank you, sir," he said with a slight head bow.

Then he turned on his heel and walked to the door. Step one of his plan had succeeded. Now he needed to get that dragon. Considering what he'd seen of the mountain so far, he didn't think that would pose much of a challenge.

All that mattered now was that he keep his focus and avoid all distractions.

He pushed the doors open and stepped out into the empty hallway. Except it was no longer empty. A small Fae female lounged against a pillar. She jumped to attention at the sound of the doors banging against the exterior walls.

His entire world plunged into darkness at the sight of her. The unruly red curls that erupted from her head and cascaded around her face and down her back like a tidal wave. The wide emerald eyes that were both mesmerizing and utterly disarming. Her pale face was spattered with freckles, with a strong jawline and pouty lips. Despite her diminutive form and the softness of her features, she had a cut in her eyebrow and a bruise had formed around it. A duality that he understood acutely.

She was soft in all the right places with a demeanor that said she brooked no bullshit. She was frankly stunning. And the biggest fucking distraction he'd ever seen in his life. *Gods.*

What was she doing here?

No, stick to the plan.

He had testing. It didn't matter who this beautiful woman was. He needed to get home, regardless of the cost.

Without saying a word, he pivoted on his heel and took off down the hallway. He'd find someone to direct him to testing. All would be well.

Then he heard scurrying feet chasing after him and a loud, "Excuse me."

He didn't slow down or stop or even look back at her. He couldn't do that. Why was she following him?

But still she trailed him. "Excuse me, Prince Fordham."

He ground his teeth together. This was not the time, but clearly *ignoring* her wasn't working. With sharp military precision, he did an about face and peered down at her with every ounce of disdain he could muster.

"Hi," she said a little breathlessly. "I'm here to be your escort. I'm Kerrigan of the House of Dragons. I'm a Dragon Blessed here in the mountain. Mistress Hellina asked me to escort you to your next assignment."

She tucked her unruly hair behind an ear. His eyes zeroed in on that motion, watching her delicate hands, which were deceptively calloused, work around the tousled hair.

And then his vision narrowed on her ears. Her faintly pointed ears. *Half*-Fae.

He balked at the realization as what she had just said registered in his mind. "You?" he asked incredulously.

"Me."

This had to be a joke or a trap of some sort. They wouldn't send a half-Fae to the prince of the House of Shadows for no reason.

"Why would they send you? Do they intend insult?"

Kerrigan stiffened. "No. I'm a Dragon Blessed."

Gods, she didn't even get it. He was going to have to spell it out. Or else she was going to follow him around under someone's inane orders for the rest of the tournament. And not only was she dangerously beautiful, but she was also anathema to his people. He needed this distraction gone.

"You are half-Fae," he snarled.

That got her attention. Her back immediately went up as if the word was an insult. And he had intended it as such. That should do it. Now she would go.

She ground her teeth together, clenched her fists and released them. But she didn't leave. "Indeed, I am. However, I'm still your escort. Right this way." She gestured in the opposite direction.

Fine. He could do better than that. He'd been raised to think half-Fae were lesser. He could give her all the reasons to have her think he hated her kind.

He took two steps toward her and looked down at her over the bridge of his nose. His shadows coiled around his body, giving off the impression that he was darker and more sinister. He towered over her, pushing into the fear.

Her bottom lip trembled slightly, but she was doing a valiant effort of trying to not look afraid.

"They pass me through to be tested and then send me *you*?" he asked.

"They let you through?" she asked with wide green eyes. "But you're not one of the twelve houses. Who sponsored you?"

She didn't even know the history of his people.

"The House of Shadows was once a recognized house of Alandria. I argued my case sufficiently that it should continue to be one. The right was granted along with sponsorship by the council, considering the debt they owe us."

"Debt?"

His anger flared at her lack of knowledge.

"So they no longer teach you our history. I'd expect nothing less from a half-breed."

The girl visibly bristled at the word. But she didn't back down. As if his insult had only made her more determined.

"Excuse me? You know nothing about me," she snapped. "Now, are we going or what? Unless you know exactly where you're going, princeling."

"Do not call me that," he seethed.

"As far as I can tell, you have no idea where you're going. So I would be *happy* to leave you here and let you fend for yourself. Maybe wandering around for the next few hours would do you some good."

He tilted his head slightly in fascination. Who was this girl?

To think that she could talk to the crown prince this way. That she would not just take insult but offer it back. *Princeling*. And why did it make him more fascinated by her? When was the last time someone had gone toe to toe with him?

No. He needed her gone. He didn't want to be interested in anyone in this godsforsaken place. Let alone a mouthy half-Fae.

"I don't want your help," he concluded.

She blew out a breath. "Well, I don't really want to help you either, but here we are…"

He turned to face the hall he had been walking down. He could continue forward down the endless hallways of an unknown mountain and hope to make it to testing in time. Or he could take the help of a half-Fae girl. A girl with the face of innocence despite the scars on her knuckles, calluses on her palms, and a cut on her eyebrow that suggested otherwise. With a mouth that could cut as surely as his indignation could and a reckless disregard for her own well-being.

"I truly am cursed," he grumbled.

She snorted as if believing him purely melodramatic. "Sure, cursed. Let's get this over with. This way."

She headed down the corridor and didn't look back to see if he followed. He could let her walk away. He *should* let her walk away. And yet…

He breathed a sigh of frustration as he followed in her wake and let her lead the way to his fate.

READ ON FOR A SNEAK PEEK
AT THE NEXT BOOK IN THE
ROYAL HOUSES SERIES

HOUSE
OF
SHADOWS

CHAPTER ONE
THE CELEBRATION

"You just won the dragon tournament. What are you going to do next?"

Kerrigan swatted at Clover. "Stop it. You're ridiculous."

"I'm not ridiculous. I'm beyond excited for my best friend." Clover leaned back against the bar, her dark bob hanging severely in front of her face, her smile the brightest Kerrigan had ever seen.

When Clover, Hadrian, and Darby had pulled her out of Draco Mountain, Kerrigan had tried to match their enthusiasm. A day earlier, she'd been fighting for her life in a tournament she hadn't entered. She had ended victorious, becoming the first half-Fae full member of the Society and a dragon rider. In two weeks' time, she was going to start a year of dragon training. It sounded miraculous. If only there weren't about a million reasons it was anything but.

"Come on, Ker," Hadrian said. His blue hair was coifed elegantly against the golden brown of his skin. The cravat at his neck, half-undone, was the only indication of his inebriation. "Don't look like that. We're celebrating."

"Agreed," Darby said. "I'm out, aren't I? If this isn't a reason to overindulge, I don't know what is."

Darby's midnight skin was coated in a gold shimmer, and her long black tresses gleamed in the dying firelight. She technically wasn't even supposed to be out with them now that she was a member of a royal Bryonican family, but she'd flouted authority and gone out to celebrate.

It wasn't every day that a Dragon Blessed from the House of Dragons became a full-fledged member of the Society—the governmental body of the city of Kinkadia and all of Alandria. Actually, it had never happened. It wasn't even supposed to happen. The House of Dragons was a feeder program for underprivileged Fae to move up in the world. It had worked for Hadrian and Darby, but Kerrigan wasn't like her friends. She was only half-Fae, and no one had wanted her.

"Seriously, you need to let the last forty-eight hours go and have another drink," Clover said, pushing an ale toward her. "Everyone else is buying anyway."

Which was true. The dragon tournament was the most lauded event in Alandrian history. The winners were treated like heroes, and everyone wanted to celebrate, which meant drink after drink after drink. Kerrigan could feel that she had overindulged.

"My head is already spinning," she said with a laugh.

Hadrian rolled his eyes. "When has that ever stopped you?"

She raised a pint to him. "Fair point."

Kerrigan tipped back the ale and took a long drink. It was the good stuff. Not the swill she and Clover normally drank in the Wastes. No, tonight, they'd had to forgo the underground pit, where Clover worked as a card dealer, for a more reputable tavern. They'd ended up in the Dragon Scales on the square in central Kinkadia. It was fancier than anywhere but a royal home but still just a tavern. The same sort of customers and the same sort of drink.

Kerrigan set her half-finished drink on the bar and forced down a yawn. She was about to suggest that they all join the dancing outside when a man sent her drink sprawling.

"Scales," Kerrigan gasped. She jumped away from the spilled ale, but it was too late. The drink coated her dress and down one side of her body.

"Hey, watch what you're doing!" Clover snarled at the man.

The man stood to his considerable height, more than a head taller than Kerrigan. His ears were severely pointed, a clear indicator that he was full-blooded Fae. His skin was creamy white and his eyes the darkest brown, and he was currently glaring at Kerrigan, having already discarded Clover's comment.

"Your kind isn't *welcome* in this establishment," he said coldly.

Kerrigan straightened up. "My *kind*?"

"We've been here all night," Hadrian said as if he hadn't heard the insinuation about her being half-Fae. "If you have a problem with that, then you can go somewhere else."

"They should never defile the Society halls with someone like you, leatha."

A sharp intake of breath was heard all around Kerrigan. A buzzing filled her ears at the horrid word. It was from the ancient Fae language, originally meaning half-Fae, but modern connotation had made it a slur, more commonly meaning half-breed bitch. It wasn't slung around in polite society.

Most people in this fancy tavern probably hadn't heard it spoken aloud except in jest. Not that Kerrigan ever found those jests funny. But Kerrigan had heard the word enough not to flinch from it.

"Creative," she crooned. She was too tipsy for this. "I'm so glad that you don't get a vote."

He took a menacing step forward, but she just laughed. It was the wrong move. She had known somewhere deep in her brain that laughing at this man would provoke him, but did he think he was frightening? She'd won the *dragon* tournament, and not that he knew this, but she was a prized fighter in the Wastes. He couldn't touch her. His overconfidence was almost endearing, if not suicidal.

"I'll give you something to laugh at," he said and then threw his fist toward her face.

She was drunk, not incapacitated.

She fluidly slid out of his reach. Her reflexes were a half second slower than normal, but it wasn't like he was Prince Fordham Ollivier. Fordham was the only person besting her four out of five bouts. This was just a Fae male who thought he was better than her.

The male overcorrected for the missed punch and tried to throw another one. She caught his fist in her hand and wrenched it sideways. He cried out.

"That isn't very nice," she slurred slightly. "Someone should teach you some manners."

She jerked the man forward, bringing her knee up to his face with a satisfying crunch. Then she threw him to the ground at her feet. She could have finished it then with the adrenaline coursing through her, but Darby put a hand on her shoulder.

"Kerrigan, everyone's watching," she whispered.

Kerrigan came back to herself then, stepping away from the man. Her hands were shaking from the fight. It had happened in a matter of seconds, and she hadn't even needed to use her magic, but this wasn't the kind of place that erupted into brawls. The room had quieted, and all eyes were on her. They hadn't seen this brute attack her, but they'd sure seen her finish it. Were they seeing a Society member enacting justice? Or a half-Fae getting revenge, knowing that no one could stop her now?

She backed away from the man on the ground. He'd earned his beating, but she couldn't be the pit fighter anymore. She had to uphold the Society laws. Gods, she'd messed up.

And the fire in the man's eyes said that he hated her all the more. Just like these entitled Fae males always did.

"Let's get out of here," Clover said.

ACKNOWLEDGMENTS

When Kerrigan first appeared in the Ascension series in *The Society* to help out the main character, Cyrene, I had no idea quite where Kerrigan was going to take me. Her inner strength still completely blows me away, and I can't wait to find out where she takes me next. I know for sure that I wouldn't have gotten to this point in the novel without some of my incredible friends, early readers, and those who worked on it with me.

Thank you to Diana Peterfreund, who helped me discover the dragons; Staci Hart, who helped keep me sane as we went through edits; Devin McCain, who drew the incredible map for the indie editions and worked as my assistant throughout the long journey that is the Royal Houses. Also, Rebecca Kimmerling, Rebecca Gibson, Katie Miller, Anjee Sapp, Jovana Shirley, Sarah Hansen, Danielle Sanchez, Nana Malone, Carrie Ann Ryan, Lexi Ryan, Sawyer Bennett, Jessica Florence, Amy Parsons, Kathryn Andrews, Tara Brown, and so many others!

My agent, Kimberly, for being my champion. Also the incredible narrator, Amy McFadden, and the team at Tantor for the audio production. And all the foreign publishers who wanted to bring this to your readers, especially Gillian at Tor.

This second edition wouldn't be possible without the incredible team at Bloom. Thank you, Shaina, for seeing my vision for this series and wanting to bring it to life. Also the rest of the team at Bloom for loving these books as much as me. I can't thank you enough for the exceptional cover design, artwork, and another round of editing. I'm so glad we're here!

Finally, of course, my husband, Joel, and my son. As well as my mom and grandma, who read everything that I write but love my fantasy series the best. Love you!

And last but never least, YOU! Thank you, dear reader, for picking up this book and taking a chance on my magical fantasy world with dragons and Fae and domestic terrorist groups. I wouldn't be able to do this without you. You're my #1!

ABOUT THE AUTHOR

K. A. Linde is a *Sunday Times* bestselling author of fantasy and romance. She has a Master's degree in political science from the University of Georgia and served as the head coach of the Duke University dance team. In her spare time, she loves reading fantasy novels, binge-watching Buffy, travelling and dancing. She currently lives in Lubbock, Texas, with her husband, son and super-adorable puppy. She is the author of the Oak and Holly Cycle novels *The Wren in the Holly Library* and *The Robin on the Oak Throne*.

www.kalinde.com
 @authorkalinde
 @authorkalinde
 @authorkalinde

DISCOVER THE ROYAL HOUSES SERIES

BRAMBLE